EX LIBRIS

VINTAGE CLASSICS

THE COMPLETE ENDERBY

Anthony Burgess achieved a worldwide reputation as one of the leading novelists of his day, and one of the most versatile. He was born in Manchester in 1917 and studied English at the university there. He served in the army between 1940 to 1956, and as a colonial education officer in Malaya and Borneo from 1954 to 1960, which proved the inspiration for *The Malayan Trilogy*. In 1959 Burgess was diagnosed as having an inoperable brain tumour and he decided to try to live by writing. He wrote over fifty books, scripts, translations, a Broadway musical, three symphonies and hundreds of book reviews. His novel *Earthly Powers* was shortlisted for the Booker Prize in 1980. Burgess was a Visiting Fellow of Princeton University and a Distinguished Professor of City College, New York. He was created a Commandeur des Arts et des Lettres by the French President and Commandeur de Mérite Culturel by Prince Rainier of Monaco. His last novel, published in the spring of 1993, was *A Dead Man in Deptford*, based around the murder of Christopher Marlowe.

Anthony Burgess died in November 1993. In the tributes that followed *The New York Times* celebrated his 'versatility and erudition', Gore Vidal said 'the Enderby series are even finer comedies than those by the so much admired Evelyn Waugh', David Lodge admired 'his tireless energy and fertility of invention' and John Updike praised his 'energy and the wide-ranging interests of a dozen writers . . . He seemed not only a prodigious intellect, but an affectionate spirit whose mind, like Ariel's, circled the globe in a few seconds.'

Novels

Abba Abba
A Dead Man in Deptford
Byrne
Earthly Powers
The Malayan Trilogy: Time for a Tiger,
The Enemy in the Blanket, Beds in the East

Autobiography

Little Wilson and Big God
You've Had Your Time

Non Fiction

Shakespeare

ANTHONY BURGESS

The Complete Enderby

VINTAGE BOOKS
London

Published by Vintage 2012

15

Inside Mr Enderby first published by William Heinemann Ltd., London.
Copyright © Anthony Burgess 1963
Enderby Outside first published by William Heinemann Ltd., London.
Copyright © Anthony Burgess 1968
The Clockwork Testament first published by Hart-Davis, MacGibbon, London.
Copyright © Anthony Burgess 1974
Enderby's Dark Lady first published by Hutchinson & Co., London.
Copyright © Anthony Burgess 1984

First published by Vintage in 2002

Vintage
Random House, 20 Vauxhall Bridge Road,
London SW1V 2SA

www.vintage-classics.info

Addresses for companies within The Random House Group Limited can be
found at: www.randomhouse.co.uk/offices.htm

The Random House Group Limited Reg. No. 954009

A CIP catalogue record for this book
is available from the British Library

ISBN 9780099541431

Penguin Random House is committed to a sustainable future for
our business, our readers and our planet. This book is made from
Forest Stewardship Council® certified paper.

Printed and bound in Great Britain by Clays Ltd, Elcograf S.p.A.

Typeset in Bembo by Palimpsest Book Production Limited,
Falkirk, Stirlingshire

Contents

Inside Mr Enderby

To D'Arcy Conyers

– Allons, dernier des poètes,
Toujours enfermé tu te rendras malade!
Vois, il fait beau temps, tout le monde est dehors,
Va donc acheter deux sous d'ellébore,
Ça te fera une petite promenade.

Jules Laforgue, *Dimanches*

Part One

1

1

Pffffrrrrummmp.

And a very happy New Year to you too, Mr Enderby!

The wish is, however, wasted on both sides, for this, to your night visitors, is a very old year. We, whispering, fingering, rustling, creaking about your bedroom, are that posterity to which you hopefully addressed yourself. Congratulations, Mr Enderby: you have already hit your ball smack over the pavilion clock. If you awaken now with one of the duodenal or pyloric twinges which are, to us, as gruesome a literature-lesson spicer as Johnson's scrofula, Swift's scatophobia, or Keats's gallop of death-warrant blood, do not fancy it is ghosts you hear sibilant and crepitant about the bed. To be a ghost one has first to die or, at least, be born.

Perrrrrp.

A posterior riposte from Mr Enderby. Do not touch, Priscilla. Mr Enderby is not a *thing* to be prodded; he is a great poet sleeping. Your grubby finger out of his mouth, please, Alberta. His mouth is open for no amateur dental inspection but to the end that he may breathe. That nose is, at forty-five, past its best as an organ, the black twitching caverns – each with its miniature armpit – stuffed and obtuse. The world of smell is visited by his early poems, remember (pages 1 to 17 of the Harvard University Press selection which is your set book). There we have washed hair, pickles, gorse, bath-salts, skin, pencil-shavings, tinned peaches, post offices, Mrs Lazenby at the corner-shop in his native slum, cloves, diabetes. But it has no existence in his maturer work; the twin ports are closed for ever. That gentle noise, Harold, is snoring. That is so, Christine; his teeth, both upper and lower, are removable: they have been removed to that plastic night-jar there. Child, child, you have spilt

denture-fluid on to Mr Enderby's landlady's carpet. No, Robin, the
carpet is neither beautiful nor rare, but it is Mrs Meldrum's property.
Yes, Mr Enderby himself is our property, the world's property, but
his carpet is his landlady's. Mrs Meldrum's.

Now. His hair goes a daily journey from head to brush, squad
by tiny squad on a one-way ticket. Here on the dressing-table are
the imitation-silver-backed brushes bequeathed by his father, the
tobacconist. The bristles are indeed dirty, Mavis, but great poets
have other things to do than attend to the calls of hygiene. See
how the bristles have trapped their day's quota of Mr Enderby's
few remaining hairs. Holy relics, children. Do not rush. One each
for everybody. There. Keep it safe, each of you, in your little diary
of posterity's present year. Shed hairs, Henry, become the property
of the picker. They are of no use to Mr Enderby, but they are
already fetching, at classical auction-rooms, a pound or so each if
nicely mounted. It is not proper, Audrey, that you should try to
pick your hair *alive*. Such a rough tug at the scalp is enough to wake
Mr Enderby.

Querpkprrmp.

You see? He's disturbed. Let him settle as one lets churned water
settle. Right. A better view of Mr Enderby, you will agree, children,
as he flops on his back cruciform and sends the bedclothes sliding
and plopping to the floor. His belly bulges in two gentle hills, one
on either side of the cutting pyjama-cord. There is a wealth of
hair, see. It is one of the abominable ironies of middle age that
hair should march down from the noble summit, the eagle's lodge,
to leave that bare as an eagle, in order that the camps and barracks
and garrisons of the warm vulgar body be crammed with a growth
that is neither useful nor pretty. The flabby chest too, see. Rich in
hair, aflame with whorls and tendrils of it. And for good measure,
chin and jowls bristling. Horrent, Milton might say.

Yes, Janice, I am constrained to agree that Mr Enderby does not
make a pretty sight when sleeping, even in total darkness. Yes, we
all remark the scant hair, the toothless jaws, the ample folds of flesh
rising and falling. But what has prettiness to do with greatness, eh?
There is something for you all to ponder on. You would not like
to have been married to him, Alberta? Might not the reverse also
have applied, even more so, you stupid giggling silly thing? Who are

you to think that you would ever be meet to mate with a great poet?

The extremities. The feet that trod Parnassus. Callosities on the intricate map of the sole, see. Torn toenails, though that of the great toe too rocky to be tearable. They could both do with a long sudsy soaking, agreed. The outstretched right hand, like a beggar's, really a king's. Gaze with reverence on those fingers that rest now from writing. Tomorrow they will write again, continuing the poem that he considers to be his masterpiece. Ah, what these fingers have produced! Each of you kiss the hand, more gently, though, than a fly crawling. I realize that the act of kissing needs an effort of will to overcome a certain natural revulsion. Here, however, is a little lesson for you in scholastic philosophy. The grubby knuckles, the nails with black borders, the deep stains of tobacco-tar (the cigarette was held interdigitally, forgotten, while the poet's mind soared above the smell of burning), the coarse skin – these are the accidents, the outer aspects of the hand, their concession to the ordinary world of eating and dying. But the essence of the hand – what is that? A divine machine that has made our lives more blessed. Kiss it, come on, kiss it. Althea, stop making that vomiting noise. Your face, Charles, is ugly enough without contorting it to a rictus of nausea. That's right, kiss it.

It has hardly disturbed him at all. He scratches it gently in his sleep, the tickle of a questing alighting moth. Listen. In his sleep he is going to say something. Your kiss has prodded a sleeping inspiration. Listen.

> *My bedmate deep*
> *In the heavy labour of unrequited sleep.*

No more? No more. There, children, what a thrill! You have heard his voice, a mumbly sleepy voice, true, but still his voice. And now let us pass on to Mr Enderby's bedside table.

Books, children, Mr Enderby's bed-reading. *Blondes Like Bullets*, whatever that means; *Who Was Who in the Ancient World*, useful, no doubt; *Raffity's Deal*, with a brutish cover; *How I Succeeded*, by a tycoon who died of arteriosclerosis; *Little Stories of the Marian Martyrs*, sensational. And here, dears, is one of Mr Enderby's own:

Fish and Heroes, his early poems. What a genius he had then! Yes, Denis, you may handle it but, please, with care. Oh, you stupid boy, you have sent a shower of things to the floor. What are these, that were hidden between the well-thumbed pages? Photographs? Don't touch, leave them, they are not for you! Merciful heavens, the weaknesses of the great. What shame we have unintentionally uncovered. Do not giggle, Brenda and Maureen, and hand that photograph back to me this instant. You will wake Mr Enderby with those obscene girlish noises. What, Charles, are they doing? The man and woman in the picture? They are minding their own business, that's what they're doing.

Bopperlop.

Rest, rest, perturbed spirit. That picture, please, Robin. I can see it in your blazer pocket. Thank you. Fellation, if you must know, is the technical term. And now, no more of that. Shall we tiptoe into Mr Enderby's bathroom? Here we are. This is where Mr Enderby writes most of his verse. Remarkable, isn't it? Here, he knows, he can be truly private. The bath is full of manuscripts and dictionaries and ink-milked ballpoint pens. In front of the W.C. is a low desk, just the right height. There is an electric heater to glow on to his bared legs. Why does he choose this meagre chamber? Poetry, he has already said in an interview, is appropriate to it; the poet is time's cleanser and cathartizer. But, one may be sure, there is much more to it than that. Some childhood agony not yet to be uncovered by us. But Educational Time Trips are already talking of pushing further back into the past. Who knows? Before you leave school you may yet visit Shakespeare struggling, in the parish of St Olave, with verse quantities and a quill. Nigel, leave those rusty razor-blades alone, stupid boy. Softly, softly, now. To the room where he eats and, when not writing, lives is but a step. No, Stephanie, Mr Enderby lives alone through choice. Love, love, love. That's all that some of you girls can think about. Mr Enderby's love-life up to this point is obscure and shrouded. His attitude to women? You have his poems, though they, admittedly, mention the sex but little.

Porripipoop.

The horns of Elfland. We have left him to his poet's peace. There is one thing, though. The poems of this year – which, of course, he has not yet written – show a shy stirring of a more than photo-graphic interest in woman. But we have no biographical evidence of an affair, a change of ménage. We have little biographical evidence of anything. He was essentially a man who lived inside himself. And this sandy seaside address is the only one we have. Can you hear the sea, children? It is the same sea that we know, cruel, green, corrupt.

And what of Mr Enderby do we find in this room? It is Mrs Meldrum, his landlady, who speaks out clear in all this ranged bric-à-brac. Yes, survey it with wonder: a geometrical series of baby ebony elephants, the sweetest of china shepherds flute-blowing to unseen lambs, a plaster toy toast-rack with ancient Blackpool gilding, a tea-caddy replica of tarnished Brighton Pavilion, an enmarbled papier-mâché candlestick, a china bitch and her china litter, a filigree sheet-iron button-box. Do you like the picture above the electric-fire mantelpiece? It shows men in rusty red preparing for the hunting morning, all men identical because, we presume, the pseudo-artist could afford only one model. And, on the opposite wall, British admirals of the eighteenth century unrolling maps of *terra incognita*, wine being poured for them in tankards that catch the fire's glow. Here, jolly monks fish on Thursday; there, they lap up their Friday feast. A pot head of a twentyish flapper, hatted and lipsticked, on that strip of wall past the kitchen door. Emily, leave your nostrils alone. To blow spittle-bubbles on your nether lip is, need I say, Charles, childish. The kitchen is hardly worth examining. Very well, if you insist.

What a strong stench of stale bread! See that fish glow in the dark. Pans on the high shelf. Do not touch, Denis, do not. Oh you damnable young idiot. The whole blasted flaming lot clanking and clashing and ringing down. You bloody young fool. You will all laugh on the other sides of your faces when I get you back to civilization. Oh God, a frying-pan has knocked the kettle over. The gas-stove is full of water. What a filthy, damnable, metal noise! Who has spilt the pepper? Stop sneezing, blast the lot of you. Aaaaaarch! Howrashyouare! Out of here, quickly.

You can't be trusted, any of you. This is the last time I arrange such an expedition. Look down on all those Victorian roofs, fish-scaled under the New-Year moon. You will never see them again.

Nor any of this town, in whose flats and lodgings the retired and
dying wheeze away till dawn. It is all very much like a great hair-
comb, isn't it? – the winking jewelled handle, the avenues of teeth
combing the hinterland of downs, the hair-ball of smoke which is
the railway station. Above us, the January sky: Scutum, Ophiuchus,
Sagittarius, the planets of age and war and love westering. And that
man down below, whom that clatter of cheap metal has aroused
from dyspeptic and flatulent sleep, he gives it all meaning.

2

Enderby awoke, aware of both noise and heartburn. Clamped to
his bedhead was a lamp in a plastic shade. He switched this on,
realized he was shivering and saw why. He picked up the tangle
of bedclothes from the floor, covered himself roughly, and lay back
again to savour the pain. It had an inexplicable note of raw turnip
about it. The noise? The kitchen-gods fighting. Rats. He needed
bicarbonate of soda. He must, he reminded himself for at least the
seven-thousandth time, remember to keep it ready-mixed and handy
by his bed. The stab of sharpened raw turnip shattered his breast-
bone. He had to get up.

He saw himself in the wardrobe mirror as he slapped stiffly out
of the room into the tiny hallway of his flat, a rheumatic robot in
pyjamas. He entered the dining-room, switching on, sniffing like
a dog as for a craftily hidden presence. Ghosts had been whimpering
around, he was sure, ghosts of the dead year. Or perhaps, he smiled
wryly at the conceit, posterity had been shyly looking in. He was
astonished at the mess in the kitchen. Such things happened, though:
a delicate balance upset by a micrometric subsidence of the old
house, an earth tremor, self-willed monads in the utensils themselves.
He took a cloudy glass from the draining-board, snowed in some
sodium bicarbonate, stirred with two fingers, then drank. He waited
thirty seconds, squinting at the glazed pane of the back door. A tiny
hand hidden beneath his epiglottis gave a come-up signal. And
then.

Delightful. Oh, doctor, the relief! I feel I must write to say thank
you for the benefits I have obtained from your product. Aaaaaaarp.

Almost immediately after the second spasm of release came a fierce and shameless hunger. He moved the three steps necessary from sink to food-cupboard and found himself freezingly sploshing in spilt water by the stove. He dried his feet in the dropped tea-towel, rearranged the fallen pans on their shelf, wincing with old man's bent pain as he picked them up. He then remembered that he needed his teeth, so he padded back to the bedroom for them, switching the living-room fire on on the way. He clacked a false gleam at the mirror when he returned to the living-room, then did a brief lumbering dance of rage at his reflection. In the food-cupboard were pellets of rocky cheddar, greasily wrapped. A lone midget cauliflower swam like a doll's brain in dense pickle. There was half a tin of sardines, soft plump knives in golden oil. He ate with fingers that he then wiped dry on his pyjamas.

Almost at once his bowels reacted. He ran like a man in a comic film, sat down with a sigh and clicked on the bathroom heater. He scratched his bare legs and read, thoughtfully, the confused draft he was working on. Pfffrumpfff. It was an attempt at allegory, a narrative poem in which two myths were fused – the Cretan and the Christian. A winged bull swooped from heaven in a howling wind. Wheeeeee. The law-giver's queen was ravished. Big with child, called whore by her husband, she went incognita to a tiny village of the kingdom, there, in a cheap hotel, to give birth to the Minotaur. But the old gummy trot who tended her would keep no secret; she blazoned it about the village (and this spread beyond to the towns, to the capital) that a god-man-beast had come down to rule the world. Prrfrrr. In hope, the anarchic party of the state was now ready to rise against the law-maker: tradition had spoken of the coming of a divine leader. Civil war broke out, propaganda flashed in jagged lightnings from both sides. The beast was evil, said King Minos: capture it, kill it. The beast was God, cried the rebels. But nobody, except the queen-mother and the toothless midwife, had ever seen the beast. Brrrrbfrrr. The baby Minotaur was growing fast, bellowing lustily, hidden away safely with its dam in a lonely cottage. But, by treachery, the forces of Minos were given knowledge of its whereabouts. Manifestly, thought Minos, when it was brought to his palace, though techni-cally a monster it was no horror: its gentle eyes were twin worlds of love. With the talisman and mascot of the rebels in his power, Minos was able to call for surrender. He had a labyrinth built, vast and marbly splendid, with the Minotaur hidden in its heart. It was a horror, unspeakable, reputedly fed on human flesh; it was the state's bogey, the state's guilt. But Minos was economical: the peripheral corridors of the labyrinth became a home of Cretan culture – university, museum, library, art gallery; a treasury of human achievement; beauty and knowledge built round a core of sin, the human condition. Prrrrf. (Enderby's toilet-roll span.) But one day, from the west, there flew in the Pelagian liberator, the man who had never known sin, the guilt-killer. Minos by now was long dead, along with his shameless queen and, long long before, the midwife. Nobody living had seen the monster and survived, so it was said. Greeted with cheers, flowers and wine, the liberator went to his heroic work. Blond, bronzed, muscular, sinless, he entered the labyrinth and, a day later, emerged leading the monster on a string. Gentle as a pet, with hurt and forgiving eyes, it looked on humanity. Humanity seized it and reviled it and buffeted it. Finally it was nailed to a cross, where it died slowly. At the moment of giving up the ghost there was a sound of rending and crashing. The labyrinth collapsed; books were buried, statues ground to chalk-dust: civilization was at an end. Brrrrp.

The poem was to be called, tentatively, *The Pet Beast*. Enderby realized that a great deal of work had to be done on it, symbols clarified, technical knots unravelled. There was the disinterested craftsman, Daedalus, to be brought into it, the anti-social genius with the final answer of flight. There was Pasiphae's pantomime cow. He tried out, in his deep woollily inept voice, a line or two on a hushed audience of hanging dirty towels:

> He, the cold king, judged cases in his dreams.
> Awake, lithe at his task,
> The other whistled, sawing pliant beams.
> Law is what seems;
> The Craftsman's place to act and not to ask.

The words, resounding in that tiny cell, acted at once like a conjuration. Just outside the flimsy door of Mr Enderby's ground-floor flat was the entrance-hall of the house itself. He heard the massive front door creak open and the hall seemed to fill with New Year revellers. He recognized the silly unresonant voice of the salesman who lived in the flat above, the stout-fed laugh of the woman who lived with him. There were other voices, not assignable to known persons but generic, voices of *Daily Mirror*-readers, ITV-viewers, HP-buyers, Babycham-drinkers. There were loud and cheerful greetings:

'Happy New Year, Enderby!'

'Prrrrrrrrp!'

The stout-fed woman's voice said, 'I don't feel well. I'm going to be sick.' She at once, by the sound of it, was. Someone called:

'Give us a poem, Enderby, "Eskimo Nell" or "The Good Ship Venus".'

'Sing us a song, Enderby.'

'Jack,' said the sick woman weakly, 'I'm going straight up. I've had it.'

'You go up, love,' said the salesman's voice. 'I'll be after you in a minute. Got to serenade old Enderby first.' There was the noise of a staggering fall against the door of Enderby's flat, a choirmaster's 'One two three', and then the vigorous ragged strains of '*Ach Du Lieber Augustin*', but with rude English words:

> Balls to Mister Enderby, Enderby, Enderby;
> Balls to Mister Enderby, ballocks to you.
> For he keeps us waiting while he's masturbating, so –

Enderby stuffed moistened pellets of toilet-paper in his ears. Locked safely enough in his flat, he now locked himself safelier in his bathroom. Scratching a warmed bare leg, he tried to concentrate on his poem. The revellers soon desisted and dispersed. He thought he heard the salesman call out, 'That's the enderby, Enderby.'

3

Cosily muffled against the sharp marine morning, Enderby walked down Fitzherbert Avenue towards the sea. It was ten-thirty by the

Town Hall clock and the pubs were just opening. He passed
Gradeleigh ('for Gradely Folk'), Kia-Ora (retired Kiwis), Ty-Gwyn
(couple from Tredegar), Channel View, White Posts, Dulce Domus,
The Laurels, Ithaca (former classics master and convicted pederast).
Converted to flats, humbled as guest-houses, all were owned by
foreigners from north and west of the downs, bemused by an image
of the glamour of the south coast: France winked at night across
the water; here the air had a fancied mildness. Not today, thought
Enderby, smacking his woolly bear-paw palms together. He wore a
scarf coloured like a Neapolitan ice; his overcoat was a tightly-belted
Melton; he was shielded from heaven by a Basque beret. The house
wherein he had a flat was, he thanked that same heaven, nameless.
Number 81, Fitzherbert Avenue. Would there ever, some day, be a
plaque to mark that he had lived there? He was quite sure not. He
was one of a dying race, unregarded by the world. Hurray.

Enderby turned on to the Esplanade, joined a queue of old
women in a cake-shop, and came out with a seven-penny loaf. He
crossed over to the sea-rail and leaned on it, tearing the loaf. The
gulls wheeled screaming for the thrown bread, beady-eyed greedy
creatures, while the sea whooped in, the green-grey winter Channel,
then grumbled back, as at the lion-tamer's whip, grudgingly rattling
many tambourines. Enderby tossed the last crumbs to the bitter
air and its grey planing birds, then turned from the sea. He looked
back on it before he entered the Neptune, seeing in it, as so often
from a distance, the clever naughty green child which had learned
to draw a straight line free-hand.

The saloon-bar of the Neptune was already half-filled with old
people, mainly widows. 'Morning,' said a dying major-general, 'and
a happy New Year to you.' Two male ancients compared arthritis
over baby stouts. A bearded lady drank off her port and slowly,
toothlessly, chewed the mouthful. 'And to you too,' said Enderby.
'If I can live to see the spring,' said the general, 'that's all. That's as
much as I can hope for.' Enderby sat down with his whisky. He
was at home with the aged, accepted as one of them, despite his
ridiculous youth. Still, his recorded age was a mere actuarial cipher;
his gullet burning as the whisky descended, his aches and pains, his
lack of interest in action – these made him as old as the crocks
among whom he sat.

'How,' asked a gentle tremulous man made of parchment, 'how,' his hand shaking his drink like a dicebox, 'how is the stomach?'

'Some quite remarkable twinges,' said Enderby. 'Almost visible, you know. And flatulence.'

'Flatulence,' said the major-general, 'ah, yes, flatulence.' He spoke of it as though it were a rare old vintage. 'Many years since I've had that. Now, of course, I eat nothing. A little bread soaked in warm milk, morning and evening. I swear it's this rum that's keeping me alive. I told you, did I, about that contretemps over the rum ration at Bruderstroom?'

'Several times,' said Enderby. 'A very good story.'

'Isn't it?' said the general, painfully animated. 'Isn't it a good story? And true. Incredible, but true.'

A plebeian crone in dirty black spoke from a bar-stool. 'I,' she said, 'have had part of my stomach removed.' There was a silence. The aged males ruminated this gratuitous revelation, wondering whether, coming from a female and a comparative stranger, it was really in the best of taste. Enderby said kindly: 'That must have been quite an experience.' The old woman looked crafty, gripped the counter's edge with papery hands that grew chalky at the knuckles, canted her stool towards Enderby and said, very loudly, 'Pardon?'

'An experience,' said Enderby, 'never to be forgotten.'

'Six hours on the table,' said the woman. 'Nobody here can't beat that.'

'Crump,' called the major-general in an etiolated martinet's voice. 'Crump. Crump.' He was not reminiscing about the first World War; he wanted the barman to replenish his rum-glass. Crump came from behind the bar, seventyish, in a waiter's white jacket, with a false smile both imbecilic and ingratiating, his grey head cocked permanently to one side like that of a listening parrot. 'Yes, General,' he said. 'Similar, sir? Very good, sir.'

'I'm always telling him,' said an ancient with the humpty-dumpty head of Sibelius, 'about that use of the word. It's common among barmen and landlords. They say you can't have the *same* again. But it is, in fact, precisely the same again that one wants. One doesn't want anything *similar*. You deal in words, Enderby. You're a writer. What's your view of the matter?'

'It *is* the same,' agreed Enderby. 'It's from the same bottle. Something similar is something different.'

'Professor Taylor used to argue that out very persuasively,' said an old man mottled like salami, a dewdrop on the hook of his nose.

'What's happened to Taylor?' asked the major-general. 'We haven't seen him for quite some time.'

'He died,' said the mottled man. 'Last week. While drawing a cork. Cardiac failure.'

'He'd just turned eighty,' said a man just turned eighty. 'Not all that old.'

'Taylor gone,' said the general. 'I didn't know.' He accepted rum from obsequious Crump. Crump accepted silver with an obsequious inclination of a broken and mended torso. 'I thought I'd go before him,' said the general, 'but I'm still here.'

'You're not all that old yourself,' said the tremulous parchment man.

'I'm eighty-five,' said the general in puffy indignation. 'I call that *very* old.'

Higher bids came from the corners. One woman confessed coyly to ninety. As if somehow to prove this, she performed a few waltz-twirls, humming from *The Merry Widow*. She sat down again to genteel shocked applause, her lips blue, her heart almost audibly thumping. 'And,' asked the Sibelius-man, 'how old might you be, Enderby?'

'Forty-five.'

There were snorts of both contempt and amusement. One man in a corner piped, 'If that's meant to be funny, I don't think it's in very good taste.'

The major-general turned sternly and deliberately towards Enderby, both hands resting on the ivory bulldog-head of his malacca. 'And what is it you do for a living?' he asked.

'You know that,' said Enderby. 'I'm a poet.'

'Yes, yes, but what do you do for a living? Only Sir Walter made a living out of poetry. And perhaps that Anglo-Indian man who lived at Burwash.'

'A few investments,' said Enderby.

'What investments precisely?'

'I.C.I. and B.M.C. and Butlin's. And local government loans.'

The major-general grunted, as though none of Enderby's replies was above suspicion. 'What was your rank in the last war?' he asked, a last throw.

Before Enderby could give a lying answer, a widow in antique tweeds, a long thin woman with black-rimmed spectacles, fell from a low stool by a wicker table. Old men reached trembling for their sticks, that they might lever themselves up and help. But Enderby was there first. 'Sho kind,' said the woman genteelly. 'Sho shorry to cauzhe all thish trouble.' She had evidently been tanking up at home before opening-time. Enderby lifted her from the floor, as light and as stiff as a bundle of celery. 'Thezhe thingzh,' she said, 'happen in the besht of familiezh.'

His hands still hooked in her armpits, Enderby was shocked to see the image of his stepmother in the big Gilbey's Port mirror on the wall opposite. Shaken, he nearly dropped his burden to the floor again. The image nodded to him, as out of some animated painting in a TV commercial, raised its glass in New Year salutation, then seemed to hobble out of the picture, into the wings, thus disappearing.

'Get on with it, Enderby,' said the peevish major-general. 'Put her back on her seat.'

'Sho very kind,' said the woman, trying hard to focus on her gin-glass. Enderby looked in the room for a source of that mirror-image, but saw only a bent back hobbling to the Gents. That might be it, a trick of the light or the New Year. It was his stepmother, strangely enough, who had told him as a child that, on New Year's Day, a man walked the streets with as many noses on his face as there were days in the year. He had gone looking for this man, thinking of him fearfully as of the family of the Antichrist that walked the world before the day of judgement. Long after he had seen through the trick, New Year's Day still possessed for him an irritating macabre flavour, as a day of possible prodigies. His step-mother was, he was pretty sure, dead and buried. She'd done her work, as far as he was concerned. There was no point in her staying alive or coming back from the grave.

'Now,' said the major-general, as Enderby sat down again with a new whisky, 'what did you say your rank was?'

'Lieutenant-general,' said Enderby. In speech a comma is as good as a hyphen.

'I don't believe you.'

'Look it up.' Enderby was almost sure he saw his stepmother leave the jug-and-bottle department, a quarter-bottle of Booth's in her bag. The Neptune was the sort of pub in which any of the three parts – saloon, public, out-door – is visible from any other. Enderby spilt whisky on his tie. An old man who had not previously spoken pointed at Enderby with shaky care and said, 'You've spilt whisky on your tie.' Enderby felt that fear would possibly make worse happen. The outer world was not safe. He must go back home and closet himself, work at his poem. He finished the driblet in his glass, buttoned himself up and donned his Basque beret. The major-general said, 'I don't believe you, sir.'

'You must please yourself, General,' said Ex-lieutenant Enderby. And, with a general salute, he left.

'He's a liar,' said the major-general. 'I always knew he wasn't to be trusted. I don't believe he's a poet, either. A very shifty look about him this morning.'

'I read about him in the public library,' said the salami-mottled man. 'There was a photograph, too. It was an article, and it seemed to think quite a lot of him.'

'What is he? Where does he come from?' asked another.

'He keeps himself very much to himself,' said the mottled man and, just in time, he snuffed up a perilous dewdrop.

'He's a liar, anyway,' said the major-general. 'I shall look up the Army List this afternoon.'

He never did. A motorist, irritable and jumpy with a seasonal hangover, knocked him down as he was crossing Nollekens Avenue. Long before spring, the major-general was promoted to glory.

4

Out in the gull-clawed air, New-Year blue, the tide crawling creamily in, Enderby felt better. In this sharp light there was no room for ghosts. But the imagined visitation had acted as an injunction to honour the past before looking, as at every year's beginning, to the future.

Enderby first thought of his mother, dead at his birth, of whom there had seemed to be no record. He liked to imagine a young woman of gentle blondeness, sweetly refined and slenderly pliant. He liked to think of her swathed in gold, in a beeswax-breathing drawing-room, singing 'Passing By' to her own accompaniment. The dying heat of a July day sang in sadness through the wide-open french windows from a garden that glowed with Crimson Glory, Mme L. Dieudonne, Ena Harkness and Golden Spectre. He saw his father, become bookish, wearing bookman's slippers, O-ing out smoke from an oval-bored Passing Cloud, nodding his head in quiet pleasure as he listened. But his father had never been quite like that. A wholesale tobacconist, ruling lines in the ledger with an ebony sceptre of a ledger-ruler, sitting in the office behind the shop in waistcoat and black bowler, always glad of opening-time. Why? To escape from that bitch of a second wife. Why in God's name had he married her? 'Money, son. Her first one left her a packet. Her stepson will, we hope, reap the benefit.' And, to some extent, it had turned out that way. Hence the few hundred a year from I.C.I., British Motors, and the rest. But had it been worth it?

Oh, she had been graceless and coarse, that one. A hundredweight of ringed and brooched blubber, smelling to high heaven of female smells, rank as long-hung hare or blown beef, her bedroom strewn with soiled bloomers, crumby combinations, malodorous bust-bodices. She had swollen finger-joints, puffy palms, wrists girdled with fat, slug-white upper arms that, when naked, showed indecent as thighs. She was corned, bunioned, calloused, varicose-veined. Healthy as a sow, she moaned of pains in all her joints, a perpetual migraine, a bad back, toothache. 'The pains in me legs,' she would say, 'is killin' me.' Her wind was loud, even in public places. 'The doctor says to let it come up. You can always say excuse me.' Her habits were loathsome. She picked her teeth with old tram-tickets, cleaned out her ears with hairclips in whose U-bend ear-wax was trapped to darken and harden, scratched her private parts through her clothes with a matchbox-rasping noise audible two rooms away, made gross sandwiches of all her meals or cut her meat with scissors, spat chewed bacon-rind or pork-crackling back on her plate, excavated beef-fibres from her cavernous molars and held them up for all the world to see, hooked out larger chunks with a soiled sausage-finger, belched like a ship in the fog, was sick on stout on Saturday nights, tromboned vigorously in the lavatory, ranted without aitches or grammar, scoffed at all books except *Old Moore's Almanac*, whose apocalyptic pictures she could follow. Literally illiterate all her life, she would sign cheques by copying her name from a prototype on a greasy piece of paper, drawing it carefully as a Chinese draws an ideogram. She provided fried meals mostly, ensuring first that the fat was tepid. But she brewed good tea, potent with tannin, and taught young Enderby the technique, that he might bring her a cup in the morning: three for each person and two for the pot, condensed milk rather than fresh, be lavish with the sugar. Enderby, sixth-form boy, would stand over her while she drank it in bed – tousled, wrinkled, puffed, ill-smelling, a wreck – though she did not really drink it: the tea seemed to soak into her as into parched earth. One day he would put rat-poison in her cup. But he never did, even though he bought the rat-poison. Hate? You've just no idea.

When Enderby was seventeen, his father went off to Nottingham to be shown over a tobacco factory, was away for the night. July heat (she showed up badly in that) broke in monsoon weather, with terrifying lightning. But it was only the thunder that scared her. Enderby awoke at five in the morning to find her in his bed, in dirty winceyette, clutching him in fear. He got up, was sick in the lavatory, then locked himself in, reading till dawn the scraps of newspaper on the floor.

Her death was reported to him when he was in the Army, L. of C. troops in Catania. She had died after drinking a morning cup of tea, brought by his father. Heart failure. The night of hearing the news, Enderby went with a woman of Catania (one tin of corned beef and a packet of biscuits) and, to her almost concealed laughter, could do nothing. Also, on arriving back at his billet, he was sick.

Well, there it was. His stepmother had killed women for him, emerging in a ladylike belch or a matchstick picking of teeth from behind the most cool and delectable façade. He had got on quite nicely on his own, locked in the bathroom, cooking his own meals (ensuring first that the fat was tepid), living on his dividends and the pound or two a year his poems earned. But, as middle-age advanced, his stepmother seemed to be entering slyly into him more and more. His back ached, his feet hurt, he had a tidy paunch, all his teeth out, he belched. He had tried to be careful about laundry and cleaning the saucepans, but poetry got in the way, raising him above worry about squalor. Yet dyspepsia would cut disconcertingly in, more and more, blasting like a tuba through the solo string traceries of his little creations.

The act of creation. Sex. That was the trouble with art. Urgent sexual desire aroused with the excitement of a new image or rhythm. But adolescence had prolonged its techniques of easy detumescence, normal activities of the bathroom. Walking towards the Freemason's Arms he felt wind rising from his stomach. Damn. Brerrrrp. Blast. He was, however, on the whole, taking all things into consideration, by and large, not to put too fine a point on it, reasonably well self-sufficient. Brrrrrp. Blast and damn.

5

Arry, head cook at the Conway, was standing by the bar of the Freemason's with a pint tankard of brown ale and bitter mixed. He said to Enderby, "Ere yar.' He handed over a long bloody parcel, blood congealed on a newspaper headline about some woman's blood. 'A said ad get it an a got it.' Enderby said, 'Thanks, and a happy New Year. What will you have?' He eased away some of the newspaper at one end, 'Missing Persons', covered with blood, and the head of a mature hare stared at him with glass eyes. 'Yer can joog it today,' said Arry. He was in a brown sports-coat that reeked of old fat, a tout's cap on his head. His upper jaw had only two canines. These were gateposts between which his tongue, car-like, occasionally eased itself out and in. He came from Oldham. 'Red coorant jelly,' said Arry. 'What a generally do is serve red coorant jelly on a art-shaped croutong. Coot out a art-shaped bitter bread with a art-cooter. Fry it in 'ot fat, quick. Boot, livin' on yer own, a don't suppose yer'll wanter go to that trooble.' He drank down his brown ale and bitter and, on Enderby, had another pint. 'Good job yer coom in when yer did,' he said. "Ave to go now. Special loonch for South Coast Association of Car Salesmen.' He swigged the pint in one lift of the tankard, had another, yet another, all in two minutes flat. Like most cooks he could eat little. He had ferocious gastric pains which endeared him to Enderby. 'Seein' yer,' he said, leaving. Enderby nursed his hare.

This bar was the haunt of all local lesbians over fifty. Most of them fulfilled the paradigms of marriage, a few were divorced, widowed or estranged. On a stool in the corner was a woman called Gladys, a peroxided Jewess of sixty with tortoise-shell spectacle-rims and leopard-skin jeans. She was kissing, more often and more passionately than seemed necessary, another woman in New-Year greeting. This woman wore a bristling old fur coat and was delicately cross-eyed. A fierce-looking thin woman in a dress as hairy and simple as a monk's habit, a nutria coat swinging open over it, crashed into the bar and greeted her too, long and gluily. 'Prudence, my duck,' she said. Prudence seemed to be a popular girl. The peculiar charm of strabismus. And then the fragments of a new poem came swimming with a familiar confidence into Enderby's head. He saw the shape, he heard the words, he felt the rhythm. Three stanzas, each beginning with birds. *Prudence, prudence, the pigeons call.* And, of course, that's what they did call, that's what they'd always called. *Act, act, the ducks give voice.* And that was true, too. What were the other birds? They weren't seagulls. The dyed-blonde Jewess, Gladys, suddenly, raucously, laughed. It was a bird like that. *Caution, caution.* Rooks, that was it. But why were they calling, giving voice, proclaiming?

He had a ball-point pen, but no paper. Only the wrapping of the hare. There was a long empty stop-press column, two forlorn football results at the head. He wrote the lines he had heard. Also other fragments that he could hear dimly. The meaning? Meaning was no concern of the poet. *The widow in the shadow. The widow in the meadow.* A voice, very clear and thin, spoke as though pressed to his ear: *Drain the sacrament of choice.* Gladys began to sing, pop garbage composed by some teenager, much heard on radio disc-programmes. She sang loudly. Excited, Enderby cried, 'Oh, for Christ's sake shut up!' Gladys was indignant. 'Who the bloody hell do you think you're telling to shut up?' she called across, with menace. 'I'm trying to write a poem,' said Enderby. 'This,' said someone, 'is supposed to be a respectable pub.' Enderby downed his whisky and left.

Walking home quickly he tried to call back the rhythm, but it had gone. The fragments ceased to be live limbs of some mystical body that promised to reveal itself wholly. Dead as the hare, meaningless onomatopoeia; a silly jingle: *widow, shadow, meadow.* The big rhythms of the nearing tide, the winter sea-wind, the melancholy gulls. A gust shattered and dispersed the emerging form of the poem. Oh, well. Of the million poems that beckoned, like coquettish girls, from the bushes, how very few could be caught!

Enderby stripped the hare of its bloody paper as he approached 81 Fitzherbert Avenue. There was a public litter basket attached to a lamp-post almost in front of the front-steps. He threw the crumpled mess of news, blood, inchoate poetry in, and got out his key. A tidy town, this. Must not let our standards relax even though there are no holiday visitors. He entered the kitchen and began to skin the hare. It would give him, he thought, stewed with carrots, potatoes and onions, seasoned with pepper and celery salt, the remains of the Christmas red wine poured in before serving, enough meals for nearly a week. He slapped the viscera on to a saucer, cut up the carcass, and then turned on the kitchen tap. Hangman's hands, he thought, looking at them. Soaked in blood up to the elbows. He tried out a murderer's leer, holding the sacrificial knife, imagining a mirror above the kitchen sink.

The water flowing from the faucet cast a faint shadow, a still shadow, on the splashboard. The line came, a refrain: *The running tap casts a static shadow.* That was it, he recognized, his excitement mounting again. The widow, the meadow. A whole stanza blurted itself out:

> 'Act! Act!' The ducks give voice.
>   'Enjoy the widow in the meadow.
> Drain the sacrament of choice.
>   The running tap casts a static shadow.'

To hell with the meaning. Where the hell were those other birds? What were they? The cuckoo? The sea-gull? What was the name of that cross-eyed lesbian bitch in the Freemason's? Knife in hand, steeped in blood to the elbows, he dashed out of his flat, out of the house, to the rubbish-basket clamped to the lamp-post. Others had been there while he had been gutting and skinning and quartering. A Black Magic box, a Senior Service packet, banana-peel. He threw it all out madly into the gutter. He found the defiled paper which had wrapped the beast. Frantically he searched page after crumpled page. THIS MAN MAY KILL, POLICE WARN. NOW THIS BOY IS LOVED. *Most people stop Acid Stomach with Rennies*. Compulsive reading. He read: 'The pain-causing acid is neutralized and you get that wonderful sensation that tells you the pain is beginning to go. The antacid ingredients reach your stomach gradually and gently – drip by drip . . .'

'What's this? What's going on?' asked an official voice.

'Eh?' It was the law, inevitably. 'I'm looking for these blasted birds,' said Enderby, rummaging again. 'Ah, thank God. Here they are. Prudence, pigeons. Rooks, caution. It's as good as written. Here.' He thrust the extended sheets into the policeman's arms.

'Not so fast,' said the policeman. He was a young man, apple-ruddy from the rural hinterland, very tall. 'What's this knife for, where did all that blood come from?'

'I've been murdering my stepmother,' said Enderby, absorbed in composition. *Prudence, prudence, the pigeons call*. He ran into the house. The woman from upstairs was just coming down. She saw a knife and blood and screamed. Enderby entered his flat, ran into the bathroom, kicked on the heater, sat on the low seat. Automatically he stood up again to lower his trousers. Then, all bloody, he began to write. Somebody knocked – imperious, imperative – at his front door. He locked the bathroom door and got on with his writing. The knocks soon ceased. After half an hour he had the whole poem on paper.

> 'Prudence! Prudence!' the pigeons call.
> 'Scorpions lurk in the gilded meadow.
> An eye is embossed on the island wall.
> The running tap casts a static shadow.'

'Caution! Caution!' the rooks proclaim.
'The dear departed, the weeping widow
Will meet in you in the core of flame.
The running tap casts a static shadow.'

The injunction of the last stanza seemed clear enough, privy enough. Was it really possible, he wondered, for him to follow it, making this year different from all others?

'Act! Act!' The ducks give voice.
'Enjoy the widow in the meadow.
Drain the sacrament of choice . . .'

In the kitchen, he could now hear, the water was still flooding away. He had forgotten to turn it off. Casting a static shadow all the time. He got up from his seat, automatically pulling the chain. Who was this blasted widow that the poem referred to?

2

1

While Enderby was breakfasting off reheated hare stew with pickled walnuts and stepmother's tea, the postman came with a fateful letter. The envelope was thick, rich, creamy; richly black the typed address, as though a new ribbon had been put in just for that holy name. The note-paper was embossed with the arms of a famous firm of chain booksellers. The letter congratulated Enderby on his last year's volume – *Revolutionary Sonnets* – and was overjoyed to announce that he had been awarded the firm's annual Poetry Prize of a gold medal and fifty guineas. Enderby was cordially invited to a special luncheon to be held in the banqueting-room of an intimidating London hotel, there to receive his prizes amid the

plaudits of the literary world. Enderby let his hare stew go cold.
The third Tuesday in January. Please reply. He was dazed. And,
again, congratulations. London. The very name evoked the same
responses as *lung cancer, overdrawn, stepmother*.

He wouldn't go, he couldn't go, he hadn't a suit. At the moment
he was wearing glasses, a day's beard, pyjamas, polo-neck sweater,
sports-jacket and very old corduroys. In his wardrobe were a pair
of flannel trousers and a watered-silk waistcoat. These, he had
thought when settling down after demobilization, were enough
for a poet, the watered-silk waistcoat being, perhaps, even, an
unseemly luxury of stockbroker-like extravagance. He had had it,
by mistake, knocked down to him for five shillings at an auction.

London. He was flooded with horrid images, some derived from
direct experience, others from books. At the end of the war,
searching for William Hazlitt's tomb in its Soho graveyard, he had
been abused by a constable and had up in Bow Street on a charge
of loitering with intent. He had once slipped on the greasy pavement outside Foyle's and the man who had helped him up – stocky,
elderly, with stiff grey hair – had begged five bob to 'elp aht a bit
cos they was on strike that week, guv. That was just after he had
bought the watered-silk waistcoat: ten bob down the drain. In the
urinal of a very foggy pub he had, unbelievably, been invited to a
fellation party by a handsome stranger in smart city wear. This man
had become nasty at Enderby's polite refusal and threatened to
scream that Enderby was assaulting him. Very unpleasant. Along
with other memories that made him wince (including one excruciating one of a ten-shilling note in the Café Royal) came gobbets
from *Oliver Twist, The Waste Land*, and *Nineteen Eighty-Four*. London
was unnecessarily big, gratuitously hostile, a place for losing money
and contracting diseases. Enderby shuddered, thinking of Defoe's
Journal of the Plague Year. And there he was – as he emptied his
cold plateful back into the saucepan – with his stepmother again.
At the age of fifteen he had bought off a twopenny stall in the
market a duo-decimo book of recipes, gossip, and homilies, printed
in 1605. His stepmother, able to read figures, had screamed at the sight
of it when he had proudly brought it home. 1605 was 'the olden days',
meaning Henry VIII, the executioner's axe, and the Great Plague.
She thrust the book into the kitchen fire with the tongs, yelling

that it must be seething with lethal germs. A limited, though live, sense of history.

And history was the reason why she would never go to London. She saw it as dominated by the Bloody Tower, Fleet Street full of demon barbers, as well as dangerous escalators everywhere. As Enderby now turned on the hot-water tap he saw that the Ascot heater did not, as it should, flare up like a bed of pain. The meter needed a shilling and he was too lazy to go and look for one. He washed his soup-plate and mug in cold water, reflecting that his stepmother had been a great one for that (knives and forks wrapped in grease as if they were guns). She had been very lazy, very stupid, very superstitious. He decided, wiping the dishes, that he would, after all, go to London. After all, it wasn't very far – only an hour by electric train – and there would be no need to spend the night in a hotel. It was an honour really, he supposed. He would have to borrow a suit from somebody. Arry, he was sure, had one. They were much of a size.

Enderby, sighing, went to the bathroom to start work. He gazed doubtfully at the bathtub, which was full of notes, drafts, fair copies not yet filed for their eventual volume, books, ink-bottles, cigarette-packets, the remains of odd snacks taken while writing. There were also a few mice that lived beneath the detritus, encouraged in their busy scavenging by Enderby. Occasionally one would surface and perch on the bath's edge to watch the poet watching the ceiling, pen in hand. With him they were neither cowering nor timorous (he had forgotten the meaning of 'sleekit'). Enderby recognized that the coming occasion called for a bath. Lustration before the sacramental meal. He had once read in some women's magazine a grim apothegm he had never forgotten: 'Bath twice a day to be really clean, once a day to be passably clean, once a week to avoid being a public menace.' On the other hand, Frederick the Great had never bathed in his life; his corpse had been a rich mahogany colour. Enderby's view of bathing was neither obsessive nor insouciant. ('Sans Souci', Frederick's palace, was it not?) He was an empiricist in such matters. Though he recognized that a bath would, in a week or two, seem necessary, he recoiled from the prospect of preparing the bathtub and evicting the mice. He would compromise. He would wash very nearly all over in the basin. More, he would shave with exceptional care and trim his hair with nail-scissors.

Gloomily, Enderby reflected that most modern poets were not merely sufficiently clean but positively natty. T. S. Eliot, with his Lloyd's Bank nonsense, had started all that, a real treason of clerks. Before him, Enderby liked to believe, cleanliness and neatness had been only for writers of journalistic ballades and triolets. Still, he would show them when he went for his gold medal; he would beat them at their own game. Enderby sighed again as, with bare legs, he took his poetic seat. His first job was to compose a letter of gratitude and acceptance. Prose was not his *métier*.

After several pompous drafts which he crumpled into the waste-basket on which he sat, Enderby dashed off a letter in *In Memoriam* quatrains, disguised as prose. 'The gratitude for this award, though sent in all humility, should not, however, come from me, but from my Muse, and from the Lord . . .' He paused as a bizarre analogue swam up from memory. In a London restaurant during the days of fierce post-war food shortage he had ordered rabbit pie. The pie, when it had arrived, had contained nothing but breast of chicken. A mystery never to be solved. He shrugged it away and went on disguising the chicken-breast of verse as rabbit-prose. A mouse, forepaws retracted like those of a kangaroo, came up to watch.

2

Enderby found Arry in white in his underground kitchen, brown ale frothing beside him, slicing pork into blade-thin shives. An imbecilic-looking scullion in khaki threw fistfuls of cabbage on to plates. When he missed he picked up the scattered helping carefully from the floor and tried again. Massive sides of beef were jocularly being unloaded from Smithfield – the fat a golden fleece, the flesh the hue of diluted Empire burgundy. Enderby said:

'I've got to go up to London to be given a gold medal and fifty guineas. But I haven't got a suit.'

'Yer'll be able to buy a good un,' said Arry, 'with that amount of mooney.' He didn't look too happy; he frowned down at his precise task like a surgeon saving the life of a bitter foe. 'There,' he said, forking up a translucent slice to the light, 'that's about as thin as yer can bloody get.'

'But,' said Enderby, 'I don't see the point of buying a suit just for this occasion. I probably shan't want to wear a suit again. Or not for a long time. That's why I'd like to borrow one of yours.'

Arry said nothing. He quizzed the forked slice and nodded at it, as though he had met its challenge and won. Then he returned to his carving. He said, 'Yer quite right when yer suppose av got more than wan. Am always doin' things for people, aren't a? Boot what dooz any bogger do for me?' He looked up at Enderby an instant, his tongue flicking out between its gateposts as if to lick up a tear.

'Well,' said Enderby, embarrassed, 'you know you can rely on me. For anything I *can* do, that is. But I've only one talent, and that's not much good to you. Nor, it seems,' the mood of self-pity catching, 'to anyone else. Except a hundred or so people here and in America. And one mad female admirer in Cape Town. She writes once a year, you know, offering marriage.'

'Female admirers,' said carving Arry, pluralizing easily. 'Female admirers, eh? That's wan thing a 'aven't got. It's *me* oo admires *er*, that's the bloody trooble. It's got real bad, that as.' He became violently dialectal. 'Av getten eed-warch wi' it,' he said. Then, as an underling sniffed towards him with a cold, 'Vol-au-vent de dindon's in that bloody coopboard,' he said.

'Who?' said Enderby. 'When?'

'Er oopstairs,' said Arry. 'Thelma as serves int cocktail bar. A new it definite ender the moonth. Bloody loovely oo is boot bloody cruel,' he said, carving steadily. 'Oo's bloody smashin',' he said.

'I don't know,' said Enderby.

'Don't know what?'

'Who's bloody smashing.'

'Oo is,' said Arry, gesturing to the ceiling with his knife. 'Oo oop thur. That Thelma.'

Enderby then remembered that two Anglo-Saxon feminine pronouns co-existed in Lancashire. He said 'Well, why don't you go in and win? Just put a few teeth in your mouth first, though. The popular prejudice goes in favour of teeth.'

'What's pegs to do with it?' said Arry. 'A don't eat. Pegs is for eatin'.
Am in loove, that's bloody trooble, and what's pegs to do with that?'

'Women like to see them,' said Enderby. 'It's more of an aesthetic
than a functional thing. Love, eh? Well, well. Love. It's a long time
since I've heard of anybody being in love.'

'Every boogger's in loove nowadays,' said Arry, ending his carving.
He drank some brown ale. 'There's songs about it ont wireless. A
used to laff at 'em. And now it's me oo's copped it. Loove. Bloody
nuisance it is an' all, what with bein' busy at this timer year. Firms
givin' loonches an' dinners till near the end of February. Couldn't
'ave coom at a worse time.'

'About this suit,' said Enderby. He faced a vast carboy of pickled
onions and his bowels melted within him. He wanted to be gone.

'Yer can do summat for me,' said Arry, 'if am to do summat for
you.' He tasted this last pronoun and then decided that his revelation, his coming request, called for *tutoyer* intimacy. 'Summat for
thee,' he amended. 'Al lend thee that suit if tha'll write to 'er for
me, that bein' thy line, writin' poetry an' all that mook. A keep
sendin' 'er oop special things as av cooked special, boot that's not
romantic, like. A nice dish of tripe doon in milk, which were always
my favourite when a were eatin'. Sent it down, oontooched, oo
did. A reet boogger. What would go down best would be a nice
loove-letter or a bitter poetry. That's where *you'd* coom in,' said
Arry, and his snake-tongue darted. ''Av a grey un, a blue un, a
brown un, a fawn un an a 'errin-bone tweed. Tha's welcome to
any wan on 'em. Thee write summat an' sign it Arry and send it
to me an' a'll send it oop to 'er.'

'How shall I spell Arry?' asked Enderby.

'With a haitch,' said Arry. 'Two a week should do the bloody
trick. Shouldn't take yer not more than a coupler minutes to write
the sort of thing that goes down all reet with women. You and
yer bloody female hadmirers,' he said.

Before going back to his flat, Enderby used – long, lavishly and
painfully – the gentlemen's lavatory on the ground floor of the
hotel. Then, shaken, he went to the cocktail bar for a whisky and
to have a look at Thelma. It would not do if he dug up old poems,
or wrote new ones, celebrating the glory of fair hair or pegs like
margarite if she should chance to be black, grey, near-edentate. The

bar seemed full, today, of car salesmen, and these chaffed and mock-courted, with ha-ha-ha and obsolete pilot's slang, a quite personable barmaid in her late thirties. She had all her front teeth, black hair, naughty eyes, ear-rings that jangled tinily – clusters of minute coins – a snub nose and a comfortable round chin. She was superbly bosomed and efficiently uplifted. She seemed to be a repository of old bar-wisdom, epigrams, radio-show catch-phrases. A car salesman bought her a Guinness and she toasted him with 'May you live for ever and me live to bury you.' Then, before drinking, she said, 'Past the teeth and round the gums, look out, stomach, here it comes.' She had a fair swallow. She had decorated her little bar with poker-work maxims: 'Laugh and the world laughs with you; snore and you sleep alone.' 'Water is a good drink when taken with the right spirit.' 'When you're up to your neck in hot water be like the kettle and sing.' There was also a Browningesque couplet (content if not technique) above the gin bottles:

> For when the last great Scorer còmes to write
> against your name,
> He writes not that you won or lost, but how you
> played the game.

Enderby doubted whether he could achieve the same gnomic tautness in anything he wrote for her. Still, that wouldn't be called for, love being essentially imprecise and diffuse. He drank his whisky and left.

3

Enderby's attitude to love-poetry was dispassionate, impersonal, professional. The worst love-poems, he had always contended, were the most sincere: the lover's palpitating emotions – all too personal, with an all too particular object – all too often got in the way of the ideal, the universal. A love-poem should address itself to an idea of a loved one. Platonism could take in ideal breasts, an ideal underarm odour, an ideal unsatisfactory coitus, as well as the smooth-browed intellectual wraith of the old sonneteers. Back in his bathroom, Enderby rummaged for fragments and drafts that would serve to start off the *Arry to Thelma* cycle. He found, mouse-nibbled:

> I sought scent and found it in your hair;
>   Looked for light, and it lodged in your eyes.
> So for speech: it held your breath dear;
>   And I met movement in your ways.

That felt like the first quatrain of a Shakespearian sonnet. It wouldn't do, of course; the sprung rhythm and muffled rhymes would strike Thelma's world as technical incompetence. He found:

> You were there, and nothing was said,
> For words toppled over the edge or hovered in air.
> But I was suddenly aware, in the split instant,
> Of the constant, in a sort of passionless frenzy:
> The mad wings of motion a textbook law,
> Trees, tables, the war, in a fixed relation,
> Moulded by you, their primum mobile,
> But that you were there really was all I knew.

He couldn't remember writing that. The reference to the war dated it within six years. The place? Probably some town with avenues, outdoor tables for drinking. Addressed to? Don't be so bloody stupid; addressed to nobody, of course; pure ideal emotion. He continued rooting, his arms deep in the bathtub. The mice scuffled to their primary home, a hole. He found half a priceless piece of juvenilia:

> You are all
> Brittle crystal,
> Your hands
> Silver silk over steel.
>
> Your hair harvested
> Sheaves shed by summer,
> Your repose the flash
> Of the flesh of a river-swimmer . . .

Then a jagged tear. He must have been, sometime, taken short. There was nothing in the bath that would do for Thelma, even an ideal Thelma. He would have to compose something new. Stripping his lower half for poetic action, he took his seat and got down to work. Here was a real problem, that of bridging the gap, of making something that should not seem eccentric to the recipient and at the same time not completely embarrass the author. After an hour he produced the following:

> Your presence shines above the fumes of fat,
>   Glows from the oven-door.
> Lithe with the litheness of the kitchen cat,
>   Your image treads the floor
> Ennobling the potato-peel, the lumps
> Of fallen bread, the vulgar cabbage-stumps.
> 'Love!' cry the eggs a-whisk, and 'Love!' the beef
>   Calls from the roasting-tin.
> The beetroot blushes love. Each lettuce-leaf
>   That hides the heart within
> Is a green spring of love. Pudding and pie
> Are richly crammed with love, and so am I.

But, after those first two painful stanzas, he found it hard to stop. He was led on ruthlessly, horrified by a growing facility, a veritable logorrhoea. At the end of the ode he had emptied Arry's kitchen and filled ten closely written sheets. One point, he thought, he had very clearly established, and that was that Arry was in love.

4

It was the day of the London luncheon. Tremulous Enderby fell out of bed early to see snow staring through the morning dark. Shivering, he snapped every electric heater in the flat on, then made tea. Snow gawped blankly at him through all the windows, so he drew the curtains, turning raw morning into cosy muffiny toast-toe evening. Then he shaved. He had washed, fairly thoroughly, the night before the night before last. He had almost forgotten what it was like to shave with a new blade, having – for nearly a year now – used the old ones stacked up by the previous tenant on top of the bathroom cupboard. This morning he slashed cheeks, underlip, and Adam's apple: shaving-soap froth became childhood ice-cream sprinkled with raspberry vinegar. Enderby found an old poem beginning *And if he did then what he'd said he'd do*, and with bits of this he stanched the flow. He started to dress, putting on a new pair of socks bought at a January sale and tucking the ends of his pyjama-trousers well inside them. He had a white shirt specially laundered, he had found a striped tie – lime and mustard – in a suitcase with the name PADMORE in marking-ink on white rag attached to its lining (who was, or had been, or might be in the unrealized future, Padmore?) and had cleaned with care his one pair of brown shoes. He had also, for show and blow respectively, saved two clean handkerchiefs. He would beat these city-slickers at their own game. The suit from Arry was sober grey, the most Eliotian one in his whole wardrobe.

He was pleasantly surprised by the decent gravity of the figure that bowed from the wardrobe mirror. Urban, respectable, scholarly – a poet-banker, a poet-publisher, teeth a flashing two double octaves in the electric firelight, spectacles drinking of the bedlamp's glow. Satisfied, he went to get his breakfast – a special breakfast today, for God knew what ghastly sauced muck he might be coldly given in the great hotel. He had bought a Cornish pasty but had, coming out of the shop, slipped on an ice-patch. This had hurt him and flattened the pasty, but its edibility was hardly impaired. It was to be eaten with Branston pickle and, as an extra-special treat, washed down with Blue Mountain coffee. He felt an unwonted exultation as he prepared this viaticum, as if – after years of struggle – he had at last arrived. What should he buy with the prize-money? He couldn't think what. Books? He had done reading. Clothes? Ha ha. There was nothing he really needed except more talent. Nothing in the world.

The coffee was disappointingly cool and weak. Perhaps he had not made it properly. Could he take lessons in that? Were there teachers of such things? Arry. Of course, he would ask Arry. At nine-fifteen (train at nine-fifty, ten minutes walk to station) he sat with a cigarette, hypnotized by the gash-gold-vermilion of the

electric fire, waiting. He suddenly caught another memory like a
flea. Far childhood. Christmas Day, 1924. Snow came down in the
afternoon, transfiguring the slum street where the shop was. He
had been given a magic lantern and, after dinner, he was to project
slides of wild animals on to the sitting-room wall. Powered by a
candle, the lantern had been fitted with a candle – a new one, its
flame much too high for the lens. His Uncle Jimmy the plumber
had said, 'We'll have to wait till it burns down. Give us a tune,
Fred.' And Fred, Enderby's father, had sat at the piano and played.
The rest of that dim gathering – only the stepmother bright in
memory, belching away – had waited for the candle to burn down
to lens level, the coloured animals suddenly to appear on the wall.

Why, wondered Enderby now, why had nobody thought to cut
the candle? Why had they all, every single one of them, agreed to
wait on the candle's convenience? It was another mystery, but he
wondered if it was really a mystery of a different order from this
other waiting – waiting on Shakespeare's time's candle to burn
down to time to dress warmly, time to leave for the station. Enderby
suddenly passionately wished he could cut the whole long candle
to its end – have written his poetry and have done. Then he
grinned as his stomach, having slyly engineered this melancholy,
plaintively subscribed to it.

Pfffrrrp. And then Brrrrrrr. But that, he realized, after surprise
at his stomach's achievement of such metallic ectophony, that, he
heard with annoyance, was the doorbell. So early, whoever it was,
and coming so inconveniently. Enderby went to his flat-door and
saw, waddling down the hallway of the house itself, his landlady,
Mrs Meldrum. Well. He paid her by post. The less he saw of her
the better. 'If I can trouble you for a moment, Mr E,' she said. She
was a woman of sixty, with pinched East Midland vowels. Her
face was modelled on that of a tired but cheerful crescent moon
in a bedtime-malted-milk-drink advertisement that even Enderby
had seen often: Punch-nose meeting cusp-chin, but no jolly Punch
plumpness. She had a full set of Tenniel-teeth of the colour of
small chips of dirty ice, and these she showed to Enderby now as
to a mirror. Enderby said:

'I've got to go up to town.' He thrilled gently, saying that, a
busy man of affairs.

'I shan't keep you not more than one minute,' said Mrs Meldrum, 'Mr E.' She waddled in past Enderby as if she owned the place, which she did. 'It's really to empty the shillings out of the electric meter,' she said, 'which is, in one way of speaking, why I called. In another way of speaking, it's about the complaints.' She went ahead of Enderby into the living-room. At the table she examined minutely the remains of Enderby's breakfast, shook her head comically at them and then, picking up the pickle-jar, read from the label like a priest muttering the Mass: 'Sugar cauliflower onions malt vinegar tomatoes carrots spirit vinegar gherkins dates salt marrow . . .'

'What complaints?' asked Enderby, as he was expected to.

'New Year's Eve,' said Mrs Meldrum, 'being a special occasion as calls for jollifications, nevertheless Mrs Bates down in the basement has complained about loud singing when she couldn't go off to sleep with the backache. Your name came into it a lot, she says, especially in the very rude singing. On New Year's Day you was seen running up and down the street with a carving-knife and all covered with blood. Well, Mr Enderby, fun's fun as the saying goes, though I must confess I'm surprised at a man of your age. But the police had a quiet word with Mr Meldrum, unbeknownst to me, and I could only get it out of him last night, him being shy and retiring and not wanting to cause trouble. Anyway, we've had a talk about it and it can't go on, Mr E.'

'I can explain,' said Enderby, looking at his watch. 'It's all really quite simple.'

'And while we're on the subject,' said Mrs Meldrum, 'that nice young couple upstairs. They say they can hear you in the night sometimes.'

'I can hear *them*,' said Enderby, 'and they're *not* a nice young couple.'

'Well,' said Mrs Meldrum, 'that's all according as which way one looks at it, isn't it? To the pure all things are pure, as you might say.'

'What, Mrs Meldrum, is this leading to?' Enderby looked again at his watch. In the last thirty seconds five minutes had gone by. Mrs Meldrum said:

'There's plenty as would like this nice little flat, Mr E. This is a respectable neighbourhood, this is. There's retired schoolmasters and captains of industry retired along here. And I wouldn't say as how you kept this flat all that clean and tidy.'

'That's my business, Mrs Meldrum.'

'Well, it may be your business, Mr E, but then again it might not. And everybody's putting the rents up this year, as you may as well know. What with the rates going up as well and all of us having to watch us own interests.'

'Oh, I see,' said Enderby. 'That's it, is it? How much?'

'You've had this very reasonable,' said Mrs Meldrum, 'as nobody can deny. You've had this at four guineas a week all through the season. There's one gentleman as works in London as is very anxious to find respectable accommodation. Six guineas to him would be a very reasonable rent.'

'Well, it's not a very reasonable rent to me, Mrs Meldrum,' said Enderby angrily. His watch-hand leapt gaily forward. 'I have to go now,' he said. 'I've a train to catch. Really,' he said, shocked, 'do you realize that that would be eight guineas more a month? Where would I get the money?'

'A gentleman of independent means,' said Mrs Meldrum smugly. 'If you don't want to stay, Mr E, you could always give a week's notice.'

Enderby saw with horror the prospect of sorting out the bathful of manuscripts. 'I'll have to go now,' he said. 'I'll let you know. But I think it's an imposition.'

Mrs Meldrum made no move. 'You go off then and catch your train,' she said, 'and think about it in your first-class carriage. And I'll empty the shillings out of the meter, as has to be done now and again. And if I was you I should stack those plates in the sink before you leave.'

'Don't touch my papers,' warned Enderby. 'There are private and confidential papers in that bathroom. Touch them at your peril.'

'Peril, indeed,' scoffed Mrs Meldrum. 'And I don't like the sound of that at all, continental papers in *my* bathroom.' Meanwhile Enderby wrapped his muffler on and fought his way – as if towards the light – into his overcoat. 'I never heard of such a thing, and that's a fact,' said Mrs Meldrum, 'and I've been in the business a fair amount of time. I've heard of coals in the bath with some of them slummy people, though I thank the Almighty God I've never harboured any of them in *my* bosom. You're going out like that, Mr Enderby, with bits of paper stuck all over your face. I can read a word there, just by your nose: *epileptical*, or something. You're not doing yourself or me or any of the other tenants any good at all, Mr E, going out in that state. Peril, indeed.'

Enderby dithered out, doubtful. He had not reckoned on having to search for new lodgings, not in the middle of *The Pet Beast*. And this town was becoming more and more a dormitory for bald young men from London. In one pub he had met the head of a news-reel company, a lavish gin-man with a light, fast voice. And there had been a processed-cheese executive heard, loud and unabashed, somewhere else. London was crawling southward to the Channel.

Enderby crawled northward to the station, picking off odd words from his razor-cuts. The snow had been trodden already, by people rushing earlier with insincere eagerness to get to work in London. Enderby teetered in tiny gavotte-steps, afraid of slipping, his rump still aching from last night's fall. Work-trains, stenographer-trains, executive-trains. Big deals over the telephone, fifty guineas nothing to them. Golfball-money. But, thought Enderby, that would provide for half a year's rent increase.

Looking up at the zinc sky he saw a gull or two flapping inland. He had neglected to feed the gulls for two days now; he was becoming careless. Perhaps, he thought vaguely, he could make it up to them by buying some special treat at the Army and Navy Stores. He passed a block of bright posters. One of them extolled domestic gas: a smiling toy paraclete called Mr Therm presided over a sort of warm Holy Family. Pentecostal therm; pentecostal sperm. Two men in dyed army overcoats marched, as in retreat, from the station, with demoralized thug faces. One said to the other, 'Can't make up its bleeding mind. Rain one day, snow the next. Be pissing down again tomorrow.' Enderby had to stop, short of breath, his heart martelling away as though he had just downed a half-bottle of brandy, his left hand clutching a snowcapped privet-hedge for support. *The pentecostal sperm came pissing down.* No, no, no. *Hissing down.* The line was dealt to him, like a card from a weighing-machine. He had a sudden image of the whole poem like a squat evil engine, weighing, waiting. The Holy Family, the Virgin Mary, the pentecostal sperm. He heard a train-whistle and had to rush.

Panting, he entered the little booking-hall and dug out his wallet from his right breast. There was still a Christmas tree by the book-stall. That was wrong: Twelfth Night was over, St Distaff's Day had set the working year spinning again. Enderby approached the stern shirt-sleeves behind the *guichet*. 'A day return to London, please,' he begged. He picked up his change with his ticket and sent a shilling over the floor. 'Don't lose that, mister,' said a lively old woman in black. 'Need that for the gas.' She cackled as Enderby chased the shining monocycle to the barrier. The ticket-collector flapped a heavy boot on to it, trapped. 'Thank you,' said Enderby. Rising from picking it up his eyes misted, and he saw a very clear and blue picture of the Virgin Mary at a spinning-wheel, a silver queen set in baby blue. This had nothing to do with *The Pet Beast* and its Mary-Pasiphae. This had something to do with his stepmother.

> In this spinning womb, reduced to a common noun,
> The pentecostal sperm came hissing down . . .

That was not it, the rhythm was wrong, it was not couplets. The couplets came from the doves in the Queen's speech in *Hamlet*. Doves, loves, leaves. Enderby clomped down the steps and up the steps to the up-train platform. The train was just arriving. There was an *-eave* rhyme somewhere. Enderby boarded the train. There were few passengers at this hour – women going up to fight in the January sales, a scholarly-looking police-inspector with a briefcase, two men looking much, Enderby thought distractedly, like himself – smart, normal, citified. Doves came from dove, dove meant paraclete. A dove in the leaves of life. Eve, leave, thieve, achieve, conceive.

'I beg your pardon?' said a woman sitting diagonally opposite to Enderby. They were the only two in the compartment. She was thin, blonde, washed-out, fortyish, smart with a mink cape-stole and a hat like a nest. 'Peeve,' said Enderby the city-man. 'Believe. Weave.' The train began to pant north-east with urgent love of

London, a sperm to be swallowed by that giant womb. 'Swallowed,' announced Enderby, with loud excitement, 'by the giant stomach of Eve. I knew Eve came somewhere into it.' The woman picked up her folio-sized handbag and silver-grey couplet of gloves and left the compartment. 'Eve leaves,' said Enderby. Where was paper? None. He had not expected this to be a working day. Inkpencil he had. He rose and followed the woman out to the corridor. She scampered, with a kitten-scream, to the next compartment, which held a trio of talking and nodding wives drably dressed for sales-battle. Enderby, a homing dove, went straight to the lavatory.

5

> In this spinning room, reduced to a common noun,
>   Swallowed by the giant stomach of Eve,
> The pentecostal sperm came hissing down.

Enderby sat, fully dressed, on the seat of the W.C., swaying as on a father's rocking knee, a cock-horse to Charing Cross. No, London Bridge. No, Victoria. An electric sperm plunging towards Our Lady of Victories, Enderby astride. He had removed the toilet-roll from its holder and scratched away on panel after panel of paper with his inkpencil. The poem was definitely a song for the Blessed Virgin.

Whence this Marianism? Enderby knew. He remembered his bedroom with its devotional pictures by Italian commercial artists: Pius XI with triple tiara and benedictory gesture; Jesus Christ with radioactive heart exposed and – for good measure – indicated by a divine delicate index-finger; saints (Anthony, John the Baptist, Bernadette); the Virgin Mary with tender smile and winsome wimple:

> I was nowhere, for I was anyone –
>   The grace and music easy to receive:
> The patient engine of a stranger son.

Outside the bedroom door had been a holy-water stoup, dried up with the drought of Enderby's boyish disbelief. All over the house, as far as the frontier of the shop's neutral or Protestant territory, there had been other stoups, also crucifixes, plaster statuettes, withered Holy-Land palm-leaves, rosaries blessed in Rome, an Agnus Dei or two, decorative pious ejaculations (done in Dublin in pseudo-Celtic script) as brief as snarls. That was his stepmother's Catholicism, imported from Liverpool – relics and emblems and hagiographs used as lightning-conductors; her religion a mere fear of thunder.

The Catholicism of the Enderbys had come from a small Catholic pocket not far from Shrewsbury, a village which the Reformation had robbed only of its church. Weak in the tobacconist-father (his pan scraped on Holy Saturday, a drunken midnight Mass at Christmas – no more), it had died in the poet-son, thanks to that stepmother. It had been too late now for more than twenty years to look at it afresh – its intellectual dignity, its cold coherent theology. He had struggled out of it with bitter tears in adolescence, helped by Nietzsche, Tolstoy, and Rousseau, and the struggle to create his own myths had made him a poet. He couldn't go back to it now, even if he wanted to. If he did, he would be seeking the converts who wrote thrillers out of a sense of damnation or who, forming an exclusive club out of the converts of Oxford and pretending that that was the Church, would not let Enderby join. Publicly known as an apostate, Enderby would have to be bracketed along with various wild Irish. It was best, therefore, to be quiet about his faith or loss of it (asked for his religion when joining the army, he had said 'Hedonist' and been made to attend parades of the United Board); the only trouble seemed to be that his art refused to be quiet.

> His laughter was fermenting in the cell,
>   The fish, the worm were chuckling to achieve
> The rose of the disguise he wears so well.

Ultimately religious belief didn't matter; it was a question of what myths still carried enough emotional weight to be used. So the Virgin Mary now spoke her final triplet, smiling faintly in elegant blue at the distaff:

> And though, by dispensation of the dove,
>   My flesh is pardoned of its flesh, they leave
> The rankling of a wrong and useless love.

There was too much love in the air, worried Enderby, as he read over this poem with displeasure. He saw that, apart from the obvious surface myth, there was something there about the genesis of the poet. He wrote on a final panel of toilet-paper: *Every woman is a stepmother*, then committed it to the lavatory-pan. That, he thought, has general validity. And now, judging from the loud darkness outside the cell where his poem had been an hour fermenting, they had arrived. Roars of seals in a circus, collapse of crates, high heels on the platform, a hiss, shudder and recoil as the train, in Elizabethan locution, died.

3

1

Some hours later Enderby sat under a magnificent ceiling, bemused by food and drink and insincere laudations. A not very choice cigar shook between fingers which, he now saw, he had neglected to pumice. In a winter afternoon's dream he failed to register many of the words of orating Sir George Goodby. Across the table and at either side twenty-odd fellow-writers were suspended from the ceiling by cigarette-smoke, their faces flapping before Enderby's eyes like two lines of drying smalls. Very solid in his stomach there pawed and pranced a sort of equestrian statue that symbolized both Time and London. He desired to pick his nose. A Hangman's Blood cocktail of all the liquids he had so far taken that day was swiftly mixed in a deep visceral shaker and then shot up to his mouth for tasting. There had been an oily mock turtle with very fresh rolls and rose-shaped butter-pats. Roast duck, of which Enderby had been served with one of the greasier segments, peas and *sauté* potatoes, acid orange sauce and a thick warmish gravy. Cranberry pie, the pastry soggy, with rich whipped cream-substitute. Cheese.

Cheese. Enderby smiled across back at some woman who had smiled at him. I have always admired your poetry but to see you in the flesh is a revelation. I bet it bloody well is. Perrrrrp.

'A revelation,' said Sir George, 'of the purest beauty. The magical power of poetry to transmute the dross of the everyday workaday world into the sheerest gold.' Sir George Goodby was an ancient man whose visible parts were made mostly of sewn bits of well-tanned skin. He had founded the firm which bore his name. This firm had become rich mainly by selling rude books which other firms had been too squeamish to handle. Knighted by Ramsay MacDonald for services to the cause of mass-literacy, Sir George had always desired to serve literature otherwise than by selling it: he had aspired from youth to be a starving poet recognized only after death. Starved poetry he had continued to write long after fate had condemned him to the making of money, and this he had blackmailed one small miserable firm into publishing, brandishing the threat of a chain-boycott of all its publications. He had paid all costs of printing, publicizing, and distributing, but the firm's reputation had been ruined. The volumes of Sir George's doggerel most memorable for badness were *Metrical Yarns of a Pipeman, A Dream of Merrie England, Roseleaves of Memory* and *An Optimist Sings.* He could not, of course, force people into buying or even reading these atrocious collections, but once a year, presenting a cheque and medal to, as he coyly termed him, a brother-singer, he would lard his speech richly with gobbets of his own work and render his auditors sick with embarrassment.

'The giants of my youthful days,' Sir George was saying, 'Dobson, Watson, Sir Edward Arnold the mystic, Bridges the revolutionary, Calverley for laughter, Barry Pain for the profounder sigh.' Enderby took a shallow draught of his cigar and felt it bite rawly. A childhood image again: the woman teacher in the elementary school explaining the soul and sin's carious effect upon it. She had chalked on the blackboard a big whitish shape like a cheese (the soul) and then, using a spit-wet finger, had spotted it like a Dalmatian (sins). For some reason, Enderby had always been able to taste that chalk-soul

– a sharp vinegary raw potato – and he could taste it strongly now. 'The soul,' said Sir George appropriately, 'which is a fair field for the poet's wandering, the sea whereon he sails his barque of rhyme, his mistress of whom he sings. The soul, which is the parson's Sunday concern, is the poet's daily bread.' His daily raw potato. Enderby felt a borborygm rising.

Brrrffffp.

'I shall inflict,' twinkled Sir George, 'one of my own sonnets on you, on a theme appropriate to the occasion.' He read out, with a voice pitched high and on one tuning-fork note, a poem of fourteen lines which was certainly no sonnet. It had verdant meads in it and a sun with effulgent rays, also – for some reason – a rosy-bosomed earth. Enderby, preoccupied with the need to suppress his body's noises, heard only fragments of an exquisitely bad poem and he nodded approvingly to show that he considered Sir George to have made a very good choice of an illustrative example of very bad poetry. As the last line scrannel-piped wretchedly out, Enderby felt a particularly loud noise coming, so he covered it with a laugh.

Ha ha (perrrpf) ha.

Sir George was rather surprised than displeased. He gaped down at Enderby for five seconds and then scanned his typescript trem-blingly, as if fearful that something scatological had stolen ambiguously in. Reassured, he frowned on Enderby, his patches of skin shaking, and then took breath for the peroration. As he opened his mouth, Enderby, with infelicitous timing, gave vent.

Brrrbrrrpkrrrk.

Shem Macnamara said, 'And as good and succinct a piece of criticism as ever I heard.' He had a double-chinned stormy Irish face and was shag-haired and black-shirted (to save laundry). Enderby, in his daily poet's garb, was seedy-looking, but this man was a barn-sleeping hedge-dragged sturdy beggar. The white tired faces of the other guests – which Enderby could see but dimly – moved in titters. And suddenly Sir George himself seemed to grow tired. He smiled weakly, frowned, opened his mouth as in silent joy, frowned, swallowed, said in *non sequitur.*

'And it is for this reason that it gives me pleasure to bestow on our fellow singing-bird here, er er Enderby, the Goodby gold medal.' Enderby rose to applause loud enough to drown three crackling intestinal reports. 'And a cheque,' said Sir George, with nostalgia of poet's poverty, 'that is very very small but, one trusts, will stave off pangs for a month or two.' Enderby took his trophies, shook hands, simpered, then sat down again. 'Speech,' said somebody. Enderby rose again, with a more subdued report, then realized that he was unsure of the exordial protocol. Did he say, 'Mr Chairman'? Was there a chairman? If Sir George was the chairman should he say something other than 'Mr Chairman'? Should he just say, 'Sir George, ladies and gentlemen'? But, he noticed, there seemed to be somebody with a chain of office gleaming on his chest, hovering in the dusk, a mayor or lord mayor. What should he say – 'Your Worship'? In time he saw that this was some sort of menial in charge of wine. Holding in wind, a nervously smiling Aeolus, Enderby said, loud and clear:

'St George.' There was a new stir of tittering. 'And the dragon,' Enderby now had to add. 'A British cymbal,' he continued, seeing with horror that orthographical howler in a sort of neon lights before him. 'A cymbal that tinkles in unsound brass if we are without clarity.' There were appreciative easings of buttocks and shoulders: Enderby was going to make it brief and humorous. Desperately Enderby said, 'As most of us are or are not, as the case may be. Myself included.' Sir George, he saw, was throwing up wide face-holes at him, as though he, Enderby, were on a girder above the street. 'Clarity,' said Enderby, almost in tears, 'is red wine for yodellers. And so,' he gaped aghast at himself, 'I am overjoyed to hand back this cheque to St George for charitable disposal. The gold medal he knows what he can do with.' He could have died with shock and embarrassment at what he was saying; he was hurled on to the end in killing momentum, however. 'Dross of the workaday world,' he said, 'as our fellow-singer Goodby so adequately disproves. And so,' he said, back in the Army giving a talk on the British Way and Purpose, 'we look forward to a time when the world shall be free of the shadow of oppression, the iron heel with its swastika spur no longer grinding into the face of prone freedom, democracy a reality, a fair day's pay for a fair day's work, adequate health services and a bit of peace hovering dovelike in the declining days of the aged. And in that belief and aspiration we move forward.' He found that he could not stop. 'Forward,' he insisted, 'to a time

when the world shall be free of the shadow of oppression.' Sir
George had risen and was tottering out. 'A fair day's work,' said
Enderby feebly, 'for a fair day's pay. Fair play for all,' he mumbled
doubtfully. Sir George had gone. 'And thereto,' ended Enderby
wretchedly, 'I plight thee my truth.'

The party broke up at once. Two men turned bitterly on Enderby.
'If,' said Shem Macnamara, 'you didn't want the bloody money you
might at least have remembered that there's others as do. Myself
included,' he mocked. He breathed, bafflingly, onions on Enderby,
for onions had not formed any part of the meal. 'I didn't mean it,'
said Enderby, near crying. 'I didn't know what I was saying.'
Enderby's publisher said, 'Want to ruin us you do?' in a sharp rising
intonation. He was a young bright man from Newport. 'Put your
foot in it you have bloody nicely, man, make no mistake about it.'
A small man moustached like Kipling, with the same beetle-
spectacles and a heavy watch-chain, came up to Enderby and took
him firmly by Arry's lapels. 'I'm Rawcliffe,' he announced. He
dragged Enderby away from the table in short dance-steps, lapels
still held hard. Rawcliffe nodded many times, stopped nodding,
cocked an ear, nodded in satisfaction, then just nodded, chewing.
'Very fibrous duck,' said Rawcliffe. 'You know me. I'm in all the
anthologies. Now then, Enderby, tell me, tell me in all sincerity
what you're doing at the present time.'

'Just writing, you know,' said Enderby. He was trying to think
who Rawcliffe was. Uneasily he heard behind him debates in small
groups on his speech and its consequences for the retail book trade.

'One would have supposed,' said Rawcliffe, tugging Arry's lapels
like cow-teats, 'mildly supposed, I suppose, that you would be
writing.' He chuckled, swallowed, and nodded. 'Now then, Enderby,
what? What are you writing? Tell me, elm,' he laughed. 'Tale told
of stem or stone, eh? James Joyce, that is. Myth-maker, what?'

'Well,' said Enderby, and, with babbling nerves, he blurted out
a detailed synopsis of *The Pet Beast*.

'And the beast is really Original Sin, eh?' saw Rawcliffe. 'Without
Original Sin there is no civilization, is that it? Good, good. And
the title, let's have that title again.' He released the lapels, found a
short pencil in a waistcoat pocket, licked the point, took out
a cigarette-packet, shook it ruefully, then block-lettered Enderby's

title on its bottom flap. 'Good,' he said again. 'Infinitely obleeged.'
And he made off nodding. Enderby sadly watched him join a group
of important poets who had not been above cynically taking a free
meal – P.S. ffolliott, Peter Pitts, Albert Death-Stabbes, Rupert Tombs,
or some such names. They had mostly murmured 'Well done' to
him at the preprandial sherry-bibbing. Now he was left alone with
his wind, companionless. Medalless also, and chequeless. Rather a
wasted trip, really.

2

'Mr Enderby?' The lady panted slightly and very prettily. 'Oh, thank
goodness I was in time.'

   'I knew,' said Enderby, 'that Sir George would realize it was all
a joke. Do, please, convey my apologies to him.'

   'Sir George? Oh yes, I know who you mean. Apologize? I
don't understand.' She was perhaps thirty, with fashionable
stallion-flared nostrils and a model-girl's swan-neck. She wore
with grace a Cardin sugar-scoop hat of beige velours, and, from
the same master, a loose-jacketed suit with only a hint of flare
to the peplum. An ocelot coat swung open over this. Chic shone
from her demurely. Such cleanness and fragrance (*Miss Dior*),
thought Enderby with deep regret, such slender and sheer-hosed
glamour. A face, he decided, devoid of all obvious sensuality
– no lusciousness of the underlip, the cat-green eyes very cool
and intelligent, a calm high forehead shaded by the sugar-scoop
brim. Enderby tightened his tie-knot and smoothed his side-
pockets, saying: 'I'm sorry.' And then, 'I thought. That is to say.'
She said:

   'Oh.' They stood looking at each other under the glowing glass-
slab signs of the hotel passage, their feet sunk in burgundy carpet.
'Well. I would like, before anything else, to tell you that I genuinely
admire your work.' She spoke with the intonation of one expecting
an incredulous snort. The voice was quiet, though the consonants
had the sharpness of some speaker too close to a microphone, and
there was the faintest tang of educated Scots. 'I wrote to you care
of your publishers, ages ago. I don't think the letter could ever

have reached you. If it had reached you I'm sure you would have replied.'

'Yes,' said flustered Enderby. 'Oh yes, I would. But perhaps that was forwarded by them to my old address because I'd forgotten to tell them about my new address and also, for that matter, the Post Office. Cheques,' said blabbing Enderby, 'are normally paid straight into my bank. I don't know why I'm telling you all this.' She stood in a model pose, listening coolly with lips parted, handbag hanging from right forearm, gloved left hand's thumb and index-finger lightly ringing ungloved right hand's ring-finger. 'I'm terribly sorry,' said humble Enderby. 'That may explain why I never got it.'

She finished her quiet listening and suddenly became brisk. 'Look,' she said, 'I had an invitation to that luncheon-party but I couldn't make it. Could we, do you think,' she suggested, with a kind of movement on the fringe of non-movement which was a sort of apotheosis of a working-girl's jigging up and down in a winter-day bus-queue, infinitely feminine, 'sit down somewhere for a few minutes, if you can spare the time, that is? Oh,' she said, 'I'm so stupid,' the gloved hand striking the lips in *mea culpa*, 'not telling you who I am. I'm Vesta Bainbridge. From *Fem*.'

'From what?'

'*Fem*.'

'What,' asked Enderby, with great and suspicious care, 'is that?' He had heard it as, though hardly believing it possible, something like *Phlegm*, and wondered what could be the purpose of an organization (if it was an organization) so named.

'Yes, of course, I see, of course you probably wouldn't know about that, would you? It's a magazine for women. And I,' said Vesta Bainbridge, 'am the Features Editress. Could we then, do you think? I suppose it's too early to have tea, isn't it, or is it?'

'If you would care for some tea,' said gallant Enderby, 'I should be only too happy, I should be only too delighted.'

'Oh, no,' said Vesta Bainbridge, 'you have to have it with me, you see, because it goes on my expense account. And this is a business thing, you see, connected with *Fem*.'

Enderby had once, as a poor soldier, been treated to a tea of poached egg on haddock and shortbread by a kind old lady in an Edinburgh restaurant. But by anyone so glamorous, so alluring as this, he had never thought, never dreamed. He was both shocked and awed. 'Do you, by any chance, come from Edinburgh?' he asked. 'Something in your voice –'

'Eskbank,' said Vesta Bainbridge. 'How remarkable! But, of course, you're a poet. Poets can always dig out things like that, can't they?'

'If,' said Enderby, 'you really like my poetry, which you said you did, I should really ask you to have tea with me, not you me with you. The least I could do,' said generous Enderby, fingering a half-crown in Arry's trouser-pocket.

'Come,' said Vesta Bainbridge, and she made the wraith of a gesture of taking Enderby by the arm. 'I *do* admire your work, really,' she insisted. She led him on sure high heels past the dainty boutiques that sold flowers and jewellery, the air-travel kiosk where there was busy telephoning about flights to New York and Bermuda, past the ugly and rich cocooned in an enchantment of wine-coloured snow underfoot, perfumed air all about, light drifting, dust-soft, from unseen sources in the delicate golds of fine white bordeaux. Here every breath, every footfall, thought thrifty Enderby, must cost at least a tanner. Vesta Bainbridge and he entered a vast room of huge scooped cubes of biscuit-coloured softness in which people lounged warmly cushioned. Laughter tinkled, teatrays tinkled. Enderby felt with horror his bowels prepare to comment on the scene. He looked up at a baroque ceiling with many fat-arsed cherubim in evidence. This did not help. They sank down, Vesta Bainbridge exhibiting the delicacy of exquisite shinlines, a fine moulding of ankle. A Roman waiter, lantern-jawed, took her order. Scots, she asked for a substantial spread: anchovy toast, egg sandwiches, pikelets, cakes, China tea with lemon. 'And,' said Enderby, 'do you manage to eat dinner after a tea like that?'

'Oh, yes,' said Vesta Bainbridge. 'I can't put on weight, however hard I try. The lemon tea's because that's the way I like tea, not for slimming reasons. Obviously,' she added.

'But,' said Enderby, drawn to the obvious weary compliment, 'you're surely perfect as you are.' Suddenly he saw himself, boulevardier Enderby, witty with women, graceful in flattery, roguish eyes atwinkle, taking tea. At the same time wind fought, as a picked-up naughty kitten fights, to be free. Tea free. A free tea. 'And,' he said, 'if I may ask, what precisely is this business with *Phlegm*?'

'Oh,' she said, 'isn't that funny? That's what Godfrey Wainwright calls it. He does covers, you know. *Fem*. Not, perhaps, a very good choice of name. But, you know, the market's saturated with magazines for women – *Feminocrat, Goodwife, Lilith, Glamourpuss*. The straightforward names with Woman in them were worked out long ago. It's so difficult for them to think of anything new, as you'll appreciate. But *Fem* isn't too bad, is it? It's short and sweet, and it sounds Frenchified and a bit naughty, wouldn't you agree?'

Enderby eyed her warily. Frenchified and a bit naughty, eh? 'Yes,' he said. 'And where would I come in with something like that?' Not very good, she'd said, and not too bad – both in the same breath. Perhaps not a very sincere sort of woman. Before she could answer his question the tea arrived. The Roman waiter laid it down gently on the fretted claw-footed low table – silver dishcovers steaming, tiny cakes oozing cream. He rose, bowing with sneering jowls, retiring. Vesta Bainbridge poured. She said:

'I thought somehow you'd prefer your tea like this – sugarless, milkless, lemony. Your poems are a little, shall we say, astringent, if that's the right word.' Enderby looked down sourly at the sour cup. He preferred stepmother's tea really, but she'd ordered without consulting him. 'Very nice,' he said. 'Just right.' Vesta Bainbridge began to eat with great appetite, showing fine small teeth as she bit into her anchovy toast. Enderby's heart warmed to this: he liked to see women eat, and this gusto mitigated, somehow, her lean perfection. But, he thought, she had no right, with such a figure, to have such an appetite. He felt a desire to invite her out to dinner, that same evening, to see how she would tuck into minestrone and pork chops. He feared her.

'Now,' said Vesta Bainbridge, and a rosy tongue-point darted out, picked up a toast-crumb, then darted in again. 'I want you to know that I admire your work, and what I propose now is entirely my own idea. It's met with some opposition, mind you, because *Fem* is essentially a popular magazine. And your poetry, as you'll be proud to admit, is not exactly popular. It's not unpopular either, of course; it's just not known. Pop-singers are known and TV interviewers are known and disc-jockeys are known, but you're not known.'

'What,' asked Enderby, 'are these things? Pop-singers and so on?' She looked askance at him and noticed that his bewilderment was genuine. 'I'm afraid,' said Enderby, 'that since the war I've rather shut myself off from things.'

'Don't you have a radio or a television set?' said Vesta Bainbridge, her green eyes wide. He shook his head. 'Don't you read newspapers?'

'I used to read certain Sunday papers,' said Enderby, 'for the sake of the book reviews. But it made me so very depressed that I had to stop. The reviewers seemed so,' he frowned, 'so very *big*, if you see what I mean. They seemed to *enclose* us writers, so to speak. They seemed to know all about us, and we knew nothing about them. There was one very kind and very knowledgeable review of a volume of mine, I remember, by a man who, I suppose, is a very good man, but it was evident that he could have written my poems so much better if only he'd had the time. Those things make one feel very insignificant. Oh, I know one *is* insignificant, really, but you've got to ignore that if you're to get any work done at all. And so I've tended to cut myself off a bit, for the sake of the work. Everybody seems to be so *clever*, somehow, if you see what I mean.'

'I do and I don't,' said Vesta Bainbridge, smartly. So far she had eaten all the anchovy toast, five egg sandwiches, a couple of pikelets and one squelchy little pastry, and yet contrived to look ethereal, mountain-cool. Enderby, on the other hand, who, because of his heartburn, had only nibbled mouse-like at a square inch of damp bread and an egg-ring, was aware of himself as gross, sweating, halitotic, his viscera loaded like a nightsoil-collector's bucket. '*I* don't feel insignificant,' said Vesta Bainbridge, and 'I'm just nothing compared with you.'

'But you don't *have* to feel insignificant, do you?' said Enderby. 'I mean, you've only to look at yourself, haven't you?' He said this dispassionately, frowning.

'For a man,' said Vesta Bainbridge, 'who's cut himself from the world, you're not doing too badly. I should have thought,' she said, pouring more tea, 'that it was very unwise for a poet to do that. After all, you need images, themes, and so on, don't you? You've got to get those from the outside world.'

'There are quite enough images,' said Enderby, speaking with firm authority, 'in half a pound of New Zealand cheddar. Or in the washing-up water. Or,' he added, with even greater authority, 'in a new toilet-roll.'

'You poor man,' said Vesta Bainbridge. 'Is that how you live?'

'Everybody,' said Enderby, with perhaps diminishing dogmatism, 'uses toilet-paper.' A man in spectacles, very tall and with an open mouth, looked across from his chair as if to dispute this assertion, thought better of it, then returned to his evening paper. *Poet Refuses Medal*, said a tiny headline which Enderby caught sight of. Some other bloody fool shooting his mouth off, some other toy trumpet singing to battle.

'Anyway,' said Vesta Bainbridge, 'I think it would be an excellent thing for you to have a wider audience. Would you try it for, say, six months, a poem every week? Preferably set in the form of prose, so as not to offend anyone.'

'I thought people didn't actually find verse *offensive*,' said Enderby. 'I thought they just despised it.'

'Be that as it may,' said Vesta Bainbridge, 'what do you say to the proposal?' She shattered a sort of macaroon with a fork and, before eating, said, 'The poems would have to be, shall I say, and I hope this is the right word, ephemeral. You know, dealing with everyday things that the average woman would be interested in.'

'The dross of the workaday world,' said Enderby, 'transmuted to sheerest gold. I suppose I could do that. I know all about household chores and dishcloths and so on. Also lavatory brushes.'

'Dear me,' said Vesta Bainbridge, 'you *have* got a cloacal obsession, haven't you? No, not that sort of thing, and not too much of this sheerest gold, either. Womankind cannot bear very much reality. Love and dreams are wanted, also babies without cloacal obsessions. The mystery of the stars would come in quite nicely, especially if seen from the garden of a council-house. And marriage, perhaps.'

'Tell me,' said Enderby. 'Are you Miss Cambridge or Mrs?'

'Bainbridge, not Cambridge. *Fem*, not *Phlegm*. Mrs. Why do you want to know?'

'I have to call you something,' said Enderby, 'don't I?' She seemed at last to have finished her meal, so Enderby offered his crumpled cigarette-packet.

'I'll smoke my own,' she said, 'if you don't mind.' She took from her handbag a packet of ship's Woodbines and, before Enderby could find an unused match in his matchbox (he saved used matches, a long unfathomable habit), she had flicked her pearl-faced lighter on and then off. Her wide nostrils walrussed out two pretty blue jets.

'I take it,' said Enderby, 'that your husband's in the navy.'

'My husband,' she said, 'is dead. It shows how cut off you are, really, doesn't it? Everybody else seems to have heard of Pete Bainbridge.'

'I'm sorry,' said Enderby. 'Very sorry.'

'What for? Because he's dead, or because you've never heard of him? Never mind,' said Widow Bainbridge. 'He died in a smash four years ago, in the Monte Carlo Rally. I thought everybody knew that. It was a great loss, the papers said, to the motor-racing world. He left behind a beautiful young widow, a bride of only two years,' she said, her tone half-mocking.

'He did,' said Enderby gravely. 'He most certainly did. Beautiful, I mean. How much?'

'How much what? How much did he leave, or how much did I love him?' She seemed suddenly tired, perhaps from over-eating.

'How much do I get for doing these poems?'

'Mr Dick sets us all right,' said Vesta Bainbridge, sighing and sitting up straighter. She brushed minimal crumbs off her lap and said, 'Two guineas a poem. It's not much, but we can't manage more. We're featuring the memoirs of a pop-singer, you see – not very long memoirs, of course, because he's only nineteen – but those are costing us a pretty penny, believe me. And the memoirs have to be written for him as well. Still, the effect on the circulation should be, to say the least, stimulating. If that princely fee is all right by you I'll send you a contract. And some back numbers of *Fem*, to show you what it's like. Please remember that the vocabulary of our readers isn't very extensive, so don't go using words like 'oriflamme' or 'inelectable'.'

'Thank you,' said Enderby. 'I'm really most grateful that you should have thought of me like this. You're really being most kind.' He had been poking into the ashtray with a matchstick, breaking up cigarette-ends; this had necessitated a sort of crouching on the chair's edge, his bald crown presented to Mrs Bainbridge. Now he looked up sincerely, his eyes rather wet behind their glasses. She smiled.

'Look,' she said, 'you don't believe me about my liking your poetry, do you? Well, I even know one or two of them by heart.'

'Say one,' begged Enderby. She took breath and recited, quite clearly but with few nuances of tone:

> 'A dream, yes, but for everyone the same.
>   The thought that wove it never dropped a stitch;
>   The Absolute was anybody's pitch
> For, when a note was struck, we knew its name'.

'Good,' said Enderby. 'This is the first time I've ever actually heard –'

> '– That dark aborted any urge to tame
>   Waters that day might prove to be a ditch
>   But then were endless growling ocean, rich
> In fish and heroes, till the dredgers came.'

'Excellent,' said Enderby. 'And now the sestet.' It excited him to hear his own verses. She went on confidently:

> '*Wachet auf!* A fretful dunghill cock
>   Flinted the noisy beacons through the shires;
> A martin's nest clogged the cathedral clock,
>   But it was morning (birds could not be liars).
> A key cleft rusty age in lock and lock;
>   Men shivered by a hundred kitchen fires.

There,' she said, taking breath. 'But I've no real idea what it means.'

'Oh,' said Enderby, 'the meaning doesn't matter all that much. I'm surprised at your liking that. It's not what I'd thought of as a woman's poem.' Suddenly the poem seemed to find its place in the real world – overseas businessmen reading financial papers, the

scent of *Miss Dior* or whatever it was, the noise of London waiting
to pounce outside the hotel. Spoken by her, it seemed suddenly
to have a use.

'And what exactly do you mean by a woman's poem?' asked
Mrs Bainbridge.

'For you,' said Enderby with disarming candour, 'something
softer and yet more elegant, something with less harshness and
thought and history in it. That, you see, is about the Middle Ages
and the coming of the Reformation. In the sestet you get Martin
Luther and the beginning of dissolution, everybody beginning to
be alone, a common tradition providing no tuning-fork of reference and no way of telling the time, because the common tradition
has been dredged away. Nothing sure and nothing mysterious.'

'I see,' said Vesta Bainbridge. 'I take it you're a Catholic, then.'

'Oh, no, no,' protested Enderby. 'I'm not, really I'm not.'

'All right,' said Vesta Bainbridge, smiling. 'I heard you the first time.'
Protestant Enderby grinned and shut up. The Roman waiter came
along, chewing gently but mournfully, with a bill. 'For me,' she said,
and notes rustled in her bag like pork crackling. She paid the bill
and, womanly, tipped the waiter merely adequately. Enderby said:

'I'd ask you to dine with me this evening, but I've just realized
that I didn't bring very much money. I expected, you see, that I'd
go straight back after lunch. I'm awfully sorry.'

'Don't be,' smiled Vesta Bainbridge. 'I'm invited out. Somewhere in
Hampstead. But it was nice of you to offer. Now,' she said, looking
at her tiny oyster watch, 'goodness, the time, where do I write to?'
She took out a small notebook and poised a pencil to record what
Enderby dictated. Somehow, the address seemed vulgar and even comic,
endited primly by that slim hand. 81 Fitzherbert Avenue. He tried to
hide from her the sound of the lavatory's flush, the crusted milk-bottles
on the doorstep, the mice scampering through the manuscripts. 'Good,'
she said, closing the book. 'Now I must go.' She settled the ocelot
over her shoulders, clipped her bag shut. Enderby stood. She stood.
'It's been awfully nice,' she said. 'Oh, that's inadequate. But it's been
quite a privilege, really it has. Now I really must fly.' She gave him an
unexpected handshake, straight from the elbow. 'Don't bother to come
to the door,' she said. Then she was off, trimly and swiftly walking a
tightrope across the carpet. For the first time Enderby caught a hint

of colour of her hair, upswept at the nape, a sort of penny-colour. He sighed, and turned to see the waiter looking at him. The waiter made a gesture – quick frogmouth, shrug – to indicate (a) that she was certainly elegant but much too thin, (b) that she was off to meet somebody handsomer than Enderby, (c) that women were fundamentally ungenerous, (d) that this was a hell of a life but there were always the consolations of philosophy. Enderby nodded, the poet at ease with all classes of men, then realized with joy that he was once more alone and free. The wind that blew through him celebrated this fact.

3

Enderby was late returning home that evening. Though his perversely independent soul – the conscious Enderby shocked and gaping – had rejected the sweets of recognition, he felt that he and London had achieved more of a *rapprochement* than he could have thought possible, scratching paper and bared legs, the day before. A smart and worldly woman admired his work and had said so frankly. Lips that had been kissed by a prominent racing-driver and, Enderby presumed, by others whose teeth habitually gleamed at cameras, had recited from the *Revolutionary Sonnets* in a rich-smelling place whose denizens had passed beyond the need for the solace of poetry. Enderby, wandering the streets, was restless and had an obscure longing for adventure. Here the snow had long disappeared, but the tang of snow on the air bit sharply from the furthermost stretch of the river. London yearned back to gasflares and geese sold cheap at the end of the trading day amid raucous Cockney voices, Sherlock Holmes in Baker Street, a widow at Windsor, all's right with the world. That was from *Pappa Pisses*. Enderby grinned sadly to himself, standing outside a music-shop, as he remembered the disastrous lecture he had once given to a Women's Institute. Victorian Literature. That was one spoonerism that his audience had passed over. But *A Sale of Two Titties* had struck Lady Fennimore as something like calculated insolence. Never again. Never, never again. He was safer in retirement, shut away in his creative lavatory. But still, this one evening, the desire for adventure was strong. Yet what did one mean by adventure these days? He gazed at the shop-window, as if for an answer. Various pictures of young louts sneered out at him from song-covers and record-sleeves − simian-foreheaded, prehensile fingers on guitar-strings, lips twisted in a song of youth. Enderby had heard of secondary modern schools and now assumed that these flat-eyed little monsters must represent their end-product. Well, for two guineas a week he was going to serve the world that these loose-lipped leerers served. What was the name of the magazine again? *Flim* or *Flam* or something. Not *Phlegm*, that was quite certain. Within the consonantal frame he tried out various vowels. And there, next door but one, outside one of Sir George Goodby's own shops, a poster put him right: 'Exclusive to *Fem*, FOR YOU, Lenny Biggs tells his own personal life story. Order your copy NOW.' And there was a picture of Lenny Biggs − a face hardly distinguishable from others of the pantheon Enderby had just viewed, though perhaps more particularly baboon-like than generally simian, with teeth as manifestly false as those of Enderby himself, sniggering with confidence at the world.

Enderby saw a man in a peaked cap dump a couple of parcels in a van lettered GOODBY'S FOR GOOD BOOKS. This van then started up contemptuously and insolently pierced the traffic. 'So,' thought Enderby, 'Sir George has already started his reprisals, has he? All copies of Enderby's poems to be withdrawn from sale, eh? Petty, a very petty-minded man.' Enderby entered the shop and was depressed to see people buying gardening books. Display studio-portraits of groomed youthful bestsellers topped piles of their bestselling novels. Enderby felt that he wanted to flee; this was as bad as reading Sunday reviews. And, to brim his misery, he realized that he had maligned Sir George: two soiled Enderby volumes sulked there on the unvisited poetry shelves. He was beneath the notice of that wealthy knight, too mean for the meanness of retaliation. Oh, well. The name Rawcliffe suddenly hurled itself, along with a pang of dyspepsia, at Enderby's breastbone. In all the anthologies, did he say? Enderby would see.

Enderby looked through *Poetry Now, A Tiny Garner of Modern Verse, Best Poets of Today, They Sing for You, Soldier's Solace* (an anthology of verse by Lieutenant-General Phipps, v.c., d.s.o., etc., sixtieth thousand), *Voices Within*, and other volumes, and found that

in all of them Rawcliffe was represented by the following artless
lyrics:

> 'Perhaps I am not wanted then,' he said.
> 'Perhaps I'd better go,'
> He said. Motionless her eyes, her head,
> Saying not yes, not no.
>
> 'I will go then, and aim my gun of grief
> At any man's or country's enemies.'
> He said. 'Slaughter will wreak a red relief.'
> She said not no, not yes.
>
> And so he went to marry mud and toil,
> Swallow in general hell his private hell.
> His salts have long drained into alien soil,
> And she says nothing still.

Enderby looked up bitterly from the tenth selected anthology, his
tenth reading of the poem. And in none of these books was there
anything by Enderby.

Enderby pulled out a spilling palmful of coin from Arry's right
trouser-pocket. Snorting, he counted it: twelve and ninepence. In his
wallet there was, he knew, one pound note. He muttered to himself
as he moved doorwards, head down to count again. He bumped into
a young salesman who said, 'Whoops, sir. See nothing you fancy, sir?'

'Books,' said Enderby, with proleptic drunken thickness. 'Waste
of time and bloody money.' He left, saying a soldier's goodbye to
Goodby's, not one of Goodby's good boys. There was a pub almost
directly opposite, shedding cosy Christmas-card lights through its
old-time bottle-glass windows. Enderby entered the public bar and
ordered whisky.

4

Enderby entered the public bar and ordered whisky. This was some
hours later, a different pub. Not the second or third pub, but

somewhere well on in the series, the xth pub or something. On the whole, benevolent and swaying Enderby decided, he had had not too bad an evening. He had met two very fat Nigerians with wide cunning smiles and many blackheads. These had cordially invited him to their country and to write an epic to celebrate its independence. He had met a Guinness-drinker with a wooden leg which, for the delectation of Enderby, he had offered to unscrew. He had met a chief petty officer of the Royal Navy who, in the friendliest spirit in the world, had been prepared to fight Enderby and, when Enderby had demurred, had given him two packets of ship's Woodbines and said that Enderby was his pal. He had met a Siamese osteopath with a collection of fighting fish. He had met a punch-drunk bruiser who said he saw visions and offered to see one then for a pint. He had met a little aggressive chinny chewing man, not unlike Rawcliffe, who swore that Shakespeare's plays had been written by Sir William Knollys, Controller of the Queen's Household. He had met a cobbler who knew the Old Testament in Hebrew, an amateur exegetist who distrusted all Biblical scholarship after 1890. He had met, seen, or heard many others too: a thin woman who had talked incessantly to a loll-tongued Alsatian; a man with the shakes who swallowed his own phlegm (*Fem*, *Fem*, remember that, *Fem*); a pair of hand-holding lesbians; a man who wore flower transfers on a surgical boot; callow soldiers drinking raw gin . . . Now it was nearing closing-time and Enderby was, he thought, fairly near to Charing Cross. That meant two stops on the Underground to Victoria. There must be a nice convenient after-closing-time train to the coast.

Enderby, paying fumblingly for his whisky, saw that he had very little money left. He estimated that he had managed to consume this evening a good dozen whiskies and a draught beer or so. His return ticket was snug in Arry's left-hand inside jacket-pocket. He had cigarettes. One more drink and he would be right for home. He looked round the public bar smiling. Good honest British working-men, salt of the earth, bloodying and buggering their meagre dole of speech, horny-handed but delicate with darts. And, on a high-backed settle at right angles to the bar counter, two British working-women sat, made placid with the fumes of stout. One said:

'Starting next week, it is, in *Fem*. With free gift picture in full colour. Smashing, he is.' Enderby listened jealously. The other woman said:

'Never take it, myself. Silly sort of name it is. Makes you wonder how they think of them sometimes, really it does.'

'If,' said Enderby, 'you are referring to the magazine to which I myself am to be a contributor, I would say that that name is meant to be Frenchified and naughty.' He smiled down at them with a whiskified smirk, right elbow on the counter, left fingers on right forearm. The two women looked up doubtfully. They were probably about the same age as Vesta Bainbridge, but they had an aura of back kitchens about them, tea served to shirt-sleeved men doing their pools, the telly flicking and shouting in the corner.

'Pardon?' said one, loudly.

'Naughty,' said Enderby, with great clarity. 'Frenchified.'

'What's French frieds to do with it?' said the other. 'My friend and me was just talking, do you mind?'

'Poetry is what I shall write for it,' said Enderby, 'every week.' He nodded several times, just like Rawcliffe.

'You keep your poetry to yourself, do you mind?' and she took a sharp draught of Guinness. A man came from the dart-playing part of the room, a single dart in his hand, saying:

'You all right, Edie?' He wore a decently cut suit of poor serge, but no collar or tie. His gold-headed collar-stud caught the light and dazzled Enderby. He had a gaunt quick face and was as small and supple as a miner. He inspected Enderby as if invited to give an estimate on him. 'You saying something to her that you shouldn't?' he said. 'Mate?' he added, provocatively.

'He was saying,' said Edie, 'about naughty poetry. French, too.'

'Was you saying naughty poetry to my wife here?' said the man. Like Milton's Death, he shook a dreadful dart.

'I was just saying,' said smirking Enderby, 'that I was going to write for it. What they read, I mean. That is to say, Edie here, your wife, as I take it to be, doesn't read, but the other one does, you see.'

'We'll have less of that about doesn't read, do you mind?' said Edie. 'And less of using my name familiar, do you mind?'

'Look here,' said Edie's husband. 'You want to keep that for the saloon bar, where they pay a penny extra for the privilege, do you mind? We don't want your sort in here.'

'Doing no harm,' said Enderby huffily. He then poured over the huff a trickle of sweet sauce of ingratiation. 'I mean, I was just talking.' He leered. 'Just passing the time of day, if you see what I mean.'

'Well,' said the dart-man, 'don't you try to pass the time with my missis, do you mind?'

'Do you mind?' said Edie, in near-unison.

'I wouldn't want to pass the time with her,' said Enderby, proudly, 'I've other things to do, thank you very much.'

'I'll have to do you,' said the man, sincerely. 'Too much bloody hoot altogether, mate, to my way of thinking, that's what you've got. You'd better get out of here before I get really nasty. Been smelling the barmaid's apron, that's your trouble.'

Prrrffffp.

'Look,' said Enderby, 'that wasn't intended, I really had no intention, that was not meant in any way to be a comment, I assure you that is the sort of thing that could happen to any man, or woman too, for that matter, even Edie here, your wife, that is to say, yourself included.' Prrrffffp.

'Do you mind?' said Edie.

'This here's my fist,' said the man, pocketing his dart. The other customers quietened and looked interested. 'You'll get it straight in the moosh, straight up you will, if you don't get out of my bleeding sight this instant, do you mind?'

'I was just going anyway,' said dignified swaying Enderby. 'If you will allow me the privilege of finishing my drink here.'

'You've had enough, you have, mate,' said the man, more kindly. From the saloon bar came the call of 'Last orders.' 'If you want to drown your secret sorrows don't do it where me and my wife is, see, because I take the sort of thing that you've been saying very hard, see.' Enderby put down his glass, gave the dart-man a glassy but straight look, then eructed strongly and without malice. He bowed and, pushing his way courteously through the long-swallowers anxious to get one last one in, made an exit that was not without dignity. Outside in the street the heady air of a Guinness-sharp refrigerated night hit him and he staggered. The dartman had followed him out and stood there, gauging and weighing. 'Look, mate,' he said, 'this is not for me really, because

I've been like that myself often enough, God knows, but my wife insists, do you mind, and this is like for a keepsake.' He bowed, and while bowing swerved his torso suddenly to the left as though listening to something from that side, then he brought left fist and torso right and up and let Enderby have one, not too hard, straight in the stomach. 'There,' he said, somewhat kindly, as if the blow had been intended purely therapeutically. 'That'll do, won't it?'

Enderby gasped. The procession of the evening's whiskies and beers passed painfully through a new taste-organ that had been erected specially for this occasion. They grimaced in pain, making painful obeisance as they passed. Gas and fire shot up as from a geyser, smiting rudely the crystalline air. Premonitions of the desire to vomit huddled and fluttered. Enderby went to the wall. 'Now then,' said the man, 'where is it you want to go, eh? Kennington you are now, see, if you didn't know.'

'Victoria,' said Enderby's stomach-gas, shaped into a word by tongue and lips. He had, at the moment, no air.

'Easy,' said the kind man. 'First to the right second to the left keep straight on brings you to Kennington Station, see. Get a train to Charing Cross, that's the second stop, Waterloo's the first, change at Charing Cross, see, Circle Line. Westminster St James's Park and then you're there, see. And the very best of luck and no hard feelings.' He patted Enderby's left shoulder and re-entered the public bar.

Enderby still gasped. This sort of thing had not happened since his student-days when he had once been beaten up by a pub pianist and his friend for being bloody sarky about the sort of pseudo-music the pub pianist had been playing. Enderby filled his coughing lungs in draught after draught, then wondered whether he really wanted to vomit. He thought, for the moment, not. The punch in the stomach still glowed and smouldered, and the name LONDON fluttered in fearful flames, a warning, as in the trailer of some film about call-girls or the end of the world. He saw himself safe in his own lavatory, at work on his poems. Never again. Never never again. Women's Institutes. Gold medals. London pubs. Traps set for poor Enderby, gins waiting for him to trip.

He reached Kennington Station without much difficulty and

booked to Victoria. In the train, sitting opposite a cross-eyed man who spoke Scots to a complacent terrier on his knee, Enderby felt a shipboard motion and knew that soon he must dash to the rails. Further along on the side where he was sitting, he had the illusion that a couple of gum-chewing teenagers were discussing a play by Calderón. He strained to listen and nearly fell on his right ear. At Waterloo he was sure that the Scotsman with strabismus said '*morne plaine*' to his dog. A drum beat and a bugle brayed in Enderby's stomach; here, perhaps, he must admit defeat, stagger off, be sick in a fire-bucket. Too late. The train and time marched on from Waterloo, under the river, and, thank God, there was Charing Cross. The charing-cross-eyed man got out here too, with terrier. 'A drop taken,' he said confidentially to Enderby and then marched off to the Bakerloo Line, dog trotting with twinkletoes behind, fat rump, joyous tail. Enderby now felt decidedly unwell and bewildered. He had a confused notion that the southbound platform of this Northern Line would take him whither he wanted. He staggered over and sat on a bench. Across the rail a poster showed an outdoor man draining a milk stout, his fine muscular throat corded with stout-drinker's strength. Next to that was a colourwash sketch, vivid with steam and laughter, of a confident young man wrestling with a delightful girl for a portion of pie made with meat-extract. Next to that a ginger child, macrocephalic, went 'Ooooo!' with pleasure, his cheek gumboiled with a slab of extra-creamy toffee. Enderby retched, but memory saved him with four lines of a drinker's poem he had written in his drunken youth:

> And I have walked no way I looked
> And multitudinously puked
> Into the gutter, legs outstretched,
> Holding my head low as I . . .

That threw his present queasiness back into the past and also depersonalized it. The solace of art. And now the distant Minotaur roar of the tube-train alerted the others waiting on that platform. One man folded his evening paper and stuck it into the side-pocket of his greatcoat. *Poet Speaks Out for Fair Play*, read Enderby. Field-day for poets, this. The tube-train slammed itself into the clearing, bringing a fine gale of Arctic air which did Enderby good. He stood and felt giddy but steeled himself to travel to Victoria, seeing that, in his muzzy state, as a very large and desirable lavatory of blasts and sulphuretted hydrogen. He straddled before a not-yet-opened double-door of the train, trying to hold the unquiet platform steady, while the passengers waiting to alight stood as though for a curtain call. Then a panic of doubt clouted Enderby as the doors slid open and the alighters flooded off. 'Is this,' he called, 'all right for Victoria?' Many of the emergent did not speak English and made apologetic gestures, but a cool woman's voice said:

'This, Mr Enderby, is most certainly not all right for Victoria.' Enderby blinked at this apparition, Mrs What's-her-name of *Fem*, racing ace's widow, in semi-formal pale apple-green taffetas, sheathed at the front, and three-quarter-length Persian lamb jacket, marcasite clip as single fine dress-embellisher, tiny hoop ear-rings of marcasite, marcasite-coloured glacé kid high-heels, penny-coloured hair cleanly glowing. Enderby's mouth opened sheepishly. 'If you got this train,' she said, 'you would be travelling to Waterloo and Kennington, Tooting Bec, ultimately Morden. From the look of you, you would probably be awakened at Morden. You wouldn't like Morden very much.'

'You,' said Enderby, 'should not be here. You should be at dinner somewhere.'

'I *was* at dinner,' she said. 'I've just come back from Hampstead.' The train-doors slid together and the train moved off into its tunnel, its wind stirring her hair and making her raise her voice, so that the Scots intonation became clearer than before. 'And,' she said, her sober green eyes appraising swaying Enderby, 'I'm on my way home to Gloucester Road. Which means we can take the same train and I can make quite sure that you alight at Victoria. From Victoria on you must be commended to the protection of whatever gods look after drunken poets.' She had in her something of the thin-lipped Calvinist; in her tone was no element of amused indulgence. 'Come,' she said, and she took Enderby's arm.

'If you don't mind,' said Enderby. 'If you'll excuse me just a moment –' Green looked at green. Enderby managed to trap the brief flow in his show handkerchief. 'Oh, God,' he said. 'Oh, Jesus, Mary and Joseph.'

'Come on,' she said. 'Walk. Take deep breaths.' She led him firmly towards the Circle Line. 'You are in a bad way, aren't you?' All her perfume could not sweeten Enderby's shame.

5

Enderby was back in 81 Fitzherbert Avenue, thoroughly sobered at last by two slips on to his bottom on the frozen way from the station. On that same sore bottom he sat on the stairs, crying. This flight ran up, starting at the side of Enderby's flat's front door, to a landing with mirror and potted palm. Then came a dark and sinister stairway, uncarpeted, to the flat above, the home of the salesman and his woman. Enderby sat crying because he had forgotten his key. He had neglected, perhaps because flustered by Mrs Meldrum's visit that morning, to transfer the key from his sports-coat pocket to the corresponding pocket of the jacket of Arry's suit. It was now after one in the morning, too late to call on Mrs Meldrum to open up for him with her master. He had no money for a hotel room; it was too cold to sleep in a shelter on the esplanade; he did not fancy begging a cell at the police station (there were criminal-looking coppers there, with wide-boy tashes). It was best to sit here on the third step up, overcoated and muffled, crying and smoking alternately.

Not that he had much left to smoke. Mrs Whatever-her-name-was of *Fem* had taken his remaining packet of ship's Woodbines (she was out of them and smoked nothing else) as a reward for her stoic Scots toleration of his wanting to be sick on the deck of the train all the way to Victoria. Enderby had five Senior Service to last him till the late winter dawn. He cried. He was weary, far beyond sleepiness. It had been a long and eventful day, excruciatingly attritive. Even on his homeward coastward train journey the entire coach had seemed to be full of wet-mouthed Irishmen singing. And now the cold stair, the long vigil. He howled like a moon-bemused hound-dog.

The door of the flat above opened creakily. 'Is that you, Jack?'

whispered the woman's voice, huskily. 'Have you come back, Jack?' Her vowels were not unlike Arry's: uvyer coom buck juck. 'I'm sorry, Jack,' she said. 'I didn't mean what I said, love. Come on to bed, Jack.'

'It's me,' said Enderby. 'Not him. Me. Without a key,' he added.

'Who are you?' asked the woman. The bulb of the landing light had long burnt out, months ago, unreplaced by Mrs Meldrum. Neither could see the other.

'Him from downstairs,' said Enderby, falling easily into demotic. 'Not him as you live with.'

'He's gone off,' came the voice down the stair-well. 'He's always said he would and now he's done it. We had a bit of a barney.'

'That's right,' said Enderby.

'What do you mean that's right? We had a bit of a barney and now he's gone off. I bet he's gone to that bitch down by the Ornamental Gardens.'

'Never mind,' said Enderby. 'He'll come back. They always do.'

'He won't. Not tonight he won't. And I'm frightened up here on my own.'

'What are you frightened of?'

'Of being on my own. Like I said. In the dark, too. It went out while we was having this barney and I couldn't see to hit him. Have you got a bob you can let me have till first thing tomorrow morning?'

'Not a sausage,' said Enderby proudly. 'I blued it all on booze in town. I think I'd better come up there,' he added, bold. 'I could sleep on the couch or something. I forgot my key, you see. It's a damn nuisance.'

'If you come up here you'd better not let Jack get hold of you.'

'Jack's gone off with this bitch down by the Ornamental Gardens,' said Enderby.

'Ah. So you seen him, did you? I thought as much. You can see the black at her roots, bitch as she is.'

'I'm coming up now,' said Enderby. 'Then you won't be frightened of being on your own. You've got a couch up there, have you?' said Enderby, rising in pain and crawling up the stairs.

'If you think you're going to get in bed with me you've got another think coming. I've finished with all men.'

'I've no intention of getting into bed with you,' said indignant Enderby. 'I just want to lie down on the couch. I don't really feel all that good.'

'You needn't be so bloody well on your bloody high horse. I've been in bed with better men than what you'll ever hope to be. Careful,' she said, as Enderby kicked the metal pot of the palm on the landing. He clambered blind up the second flight, hugging the banister. At the top he collided with a warm bosomy shape. 'You can cut that out for a start,' she said. 'A bit too forward you are for a start.' She sniffed briskly. 'That scent's very expensive,' she said. 'Who you been with, eh? Still waters run deep, if you're really who you say you are, meaning him that lives down there.'

'Where is it?' groped Enderby. 'I just want somewhere to lie down.' His hands felt the softness and width of a sofa, the continuum broken by bottle-shapes (they clanked) and a half-full chocolate box (rustled). 'Lay down,' he corrected himself, to be more matey.

'Make yourself comfortable,' she said, bloody sarky. 'If you want anything don't hesitate to ring. At what hour of the morning would you like your morning tea?' she said, in a hot-potato chumble. 'Men,' she said, going apparently, to her bedroom. She made a contemptuous noise, worthy of Enderby himself, leaving him to the dark.

4

1

He awoke with first light to the xylophone of milk bottles and impotent rasping of self-starters. He smacked his lips and clacked his tongue on his hard palate, feeling his mouth like – the vulgar simile

swam up from his vulgar pub-crawl – an all-in wrestler's jock-strap.
The vulgar simile put fingers to its nose in the gesture his stepmother
had called 'fat bacon', made the old Roman sign, raspberried, and
clambered off up the wall like a lizard. Enderby in his overcoat felt
cold and grubby, matching the room that now emerged like a picture
on a television screen when the set has at last warmed up. With the
picture, noise: that woman's snoring from the next room. Enderby
listened, interested. He had never realized that women could snore
so loud. His stepmother had, of course, been able to blast a roof off,
but she had been unique. Unique? He remembered some lavatorial
writing or other about all stepmothers being women or all women
stepmothers or something, and then the whole day came back,
certainly not a dull day, and he caught quite clearly the name of the
widow who had given him tea and taken him to the Victoria tube-
stop: Vesta Bainbridge. Shame warmed all Enderby's body and then
hunger hammered at him, as at a door. The shameful day marched
by briskly, its nostrils widened in a silly smirk, and it carried a banner
of St George. It noisily tramped off to stand at ease behind the
gimcrack sideboard. Enderby put on his spectacles, seeing beer bottles
and old *Daily Mirrors* with painful clarity, then creaked, groaning, to
the kitchenette. This was full of small square platters that had held
TV meals, also empty milk bottles with crusty archipelagoes inside
them. Enderby drank water from the tap. He opened the cupboard,
wiping his mouth on a dish-cloth, and found gherkins. He ate some
of these crisp slugs and soon felt better.

Before leaving he called on his hostess, but she lay sprawled
over the double bed, uncovered, working hard at sleep. Her bubs,
like blancmanges not properly set, shivered gently under the translucent nightgown as a lorry went by. Black smoke of hair over her
face lifted and fell, obedient to her snore. Enderby covered her
with the eiderdown, bowed, and left. She was not so old, he decided.
A fat stupid girl not really capable of ill-nature. She had given
Enderby shelter; Enderby would not forget.

As Enderby went downstairs he met his own milkman: a pint
for Enderby's door, a half-pint for the foot of the stairs. The milkman
leered and double-clacked his tongue. So many dawns, so many
betrayers. Enderby had an idea. 'Had to sleep up there,' he said.
'Locked myself out. Do you know anything about locks?'

'Love laughs at locksmiths,' said the milkman sententiously. 'I'll just see if I've got a bit of wire.'

A minute later the postman came with Littlewood's coupons for upstairs, nothing for Enderby. 'That's not quite the way,' he said critically. 'Let me have a try.' He breathed heavily over the lock, probing and fiddling. 'Coming,' he panted. 'Half a tick.' The lock sprang, Enderby turned the knob, the door opened.

'Very much obliged,' he said, 'to both you gentlemen.' He had not relished the prospect of going to see Mrs Meldrum. He gave them his last coppers and entered.

Ah, but it was a relief to be back. Enderby stripped off his overcoat and hung it by its left shoulder on the hook in the tiny hall. He took off, with slightly greater care, the suit he had borrowed from Arry and rolled it neatly in a ball. He placed this, pending the returning of it, on the unmade bed, and then he put on his turtle-neck sweater. He was dressed now for work. His bare legs twinkled into the living-room and at once he scented change. There was a letter on the table, unstamped, and the table itself had been cleared of yesterday morning's dirty dishes. Enderby kicked on the electric fire and sat down to read, his brow troubled. The letter was from Mrs Meldrum.

Dear Mr E,

You will forgive me taking a look round when you was out, as I have every right being the landlady when all said and done. Well, you have got the place disgraceful no two ways about it, what with the bath full of pieces of poetry which was never the intention of them who make baths and have them fitted in. And the carpets not swept neither, I would be ashamed to have to show anybody round it. Well, what I said still hold water, that the rent goes up from next month and you been lucky to have it so cheap for so long, what with prices of things going up everywhere. If you dont like it you know what to do, I have others who will *keep the place proper* only too anxious to move in next week. You need somebody to look after you and no mistake, it is not natural for a man of your age and with your education as you say you have, living on his own and nobody to look after the house. To be blunt about it and not to shut up about what needs to be spoke out loud you need to get married before you sink to rack and ruin, which is the true opinion of many as I have spoke to.

Yours respctfly
W. Meldrum. (Mrs)

So. Enderby scratched his knee bitterly. That's what they wanted, was it? Enderby looked after, the dishes washed properly, the beds made regularly, the bathroom a pretty dream of a place with glaucous curtains and brushes for back and nails, nylon bristles with plastic fish-shape handles, the bath always waiting for a pink healthy tubber singing la-la-la through the steam. And, for hubby Enderby, a den to write his precious poetry in, a hobby for hubby. No. Bird-voices started in his head: prudence-preaching pigeons, cautioning rooks: beware of meadows, widows. Act act act, called the ducks: drain the sacrament of choice. 'This is my choice,' said Enderby firmly, as he went to the kitchen to get breakfast (that bitch Mrs Meldrum had washed his dishes!) and brew up stepmother's tea. He would be true to that archetypal bitch, his father's second wife. She had made his life a misery; he would give no other woman that privilege.

And yet. And yet. Enderby had his breakfast of dry bread, strawberry jam, and tea, then went to his workshop. His papers lay untouched by Mrs Meldrum; his table with its legs specially shortened awaited him by the hollow seat. *The Pet Beast* was growing slowly; the volume of fifty poems, planned for the autumn, was nearly complete. The first job to be cleared out of the way was the composing of a new love lyric for the *Arry to Thelma sequence.* Enderby felt guilty about the state of Arry's suit. It had, inexplicably, collected mud round the knees; a lapel had been incontinently soiled; the knife-crease had, with incredible speed, become blunted. Arry should be mollified with something really good. He had been complaining about the subject-matter of Enderby's offerings: too many kitchen similes, the appeal to her hard heart too indirect. She had, Arry swore, been reading these poems aloud to the car salesmen, and they had been yak-yakking at them. Enderby must write something very direct, not crude, mind, but direct, telling her what Arry desired to do with her, something that she would keep under her pillow and blush when she drew it (scented with her scent) out. Enderby thought, sitting on his throne, that he might have something suitable in stock. He rummaged in the bath and found certain very early lyrics. Here was one he had written at the age of seventeen. 'The Music of the Spheres', it was called.

> I have raised and poised a fiddle
>   Which, will you lend it ears,
> Will utter music's model:
>   The music of the spheres.
>
> By God, I think not Purcell
>   Nor Arne could match my airs.
> Perfect beyond rehearsal
>   My music of the spheres.
>
> Not that its virtue's vastness –
>   The terror of drift of stars.
> For subtlety and softness
>   My music of the spheres.
>
> The spheres that feed its working,
>   Their melody swells and soars
> On thinking of your marking
>   My music of the spheres.
>
> This musing and this fear's
> Work of your maiden years.
> Why shut longer your ears?
> Look, how the live earth flowers!
> The land speaks my intent:
> Bear me accompaniment.

That, addressed to a supposed virgin, was manifestly absurd for Thelma. And was not that spherical imagery perhaps too gross for a barmaid brought up, one presumed, respectably? Dirty jokes in the bar were one thing, but dirty literature, even the most factitious suggestion of its presence, was another. His stomach, still sore, attested this.

Seventeen. The date of composition was at the foot of the manuscript. To whom had he written that? He brooded, scratching. To nobody, he decided glumly. But had he not dreamed, at that romantic age, of some willow-wand creature who, though of infinite refinement and smelling sweet as May, would not be offended by this all too decipherable symbolism of importunacy? He had shaped this girl in his heart, as mystics shape God, in terms of what she should not be, namely his stepmother; then her positive image had arisen by dint of long brooding on her negative attributes. She had come in a dream then, slender and laughing and, above all, *clean. Not* a widow: he refused to allow this re-issue of the image to take on the colours and scents of Mrs Bainbridge.

He sighed, then began, very deliberately and coldly, as a pure poetic exercise, to write a very erotic poem from Arry to Thelma, full of breasts and thighs and panting longing. When he had finished he set it aside to cool, then he went on with his building of the labyrinth, home of the Pet Beast.

2

This was the order of a usual Enderby day: he would rise at dawn or just after, winter and summer alike; he would breakfast, defecate, and then work, sometimes beginning his work while actually defecating; at ten-fifteen he would shave and prepare to go out, sometimes with a shopping-reticule; at ten-thirty he would leave the flat, walk seawards, buy a loaf, feed the gulls; immediately after that he would take his morning whisky with the aged and dying or, if Arry were not at work, with Arry in the Freemason's Arms; sometimes he would visit Arry in his kitchens, and Arry would give him scraps for his larder – a turkey-carcass, a few slices of fat pork, a bit of scrag-end for Sunday's meal; Enderby would then do such shopping as was needed – a loaf for himself, potatoes, ten cigarettes, pickles, a small meat-pie, a fourpenny custard; back home he would prepare his meal, or, if something cold was left over from the day before, eat at once, working while he ate; he would then loll somnolent in a chair or even, rolling dressed into bed, deliberately sleep. Then back to the lavatory for the last long stint of the day; after that the remains of his earlier meal, or bread with some cheap relish; stepmother's tea as a nightcap; bed. A way of life which harmed no one. Sometimes the caprices of the Muse would disrupt this pattern by hurling poems – fragmentary or fully-formed – at Enderby; then, in mid-whisky, in bed, cooking, toiling at the structures of non-lyrical works, he would have to write down at once to her hysterical or coldly vatic or telegraphic dictation. He respected his Muse but was frightened of her whims: she could be playful kitten or tiger fully-clawed, finger-sucking idiot child or haughty goddess in Regency ball-gown; her moods, like her visits, were unpredictable. More predictable were his other visitants – dyspepsia in its various forms, wind, hiccoughs. Between dispensations of celestial and visceral afflation he lived his quiet days, a solitary man, harmless. Letters and visitors rarely disturbed his door, news from the dangerous world never intruded. His dividends and tiny royalties were paid straight into the bank; the bank he visited once a month only, humbly waiting with his cash cheque made out neatly for twenty-odd pounds behind bull-necked publicans and ascetic-faced butchers who paid in, inexplicably, dull mounds of copper that took long to count. He envied nobody except the great proved dead.

His routine, already disturbed by the disastrous London trip, was further disturbed by a consequence of that trip, namely the arrival of a big parcel. The address-panel had *Fem* printed on it and the picture of a well-groomed though moronic-faced young woman, evidently a typical *Fem*-reader. Enderby, who had been deep in his poem, received the parcel trouserless and open-mouthed, then ran into the living-room with a thudding heart to open it up. There was a contract for him to sign and a brief letter from Mrs Bainbridge telling him that here was a contract to sign and here were copies of past issues of *Fem*. She wrote in thick long-strokes, was formal and business-like, but had allowed her scent to inspissate, most delicately, the writing-paper. Enderby had little nose, but he caught her very feminine image very clearly. So.

Enderby knew little of magazines. As a boy he had read *Film Fun* and *Funny Wonder*. As a young man he had known poetry

periodicals and waspish left-wing week-end reviews. In the Army
he had seen such things as the troops read. In professional waiting-
rooms he had sat stony-faced over *Punch*. He was aware of a
post-war rash of cheap journals and wondered at their range of
specialization and at the number of cults they seemed to serve.
There were two or three, he knew, wholly devoted to some dead
filmstar who had become a sort of corn-god; he had seen others
which, severally, glorified young living louts with guitars – presumably what Mrs Bainbridge had called pop-singers. There was
evidently a strong religious hunger among young girls which these
poor simulacra and their press-priests alone seemed available to
feed. There was also, among these same young girls, money crying
to be spent, for it seemed that in this age of specialists only the
unskilled and witless were at a premuim. But the dreaming wives
had money also. *Fem* fought screaming for their sixpences, trying
to elbow out *Womanly*, kick *Lovely* in the teeth, rip the corsets off
Wifey and tear out the hair of *Blondie* by its black roots.

He sat down eagerly to read *Fem*. Time passed, lost for ever,
never to be redeemed, as he snorted adenoidally over its contents.
The cover had a girl's face, generically and boringly lovely. The
cover of each issue, he noted, flicking through the pile on his knees,
had a young woman's face, probably always the same one, though
he could not be certain. The covers of magazines for men, he
fancied, preferred to exploit woman from the neck down. A fair
division. Enderby read readers' letters: somebody's little girl asked
if God lived in an aeroplane; how to turn an old jam-jar into an
elegant vase by using four different shades of nail-varnish (total
cost 8*s*. 6*d*.); that sweet grateful smile was all the reward she could
ask for her act of charity; the budgerigar of Mrs F. (Rotherham)
could say 'Dolly loves Mummy'; how stupid men could be, couldn't
they, wanting to keep potatoes in a kitchen-drawer! (Enderby read
this gravely puzzled: why was that stupid?) There was a serial story
called 'For Ever and a Day', illustrated opulently with a ravishing
but doubtful bride. A five-page article demonstrated that it did not
cost *very* much more to make your own disc-cabinet (or to get
husband or boyfriend to make it) than to buy it in a shop. There
were short stories called 'Heart Afire', 'Why Did You Leave Me?',
'I Thee Wed', 'Hello, Romance', mostly garnished with pictures of

couples glued together, upright. A vital-warming religious column by a popular young pop-singing parson was followed by a feature on 'Our Queen's Dogs'. There was a chilling clinical chat on tumours, there were articles on stiletto heels, marmalade-making, being a radiant bride. Enderby sat absorbed for a long time in a Special Cookery Supplement, seeing at last a means of improving his diet (he would try Orange Goody tomorrow). He was shocked and touched by letters sent to Millicent Goodheart, a blue-haired lady with sharp red talons and a gentle smile: 'He said it was artificial respiration, but now I find I am to have his child'; 'I have only been married three months but I have fallen in love with my husband's father'. Enderby nodded approvingly at the good sense of the replies. She should not have done it; I'm terribly sorry for you, my dear, but you must remember marriage is for keeps.

Dusk fell while he was still reading, with much more reading still to do. He stole to the light-switch, feeling guilty, excusing himself for this long soaking: after all, he was going to write for them, he had to know their tastes. His belly growled its neglect. Enderby had nothing in the flat except bread, jam, pickles; he must go out and buy something. He rather fancied a dish concocted by Gillian Frobisher, Head of *Fem*'s Cookery Department: Spaghetti Fromaggio Surprise.

Enderby went out with his shopping-net and returned with a pound of spaghetti, a quarter of cheese, and a large garlic for fourpence. (The recipe gave the alternative of two large onions, but Enderby had an obscure repugnance to entering a green-grocer's just to ask for two onions; garlic was a different matter, being exotic.) Panting with excitement, he took the relevant issue of *Fem* into the kitchen and followed the instructions slavishly. 'Enough for four', he read. He was but one man alone, himself, he, hungry Enderby. He must divide everything, then, by four. He took the pound of spaghetti and broke the brittle sticks into small pieces. He took his frying pan (pity that the recipe asked for a large deep one; still, never mind) and poured one tablespoonful of olive oil. (He had about a cupful of this in his cupboard, saved from sardine tins.) He threw in about a quarter of the spaghetti, lit the gas, and cooked it slowly, turning and stirring. He then added two cupfuls of water, remembering that he was to divide by four, so threw some of the water out again. He turned, breathing heavily, to *Fem*, while the pan gently simmered. Grated cheese. He grated some with Mrs Meldrum's nutmeg-grater and threw it into the mixture. Now this question of onion or garlic. 'Two large onions chopped', said Gillian Frobisher, or 'garlic to taste'. Enderby looked at his garlic, stronger, he knew, than onions; perhaps this one would be equivalent to two of those. Should he skin it? No. The goodness was in the skin: potatoes, for instance. He sliced the garlic warpwise, then woofwise, then threw the bits into the simmering pan. And now. A greased dish. He found a cloudy Pyrex on the shelf, and he liberally coated its inside with margarine. He now had to transfer the stuff from the pan into the Pyrex. He had some difficulty in turning it out: it had stuck to the pan for some reason, and he had to gouge vigorously to detach what was willing to be detached. He flopped the mixture into the dish. 'Top with sour cream', said Gillian. There was no sour cream, but plenty of sour milk, greenish on top. He crowned the dish with generous curds, then lit the oven. It had to cook to a slow heat therein, about twenty minutes. Groaning, he placed the dish on the oven shelf, kicked the black door shut, wiped one hand on the other. There.

Damn. He had not, he realized, consistently divided by four. Never mind. And perhaps the spaghetti was meant to turn black. He had heard of smart restaurants where things were deliberately burned before one's eyes, as one sat cool and well-dressed at table. He went back to the electric fire to continue his reading of yet another issue of *Fem*. After gazing transfixed at a soup advertisement showing a cup of cold blood, and an egg advertisement in which a pallid yolk hung over the edge of the fish-slice that lifted it aslant from the pan, ready to flop in pale yellow, Enderby settled to a story called 'You're Not My Darling'. This was about an air-hostess who fell in love with the captain of her aircraft, a theme new to Enderby. He gawped on long past Gillian Frobisher's twenty minutes of cooking time, came to with a hiccoughing start, then drew his Spaghetti Fromaggio Surprise out of the oven. Its name was not inept. He sat down to it, and savoured mingled hues of burnt farinacity and shouting brutal garlic, loud and hot as an acetylene blast; the tone of these hues was a tired tepidity. He had not quite expected this; still presumably Gillian Frobisher knew what she was doing. He ate dutifully, with many draughts of cold water. He must learn the tastes of his prospective readers.

3

Enderby awoke in the middle of the night, jerked with sergeant's roughness out of an odd dream about pokers. The pain was ghastly though it did not feel dangerous. Enderby's head was clear enough as he crawled out; he even remembered the name of the bloody woman. Gillian Frobisher. There was a photograph of her in one of the Cookery Supplements: a crisp handsome Jewish girl with an impossibly clean frying-pan. If he ever got hold of her, Enderby vowed, he would dirty that frying-pan and no mistake. He had been taken advantage of.

Bicarb shattered the pain and sent its fragments flying on the wind. Enderby sat down in his living-room and switched on the electric fire. It was, said his watch, three-ten. A ghastly hour. There was noise upstairs, a woman's voice shouting as through a muslin strainer, 'Get out, do you hear? Get out, you pig.' Then the rumble of a man's voice and the tread of heavy shoes. Jack was, apparently, back. Soon the woman's abuse grew fainter and was curiously articulated, as though from the side of the mouth, in brief bursts. Later the springs began to bounce. Enderby picked up the contract from the sofa, wondering whether he ought to sign or not. To produce a block of rhymed clichés weekly, sententious vapourings about the stars so far away, the feel of chubby baby arms round mummy's neck, being kind to those in trouble – was not this prostitution? The poems he was writing to Thelma from Arry were not that, whatever they were. Where they were not straight-forwardly sensual they were gently ironical: he needn't be ashamed of them. But this proposal of Mrs Bainbridge – was it not the fiend luring him away from proper art with the chink of guineas that, anyway, would be all for Mrs Meldrum? Enderby walked into the bathroom to survey all the tumbled years' work in the bath. He had moved, over the last decade and a half, from town to town and flat to flat, but he had thought that here he could settle it. It was not good to change one's workshop in the middle of a major creation. The mood altered under the subtle influence of a new place, the continuity was broken. And then the thought of packing all this bathful into suitcases – mice, breadcrusts and all. One lost things, one was tempted to throw things away. But Enderby, standing in bare feet, thinking hard, wondered whether perhaps he ought to make the sacrifice, move on up or down the coast, away from Mrs Meldrum and – a much more dangerous person, the widow to be enjoyed in the meadow – Mrs Bainbridge, coolly elegant, self-confessed admirer of his poems.

He saw that to some extent he was rationalizing his fear of a relationship with a woman, the possibility that what was now finishing upstairs might soon start downstairs. And yet a worry that had often nagged him – especially after scurrying away from the verge of other relationships – was that this very desire to remain uncommitted might impair his work. Love of woman had always, traditionally, played a large part in the lives of the poets. Look at Goethe, for instance, who had to have a new love affair before he could begin a new lyric. Enderby, in so far as German culture had played any part in his development, had chosen to be influenced by a much dourer personality – Schopenhauer. Spengler, too, with his promise of the undergoing of evening lands, had had something to say to him. He had needed to invoke both philosophers before writing a poem about sex and other people. He remembered the typical evening of wartime, blackout in the garrison town, horny hands groping for giggling bodies in the dark.

Nymphs and satyrs, come away.
  Faunus, laughing from the hill,
  Rips the blanket of the day
  From the paunch of dirty Will.

Each projector downs its snout,
  Truffling the blackened scene,
Till the *Wille's* lights gush out
  Vorstellungen on the screen.

Doxies blanch to silverwhite;
  All their trappings of the sport,

Lax and scattered, in this light
   Merge and lock to smooth and taut.

See! The rockets shoot afar!
   Ah! The screen was tautest then.
Tragic the parabola
   When the sticks reel down again.

That was no romantic attitude to sex. Love, Schopenhauer had seemed to say, was one of the perpetual cinema performances or *Vorstellungen* organized by the evil Will, projectionist as well as manager, and these slack bodies of gum-chewing gigglers were made into stiff shining screens for the projection of what looked like reality, value. But the deflation, the reeling to earth after coitus, was frightful, and one saw the inflated words of desire − so soon after their utterance − for what they really were. The casual images of onanism could not be hurt, could not be lied to.

Enderby went back to the living-room. Heartburn, like labour pains, had started again. There was plenty of bicarbonate solution still in the glass, so, in less than half a minute, Enderby was able to growl it away hollowly:

Grerrrbrogharrrgawwwwwwpfffffh.

There was an immediate response from upstairs: a shoe of admonition was banged three times. Enderby looked up to the noise meekly, as to chiding God. It was time that he left. He heard what sounded like, 'Shut up, Enderby,' and then the woman's voice said, 'Leave him alone. He can't help it.' A row of indistinguishable words then began, ending with Jack shouting, 'Oh, he did, did he? And whose idea was that? False little bitch, aren't you?' The sadness, see, after coition. Enderby shook his head sadly and went back to bed. He would give a week's notice to Mrs Meldrum; he would sign no contract with Mrs Bainbridge. Mrs Meldrum could have her smiling bald bath-taking young man on an expense account; if there was no weekly poem from Enderby it was not likely that the strong-stomached readers of *Fem* would pine away.

4

That settled it. Morning brought a letter from Vesta Bainbridge:

Dear Mr Enderby,

Well, you do seem to have been beating it up pretty tidily on your visit to London. I have only now managed to get hold of an evening paper of that memorable day which, albeit briefly, makes it reasonably clear that you went out of your way to antagonize a certain knightly patron of your art. I must confess that, in some ways, I admire your independent attitude, though God knows how any poet nowadays can afford that Byronic luxury. Sir George, I hear, is very angry and hurt. What came over you? I just don't understand, but then I'm only a very ordinary person with no great claim to intellect, and I would never be so presumptuous as to think myself capable of fathoming a poet's brain. The fact is, and I daresay you'll hear this from your own publisher fairly soon, that your name smells to heaven with Goodby's for Good Books, so watch out.

In the circumstances, I think it would be a good plan to print your weekly effusion under or over a pseudonym. This would also give us a chance to prettify the feature with a photograph of some long-haired male model with a quill in his hand and his dreamy eyes up to heaven – you know what I mean: *The Poet*: what every housewife thinks a poet ought to look like. Can you suggest a pseudonym? Do sign that contract and return it. I *did* enjoy our tea together.

Yours,

Vesta Bainbridge

Enderby trembled with rage as he crushed the good quality writing-paper. He hurled the letter into the lavatory-pan and then pulled the chain, but the thing was too thick to flush down. He had to pick it out wet and then take it into the kitchen and put it in an old cardboard rubbish-box along with condensed-milk tins, fishbones, potato peelings and tea leaves. After an hour of brooding and trying to carry on with his work, he felt a compulsion to read it again and did so, all smothered with tea-leaves as it was. Beating pretty tidily London memorable day albeit briefly independent attitude Byronic what every housewife thinks Vesta Bainbridge. He stood frowning, reading it in the tiny hallway, squinting at the words because it was dark there. There was a sudden double-beating on the door, as on a gorilla's chest, and Enderby looked up, surprised. 'Come out, Enderby,' cried the voice of Jack. 'I want a word with you, Enderby, you bloody poet.'

'For cough,' snarled Enderby, with much of his stepmother's spirit and intonation.

'Come out of there, Enderby. Come out and fight like a man. Open that door and let me bash you, you bastard.'

'No,' said Enderby, 'I won't. If I opened that door I'd regret it. I know I would. I don't want your blood on my hands.'

'Enderby,' shouted Jack, 'I'm giving you fair warning. Open up there and let me do you in, you fornicating poet. I'll give you sleeping with my wife, you false sod.'

'It's not your wife,' said Enderby. 'And I slept on the couch. Somebody's been telling lies about me. Now you clear off before I get angry.'

'Open that door, Enderby, please,' pleaded Jack's voice. 'I want to do you in, it's only right and fair as I should, you bastard, and I'm already late for work. Open up and let's get it over.' And he thumped with both hands on the door. From above the woman's voice could be heard, and there was something about it to show clearly the image of a woman in nightdress and curlers. 'Stop it, Jack,' she cried. 'You're only making a fool of yourself.'

'Fool of myself, eh? We'll soon see. Now you shut up. You've had your turn and now it's going to be Enderby's turn.' He renewed the thundering. Enderby went to the kitchen and came back with his hare-eviscerating knife. 'Open up, Enderby. Time's getting on, you bastard.' Enderby opened up.

Jack was a youngish tough man with lined cheeks and eyes the colour of urine. If hairs be wires, black wires grew in his head. He had both fists ready, with the thumbs pitiably tucked inside. Enderby had been punched in London; he was not going to be punched here. He raised his knife. 'For cough,' he said.

'That's playing unfair,' said Jack. 'I meant clean bashing. That's not right when you get on to that stabbing lark. All I'm saying is, you leave her upstairs alone, see, and one bloody good bash in the chops and call it a day. You've no call to go fornicating with what's mine, as you ought to be first to admit. Now put that knife down like a man and take what's coming to you.'

'For cough,' said Enderby, in a murderer's stance. 'I hadn't got my key, that was all, and she let me sleep on the sofa. If you don't believe that you'll never believe anything.'

'I'll believe what I want to believe,' said Jack with great candour. 'I'm coming back to see you again. Don't think you've got away with this, because you haven't, Enderby, poet or no poet. I tell you that straight. I'm off to work now and late too, which is your fault and makes things worse.' With a sudden brisk jerk and stylish follow-through he wrested the knife from the grasp of Enderby. 'There,' he said proudly. 'Now you've had it.' Enderby swiftly slammed the door. 'I'll be back, Enderby,' called Jack. 'Make no mistake about it. You'll be done, no two ways about that, as you'll see.' He kicked Enderby's door and then thumped out of the house, crashing the great outer portal shut.

Enderby locked himself in the lavatory, trembling. *Canaille, canaglia*, with their bloody sex and blasted jealousy. Well, the time had come; all things pointed to it: out, out, out. Where to now? He sat on the seat and began to scribble: (a) Draw cash from bank; (b) Get map of south coast; (c) Send cheque and week's notice Mrs M.; (d) Write to Mrs B.; (e) see Arry. With this need to plan and the thought of the nightmare of packing still to come, he grew flustered. He tried to calm himself by writing a final consummatory poem for Arry, the end of the whole cycle. It reeked with hot hands, white flesh, hoarse desire, love, love, love. It had a certain cathartic effect on Enderby, like loud blasphemous obscenities.

> . . . And in that last delirium of lust
> Your image glows. Love is a blinding rain,
> Love crow all the cocks, love lays the dust
> Of this cracked crying throat whose thirst is pain . . .

He wrote out a cheque for Mrs Meldrum, composed the curtest of farewells: 'Thank you for your unwanted solicitude. Take a week's

notice. Yours etc.' To Mrs Bainbridge he wrote a courteous acknowl-
edgement of her communications and regretted that, on maturer
consideration, he found himself unable to find it in himself to meet
the meagre poetic needs, if even these existed, of the readers of
Fem. His compliments to Miss or Mrs Frobisher, if Mrs Bainbridge
would be good enough to pass them on, and congratulations on
possessing so tough-stomached a gang of followers of her culinary
columns. He, Enderby, had, if it was of any interest to anyone,
suffered greatly from her Spaghetti Fromaggio Surprise. He
proposed to destroy the contract and distribute the copies of *Fem*
to the poor. He was hers sincerely. P.S. He was moving from the
above address forthwith, whither he knew not yet. No point in
her replying. Calmer now, Enderby shaved and prepared to go out.
He would be safe so long as that shouter Jack was still at work.

5

Arry, in grubby cook's white, complete with white necktie and
white mushroom hat, stood at the bar of the Freemason's Arms,
taking time off from his kitchens. He greeted Enderby with no
enthusiasm but, without asking or being asked, ordered a double
whisky for him. 'That suit,' he said, 'were a right bloody mess. Ad
to send it tert cleaner's.' He drank off a good three-quarters of a
pint of brown ale mixed with bitter.

'I'm sorry,' said Enderby. 'It won't happen again. I shan't have
to borrow from you again. I'm leaving.'

'Leavin'? Goin'? Not coomin' back 'ere naw mawr?'

'That's right.'

Arry looked solemn, but that stiff crust of his expression seemed
to be hiding a tiny feeling of relief; a whiff of relief escaped as
through a steam-hole in the crust. He said:

'Where to?'

'I don't know,' said Enderby. 'Somewhere else along the coast.
It doesn't matter where, really.'

'Thee gets as far aweeeeeh,' advised Arry, prolonging his vowels,
as in some primitive language, 'far aweeeeeh,' to emphasize the
distance, 'far aweeeeeh,' by onomatopoeic suggestion, 'as tha can

bloody get. That's naht 'ere, naht for nobody. Coom back 'ere,'
he said, 'never naw mawr.' He looked with gloom at the lesbians
in the corner – Gladys in glasses and leopard-skin pants sly-
cuddling cross-eyed Prudence – and then with compassion at
Enderby.

'This is to say good-bye, really,' said Enderby, 'and to hope that
your suit prospers.'

'It'll be aw right when it cooms back fromt cleaner's.'

'I meant the other suit,' said Enderby, 'the Arry to Thelma suit.
I've brought one more poem for you, the very last of the cycle. If
this doesn't do the job, nothing will.' He took the folded sheet
from his pocket.

Arry shook his head. 'Naht doin',' he said, 'naht doin' at all. It
were a bloody wester mah tahm.'

'My time, too,' said Enderby.

'Wan 'and int till,' said Arry, 'and toother betwinner legs. No
good to man nor flamin' beast that Thelma. Oo's tecken no notice
er naht av doon forrer.'

'Well,' sighed Enderby, 'that's how it is. Nobody wants poetry
nowadays. All wasted.' He prepared to rip up his final fiery
offering.

'Weren't wested,' said Arry. 'Ot stooff, wan or two were. *Ah*
lakhed 'em. Boot oo,' he said, 'didn't 'ave bloody intelligence.' He
put out a clean cook's hand to rescue Enderby's poem. He took
the folded sheet and unfolded it with wan interest. He pretended
to read it, then put it into his trouser-pocket. Enderby bought
him a pint of brown ale and bitter. Enderby said:

'Since I've lived here you're the only one I've been in any way
friendly with. That's why I wanted to shake hands with you before
I go.'

'All sheck 'ands wi' thee,' said Arry, and did so. 'When will yer
be clearin' off?'

'I've got to pack,' said Enderby. 'And then I've got to decide
where I'm going to. Tomorrow, I should think. While Jack's out at
work.'

'Oo's Jack?'

'Oh, yes, sorry. The chap who lives upstairs. He thinks I've been
carrying on with the woman he lives with.'

'Ah,' said Arry, shaking his head, then looking at Enderby with renewed compassion. 'Get away as soon as yer can,' said Arry. 'Shoove yer things in a bag and then get to Victoria Station. On Victoria Station there's nameser places stoock oop on indiketters. Teck thy choice, lad. There's plenty on 'em. You choose wanner them and go straight to it. All places is the same nowadays,' he said. 'The big thing to do is to kip movin'. And,' he asked, 'what will yer do when yeu've getten wherever yer goin'? Wilt kip on wi' same game?'

'It's all I can do,' said Enderby. 'Writing verse is all I'm cut out for.'

Arry nodded and finished his pint, the fourth since Enderby's entrance. 'Dawn't write too mooch abaht spaghetti, then,' he said, frothily. 'Leave spaghetti to them as knaws summat abaht it.' He shook hands with Enderby once more. 'Moost get back now,' he said, 'tert bloody job. Special loonch for Daughters of Temperance.' He spaced out the words like a poster. 'Luke after yerself,' said Arry. He waved a white cook's arm from the door and then went out. Spaghetti coiled, puzzled, in Enderby's brain. Then a horrid thought struck him. He finished his whisky palpitating but then calmed down. He might have sent it to Mrs Meldrum. But no, he distinctly remembered pinning a cheque to a quarter-sheet of writing-paper. But that made no difference, did it? That might still have got into the wrong envelope. He'd better get out of here very, very quickly.

As he panted towards his packing down the esplanade, the gulls wheeled and wailed and climbed the blue wall of the marine winter day. For two days now he had forgotten to feed them. They planed, complained. Greedy beady eyes. Ungrateful birds. They mewed no farewell to Enderby; they would be there, waiting for his doles of bread, further up or down the coastline.

5

1

Of what the world would call essentials, Enderby had few to pack. It was the bathful of verse that was the trouble. Kneeling in front of it, as though – and here he laughed sardonically – he worshipped his own work, he began to bundle it into the larger of his two suitcases, separating – with reasonable care – manuscripts from sandwich-crusts, cigarette-packets, and the cylinders of long-used toilet-rolls. But he found so many old poems which he had quite forgotten that he could not resist reading them through, open-mouthed, as afternoon ticked on towards dusk. He had modified drastically his original plan of departure, his aim now being to catch some evening train (Jack permitting) to Victoria, spend the night in a hotel, and then, about midday, follow some new spoke to the south coast. He had, he felt, to live near the sea, this being a great wet slobbering stepmother or green dogmatic Church which he could keep his eye on; nothing, at least, insidious about it.

It was amazing what things he had written, especially in his youth: pastiches of Whitman, Charles Doughty, an attempted translation of the *Duino Elegies*, limericks, even the beginning of a verse-play about Copernicus. There was one sonnet in sprung rhythm and Alexandrines which dated from the days of his love and envy of the proletariat. He read the sestet with horror and wonder:

> When the violet air blooms about him, then at last he can wipe
> His hands sheerfree of swink, monarch of hours ahead;
> Hearty he eats and, full, he sits to pull at his pipe,
> Warm at the kitchen glow. The courts- and sports-news read,

He argues, sups, in the Lion vault; to a plate of tripe
Or crisp chips home returns, then climbs to a dreamless bed.

Dead on this homecoming cue Jack came home, his hands sheerfree
of salesman's swink, ready for Enderby. Enderby was aroused from
the past by the gorilla two-fist beat on the door.

'Come on, Enderby, out of it. On the job, Enderby. Come and
be bashed, you poetic bloody nuisance.'

'Have you got my knife?' asked Enderby, standing now behind
his punished door.

'Your knife, eh? That's been put in a refuse-bin, you dirty mess
as you are, you. There's going to be clean bashing only, you nasty
deceitful thing. I'm giving you fair warning, Enderby. If you don't
open up I'm going to get old Ma Meldrum's key. I'll say that you
lost yours, lying like you lied, you nasty liar. Then I'll come in and
do you. So open up like a sportsman and play the game and be
bashed, you bugger, you.'

Enderby shivered with rage and immediately began to roam
the flat, trembling, looking for some weapon. Meanwhile Jack,
who should, by rights, have been fatigued by his work, hammered
at the door and execrated nastily. In the bathroom Enderby cast
around and his eyes momentarily softened as they lighted on his
old friend, the lavatory-seat. It had always been somewhat loose;
it was not difficult to wrench it from the pin that had held it
to the pedestal. 'Coming,' called Enderby. 'Shan't be a minute.'
He apologized to the wooden O as he pulled it roughly away,
promising that soon he would write it a small ode of reparation.
Armed with it he went to the door, pulled the door open and
saw Jack's thumb-protecting fists ready for a fierce double-bang
at the empty air.

'That's not fair,' he said, backing. 'You're not playing the game,
Enderby. All I ask is a fair apology for ill-treating me as regards
my own property.' ('Is that you back, Jack?' came the voice from
above. 'Don't hurt him too hard, love.')

'There's nothing to apologize for,' said Enderby. 'If you don't
believe what I told you you must take the consequences of your
disbelief. I'm going to clonk you on the head with this seat
here.'

'Not that,' said Jack, trying, on dancing feet, to get in odd punches. 'That's comic, that is, that's not decent. That's making a farce out of the whole thing.' Enderby parried the weak blows, slamming Jack's wrists hard with his wooden weapon. He drove him down the hallway towards the front door of the house, past the two spotted pictures on the wall, both of Highland scenery in wretched weather. Enderby raised the seat high, intended to hit Jack's wiry head with its hard border. He misjudged somewhat, and the seat came down to encircle Jack's face, so that Jack was framed like a most animated portrait in a bottom-shaped ring. His hands clawed at it, forgetting to chop at Enderby's own, which tugged down and down, Enderby's obscure aim being to pull Jack to the floor and then stamp on him. 'You bastard, you,' cried Jack. 'This isn't funny, this isn't, you sod.' He tried to lift off the wooden lei of bottom-polished smoothness, but Enderby's weight pulled down and down. 'All I ask,' panted Jack, 'is an apology for what you done, did. Give me that and I'll let you go.' Enderby swung round, still clinging to Jack's round pillory, and saw Jack's woman at the foot of the stairs. She was dressed like Hamlet in black tights, a black sweater above, inside which her bubs danced still from her descent.

'You,' sobbed Enderby, at his last gasp with all this effort, 'started all this. Tell him the truth.'

'He bashed me,' she said, 'and I did nothing wrong. Now it's only right that you get bashed.'

'Tell him the truth,' cried Enderby's dying voice.

'That won't make no difference to Jack,' she said. 'You've got to get done by Jack. Jack's like that, you see.'

'I want him to apologize,' cried Jack, still framed.

'There's nothing to apologize for,' gurgled Enderby's fading ration of air.

'Apologize for what you're doing now, then.'

'I'll stop it,' said Enderby. He let go of the wooden seat, and Jack, now pulling at nothing, went hurtling back to the hallstand, crashing into it and sending it over, still horse-collared. The little inlaid mirror tinkled; from the glove-drawer, suddenly opened, there issued letters, unforwarded, for people long shadily departed, and also highly coloured coupons representing, each, a fivepence rebate off a packet of soap-powder.

'Call it,' Enderby, bent double as though air were something to be sucked up from the floor, tried to say, 'Call it,' seeing Jack on the floor with lavatory collar still on lying beside, as a wooden mate, the crashed hall-stand, 'a day.'

'You come upstairs, love,' said the woman to Jack. 'You'll be tired after your hard day's work. I'll make you a nice cuppa.'

Jack got up, removed the collar and, panting still, handed it to Enderby. 'You got what was coming to you,' he said. 'I'm not one of those vindictive buggers, Enderby. Fair's fair's what I stand or fall by.' He dusted himself down with the hall-stand brush, still in his overcoat which was of a dull plum colour. 'Don't do it again, that's all I'm going to say now, and let it be a warning.' The woman, soothing, put her arms about him and began to lead him upstairs. Enderby, exhausted, entered his own flat, holding the lavatory-seat like a victor's wreath. It was a long long time since he'd exerted himself so much. He lay down for at least an hour on the floor of the living-room, seeing how dirty the carpet was. Under the couch were walnuts and bits of paper. He lay until the town-hall clock struck, from afar, over the chill evening air of late January, the hour of seven. There was now no hope of leaving tonight.

When he felt better he got up from the floor and went into the kitchen to examine his store-cupboard. There was little point in, and little room for, taking these half-empty jars and bits of lard in paper, potatoes, cut spaghetti-sticks, mustard. He took down Mrs Meldrum's largest saucepan and prepared a stew of meat-paste, Oxo cubes, spaghetti, olive oil, spuds in jackets with dirt and all, pickled onions, cheese-heels, bread-crusts, dripping, half a meat pie, Branston sweet pickle, margarine, celery salt, water. At the back of the fast-emptying cupboard he found a neglected chicken carcass, a gift from Arry, which would go well. He left the stew to bubble, thrifty Enderby, and went back to the sorting and packing of his papers.

2

Enderby, fagged out by fighting, packing, and the thin and over-savoury stew he had cooked, slept later the following morning than he had intended. The work of packing and clearing-up was not yet finished. Both suitcases were crammed, but there were still many manuscripts to bundle together and put safe somewhere. Enderby, yawning, creased, and with hair in sleepy spikes, made tea with the remaining half-packet of Typhoo and coffee with the last few spoons of Blue Mountain. Taking in the milk he left a note of farewell for the milkman, several empty bottles, and a cash cheque for five shillings and fourpence. He then drank one cup of tea and emptied the rest down the lavatory, feeling the sense of virtue he always felt when he knew he had used what another man might well have wasted. Then he heated up last night's stew and felt further virtue when the gas failed half-way through the process. No waste there either. He switched on all the electric fires in the flat, ate breakfast, drank coffee, smoked. Then, in shirt and underpants (last night's nightwear, his pyjamas having been packed) he emptied the rubbish out of its cardboard box into a small dustbin outside the backdoor. (Sunny, piercingly cold, gulls high-screaming.) He cleaned out this box with a copy of *Fem*, finding difficulty in dislodging corner-hugging mush of decayed peel and odd tea-leaf hieroglyphics, then lined it with two or three copies of the same magazine, collected handfuls of poems from the bath and packed them in tightly, covered with further *Fems* then tied the box about with a discarded pair of braces and a long knotty link he made out of odd pieces of string that were lying around. He washed all dishes in (necessarily) cold water and packed them on their shelves. Then he had a cold and excruciating shave, washed quickly, and dressed in his daily working garb with corduroy trousers and a tie. The time was eleven-thirty. He could, he thought, soon now be off. The keys, of course. He went out into the hallway of the house, found that someone, probably Jack, had righted the crashed hallstand, and then he put the keys in the glove-compartment. On a letter addressed to a long-left Mrs Arthur Porceroy (postmark 8.vi.51) he wrote, in inkpencil, KEYS ENDERBY, and leaned this notice upright on the hallstand. While he was doing this the front door opened. A man looked in. He seemed to play an elaborate game of looking for someone everywhere except where someone was, his sad eyes roaming the entire hallway and then appearing at last to find Enderby. He nodded and smiled bleakly, as in modest self-congratulation on his success, and then said, 'Would I be addressing one of the name of Enderby?' Enderby bowed. 'Could I have the pleasure of a word with you?' the man asked. 'A question of poetry,' he added. He had a thin Uriah Heep voice. He was of less than medium height, had a long face and a fluff of whitish hair, wore a raincoat, was about Enderby's age.

'Who are you from?' asked Enderby sharply.

'From?' repeated the man. 'From nobody except me. Me being the name of Walpole. And coming to see you on a question of poetry. It's cold here in the hall,' he said. Enderby led the way into the flat.

Walpole sniffed the warm dry air, the lingering sour stew-smell, the raised dust, and then noticed Enderby's packed bags. 'Leaving, eh?' he said. 'Well, I only just got you in time, didn't I?'

'I've got to catch a train,' said Enderby, 'any minute now. Would you –?'

'Oh, I'll be quick,' said Walpole, 'very quick. What I want to say is that I won't have you writing poetry to my wife.'

Enderby saw rush and then fade a quite unreasonable possibility. Then he smiled and said, 'I don't write poetry to anybody's wife.'

Walpole drew from his raincoat pocket a carefully folded and smoothed sheaf of sheets. 'This poetry,' he said. 'Look at it carefully and then tell me whether or not you wrote it.'

Enderby looked at it quickly. His handwriting. The Thelma poems. 'I wrote these, yes,' he said, 'but not on my own behalf. I wrote them at the request of another man. I suppose you could call him a client, really. You see, poetry is my profession.'

'If it's a profession,' said Walpole in all seriousness, 'does it have what you might call rules of professional etty kwett? More important than that, in a way of speaking, does it have a union?'

Enderby suddenly saw that he had been made a party to a proposed bed-breach. He said that he saw, ignoring Walpole's questions, saying, 'I see, I see. I'm really very sorry about all this. I knew nothing about it. I'm even more innocent than Arry. It just never crossed my mind – and I take it that it never crossed Arry's – that Thelma was a married woman.'

'Mrs Walpole,' said Walpole tautologically, 'is my wife. Thelma may or may not be her name, all according to whether she is on duty or not. At the moment she is not on duty. And this question of *Harry*' – he stressed the aitch pedantically – 'is a question that brings you in as a hypocrite and a liar, if you don't mind me saying so.' Walpole held up his hand as if taking the oath. 'I make use of those terms,' he said, 'out of reference to the conventionalities you yourself, as a boor Joyce, probably uphold. To me, in one manner of speaking, they have no proper relevance, being relics of boor Joyce morality.'

'I,' said Enderby warmly, 'object very strongly to being called a hypocrite and a liar, especially in my own house.'

'Clear your mind of cant,' said Walpole, whose reading was evidently wide. He straddled comfortably, raincoat-tails spread, in front of the electric fire. 'You are just leaving this place which is not a house and not, I presume, your property, and, moreover, what difference should it make to the effect of certain words on the individual brain whether those words are spoke in a church or in a lavatory, if you'll pardon the term, or, as it might be, here?' He made the knees-bend gesture of freeing a trouser-seat stuck in a rump-cleft.

The mention of church and lavatory went straight to Enderby's heart, also the invocation of logic. 'All right, then,' he said. 'In what way am I a hypocrite and a liar?'

'A fair question,' admitted Walpole. 'You are a hypocrite and a liar' – he pointed a *j'accuse* finger with forensic suddenness – 'because you hid your own desires under another man's cloak. Ah, yes. I have spoke to this man Harry. He admits to having sent up to Mrs Walpole plates of stewed tripe and, on one occasion, eels – both dishes to which she is not partial – but it was clear that that was in the way of colleagual friendliness, them both working in the same establishment. Both are workers, even though the place of their work is boor Joyce. Can you say the same for yourself?'

'Yes,' said Enderby, 'no.'

'Well, then,' continued Walpole, 'I have it on the word of Harry, who is a worker, that he had no adulterating intention in mind. To him it came as a shock, and I was there and I saw the shock as it came, that another man should be sending poetry to a married woman and signing it with another man's name, the name of a man who, still living in a capitalist society, is not in the same position to hit back as what *you* are.' Again the accusatory finger darted out like a chameleon's tongue.

'Why,' said stunned Enderby, aghast at such treachery on Arry's part, 'should not *he* be the liar and hypocrite? Why should you not believe me? Damn it all, I've only seen this woman once, and that was only to order a single whisky.'

'Single or double makes no difference,' said Walpole sagely. 'And there have been occasions when men, especially poets, have only seen a woman once (and I will thank you not to use that term in connexion with Mrs Walpole) or even not at all, and yet they have written reams and reams of poetry to her. There was the Italian poet who you may have heard of who wrote about Hell, and there again it was a married woman. He wrote about Hell, Mr Enderby, and not what you wrote in those shameful verses you have there and I would trouble you to hand back. There you have wrote about buttocks and breasts, which is not decent. I spent some time reading those poems, putting aside my other reading work to do so.' Enderby now detected, surfacing from the thin starved East Midland accent, the stronger tones of Anglo-Welsh. 'Indecencies,' said Walpole, 'that any man using to a married woman should be heartily ashamed of and should fear a judgement for.'

'This is absurd,' said Enderby. 'This is bloody nonsense. I wrote those poems at Arry's request. I wrote them in exchange for the loan of a suit and a few gifts of chicken and turkey carcasses. Does that not sound reasonable?'

'No,' said Walpole reasonably. 'It does not. You wrote these poems. You wrote of breasts and buttocks and even navels in connection with Mrs Walpole and nobody else. And there the sin lies.'

'But damn it,' said angry Enderby, 'she's got them, hasn't she? She's the same as any other woman in that respect, isn't she?'

'I do not know,' said Walpole, stilling Enderby's rage with a choir-conductor's hand. 'I am no womanizer. I have had to work. I have had no time for the fripperies and dalliances of poetry. I have had to work. I have had no time for the flippancies and insincerities of women. I have had to work, night after night, after the labours of the day, reading and studying Marx and Lenin and the other writers who would lead me to a position to help my fellow-workers. Can you say as much? Where has your poetry led you? To this.' He swept a hand round Enderby's dusty living-room. 'Where have my studies led me?' He did not answer his own question; Enderby waited, but the question was definitely established as rhetorical.

'Look,' said Enderby, 'I've got to catch a train. I'm sorry that this has happened, but you can see it was all a misunderstanding. And you must take my assurance that I've had nothing to do socially with Mrs Walpole and very little more professionally. By "professionally",' added Enderby carefully, spying a possible misin-terpretation, 'I mean, of course, in connection with her profession as a barmaid.'

'That,' said Walpole, shaking his head, 'is not salaried, it is not a profession. Well,' he said, 'the question of a punishment arises. I think, to some extent, that should be a matter to let rest between you and your Maker.'

'Yes, yes,' said Enderby, too eagerly, with too much relief, 'I agree.'

'You agree, do you?' said Walpole. 'A more intelligent and more well-read man and who follows political theories would there be tempted to ask a certain simple question. What would that certain simple question be, Comrade Enderby?'

The chill honorific, with its suggestion of brain-washing and salt-mines, made Enderby's bowels react strongly: they seemed to liquefy; at the same time a solid blast prepared itself for utterance. Nevertheless he said bravely, 'People who accept dialectical materialism don't usually accept the proposition of a divine first cause.'

'And very well put, too,' said Walpole, 'though a bit old-fashioned in its circumloquaciousness. God is what you mean, Comrade Enderby, God, God, God.' He raised his eyes to the ceiling, his mouth opening and shutting on the divine name as though he were eating it. 'God, God, God,' said Walpole. As in response to a summons there was a knock on the flat-door. 'Ignore it,' said Walpole sharply. 'Here we have important things on hand and not the frip-peries of visitors. I have done it,' said Walpole, with sudden craftiness.

'I have achieved it,' he said more softly, his eyes shining with bright dementedness. 'I have discovered the sin thesis.' The knock came again. 'Ignore it,' said Walpole. 'Now then, Comrade Enderby, you should now by rights ask the question "What sin thesis?" Go on,' he said, with clenched fierceness, '*ask it*.'

'Why aren't you at work?' asked Enderby. Again the knock.

'Because,' said Walpole, 'today is Saturday. Five days shalt thou labour, as the Bible says. The seventh day is the Lord thy God's. The sixth day is for football and spreading the word and punishing and suchlike. Go on. *Ask it*.'

'What sin thesis?' asked Enderby.

'A sin thesis of *everything*,' said Walpole. 'The others left God out, but I put Him in. I found a place for Him in the universe.'

'What place?' asked Enderby, fascinated despite his bowels, his fear, the knock at the door.

'What place could it be,' said Walpole, 'except *His own place*? God's place is God's place, and you can't say fairer than that. Now,' he said, 'on your knees, Comrade Enderby. We're going to pray together to this same God, and you're going to ask for forgiveness for all sins of fornication.' The knock came again, louder. 'QUIET,' bawled Walpole.

'I won't pray,' said Enderby. 'I've committed no fornication.'

'Who hasn't,' said Walpole, 'in his heart?' And, like Enderby's boyhood picture of the Saviour, he pointed to his own. 'On your knees,' he said, 'and I shall pray with you.'

'No,' said Enderby. 'I don't accept the same God as you. I'm a Catholic.'

'All the more reason,' said Walpole. 'THERE IS ONLY ONE GOD, COMRADE!' he suddenly bawled. 'On your knees and pray and you will be let off by me, if not by the Comrade Almighty. If you don't pray I shall be the Hound of Heaven and get some of the lads from the works on the job, and bloody quick, too, even if you do think you're going off this morning. ON YOUR KNEES! he ordered.

Enderby sighed and obeyed. His knees were stiff. Walpole knelt with the stage-fall ease of more practice. He did not close his eyes; he kept them full on Enderby. Enderby faced the electric fire's tabernacular gold. Walpole prayed:

'Comrade God, forgive the boor Joyce transgressions of Comrade Enderby here, who has been led astray by the lusts of his own body into writing phonographic poetry to Mrs Walpole, who You know, though she is stiff-necked and not one of Thy chosen. Let Your light shine upon him to make him a decent worker and good member of his union, when, him being a poet, such shall be formed. Better still, make him stop writing filthy poetry altogether and take up some decent trade at correct union rates and live in Godly righteousness, if that be Thy holy will, with some decent woman of Thy choosing in the state of holy matrimony, till such time as this boor Joyce institution is replaced by something better and more in keeping with what the proletariat will require.' Enderby now saw Walpole smile winningly at some apparition to his left, behind Enderby, at about picture-rail level. Enderby, presuming that this was God, felt no new fear. 'Just a tick,' said Walpole. 'Marvellous what prayer can do, innit? A bloody miracle, that's what it is. To finish up with, then,' he prayed, eyes now back on Enderby, 'stop this Thy comrade servant womanizing and messing about and bring him back to Your holy ways in the service of the classless society which Thou hast promisedest in the fullness of the workers' time. Thank you, Comrade God,' he said finally. 'Amen.'

Enderby, with much groaning and a posterior blast or two, got creaking to his feet. At that moment the electric fire, like some Zoroastrian deity now, having been prayed at, done with, went out. Enderby, standing, turned, blowing, and saw Mrs Bainbridge. She dangled Enderby's key in explanation of her entrance without Enderby's more direct agency, saying, 'Well, I never in all my life knew a man more capable of surprises.' She was a dream of winter bourgeois elegance: little black town suit with tiny white jabot of lace-froth; pencil skirt; three-quarter-length coat with lynx collar; long green gloves of suède; suède shoes of dull green; two shades of green in her leafy velvet hat: slim, clean, lithe-looking, delicately painted. Walpole, Marx-man of God, was clearly entranced. He handed her a small yellow throwaway poster and then, as a second thought, gave one to Enderby as well. 'GOD OR CAPITALISM?' it read. 'You Can't Have Both. H. Walpole will speak on this VITAL topic at the Lord Geldon Memorial Hall, Thursday, February 11th. All Welcome.'

'You come to that, lady,' said Walpole, 'and bring him along. There's good in him if only we can get at it, as you yourself will know well enough. Work on him hard, make him a decent man and stop him sending poetry to women, that's your job, I would say, and you look to me capable of tackling it.'

'Poetry to women?' said Vesta Bainbridge. 'He makes a habit of that, does he?' She gave Enderby a hard-soft green womanly look, holding her large shovel handbag in front of her, legs, as in a model pose, slightly astride.

H. Walpole was, for all his theophanic socialism, a decent man of bourgeois virtues who, now that Enderby had been thoroughly prayed for, did not want to put him in the bad with this fiancée of his here. 'That's only in a manner of speaking, as you might say,' he said. 'A very sexual man, you might say Mr Enderby is, with strong desires as must be kept down, and,' he said, 'you look to me like the one capable of doing it.'

'Thank you very much,' said Vesta Bainbridge.

'Look here,' said Enderby. The other two waited, listening. Enderby had really nothing to say. Walpole said:

'Right. In his poetry if not in his private life, if you see what I mean. That's where you'd come in, comrade madam, and would give him a bigger sense of reality. May the blessings of the God of all the workers bless your union till such times as society makes something better come about.'

'Thank you very much,' said Vesta Bainbridge.

'And now,' said Walpole cheerfully, 'I take my leave. I've enjoyed our little dialectical conversation together and hope to have many more. Don't show me out, I know the way. God keep you in His care,' he said to Enderby. 'You have nothing to lose but your chains.' He blessed Enderby and his putative betrothed with a clenched fist, smiled once more, then went out. Enderby and his putative betrothed were left together, listening to Walpole's marching footsteps and cheerful whistle recede.

'Well,' said Vesta Bainbridge.

'This,' said Enderby, 'is where I live.'

'So I see. But if you live here why are you moving?'

'I don't quite get that,' said Enderby. 'Would you say that again?'

'I don't quite get *you*,' said Vesta Bainbridge. 'You send me what

I suppose you'd call a verse-letter, straining at the leash with quite unequivocal suggestions, then you take fright and decide to run away. Or is it as simple as that? Obviously you thought I wouldn't get the letter till Monday morning, so it seems as though you planned to attack and retire at the same time. Actually, I always go into the office on Saturday mornings to see if there's any mail, and there I found the letter-rack practically sizzling with your little effort. I got a train right away. I was puzzled, intrigued. Also worried.'

'Worried?'

'Yes. About you.' She sniffed round the living-room with a wrinkle of distaste. 'I can see one would have cause to be worried. This place is absolutely filthy. Does nobody come in to clean it?'

'I do it myself,' said Enderby, suddenly and shamefully seeing the squalor of his life more clearly against the foil of her frightful wholesomeness. 'More or less.' He hung his schoolboy head.

'*Exactly*. And what, Harry, if I may call you that – indeed, I *must* call you that now, mustn't I? – were you proposing to do? Where were you proposing to go?'

'Harry's not my name,' said Not-Harry Enderby. 'It's just the name at the end of the poem.'

'I know, of course, it can't really be your name, because your initials don't have an aitch in them. Still, you signed yourself Harry and Harry seems to suit you.' She surveyed him with a cocked parrot head, as though Harry were a hat. 'I repeat, *Harry*, what are you going to do?'

'I don't know,' said pseudoharry wretched Enderby. 'That was all to be thought out, you see. Where to go and whatnot. What to do and so on and so forth.'

'Well,' said Vesta Bainbridge, 'a few days ago I gave you a tea and you offered me a dinner which I couldn't accept. I think it would be a good idea if you took me out to lunch somewhere now. And after that –'

'There's one place I shan't take you,' said Enderby, betrayed and angry. 'That's quite certain. It would poison me. It would choke me. Every mouthful.'

'Very well,' soothed Vesta Bainbridge. 'You shall take me wherever you choose. And after that I'm taking you home.'

'Home?' said Enderby with sudden fear.

'Yes, home. Home, home home. You know, the place where the heart is. The place that there's no place like. You need looking after. I'm taking you home, Harry.'

Part Two

1

1

Errrrrrrrp.

Enderby was in a very small lavatory, being sick. He was also married, just. Enderby the married man. A vomiting bridegroom.

When his forehead was cooler he sat, sighing, on the little seat. All below him was June weather, June being the month for weddings. Alone in this buzzing and humming tiny lavatory he had his first leisure to feel both gratified and frightened. The bride, though only in a severe suit suitable for a registry office, had looked lovely. Sir George had said so. Sir George was friendly again. All was forgiven.

Almost the first thing she had insisted on was an apology to Sir George. Enderby had written: 'So sorry I should seem to rate your sirship as a stupid dolt, but thought you would appreciate that feeble gesture of revolt. For you yourself have tried, God wot, the awful agonizing art, and though, as poet, you are not worth the least poetaster's fart, yet you're equipped to understand what clockwork makes the poet tick and how he hates the laden hand below the empty rhetoric . . .' That, she had said, was not really suitable, so he had tried something briefer in genuine prose, and Sir George had only been too delighted to accept the formal creaking apology.

Oh, she had begun to reorganize his life, that one. From the start, taking breakfast together in the large dining-room of her large flat, February Gloucester Road sulking outside, it was clear that things could only go one way. For what other relationship could be viable in the world's eyes than this one they were begin-ning now? Enderby had been forced to reject that of landlady and tenant, for he had paid no rent. The step-relationship was, with women, practically the only other one he had experienced. She was, he knew, and for this he valued her, antipodeal to a stepmother, being clean and beautiful. His father's remarriage had introduced brief squibs of step-aunts-in-law and the fable of a paragon step-sister, too good for this world and hence soon dead of a botulism, whom Enderby had always visualized as a puppet doll-dangling parody of his stepmother. Vesta was not, he had felt, a stepsister. A female Friend? He had rung that on his palate several times, upper case and all, and savoured a melancholy twilit aquarelle of Shelley and Godwin, with chorusmen's calves as if limned by Blake, holding reading-parties in a moored boat with high-waisted rather silly ladies, lovers of Gothic romances, while midges played fiddles in the sad air. Epipsychidion. Epithalamion. Ah God, that word had really started things off, for it had started off a poem.

> The cry in the clouds, the throng of migratory birds,
> The alien planet's heaven where seven moons
> Are jasper, agate, carbuncle, onyx, amethyst and blood-ruby and
>   bloodstone.
> Or else binary suns
> Wrestle like lions to a flame that we can stand,
> Bound, twisted and conjoined
> To an invertebrate love where selves are melted
> To the primal juice of a creator's joy,
> Before matter was made,
> Two spheres in a single orbit . . .

They had drunk Orange Pekoe with breakfast and she, in a rust-coloured suit with a heavy clip of hammered pewter on the left lapel, had just gone off to work. Enderby, in the kitchenette whose pastel beauty made him feel particularly dirty and gross, had put on the kettle for stepmother's tea, and the word 'epithalamion', like the announcement of a train's approach, had set the floorboards trembling with thunder. Panting at the dining-table, he had set down words, seeing his emergent poem as a song for the celebration of the consummation of the passion of the mature – Gertrude and Claudius in *Hamlet*, red-bearded lips on a widow's white neck. The leafy tea had cooled beside him. Mrs Opisso the daily woman had come in, dusky, hippy, bosomy, garlicky, moustached, leering brilliantly, a wartime Gibraltarian evacuee in whose blood seethed Genoese, Portuguese Jewish, Saracen, Irish, and Andalusian corpuscles, to say, interrupting sweeping, 'What are you in this house, eh? You not going out, not doing work, true? What are you to her, eh? You tell.' It had not been easy to tell; it was not enough to say that it was none of her business.

> . . . Swollen with cream or honey,
> The convalescent evening launches its rockets,
> Soaring above the rich man's gala day,
> In the thousand parks of the kingdom
> Which radiate from this bed . . .

Vesta would not necessarily think that this epithalamion was intended for her and her guest-Male Friend-protégé, for she had already said sardonically, 'if you intend to write any love poetry this morning make sure you don't send it to Sir George by mistake. This carelessness of yours will land you into big trouble one of these days, you mark my words.' Enderby had hung his head. She had been irritable that morning, tired, rubbing her brow tiredly, as in a TV commercial for some quack analgesic, under her green eyes delicate blue arcs of tiredness. She had stood by the door, in neat rust, a chiffon scarf in two tones of green, a minute brown beret aslant, brown suède gloves to match her shoes, slender, elegant and (so Enderby had divined) menstruating quietly. Enderby had said:

'Menstruation hits some women more than others, you know. Try gin and hot water. That's said to work wonders.'

She had blushed faintly and said, 'Where did you learn that?'

'In *Fem.*'

Sighing, she had said, 'It's all very confusing. I must work out, when I have time, the precise nature of our relationship.'

> Anoint the ship with wine! On ample waters,
> Which always wear this ring, that the earth be humbled
> Only away from cities, let it dance and ride . . .

And again, another time, the precise nature still not worked out, 'The question is, what's to be done with you?'

'Done with me?'

'Yes, that's the question.'

'Nothing is to be done with me.' He had looked across at her in fear, over the shattered fragments of toast which he had been feeding, as to a pet bird, to his mouth. 'I am, after all, a poet.' A lorry had backfired the world's answer.

'I want to know,' Vesta had said, chill morning hands round her breakfast-cup, 'exactly how much money you've got.'

'Why do you want to know that?' cunning Enderby had asked.

'Oh, please. I've got a busy day ahead of me. Let's not have any nonsense. Please.' Enderby had begun to tell out the contents of his left trouser-pocket. 'Not that sort of money,' she had cut in, sharply. Enderby had said, with care:

'Ten thousand pounds in local government loans at five and a half per cent. For dividends. Two thousand pounds in ICI, BMC, Butlin's. For capital appreciation.'

'Ah. And what income does all that yield?'

'About six hundred. Not a lot, really, is it?'

'It's nothing. And I suppose your poetry brings in less than nothing.'

'Two guineas a week. From *Fem*, God bless it.' For he had at last signed the contract and already seen in print, over the name of Faith Fortitude, hogwash beginning, 'A baby's cheeks, a baby's limbs are prayers to God and holy hymns; a little baby's toothless smile does the holy saints beguile . . .'

'An income like yours isn't worth having, really it isn't. So we've got to work out what's to be done with you.'

'Done with me?' prompt Enderby had flashed.

'Look,' she had said, 'I know you're a poet. But there's no need to regale us with poetic drama in the style of early Mr Eliot, is there? Not at breakfast there isn't.'

'Stichomythia,' had been learned Enderby's comment. 'But it's you who keep starting it off.'

Well, that was something not yet started off: useful employment, a *deuxième métier* for a poet. From Valentine to Pentecost he had been allowed, though not in the lavatory, to work at *The Pet Beast* peaceably. But after the honeymoon things would have to be different.

And you whose fear of maps
Set buzzing the long processes of power,
Resign your limbs at length to elements
Friendly or neutral at least,
Mirrors of the enemy . . .

His own bit of money had not, even before they'd started on capital purchases, been going very far ('Call in at the Lion, will you, and buy a couple of bottles of gin. Pay Mrs Opisso; I'm clean out of cash.'). And the greedy maws of Fortnum and Mason and the Army and Navy Stores. And a new wardrobe for himself, London not really favouring the casual valetudinarian garb of the seaside. Enderby's capital was going now. She, a thriftless Scot, did not believe in money, only in things. Hence the seven-thousand-pound house in Sussex in her name, this being his marriage settlement, also furniture, also a bright new Velox for Vesta to drive, Enderby when most sober managing a car like the drunkest drunk. And a mink coat, a wedding present.

Who had proposed marriage, and when? Who loved whom, if at all, and why? Enderby, in thinker's pose on the lavatory seat, frowned back to an evening when he had sat finishing his epithalamion in her twin dining-room, facing a piece of furniture he admired – a sideboard, massive and warped, proclaiming its date (1685) among carved lozenges and other tropes, fancies of the woodworker signifying his love of the great negroid ship-oak he had shaped and smoothed. Above that sideboard hung a painting of Vesta done by Gideon Dalgleish, she pearly-shouldered and haughty in a ballgown, seeming about to fly off, centrifugally, back into waiting but invisible paint-tubes. Above open book-shelves was a photograph of the late Pete Bainbridge. He grinned handsomely in a helmet, seated at the wheel of the Anselm 2.493 litre (six-cylinder; 250 b.h.p. Girling disc brakes; Weber 58 DCO carburettors, etc.) in which he had met his messy death. Enderby had started his last stanza:

And even the dead may bring blue lips to this banquet
And twitter like mice or birds down their corridors
Hung with undecipherable blazons . . .

He had felt a sudden and unwonted surge of personal, as opposed
to poet's, strength: he, unworthy and ugly as he was, was at least
alive, while this bright and talented handsome one had been blown
to pieces. He had grinned, borrowing the shape of the grin from
the dead man, in a sort of triumph. Vesta, reading some new brilliant
novel by an undergraduate, had looked up from her Parker-Knoll
and caught the grin. She had said:

'Why are you grinning? Have you written something funny?'

'Me? Funny? Oh, no.' Enderby had covered his manuscript with
clumsy paws, as one protects one's dinner-plate from an importunate
second scooping of mashed potato. 'Nothing funny at all.'

She had got up, so graceful, to see what he was writing, asking:
'What are you writing?'

'This? Oh, I don't think you'd like it. It's – Well, it's a sort of –'

She had picked up the sheet of scrawled lines and read aloud:

'. . . For two at least can deny
That the past has any odour. They can witness
Passion and patience rooted in one paradigm; in this music
   recognize
That all the world's guilt can sit like air
On the bodies of these living.'

'You see,' Enderby had said, over-eagerly, 'it's an epithalamion.
For the marriage of two mature people.' Inexplicably she had
lowered her head with its sweet-smelling penny-coloured hair and
kissed him. Kissed him. Him, Enderby.

'Your breath,' she had said, 'is no longer unhealthy. Sometimes
it's hard for the body and mind to come to terms. You're looking
better, much better.' What could he say but, 'Thanks to you'?

Airsick, seated in this aerial lavatory, he had to admit that a new
Enderby had emerged out of the spring and early summer – a
younger Enderby with less fat and wind, new teeth imperfect
enough to look real, several smart suits, hair cunningly dressed by

Trumper's of Mayfair and breathing delicately of Eucris, less gauche in company, his appetite healthier with no dyspeptic lust for spices and bread-and-jam, more carefully shaven, his skin clearer, his eyeballs glassy with contact lenses. If only Mrs Meldrum could see him now!

Who had mentioned love? Had anybody mentioned love? They had lived under one roof chaste, vestal, phoenix, and turtle, with Pete Bainbridge grinning from some Elysium of racing-drivers at the strange ménage of Friends. But one had only to chuck and see spin that worn coin on the polished floor for it to chink louder and louder music and revolve into a world. Had it been pocket or handbag? Enderby could not remember, but he was sure that one evening one of them had spoken the word in some connection or other, perhaps denouncing its inflation in popular songs or in the hoarse speech of immediate need, perhaps discussing its personified identification with, in seventeenth-century religious poetry, the Lord. Then, by a swift process too subtle and irrational for analysis, one or other of them had whistled down the dove-hawk from safe heights of speculation to perch, blinking, on a pair of joined hands.

'I've been so lonely,' she had said. 'I've been so cold at night.'

Enderby, potential bedwarmer, still potential on this brief flight to the honeymoon, for they had been chaste till now. Till tonight. Tonight in the Albergo Tritone on the Via Nazionale. Something, gulped Enderby, to look forward to.

'Look,' said a voice, meaning 'Listen'. Enderby started from the tiny seat, listening. 'Your ticket does not entitle you to undisputed monopolization of the john.' That, Enderby considered, was well put. The voice was American and authoritative and Enderby hastened to give place, fairly sure now that he felt better. Outside the folding doors he breathed deeply, taking in a large touristy man who nodded at him, edging past. He had a steak complexion and two cameras – still and movie respectively – on his stomach at the ready. Enderby wondered if he would photograph the john. Through a porthole summer cloud shone up. Enderby walked down the aisle to his bride who sat, cool and lovely, gazing at summer cloud beneath. She looked up and smiled, asking if he felt better. She gave her hand to him as he sat. It seemed to be a new life beginning.

2

As if he were in a well-appointed bath, Enderby was struck by various liquid sensations as they descended to Rome (going down. Eternal City: pasta, old junk, monumental remnants, figleaved stone stalwarts, veal, Vatican, staircases to basement and bones of martyrs. The whole roofed in ringing silver and refreshed by fountains. And the very best of luck). He felt cold sweat as his stomach, tardy in descending, encouraged its master to view Rome in a sort of stepmother-context (Pope in picture on bedroom wall, blessing seven hills; translucent image of St Peter's embedded in cross of blancmange-coloured rosary; missal bookmark of Holy Family as middle-class spaghetti-guzzlers, printed in Rome). Then he was warmed by thrilling gushes, the chicken-skinned hand that held the hand of the bride growing smooth again, as there swam up from the *News of the World* a picture of a heavy-breasted starlet sploshing, for a lark, in the Trevi fountain. There were also weary handsome princes in sordid divorce cases and Cinecittà was greater than the Vatican. It was all right really, it would be all right, sensual, thrilling. He looked with pride on his bride and, like a distant rumour of war, felt a prick of desire, legitimate desire; she was, in a flash, identified with this new city, to be, all so legitimately, sacked and pillaged. He said to her, a few words coming back from his L. of C. days, '*Io ti amo.*' She smiled and squeezed his hand. Enderby, Latin lover.

The warmth, the excitement, the sense of rejuvenation, survived the landing (the stewardess smirked at the exit as though she herself, after the aerial gestation, had given birth to the airport; the American who had ousted Enderby from the john began clicking away desperately). In the ragged procession to the buildings, Ciampino stretching in hot honeymoon weather, Enderby felt the barren flat airfield express, like a blank page, his new freedom, this being a freedom from his old freedom. A Cassius-lean and Casca-sullen Roman customs-man zipped open roughly the overnight bag of Vesta and held up for the whole shed to see a new nightdress. He winked sullenly at Enderby, and this to Enderby was a good omen, even though the man was starved-jawed and hence untrustworthy. The fat bus-driver sang some plangent oily aria with *amore* in it, jolting up the Appian Way, thus inspiring confidence. And then, whoosh, came the cold water again as the sun clouded over above a mossy aqueduct growing in ruins out of the dry grass, over an old plinth lying like a large merd under a comic-strip-coloured petrol poster. The American from the john fed his cameras like lapdogs. Meanwhile Enderby grew oppressed with a sense of travelling through a butcher's shop of mean history, between the ribs of carcasses, already being force-fed with chunks of the carrion empire. Rostra were quietly set up just beyond his line of vision and on them settled a sort of Seneca chorus of smirking noseless ancient Romans, fat on Sicilian corndoles and gladiator's blood. They would be present at the honeymoon; it was their city.

The sun suddenly exploded, a fire in a syrup factory, as they arrived at the airline terminal on the Via Nazionale. A dwarf porter of great strength carried their cases the few doors down to the hotel and Enderby gave him a tip of over-light suspect coins. They were bowed at and greeted with insincere golden smiles in the hotel lobby. 'Signor Enderby,' said Signor Enderby, 'and Signora Bainbridge.' 'No, no, no,' said Signora Enderby. Enderby smiled. 'Not used to it yet, you see. Our honeymoon,' he explained to the receptionist. He, a dapper Roman elf, said:

'Honeymoon, eh? I maker sure everythinger quiet forer honeymoon. A long time since I have a honeymoon,' he said regretfully. Vesta said:

'Look, I don't feel all that well. Do you think we could be taken to our –?' There were immediate calls and dartings and hoistings of bags.

'Darling,' said Enderby, concerned. 'What is it, darling?'

'Tired, that's all. I want to lie down.'

'Darling,' said Enderby. They entered a lift that was all rococo filigree-work, an airy frail cage that carried them up to a floor paved with veiny marble. Enderby saw, with interest, an open Roman lavatory, but he waved the interest away. Those days were over. They were shown into their room by a young man in a wine-coloured coat, his nose squashed flat as in desperate contradiction of the myth of Roman profiles. Enderby gave him several worthless slips of metal and asked for *vino*. (Enderby in Rome, ordering *vino*.) The young man shook hands with himself fiercely, then tensely raised the upper hand, teeth clenched as though lifting a killing weight, showing the space between to Enderby – a bottle of air with a hand-bottom and hand-top. 'Frascati,' he nodded direly, and went out, nodding. Enderby turned to his wife. She sat on the window-side of the double bed, looking out at the Via Nazionale. The little room was full of its noise – tram-clanks, horse-clops, Fiats and Lambrettas. 'Tired, tired, tired,' said Vesta, blue arcs back under her eyes, her face weary in the sharp Roman light. 'I don't feel at all the thing.'

'It's not –?' asked Enderby.

'No, of course it's not. This is our wedding-day, isn't it? I'll be all right when I've had a rest.' She kicked off her shoes and then, as Enderby gulped, swiftly unhitched her stockings. He turned to the dull sights of the street: metropolitan dourness, no flashing Southern teeth, no song. Across the road a shop, as though for Enderby's own benefit, had a special display of holy pictures going cheap, ill-painted hagiographs festooned with rosary-beads. When he turned back towards the bed Vesta was already in it, her thin arms and shoulders uncovered. Not a voluptuous woman; her body pared to a decent female minimum. That was as it should be. Enderby had once caught his stepmother stripped off in the bathroom, panting with the exertion of one of her rare over-all washes, flesh-shaking, fat tits swinging like bells. He shuddered at the memory, his burring lips becoming, for the moment, those of his stepmother flinching at the cold sponge. There was a knock. Enderby had read Dante with an English crib; there was, he knew, a line which contained the word for 'come in'. He delved for it, and it came up just as the door opened. 'All hope abandon,' he called in fine Tuscan, 'you who –' A long-faced waiter peered in, doubtful, then entered with his tray, leaving without waiting (a non-waiting waiter) for a tip. Enderby, a mad Englishman, sighed and poured wine. He shouldn't have said that. It was a bad omen. It was like Byron waking on his wedding-night and thinking that the bedroom fire was hell. He said:

'Darling. Would you care for a glass of this, darling?' He gulped some thirstily. A very nice little wine. 'Help you to sleep if you're going to sleep.' She nodded tiredly. Enderby poured another glass, the urine-gold flashing in the clear light, belching as it left the

bottle. He gave the glass to her and she sat up to sip it. Fair down
on her upper lip, Enderby noticed in love and pity, his arm round
her shoulders to support her sitting up. She drank half a glassful
and at once, to Enderby's shock and horror, reacted violently.
Pushing him and the glass away, she fought to leave the bed, her
cheeks bulging. She ran on bare feet to the washbowl, gripped its
sides, groaned and started to vomit. Enderby, much concerned,
followed and stood by her, slender, defenceless in her minimal
unalluring summer underwear. 'That's your lunch coming up,' said
Enderby, watching. 'A bit fatty, wasn't it?' With a roar more came
up. Enderby poured water from the water-bottle.

'Oh God,' she groaned. 'Oh Jesus.' She turned on both taps and
began to retch again.

'Drink this,' said Enderby. 'Water.' She gulped from the proffered
glass and vomited again, but this time mostly water, groaning
between spasms blasphemously. 'There,' said Enderby, 'you'll be
better now. That was a nasty sort of pudding they served up. All
jammy.'

'Oh Jesus Christ,' retched Vesta (All jammy). Enderby watched
kindly, a past master on visceral dysfunctions, as she got it all up.
Then weak, wet, limp, spent, she staggered back to the bed. 'A
good start,' she gasped. 'Oh God.'

'That's the worst of meals on aircraft,' said Enderby, sage
after his first flight. 'They warm things up, you see. Have some
more wine. That'll settle your stomach.' Fascinated by the near-
rhymes, he began softly to repeat. 'That'll settle, that'll settle,'
pacing the room softly, one hand in pocket, the other holding
wine.

'Oh, shut up,' moaned Vesta. 'Leave me alone.'

'Yes, darling,' said Enderby, accommodating. 'Certainly, darling.
You have a little sleep, darling.' He heard himself wheedling like a
foreign whore, so he straightened up and said more gruffly, 'I'll go
and see about traveller's cheques.' Saying that, he was standing up
against the door, as if challenging it or measuring himself against
it. When a knock came he was able to open it at once. The long-
faced boy looked startled. His arms were full of roses, red and
white. '*Fiori*,' he said, '*per la signora.*'

'Who from?' frowned Enderby, feeling for an accompanying

card. 'Good God,' he said, finding it. 'Rawcliffe. And Rawcliffe's in the bar. Darling,' he called, turning. But she was asleep.

3

'Ah,' said Rawcliffe. 'You got the message, got the flowers? Good. Where,' he asked, 'is Mrs Enderby?' He was dressed as when Enderby had last seen him, in an old-fashioned heavy suit with a gold watch-chain, Kipling-moustached, beetle-goggled, drunk.

'Mrs Enderby,' said Enderby, 'is dead.'

'I beg your pardon,' said Rawcliffe. 'Already? Roman fever? How very Jamesian!'

'Oh, I see what you mean,' said Enderby. 'Sorry. She only became Mrs Enderby today, you see. It takes some getting used to. I thought you meant my stepmother.'

'I see, I see. And your stepmother's dead, is she? How very interesting!' Enderby shyly examined the bar, the shelves massed with liquors of all countries, the silver tea-urn, the espresso apparatus. Behind the bar a short fat man kept bowing. 'Have some of this Strega,' said Rawcliffe. 'Dante,' he said, and the fat un-Dantesque man came to attention. Rawcliffe then spoke most intricate Italian, full, as far as Enderby could judge, of subjunctives, but with a most English accent. 'Strega,' said Dante. 'Are you,' said Enderby nastily, 'in all the Italian anthologies, too?' He was given, with flourishes, a glass of Strega.

'Ha, ha,' said Rawcliffe, without much mirth. 'As a matter of fact, there's a very good Italian translation of that little poem of mine, you know. It goes well into Italian. Now, tell me, tell me, Enderby, what are you writing at the moment?'

'Nothing,' said Enderby. 'I finished my long poem, *The Pet Beast*. I told you about that.'

'You most certainly did,' said Rawcliffe, bowing. Dante bowed too. 'A very good idea, that was. I look forward to reading it.'

'What I'd like to know,' said Enderby, 'is what you're doing here. You don't look as though you're on holiday, not in those clothes you don't.'

Rawcliffe did something Enderby had read about but never

before seen: he placed a finger against his nose. 'You're right,' he said. 'Most certainly *not* on holiday. At work. Always at work. Some more Strega?'

'With me,' said Enderby. Dante bowed and bowed, filling their glasses. 'And one for you, too,' said Enderby, expansive, on his honeymoon. Dante bowed and said to Rawcliffe, '*Americano?*'

'*Inglese,*' said Rawcliffe.

'*Americani,*' said Dante, leaning forward, confidential, 'fack you. *Mezzo mezzo.*'

'*Un poeta,*' said Rawcliffe, 'that's what he is. *Poeta.* Feminine in form, masculine in gender.'

'I beg your pardon,' said Enderby. 'Did you by any chance mean anything by that?'

'As a matter of fact,' said Rawcliffe, 'it's my belief that all we poets are really a sort of a blooming hermaphrodite. Like Tiresias, you know. And you're on your honeymoon, eh? Have some more Strega.'

'What exactly do you mean by that?' said Enderby, wary.

'Mean? You are a one for meaning, aren't you? The meaning of meaning. I. A. Richards and the Cambridge school. A lot of twaddle, if you ask my opinion. All right, if you won't have more Strega with me I'll have more Strega with you.'

'Strega,' said Enderby.

'Your Italian's coming along very nicely,' said Rawcliffe. 'A couple of nice vowels there. A couple of nice Stregas,' he said, as these appeared. 'God bless, all.' He drank. He sang, 'Who would an ender be, let him come hither.'

'How did you know we were here?' asked Enderby.

'Air terminal,' said Rawcliffe. 'Today's arrivals from London. Always interesting. Here, they said honeymoon. Remarkable, Enderby, in a man of your age.'

'What do you mean by that?' asked Enderby.

'You gentlemen ave Strega on the ouse,' said Dante, pouring.

'*Tante grazie,*' said Rawcliffe. 'There you go, Enderby, worrying about meaning all the time.' He sang, standing to attention. 'Would you a spender be, would you a mender be, God save the Queen. No meaning there, is there? Would you a fender be. That's better still. Too much meaning in your poetry, Enderby. Always has been.'

His words rode over a few drinker's belches. 'Pardon, as they say.'
He drank.

'Strega,' said Enderby. '*E uno per Lei, Dante.*'

'You can't say that,' said Rawcliffe, hiccoughing. 'What bloody
awful Italian you speak, Enderby! Bad as your poetry. Pardon. Fair
criticism. But I will say that the monster idea of yours was a bloody
good one. Too good to make a poem out of it. Ah, Rome,' he said,
lyrically, 'fair, fair Rome. Remarkable place, Enderby, no place like
it. Listen, Enderby. I'm going to a party tonight. At the house of
the Principessa Somebody-or-other. Would you like to come? You
and your missus? Or does it behove you to retire early this fair
nuptial night?' He shook his head. 'La Rochefoucauld, or some
other bloody scoundrel, said you mustn't do it on the first night.
What did he know about it, eh? Homosexuals, the lot of them.
All writers are homosexuals. They have to be. Stands to reason. To
hell with writing.' He poured his last few drops of Strega on to
the floor. 'That,' he said, 'is for the Lares and Penates to come and
lap up. A potation, that is to say a libation. They come to lap it
up like bloody big dogs. More Strega.'

'Don't you think?' said Enderby cautiously. 'I mean, if you're
going to a party –'

'Not for hours yet,' said Rawcliffe. 'Hours and hours and hours.
Plenty of time for you to get it over and done with several times over
before it starts. If you can, that is. Shellfish are bloody good, you know.
Magnificent augmenters of male potency. Scampi. Dante,' he cried,
'send for some scampi for this here signore. He is a newly married
man, God bless him.' Rawcliffe swayed on his stool. Dante said:

'Today you are married? Very good. You ave Strega on the ouse.'
He poured. '*Salute*,' he toasted. '*Molti bambini*,' he winked.

'Lovely grub,' said Rawcliffe, drinking. Enderby drank and said:

'What you've been saying is very indelicate. You ought by rights
to be bashed.'

'Oh dear dear dear me, no,' said Rawcliffe, shaking his head, his
eyes shut. 'Not on a day like this. Much too warm. *Pace, pace*, this
is a city of peace.' He began to fall asleep.

'*Troppo*,' confided Dante. 'Too mash. You get im ome.'

'No,' said Enderby. 'Damn it all, I'm on my honeymoon. I don't
like him, anyway. Nasty bit of work.'

'Jealous,' mumbled Rawcliffe, eyes still shut, head drooping to the counter. 'I'm in all the anthologies. He's not. Popular poet, me. Known and loved and respected by all.' He then neatly, as in a professional tumbling act, collapsed with the stool on to the deep carpet of the bar, falling, it seemed, quite slowly, in a rotary figure. The noise, though muffled, was loud enough to summon men in skimpy suits from the hotel lobby. These spoke very fast Italian and looked with hate upon Enderby. Enderby said:

'Nothing to do with me. He was drunk when I met him.' Surlily he added, 'Damn it all, I'm on my honeymoon.' Two men bent over Rawcliffe and Enderby was afforded an intimate, non-tourist's, glimpse of the city, for one man had dandruff and the other boil-scars on his nape. Rawcliffe opened one eye and said, very clearly:

'Don't trust him. He's a spy pretending to be on his honeymoon. Made me drunk to shteal official shecretsh. Overthrow of Italian government plot dishcovered, alleged. Bombs shecreted in Foro Traiano and Tempio di Vesta.'

'You leave my wife out of this,' threatened Enderby.

'Ah, wife,' said one of the men. '*Capito*.' All was clear. Enderby had knocked Rawcliffe down in wronged husband's legitimate anger. A matter of honour. Rawcliffe now snored. The two men returned to their lobby to see about a taxi for him. Dante said to Enderby, tentatively: 'Strega?'

'*Si*,' said Enderby. He signed the chit and counted the number of other chits he had signed, all for Strega. Amazing. He would have to go easy, he hadn't all the money in the world. But, of course, he reflected, after this honeymoon he would start *earning* money. The capital was there to be spent; Vesta had said so.

Rawcliffe ceased snoring, smacked his lips, and said: 'Thou hast wrongedst me, O Enderby.' His eyes did not open. 'I wished no harm. Merely desired to crown your nuptials in appropriate manner.' He then gave a loud snore. A taxi-driver with a square of moustache dead under his nose entered, shook his head tolerantly, and started to lift Rawcliffe by the shoulders. Members of the hotel staff appeared, including menials in off-white jackets, and Dante struck a pose behind the bar. All were waiting for Enderby to lift Rawcliffe's feet.

Enderby said: 'I know he's *Inglese* and I'm *Inglese*, but it bloody

well stops there. I can't stand him, see? *Io,*' he said, piecing the
sentence together painfully, '*non voglio aiutare.*' Everybody inclined,
with smiles, to show that they appreciated this attempt on the part
of an Englishman to use their beautiful language, but they ignored
the meaning, perhaps having been well schooled by this snoring
Rawcliffe. 'I won't help,' repeated Enderby, picking up Rawcliffe's
feet. (There was a hole in the left sole.) 'This is no way to be
spending a bloody honeymoon,' said Enderby, helping, very
awkwardly, to carry Rawcliffe out. 'Especially in Rome.' As he
passed, now panting, the ranked officials of the hotel, these bowed
fully or gently inclined, all with smiles.

The Via Nazionale was afire with sun and brilliant with people.
The taxi throbbed, waiting, by the kerb, Enderby and the driver
sweated as they pushed their way, Rawcliffe still snoring. A sort of
begging friar rattled his box at Enderby. 'For cough,' said Enderby.
An American, not the john one, poised his camera to shoot. 'For
cough,' snarled expiring Enderby. The driver, raising his knee to
support the snoring body, freed his hand to open the passenger-
door. Rawcliffe, like six months' laundry, was bundled in. 'There,'
said Enderby. 'All yours.'

'*Dove?*' asked the driver.

'Oh, God, yes, where to?' Enderby manhandled, still panting,
the loud, still Rawcliffe, trying to shout, 'Where do you live, you
bastard? Come on, tell us where.'

Rawcliffe came awake with startling briskness, as though he had
merely pretended to pass out so that he might be carried. His blue
eyes, quite clear, flashed patches of Roman sky at Enderby. 'Tiber,
Father Tiber,' he said, 'on whom the Romans prey. The Via Mancini
by the Ponte Matteotti.'

The driver eagerly drank that in. 'O world, O life, O time,'
intoned Rawcliffe. 'Here lies one whose name was *not* writ in
water. In all the anthologies.' He returned to a heavy sleep with
louder snores than before. Enderby hesitated, then, since the whole
waiting world seemed to expect it of him, roughly made room
next to Rawcliffe. They drove off. The driver honked down the
Via Nazionale and turned abruptly into the Via IV Novembre.
Then, as they sped north up the Via del Corso, Rawcliffe came
quite alive again, sat up sedately, and said:

'Have you such a thing as a cigarette on you, my dear Enderby? An English cigarette, preferably.'

'Are you all right now?' asked Enderby. 'Can I get out here and let you go home on your own?'

'Over there on the left,' pointed Rawcliffe, 'you'll find the Pantheon if you look carefully. And there' – his hand swished right, striking Enderby – 'down the street of humility, at the end, is the Fontana di Trevi. There you will throw your coin and be photographed by touts in berets. Do give me a cigarette, there's a good fellow.' Enderby offered a single crushed Senior Service. Rawcliffe took it steadily without thanks, lighting up as firm as a rock. 'We come now, Enderby, to the Piazza Colonna. There it is, the column itself, and at the top Marcus Aurelius, see.'

'I could get off here,' suggested Enderby, 'and go back to the hotel. My wife isn't too good, you know.'

'Isn't she?' said Rawcliffe. 'Not too good at what? A great admirer of poets, though. I'll say that for her. She always liked my little poem in the anthologies. It's quite likely, you know, Enderby, that you're going to be a great man. She likes to back winners. She backed one very good one, but that was in the field of sport. Poets don't get killed as racing-drivers do, you know. Look, the Piazza del Popolo. And now we're coming up to the Via Flaminia and there, you can just see, is Father Tiber himself, into whom the Romans spit.'

'What do you know about my wife?' asked Enderby. 'Who told you I'd married Vesta Bainbridge?'

'It was in the popular papers,' said Rawcliffe. 'Didn't you see? Perhaps she kept them from you. Pete Bainbridge's widow to remarry, they said. The popular papers didn't seem to know very much about you. But when you're dead there'll be biographies, you know. There haven't been any biographies of Pete Bainbridge, so there's a lot to be said for not being known to the readers of the *Daily Mirror*. Ah, here is the Via Mancini.' He banged the glass partition and made grotesque boxing gestures at the driver. The driver nodded, swerved madly, and came to rest before a small drinking-shop. 'This is where I have my humble lodging,' said Rawcliffe. 'Above here.'

'Do you really believe that?' asked Enderby. 'I thought perhaps

I appealed to a sort of protective instinct in her. And I'm very fond of her. Very, very fond. In love,' said Enderby. Rawcliffe nodded and nodded, paying the driver. He seemed to have recovered completely from his Strega-bout. The two poets stood in the warm street, cooled by river air. Enderby let the taxi go and said, 'Damn. I've let that taxi go. I ought to get back to my wife.' He reminded himself that he disliked Rawcliffe because he was in all the anthologies. 'It strikes me,' said Enderby, 'that you were swinging the bloody lead. I needn't have come with you at all.'

'Strega,' said Rawcliffe, nodding, 'passes through my system very quickly. I think, now we're here, we'll have some more. Or perhaps a litre or so of Frascati.'

'I must get back. She may be all right now. She may be wondering where I am.'

'There's no hurry. The bride's supposed to wait, you know. Supposed to lie in cool sheets smelling of lavender while the bridegroom gets drunk and impotent. The Toby night, you know. That's what it used to be called. After Tobias in the Apocrypha. Come on, Enderby, I'm lonely. A brother poet is lonely. And I have things to tell you.'

'About Vesta?'

'Oh, no. Much more interesting. About you and your poetic destiny.'

They entered the little shop. It was dark and warm. On the walls were vulgar mosaics, pseudo-Etruscan, of prancing men and women in profile. There were glass jars of wine and cloudy tumblers. An old man from the age of Victor Emmanuel sucked an ample moustache; two sincere-eyed rogues, round-faced and, despite the heat, in overcoats, whispered roguery to each other. A champing old woman, each step an effort, brought a litre of urine to two English poets. 'Salute,' said Rawcliffe. He shuddered at the first draught, found the second blander. 'Tell me, Enderby,' he said, 'How old would you say I am?'

'Old? Oh, about fifty.'

'Fifty-two. And when do you think I stopped writing?'

'I didn't know you *had* stopped.'

'Oh, yes, a long time, a long, long time. I haven't written a line of verse, Enderby, since I was twenty-seven. There, that surprises you, doesn't it? But writing verse is so difficult, Enderby, so so difficult. The only people who can write verse after the age of thirty are the people who do the competitions, you know, in the week-end papers. You can add to that, of course, the monkey-gland boys, of whom Yeats was one, but that's not playing the game, by God. The greatest senile poet of the age, by God, by grace of this bloody man Voronoff. But the rest of us? There are no dramatic poets left, Enderby, and, ha ha, certainly no epic poets. We're all lyric poets, then, and how long does the lyric urge last? No bloody time at all, my boy, ten years at the most. It's no accident, you know, that they all died young, mainly, for some reason, in Mediterranean lands. Dylan, of course, died in America, but the Atlantic's a sort of Mediterranean, when you come to think of it. What I mean is, American civilization's a sort of sea-board civilization, when you come to think of it, and not a river civilization at all.' Rawcliffe shook his head in a fuddled gesture, the Frascati having wakened the sleeping Strega. 'What I mean is, Enderby, that you're bloody lucky to be writing poetry at all at the age of – what is your age?'

'Forty-five.'

'At the age of forty-five, Enderby. What I mean is, what are you looking forward to now? Eh?' He let more Frascati stagger into his glass. Outside, the Roman daylight flashed and rippled. 'Don't kid yourself, my dear boy, about long bloody narrative poems, or plays, or any of that nonsense. You're a lyric poet, and the time is coming for the lyric gift to die. Who knows? Perhaps it's died already.' He looked narrowly at Enderby over the glass flask of Frascati swimming and dancing in his grip. 'Don't expect any more epiphanies, any more mad dawn inspirations, Enderby. That poem of mine, the one in the anthologies, the one I'll live by if I'm going to live at all, I wrote that bugger, you know, Enderby, at the age of twenty-one. Youth. It's the only thing worth having.' He nodded sadly. As in a film, an easy symbol of youth orchestrated his words, passing by outside, a very head-high girl of Rome with black hair and smoky sideburns, thrust breasts, liquid waist like Harry Ploughman's, animal haunches. 'Yes, yes,' said Rawcliffe, 'youth.' He drank Frascati and sighed. 'Haven't you felt, Enderby, that your gift is dying? It's a gift appropriate to youth, you know, owing nothing to experience or learning. An athletic gift, really, a *sportif* gift.' Rawcliffe dropped his jaw at Enderby, disclosing crooked teeth of various colours. 'What are you going to do, Enderby, what are you going to do? To the world, of course, all this is nothing. If the world should enter and hear us mourning the death of Enderby's lyric gift, the world, Enderby, would deem us not merely mad. They would consider us, Enderby, to be, Enderby' – he leaned forward, hissing – 'really talking about something else in the guise of the harmless. They would think us, perhaps, to be *Communists*.'

'And,' said Enderby, frightened by this vision of coming impotence, impotence perhaps already arrived, 'what do *you* do?'

'I?' Rawcliffe was already drunk again. He shoulder-jerked spastically and munched the air like spaghetti. 'I, Enderby, am the great diluter. Nothing can be taken neat any more. The question is this: do we live, or do we partly live? Or,' he said, 'do we,' and he was suddenly blinking in the killing lights, before the cranking cameras, jerking upright to stand against the wall, as against, with spread thin arms, a rockcliff, a rawface, 'die?' He then collapsed on the table, like a Hollywood absinthe-drinker, but none of the Romans took any notice.

4

'And,' said Vesta, 'what exactly do you think you've been doing? Where exactly do you think you've been?' Enderby felt a sort of stepson's guilt, the only kind he really knew, looking at her, head hung. She was brilliant in a wide-skirted daffodil-yellow dress, penny-coloured hair smooth and shining, skin summer-honeyed, healthy again, her eyes green, wide, nasty, a most formidable and desirable woman. Enderby said, mumbling: 'It was Rawcliffe, you see.'

She folded her bare arms. 'You know Rawcliffe,' chumbled Enderby and, a humble and hopeful attempt at palliation of his crime or crimes, 'he's in all the anthologies.'

'In all the bars, most likely, if I know anything about Rawcliffe. And you've been with him. I'm giving you fair warning, Harry. You keep out of the way of people like Rawcliffe. What's he doing in Rome, anyway? It all sounds very suspicious to me. What did he say? What was he telling you?'

'He said that being a lyric poet was really like being a racing motorist and that you've only lowered yourself to marry me because you'll be in all the biographies and will share in my eternal fame and glory, and he said that my poetic gift was dying and then what was I going to do? Then he passed out and I had to help carry him upstairs and that made me very thirsty. Then I couldn't find a taxi for a long time and I couldn't remember the name of the hotel. So that's why I'm late. But,' said Enderby, 'you didn't say anything about what time to be back, did you? You didn't say anything at all.'

'You said you were going to cash traveller's cheques,' said Vesta. 'It was your duty to stay here, with me. A fine start to a honeymoon this is, isn't it, you going off with people like Rawcliffe to get drunk and listen to lies about your wife.'

'What lies?'

'The man's a born liar. He was always trying to make passes at me.'

'When? How do you know him?'

'Oh, he's been a journalist of sorts,' said Vesta. 'Always messing round on the fringes of things. He's probably here in films, I should think, just messing round. Look,' she said very sternly, 'in future you're not to go anywhere without me, do you understand? You just don't know the world, you're just too innocent to live. My job is to look after you, take charge of things for you.'

'And *my* job?' said Enderby.

She smiled faintly. Enderby noticed that the bottle of Frascati, three-quarters full when he had left the bedroom, was now empty. She had certainly recovered. Outside was gentle Roman early evening. 'What do we do now?' asked Enderby.

'We go and eat.'

'It's a bit early for that, isn't it? Don't you think we ought to drink a little before eating?'

'You've drunk enough.'

'Well,' said Enderby, looking again at the empty Frascati bottle, 'you haven't done too badly yourself. On an empty stomach, too.'

'Oh, I sent down for some pizza and then a couple of club

sandwiches,' said Vesta. 'I was starving. I still am.' She took from the wardrobe a stole, daffodil-yellow, to cover her bare shoulders against evening cold or Italian lust. She had unpacked, Enderby noticed; she couldn't have been ill for very long. They left the bedroom and went down by the stairs, mistrusting the frail filigree charm of the lift. In the corridors, in the hotel lobby, men frankly admired Vesta. Bottom-pinchers, suddenly realized Enderby, all Italians were blasted bottom-pinchers; that raised a problem. And surely duels of honour were still fought in this backward country? Out on the Via Nazionale, Enderby walked a pace behind Vesta, smiling sourly up at the SPQR shields on the lamp standards. He didn't want any trouble. He hadn't before quite realized what a responsibility a wife was. 'I was told,' said Vesta, 'that there's a little place on the Via Torino. Harry, why are you walking behind? Don't be silly; people are looking at you.'

Enderby skipped to her side, but, invisible to her, his open hand was spread six inches behind her walking rump, as though warming itself at a fire. 'Who told you?'

'Gillian Frobisher.'

'That,' said Enderby, 'is the woman who nearly killed me with her Spaghetti Surprise.'

'It was your own fault. We turn right here.'

The restaurant was full of smeary mirrors and smelt strongly of cellar-damp and very old breadcrumbs. Enderby read the menu in gloom. The waiter was blue-jawed, lantern-jawed, untrustworthy, trying to peer, slyly, into Vesta's *décolletage*. Enderby wondered why such glamour surrounded the Italian cuisine. After all, it consisted only of a few allomorphs of paste, the odd sauce or so; the only Italian meat was veal. Nevertheless Enderby read 'bifstek' and, with faint hope, ordered it. Vesta, starving, had worked through mine-strone, a ravioli dish, some spaghetti mess or other, and was dipping artichoke leaves into oily vinegar, Enderby had begun to glow on a half-litre of Frascati when the alleged steak arrived. It was thin, white, on a cold plate. Enderby said to the waiter:

'*Questo é vitello.*' He, who had, before his life with Vesta, subsisted on ghastly stews and dips in the jampot, now became steak-faced with thwarted gastronome's anger.

'*Si, é vitello, signore.*'

'I ordered beefsteak,' cried furious Enderby, uncouth Englishman abroad, 'not bloody veal. Not that it is bloody veal,' he added, with poetic concern for verbal accuracy. 'Fetch the manager.'

'Now, Harry,' rebuked Vesta. 'We've had enough naughtiness for one day, haven't we? See, people are looking at you.' The Roman eaters all round were shovelling away, swollen-eyed, sincerely voluble with each other. They ignored Enderby; they had seen his type before. The manager came, fat, small, shiftily black-eyed, breathing hard with suppressed indignation at Enderby.

'I ordered,' said Enderby, 'a steak. This is veal.'

'Is a same thing,' said the manager. 'Veal is a cow. Beef is a cow. Ergo, beef is a veal.'

'Are you,' said Enderby, enraged by this syllogism, 'trying to teach me what is a beefsteak and what is not? Are you trying to teach me my own bloody language?'

'Language, Harry, language,' said Vesta ineptly.

'Yes, my own bloody language,' cried Enderby. 'He thinks he knows better than I do. Are you going to stick up for him?'

'Is a true,' said the manager. 'You not a eat, you pay just a same. What a you a order you a pay.'

Enderby stood up, saying, 'Oh, no. Oh, most certainly bloody well no.' He looked down at Vesta, before whom frothed a zabaglione. 'I'm not,' he said, 'paying for what I didn't order, and what I didn't order was that pallid apology down there. I'm going to eat somewhere else.'

'Harry,' she ordered, 'sit down. Eat what you're given.' She pinged her zabaglione glass pettishly with her spoon. 'Don't make such a fuss over nothing.'

'I don't like throwing money away,' said Enderby, 'and I don't like being insulted by foreigners.'

'You,' said Vesta, 'are the foreigner. Now *sit down.*'

Enderby grumpily sat down. The manager sneered in foreigner's triumph, ready to depart, having resolved the stupid fuss, meat being veal anyway, no argument about it. Enderby saw the sneer and stood up again, angrier. 'I won't bloody well sit down,' he said, 'and he knows what he can do with his bloodless stuff here. If you're staying, I'm not.'

Vesta's eyes changed from expression to expression rapidly, like

the number-indicator of a bus being changed by the conductor.
'All right,' she said, 'dear. Leave me some money to pay for my
own meal. I'll see you in fifteen minutes in that open-air café
place.'

'Where?'

'On the Piazza di what's-its-name,' she said, pointing.

'Repubblica,' said the waiter, helpful.

'You keep your bloody nose out of this,' said Enderby. 'All right,
then. I'll see you there.' He left with her a large note for several
thousand or million lire. From it the face of some allegorical lady
looked up at Enderby in mute appeal.

Fifteen minutes later Enderby, gazing glumly at the colour-lit
fountain, watching the Vespas and the Fiats and the sober crowds,
sat near the end of a bottle of Frascati. It had come to him warm,
and he had said to the terrace waiter, '*Non freddo.*' The waiter had
agreed that the bottle was *non freddo* and had gone off smiling.
Now the bottle was less *freddo* than ever. It was a warm evening.
Enderby felt a sudden strong longing for his old life, the stewed
tea, the poetry in the lavatory, onanistic sex. Then, wanting to
blubber, he realized that he was being very childish. It was right
that a man should marry and be honeymooning among the fountains of Rome; it was right to want to be mature. But Rawcliffe
had said something about poetry being a youthful gift, hence
immature, cognate with the gifts of speed and alertness that made
a man into a racing-driver. Was it possible that the gift was already
leaving him, having stayed perhaps longer than was right? If so,
what was he, what would he turn into?

Vesta arrived, a *Vogue* vision of beauty against the floodlit fountain. Fluttered and suddenly proud, Enderby stood up. She sat down,
saying, 'I was really ashamed of you in there. You behaved absolutely
disgracefully. Naturally, I paid for the meal you ordered. I hate
these petty wrangles over money.'

'My money,' said Enderby. 'You shouldn't have done it.'

'All right, your money. But, please remember, *my* dignity. I don't
allow you or any man to make a fool out of me.' She softened. 'Oh,
Harry, how could you, how could you behave like that? On the first
day of our honeymoon, too. Oh, Harry, you upset me dreadfully.'

'Have some wine,' said Enderby. The waiter inclined with a

Roman sneer, bold eyes of admiration for the *signora*. 'That last lot,' said Enderby, 'was bloody *caldo*. This time I want it *freddo*, see? Bloody *freddo*.' The waiter went, sneering and leering. 'How I hate this bloody town!' said Enderby, suddenly shivering. Vesta began to snivel quietly. 'What's the trouble?' asked Enderby.

'Oh, I thought things would be different. I thought you'd be different.' Suddenly she stiffened, staring straight ahead of her, as though waiting for some psychic visitation. Enderby looked at her, his mouth open. Her mouth opened, too, and, as from the mouth of a spiritualistic medium, there was emitted what sounded like the greeting of a Red Indian 'control':

Haaaaooooo.

Enderby listened in silent wonder, his mouth open wider. It was a belch.

'Oh,' she said, 'sorry. I couldn't help that at all, really I couldn't.'

'Let it come,' said Enderby kindly. 'You can always say excuse-me.'

Barrrrrp.

'I *do* beg your pardon,' said Vesta. 'You know, I don't think I feel frightfully well. I don't think this change of food is agreeing with me.' Rorrrrp. Auuuuu.

'Would you like to go back to the hotel?' asked Enderby eagerly.

'I think I'll have to.' Borrrrphhh. 'We're having the most unfortunate day, aren't we?'

'The Toby night,' said Enderby with relief. 'Like Tobias in the Apocrypha.' He took her arm.

2

1

'Piazza San Pietro,' said the guide. 'St Peter's Square.' He was a young Roman with a crewcut, insolent, bold eyes for the ladies.

'Place Saint Pierre. St Peter's Platz.' Vulgar, decided Enderby. Pretentious. The guide saw Enderby's sourness, saw that he was not impressed. 'Plaza San Pedro,' he said, as though playing a trump card.

It was a real scorcher, and Vesta was dressed for a real scorcher in beige linen, something austere and expensive by Berhanyer. She had amazing powers of recuperation. Last night her stomach upset had jabbered and frothed away like an idiot child even when, eventually, she had got to sleep. Enderby had lain in clean pyjamas listening tolerantly, her slim back and haunches visible through the diaphanous nightdress, neat but unseductive, heaving occasionally with new accessions of wind, the bedclothes having been kicked away by Enderby because of the warmth of the night. The bedside lamp out, she had become a mere parcel of noises which had filled Enderby with weak nostalgia for his single days, so that he had gone to sleep to dream of stewpans and the craft of verse, the sea. At three-thirty by his luminous wristwatch (a wedding-present), he had awakened with his heart punch-balling desperately because of Strega and Frascati to hear her still fizzing and pooping healthily away. But, waking at nine o'clock to the peevish traffic of the Via Nazionale, he had seen her at the window, eating.

An essential task had not yet been accomplished. Enderby, blinking and squinting, noting that he had slept with his teeth in, wondering where he had put his contact lenses, was emboldened by morning chordee to say, 'Oughtn't you to come back to bed for a while? What I mean is, you ought really.' Impromptu verses, wittily gross, came into his head to give the lie to Rawcliffe's raised finger of doom; the Muse was still very much with him:

> The marriage contract was designed,
>   Despite what all the notaries think,
> To be by only one pen signed,
>   And that is mine, and full of ink.

Enderby hesitated about saying these verses aloud. Anyway, Vesta said:

'I've been up for hours. I had a ham omelette in the restaurant and now I'm eating the breakfast I ordered for you. But it's only *croissants* and jam and things. Look, we're going on a little excursion. I thought it might be fun. We're going to see Rome. The coach calls here at nine-thirty, so you'd better hurry.' Waving the excursion tickets in a shaft of Roman sun, then cracking a kind of hard bread: 'You don't seem very enthusiastic. Don't you want to see Rome?'

'No.' Ask a straight question and you get a straight answer.

'You call yourself a poet. Poets are supposed to be full of curiosity. I don't understand you at all.'

Anyway, here they were, stepping out of the coach in full noon, to inspect the Obelisk of Nero's Circus. The guide, who had decided that Enderby was a Spaniard, said ingratiatingly, 'Obelisco del Circo de Nerón.' '*Si*,' said Enderby, unenticed, 'Look,' he said to Vesta, 'I'm parched. I must have a drink.' It was all the solids they'd been forced to eat – the Pincian Gate and the Borghese Gallery and the Pincio Terrace and the Mausoleum of Caesar Augustus and the Pantheon and the Senate House and the Palace of Justice and the Castle of St Angelo and the Via della Conciliazione. Enderby remembered what the great poet Clough had said about Rome. Rubbishy, he had called it. Enderby was always ready to defer to the judgement of a great poet. 'Rubbishy,' he quoted.

'You know,' said Vesta, 'I do believe you're really quite a philistine.'

'A thirsty one.'

'All right. It's nearly the end of the tour, anyway.' Enderby, who had developed in less than a day a sightless instinct for drinking shops, led Vesta down the Road of Conciliation. Soon they were sitting very cool and drinking Frascati. Vesta sighed and said:

'Peace.'

Enderby choked on his wine. 'I beg your pardon?'

'That's what we all want, isn't it? Peace. Peace and order. Certitude. Certainty. The mind quiet and at peace in the presence of order.' Her skin was so clear, so youthful, under the wide-brimmed hat (also from the Madrid workshop of the crafty young Berhanyer), and her body so elegantly decked; exquisite the stallion-flared nostrils and honest and yet clever the green eyes. 'Peace,' she said again, then sighed once more. 'Och.'

'What was that word?' asked Enderby.

'Peace.'

'No, no, the one after.'

'I didn't say anything after. You're hearing things, Harry boy.'

'What did you call me then?'

'Really, what *is* the matter with you? Rome's peculiar magic seems to be having a curious influence . . . And you're drinking far far more than you drink in England.'

'You cured my stomach,' said Enderby ungrudgingly. 'I find I can down any quantity of this stuff without any ill effects. That diet you put me on certainly worked wonders.' He nodded cheerily at her and poured more wine from the flask.

Vesta looked slightly disgusted; she flared her nostrils further, saying, 'I talk about peace and you talk about stomachs.'

'One stomach,' said Enderby. 'Poets talk about stomachs and *Fem* editors talk about peace. That seems a fair division.'

'We can look forward to so much peace,' said Vesta, 'the two of us. That beautiful house in Sussex, overlooking the downs. It breathes peace, doesn't it?'

'You're too young to want peace,' said Enderby. 'Peace is for the old.'

'Och, we all want it,' said Vesta fiercely. 'And I feel it here, you know, in Rome. A big big peace.'

'A big piece of peace,' said Enderby. '*Pax Romana*. Where they made a desolation they called it a peace. What absolute nonsense! It was a nasty, vulgar sort of civilization, only dignified by being hidden under a lot of declensions. Peace? They didn't know what peace was. The release of the vomitorium after fieldfares in syrup and quail's brains in aspic and a go at a little slave-boy between courses. They knew that. They knew the catharsis after seeing women torn apart by mangy starved lions in an arena. But they didn't know peace. If they'd been quiet and reposeful for thirty seconds they'd have heard too many voices telling them that the Empire was all a bloody swindle. Don't talk to me about the bloody *pax Romana*.' Enderby snorted, not quite knowing why he was so moved.

Vesta smiled in tolerance. 'That's not real Rome. That's Hollywood Rome.'

'Real Rome *was* Hollywood Rome, only more so,' said Enderby.

'And what's really left of it now? Mouldering studio-lots. Big vulgar broken columns. The imperial publicity of P. Virgil Maro, yes-man to Augustus and all his triumphal arches, now dropped. Boots boots boots boots marching up and down again. Rome.' Enderby made, appropriately but vulgarly, the old Roman sign. 'A big maggoty cheese, with too many irregular verbs.'

Vesta was still smiling, somewhat like Our Lady in the vision Enderby had had that slippery day, travelling to London with a poem to give birth to. 'You just don't listen, do you? You just don't give me a chance to say what I want to say.'

'Bloody Roman peace,' snorted Enderby.

'I didn't mean that Empire. I meant the other one being nourished in the catacombs.'

'Oh God, no,' murmured Enderby.

Vesta drank some wine and then, quite gently, belched. She did not say excuse me; she did not seem to notice. Enderby stared. She said, 'Doesn't it seem to you to be a bit like coming home? You know – the return of the prodigal? You opted out of the Empire and have regretted it ever since. It's no good denying it; it's there in your poems all the time.'

Enderby breathed deeply. 'In a way,' he said, 'we all regret the death of universal order. A big smile of teeth. But that smile is a smile of dead teeth. No, not even just dead. False. It never began to be alive. Not for me, anyway.'

'Liar.'

'What do you know about it?' said Enderby, truculent.

'Oh, more than you think.' She sipped her Frascati as though it were very hot tea. 'You've never been much interested in me, have you? Not really. You've never troubled to find out anything about me.'

'We haven't known each other very long,' said Enderby, somewhat guiltily.

'Long enough to get married. No, be honest. To Enderby, Enderby's always been the important thing. Enderby the end of Enderby.'

'That's not really true,' said Enderby doubtfully. 'I've regarded my work as important, I suppose. But not myself. I've not cared very much for my own comfort or honour or glory.'

'Exactly. You've been too interested in yourself to be interested in those things. Enderby in a void. Enderby spinning round and round in an eternal lavatory.'

'That's not fair. That's not true at all.'

'You see? You're getting really interested. You're prepared for a good long talk about Enderby. Supposing we talk about me instead.'

'Gladly,' said Enderby, settling himself in resignation. Vesta pushed her wine-glass away and, with slim hands folded on the table, said:

'How do you think I was brought up?'

'Oh,' said Enderby, 'we know all about that, don't we? Good Scottish home. Calvinist. Another imperial dream to be opted out of.'

'Oh, no,' said Vesta, 'not at all. Not Calvinist. Catholic. Just like you.' She smiled sweetly.

'What?' squawked Enderby, aghast.

'Yes,' said Vesta, 'Catholic. There are Catholics in Scotland, you know. Lots and lots of them. It was intended that I should be a nun. There, that's a surprise for you, isn't it?'

'Not really,' said Enderby. 'Granted that original premiss, which I'm still trying to digest, not at all a surprise. You wear your clothes like a nun.'

'What a very odd thing to say!' said Vesta. 'What, I wonder, do you mean by that?'

'Why didn't you tell me before?' asked Enderby, agitated. 'I mean, we've lived under the same roof for, oh, for months, and you've never breathed a word about it.'

'Why should I have done? It never seemed relevant to anything we ever talked about. And you never showed any curiosity about me. As I've already said, you have, for a poet, surprisingly little curiosity.'

Enderby looked at her, definitely curiously: by rights, this revelation should have modified her appearance, but she still seemed a slim Protestant beauty, cognate with his adolescent vision, an angel of release.

She said, 'Anyway, it makes no difference. I left the Church when I was, oh, when I married Pete. He, as everybody but you knows, had already been married and divorced. I was drifting anyway; I didn't believe any more. Pete believed in motor engines, I'll say that for him, and he used to pray before racing, though I don't know what to; perhaps to some archetypal internal combustion engine. Pete was a nice boy.' She drained her glass.

'Have some more wine,' said Enderby.

'Yes, I will, just a little. Rome has a peculiar atmosphere, hasn't it? Don't you feel that? It makes me, somehow, feel that I'm empty, empty of belief and so on.'

'Be careful,' said Enderby, very clearly, leaning across. 'Be very careful indeed of feeling like that. Rome's just a city like anywhere else. A vastly overrated city, I'd say. It trades on belief just as Stratford trades on Shakespeare. But don't you start thinking that it's a great pure mother calling you home. You can't go home, anyway. You're living in sin. We were only married in a registry office, remember.'

'And are we living in sin?' asked Vesta coolly. 'I haven't noticed particularly.'

'Well,' said Enderby, confused, 'that's what the world would think if the world happened to know and to be Catholic. We're not, of course, really, as you say, living in sin at all.'

'You've contracted out of everything in your time, haven't you? Out of the Church, out of society, out of the family –'

'Damn it all, I am, after all, a poet –'

'Everything goes into the lavatory, everything. Even the act of love.'

Enderby flushed flea-coloured. 'What do you mean by that? What do you know about that? I'm just the same as anybody else, except that I'm not accustomed, except that it's been a long time, except that I'm ugly and shy and –'

'Everything's going to be put right. You just wait. You'll see.' She gave him, forgiving, a kind cool hand. Anything he might then have wanted to say was snatched from his very lungs by a massive silver plunging of claws, swallowed, as all sounds of angelic noontime were swallowed, by a sudden boisterous revelry of bells, huge throats of white metal baying, snarling, hurling, fuming at the sky, the heavens of Rome a nickel and aluminium flame of bells.

2

After sauced pasta and a straw-harnessed globe of Chianti, Vesta's proposal seemed reasonable enough. Because she spoke of the process rather than the end: cool breezes stirred by the fan of the moving coach; the stop for tasting the wines of the Frascati vineyards; the wide sheet of lake and the *albergo* on its shore. And then the rolling back to Rome in early evening. It was more than a proposal, anyway. When Enderby said yes she promptly pulled the tickets out of her handbag. 'But,' said Enderby, 'are we to spend all our time in Rome riding in coaches?'

'There's a lot to see, isn't there? And you'd better see it all just so you can confirm that it's rubbishy.'

'It is rubbishy, too.' And Enderby, in after-lunch somnolence, thought particularly of that ghastly Arco di Costantino which was like a petrified and sempiternal page of the *Daily Mirror*, all cartoons and lapidary headlines. But a lake would be, especially in this cruel mounting heat, different altogether. Rome was really best taken in liquid form – wine, fountains and Aqua Sacra. Enderby approved of Aqua Sacra. Charged with a wide selection of windy chemicals, it brought the wind up lovely and contrived a civilized evacuation of the bowels. In these terms he recommended it seriously to Vesta.

Enderby was surprised that this lake was to be visited by so many. Boarding the coach at the hotel, he had immediately prepared for sleep; almost at once they, and the jabbering polyglot others, had been told to get out. They were at some nameless piazza, sweltering and bone-dry, mocked by a fountain. There, their metal blistering in the sun, stood a fleet of coaches. Men with numbered placards stuck on sticks yelled for their squads, and obedient people, frowning and wrinkling in the huge light, marched on to markers. 'We're Number Six,' said Vesta. They marched.

Heat was intense in the coach; it had cooked to a turn in a slow oven. Even Vesta glowed. Enderby became a kind of fountain, his bursting sweat almost audible. And a worried man came on to the coach, calling, 'Where is Dr Buchwald?' in many languages, so that a kind of fidgety sense of responsibility for this missing one pervaded the coach and engendered scratchiness. In front of Enderby a Portuguese snored, his head on the shoulder of a Frenchman, a stranger; Americans camera-recorded everything, like the scene of a crime; there were two chortling Negroes; a large ham-pink German family spoke of Rome in serious and regretful cadences, churning the sights and sounds into long compound sausage-words. Enderby closed his eyes.

Vaguely, through the haze of his doze, he was aware of comforting wind fanned in by the movement of the coach. 'A very popular lake,' he said sleepily to Vesta; 'must be. All these people.' The convoy was rolling south. Through the coach loudspeaker came the voice of the guide, in Italian, French, German and American, and the intermittent drone was finneganswaked by lightly sleeping Enderby into a parachronic lullaby chronicle, containing Constantine the grandgross and battlebottles fought by lakes which were full of lager. He awoke, laughing, to see villas and vineyards and burning country, then slept again, carrying into deeper sleep a coin-image of Vesta looking on him protectively with the protectiveness of a farmer's wife carrying a pig to market.

He was awakened, smacking dry lips, to a small town of great charm and cleanliness, napkin-carrying waiters waiting on a wide terrace full of tables. Stiff stretching coach-loads got out to drink. Here, Enderby understood, they were very near to Frascati, and that wine that was so shy of travel had travelled the least possible distance. White dust, heat, the shimmering flask on the table. Enderby felt suddenly well and happy. He smiled at Vesta and took her hand, saying:

'Queer that we're both renegade Catholics, isn't it? You were right when you said that it's a bit like coming home. What I mean is, we understand a country like this better than the Protestants. We belong to its traditions.' He indicated, with a kind smile, a couple of hungry-eyed children at the foot of the terrace steps, the elder of the two solemnly nose-picking. 'Even if you don't believe any longer,' said Enderby, 'you're bound to find England a bit strange, a bit inimical. I mean, take all the churches they stole from us. I mean, they can keep them for all I care, but they ought to be reminded occasionally that they're really still ours.' He looked round the full drinking terrace happily, soothed by the jabber of alien phonemes.

Vesta smiled somewhat sourly and said: 'I wish you wouldn't talk in your sleep. Not in public, anyway.'

'Why, what was I saying?'

'You were saying, "Down with the Pope", or words to that

effect. It's a good thing that not many people on this trip can understand English.'

'That's funny,' said Enderby. 'I wasn't even thinking of the Pope. That's very curious. Amazing what the subconscious mind can get up to, isn't it?'

'Perhaps you'd better stay awake on this leg of the journey,' ordered Vesta. 'It's the last leg.'

'I mean, it isn't as though anybody mentioned the Pope, or anything, is it?' puzzled Enderby. 'Look, people are climbing aboard.'

They followed the chatter, smiling faintly at their fellow-passengers as they moved down the aisle of the coach. There had been some changing-round of seats, but that didn't matter: at the very furthest, you could not be more than one seat away from the window. A paunched small cocky Frenchman, however, linen-suited and with panama as though resident in a colony, hurled and fluted sharp words at a German who, he alleged, had taken his seat. The German barked and sobbed indignant denial. A tipsy lean Portuguese, thus encouraged by a fellow-Latin, started on an innocent red cheese of a Dutchman: a claim had, at the outset, been staked to that seat nearest the driver and renewed at this stop for refreshment – see, your fat Dutch arse is sitting on it, my map of Rome and environs. Europe now warred with itself, so that a keen-eyed Texan called, 'Aw, pipe down.' The guide came aboard and spoke French, saying that as a little infant at school he had been taught to keep to the first seat allotted to him. Enderby nodded; in French that sounded reasonable and civilized. The guide translated into American, saying, 'Like you were in school, stick to your own seat and don't try and grab somebody else's. Okay?'

Enderby felt himself growing instantly red and mad. He cried: 'Who the hell do you think you are – the Pope?' It was an Englishman's never-never-never protest against foreign overbearingness. Vesta said, 'Why don't you keep your big mouth –' The words of Enderby were translated swiftly into many tongues, and faces turned to look at Enderby, some wondering, others doubtful, yet others fearful. But one elderly man, a grey and dapper *raisonneur*-type, stood to say, in English. 'We are rebuked. He reminds us of the purpose of our journey. Catholic Europe must not be divided.' He sat down, and people began to look more warmly on Enderby, one wizened brownish woman offering him a piece of Belgian chocolate. 'What did he mean by that?' asked Enderby of Vesta. 'The purpose of our journey,' he said. 'We're going to see this lake, aren't we? What's a lake got to do with Catholic Europe?' 'You'll see,' soothed Vesta, and then, 'I think, after all, it might be better if you *did* have a little sleep.'

But Enderby could not now doze. The countryside slid past, brilliant distant townships on high sunlit plateaux, olive, vine, and cypress, villas, browned fields, endless blue sky. And at length came the lake, a wide white sheet of waters in laky air, the heat of the day mitigated by it, and the little inn close by. The guide, who had sulked and been silent since Enderby's blast of brash Britishry in rebuke, now stood up to say, 'We stay here two hours. The coach will be parked in the parking-place for coaches.' He indicated, with a sketchy squizzle of his Roman fingers, roughly where that might be. He frowned at the Enderbys as they came down the coach-aisle, a blue-jawed lean Roman's frown despite Enderby's 'No hard feelings? Eh?' He was even stonier when Enderby said, '*Ma é vero che Lei ha parlato un poco pontificalmente.*' 'Come on,' said Vesta.

The wide silver water breathed coolness. But, to Enderby's fresh surprise, nobody seemed anxious to savour it. Crowds were leaving coaches and toiling up a hill towards what seemed to be a walled township. Coach after coach came up, disgorging unfestive people, grave, some pious with rosaries. There were carved Africans, a gaggle of Chinese, a piscatorium of Finns, a rotary chew of Americans, Frenchmen haussing their *épaules*, rare blond Vikings and their goddesses, all going up the hill. 'We,' said Vesta, 'are also going up there.'

'What,' asked Enderby carefully, 'lies up yonder hill?'

'Come on.' Vesta took his arm. 'A little poetic curiosity, please. Come and find out.'

Enderby now half-knew what lay at the top of the hill-street they now began to ascend, dodging new squealing arriving coaches, but he suffered himself to be led, passing smiling sellers of fruit and holy pictures. Enderby paused for a moment aghast, seeing a playing-card-sized portrait repeated more than fifty-two times: it seemed at first to be his stepmother in the guise of a holy man blessing his portrait-painter. And then it was not she.

Panting, he was led up to massy gates and a courtyard already thronged and electric. Behind himself and Vesta crowds still moved purposefully up. A trap, a trap: he would not be able to get out. But now there was a holy roar, tremendous, hill-shaking, and an amplified voice began to speak very fast Italian. The voice had no owner: the open ecstatic mouths drank the air, their black eyes searching for the voice above the high stucco buff walls, the window-shutters thrown open for the heat, trees and sky. Joy suffused their stubbled faces at the loud indistinct words. The cry started – '*Viva, viva, viva!*' – and was caught up. 'So,' said Enderby to Vesta, 'it's him, is it?' She nodded. And now the French became excited, ear-cocking, lips parted in joy, as the voice seemed to announce fantastic departures by air: Toulon, Marseilles, Bordeaux, Avignon. '*Bravo!*' The vales redoubled to the hills, and they to heaven. '*Bravo, bravo!*' Enderby was terrified, bewildered. 'What exactly is going on?' he cried. Now the voice began to speak American, welcoming contingents of pilgrims from Illinois, Ohio, New Jersey, Massachusetts, Delaware. And Enderby felt chill hands clasp his hot body all over as he saw the rhythmical signals of a cheer-leader, a young man in a new jersey with a large blue-woven P.

'Rhode Island,' said the voice. 'Kentucky, Texas.'

'Rah, rah, rah!' came the cheers. 'The Pope, the Pope, the Pope!'

'Oh God, no,' moaned Enderby. 'For Christ's sake let me get out of here.' He tried to push, with feeble excuse-mes, but the crowd behind was dense, the eyes up to the hills, and he trod on a little French girl's foot and made her cry. 'Harry,' said Vesta sharply, 'you just stay where you are.'

'Mississippi, California, Oklahoma.' It was like something from a sort of holy Walt Whitman.

'Rah, rah, rah! The Pope, the Pope, the Pope!'

'Oh Christ,' sobbed Enderby, 'please let me get out, please. I'm not well, I'm ill, I've got to get to a lavatory.'

'The Church Militant is here,' said Vesta nastily, 'and all you want is a lavatory.'

'I do, I do.' Enderby, his eyes full of tears, was now grappling with a redolent Spaniard who would not let him pass. The French child still cried, pointing up at Enderby. Suddenly there was a soft of exordium to prayer and everybody began to kneel in the dust of the courtyard. Enderby became a kind of raging schoolmaster in a sea of stunted children. She too knelt; Vesta knelt; she got down on her knees with the rest of them. 'Get up!' bawled Enderby, and, like a sergeant, 'Get off your bloody knees!'

'Kneel down,' she ordered, her eyes like powerful green poisons. 'Kneel down. Everybody's looking at you.'

'Oh my God,' wept Enderby, praying against the current, and he began to try to get out again, lifting his legs as though striding through treacle. He trod on knees, skirts, even shoulders, and was cursed roundly even by some who prayed with frightening sincerity, their eyes dewy with prayer. Stumbling, himself cursing, goose-stepping clumsily, laying episcopal palms on heads, he cut through the vast cake of kneelers and reached, almost vomiting, blind with sweat, the gate and the hill-road. As he staggered down the hill, past the smiling vendors, he muttered to himself, 'I was a bloody fool to come.' From the top of the hill came the sound of a great Amen.

3

'*Cefil Uensdi*,' said the man. '*Totnam Otispar. Cardiff Siti.*' He had a surprised lion-face, though hairless, with a few wavy filaments crawling over his otherwise bare scalp. Staring all the time at Enderby as though convinced Enderby wished to mesmerize him and too polite (a) to object that he did not wish to be mesmerized and (b) to announce that the mesmerism was ineffectual, he ever and anon brought, with a bold arm gesture, a cigarette-end to his lips, drawing on this with a desperate groan as if it were a sole source of oxygen and he dying.

'*Tutti buoni*,' nodded Enderby over his wine. 'All football very good.'

The man gripped Enderby's left forearm and gave a mirthless grin of deep deep blood-brotherhood's understanding. They were sitting at rough trestle-tables in the open air. Here Frascati had reached its last gasp of cheapness – golden gallons for a few bits of tinkly metal. '*Ues Bromic*,' the man went on in his litany. '*Mancesita*

lunaiti. Uolveramiton Uanarar.' This, though more heartening than
the geographical manifests up the hill, was beginning to weary
Enderby. He wondered vaguely if perhaps that was what Etruscan
had sounded like. Up on the main road, beyond the dark and
nameless trees that were a wall to this sky-roofed tavern, the pilgrims
could be heard coming back to their buses, walking slowly and
with dignity now after the comic freewheeling down the hill. If
Vesta had any sense at all she would know where to find him. Not
that, in his present mood, he cared much whether she found him
or not. Next to the lion-faced man with the football litany lolled
a patriot who did not believe that Mussolini was really dead: like
King Arthur he would rise with unsheathed sword to avenge his
country's new wrongs. This man said that the English had always
been the friends of Mussolini; Italian and Briton together had
fought to expel the foul Tedesco. He bunched one side of his face
often at Enderby, raising his thumb like an emperor at the games,
winking in complicity. There were other drinkers on the periphery,
some with bad unsouthern teeth, one carrying on his shoulder an
ill-kempt parrot that squawked part of a Bellini aria. There was
also a very buxom girl, a country beauty called Bice, who brought
round the wine. Enderby did not, would not, lack company. He
only wished his Italian were better. But 'Blackburn Rovers' he fed
to the litanist and 'Newcastle United'; to the patriot 'Addis Ababa'
and 'La Fanciulla del Golden West'. Meanwhile thunder flapped
with extreme gentleness on the other side of the lake. 'Garibaldi,'
he said. 'Long live Italian Africa!'

When Vesta at last arrived the pleasant dirty drinking-yard at
once was disinfected into a background for a *Vogue* fashion pose.
She looked tired, but her calm and elegance fluttered all present,
making even the roughest drinkers consider removing their caps.
Some, remembering that they were Italian, said dutifully, '*Molto
bella*' and made poulterer's pinching gestures to the air. Without
preamble she said to Enderby, 'I knew I'd find you in some such
place as this. I'm fed up. I'm sick to death. You seem to be doing
your utmost to make a farce out of our honeymoon and a fool
out of me.'

'Sit down,' invited Enderby. 'Do sit down. Have some of this
nice Frascati.' He bowed her towards a dry and fairly clean part of

the bench on which he had been sitting. The litanist, grasping that she was *Inglese*, assuming a passion for football in her accordingly, said, ingratiatingly, 'Arse an all,' meaning a football team. Vesta would not sit. She said:

'No. You're to come with me and look for this coach. What I have to say to you must wait till we get back to Rome. I don't want to risk breaking down in public.'

'Peace,' mocked Enderby. 'Peace and order. You played a very mean trick on me, and I shan't forget it in a hurry. A really dirty trick.'

'Come on. Some of the coaches are going already. Leave that wine and come on.' Enderby saw that there still remained a half-litre of this precious golden urine. He filled his glass and said, '*Salute.*' His swallow excited cries of '*Bravo*', as enthusiastic as those heard up the sacred hill, though not then for Enderby. 'Right,' said Enderby, waving farewell. 'We're late,' said Vesta. 'Late for that coach. We wouldn't have been late if I hadn't had to come looking for you.'

'It was a mean trick,' repeated Enderby. 'Why didn't you tell me that we were being taken to the Vatican?'

'Oh, don't be so stupid. That's not the Vatican; that's his summer residence. Now where on earth is this coach?'

There was a bewildering number of coaches, all looking alike. The pilgrims had nestled snugly and smugly in them; some of them were impatiently roaring off. Coaches had settled everywhere – by the roadside, down small hilly streets – like big bugs in bed-crevices. Vesta and Enderby began to examine coaches swiftly but intently, as though they proposed to buy them, passengers and all. None looked familiar, and Vesta made noises of distress. Listening through his thick curtain of wine, Enderby thought he heard the veneers and inlays of Received English stripped roughly off, so that something like raw Lallans became audible, as spicy as home-pickled onions with its gutturals and glottal stops. She was really worried. Enderby said:

'Damn it all, if they do leave us behind there's no great harm done. There must be a bus service or trains or taxis or something. It's not as though we're lost in the jungle or anything.'

'You insulted him,' complained Vesta. 'It was blasphemous, too. These people take their religion very seriously, you know.'

'Nonsense,' said Enderby. Stealthily the sky had, above their searching heads, been clouding over. There was a greenish look in the atmosphere as though the atmosphere proposed, sooner or later, to be sick. From beyond the lake came renewed gentle drummings, as of finger-tips on timpani. 'It's going to rain,' wailed Vesta. 'Och, we'll be caught in it. We'll be drenched.' But Enderby, in impermeable of wine, said not to worry, they would catch that blasted bus.

But they did not catch it. As soon as they approached a coach, the coach skittishly started up, its gears grinding a derisive expletive all for Enderby. Faces looked down, grinning pilgrims, and some hands waved. It was as though Vesta and Enderby were host and hostess after some huge party, seeing off loads of quite unappreciative guests. 'He's done it deliberately,' cried Vesta. 'He's getting his own back. Oh, you *are* a nuisance.' They hurried towards another coach and, like a kitten in chase-me play, it at once began to move off. There were very few left now, but Enderby was fairly sure that, from one of these few, a Roman face, the ignoble face of a Roman guide, leered and Roman fingers made a complicated gesture of mean triumph.

The timpanists across the lake picked up their felt sticks and rolled for a few bars, while the coaches, as though they could thus escape from bad weather, sang off to the city. The lake underwent complex metallurgical changes and the sky, cloaking hot and fearsome lights, began to sweat, then cry. 'Oh Jesus,' called Vesta, 'here it comes.' And indeed there it came while they were still half a mile from shelter other than that of trees: the sky cracked open like a waterbutt, and the air became vertical glass down which pail after pail was poured. They dashed blindly towards the lake-side inn, Vesta tottering on her smart spikes, Enderby gripping her elbow as though her arm were a pair of blackboard dividers, already too wet really to be all that urgent about seeking shelter. The deluge made Enderby's scalp prickle with dandruff, and his fawn summer suit was soaked. But she, poor girl, was already a wreck: hat comically flopping, hair in rat-tails, mascara running, her face that of a crying old crone as though she wept over the disintegration of her *chic*. 'In here,' gasped Enderby, steering her straight into a room smelling of size and new paint, empty chairs and tables in it, a sleek boy-waiter admiring the free show of the rain. 'I think,' panted

Enderby, 'that we'll have to take a room, if they have one. The first thing to do is to get dry. Perhaps they'll —' The waiter called a name, then turned his young empty face back on these two wet ones. Enderby said, '*Una camera. Si é possible.*' The boy called again, an unbroken boy's yelp under the drumming water. A woman came, creamily fat in a flowered frock, clucked commiseration, took in in a swift look Vesta's ringed finger, said there was a *camera* with one *letto*. Beside her smiling hugeness Vesta looked a snivelling waif. '*Grazie,*' said Enderby. Lightning cracked momentarily the late-sky, the timpanists counted half a bar and came in with a fine peal, rolling cosmic Berlioz chords. Vesta made the sign of the cross. She was shivering.

'What,' asked Enderby, 'did you do that for?'

'Oh God,' she said, 'it scares me. I can't stand thunder.' Enderby felt his stomach turn over when she said that.

4

Up in the bedroom they confronted each other naked. Somehow, for some reason, Enderby had not expected that, when they had stripped off their drenched clothes and dumped them outside the door, they would confront each other naked. Naked confrontation was supposed to come about otherwise: deliberately, in desire or duty. Enderby had been trying to digest too many other things to foresee this prelapsarian picture (and there up the hill, so neatly fitting into the pattern, was a great postlapsarian witness), for the room was very much like his own as a boy – pictures of St John the Baptist, the Sacred Heart, the B.V.M., a melodramatic Golgotha; a smell of unclean bedclothes, dust, boots, and stale holy water; a stringy unbeaten carpet; a narrow bed. This reproduction of the main stage-set for so many adolescent monodramas, here in Italy under rain, did not depress him: that bedroom had always been an enclave of revolt in stepmother country. Very clearly, lines of an unpublished poem came back to him:

> . . . There were times, misunderstood by the family,
> When you, at fifteen, on your summer evening bed

Believed there were ancient towns you might anciently visit.
    There might be a neglected platform on some station
And a ticket bought when the clock was off its guard.
    Oh, who can dismember the past? The boy on the friendly bed
Lay on the unpossessed mother, the bosom of history,
    And is gathered to her at last. And tears I suppose
Still hunger for that reeking unwashed pillow,
    That bed ingrained with all the dirt of the past,
The mess and lice and stupidity of the Golden Age,
    But a mother and loving, ultimately Eden . . .

He nodded several times, standing there naked in rainy Italy, thinking that it was a mother he had always wanted, not a stepmother, and he had made that mother himself in his bedroom, made her out of the past, history, myth, the craft of verse. When she was made she became slimmer, younger, more like a mistress; she became the Muse.

Lightning again shivered the firmament and then, after a careful count, the laughing drummers knocked hell out of their resonant membranes. Vesta gave a little scream, put her arms round Enderby's trunk, and then seemed to try to push herself inside him as though he were a deviscerated rabbit of great size and she a mound of palpitating stuffing. 'There, there,' said Enderby, kindly but disturbed: she had no right to bring these stepmother terrors into his adolescent bedroom. Then he sweated, seeing more than a mere fear of thunder. Still, he clasped her to him and soothed her shoulder-blades, thinking how such naked contacts had an essential unalluring core of *heartiness*: the slap of palm on buttock; the jelly sound of two moist segments of flesh drawing apart. She shivered: the air had cooled considerably.

'You'd better,' said Enderby, 'get into bed.'

'Yes,' she shuddered, 'yes. Into bed.' And she pulled him towards bed, her grip on him unrelaxed, so that they shambled to it as though clumsily dancing. As soon as they were in it, a skein of lightning lay an instant against the sky, like a stunned man against a cliff, and then the drums whammed out from hi-fi loudspeakers all over the heavens. She again seemed to try to enter him in fear, a rather soft rock of ages, and he smelt her terror, as familiar a smell as that faintly oily one of the coverlet.

'There,' he said again, clasping her, stroking and soothing. It was a very narrow bed. This, he kept reminding himself, was his bride, an intelligent and desirable young woman and it was time, under the thunder and rain, to be thinking of performing, that is to say consummating, that is to say. He stealthily felt his way down to find out what was his body's view of this constatation, but all was quiet there, as though he were calmly reading Jane Austen.

The rain eased and the thunder was trundled, grumbling, off. Enderby felt her body relax and seem, somehow, to grow moister and more expectant. She gripped him still, though there was no more thunder to fear. Enderby's engines, rusty and sluggish, tried to wake up and respond to various quite unoriginal ganglionic stimuli, but there were certain difficulties which were secret and shameful. Enderby had been spoiled by too many pictures; it was a long time since he had held a real woman in his arms like this; he had possessed in imagination houri after houri of a beauty, passivity, voluptuousness no real woman could ever touch. Perhaps, he now felt, if this body he held could become – just for twenty or thirty seconds – one of those harem dreams of his, pampered, pouting, perfumed, steatopygous, he could, he was sure, achieve what it was a plain duty, apart from all questions of gratification, to achieve. But the body of his bride was spare, barely cushioned. With a desperate effort he conjured a gross tit-swinging image, saw whose image it was, then, making the retching noises of a child trying to disgust, he swung out of the bed with unwonted agility and stood shivering on the worn mat. 'What's the matter?' she called. 'What is it? Don't you feel well?' Forgetting that he was naked, Enderby dashed out of the room without replying. Two doors down the corridor was the sign *Gabinetto*, and Enderby, re-living the past, entered it and locked its door. To his horror he found that the lavatory was not a sane comfortable English WC but a Continental crouch-hole with a right-hand hand-rail and a toilet-roll-fitting on the same side. Once, many years ago, he had fallen into one of these holes. He almost cried for the security of his old seaside lavatory but, unlocking the door to leave, the tears froze as he heard two female Italian voices on the corridor. One of these, saying loud passing greetings to the other, was now right up against the *gabinetto* door and trying the handle. Enderby swiftly re-locked himself in. The voice spoke urgently, saying, for all Enderby knew, that its owner was in a bad way, desperate, and couldn't wait too long. Enderby seated himself on the edge of the low crouch-hole dais, saying, 'Go away. Go away,' and, as an after-thought, '*Io sono nudo, completamente nudo*', wondering if that was correct Italian. Correct or not, the voice was silenced and appar-ently carried back down the corridor. Enderby the completely naked sat on, in thinking pose, feeling at his lowest ebb.

5

Like an Arab thief, though not so slippery, Enderby darted back to the bedroom. Vesta was sitting up in the bed, smoking a ship's (or export) Woodbine through a holder and, because of that, looking more naked than she was, though this, reflected Enderby, was not really possible. 'Now then,' she said. 'We're going to have this whole thing out.'

'No,' mumbled Enderby. 'Not like this.' He sat shamefacedly down on the cane chair in the corner, wriggling and wincing as odd prickly cane thorns assaulted his bottom. 'Not,' said Enderby, 'with no clothes on. It's not right.' He joined his hands as for prayer and, with this frail cage of fingers, hid his genitals from the smoking woman in the bed. 'I mean,' said Enderby, 'one can't really talk about anything naked.'

'Who are you to say that?' she said fiercely. 'What do you know about the world? My first husband and I once belonged to a nudist camp —' (Enderby whimpered at the sudden formality of 'first husband') '— and there used to be *really* prominent men and women there, and they didn't have any *pudeur* about talking. And they, I might add,' she added acidly, 'could talk about rather more than lavatories and stomachs and how rotten the Roman Empire must have been.' Enderby gazed glumly out of the window, seeing that the rain had stopped and the June warmth, encouraged, was creeping back into the Italian evening. Then he was granted a brief image of a fat sack-bellied middle-aged female nudist don, breasts hanging like tripe, discoursing on aesthetic values. This cheered him up a little, so he turned boldly on Vesta to say:

'All right then. Let's have it out, the whole damned thing. What exactly do you think you're playing at?'

'I don't understand you,' she said. 'I'm playing at nothing. I'm working hard, with absolutely no co-operation from you, to try and build a marriage.'

'And your idea of building a marriage is to try to drag me back into the Church, is that it?' said Enderby, half-uncovering his genitals so as to gesticulate with one hand. 'And in a nasty sly way too. Not saying anything about being a Catholic yourself, and even being quite ready to have a registry office wedding, even though you know that that sort of wedding means nothing at all.'

'Oh,' she said, 'you admit that, do you? You admit that it means nothing at all? In other words, you admit that a Catholic wedding is the only valid one?'

'I don't admit anything,' cried Enderby. 'All I'm saying is that I'm confused, completely confused about what's supposed to be going on. What I mean is, we've only been married a couple of days, and everything seems to have changed. You weren't like this before, were you? You weren't like this when we were living in your flat in London, were you? Everything was all right then. You were on my side, and you were getting on with your job and I was getting on with mine, and it was all nice and pleasant and not a care in the world. But now look at things. Since we got married, and that's only a couple of days ago, mind you, only a couple of days –' (two fingers held up, five on his genitals) '– you've been doing your damnedest to turn into my stepmother.'

Vesta's mouth opened and smoke wandered out. 'To what, did you say? To turn into what?'

'My stepmother, bitch as she was. You're not fat yet, but I suppose you soon will be. You keep belching away all the time and saying "Och" and going on at me – natter and nag, nag and natter – and you're scared of the bloody thunder and you're trying to get me to go back into the Church. Why? That's what I want to know. Why? What's your motive? What are you getting at? What are you trying to do?'

'This,' she said heavily, 'is fantastic. This is the most incredible – this is the most incredible fantastic –' She started to get out of bed. Enderby, seeing this, saw that there would be too much visible nakedness about the room, so he lunged across from the cane chair, genitals swinging, and pushed her back into bed and pulled the clothes over her. He said:

'We'll have less frivolity, if you don't mind, and less nonsense. Before we got married – listen to me, I'm talking – before we got married you were what I'd dreamed of, ever since I was a boy. You were everything she wasn't; you were a release; you were a way out. You were something that would kill her for good and all. And now look at you.' He pointed sternly. She, as though he were a stranger who had just broken in, pulled the grey sheet over her bosom and looked fearful. 'You're trying to drag me back into that old world, aren't you? Back to the bloody Church and female smells all over the place –'

'You're drunk,' she said. 'You're mad.' There was a knock at the door and Enderby, gesticulating, went to answer it, now wearing his nakedness as unconsciously as if it were a suit. 'Drunk, eh?' he said. 'Mad, eh? You've made me drunk, that's what it is.' He opened the door, and the lady of the house presented a pressed pile of dried clothes. '*Tante grazie*,' said Enderby, and then, turning back on his wife, he presented his bottom to the *signora*; she slammed the door and went off speaking loud Italian. 'Things,' said Enderby, 'already,' dumping the clothes on the bed, 'have not worked out at all as I expected. It's been a bloody big mistake, that's what it's been.'

She reached over for her clothes, angrily fussily trembling, saying, 'A mistake, you say? That's gratitude, I must say, gratitude.' She paused, one hand on her clothes, breathing deeply as if a stethoscope had begun to wander down her back, eyes downcast, seeking self-control. Then she said, calmly, 'I'm keeping my temper, you notice. Somebody has to be rational.' Enderby began, in a sort of hopping dance, to put on his underpants. 'Listen to me,' she said, 'listen. You're like a child, you know so little about life. When I first met you, it looked horrible that a man of so much talent should be living the way you did. No, let me speak, let me keep my temper.' Enderby, from inside his shirt was mumbling something. 'You had nothing to do with women,' she continued, 'and no faith in anything, and no sense of responsibility to society. Oh, I know you had substitutes for all those things,' she said bitterly. 'Dirty

photographs instead of flesh and blood.' Enderby repeated the
hopping dance, this time with his trousers, scowling and blushing.
'Society,' she said, with loud eloquence, 'shrunk to the smallest
room in the house. Is that any life for a man?' she asked strongly.
'Is that any life for a poet? Is that the way you expect to make
great poetry?'

'Poetry,' said Enderby. 'Don't you start telling me about poetry.
I know all about poetry, thank you very much,' he said with a
bull-snort. 'But let me tell you this. There's no obligation to accept
society or women or religion or anything else, not for anyone
there isn't. And as for poetry, that's a job for anarchs. Poetry's made
by rebels and exiles and outsiders, it's made by people on their
own, not by sheep baaing bravo to the Pope. Poets don't need
religion and they don't need bloody little cocktail-party gossip
either; it's they who make language and make myths. Poets don't
need anybody except themselves.'

Vesta picked up her brassière and wearily dropped herself into
it as though it were some necessary instrument of penance. 'You
seemed,' she said, 'to like going to parties. You seemed to think it
was a good thing to wear a decent suit and talk with people. You
said it was civilized. You gave me, one evening you may have
forgotten, a long dull lecture on the Poet and Society. You even
went to the trouble of thanking me for having rescued you from
your old life. Some day,' she sighed, 'you'll make it absolutely clear
to people what exactly you *do* want.'

'Oh,' said Enderby, 'it was all right, I suppose. It made a nice
change. It was nice to be clean and smart, you see, and hear educated
accents. It was, you see, so different from my stepmother.' Now
fully dressed, he sat with greater confidence on the cane-bottomed
chair in the corner. 'But,' he said, 'if society means going back to
the Church, I don't want anything to do with society. As far as
I'm concerned, the Church is all tied up with that bitch, superstitious and nasty and unclean.'

'Oh, you're so stupid,' said Vesta, having put on her dress swiftly
and neatly. 'You're so *uneducated*. Some of the best modern brains
are in the Church – poets, novelists, philosophers. Just because a
silly illiterate woman made a nonsense out of it for you doesn't
mean that it *is* a nonsense. You're a fool, but you surely aren't such

a fool as all that. Anyway,' she said, clicking her handbag open and rummaging for a comb, 'nobody's asking you to go back into the Church. The Church, presumably, can get on very well without you. But if I'm going back, you might at least have the courtesy and decency to go through the form of going back with me.'

'You mean,' said Enderby, 'that we'll have to get properly married? By a priest in a church? Look,' he said, folding his arms and crossing his legs, 'why didn't you think about all this before? Why do you have to wait till our honeymoon before you decided to baa back to the fold? Don't answer, because I know the answer. It's because you want to go down to posterity as the woman who reorganized Enderby's life, faith and works. It's what Rawcliffe said, and I hadn't thought of it before, because I really believed that you had some affection for me, but, looking at it more soberly, I can see now that was impossible, me being ugly and middle-aged and, as you're kind enough to say, stupid. All right, then; now we know how we stand.'

She was combing her hair, gritting her teeth at the tangles, and the penny-colour shone out, crackling, renewed after its rat-tailed dullness. 'Fool, fool,' she said. 'My idea was that we could make a go of marriage. We still can. Of course, if you think that Rawcliffe's more trustworthy than I am (and remember that Rawcliffe's jealous as hell of you) then that's your own affair and you can get on with it. The fact is that, for all your stupidity, I'm very fond of you and, at the same time, I feel that I can make you happy by making you more normal, more sane.'

'There you are, you see,' said Enderby in triumph.

'Oh, nonsense. What I mean is this: an artist needs a place in the world, he needs to be committed to something, and he needs to be in touch with the current of life. Surely the trouble with all your work is that it reads as though it's cut off from the current?'

'Very interesting,' said Enderby, his arms still folded. 'Very, very fascinating.'

'Och,' she said, drooping as though suddenly very weary. 'What does it matter? Who's going to care whether you write great poetry or not? The feeblest teenage pop-singer is a million times more regarded than you are. You sell only a handful of copies of every book you write. There's going to be a nuclear war and the libraries will be destroyed. What's the use? What good can it all possibly be if one doesn't believe in God?' She sat on the bed, quite dispirited, and began to cry softly. Enderby came softly over to her and said:

'I'm sorry, I'm terribly sorry. But I think I'm too old to learn really, too old to change. Perhaps we'd better admit it's all a mistake and go back to things as they were before. No real harm's been done, not yet, has it? I mean, we're not even properly married, are we?'

She looked up sternly and said, 'You're like a child. A child who doesn't like his first morning at school so says he doesn't think he'll go back in the afternoon.' She wiped her eyes and became hard, self-possessed again. 'Nobody makes a fool of me,' she said. 'Nobody throws me over.'

'You could have the marriage annulled,' said Enderby. 'On the grounds of non-consummation. Because it won't ever be consummated, you know.'

'You think,' said Vesta, 'that you'll go back to living on a tiny but adequate income, writing your poetry in the lavatory. But you won't. What little bit of capital you've got left I shall have. I'll make sure of that. And the things you've bought are on my name. Nobody makes a fool out of me.'

'I can get a job,' said Enderby, growing angry. 'I'm not reliant on anybody. I can be independent.' Then he felt tears of self-pity coming. 'The poet,' he said, whimpering, 'is best left to live on his own.' Through his tears he had confused images of Dantesque eagles flitting round lightning-shot peaks. He left the edge of the bed and went to stand in a corner. 'The poet,' he said, blubbing like that seven-year-old Elizabethan bridegroom who had cried to go home with his father.

3

1

'My main purpose,' said swaying Rawcliffe, 'was to present you with —' He swayed and fumbled in various pockets, drawing out filthy old papers decaying at their folds, two half-used tubes of stomach tablets which were dust-fluffy, a referee's whistle, a dry rattle of ball-points, finally a quite clean envelope. '– these. Tickets for a première. I think, my dear old Enderby, you should be reasonably amused. I have no further interest in the film in question, having been so closely involved in it. And, let me tell you, Enderby, it is a cheap film, a film made on a shoestring, a film made very quickly, with bits borrowed – quite without permission, you know – from other films. Strega,' he said suddenly to Dante behind the bar. The bar was, as at their first meeting in it, empty except for them. Enderby felt worn and old, his mouth seeming to taste of cascara-coated motoring chocolate. It was mid-morning, the day after the day of their return from the papal township by the lake, and Vesta had gone to see a woman called Princess Irene Galitzine, a Roman lady famed for her boutique models or couture designs or something. Vesta was spending money fast. 'And,' said Rawcliffe, 'there are, of course, for this the world expects of Italy, several *sfacciate donne Fiorentine*, except that they're not Florentine but Roman, *mostrando con le poppe il petto*. There, Enderby, you see: brazen-faced bitches showing breasts with paps. Dante was a great prophet; he foresaw the Italian film industry. Dante.'

Dante behind the bar bowed. 'Same a name,' he said confidentially to Enderby.

'Bloody big coincidence, eh?' swayed Rawcliffe. 'You'll find everything in Dante, Enderby, if you look long enough. Even the film you're going to see derives its title from the *Purgatorio*. I found that title, Enderby, I, an English poet, for none of these unholy Romans has even so much as glanced at Dante since leaving school, if any of them ever went to school.' Enderby took from the envelope the cards of invitation and saw that the film was named *L'Animal Binato*. It meant nothing to him. He turned to the bottle of Frascati on the counter and poured himself a tumbler. 'Drinking hard, I see, Enderby,' said Rawcliffe. 'If I may make so lewd a guess, it is because you are using muscles you never used before. Venus catches cold without Bacchus and Ceres, although you can leave out that goddess of breakfast foods for all I care. Strega,' he called again, nodding vigorously.

'Look,' said Enderby, 'I'm not taking you home again. You were

a damned nuisance last time, Rawcliffe, and you made a real fool
out of me. If you're going to pass out here, you can stay passed
out, is that clear? I've got worries of my own without having to
look after –'

'He talks in rhyme,' said Rawcliffe in exaggerated wonder. 'He
is still very much the poet, is he not? But for how much longer
now, eh?' he said sinisterly, slitting his eyes. 'The Muse, O Enderby.
Has the Muse yet been in to tell you that she has booked her
one-way flight to Parnassus or wherever Muses live? She has done
her long stint with Enderby and the time has come for Enderby
to abjure this rough magic and pack it in, the Muse, unlike Ariel,
being no airy slave of indeterminate sex but a woman, very much
a woman.' Rawcliffe now made himself look shrunken and very
old. 'Perhaps, Enderby, I was destined never to be much of a success
with that particular woman because of – you know, because of
– that is to say, a certain, shall I say, indeterminate attitude towards
sex.' He sighed in a litre or so of Roman bar air. He drank down
a centilitre or less of Strega. 'And now, you see, Enderby, I'm on
the move again. This afternoon, to be precise. So, you see, you
won't have to carry me home or anywhere. The BEA men will
come and collect me, excellent fellows. They will get me on that
plane. Where am I going, Enderby?' He leered roguishly, wagging
a finger. 'Ah, I'm not telling you. I am, suffice it to say, on my way
further south. I have picked up my little packet here.' He tapped,
winking, the right breast of his coat. 'And now little Marco and
Mario and that bloody Piedmontese, to quote Milton, can go and
stuff themselves. I have finished, Enderby, with the lot. Finish,
Enderby,' he said loudly and with emphatic fists on the counter,
'with the lot. You, I mean. Get wise to yourself, as they say. Wake
up. A poet must be alone.'

Enderby pouted, pouring himself the last of his bottle. He felt
that it was not up to Rawcliffe to tell him that he must be alone.
He took from his inside jacket-pocket a piece of paper on which he
had been doing sums. 'Did you know,' he said, 'how much mink
costs? Mink,' he repeated. 'I have it here,' he said carefully. 'One
Black Diamond mink coat: one thousand four hundred and ninety-
five pounds. One hip-length jacket: five hundred and
ninety-five pounds. One pastel mink bolero: three hundred

and ninety-five pounds. We leave out of account,' said Enderby, 'as being too inexpensive for serious consideration, a pastel stole at two hundred pounds. That's a frippery, a mere nugacity.' He smiled sillily. 'What,' he asked, 'can a poet do with no money, eh? How does a poet live?'

'Well,' said Rawcliffe, both hands round his new Strega as if it were something to be strangled, 'there are jobs, you know. All sorts of jobs. Only the very luckiest of poets can be professional poets. You could teach or write for the papers or do film scripts or advertising slogans or lecture for the British Council or get unskilled work in a factory. Lots of things to be done.'

'But,' objected Enderby, 'suppose one is no good at anything except writing poetry? Suppose one makes a bloody fool of oneself at anything else?'

'Oh,' said Rawcliffe reasonably, 'I don't think that anybody could make such a bloody fool of himself that it would really matter. Now, if I were you, I should leave everything in the hands of Auntie Vesta. She'll fix you up with something nice and easy.'

'But,' protested Enderby, 'only a minute ago you were telling me that I've got to be alone.'

'I see,' said Rawcliffe, seeing into his Strega. 'Well, in that case it's all a bit of a mess, isn't it, Enderby? But don't worry me with your worries, Enderby, because I've got worries of my own, you see. You sort out things for yourself.' He seemed suddenly sober and rather cold despite the June warmth. He downed his Strega and shivered exaggeratedly, as if he had taken a wholesome but bitter medicine. 'Perhaps,' he said, 'I should have started this heavy drinking business earlier. I might possibly be dead by now instead of having putatively fathered or foster-fathered or helped with the illegitimate fathering of *L'Animal Binato*, alive and healthy and almost impervious to the more deadly effects of alcohol. I should, by rights, Enderby, have considered seeing myself off when I found that the lyric gift had departed from me. I could at least have contrived to be careless crossing the road, couldn't I? And, instead of that propaganda job during the war, I could perhaps have volunteered for something more genuinely lethal.'

'What,' asked Enderby morbidly, 'did it feel like? I mean, when the lyric gift departed?' Rawcliffe looked up so morosely, fixing

Enderby with an eye so baleful, that Enderby began to smile nervously. Rawcliffe said:

'Blast your mean little soul, it's no laughing matter, even in
retrospect.' Then he came nearer to Enderby and gave him a close-
up of bad teeth and worse breath. 'It was like everything going all
dead,' said Rawcliffe. 'It was like going dumb. I could see quite
clearly what had to be said, but I couldn't say it. I could perceive
that an imaginative relationship existed between disparate objects
but I couldn't tell what the relationship was. I used to sit for hours
with paper in front of me, hours and hours, Enderby, and then I
would at last get something down. But what I got down somehow
– don't laugh at me – had a smell of decay about it. What I got
down was *evil*, and I used to shudder when I crumpled it up and
threw it in the fire. And then, at night, in bed, I used to wake up
to hear mocking laughter. And then,' tottered Rawcliffe, 'one night
there was the sound of an awful *click*, and then everything in the
bedroom seemed cold, somehow, cold and obscene. I knew, Enderby,
it was all over. Thenceforward I should be outside the Garden,
useless to anyone, a mess and, moreover, Enderby, in some indefin-
able way *evil*. Like an unfrocked priest, Enderby. The unfrocked
priest does not become a mere neuter harmless human being; he
becomes *evil*. He has to be used by something, for supernature
abhors a supervacuum, so he becomes *evil*, Enderby.' He swigged
more Strega and staggered, as it were, against the ropes, saying, 'And
all that is left for the poet, Enderby, when the inspiration is departed,
Enderby, is the travesty, the plagiarism, the popularization, the
debasement, the curse. He has drunk the milk of paradise, but it
has long passed through his system, Enderby, and, unfortunately for
him, he remembers the taste.' Rawcliffe shut weary eyes, saying,
'*Ara vos prec*,' and then, 'be mindful in due time of my pain. I
translate, Enderby, because you would not understand the original
Provençal. That is the poet Arnaut Daniel in Purgatory. He was a
lucky bugger, or is, Enderby, a lucky bugger to be in Purgatory.
Not like some of us.' At this point, Rawcliffe went quite gently to
sleep standing up, his head reposing on arms he had folded on the
counter. Dante said: 'Better e slip.' There was a plum-plush settee
against the wall; to this Dante and Enderby carried, led, pushed,
dragged Rawcliffe. 'Too mash facking Strega,' diagnosed Dante.

Sighing, Enderby sat next to Rawcliffe, a fresh bottle of Frascati
and a tumbler on the table in front of him, and he continued to
do sums on bits of paper. At intervals Rawcliffe gave gnomic utterance, often obscure, from his sleep; reports from the first crazed
space-traveller:

'No expense of breath in falling downstairs.'

'Mario, put that bread-knife away.'

'You are a naughty boy, but not undelectable.'

'In all the antholololologies.'

'This will make Enderby feel very sick.'

Indeed, Enderby felt very sick when he had worked out his
sums and found that his credit balance in the bank stood at, taking
the most liberal computation, little more than four hundred and
ninety pounds. It was pointless asking himself where the money
had gone to, for he knew all too well: it had flowed back to its
source: his stepmother had given and his stepmother had, in a
youthful well-spoken, dove-soft, spring-smelling, highly improbable
disguise, taken away again. From his sleep Rawcliffe called:

'Aha! Man not the boats, but woman-and-child them. I'll shoot
all else. Back, you brute, back. The rash, smart, sloggering
Hopkinsian brine. Enderby was a very inferior poet. Very wise of
him to pack up.'

Enderby spoke sternly to this dark voice. 'I am not packing up,'
he said. This silenced Rawcliffe's sleep-persona temporarily. To
himself Enderby said, 'If I can keep the relationship on the most
superficial of levels, for superficially I am quite fond of her, then it
should be possible to contrive some sort of satisfactory co-existence.
But I will not be ordered about. And she has, after all, a good job
and I could, at a pinch, refuse to get a job of my own or have a
job found for me. The Sussex house has many rooms. My stomach
is better.' Rawcliffe's sleeping voice spoke again from outer space:

'You will do as I say, Vincent. I will not have you calling Reggy
an old queen. He is not old.' And then, 'God should feel highly
flattered that we have invented Him.' And finally, before falling into
serious speechless sleep, in the voice of Yeats speaking with the
voice of Swift speaking with the voice of Job: '*Let the day perish
wherein I was born.*' Enderby shuddered, the wine seeming sharper
than usual.

2

They arrived late for the film première. The cinema was in an obscure street somewhere off the Viale Aventino, and the taxi-driver had difficulty in finding it. He at first denied, in the manner of taxi-drivers, the existence of what he himself did not know existed, until Enderby waved a ticket of invitation in his moustached face. The façade of the cinema rather let down the rest of Rome, thought Enderby, as he helped Vesta out of the cab.

Sculpturally and architecturally, the rest of Rome was rubbishy, yet rubbishy on a baroque and hypnotic scale, like the delusions of grandeur of some gibbering G.P.I. patient. But here was authentic fleapit, from the look of it, epitome of every bughouse that Enderby had, as a child, queued outside on Saturday afternoons, sticky paw clutching twopence, filthy-jerseyed other children clinging to him aromatically lest they lose him in the scrimmage of entrance, Enderby being the only one of their lot who could read. The old silent film had, Enderby reflected, been, in one facet, an extension of literature. He said now to Vesta, 'This is one of those places where you go in with a blouse and come out with a jumper.' He tweaked her elbow jocularly, but she looked queenily blank. 'Blouse?' she said. 'I'm not wearing a blouse.' She was, in fact, wearing black silk from her Roman-lady *couturière*, sleeveless, the back *décolleté*, the skirt slim, tails of mink dripping from her shoulders against the night's cool. Enderby was in white tuxedo, black silk in breast pocket to match tie. But it looked as though he needn't have taken so much trouble: there were no adoring crowds, no gleaming stars' mouths of coral and ivory in maniacal abandon to the flashbulbs, no jostle of Cadillacs and Bentleys. There were a few decent Fiats, unattended, evidently owner-driven; a painted banner across the deplorable rococo façade said, in the midst of cheap coloured bulbs, L'ANIMAL BINATO. The man who took their cards of invitation chewed something morosely and his lantern-jaw was ill-shaven. It let down Vesta as much as it let down Rome. Little, of course, thought Enderby, could let down Enderby.

They were flashlamped to their seats. Enderby felt torn cheap plush beneath him and smelt a strong citrus tang through the dark. Orange, too, bloodless orange, was the light which warmed the

worn stage curtains. These now, as if they had been waiting only
for Enderby and his wife, parted to the noise of loud cinema music,
banal, conventionally sinister. Enderby peered through the dark:
there did not, by the feel and sound of things, seem to be a very
large audience. The screen said L'ANIMAL BINATO and followed
this with jerkily dissolved frames of the names of the conspirators:
Alberto Formica; Giorgio Farfalla; Maria Vacca; A. F. Corvo; P.
Ranocchio; Giacomo Capra; Beatrice Pappagallo; R. Coniglio;
Giovanni Chiocciola; Gina Gatto. Rawcliffe's name appeared near
the end, Italianized to, as far as Enderby could tell, something like
Raucliffo. 'Serve him right,' thought Enderby, and told Vesta so. She
said shhhhh. The film began.

Night, very much night, with tortured cypresses lit by lightning.
Thunder (Vesta dug her nails into Enderby's hand). Tempestuous
wind. Camera tracks to steps of terrace, handsome woman standing
thereon, much of Italian bosom exposed to lightning. She raises
arms, cornily, to stormy heavens in a crash of thunder. Camera
swings up towards sky. Another stock shot of lightning cracking
cloud like a teacup. Thunder (Vesta's nails). New camera angle
shows a something speeding down the firmament, a white flashing
something. Cut to wooden effigy of cow, lightning-lit. Handsome
bosomed woman seen walking through tempest, statelily, towards
wooden cow. Lightning shows her doing something obscure, pulling
some lever or other, then creaking music accompanies shot of
wooden cow opening, two hollow half-cows, woman climbing into
upright half, cow closing up, woman imprisoned in cow. Cut to
white bull, snorting against the thunder, tearing down the sky,
bull-lust from heaven.

'You know,' said Enderby with wonder, 'this is really an astonishing
coincidence.'

'Shhhhh,' said Vesta. Enderby, his eyes now accustomed to the
dark, looked round to find the cinema half-empty, but next to him
was a huge man, jowled and bag-eyed in lightning from the screen,
a cigar burning towards his fingers, already asleep and snoring
slightly.

Day. Ruritanian palace, moustached handsome king in late
middle age conferring with deferential bearded (false-bearded)
counsellors. Fanfare. Palaver is ended. One counsellor stays behind,

ingratiating Iago-type, to talk to the king. The king's eyes cornily cloud with suspicion. Odd Italian words that Enderby can understand snap out from the sound-track: queen, cow, Dedalo. Dedalo ordered to be brought in. Cut to Dedalo's workshop. Dedalo and Icaro, Dedalo's crisp-haired son, are building aeroplanes. Dedalo very old skinny man. Summoned by servant, he pulls down shirt-sleeves, dons jacket period 1860, follows down labyrinthine corridors, a kind old man with clever eyes and deep face-furrows. He enters royal presence. Long unintelligible Italian colloquy with much eloquent arm-waving. Dedalo struck on aged face by angry king. Iago-type goes off, bowing, oily, leaving royal face in royal hands. Dedalo hauled off for torture.

Enderby now began to feel an emotion other than wonder; his stomach heaved and pricked with apprehension: this was more than coincidence. 'Don't you think,' he said to Vesta, 'this is just a little too much like my poem? Don't you think –'

'Shhhhh,' she said. The snoring man next to Enderby said, in his sleep, '*Tace*.' Enderby, reminded of the sleep-talking Raucliffo, said, '*Tace* your arse.' And to Vesta, 'This is just like *The Pet Beast*.' He then remembered that she hadn't yet read it, had not, in fact, yet shown any desire to read it. He grimly watched the screen, the further unwinding of Raucliffo's infamy.

Day. Pregnant queen in exile, sitting in mean cottage with old crone. Colloquy. Labour-pains. Then dissolve to shot of doctor galloping in from afar. He enters cottage. From bedroom door come bellowing noises. He enters bedroom. Close-up of doctor's face. Horror, incredulity, nausea, syncope. Close-up, with foul discord of what doctor sees: head of bull-calf on child's body.

'That's mine,' said Enderby. 'It's mine, I tell you. If I find that blasted Rawcliffe –'

'It's nobody's,' said Vesta. 'It's just a myth. Even I know that.'

'*Tace*,' snored Enderby's pone.

Calf-child, in montage series, grows to bull-man, hideous, muscular, fire-breathing, gigantic. Having stolen piece of raw meat from kitchen, bull-man makes discovery of carnivorous nature. Kills old crone and eats her. Tries to kill mother, too, but mother escapes, falls over cliff screaming but uneaten. Good clean fun. Bull-man totters, tall as ten houses, to capital city, leaving bone-trail behind.

Cut to palace gardens where Princess Ariadne, with sizeable bosom-show, is playing ball with giggling bosom-showing alleged maidens. Close-up of beast drooling through thicket. Screams, scatter, Ariadne carried off on beast's back. Beast, drooling, carries her, screaming, to cellars of metropolitan museum. Shots of priceless pictures, rare books, stately sculptures, sounds of great music as bull-man bellows his-its way to hide-out deep beneath eternal monuments of culture. Ariadne shows more bosom, screams more loudly. Bull-man does not, however, wish to eat her, not yet anyway.

Enderby clenched his fists tight, their knuckles gleaming in the light that flashed, intermittently, from the screen.

Dénouement. Alpine-Italian hero, Mussolini-headed, crashes into deep cellars, wanders through dark, hears bull-bellow and princess-scream, finds monster and victim, shoots, finds bullets of no avail as bull-man is, on sire's side, thing from outer space. Ariadne escapes, screaming, showing allowable limit of Roman bosom, as howling chest-beating beast advances on hero. Hero, like Count Belisarius, has pepper-bag. He hurls its contents, temporarily blinding beast. To sneezes-bellows-howls, hero escapes. Lo, a prodigy: Dedalo and Icaro in flying-machine some decades ahead of its time drop bomb on metropolitan museum. Howls of dying bull-man, crash of statuary, flap and rustle of books caught alight, Mona Lisa with burnt-out smile, harp-strings pinging as they crack. Death of culture, death of the past, a rational future, embracing lovers. Dedalo and Icaro have engine-trouble. They crash in sea, against glorious sunrise. Heavenly voices. End.

'If,' trembled Enderby, 'I could lay my hands on that bloody Rawcliffe —'

'Stop it, do you hear?' said Vesta very sharply indeed. 'I can't take you anywhere, can I? Nothing satisfies you, nothing. I thought it was quite a nice little horror film, and all you can do is to say that it's been stolen from you. Are you getting delusions of grandeur or something?'

'I tell you,' said Enderby, with angry patience, 'that that bastard Rawcliffe —' The house-lights, all sick sweet orange, came gently up, disclosing applauding people crying *bravo, brava*, and *bravi*, as for the Pope's whole family. The fat man next to Enderby, now radiantly awake, lighted his long-gone-out cigar and then openly laughed at Enderby's clenched fists. Enderby prepared twelve obscene English words as a ground-row (variations and embellishments to follow), but, like a blow on the occiput, it suddenly came to him that he had had enough of words, obscene or otherwise. He smiled with fierce saccharinity on Vesta and said, so that she searched his whole face for sarcasm, 'Shall we be going now, dear?'

3

Late at night, thought Enderby, meant in England after the shutting of the pubs. Here there were no pubs to shut, so it was not yet late. He and Vesta picked up a horse-cab or *carrozza* or whatever it was called on the Via Marmorata, and this clopped along by the side of the Tiber while Enderby fed sedative words to his wife, saying, 'I'm honestly going to make an effort, really I am. My maturity's been much delayed, as you realize. I'm really terribly grateful for everything you've done for me. I promise to try to grow up, and I know you'll help me there as you've helped me in everything else. That film tonight has convinced me that I've got to make a real effort to live in public.' Vesta, beautiful in the June Roman aromatic night, her hair stirred but gently by the bland wind of their passage, gave him a wary look but said nothing. 'What I mean is,' said Enderby, 'that it's no use living in the lavatory on a tiny income. You were quite right to insist on spending all my capital. I've got to *earn* a place in the world; I've got to come to terms with the public and give the public, within reason, what it wants. I mean, how many people would want to read *The Pet Beast*? A couple of hundred at the outside, whereas this film will be seen by millions. I see, I see it all.' He reminded himself of the main protagonist of a drink-cure advertisement in *Old Moore's Almanac*: the medicine cunningly mixed with the drunkard's tea; the immediate result – the drunkard's raising a hand to heaven, wife hanging, sobbing with relief, round his neck. Too much ham altogether. Vesta, still with the wary look, said:

'I hope you mean what you say. I don't mean about the film; I mean about trying to be a bit more *normal*. There's a lot in life that you've missed, isn't there?' She gave him her hand as a cool token. 'Oh, I know it must sound a little pretentious, but I feel that I've got a duty to you; not the ordinary duty of a wife to a husband, but a bigger one. I've been entrusted with the care of a great poet.' The horse should, rightly, have neighed; massed trumpets should have brayed from the Isola Tiberina.

'And you were quite right,' said Enderby, 'to bring me to Rome. I see that too. The Eternal City.' He was almost enjoying this. 'Symbol of public life, symbol of spiritual regeneration. But,' he said, slyly, 'when are we going back? I'm so anxious,' he said, 'to go back, so we can *really* start our life together. I long,' he said, 'to be with you in our own home, just the two of us. Let's,' he said, bouncing suddenly with schoolboy eagerness, 'go back tomorrow. It should be possible to get a couple of seats on some plane or other, shouldn't it? Oh, do let's go back.'

She withdrew her hand from his, and Enderby had a pang of fear, not unlike heartburn, that perhaps she was seeing through this performance. But she said:

'Well, no, we can't go back. Not just yet. Not for a week or so, anyway. You see, I have something arranged. It was meant to be a surprise, really, but now I'd better tell you. I thought it would be a good idea for us to be married, here in Rome, married properly. I don't mean a nuptial mass or anything, of course, but just the plain ceremony.'

'Oh,' gleamed Enderby, swallowing bolus after bolus of anger and nausea, 'what a very good idea!'

'And there's a very good priest, Father Agnello I believe his name is, and he'll be coming to see you tomorrow. I met him yesterday at Princess Vittoria Corombona's.' She trilled the name with relish, dearly loving a title.

False Enderby breathed hard with the effort of pushing True Enderby back into the cupboard. 'What,' he asked, 'was a priest doing in a dress-shop?'

'Oh, silly,' smiled Vesta. 'Princess Vittoria Corombona doesn't run a dress-shop. She does film-gossip for *Fem*. Father Agnello is very intellectual. He's spent a lot of time in the United States and he speaks English perfectly. Strangely enough, he's read one of your poems – the blasphemous one about the Virgin Mary – and he's very anxious to have a couple of good long talks with you. Then, of course, he'll hear your confession.'

'Well,' smiled Enderby, 'it's good to know that everything's being taken care of. It's such a relief. I am really, you know, most grateful.' He squeezed her hand as they turned into the Via Nazionale: lights, lights; the Snack Bar Americano; the Bank of the Holy Spirit; shop after shop after shop; the air terminal, alight and busy; the hotel. The fat horse clomped to a ragged halt and snorted, not specifically at Enderby. The driver swore that his taxi-meter was wrong, a mechanical fault hard to repair, it showed too little. Enderby would not argue. He gave five hundred lire more than the clocked amount, saying 'Sod you too' to the driver. Rome; how he loved Rome!

Enderby watched and waited carefully in the hotel bar. There were late coffee-drinkers at the little tables, voluble speakers of fast foreign tongues, ten or a dozen all told, and Enderby would have given them all for Rawcliffe. He wished yesterday morning could be shunted back for just five minutes, he and Dante and Rawcliffe alone in the bar, one damned good crack on the proleptically bloody nose. L'Animal Binato, indeed. The Muse would be very annoyed now, fuming, a harpy, with all that work wasted. Enderby watched Vesta lovely over her glass of Pernod, waited till his third glass of Frascati, then writhed in simulated stomach-ache. 'Uggggggh,' said Enderby, 'blast it. Arrrrgh.' Vesta said:

'You've been drinking too much, that's your trouble. Come on, we're going to bed.' Enderby, artist to the end, made a harrowing borborygm, just like old times. Grerrrrkhrapshhhhh. She rose in concern. Enderby said:

'No. You wait here. There's a lavatory on the ground floor. Really, it's nothing.' He smiled, the liar, through his agony, motioning her to sit down again. He gargoyle-bulged his cheeks, nodded vigorously to show that this showed what it seemed to show, then left the bar smartly, urrping and arrrkhing to the surprise of the coffee-drinkers, into the lobby. To the insincerely gold-grinning dapper receptionist, framed in tubes of light at his desk, Enderby said urgently, 'I have to return to London. Just for a couple of days. Business. My wife will stay on here. I don't want you to think,' added Enderby guiltily, 'that I'm running away or anything like that. If you wish, I'll pay my bill up to date. But I'm leaving my luggage. All except one small overnight case. I take it that that will be all right, will it?' He almost prepared to give the receptionist a thousand-lire note of hush-money but, in time, thought better of it. The receptionist, with a graceful head-inclination as of one bending to hear the tick of a watch in an invisible man's waistcoat pocket, said that everything would be quite all right, but Signor Enderby must understand that there could be no rebate in respect of the time that Signor Enderby would be away. Signor Enderby gladly understood. 'I want,' he said, 'to ring up the air terminal, the one on this street. Could you give me the number?' The receptionist would be only too pleased to ring up for him; he could take the call in one of those boxes over there.

From the box Enderby could just see Vesta eating a ham sandwich. It must be ham, because she was stroking each sliver with what must be, from the shape of the jar, mustard. Enderby tried, which was not difficult, to look very ill in case she should glance up and see him. If she came over he would have to pretend that he had blindly dashed in here because it had the outward appearance of a lavatory; if she saw him urgently mouthing into the telephone he would have to pretend he was calling a doctor. A voice now spoke in English to Enderby, and Enderby said furtively, 'Enderby here.' The name, understandably, meant nothing to the suave clerkly voice. Enderby said, 'I want to travel to London by the next possible plane. Very urgent. I already have a first-class ticket, but my booking, you see, is for the twenty-fifth or twenty-sixth or something – I can't quite remember the exact date. This is very very urgent. Business. And my mother's dying.' There was no cluck of condolence: hard bastards these Romans. The voice said, above the rustle of ledger-pages, that it thought there might be empty seats on the BOAC plane from Cape Town, due at Rome at five-thirty in the morning. The voice would ring back to confirm or deny. 'A matter of life and death,' said Enderby. The voice, however, seemed to know that Enderby was about to run away from his wife.

Vesta had finished her sandwiches and was picking her front teeth with an old London tube ticket she had taken from her bag. The bag was open, very untidy, but in it Enderby saw a bunch of keys. Those keys he would require: in the Gloucester Road flat were certain things he needed. Seeing the teeth-picking, Enderby nodded: another thing marshalling him the way that he was going. 'How do you feel now?' she asked.

'A good deal better,' smiled Enderby. 'I got a lot of it up.' With what was still in the bank, with what he thought he could legitimately filch from her (mink, chiefly), he considered it was possible for him to return for a year or two to something like his old life: the lone poet in some sordid attic or other with thin stews and bread, trying to make it up to his Muse. He did not repine at the loss of his capital. Not any longer. It was, after all, his stepmother's money, and here, now pulling a ham-fibre from her molars, though with grace and without ostentation, sat his stepmother, all too able to use that money. The interest, of course, was another matter. The Church had always condemned the lending out of money at interest, so no good Catholic had a right to claim the increment it had earned when the return of the loan was made. Enderby, though determined to be just, was also determined to be strictly Protestant here. As he smiled to himself he was suddenly jolted by the calling of his name over a loudspeaker.

'Who on earth,' said Vesta, 'can be ringing you up at this hour of the evening? You stay there, I'll take it. You're still looking a bit pale.' And she rose.

'No, no, no,' protested Enderby, pushing her roughly back into her cane armchair. 'It's something you're not supposed to know about. A surprise,' he tried to smile. She grimaced and, taking a hair-clip from her bag, began to clean her left ear. Enderby was delighted to see that.

The clerkly voice was pleased to be able to confirm a booking on the plane from Cape Town. Enderby was to report at the terminal at four; the clerk then on duty would alter his ticket for him. '*Deo gratias*,' breathed Enderby, meaning *grazie*. But only that liturgical gratitude, he reflected, could express his relief at the prospect of getting out of, with all its detonations and connotations, Rome.

'It's arranged,' he smirked at Vesta. 'Don't ask me what, but it's all arranged.' As they rose to go to their room he saw on the table a hair-clip; its bend of bifurcation was stuffed with ear-wax. He took Vesta's arm with something like love.

4

Staying awake till three-thirty was not really difficult. Really difficult was getting the packing done on a night when Vesta, normally a good solid Scots sleeper, had decided to be restless and somniloquent. Enderby watched her warily as she lay prone, having kicked the clothes off the bed, her nates silvered by the Roman moonlight to the likeness of a meringue. Delectable, yes, but from now on for somebody else's delectation. Enderby stole about the silvered room in his socks, suddenly stiffening as in a statue dance each time she burbled in her sleep, rushing to the dark corner by the window to stand as if for his height to be taken when she pettishly whisked from the prone to the supine. Supine, she uttered strange words to the ceiling and then chuckled, but Enderby would not permit himself to be scared. Taking his passport and air ticket from the top drawer of the chest of drawers he also, after a few seconds of ethical thought, decided to take hers. Thus, if she woke to a realization of Enderby's desertion, she would not be able to follow at once. But he placed several thousand or million lire on the mantelpiece, and he knew that she had traveller's cheques of her own. Although she and Rome went so beautifully together, he could not, in all decency, condemn her to too long an enforced stay; he hoped he still had enough humanity not to wish that on his worst enemy.

One suitcase was enough for Enderby's clothes and shaving gear. The lotions and creams and sprays she had made him buy – these he decided to leave behind: no one would ever want to smell him any more. Now there was the question of that key to the flat; he had left a couple of boxes there, stuffed with drafts and notes. The typescript of *The Pet Beast* was locked in the drawer of her own escritoire, and there it could stay. Its interest, he admitted glumly, was one of content more than form, and the content had been filched and distorted. Let that be a lesson to him. Enderby now squinted in the moonlight for Vesta's bag, a flat silver envelope into which, that evening, she had poured the entire load of rubbish from a black bag from a grey bag from a white bag from a blue bag, a woman who, with residual Scots thrift, could not bear to throw anything away. Enderby saw this silver bag, further silvered by the light, lying on her bedside table. He stalked over for it, like some clumsy ballerina on her points, and, as he made to pick it up, Vesta swiftly pronated, diagonal across the bed, and a bare slim arm flopped over the table to hold the bag down like a silver bar. Enderby hesitated now, standing with breathing suspended, wondering whether he dare risk. But then she, with the same swiftness, lurched her body to the supine, though with her left arm still across the table, and began to speak out of some profound dream. She said:

'Pete. Do it again, Pete. Och, Pete, that was bloody marvellous.' It was a coarse accent, suggesting the Gorbals rather than Eskbank, and, to match it, the sleeping Vesta began to use coarse terms suggesting an extremity of abandon. Enderby listened horrified, at last calming his nerves by reflecting that anything, even necrophily, was allowed to the dreamer. He did not now try to extract the bag from under her silver arm; he could perhaps get into the flat without a key. Effect an entrance, as they say. He now wished to effect an exit, and quickly.

As he fumbled at the door-handle, hidden under the mink coat that hung from the door-hook, he had the impression that she was about to lift herself out of sleep, some warning bell having shrilled at the end of one of the long corridors of the cerebral cortex. He calmed her with words and a noise:

'Brarrrkh. Just going to the lavatory.' His last words to her as he softly folded the mink over his arm. She grunted, smacked her lips, then, seeming satisfied, started to lower herself into deeper levels of sleep. Enderby opened the door and went out. Standing an instant to quieten his loud heart, he felt cautiously elated that soon, on the aircraft, he would be able to feel fully and uninhibitedly elated.

A poem began to twitch as he weighed his suitcase and paid his embarkation fee and bought his bus ticket:

Stepmother of the West . . .

Enderby waited with excitement for the images to come into focus – Emperor and Pope the same pantomime dame, no more red meat since spate of it in snaring arena, old bitch she-wolf with

hanging dugs, the big backyard of broken columns for the refuse-
collector; Enderby waited with impatience for the rhymes to line
up. City, titty. Beyond that was nothing.

Stepmother of the West, of venal cities
  Most venal something something she-wolf bitch
Romulus Remus something something titties
  Something something something something rich which ditch
    pitch

On the bus to Ciampino Enderby, frowning, called on his Muse
to do something about this ragged *donnée*. On the aircraft, placed
next to a Negro clergyman, Enderby muttered and grimaced so
that the stewardess came up to ask if everything was all right. A
suspicious character, muttering and frowning, a mink coat on the
luggage rack overhead, Enderby looked down on Rome. He had
forgotten all about Vesta already. He had expected that he would
be able to recite, under his breath, at least a stanza of this poem
in valediction. Thwarted and somewhat apprehensive, remembering
the prophecy of the traitor Rawcliffe, he could only devise a farewell that went beyond words but which the Negro clergyman
apparently took to be an adverse comment on his colour.

Fffffrrrrrerrrrrpshhhhhh.

Part Three

1

1

'You've got absolutely nothing to worry about there,' said Dr Preston Hawkes. 'The plates are negative: no TB, no carcinoma, nothing.' He held up a couple of cloudy portraits of the inner Enderby. 'That's the lot, then.' He had a loud Northern voice, some of the vowels home-made approximations to Received Standard. 'You can go away with a contented mind.' He was young and highly dentate, tanned, and tousled as though to advertise, for a side-line, the healthful properties of the resort where he practised. 'If bicarb helps that dyspepsia, you just stick to bicarb. But fundamentally your stomach and guts are perfectly sound.'

'You would say, would you,' said Enderby, 'that I'm quite unlikely to die in the near future?'

'Oh, my dear fellow,' said Dr Preston Hawkes, 'none of us can ever know that. Apart from the normal hazards of living – getting run over or electrocuted or slipping in the bathroom – there must always be some unknown factor that doesn't yield to examination. We know a lot,' he confided, 'but we don't know everything. But, as far as I can see, you're physically sound and likely to live for many years.' He glowed at Enderby like a frying slice of potato. 'Of course,' he said, 'your tone isn't as good as it might be. Take exercise: tennis, golf, walks. You could do with paring yourself down a bit. Keep off fried things; don't eat too much starch. You're a sedentary worker, aren't you? A clerk or something?'

'Perhaps in the older sense,' said Enderby. 'I am,' he explained sadly, 'a poet.'

'You mean,' said Dr Preston Hawkes incredulously, 'that's your job?'

'It was,' said Enderby. 'That's really why I came to see you. You see, I'm not writing any more poems.'

'Oh.' Dr Preston Hawkes became agitated; he tapped contrary-motion five-finger exercises on his desk, his smile fixed and nervous. He spoke now slackly, bubbling. 'Well, I hardly think – I mean, that's nothing to do with me, is it? I mean, I should have thought – That is to say, if you don't propose writing any more poetry, well, good luck to you. The very best of luck and all that sort of thing. But that's entirely your own affair, isn't it? That's what I'd say, anyway.' He now began to perform, though ineptly, the ritual of a man whose time is valuable: a syndrome of nervous grubbing among papers, looking at his watch, peering exophthalmically above Enderby's head as though the next patient was due to squeeze in between door and lintel.

'No,' said Enderby, 'you've got that wrong. What I mean is that I can't write poetry any more. I try and try, but nothing happens, nothing will come. Can you understand what I mean?'

'Oh, yes,' said the doctor, smiling warily. 'I quite see that. Well, I shouldn't worry too much about it if I were you. I mean, there are other things in life, aren't there? The sun is shining, the children are playing.' That was literally true; Dr Preston Hawkes lifted a hand as if he himself were conjuring the warm evening shaft through the window, the noise of an infant squabble on the road to the beach. 'I mean, writing poetry isn't the whole of life, is it? You're bound to find something else to do. Life is still all before you. The best is yet to be.'

'What,' asked Enderby, 'is the purpose of life?'

The doctor brightened at this question. He was young enough to have answers to it, answers clearly remembered from pipe-puffing student discussions. 'The purpose of life,' he said promptly, 'is the living of it. Life itself is the end of life. Life is here and now and what you can get out of it. Life is living by the square inch and the round minute. The end is the process. Life is what you make it. I know what I'm talking about, believe you me. I am, after all, a doctor.' He smiled towards something framed on the wall, his duly certified twin baccalaureate.

Enderby shook his head in vigorous gloom. 'I don't think Keats would have given you that answer. Or Shelley. Or Byron. Or

Chatterton. Man,' said Enderby, 'is a tree. He bears fruit. When he stops bearing fruit life cuts him down. That's why I wanted to know whether I was going to die.'

'Look,' said the doctor sharply, 'this is all a lot of morbid nonsense. It's everybody's duty to *live*. That's what the National Health Service is for. To help people to live. You're a healthy man with years of life ahead of you, and you ought to be very glad and very grateful. Otherwise, let's face it, you're blaspheming against life and God and, yes, democracy and the National Health Service. That's hardly fair, is it?'

'But what do I live for?' asked Enderby.

'I've told you what you live for,' said the doctor, more sharply. 'You weren't paying attention, were you? You live for the sake of living. And, yes, you live for others, of course. You live for your wife and children.' He granted himself a two-second smirk of fondness at the photograph on his desk: Mrs Preston Hawkes playing with Master Preston Hawkes, Master Preston Hawkes playing with teddy-bear.

'I had a wife,' said Enderby, 'for a very short time. I left her nearly a year ago. In Rome it was. We just didn't get on. I'm quite sure I have no children. I think I can say that I'm absolutely sure about that.'

'Well, all right then,' said the doctor. 'But there are lots of other people who need you, surely. Friends and so on. I take it,' he said cautiously, 'that there are still people left who like to read poetry.'

'That,' said Enderby, 'is written. They've got that. There won't be any more. And,' he said, 'I'm not the sort of man who has friends. The poet has to be alone.' This platitude, delivered rhetorically in spite of himself, brought a glassy look to his eyes; he got up stiffly from his chair. The doctor, who had seen television plays, thought he descried in Enderby the lineaments of impending suicide. He was not a bad doctor. He said:

'You don't propose to do anything silly, do you? I mean, it wouldn't do anybody any good, would it, that sort of thing? I mean, especially after you've been to see me and so on. Life,' he said, less certainly than before, 'has to be lived. We all have a duty. I'll get the police on to you, you know. Don't start doing anything you shouldn't be doing. Look, I'll arrange an appointment with a psychiatrist, if you like.' He made the gesture of reaching at once for the telephone, of being prepared to tap, at once, all the riches of the National Health Service for the benefit of Enderby.

'You needn't worry,' said Enderby soothingly. 'I shan't do anything I'd consider silly. I promise you that.'

'Get around a bit,' said the doctor desperately. 'Meet people. Watch the telly. Have the odd drink in a pub, all right in moderation. Go to the pictures. Go and see this horror film round the corner. That'll take you out of yourself.'

'I saw it in Rome,' said Enderby. 'The world première.' Here in England *L'Animal Binato* or *The Two-Natured Animal* had become *Son of the Beast from Outer Space.* 'As a matter of fact,' said Enderby, 'I wrote it. That is to say, it was stolen from me.'

'Look,' said Dr Preston Hawkes, now standing up. 'It would be no trouble at all for me to fix up an appointment for you. I think you'd feel a lot happier if you talked with Dr Greenslade. He's a very good man, you know, very good, very sympathetic. I could ring up the hospital now. No trouble at all. He could probably see you first thing in the morning.'

'Now,' said Enderby, 'don't worry. Take life as it comes. Live it by the square yard or whatever it was you said.'

'I'm not at all happy about what you might do,' said Dr Preston Hawkes. 'It wouldn't be fair for you to go back home and do yourself in straight after coming to see me. I'd feel happier if you'd see Dr Greenslade. I could ring up now. I could get a bed for you straight away. I'm not sure that it's right for you to be going off on your own. Not in your present state of mind, that is.' He stood confused and young, mumbling, 'I mean, after all, we've all got a duty to each other –'

'I'm perfectly sane,' soothed Enderby, 'if that's what you're worrying about. And I promise you again not to do anything silly. You can have that in writing if you like. I'll send you a letter. I'll write it as soon as I get back to my digs.' Dr Preston Hawkes bit his lip from end to end and back again, as though testing it for durability. He looked darkly and uncertainly at Enderby, not liking the sound of 'letter' in this context. 'Everything,' said Enderby, with a great smile of reassurance, 'is going to be all right.' They had exchanged roles. It was with a doctor's jauntiness that Enderby said, 'Nothing to worry about at all.' Then he left swiftly.

He passed through a waiting-room full of people who, from the look of them, could not write poetry either. Some were in sporting kit, as if prepared to be tried out at the nets by Dr Preston Hawkes, wearing their ailments as lightly as a blazer-badge; others, dressed more formally, saw disease as a kind of church. Enderby had to squint his way out. He lost his contact-lenses some-where; the glasses he had formerly worn were, he supposed, still in the Gloucester Road flat. Unless, of course, she had thrown out all that was his. Walking through the rich marine light he regur-gitated the word 'police'. If this doctor proposed to put the police on to him it would be necessary to act quickly. In imagination he heard what the world called sanity as something in heavy clumsy hoofing boots. He remembered the boots that chased him when, just back from Rome, he had tried to break into the flat by the window and been suddenly transfixed in the beam of a copper's lantern. He could have stayed to explain, of course, but the police might well, with their professional tendency to suspicion, have held him till the eventual arrival of Vesta. That mink coat, left behind in the scamper, would have taken some explaining away. So he had swung his suitcase into the constable's groin and, between a starting-line and finishing-tape of whistles, dodged about till – to his surprise, for he had thought such things only possible in films – he had managed to escape by skidding down a sidestreet and into an alley, waiting there till the whistles peeped, like lost tropical birds, forlornly in the distance.

The May sun whizzed over the sea, and spread over the sea was a sort of blinding silver-shred marmalade. It was not the sea near to whose roar he had laboured, to so little purpose, at *The Pet Beast*, but its north-western brother. It fed a louder and more vulgar resort than Enderby's former Channel home: there was more gusto in the pubs, the vowels were broader, jugs of tea could be bought to take on the sands, a pleasure-beach was hysterical with violent machines of pleasure, an open-air concert party had a comedian who told his feed that if his brains were elastic he wouldn't have enough to make a canary a pair of garters. 'I've got blue blood in my veins,' said the feed. 'What do you think I've got in mine?' said the comedian. 'Dandelion and burdock?' It was an odd place, so posterity might think, in which to choose to die.

On this lovely evening there were queues, Enderby peeringly noticed, for *Son of the Beast from Outer Space*. Next door but two to the cinema was a cool cavern of a chemist's, full of the smell of soap, holiday laughter in a place of medicines, the prints of beach snapshots being collected, sunburnt arms and necks. Enderby had to wait till a holiday woman had been served with hair-clips, skin-cream, hydrogen peroxide and other life-enhancers before he could ask for the means of death. At last the white-coated girl put her head on one side at him:

'Yes, sir?'

He felt as embarrassed as if he were buying condoms. 'Aspirin, please.'

'Which size, sir?' There were, it seemed, various sizes. Enderby said:

'Fairly small ones, please. I have to take rather a lot.' She opened her mouth at him so he said, 'Not a lethal dose, of course.' He smiled winningly.

'Ha ha, sir. I should hope not. Not on a lovely evening like this.' He was quite a one.

Enderby went out with a bottle of a hundred. He had exactly twopence left in the world. 'Good,' he thought, 'timing.'

2

'A queer year,' reflected Enderby, potential death in his pocket, turning off the warm gay beery candy-flossy promenade into Boggart Road. It had been a queer empty year, or near-year.

June had been the month of marriage, honeymoon, desertion. He had drawn out from his London bank ninety pictures of clavigerous lions. He had bought a sponge-bag, stuffed the lions into it, wound the string of the bag round a trouser-button, then hung the bag inside his trousers. There it had walked and sat with him, a big comforting scrotum. Every man's fly his own bank; cheerful disbursements at all hours; no interest (though, of course, no overdrafts); frugal needs met without formality. He had travelled to this

Northern resort once mentioned with approval by Arry (far from South, London, Vesta). He had found a homely attic with a gas-ring (share lavatory and bathroom) at Mrs Bamber's, Butterworth Avenue, a permanent apex above the transient holiday guests.

In July and August he had put together laboriously a volume of fifty lyric poems (the fair copies and late drafts had fortunately been in his suitcase taken to and from Rome; a mass of other, rougher, material was still in, or else had been thrown out of, the Gloucester Road flat and was, presumably, no longer recoverable). The title of the volume was *The Circular Pavane*. Having been turned into typescript by a little woman at a typing bureau in Manchester, it had been delivered to, and received with little enthusiasm by, his publisher. In public lavatory cabinets, where privacy could be bought for a penny, he had planned a long autobiographical poem in blank verse, a sort of *Prelude*. The spongebag inside trousers still fat, he was able to afford to wait for the torpid or sulking Muse to wake up and see sense. The few autobiographical poetic lines achieved had been destroyed, re-written, destroyed, re-written, destroyed, re-written, slept on, read, re-read, re-written, destroyed. Through August and September the resort had been big-mouthed with cheerful visitors wearing comic caps with slogans (Try Me I'm The Easy Sort; Have A Go Joe Your Mother Won't Know), sticky with kisses, brine, ale, candy, rock. There had been no news of Vesta or anyone. Sitting in a public lavatory one sunny morning, hearing the cheerful bucket-and-spade-clanking children on their way to the beach, he had savoured, like Frascati, his renewed aloneness. It was a pity he could not write anything, however. He had abandoned the idea of the long autobiographical poem; how about an epic on King Arthur or Lord Rutherford or Alcock and Brown? A verse drama, perhaps? He had spent long grubbing hours in the public library, pretending that he was really working, building foundations, gathering material. He had written nothing.

October, November, brought a whiff of foreboding. This was getting past a joke. He had money enough still, of course, but less and less to do with his time. Walking through the sea-deafening deserted streets, overcoat-collar round his ears, trying to crank up a poem, returning to hopelessness, stew, Mrs Bamber insisting on coming up to his attic, sitting there, talking about her own past redolent of oyster-bars and Yates's Wine Lodge.

If, he vowed at Christmas, if he were given some sort of token of assurance that he would be able to start writing again, then, when his money ran out, he would willingly take some futile occupation or other, becoming a part-time poet, keeping alive for his Muse.

Towards the end of January he awoke to a morning clamped in frost, a poem singing in his ears. Thank God, the relief. He wrote the gnomic telegraphic message down and spent the morning refining it to a final shape:

> You being the gate
> Where the army went through
> Would you renew the triumph and have them decorate
> The arch and stone again?
> Surely those flowers are withered, the army
> Now on a distant plain.

Reading it, he saw, his hair bristling, that it was a private message, a message from her to himself.

> But some morning when you are washing up,
> Or some afternoon, taking a cup
> Of tea, possibly you will see
> The heavens opening and a lot
> Of saints singing, with bells swinging.
> But then again, possibly not.

He had felt a clammy glair of sweat settle on him, his diaphragm start to liquefy. A poem of farewell.

In March came publication of *The Circular Pavane*. Reviews followed: '. . . Pleasant and lucid verse in the tradition . . .'; 'Mr Enderby has lost none of his old cunning; it is a pity, however, that we see no signs of new cunning, new directions. It is a cunningly blended mixture, but it is very much the mixture as before . . .'; '. . . One remembers with a sigh the old lyrical perfection. It is a relief to turn to the work of two young Oxford poets . . .' And one that was surely by Rawcliffe: 'Mr Enderby is undoubtedly enough of a realist not to regret the passing of the lyric gift. It cannot last for ever, and with Mr Enderby it has lasted longer than with most. Many of his contemporaries have already elected for the dignified silence of remembered achievement, and one may predict that Mr Enderby, after this not unexpectedly disappointing volume, will join their cloistral seclusion . . .' In *Fem* there was, of course, no review.

Enderby had spent April brooding over a pain in his chest. In May, now, this month, three days ago, he had decided to go to a doctor. The doctor, after palpation and auscultation, had more or less decided that nothing was really wrong but, to be on the safe side, had sent Enderby to the hospital for radiography. But, before that, with 'nothing wrong' in his ears, Enderby had sat down in his warm attic to write out a list of possible ways to die:

> Slash wrists in warm bath
> Overdose of sedative
> Hang from picture rail in dining-room
> Jump in sea from jetty

This was early summer, and Mrs Bamber's house had a fair number of early summer visitors, mostly, as far as Enderby could judge from the noise, teams of galloping children ineptly driven by whoaing but disregarded young parents. It would not be right, Enderby thought, to make his suicide a public affair. It was no way to start a holiday morning to find a corpse swinging with its tongue out at the cornflakes laid the night before, or else dreaming cold in a bath of cold red ink. Too public, of course, to upset anyone might have been the jump from the jetty at the end of Central Pier, but some swimmer, bored already with his holiday, might have splashed too swiftly to the rescue. The overdose was best: clean and quiet, clean and quiet, by something something and dreamy something. Kingsley, jocular Christian.

Enderby, non-Christian stoic, climbed the vanilla-coloured steps of 17 Butterworth Avenue. The front door was open and on the hat-stand were buckets and spades, the smell of feet and sand in the whole dark seaweedy hall. All the guests were out, perhaps at

Son of the Beast from Outer Space, but from her kitchen Mrs Bamber sang, the merry widow of a tram-driver, a song smelling of oysters and ruby port. Mounting the stairs, Enderby was suddenly transfixed by a line from, he thought, *Ulysses*, which seemed to him, with his lethal dose in his pocket, to be the most poignant line (though it was not really a line – only, so far as he could remember, a splinter of Bloom's interior monologue), the most pregnantly regretful line he had ever heard:

. . . And lie no more in her warm bed.

He shook his head as images clustered round it, images he was no longer capable of translating into words and rhythms: the horses under starter's orders, the champagne tent, the sun on the back of the neck, the omelette made with a hundred eggs and a bottle of Napoleon brandy, life.

. . . And lie no more in her warm bed.

Enderby climbed higher, climbed to the top, where there was only a roof between him and the sun. This garret of his was, like the sea, warming up for the summer. He entered and sat on his bed, panting after the climb. Then his stomach, living its own life, decided it was hungry, so Enderby put to warm on the gas-ring the remains of a simple stew. While it bubbled, he turned over and over the sizeable bottle of aspirin he had bought: he had read, or heard, that a hundred should be enough. Mrs Bamber, he felt sure, would be efficient at coping with the unexpected corpse of Enderby: she was a Lancashire woman, and Lancashire people rather enjoyed death. It would, anyway, be a clean corpse lying, jaw dropped as in astonishment at being dead, between the sheets. (He reminded himself to effect, as far as was possible, a total evacuation of his body before making it a corpse.) The holiday guests would not be disturbed; the Chief Constable and the Town Clerk would want no publicity; everything would be done quietly at night, and then cornflakes would be shuffled on to plates for the morning. Enderby now sat down, with something like appetite, to his last supper, a thin but savoury viaticum. He felt excited, as though after supper

he were going to see a film that everybody had been talking about
and the critics had highly praised.

3

Enderby was in his pyjamas. It was still light, a May evening, and
he had a fugitive impression of being a child again, sent to bed
while the life of day was beating strongly without. He had washed
his feet and scrubbed his dentures, scoured his few pots and pans,
eaten a piece of chocolate left over from some weeks back, and
poured water from the jug on the wash-stand into a clean milk-
bottle. (He had no tumbler, and would need a good long draught
to speed the aspirin down.) Now, with the cottonwool stopper
removed and the tablets clinking discreetly, the aspirin bottle began
to dramatize itself, drawing evening light from all angles, becoming
almost grail-like, so that the hand that held it shook. Enderby
carried it over to his bed, and it made a tiny dry castanet-noise
all the way. From the bed, which he now entered, he could look
down on Mrs Bamber's back-yard. He dredged it hungrily, squinting,
for symbols of life, but there were only a dustbin, a cardboard box
full of cinders, dandelions growing up from the flag-cracks, an old
bicycle discarded by Mrs Bamber's son, Tom. Beyond were three-
storey houses with bathing costumes drying on window-sills, beyond
again the sea, above all a primrose sky. 'Now,' said Enderby aloud.

One shaking hand shook out a shaking palmful of aspirin. He
gave the white seeds to his mouth like a golly-wog money-box
feeding in a penny. He drank water from the milk-bottle, still
shaking. Aspen, aspirin. Was there a connection?

An aspen hand aspiring now to death

He finished off the bottle in six or seven more handfuls, washing
them down carefully. Then, sighing, he lay back. There was nothing
to do now except wait. He had committed suicide. He had killed
himself. Self-slaughter was of all sins the most reprehensible, being
the most cowardly. What punishment awaited suicide? If Rawcliffe
were there now he would be able to quote from the *Inferno*, lavishly,

that man who had added to Italian art. Enderby could vaguely remember that suicide belonged to Nether Hell, the Second Ring, between those who had been violent against their neighbours and those who had been violent against God and art and nature. There, in that Third Ring, Rawcliffe rightly belonged, perhaps there already. All these were, Enderby thought, Sins of the Lion. He closed his eyes and saw, quite clearly, the bleeding trees that were the suicides, harpies fluttering about with a rattle of dry wings like the magnified noise of a shaken aspirin bottle. He frowned. All this seemed very unfair. He had, after all, chosen the way of the Second Ring to avoid the way of the Third, and yet both sins were tucked together in the same round slice of Nether Hell.

With infinite care and delicacy the day wormed itself through a continuum of darker and darker greys. The watch on his wrist ticked on healthily, the too-efficient servant that would announce death as coldly as day and breakfast. Enderby began to feel a great tiredness and to hear a loud buzzing in his ears.

A fanfare of loud farts, a cosmic swish of lavatory-flushings. The dark in front of his eyes was cut away in rough slice after rough slice, like black bread, right down to the heel of the loaf. This then began to turn slowly, brightening with each revolution until it became blinding like the sun. Enderby found it an insuperable effort to interpose blankets or hands or eyelids. The circle cracked with intolerable luminosity, and then Enderby seemed to be dragged, with hearty, though somehow archangelic, tug-of-war cries towards some ineffable hidden Presence. Suddenly this Presence, at first humorously offering Itself as a datum for mere intellection, erupted into a tingling ultimate blow at all the senses, and Enderby staggered back.

There she was, welcoming him in, farting prrrrrrp like ten thousand earthquakes, belching arrrp and og like a million volcanoes, while the whole universe roared with approving laughter. She swung tits like sagging moons at him, drew from black teeth an endless snake of bacon-rind, pelted him with balls of ear-wax and snuffled green snot in his direction. The thrones roared and the powers were helpless. Enderby was suffocated by smells: sulphuretted hydrogen, unwashed armpits, halitosis, faeces, standing urine, putrefying meat – all thrust into his mouth and nostrils in squelchy balls. 'Help,' he tried to call. 'Help help help.' He fell, crawled, crying, 'Help, help.' The black, which was solid laughter and filth, closed on him. He gave one last scream before yielding to it.

2

1

'And,' said Dr Greenslade the psychiatrist, 'we won't try that sort of thing again, will we? For, as we can now see, it only causes lots and lots of worry and trouble to other people.' He beamed, a fat youngish man in a white coat not too clean, with the unhealthy complexion of a sweet-eater. 'For example, it didn't do our poor old landlady's heart any good, did it? She had to run up the stairs and then down the stairs' – he illustrated this with up-and-then-down-the-air wiggling fingers – 'and she was most agitated when the ambulance finally got there. We must consider others, mustn't we? The world wasn't made just for us and nobody else.'

Enderby cringed from the nanny-like substitution of first plural for second singular. 'Everybody gives trouble when they're dying,' he mumbled. 'That can't be avoided.'

'Ah,' pounced Dr Greenslade, 'but you didn't die. When people die in the normal decent way they give a normal decent *leisurely* kind of trouble which harms no one. But you were just caught more or less in the act of sailing off. That meant rushing about and worry for everybody, particularly for your poor old landlady. Besides' – he leaned forward, hushed – 'it wasn't just a matter of straight-forward dying with you, was it? It was' – he whispered the dirty words – '*attempted suicide*.'

Enderby bowed his head, this being the required stock response. Then he said, 'I'm sorry I made a mess of it. I don't know what came over me. Well, I do in a way, of course, but if I'd been braver, if I'd stuck it out, I think I could have sailed straight through, if you see what I mean. What I mean is that that was just a vision of Hell meant to frighten me. Bogies and so on. It wasn't real.'

Dr Greenslade rubbed his hands discreetly. 'I can see,' he said, 'that a lot of fun lies ahead. Though not for me, unfortunately. Still, I'll be getting Wapenshaw's reports. It's a lovely place,' he said dreamily, 'especially lovely at this time of year. You'll like it.'

'Where?' said Enderby with suspicion. 'What?' Dr Greenslade had sounded like some Dickens character talking about a beloved idiot-child's grave. 'I thought I was being discharged.'

'Oh, dear me, no,' said shocked Dr Greenslade. 'Healthy people don't try to commit suicide, you know. Not coldly and deliberately they don't. And you'd planned this, you know. Preston Hawkes told me you'd planned it. It wasn't just a mad impulse.'

'No, it wasn't,' said Enderby stoutly. 'It was logical. I knew perfectly well what I was doing and I've given you perfectly logical reasons for doing it.' He belched acidulously: Greeeeekh. 'This hospital food's bloody awful,' he said.

'The food at Flitchley is excellent,' dreamed Dr Greenslade. 'Everything's excellent there. Lovely grounds to walk in. Table tennis. Television. A library of sedative books. Congenial company. You'll be sorry to leave.'

'Look,' said Enderby quietly, 'I'm not going, see? You've got no right to keep me here or send me anywhere. I'm perfectly all right, see? I demand my freedom.'

'Now,' said Dr Greenslade harshly, changing from nanny to schoolmaster, 'let's get one or two things absolutely clear, shall we? There are certain laws in this country appertaining to mental derangement, laws of restraint, certificates and so on. Those laws have, in your case, already been invoked. We can't have people wandering all over the country trying to kill themselves.' Enderby closed his eyes to see England swarming, as a log swarms with woodlice, with peripatetic suicides. 'You're a danger to yourself,' said Dr Greenslade, 'and a danger to the community. A man who doesn't respect his own life isn't likely to respect anybody else's. That's logical, isn't it?'

'No,' said Enderby promptly.

'Oh, well,' said Dr Greenslade sarcastically, 'you, of course, are the big expert on logic.'

'I don't pretend to be anything,' said Enderby loudly, 'except a poet whose inspiration has departed. I'm an empty eggshell.'

'You are,' said Dr Greenslade sternly, 'a man of education and culture who can be of great value to the community. When you're made fit again, that is. Empty eggshells, indeed,' he poohed. 'Poets,' he near-sneered. 'Those days are past, those wide-eyed romantic days. We're living in a realistic age now,' he said. 'Science is making giant strides. And as for poets,' he said, with sudden bubbling intimacy, 'I met a poet once. He was a nice decent fellow with no big ideas about himself. He wrote very nice poetry, too, which was not too difficult to understand.' He looked at Enderby as though Enderby's poetry was both not nice and not intelligible. 'This man,' said Dr Greenslade, 'didn't have your advantages. No private income for him, no cosy little flat in a seaside resort. He had a wife and family, and he wasn't ashamed of working for them. He wrote his poetry at week-ends.' He nodded at Enderby, week-day poet. 'And there was nothing abnormal about him, nothing at all. He didn't go about with a lobster on a string or marry his own sister or eat pepper before drinking claret. He was a decent family man whom nobody would have taken for a poet at all.' Enderby groaned frightfully. 'And,' added Dr Greenslade, 'he had a poem in all the anthologies.' Enderby held back a loud howl. Then he said:

'If he was so normal, why did you have anything to do with him?'

'This,' smiled Dr Greenslade in large triumph, 'was a purely social acquaintance. Now,' he said, looking at the clock above Enderby's head, 'you'd better get back to your ward.' Enderby stood up. He was in hospital pyjamas, dressing-gown, slippers, and felt grey, shrunken, a pauper. He shambled out of the electro-cardiogram room into the corridor, hesitated at the stairs with their WAY OUT notice, remembered that they had locked his clothes away, and then, resigned, shuffled into the Medical Ward. He had been brought here to sleep it off after the stomach-pumping in the Emergency Ward, had lain for two days starved in a sort of big cot with iron bars at the sides, and now was allowed to pout about the ward in his dressing-gown. If a fellow-patient said, 'What's wrong with you, mate?' he replied, on the ward sister's instructions, 'Acetylsalicylic poisoning.' But these rough men, all with impressively visible illnesses, knew better than that. This here one had had a go at doing himself in. As Enderby, hands in dressing-gown pockets, bowed towards his bed (ring-worm to the left of it, to the right a broken femur), a dwarf of a working-man hopped towards him on crutches. ''Ere,' said the dwarf.

'Yes?' said Enderby. The dwarf cleared his nasopharynx via his oesophagus and said, conspiratorially:

'Trick cyclist been 'avin a go at you, eh? I seen 'im come in. Ridin' all over you, eh?'

'That's right,' said Enderby.

'Should be a law against that, I reckon. Draggin' out secrets from the back of your mind, like. Not decent, way I see it. 'Ad a go at me once. Know what that was for?'

'No,' said Enderby. The dwarf hopped nearer, his eyes ashine. He said, low:

'Wife and kids was out at the pictures, see. I 'ad nowt to do, not bein' much on the telly, and I'd washed up after my supper and put the kitchen straight. I'd read the paper too, see, and there wasn't much in that, all murders and suchlike and these 'ere summit conferences. Anyway, know what I'd got in my overall pocket?'

'No,' said Enderby.

'One of these big nuts,' said the dwarf. 'Don't know 'ow it got there, but there it was. Big one,' he insisted, making an illustrative ring with thumb and finger. 'A nut, you know. Not a nut you can eat, but one of these nuts you put a bolt through.' He showed, with the index-finger of his other hand, how exactly this was done. 'Do you see my meaning?' he asked.

'Yes,' said Enderby.

'Well,' said the dwarf, 'I got to lookin' at it and thinkin' about it, and then an idea come into me 'ead. Know what the idea was?'

'No,' said Enderby.

The dwarf came very close, awkward on his crutches, and seemed about to eat Enderby's ear. 'Put it in,' he said. 'Wife was out, see, and there was nowt else to do. It fitted real snug, too, you'd be surprised. Anyway, there it was, and you know what 'appened then?'

'No,' said Enderby.

'Wouldn't come out,' said the dwarf, reliving the horror in his eyes. 'There it was, stuck in, and it wouldn't come out. Right bloody fool I must 'ave looked to the cat when it come in through the window. A 'ot night, see, and the window was open. There I was, with this thing of mine stuck in this nut, and it wouldn't come out. I tries all sort of things – puttin' it under the cold water tap and gettin' a file at it, but it wasn't no good. Then the wife comes back from the pictures and she sees what I've done and she sends the kids straight upstairs. Bad enough the cat seein' it, but it wasn't right the kids should know what was goin' on. So you know what she does?'

'No,' said Enderby.

'She sends for the ambulance and they takes me to 'ospital. Not this one, though. We was livin' somewhere else at the time. Well, they tries and tries, but it's no good. All sorts of things they tries. Know what they 'as to do at the finish?'

'No,' said Enderby.

'Send for the fire brigade. I'm not tellin' you a word of a lie, but they 'as to do that. On my God's honour, they send for the fire brigade, and you know what the fire brigade 'as to do?'

'No,' said Enderby.

'They gets one of their special saws to saw through metal and they as a 'ose-pipe playin' on it all the time. Know why that was?'

'To keep it cool,' said Enderby.

'You've got it,' said the dwarf. 'There's not many as would give the right answer like you done. To keep it cool. Anyway, they gets it off, and that's when they ask me to see this trick cyclist like what you've seen. Didn't do no good though.' He looked gloomy.

'Is that why you're back in again?' said Enderby.

'Naw,' said the working-dwarf with scorn. 'Broke my leg at work this time. Always somethin' though, int there?'

From this moment Enderby thought that, with a certain measure of help and encouragement, he might conceivably decide that it might be possible for him to want, with certain inevitable reservations, to go on living. He woke up in the middle of the night laughing at some dream-joke. The sister had to give him a sedative.

2

Flitchley, surrounded by the pink snow of apple-blossom, cuckoo-
(appropriately)-echoing, green, quiet with a quiet that the clack
and clock of table-tennis only emphasized the more, Flitchley was
all that Dr Greenslade had said it would be. Several weeks later
Enderby sat on a bird-loud terrace reading a harmless boy's book
of violence ('. . . The Chink, with a sinister Oriental smile on his
inscrutable yellow countenance, wrenched the knife from the back
of his dead companion and threw it straight at Colonel Bill. Bill
ducked, hearing the evil weapon twang in the door. He had ducked
only just in time. "Now," he said, a cold smile on his clean-cut
features, "I think I've had more than enough of your treachery
for one day, Mr John Chinaman." He advanced on the Chink,
who now gibbered in his own outlandish language what was
evidently a prayer for mercy . . .'). In the day-room was the cheerful
music of the table being set for luncheon. Beyond the haha a
gardener bent at work. Fellow-patients of Enderby walked the
grounds or, like himself, sat at rest with sedative literature.
Occasionally Enderby would lower his book to his lap, close his
eyes, and say softly to himself, many times over, 'My name is
Enderby-Hogg, my name is Enderby-Hogg.' It was part of the
process of his cure; a gently contrived change of identity. Hogg
had been his mother's maiden name; soon, the Enderby silenced,
it would be altogether his.

The bell rang for luncheon and, from the day-room radio, news
refinedly boomed. Enderby-Hogg sat down, one of a mess of six,
having first shaken hands with a Mr Barnaby. Mr Barnaby, like a
dog, insisted on shaking hands with everybody at all hours of the
day and sometimes, waking everybody gently up for the purpose,
in the night. He had a sweet wrinkled face and, like that Enderby
soon to disappear, was something of a poet. He had written verses
on the Medical Superintendent beginning:

You have certainly got it in for me and no
Question about that, you fierce-eyed man.
Your wife no more loves you than that black crow
Up in the tree loves you, or that can

Which whilom held baked beans of the brand of Heinz,
Or that dog belonging to the lodge-keeper which so sorely whines

At the same table was Mr Trill, one of the symptoms of whose derangement was an ability to name the winner of any major horse-race run in the last sixty years. He was a man of venerable appearance who, he swore, hated racing. Enderby-Hogg now said to him, in automatic greeting, 'Thousand Guineas, 1910.' Mr Trill looked up mournfully from his soup and said, 'Winkipop, owned Astor, trained W. Waugh, ridden Lynham. Starting price five to two.' There was Mr Beecham, a master plumber who, on psychiatric instructions, spent all his day painting pictures: black snakes, red murder, his wife with three heads. Mr Shap, insurance agent, with dark glasses and a black hole for a mouth, said nothing, did nothing, but at times would scream one word: PASTE. Finally there was Mr Killick who preached, in an undertone, to the birds. He had the look of a successful butcher.

This company of six drank its soup and then was served, by two cheerful nurses of radiant complexion, with slabs of meat pie and scooped spuds. There were spoons and forks, but no knives. The meal chewed itself by pleasantly and quietly, except that at one point a dressing-gowned man at another table cried to the ceiling:

'Sink her, Number One!'

He was soothed quickly by one of the nurses, a homely Lancashire lass with a strong sense of humour. She said, 'You sink that meat pie quick, my lad. Treacle duff's coming alongside.' Enderby-Hogg laughed with the rest at this typical bit of Lancashire badinage. The treacle duff, with liberal custard, was then wheeled in, and Mr Killick, hungry after a morning preaching to the birds, had three helpings. After the meal some went back to bed, while Enderby-Hogg and others sat in the solarium. Enderby-Hogg had no money, but some obscure charitable fund invoked by the almoner supplied him with a sufficiency of cigarettes. A nurse came round with matches to light up for the smokers: no patient was allowed matches of his own, not since one Jehovah-minded G.P.I. sufferer had called Flitchley Sodom and set fire to it.

After a quiet smoke and lazy rambling chat, Enderby-Hogg went to the lavatory. The little cabinets, without doors, could be looked in on from the corridor through a thick glass wall: even here there was no sense of aloneness. After an ample healthy movement, Enderby-Hogg went to the ward he shared with eleven others, there to lie on his bed till summoned for his afternoon session with Dr Wapenshaw. He finished his boy's book ('... "And," grinned Colonel Bill, "despite all the dangers and hazards, it was a jolly good adventure which I'd be happy to undertake again." But, as he pulled the throttle and the mixture exploded sweet and strong, little did he think that adventure of an even more thrilling kind awaited him. That adventure, chaps, we shall learn about in our next story – the ninety-seventh! – of Colonel Bill and the faithful Spike.'). Enderby-Hogg looked forward, without undue excitement, to reading that story.

At three o'clock a smiling nurse summoned him to Dr Wapenshaw. Dr Wapenshaw said, 'Ah, hallo there, old man. Things going all right, eh? Jolly good, jolly good,' for all the world like Colonel Bill or his creator. Dr Wapenshaw was a big man whose superfluous fat proclaimed, like medals, his former Rugby football triumphs. He had large feet and a moustache and a voice like Christmas pudding. But he was a clever and original psychiatrist. 'Sit down,' he invited. 'Smoke if you want to.' Enderby-Hogg sat down, smiling shyly. He adored Dr Wapenshaw.

'Enderby-Hogg, Enderby-Hogg,' said Dr Wapenshaw, as though beginning a nursery rhyme. A thick file was open on the desk before him. 'Enderby-Hogg. Bit of a mouthful, isn't it? I think we might drop the Enderby, don't you? Keep it, of course, in the background as an optional extra if you like. How do you feel about the Hogg?'

'Oh, fine,' said Hogg. 'Perfectly all right.'

'What do you associate the name with? Pigs? Filth?' smiling. 'Gluttony?' Humorously, Dr Wapenshaw pig-snorted.

'Of course not,' said Hogg, smiling too. 'Roses. A lawn in summer. A sweet-smelling woman at the piano. A silver voice. The smoke from a Passing Cloud.'

'Excellent,' said Dr Wapenshaw. 'That will do very well indeed.' He sat back in his swivel-chair, swivelling boyishly from side to side, looking kindly at Hogg. 'That beard's coming along all right,' he said. 'You should have a pretty good one in a couple of weeks. Oh, yes, I've made a note about glasses. We're sending you to the oculist on Thursday.'

'Thank you very much,' said Hogg.

'Don't thank me, my dear fellow,' said Dr Wapenshaw. 'After all, it's what we're here for, isn't it? To help.' Tears came into Hogg's eyes. 'Now,' said Dr Wapenshaw, 'I've explained to you already just what it is we're trying to do and why we're trying to do it. Could you recap' – he smiled – 'in your own words?'

'Enderby,' said Hogg, 'was the name of a prolonged adolescence. The characteristics of adolescence were well-developed and seemed likely to go on for ever. There was, for instance, this obsession with poetry. There was masturbation, liking to be shut up in the lavatory, rebelliousness towards religion and society.'

'Excellent,' said Dr Wapenshaw.

'The poetry was a flower of that adolescence,' said Hogg. 'It still remains good poetry, some of it, but it was a product of an adolescent character. I shall look back with some pride on Enderby's achievement. Life, however, has to be lived.'

'Of course it has,' said Dr Wapenshaw, 'and you're going to live it. What's more, you're going to enjoy living it. Now, let me tell you what's going to happen to you. In a month's time – perhaps less if you continue to make the excellent progress you're already making – we're sending you to our Agricultural Station at Snorthorpe. It's really a convalescent home, you know, where you do a little gentle work – not too much, of course: just what you feel you *can* do and nothing more – and lead a very pleasant simple social life in beautiful surroundings. Snorthorpe,' said Dr Wapenshaw, 'is a little town on a river. There are summer visitors, swans, boating, nice little pubs. You'll love it. A group of you – under supervision, of course, if you can really call it supervision – will be allowed out to pubs and dances and cinemas. In the home itself there'll be chess competitions and sing-songs. Once a week,' smiled Dr Wapenshaw, 'I myself like to come down and lead a sing-song. You'll like that, won't you?'

'Oh yes,' breathed Hogg.

'Thus,' said Dr Wapenshaw, 'you'll gradually adjust yourself to living in society. You'll even meet women, you know,' he smiled.

'Some day, you know, I look forward to your making a *real* go of marriage. Enderby made rather a mess of that, didn't he? Still, it's all over now. The annulment's going through, so they tell me, quite smoothly.'

'I can't even remember her name,' frowned Hogg.

'Don't worry about that,' said Dr Wapenshaw. 'That's Enderby's affair, isn't it? You'll remember it in your own good time. And, moreover, you'll remember it with amusement.' Hogg smiled tentatively, as in anticipation. 'Now, as far as your future generally is concerned, I don't want you to think about that at the moment. There's going to be no worry about getting a really congenial job for you – we have our own department, you know, which sees to all that, and very efficient they are. The thing for you to do at the moment is to *enjoy* being this new person we're trying to create. After all, it *is* great fun, isn't it? I'm getting no end of a kick out of it all, and I want you to share that kick with me. After all,' he smiled, 'we've grown very close, haven't we, these last few weeks? We've embarked on a real adventure together, and I'm enjoying every minute of it.'

'Oh, me too,' said Hogg eagerly. 'And I'm really most awfully grateful.'

'Well, it's really awfully nice of you to say that,' said Dr Wapenshaw. 'But you've helped no end, yourself, you know.' He smiled once more and then became genially gruffly business-like. 'I'll be seeing you,' he said, looking at his diary, 'on Friday morning. Now off you go and have your tea or whatever it is and leave me to see my next victim.' He sighed humorously. 'Work, work, work.' He shook his head. 'No end to it. Run along now,' he grinned. Hogg grinned back and ran along.

For tea they had Marmite sandwiches, fish-paste sandwiches (Mr Shap cried out PASTE with such exquisite appropriateness that everybody had to laugh), fancy cakes and a small plum cake to each mess of six. After tea Hogg walked the grounds and surprised Mr Killick whispering to some bread-guzzling starlings beyond the haha, 'Come on now, you birdies, be good and kind to each other and love God who made you all. He was a bird just like you.' Hogg returned to the sunny solarium to find Mr Barnaby triumphantly finishing another stanza of his Ode to the Medical

Superintendent. He read this aloud with great feeling, having first
shaken hands heartily with Hogg:

> I saw you the other night out on the field
> Walking with a big stick with which you struck the grass
> Repeatedly, but the dumb grass would not yield
> To your importunities. So it will come to pass
> That that piece of china standing on your shelf
> Will fall on your head and give quite a shock to your
>   evil-smelling self.

For dinner there were fish and a rice pudding with sultanas
embedded in it. Mr Beecham, his hands vermilion from his day's
work on a large symbolical canvas, slowly picked out all the sultanas
from his portion and arranged them in a simple gestalt on his
bread-plate. After dinner there was television: amateur boxing which
excited two patients so much that one of the nurses had to switch
over to the other channel. On the other channel was a simple
morality of good and evil set in the West of North America in the
eighteen-sixties. It was interrupted at intervals by asthenic women
demonstrating washing-machines, though some patients evidently
could not see these as interpolations, taking them rather as integral
to the plot. Integration was the theme: the building of a new
human society under the sheriff's steadfast bright star. Hogg nodded
frequently, seeing all this (conquest of new territory, death to the
evil antisocial) as an allegory of his own reorientation.

3

High summer in Snorthorpe. Boats for hire by the bridge, by
the bridge a hotel called the White Hart, much favoured by
summer visitors. Drinkers squinting happily in moonlight on the
terrace. Dogs yapping in glee, chased by children. Ducks and
swans, fullfed, pampered. Willows. An old castle on a height far
above the river.

   A knot of men came walking, in loose formation though
evidently a supervised gang, in the direction of the little town

from the sunbrown fields of the Agricultural Station. They were men who looked as burnt and fit as the boating visitors, each carrying some such tool as a hoe or fork. By the bridge they halted at the cheerful command of their leader. 'All right,' he called. 'Rest for five minutes. Old Charlie here says he's got a stone in his boot.' Mr Peacock was a decent brown man, squat and upright, who treated his charges like young brothers. Old Charlie sat on the parapet and Mr Peacock helped him off with his road-dusty boot.

'Fag?' said Piggy Hogg (as he was jocularly called) to his companion. Bob Curran took one, nodding his thanks. He pulled out a cheap cylindrical lighter and struck it, the flame invisible in noon air that was all flame. Piggy Hogg bent over, sucking his fag alight.

'Won't be long for you now,' said Bob Curran.

'Won't be long,' said Piggy Hogg, taking in the long receding bank of willows. 'Next week, they reckon.' He detached a tobacco fibre from his lower lip. The lips were framed in brown beard pied with grey; his skin was tanned; he wore steel spectacles. He had something of the look of Hemingway, but there his association with literature ended. A moderately well-spoken middle-aged man evidently not used to manual work, but a good trier, respected by his ward-mates, helpful as a letter-writer. Some had said that it was a waste of an educated man, putting him like they said they were going to as bar-tender in training at a Midland hotel. But Piggy Hogg knew it was no waste.

A couple of nights back he had, after lights out, slipped on his bedroom headphones. Rejecting, with a click of the plastic dial on the wall, first the Light, then the Home, he had notched into the Third. A bored-sounding young man had been talking about Modern Poetry: '. . . Enderby, before his unaccountable disappearance . . . established as a good minor poet in the tradition . . . perhaps little to say to our generation . . . the more significant work of Jarvis, Sime and Cazalet . . .' He had listened with absolutely no interest. One was used, one was thrown away; Enderby had come out of it better than many; Hogg was looking forward to being a bar-tender. A bar-tender, moreover, who would be different from most, quite a character with his odd lines of poetry thrown out over the frothing pints. Behind the words and rhythms lay the sensations. Time for those.

'What did the old sky-pilot have to say to you?' asked Bob Curran.

'Him?' said Piggy Hoggy vaguely. 'Oh, I thought he made out quite a reasonable case for the Church of England. It's a communion of sorts. It doesn't make too many demands. He lent me some books to read, but I told him I'm not much of a reading man. If it'll give him any pleasure, I'll join.'

'I've never been much of a man for religion myself,' said Bob Curran. 'My dad was a tinker and all tinkers are atheists. We used to have a lot of fun, I remember, on Thursday evenings in the old days. You know, belly of pork and cider and somebody would give a talk about Causal Necessity and then there'd be one hell of a discussion afterwards. All in our front parlour, you know, with The Death of Nelson above the joanna.' Bob Curran was a very lean man of fifty-seven, a radio salesman recovering from schizophrenia. 'It seems to me,' he said, 'that people had more faith in those days. They *believed* more. Why, I do believe that my old man, who was nothing more than an ignorant old tinker, believed more in there not being a God than some of these religious sods today believe in there being one. It's a funny old world,' he concluded, as he always did.

'Oh, yes,' agreed Piggy Hogg, 'but it's not without interest.' After lunch there was to be a cricket match between the Home and the local St John Ambulance. Piggy Hogg had been persuaded to umpire. He had always been flustered by l.b.w. but, he had decided, when in doubt over any appeal except an obvious clean bowl or catch, always to say, 'Not out'. That night there was to be a sing-song led by Dr Wapenshaw, with beer from the canteen − two bottles a man. Piggy Hogg led the winning quiz-team. He had beaten Alfred Breasley at chess.

'Right, my tigers,' called Mr Peacock. 'Old Charlie's boot's free from stones.' (Old Charlie grinned without teeth.) 'God's in his heaven, all's right with the etcetera etcetera. On our merry way. Let me see, it's Saturday, isn't it? Corned beef and mashed and beetroot and treacle tart to follow. Right, Piggy old man, stop slavering at the chops. Let's march.'

Piggy Hogg glanced up at the tiny clouds (cotton-wool stoppers from heavenly aspirin-bottles) and down at the sun-warmed boats on the shore that looked like chicken-carcasses. A swan opened an archangelic wing. Shouldering his hoe, chucking away his fag-butt, he marched.

Enderby Outside

To Deborah

Esperad todavía.
El bestial elemento se solaza
En el odio a la sacra poesía
Y se arroja baldón de raza a raza.

– Rubén Darío

Part One

1

1

'It's,' said this customer at the bar, 'what I personally would want to call – and anyone else can call it what the hell they like for all I care –' Hogg listened respectfully, half-bowed, wiping dry a glass from which a noisy woman, an actress or something, had drunk and eaten a Pimm's Number One. 'But it's what I, speaking for myself, would call –' Hogg burnished an indelible veronica of lipstick, waiting for some highly idiosyncratic pay-off, not just the just word but the word just with just this customer's personal brand of justness. 'A barefaced liberty.' Hogg bowed deeper in tiny dissatisfaction. He had been a wordman himself once (nay, still – but best to lock all that up: they had said those days were past, trundled off by time's rollicking draymen, empties, and they knew best, or said they did. Still –) 'A man's name's his name, all said and done.' You couldn't say what this man had just said. A liberty was diabolical; it was lies that were barefaced. Hogg had learned so much during his season with the salt of the earth, barmen and suchlike. But he said blandly:

'It's very kind of you, sir, to feel that way about it.'

'That's all right,' said this customer, brushing the locution towards Hogg as though it were a tip.

'But they didn't call it after me, sir, in a manner of speaking.' That was good, that was: genuine barman. 'They brought me in here, as you might say, because the place was already called what it is.'

'There's been plenty named Hogg,' said the customer sternly. 'There was this man that was a saint and started these schools where all these kids were in rags. They had to be in rags or they wouldn't have them in. It was like what they call a school uniform.

And there's this Hogg that was a lord and gave it up to be prime minister but he didn't get it so he goes round ringing bells and telling them all off.'

'There was also James Hogg, the poet,' said Hogg unwisely.

'You leave poets out of it.'

'The Ettrick shepherd he was known as, in a manner of speaking. Pope in worsted stockings.'

'And religion as well.' This customer, who had had no lunch except whisky, grew louder. 'I might be an Arsee, for all you know. Respect a man's colour and creed and you won't go far wrong. I take a man as I find him.' He spread his jacket like wings to show green braces. Hogg looked uneasily across the near-empty bar. The clock said five to three. John, the tall sardonic Spaniard who waited on, the Head Steward's nark, he was taking it all in all right. Hogg sweated gently.

'What I mean is,' said flustered Hogg, 'this bar was called Piggy's Sty because of the man that was here before me.' John the Spaniard sneered across. 'Sir,' added Hogg.

'And you won't go far wrong is what I say.'

'It was to do with the people that started these hotels,' said Hogg urgently. 'They had a Hogg over there when they started. He brought them luck and he died. Americans they were.'

'I can take them or leave them. We fought side by side in both lots. They did as much good as harm, and I hope they'll say as much about you.' He slid his empty glass towards Hogg, impelling it as though it were a child's match-box ten-ton truck.

'Similar, sir?' asked Hogg, barman's pride pushing through the fluster.

'No, I'll try one of theirs. If the Yanks run this place then they'll likely know what's what.' Hogg didn't get that. 'What they call bourbon. That bottle there with the nigger on.' Hogg measured out a double slug of Old Rastus. 'With branch-water,' said this customer. Hogg filled a little pig-shaped jug from a tap. He rang up the money and said:

'They wouldn't have false pretences, that being their policy, as you might say. They said that customers like things genuine in the States and it's got to be the same here too. So it had to be a Hogg.'

The customer, as though testing his neck for fracture, swivelled

his head slowly, taking in Piggy's Sty. It was one of many whimsi-
cally named bars in this tall but thin hotel, London's new pride.
This bar and the Wessex Saddleback, where at this moment there
were a lot of thick-necked Rotarians sweating on to charred
gristle, made up nearly the whole of the tenth floor. You could
see much of autumn London from the windows of the bar (on
which artificial trotter-prints were like a warning). You could see
an ape-architecture of office-blocks, the pewter river, trees that
had scattered order-paper leaves all about Westminster, Wren and
his God like babes in the wood, the dust of shattered Whig resi-
dences thrown by the wind. But this customer looked only on
the frieze of laughing tumbling porkers, the piggy-banks with
broken saddles to make ashtrays, little plastic troughs with plastic
chrysanthemums in them. He turned back to Hogg to nod at
him in grudging admiration as though he, Hogg, had made all
this.

'Closing now, sir,' said Hogg. 'One for the road, sir?'

'You wouldn't catch them daring to take the mike out of *my*
name,' said the customer. He now winked pleasantly at Hogg. 'Not
that I'd give them the chance. A man's name is his own.' He laid
a finger to his nose, as though to cool the inflammation which
Hogg's stepmother had used to call Harry Syphilis, winking still.
'Catch *me*.' He smirked, as though his name was something he had
won and was going to hug greedily to his chest till he got home.
'I'll have some of our own now after that nigger stuff. A wee
drappie. Och aye. There's a wee wifey waiting.' Hogg daringly
poured Scotch into the glass that had held bourbon. John had his
eyes on his two leaving customers.

'Electric shepherds,' said one of these, a man who might well
be a pig-farmer and yet had not seemed really at home in Piggy's
Sty. 'It'll come to that, I daresay.' He was with a man in clerical
grey, etiolated as by a life of insurance. They both nodded at Spanish
John and then went out. John showed them a baroque shrine of
golden teeth and said: 'Zhentilmen.' Then he picked up their glasses
and brought them to the counter for Hogg to wash. Hogg looked
on him with hate.

'But what I say is,' said the one customer left, 'it's an insult to
the name of your old dad. That's the way to look at it.' He descended

his stool with care. John bowed and bowed, his gob all bits of fractured doubloon. The customer grunted, dived into his trouser-pocket, and brought up a half-crown. This he gave to John; to Hogg he gave nothing. John bowed and bowed, baring deeper and deeper gold deposits. Hogg said:

'Actually, it was my mother's.'

'Eh?' The customer squinted at him.

'What I mean is, Hogg was my mum's name, not my dad's.'

'I don't come in here,' said the customer, 'to have the piss took.' A certain lowness was coming out now. 'You watch it.'

Hogg sulked. He had gone too far again. And this horrible John had, as before, been a witness. But Hogg had spoken truth. Hogg had been the maiden name of that barely imaginable sweet woman, singing 'Passing By' to her own accompaniment, Banksia and Macartney and Wichuraiana vainly opposing their scents to hers through the open french-window. His father O-ing out the smoke of a Passing Cloud while he listened, his father had been called –

'I like a laugh same as the next one, but watch it, that's all.' And the customer left, going aaarkbrokhhh on his stomach of whisky. Hogg and Spanish John faced each other.

'*Puerco*,' said John, for so he translated Hogg's mother's name. 'You speak other time of poetry, not good. Get on with bloody job is right way.'

'Nark,' growled Hogg. 'Tell Holden if you want to. A fat lot I care.' Holden was the Head Steward, a big man hidden behind secretaries and banks of flowers, an American who sometimes pretended he was Canadian. He would talk about cricket. It was something to do with American trade policy.

'I say bugrall this time,' promised John generously. 'This time not big. Last time very big.'

Well, it hadn't really been Hogg's fault. A group of young fattish television producers had been there for dinner, cramming down peanuts with the martinis, going '*Ja*' when they meant 'yes'. They had talked loudly of the sexual *mores* of certain prominent actresses and, by a natural transition, had been led on to a discussion of poetry. They had misquoted something by T. S. Eliot and Hogg, off his guard, had put them right. This had interested them, and they had tried him on other poets, of all of whom – Wunn, Gain, Lamis, Harkin, some such names – Hogg had never heard. The television men had seemed to sneer at him, a common barman, for knowing; now they sneered at him for not knowing. The leader of the *ja*-sayers fed himself, in the manner of a Malaysian rice-eater, with a shovel-hand loaded with salty peanuts, sneering at the same time. He said indistinctly, 'Wenggerggy.'

'Who?' said Hogg. He had begun to tremble. There was a phantom girl hovering near the pig-pink (chopped-ham-and-pork-pink, to be accurate) ceiling, a scroll in her hand, queenly shoulders nacreous above a Regency ball-gown. Hogg knew her all too well. Had she not deserted him a long time ago? Now she smiled encouragingly, unrolling her scroll coquettishly though, an *allumeuse*. 'Did you say *Enderby*?' asked Hogg, shaking beneath his barman's white bum-freezer and frowning. The girl swooped down to just behind him, flat-handed him on the nape, and then shoved the wide-open scroll in front of his eyes. He found himself reciting confidentially, as in threat:

> 'Bells broke in the long Sunday, a dressing-gown day.
> The childless couple basked in the central heat.
> The papers came on time, the enormous meat
> Sang in the oven. On thick carpets lay
> Thin panther kittens locked in clawless play –'

'Ah, Jesus –'
'A *sonnet* yet –'
Hogg glowered at this one, a small gesturing man, and prepared to say 'For cough'. But instead he went stoutly on:

> 'Bodies were firm, their tongues clean and their feet
> Uncalloused. All their wine was new and sweet.
> Recorders, unaccompanied, crooned away –'

At this moment another television man came in, one they had apparently all been waiting for. He was much like the others, very pasty. They clawed at him passionately, shouting.
'The Minetta Tavern –'

'Goody's on Sixth Avenue —'

There was a solitary man at the counter, one who had ordered by pointing; he wore dark glasses; his mouth had opened at Hogg and let cigarette-smoke wander out at him. The tabled customers, aware of the intrusion of verse-rhythm into the formlessness of chat, had all been looking at Hogg. Spanish John stood shaking his head, nastily pleased.

'No more verse-fest,' said the chief peanut-eater to Hogg. 'More martinis.'

'Wait,' said Hogg, 'for the bloody sestet.'

'Oh, let's go in,' the newcomer said, 'I'm *starving*.' And so they all shouted off to the Wessex Saddleback, clawing and going *ja*. Hogg turned gloomily to the man in dark glasses and said:

'They could have waited for the bloody sestet. No manners nowadays. It's a miracle, that's what they don't seem to realize. I tried for years to get that thing right, and only then it just came to me.' He suddenly felt guilty and began to excuse himself. 'Another man, though. Not really me. It's a long story. Rehabilitation they call it.' The man had said:

'*Nye ponimai*.' That was why he had started pointing again. Hogg, sighing, had measured out a large globule of an Iron Curtain glycerine-smelling apéritif. Must watch himself. He was happy now, wasn't he? Useful citizen.

It was after that occasion that he had been summoned to see Mr Holden, a man desperately balding as though to get into *Time* magazine. Mr Holden had said:

'You were on a sticky wicket there, *ja*. A straight bat and keep your eye on the pitcher. This is a respectable hotel and you are a sort of gliding presence in white, that's your image, *ja*. You've done well to get here after so short an innings in the profession. Self-employed before, that's what it says on your dossier. Well, whatever it was is no concern of the management. Though it's beginning to sound as though it wasn't quite com eel foe. Still, the pairst is pairst. The cream of global citizenry pairsses through these portals. They don't want bartenders telling them to keep their tongues clean. And you said something about our cellar that was libellous, but he may have balled that up, so we'll let it pairss. It's your name that's your asset, remember that. Carry your bat, brother, or you'll find yourself no-balled PDQ.'

Past, was it? The past, that is. He did something there was no law against doing shortly after. If anybody found out they would have him on television, sandwiched between a dustman who collected Meissen and a bank-clerk who had taught his dog to smoke a pipe. A curiosity at best. At worst a traitor. To what, though? To what a traitor would he be regarded as? And now, a month later, he was frowning while he compared his takings with the roll in the till that recorded each several amount rung. He would have to take the money in a little box to the huge clacking hotel treasury full of comptometers that – so Larry in the Harlequin Bar upstairs had asserted – if programmed proper could be made to see right through to your very soul. And then he had an appointment. In (his breast swelled minimally) Harley Street. To your very soul, eh? He felt uneasy. But, damn it, he had done no real wrong, surely? When John Milton clocked in to do his daily stint of translation of Cromwell into Latin, had they not perhaps used to say: 'All right that was, that thing you pinned up on the wall about Fairfax and the siege of Colchester. You carry on'? He, Hogg, had not pinned anything up, though, by God, one of these days – He had merely –

'My brother,' John was saying, 'now he work in Tangier. At Big Fat White Doggy Wog, bloody daft name for bar. Billy Gomez, everybody know him. Good on knife if trouble, ah yes, man.' He made a bloodthirsty queeeeeking noise and drove a ghost-stiletto at Hogg's hidden puddings. 'He say poetry, but now not. *Good* poetry. *Spanish* poetry. Gonzalo de Berceo, Juan Ruiz, Ferrant Sanchez Calavera, Jorge Manrique, Gongora – *good* poetry. England too fackin cold for good poetry. English man no *fuego*. Like bloody fish, *hombre*.'

'I'll give you no *fuego*,' said Hogg, incensed. 'We gave you *mucho* bloody *fuego* in 1588, bastards, and we'll do it again. Garlicky sods. I'll give you no good poetry.' A ruff went round his neck. He stroked a spade-beard, enditing. The sky was red with fireships. Then he saw himself in the gross reredos mirror, his cross reflection framed in foreign bottles, a decently shaven barman in glasses, going, like Mr Holden, rapidly bald.

'We go eat now,' said John. In the hotel's intestines steamed an employees' cafeteria, full of the noise of shovelled chips and heady with Daddies Sauce. A social organizer walked regularly between the tables, trying to get up table-tennis tournaments. John's empty stomach castanetted dully.

'I don't want to eat,' sulked Hogg. 'I'm full up already. Chocker, that's what I am.'

2

Hogg walked to Harley Street, much set upon by leaves and blowing bits of paper. He knew his way about these defiled streets, London Hogg as he was. His stepmother in purgatory or wherever she was would have a fit to see how well he knew London. Bruton Street, New Bond Street, across Oxford Street, then through Cavendish Street and across Cavendish Square, then into Harley Street, knowing also that Wimpole Street was the next one, where Robert Browning had read bits of *Sordello*, a very obscure and long poem, to that woman who had looked like and, indeed, possessed a spaniel, and under the bed there had been big spiders. Her father had made her drink black stout. Hogg tried to pretend that he did not know these things, since they were outside his barman's province, but he knew that he knew them. He frowned and set his shoulders in defiance. A man who sold newspapers and dirty magazines said, 'Cheer ap, gav.'

Hogg, in working trousers and decent dogtooth-patterned sports-jacket, was soon seated in Dr Wapenshaw's waiting-room. He had received, some three days before, a curt summons from Dr Wapenshaw, chief agent of his rehabilitation from failed suicide to useful citizen. He could think of only one possible reason for the curtness, but it was a reason so unlikely that he was fain to reject it. Still, when you thought about these cybernetic triumphs and what they were capable of, and how a psychiatrist as cunning as Dr Wapenshaw would be quite likely to have banks of electronic brains working for him (and all at National Health expense), then it was just about possible that the summons might be about this particular hole-in-the-corner thing that Hogg had done, an act of recidivism, to use the fashionable jargon. Otherwise, he, Hogg, and Dr Wapenshaw had achieved a condition of mutual love and trust that, however official and Government-sponsored, had been looked on as a wonder in that green place of convalescence. Had not Dr Wapenshaw shown him, Hogg, off as an exemplary cure, inviting colleagues of all nations to prod and finger and smile and nod and ask cunning questions about Hogg's relationship with his Muse and his stepmother and his lavatory and his pseudo-wife, cooling all that turbulent past to the wan and abstract dignity of a purely clinically interesting case to be handled by fingers smelling of antiseptics? Yes, that was so. Perhaps that curtness was, after all, the official wrapping that enclosed warmth and love and protected them from the eyes of strangers. Still and nevertheless.

The waiting-room had a gasfire, and the only other waiting patient was crouching over it, as though it were a wicket and he its keeper. The chill of autumn was reflected in the covers of copies of *Vogue* and *Vanity Fair* that lay on the polished table that turned the vase of real, not plastic, chrysanthemums into a kind of anti-podeal ghost. These covers showed thin young women in mink against the falling of leaves. Something like winter cold struck Hogg as he noticed a deck of copies of *Fem*. Those days, not so long ago, when he had actually written ghastly verses for *Fem*, set as harmless prose ('I lift my baby to the air. He gurgles because God is there') and pseudonymously signed Faith Fortitude; those incredible days when he had actually been married to its features editress, Vesta Bainbridge; those days should, officially, be striking him with little more than mild and condescending curiosity. That had been another man, one from a story read yawning. But the past was fastening its suckers on him once more, had been doing ever since that night of the goddess and the television *ja*-sayers and unpremeditated chrysostomatic utterance. Hogg nodded, sighing heavily. Dr Wapenshaw knew; he knew everything. That was what this interview was going to be about.

'For a load of blasphemous balderdash,' said the man by the gasfire, 'you ought to read this lot.' He turned to Hogg, waving a thin little book. He had, then, been holding it to the gasfire, as if, as with bread in some sturdy feed in some school story of pre-electric days, deliberately toasting it. He was a man with wild grey hair who spoke with a cultivated accent which made his demotic vocabulary seem affected, which, if he was, as he evidently was, one of Dr Wapenshaw's patients, being rehabilitated in the same modes as Hogg himself had been, if he really had been, it probably was. 'And they say it's *us* that are crackers,' he said. 'You and me,' he clarified, 'are supposed to be the barmy ones.' Hogg prepared to dissociate himself from that predication, but he let it pass. The man launched wild fluttering wings of paper at Hogg and Hogg deftly caught them. The man did not say 'Fielded'; that was rather for Mr Holden or for Dr Wapenshaw himself, at least the Dr Wapenshaw of the chimney green days with his 'Good show' and 'That's the ticket.' Hogg leafed through the little book, frowning. He caught the title and further frowned: *The Kvadrat's Kloochy*. He said, with care:

'What does it mean, then?'

'Oh,' said the man, irritably, 'what does *anything* mean? It's all a *merde universelle*, as that French Irishman says. You read it, that's all.' Hogg read, at random:

> The miracle of this uncomplicated monody with its minimal chordal accompaniment is not diminished by our hindsight knowledge that it had been there waiting, throughout recorded history, yet unnoticed by the bearded creaking practitioners of the complex. They built up their multivocal counterpoint, their massive orchestras, their fugal and sonata forms, seeking a perfection that, if they could have cleansed the rheum from their old-man's eyes, they would have known had to lie in the simple and direct rather than the periphrastic and complicated. And yet it is in the error of the traditional equating of age with wisdom that one may find the cause of their blindness or, to be kind, presbyopia. The answer to all problems, aesthetic as much as social, religious, and economic, resides, in a word, in Youth.

'I don't see what all this is about,' said Hogg. He frowned still, turning over the page to find a photograph of four common louts who leered up at him, one bearing a guitar from which electrical flex sprouted, the others poising sticks over gaudy sidedrums.

'Ah,' growled the man, 'don't bother *me* with it. You stick to your world and I'll stick to mine.' And then he cried, very loud:

'Mother you've forsaken your son.' Hogg nodded without fear. Had he not spent an entire summer among men given to sudden despairing ejaculations or, worse, quiet confident assertions about the nature of ultimate reality, often delivered, Hogg and other patients shaken awake for the intimation, in the middle of the night? He read on:

Jack Cade and the Revolters established the fruitful device of a heavy ictus on the fourth beat in their disc *Like He Done That Time*, pressed in April 1964. In May of the same year this was further developed by Nap and the Bonies, who, in their *Knee Trembler*, transferred it to the quaver between the third beat and the fourth. Needless to say, this was achieved instinctually, these youthful performers being unburdened by traditional technical knowledge. In June both groups were superseded by the Tumers who, intuitively aware of a new shift in the *Zeitgeist*, perhaps wisely reverted to a greater simplicity of rhythmical texture and . . .

'Ah, Hogg!' cried a voice both fierce and plummy. Hogg looked up to see a different Dr Wapenshaw from the one he remembered – an urban Dr Wapenshaw in a natty suit of charcoal grey with discreet stripes, more formidable than the one who, in that country retreat, had dressed for his consultations as if for outdoor games. The chubby face was stern. Meekly Hogg went into the consulting-room. 'Sit you down,' said Dr Wapenshaw. Hogg sat on the seat nearest the door, a sort of creepy-stool. 'Here,' said Dr Wapenshaw, throwing a fierce fistful of air at a seat drawn up to the desk, a desk massive enough to contain any number of small secret electronic monitors. He himself went round the desk to its window-side and stood behind his swivel-chair, grey Harley Street framed behind him, while he watched Hogg, who still had *The Kvadrat's Kloochy* in his hand, shamble over. 'Very well, then,' said Dr Wapenshaw, in the manner of a sour grace. Consultant and patient sat simultaneously.

'Soon be winter now,' said Hogg in a conversational manner. 'The nights are drawing in very fast. Could do with a fire, really, in a manner of speaking.' Suddenly noticing that Dr Wapenshaw's consulting-room had a grate conspicuously empty, he added, 'Not that I meant that in any spirit of criticism, as you might say. All I meant was that it gets a bit chilly at nights.' Dr Wapenshaw held him with a disgusted look; Hogg grew flustered. 'What I mean is, some feel the cold more than others, so to speak. But' – and he struck hard at Dr Wapenshaw's flint, desperately seeking some of that old warmth – 'nobody can deny that it's late autumn now, and after autumn, if you'll pardon the observation –'

'Shut up!' cried Dr Wapenshaw. ('No, no, don't,' whimpered the patient in the waiting-room.) 'I'll do all the talking.' But all he did was to hurl a thick book bound in green paper across at Hogg. Hogg was already growing tired of having books hurled at him; still, he caught it deftly, just like the other one, which was now on his knee. 'Look at that,' ordered Dr Wapenshaw. 'Page 179. Read it, man.'

Hogg fingered the book rather tenderly. It was, he saw, a proof copy. He had, in the remote past when he was another man altogether, handled proof copies of his own work, very slim proof copies, poems. He flicked through the massive prose-work with a certain envy, then admired the title. '*Rehabilitations*,' he read out. 'There used to be a lot like that in the old days. F. R. Leavis and such people. The New School of Criticism, they called it. But it's all changed now. They have different ideas now and more flowery titles. *The Romantic Orgasm* was one I saw in a shop. And *The Candle in the Thigh* was another. They get a lot of the titles from poor Dylan, you know, who died. It's nice to see a good old-fashioned title like this again. That,' he said diffidently, though with a wisp of ancient authority, when he had lighted at last on page 179, 'isn't the right symbol for a deletion and close up, if you'll pardon the correction. It should be like a little balloon on the tip of a stick –'

'Read it, man, read it!' And Dr Wapenshaw thumped his desk thrice. Hogg read where he was ordered, wonderingly. Dr Wapenshaw tattooed the desk-top softly, as though his fingers at least were appeased – three beats in the left hand against two beats in the right, as though playing in some children's nonsense by Benjamin Britten, with tuned tea-cups and tin-whistles but also Peter Pears as an old man. 'Well?' he said at length.

'You know,' said Hogg, 'this case seems pretty close to what my own was. This chap here, K you call him, was a poet, and that made him into a protracted adolescent. He spent a lot of his time writing verse in the lavatory – a kind of womb you say it is here, but that's a lot of nonsense, of course – and this woman made him marry her and it was a mess and he ran away and then tried to go back to the old life, writing poetry in the lavatory and so on, and it didn't work so he attempted suicide and then you cured him by reorientating his personality, as it's called here, and then he became a useful citizen and forgot all about poetry and – Well,' Hogg said, 'that, if I may say so, is an astonishing coincidence, you might call it.' He tried to beam, but Dr Wapenshaw's black look was not irradiable. Dr Wapenshaw leaned across the desk and said, with terrible quietness and control:

'You bloody fool. That *is* you.'

Hogg frowned slightly. 'But,' he said, 'it can't be. It says here that this K had delusions about other people stealing his work and making horror-films out of his poetry. That's not quite the same, is it? I mean, this bloody man Rawcliffe did pinch the plot of my *Pet Beast* and make a bloody awful Italian picture out of it. I even remember the name. *L' Animal Binato* it was called in Italy – that's from Dante, you see: The Double-Natured Animal or something like it – and in England it was called *Son of the Beast from Outer Space.*' He read more intently, frowning further. 'What's all this,' he said, 'about a sexual fixation on this bloke K's stepmother? That can't be me, this bloke can't. I hated her, you know how much for I told you. And,' he said blushing, 'about masturbating in the lavatory. And about this woman being very refined and trying to make a real married man out of him.' He looked up, his sternness a remote (fourth or fifth or some-thing) carbon copy of Dr Wapenshaw's own. 'That woman,' he said clearly, 'was *not* refined. She was a bitch. She wanted my bit of money, which she got, and she wanted a bit of my honour and glory. When I was dead, that is,' he said, less assertively. 'In my biography, if such should come to be written.' The great expensive consulting-room tasted that, shrugged, grimaced, swallowed it.

'Can you see it?' said Dr Wapenshaw, his upper lip lifted. 'Can you honestly say that you see it, man? The most elegant woman in Europe, controller of the best pop-groups in the business?' Hogg stared at this wink of evidence of knowledge of a very vulgar world (he knew it all; he read the *Daily Mirror* doggedly every morning before opening his bar) in an eminent consultant. He said:

'I've not seen her name in the papers —'

'She's married again. A *real* marriage. A man with *real* money and *real* talent, also younger than you and, moreover, handsome.'

'— But that confirms what I always thought, what you said then I mean. I mean *not* refined. A bitch.' *The Kvadrat's Kloochy* fell off his knees, as in conscious failure to convert. Dr Wapenshaw said harshly:

'Right. Now look at this.' And Hogg had hurled at him his third fluttering paper bird of the afternoon. He caught it without much skill; he was already weary; it was a journal he at once recognized; it was called *Confrontation*, a cisatlantic quarterly trans-atlantically financed and of, he understood, little general appeal. He nodded, unsurprised. Dr Wapenshaw knew everything, then. Hogg understood all. He knew now what it was all about. This was it. He turned the page where the sestet of that sonnet, which the *ja*-sayers had not wished to hear, spoke to no frequenters of expensive bars, though the octave certainly had:

> Coiled on the rooftree, bored, inspired, their snake
> Crowed Monday in. A collar kissed the throat,
> Clothes braced the body, a benignant ache
> Lit up a tooth. The papers had a note:
> 'His death may mean an empire is at stake.'
> Sunday and this were equally remote.

And it was signed with that former, forbidden, name. Hogg said, stuttering:

'I can explain everything. I started that before, you see, before you got hold of me. Cured me, I mean. Of antisocial activities, that is. But I couldn't finish it. And then one night when I was working in the bar it just came. It had sort of tidied itself up behind my back. It was perfect, if you'll pardon the expression. So I sent it off and they published it. A kind of last fling, as you might term it. Or posthumous, perhaps you could even say. And then no more poetry, not never no more.' That last phrase was perhaps too ingratiating, too consciously the old-time barman. Dr Wapenshaw did not fall for it. Instead, he rose in wrath and cried:

'That's right, that's right, indulge yourself at my expense.' He strode across to a little table near the empty grate, picked up a human skull from it, and then waved it threateningly at Hogg. 'What you won't or can't realize, *you traitor*, is that that treacherous effusion of yours has been seen, yes, seen. Shorthouse saw it, Dr Shorthouse to you. You wouldn't know who Dr Shorthouse is, in your wilful treachery, but Dr Shorthouse is the author of *The Poetic Syndrome* and *Art and the Spirochaete* and other standard clinical works. Shorthouse saw it and Shorthouse showed it to me.' He crept towards Hogg, his eyes blowlamping in shame and anger, holding the skull in both hands like a pudding. 'And,' he cried, 'I felt a fool, because I'd already discussed your case with Shorthouse.'

'Dr Shorthouse,' kindly emended Hogg.

'Now do you see? *Do you see?* I boast about you as a cure, and here you are again with your bloody poetry.' Thumbs in skull's eye-sockets, he tore outwards in his anger, though the skull stayed firm.

'If it's the page-proofs of that thing of yours you're worried about,' said Hogg, still kindly, 'I'd be only too pleased to help you to correct them. What I mean is, to say that I wasn't cured after all and that my case was a failure. If that would be of any use,' he added humbly. 'You see,' he explained, 'I know all about altering things when they're in proof. I was a writer by profession, you see, as you know (I mean, that's what you tried to cure me of, isn't it?), and to you, who are really a doctor, it's only a sort of hobby when all's said and done.' He tried to smile at Dr Wapenshaw and then at the skull, but only the latter responded. 'Or if you like,' suggested Hogg, 'I'll tell everybody that I'm really cured and that that sonnet was only a kind of left-over from the old days. Or that that bloke K isn't really me but somebody else. In any case, that Shorthouse man won't say anything to anybody, will he? I mean, you doctors stick together, you have to, don't you? In one of those papers of yours I could do it,' expanded Hogg. '*The Lancet* and *The Scalpel* and all those things.'

Dr Wapenshaw tore at the skull with his tense strong-nailed hairy fingers, but the skull, as though, it shot into Hogg's mind, remembering Housman's line about the man of bone remaining, grinned in armoured complacency. Dr Wapenshaw seemed about to weep then, as though this skull were Yorick's. After that, he made as to hurl the skull at Hogg, but Hogg got down to the floor to pick up the copy of *The Kvadrat's Kloochy*. Dr Wapenshaw put the skull back on its table, took a great breath and cried:

'Get out! Get out of my bloody consulting-room!'

'I,' said Hogg, still on his knees, mildly, 'only came here because you told me to.'

'Go on, get out! I expended skill and time and patience and, yes, bloody love on your case, and this is the thanks I get! You want to ruin my bloody career, that's what it is!'

Hogg, who had forgotten that he was still kneeling, said with continued mildness: 'You could always put what they call an erratum slip in the book, you know. I had one once. The printers had printed "immortal" instead of "immoral". It'll be a great pleasure to help you, really and truly. In any case, if the worst comes to the worst, they can always take that whole section out of the book and you can put something else in. Although,' he added seriously, 'you'll have to make sure it's exactly the same length. You could sit down tonight and make something up.'

Dr Wapenshaw now stomped over to kneeling Hogg and began to lift him by his collar. 'Out!' he cried again. 'Get out of here, you immoral bastard!' He thumped to the door, opened it and held it open. The patient by the gasfire was weeping quietly. 'As for you, you scrimshanker,' Dr Wapenshaw cried at him, 'I'll deal with you in a minute. I know you, leadswinger as you are.' Hogg, in sorrowful dignity that would, he foreknew, become a brew of rage when he could get to somewhere nice and quiet, walked to the door and said:

'You take too much on yourselves, if you don't mind me saying so.' He waved *The Kvadrat's Kloochy* in a kind of admonition. 'I'd say it was the job of people like you to set the rest of us a good example. It's you who want a good going over, not this poor chap here.'

'Out!'

'Just going,' said Hogg, just going. He went, shaking his head slowly. 'And,' he said, turning back to Dr Wapenshaw, though from a safe distance, 'I'll write what poetry I want to, thanks very much, and not you nor anybody else will stop me.' He thought of adding 'So there,' but, before he could decide, Dr Wapenshaw slammed his consulting-room door; the patient by the gasfire went 'Oh!' as though clouted by his mother. Not a very good man after all, thought Hogg, leaving. He ought to have suspected that heartiness right at the beginning. There had always, he felt, been something a bit insincere about it.

3

Some short time later, Hogg sat trembling in a public lavatory. He could actually see the flesh of his inner thighs jellying with rage. Up above him diesel trains kept setting off to the west, for this was Paddington Station, whither he had walked by way of Madame Tussaud's, the Planetarium, Edgware Road, and so on. He had put a penny in the slot and was having more than his pennyworth of anger out. The whole poetry-loathing world had the face of Dr Wapenshaw but, he felt, having soundly and legitimately bemerded that face in imagination and micturated on it also, the world was content merely to loathe, while Dr Wapenshaw had had to go further, deliberately liquidating the poet. Or trying to. He, Hogg, was maligning the world. The world was very bad, but not as bad as Dr Wapenshaw. But then again, was not the bloody Muse bad too, withholding her gifts as she had done and then coming forward with a most ill-timed bestowal? The point was, what was the position? What precisely and the hell did she want him to do? He caught a most agonizing and fragrant whiff of himself as he had once been, seated like this in the workroom of his seaside flat, scratching bared legs that were mottled by the electric fire, working away steadily at his verse, the Muse and he set in a calm and utterly professional relationship. Would she, coaxed (which meant, among other things, not calling her bad or bloody as he had done just then), be willing to return on a sort of chronic basis? An acute spasm

like that one which there had just been the row about really
did nobody anything but harm.

But, of course, in those days, before that bloody woman had
married him and made him squander his capital, it had been possible
for him to be a professional (i.e. non-earning, or earning very little)
poet. Now he had to have a wage. Even if the gift returned properly it would have to be expended in the form of what was called
a nice hobby. Of course, he had been able to save a little. He had
a little bedroom in the hotel, his food, a few tips. His trousers
being down, he was able to find out at once how much he had
saved. He kept his money in cash in a sponge-bag whose string
was wound about a fly-button. He trusted neither banks nor his
colleagues at the hotel. Keys there were a mockery, because of
pass-keys. Once he had entered his little bedroom to find Spanish
John in it, with a shirt of Hogg's in one hand and one of Hogg's
razor-blades in the other, and Hogg had been quite sure he had
locked his door. John had smiled falsely and said that he had found
the door unlocked and had entered to borrow a razor-blade, he
being out of them, and at the same time had been filled with a
desire to admire Hogg's shirts, which he considered to be very
good ones. Hogg did not believe that. Anyway, he kept his money
in a bag in his trousers. It was a kind of testicle-protector, for there
were some dirty fighters among the Maltese and Cypriot commis
waiters. He now took his roll of five-pound notes out of the bag
and counted them earnestly. A crude drawing of a man, a sort of
naked god of fertility, looked down without envy.

Twenty-five drawings of a clavigerous lion guarding a rather
imbecile teenage Britannia. That was not bad. That was one hundred
and twenty-five pounds. And, in his trouser pocket, there was about
thirty shillings in silver, made up of mostly very mean gratuities.
The value of certain other gratuities, dispensed in foreign notes,
he had not yet troubled to ascertain. These – dirhams, lire, new-
francs, deutschmarks, and so on – he kept folded in his passport,
which was in the inside pocket of his sports jacket, now hanging
from the door-hook. It was necessary, he had learned, for every
employee of the hotel to keep close guard on his passport, because
of the thievery and shady trade in passports that went on among
the dark scullions, outcasts of the islands, creatures of obcure ethnic

origin, cunning, vicious, and unscrupulous. Despite Britain's new despised status in the world, a British passport was still prized. So there it was, then. Enough to buy time to write, say, some really careful sestinas or rambling Pound-type cantos, if the Muse would be willing to cooperate. He blew very faint wind. That was not, he told her, in case she were around, acting silly, meant in any spirit of acrimony or impatience: it was legitimate efflation, paid for in advance.

He was calmer now. He looked with sympathy at the graffiti on the walls and door. Some of these must, he thought, be considered a kind of art, since they were evidently attempts to purge powerful emotion into stylized forms. There were also wild messages, pleas for assignations at known places, though the dates were long gone; there were boasts too extravagant to be capable of fulfilment, also succinct desiderations of sexual partners too complaisant to be of this world. Sex. Well, he, Hogg, had tried, following the rehabilitatory pattern imposed by Dr, now bloody, Wapenshaw, to go in for sex like everybody else, but it had not been very successful. In any case, you really had to be young nowadays to go in properly for sex: that had been made fairly clear to him by such of the young – Italian chambermaids and so on – as he had met, as also by some of the popular art he had, again in fulfilment of the Wapenshaw bloody pattern, tried glumly to appreciate. So there it was, then. He must stop himself saying that to himself all the time.

On the walls there were also little verses, most of them set – like those works of Faith Fortitude – as prose. They were all traditional verses, mostly on cloacal subjects, but it was somehow warming to find that verse was still in regard for its gnomic mnemonic properties. Among the common people, that was. He could not imagine bloody Wapenshaw writing or drawing anything in a lavatory. There was, Hogg noticed, a nice little patch of naked wall by his right arm. He did not need his Muse for what he now took out his ballpoint pen to write. He wrote:

> Think, when you ease your inner gripe
> Or stand with penis in your paw,

A face is lodged within the pipe
And it belongs to Wapenshaw.

That, perhaps, would be learned by heart and reproduced elsewhere underground, imperfect memory blurring the sharp elegance
but perhaps not wholly losing that name, in some allomorph or
other. Enderby, folk poet. Enderby, not Hogg. And Wapenshaw
given proper immortality.

Hoggerby now felt hungry. He girded himself, pulled the
chain, donned his jacket, and went out. He nodded kindly at
the wash-and-brush-up man, who was reading the *Evening
Standard* by his glazed partition, then mounted to the light. He
walked out of the station and found a sufficiently dirty-looking
little eating-hell in a side-street, nearly filled with slurping men.
He knew the sort of meal he wanted: a rebellious meal. From
the tooth-sucking man with glasses behind the counter he ordered
a mug of very strong tea, eggs and fat bacon, marged doorsteps.
He was going to give himself indigestion. That would show
bloody Wapenshaw.

2

1

'A great honour, *ja*,' said Mr Holden from behind massed flowers
of the season. In the adjoining office typewriters clacked. Standing
before Mr Holden were Hogg and John the Spaniard, respectively
flashing gold-and-caries and looking dour about the great honour.
'Smallish and very select, and the Saddleback is just about the
right-sized pitch, *ja*. So it'll be cocktails in the Sty, and this is where
you, brother Hogg, show your batting strength. We'll be having
some waiters from the Sweet Thames Run Softly bar, sort of extra
cover. You'd better start boning up on your cocktails, fella, read up

your sort of bartender's Wisden. Horse's necks, sidecars, manhattans, snowballs, the lot. You reckon you can carry your bat?'

'I know them all,' said Hogg, 'including some that haven't been thought of yet.'

'I show him,' said John, 'if he not know.'

'A pop-group, you say?' said Hogg.

'You ought to know these things,' said Mr Holden. 'You get plenty of time for reading the papers. A sort of belated celebration, a kind of late cut to the off. They've been making this movie in the Bahamas, as you should know, and only now have they been able to get this fixture organized. There's a lot to celebrate. A new golden disc, the birthday honours, and now Yod Crewsy gets this F.L.R.S. thing. *Ja*, plenty to celebrate. *Mucho*,' he added for John's benefit.

'*Usted habla bien español.*'

'F.R.S.L.?' Hogg queried. 'Fellow of the Royal Society of Literature?'

'Not bad, not bad, fella. Keep on like that, eye on the ball and all that palooka. *Ja*, he got the Hangman award for some book of poems he wrote and the F.S. thing sort of automatically followed.'

'Heinemann award?' frowned Hogg. 'And what do you say this lot are called?'

'Ah, Jesus, you'll never get off the reserve list,' said Mr Holden. 'The Crewsy Fixers. You mean to say you never heard of the Crewsy Fixers? England's best ambassadors they've been termed, a little Test team all on their own, *ja*, doing all in their power to protect the wicket of your shattered economy. Foreign earnings, that is, an export drive to the boundary, and Her Majesty the Queen' (Mr Holden bowed his head) 'is no doubt dooly grateful. Hence, fella, those medals. So now you know, but I guess you should have known already.'

'*Sí sí sí sí,*' agreed John. 'Already he should know.'

'I would call that a very blasphemous name,' said Hogg coldly. 'Not,' he added hastily, 'that I'm at all a religious man, you understand. What I mean is, it seems to me in very bad taste.'

'To the pure,' said Mr Holden, 'all things are pure. There's Yod Crewsy and his Fixers, so they become the Crewsy Fixers. Right? If you're thinking it sounds like something else, then you're on a very shaky wicket yourself, fella, so far as taste goes. And they're very very religious boys, which again you should have known. *Molto religioso,*' he added to John.

'*Lei parla bene italiano.*'

'I bet,' divined Hogg, 'that he called himself Crewsy just so he could make up that blasphemous name. And that Yod bit doesn't sound Christian to me. Yod,' he told Mr Holden, 'is a letter of the Hebrew alphabet.'

'Now you'd better watch that,' said Mr Holden very sternly. 'Because that sounds to me very much like racial prejudice. And if there's one thing the policy of this hotel group says out out out to, it's racial prejudice. So watch it.'

'He say too,' intimated John, 'about Spanish people not good.'

'Right, then,' said Mr Holden. 'We'll have harmony, efficiency, and team spirit. A very special luncheon for very special people. The confectionery chefs are working out a very special ice pudding for the occasion. And there's going to be a very exotic dish not before served here. It's called −' He consulted a draft menu on his desk. '− *lobscouse*. Something Arabic, I guess. Those boys sure scored big in Saudi-Arabia.'

Hogg stood transfixed. 'Ice pudding,' he said. 'In Saudi-Arabia. It melts as it is made. Like time, you know.'

'You feeling all right, Hogg?' While Mr Holden frowned, John the Spaniard poked his right temple with a brown finger, shaking his head in sad glee. 'You sure you feel up to this, fella? If not, we can always get Juanito here to take over. I reckon he can face the bowling if you can't.'

'It has to be Hogg,' said Hogg, distracted. 'He may be a pig but he's not a Hogg. It's coming,' he added. 'There's something there all right. The gift's coming back. Something special. I'll have to go and put it down on paper.' Somebody else seemed to be in the room. She?

'Ah, a cocktail,' nodded Mr Holden, relieved. 'That's okay, then. Something special, eh? You go right off and get it down, fella. And don't forget that we own the copyright. One more thing. Wigs. There's got to be wigs. They needn't fit too good, but there's got to be wigs. Okay. Back to the pavilion.'

Hogg left in a small daze. 'Useless to hope to hold off,' he muttered, 'the unavoidable happening.' What the hell was it all about? She was there all right; she was playing silly hide-and-seek, finger in mouth, up and down the corridors. She was wearing a very short dress. John the Spaniard said:

'What you mean, *hombre*? You call me pig.'

'Big, I said big,' said Hogg, distracted. 'Look, the bar doesn't open for another hour. I've got to go to my room.'

'Big pig, you say? I hear. Not bloody daft, man.'

Hogg made a dash for the staff lift which, he saw, was just about to land. It opened, and a very natty though puffy young man came out, bearing what looked like the disgorgements of one of the hotel computers. He seemed to look direly at Hogg, as though it was his character that had been programmed. Hogg got in frowning, his brain full of words that were trying to marshal themselves into an ordered, though cryptic, statement. John the Spaniard tried to follow, but the puffy young man was in the way. Hogg pressed the right button and saw the door slice fist-shaking John laterally until there was nothing left of him save the after-image of the glow of his fillings. The lift-car seemed to remain where it was, and only the flash of the floor-numbers spoke of rising to 34A, a floor not accessible to the hotel guests. A high-powered car rushing on to it, whether you will or not. Hogg nearly fainted.

He got out blindly when the door automatically opened, fumbled for his key, almost tumbled into his cheerless cell. Paper. He had a lined writing-pad, in keeping with his new image. He sat panting heavily on his cot and began to scribble. She breathed hard into his left ear; her voice had become, for some reason, a lisping child's one. He wrote:

> Useless to hope to hold off
> The unavoidable happening
> With that frail barricade
> Of week, day or hour
> Which melts as it is made,
> For time himself will bring
> You in his high-powered car,
> Rushing on to it,
> Whether you will or not.

And then sudden silence. What was it all about? What did it mean? Too much meaning in your poetry, Enderby. Someone had said that once. You worry, my dear Enderby, far too much about meaning. Rawcliffe, one of the special trinity of enemies. And there was Wapenshaw, trying to crush his skull. He saw the strong hairy fingers, but the skull only grinned. The consolation of bone, the bone's resignation. But what thing was going to happen that he had to resign himself to? A handshake of finality, the welcome of whole fields of empty time. No, no, it was not quite that. With a rush like blood it came:

> So, shaking hands with the grim
> Satisfactory argument,
> The consolation of bone
> Resigned to the event,
> Making a friend of him,
> He, in an access of love,
> Renders his bare acres
> Golden and wide enough.

The prophetic tingling, as of something thrilling to welcome and then to lose and not to mind losing. He could have wept. The Muse stood by his wash-basin. What, then? What was the covenant to be? He might have to wait for a dream for the full disclosure. There was a hammering on the door. She hid, sliding through its door, in his tiny clothes-cupboard.

'*Puerco, puerco!*' called John the Spaniard. 'You get tonic water for bloody bar, man!'

'For cough!' cried Hogg. 'Go away, you garlicky bastard!' And then, radiating from the clothes-cupboard, it announced itself as the last stanza:

> And this last margin of leaving
> Is sheltered from the rude
> Indiscreet tugging of winds.

'*You* bastard! You pull pudding in there! I bloody *know*!' Hogg wrote, like a dying message:

For parting, a point in time,
Cannot have magnitude
And cannot cast shadows about
The final

John's thudding drowned the final whatever it was. The Muse, hidden in the cupboard, shook her sad child's head. Hogg-Enderby, enraged, got up and unlocked his door. Then he pulled it open. John almost fell in.

'Right,' Hogg-Enderby clenched. 'You've had this coming a long time, bloody *hombre*. You and bloody Franco and wanting bloody Gibraltar. Right.' Well, Wapenshaw and the rest wished him to be involved in the world, didn't they – low, vulgar, an ordinary citizen ungiven to civilized restraints? John grinned dirty gold and put out mean claws. Hogg, as low barman, at once kicked him on the shin. While John was hopping mad, Hogg pushed him on to the bed. John sat there nursing his pain and trying to kick at the same time, mouthing the foulest bodega provincial Spanish with no refined lisp in it. Hogg looked for something to hit him with and picked up the cheap bedroom chair from near the clothes-cupboard. By the time he had raised it John was on his feet again. He leered very terribly and said:

'*Momento de verdad.*' Hogg thought he saw peasant's muscles underneath the cheap bar-waiter's clothes; his heart failed; he was too old; he shouldn't have started this. He put the chair gently down on the floor again. He said:

'All right. Here's my bloody throat.' And he proffered it. John did not expect this. He said:

'You give kick on flaming leg, *hombre*. Not good.'

'Listen,' said Hogg, 'listen.' He, who had done Latin at school, who had spoken soldier's Italian in Catania but also read Dante with a crib, for some reason was now impelled to draw on this Romance equipment and create, nearly from scratch, not merely a language for Spain but a literature as well. '*La consolación del osso,*' he suggested. John cocked an ear and said:

'*Hueso.*'

'That's right,' Hogg agreed. '*La consolación del hueso resignado al evento.*' He didn't know whether that was right or not, but he felt it ought to have a place somewhere along the line of colonial deformation of Latin. In any case, John went pale. It was Orpheus with his lute, by God, who (so Hogg as schoolboy Enderby had believed, taking the first line of the song as a semantic entity) made trees. 'And,' said Hogg, very recklessly now, '*adiós, no è que un punto temporal.*'

'*Sí sí.*'

'*Y un punto* can't have a bloody *ombra.*'

'*No puede tener sombra, sí, claro.*'

'And so there can't be any *sombras* around the something *final.*' (There was a rhyme there, wasn't there? He was actually rhyming in Spanish.)

'Ah,' and as though they were both merely trying to remember a Spanish poem that actually existed, '*el beso.*'

Beso, baiser, bacio. Kiss.

> And cannot cast shadows about
> The final kiss

Tears came into Hogg's eyes. He felt unutterably wretched. He said to John, tearfully, 'You can have the job any time you like. I don't want it. I want to be poet again, that's all.'

John nodded. Garlicky sod as he was, he understood. 'Poetry no money,' he said. 'Go on National Assistance, man.' Like most immigrants, he knew everything about the resources of the British Welfare State. And then he said: 'No, no good. Wait is best. Wait!' He knew all about destiny too, being a foreigner. 'Wait for,' he said, '*el acaso inevitable.*'

Hogg looked at him in wonder. The unavoidable happening.

2

They got on a good deal better after that, though John exaggerated the limp from Hogg's shin-kick. When the day for the luncheon arrived, they were working in accord, and Mr Holden was pleased. '*Ja,*' he said, 'all we want here is harmony. Like a real good opening pair. Hobbs and P. G. Grace, or two guys like that.' But Mr Holden fussed in nervousness at midday on the day. Everything had to be just right. Out of stereophonic speakers there excreted (Hogg could think of no other word) pseudo-music composed and performed by the guests of honour, and Mr Holden tried to adjust the volume so as to secure the correct balance between the subliminally insinu-ating and the overtly assertive. Furniture-music, like Erik Satie, but set cunningly for the barking of ears: that was the aim. Hogg considered that he had never in his whole life heard anything so, at the same time, obscene, noisy, and insipid. He was mixing cock-tails in big crocks, selecting the ingredients aleatorically. After all, poetry was compounded of chance elements, and cocktail-making was by far the inferior art. He set out now to blend his special, intended for people he already disliked, like this blasphemous gang that was a collective guest of honour, and those he would dislike when he saw them. He threw together Scotch whisky and British port-type wine, adding flat draught bitter beer, grenadine, angostura, and some very sour canned orange juice which the management had bought up cheap some months before. As the resultant colour seemed rather subfusc for a festive drink, he broke in three eggs and electrically whisked all up to a yellowy pinkish froth. He tasted a little gingerly from a dram-measure and found it tasted of nothing. It left, however, a sickish residual gust that would do very well. Nodding, he put it in the refrigerator to keep cold with the other crocks.

'You better get your wig on, fella,' said Mr Holden. Hogg looked around, seeing John the Spaniard and the three Albanian waiters from the Sweet Thames Run Softly bar downstairs all looking terrible in coarse golliwog toupees that were meant to be a kind of homage, so Hogg understood, to an enviable aspect of youth typified by those blasphemous obscenities – namely, a riotous and sickening excess of head-hair. Hogg picked up his own wig and crammed it on. He did not like what he saw in the mirrored reredos. He seemed to resemble very much his stepmother surfacing from blurred after-stout sleep, taken with her glasses on and teeth in, her head a very unsavoury Medusa-tangle.

The first man to arrive seemed to be the man who had been deputed to organize this luncheon by the various interests concerned. Hogg frowned: the face seemed familiar. It was a stormy Irish face that appeared to fight against its London sleeking. The lapelless jacket and tapering trousers were a kind of healthy stirabout colour.

'You'll find everything in order,' said Mr Parkin, a very much more important man than Mr Holden. He was British, not American, and he wore striped trousers and a short black jacket, like a member of parliament meeting his constituents in the lobby. He had obviously, considered Hogg, been cast rather than appointed. He was distinguished greying butler-talking British, which meant, thought Hogg, that he was probably a con-man reformed out of fear of another stretch. He was in charge of banquets and luncheons for the distinguished and the like. He was above knowing Hogg's name. 'Barman,' he said, 'a drink for Mr Macnamara.'

So that was who it was. Shem Macnamara, once a poet himself but now, analogously to Mr Parkin, reformed. 'Scatch on the racks,' said Shem Macnamara, like an American. He did not recognize Hogg. He breathed a kind of mouthwash as he opened meaty lips for the drink. Hogg remembered that luncheon long ago that had been given for him, himself, Enderby as he had been, when he had won the Goodby Gold Medal for poetry. Then Shem Macnamara had been very poor, only too ready for a free meal and a quiet sneer at the success of a fellow poet. Then, instead of expensive mouthwash, he had breathed on Hogg-Enderby, bafflingly (for no banquet would serve, because of the known redolence of onions, onions) onions.

'Onions,' said Hogg. He was frowned on in puzzlement. 'Cocktail onions,' he offered. Well, just imagine. Shem Macnamara deepened his frown. Something in that voice saying 'Onions'? He did not take any onions.

The guests began to arrive. There were ugly tall girls, very thin, showing bony knees, whom Hogg took to be photographer's models, or some such thing. He filled out trayloads of his special cocktail for them, and told the waiters to say it was called a Crucifier. It seemed to do none of these girls any harm, blasphemous bitches as they were. There were young men who seemed to be literary men, and some of these ordered drinks that had to be freshly made up and were very complicated. Hogg cursed under his wig when one young man stood over him at the bar while some exotic nonsense called a Papa Doc was painfully put together – rum, lemon juice, vermouth, tabasco (two drops), stir with a cock's feather. 'This,' groused Hogg, 'is a hen's feather. Does it make much difference?' Mr Holden hovered, looking black. Some very important New York Jews came in, all stroking some of the model-girls as if thereby to conjure humps of voluptuousness. A most insolent Negro in native robes was made much of; Hogg had a large helping of the Crucifier ready for him, but he asked for plain milk, and this had to be sent downstairs for, and then, when it had been handed to him, he merely carried it round unsipped, as if to demonstrate that he was not totally anti-white. Photographers struck with flashes from opposed corners, like a little war, and there were, though not practising their art today, some, so Hogg heard from John, very great photographers among the guests.

The Crucifier was, to Hogg's annoyance, rather popular. Atrophy of the gustatory sense or anaesthesia of the stomach lining, or something. He prepared a sicklier version – whisky and port-style British wine diluted with warm water from the washing-up tap – and this too was well appreciated. It was the name, that was what it was: it was a small and unbargained-for poetic victory. Suddenly, while Hogg was sucking on the sour lozenge of an image of himself, sweating under a dyed-wool wig into the American-type martinis he was pouring from the gin bottle, there was a reverent hush. The Prime Minister had arrived. He was a little bumptious man in a baggy suit to show he had just come from work, and he was at his ease with everyone and full of little pleasantries. Hogg begged John the Spaniard to make sure he got a Crucifier, but the Prime Minister asked for orange juice. Hogg was happy to serve some of the cheap acid variety. Then he got down to a batch of champagne cocktails for a bunch of exquisite young men who grinned at his wig, himself longing for a mug of very strong, or stepmother's, tea. There was a lot of loud chatter and some giggles (as though the session were proceeding at once, without the interim of a meal, towards seduction); under it the ghastly pseudo-music swelled up, reached its sonic level, then rose above to drown it. It was a fanfare. There were cheers. The guests of honour had come at last, embraced and worshipped from their very entrance. Hogg stopped mixing to have a good look at them.

They were, he thought, about as horrible in appearance as it was possible to imagine any four young men to be. The one Hogg knew to be their leader, Yod Crewsy, received, because of his multiple success, the most homage, and he accepted this as his due, simpering out of a lopsided mouth that was too large to be properly controlled and, indeed, seemed to possess a kind of surrealist autonomy. The other three were vulgarly at home, punching each other in glee and then doing a kind of ring-a-roses round the Prime Minister. The working photographers flashed and flashed like an epidemic of sharp sneezes. With the four, Hogg now noticed, there was a clergyman. He was small, old, and vigorous, and he champed and champed, nodding at everyone and even, before he came up to Hogg at the bar, sketching a general blessing. He said, nodding:

'If there's such a thing as a Power's among that heathen army you have up there on your shelves, then I'll have a double Power's. And I'll trouble you for a glass of fresh water.'

Hogg surveyed his small stock of Irish. 'Will a Mick Sullivan do?'

'Ah, well then, I'll try it. Such a big place as you are and divil a drop of Power's to bless yourself with.'

'If you'd like something for a change,' said Hogg, 'there's this special cocktail here I've mixed in honour. A Crucifier, it's called.' He at once realized that that must sound like a deliberate insult to this man's cloth. 'Blasphemous, I know,' he said. 'I apologize. But I consider that the name itself. Of those four, I mean. The guests of honour, that is. Father,' he added.

'Well now, shouldn't we all be sticking to our own vocations and not stepping outside the lines to deliver judgements on what isn't our proper province at all? Perhaps you'd be willing to allow that it's myself as would be the proper and qualified judge of what's blasphemous and what isn't, me being the chaplain to those boys?' While he spoke his eyes roamed everywhere in Irish neurosis. In the corner there was the sound of someone being sick, a woman from the pitch of the retchings. Hogg showed minimal satisfaction, then swiftly shut it off. The chaplain saw. 'Taking pleasure itself, is it, in the misfortune of some poor body's weak and delicate stomach and it fasting from dawn maybe?' The Prime Minister was heard to say:

'Well, as long as nobody blames it on the Government.' There was dutiful laughter, though one man, standing alone by the bar, nodded seriously. He had, like the Crewsy Fixers, very long hair, but it seemed as seedy as Hogg's own wig. His suit was not new; the side-pockets bulged. The chaplain poured himself another measure from the whiskey-bottle. Yod Crewsy and one of his group, a guffawing youth with very white dentures, came over to the bar, bearing glasses, Hogg was glad to see, of the later version of the Crucifier. Yod Crewsy said to Hogg:

'What you on then, dad?' Before Hogg could make an evasive reply, Yod Crewsy feigned to be surprised and overjoyed by the sudden sight of the seedy-maned young man with the bulging pockets. He put on a large record-sleeve smile and then embraced him with arms whose thinness the cut of his serge jerkin did nothing to disguise, saying: 'Jed Foot. Me old Jed, as ever was. Glad like you could make it, boy.' Jed Foot, mouth closed, smiled with his cheek-muscles. Hogg could not remember whether Jed belonged to the same alphabet as Yod. Yod Crewsy said to his chaplain: 'Look who's here, Father. We're back to the old days. Happy times them was,' he said to Jed Foot. 'Pity you got out when you did. What they call a miscalculation. Right?' he said to Hogg cheekily.

'A memento mori,' said Hogg, with poet's acuity. The chaplain chewed darkly over that before taking more whiskey, as though Hogg had revealed himself as an anti-vernacularist.

'You got your mementos,' said Jed Foot to Yod Crewsy. 'Them songs. Pity I never learned how to write down music.'

'Every man to his like opinion,' said Yod Crewsy. 'You said the groups was finished. What you been on – the Western Australia run? Dead horrible, I know. Collie and Merredin and Bullfinch. They've been working you hard, boy. I can see that.'

'I've been doing the clubs. The clubs is all right.'

'Have another of these,' said Hogg to Yod Crewsy. 'A *big* one. A Crucifier, it's called.'

'What I want,' said Yod Crewsy, 'is me dinner. Her ladyship here yet?'

'Herself will be the last to come,' said his chaplain. "Tis a lady's privilege. You,' he said to Hogg, 'have the face of a man who's been a long time away from the altar. A Catholic face I said to meself as soon as I clapped eyes on it, and very guilty and shifty too with your self-knowledge of being in the presence of a priest of your Church and you with the boldness to be speaking of blasphemy and many a long year between yourself and the blessed sacrament.'

'Look here,' said Hogg. Swirls of toothed worshippers were about Yod Crewsy and his accomplices, but this Jed Foot drank bitter gin alone. 'You,' said Hogg, 'and your bloody ecumenical nonsense.'

'It is yourself as would be daring to flaunt the shame of your apostasy in the face of a priest of your Church and spitting venom on the blessed enactments of the Holy Father himself?' He took more whiskey. 'I'll be troubling you,' he said, 'for another glass of fresh water.'

It had been part of Hogg's cure to attend the services of the Church of England, a means of liquidating for ever his obsession with his dead stepmother who, Dr Wapenshaw had said, was really the Catholic Church. He was about to tell this chaplain that the liturgy of traditional Anglicanism was superior to that of reformed Papistry when the chaplain turned his face towards the entrance with mouth open in joy. Everybody else turned too. A lady was entering and, with her, a handsome and knowing Jewish man in his thirties. Hogg's heart turned over several times, as on a spit. Of course, of course, blast it: he should have known. Had not bloody Wapenshaw said something about her running the best pop-groups in the business? This was too much. He said to Mr Holden, who was standing by the bar, though not drinking:

'I've got to get out of here, I've *got to*.'

'You stay where you are, fella, on the crease.'

'But I've got to get to a lavatory.'

'Now listen,' said Mr Holden, his tea-coloured eyes very hard. 'I've had about enough from you, fella, that I have. Obstruction for its own sake and going against the rules. You stay in till you're given out, right? And another thing, there's too many been made sick, and hard drinkers too from the look of them. See, they're taking that poor girl off now. I reckon those drinks you've been mixing will have to be looked into. Now what in hell's name –' For Hogg had pulled his wig down over his eyes like a busby. Even so he could see her clearly enough through the coarse fringe.

'Vesta, me dear,' the chaplain was saying. 'Five Our Fathers and five Hail Marys for being late.' She smiled from her clever green eyes. She, never behind in the fashions, was in a new long-length skirt of palest pink and brown biki-jacket. On the shining penny-coloured hair was a halo hat of thrushes' feathers. Her purse and shoes were quilled. All the other women at once began to look dated in their bright reds and greens. Hogg moaned to himself, desperately washing a champagne-glass below the level of the counter-top.

'You know my husband, I think,' Vesta said.

'And isn't it meself he's been coming to for his preliminary instruction? Well, praise be to God, as one goes out another comes in.' He swivelled his long Irish neck to frown at Hogg.

'What a strange little man,' Vesta said. 'Is he serving only from the top of his head, or something?' And then she turned to greet the Prime Minister with every sign of ease and affection. Her chief pop-group came over whooping to kiss her cheeks extravagantly, calling her, though in evident facetiousness, 'mum'. The photographers opposed fresh lightnings at each other.

'Oh God God God,' groaned Hogg.

'Repentance, is it?' the sharp-eared chaplain said. 'Well, you have a long penance in front of you for scoffing at the True Church itself.'

A man with glasses, dressed in hunting pink, came to the door to shout that luncheon was served. There was a ragged shouting exodus towards the Wessex Saddleback. Some, though, as Hogg saw, with very little satisfaction now, on the clearing of the bar, would not be wanting any lunch. Himself included. Shem Macnamara was one of the last to leave. He turned frowning to look at Hogg, mouthing the word 'onions'. He had, he was sure, heard that voice somewhere before.

3

Hogg and John the Spaniard washed glasses companionably together, Hogg in a daze though, though he responded to John's excited comments on the event still proceeding with his usual courtesy. John had been swigging from half-empty glasses and was more garrulous than usual.

'You see that bloody thing, *hombre*? All ice cream and done like big *monumento*.' It appealed to John's baroque taste and prompted memories of the victorious group-effigies erected by the Caudillo: the Crewsy Fixers, with drums and guitar, in highly compressed frozen confectioner's custard – whether really to be eaten or not was not clear, though the sound of laughing chiselling was coming through at that moment.

'Oh?' said Hogg.

'See this bloody *vaso*? One *párpado* dropped in. Daft, *hombre*.' It was not so much a false eyelid as a set of false eyelashes for one eye.

'Ah,' said Hogg. Some of the glasses were very filthy.

'One thing,' said John. 'We not serve no *coñac* from in here. Bottles on the *mesa* already. *Vasos* too. Not bar job, *hombre*.'

'No.'

John sang. It was a kind of flamenco without words. Soon he desisted. The rhythms, if not the sense, of an after-lunch speech were coming through. It was the Prime Minister. 'He speak bloody good, man. But always same thing. I hear on telly.' Hogg could tell exactly what the Prime Minister was saying: selling country short; legacy of misrule; determination to win through to solvency despite treacherous and frivolous opposition of opposition; team-work of these four boys here, not unfortunately his constituents but he would be proud to have them, example to all; people's art; art of the people; the people in good art, heart; struggles to come; win through to solvency; legacy of misrule. After long clapping there was the sound of a kind of standing ovation. Suddenly the door of Piggy's Sty was burst open. It was Jed Foot lurching in, very white. He said:

'Give us something strong. Can't stand it, I tell you. The bastard's on his feet.' Sympathetic, Hogg poured him a large brandy. Jed

Foot downed it in one. 'Taught him all he knows,' he whined. 'Bloody treachery. Give us another one of them.' Hogg poured an even larger brandy. Jed Foot gave it, in one swig, to his gullet. John tut-tutted. He said:

'We finish now here, *hombre*. I go see.'

'I'm getting out,' said Hogg. 'Out. Bloody fed-up, that's what I am.'

'Bloody fed-up, mate?' said Jed Foot, his mouth quivering. 'You don't know what bloody fed-upness is, I'll have another one of them.'

'I'm off duty now,' Hogg said. He had already discarded that shameful wig. Now he took off his barman's coat. His own mufti jacket was in the little store-room at the back of the bar. He went to get it. John was just opening the door that led to the exit-corridor; the door of the Wessex Saddleback was opposite. When Hogg, decently jacketed, was making his way out, he found that that door had been thrown wide open so that hotel employees could listen and look. The whole of Europe was represented there among the chambermaids and small cooks who, with open mouths, worshipped this global myth. Jed Foot was at the back of them; John had pushed to the front. Hogg, shambling in wretchedness towards the staff lift, suddenly heard familiar noises:

> 'And so the car plunged in the singing green
> Of sycamore and riot-running chestnut and oak
> That squandered flame, cut a thousand arteries and bled
> Flood after summer flood, spawned an obscene
> Unquenched unstanchable green world sea, to choke
> The fainting air, drown sun in its skywise tread.'

It was being read wretchedly, as though the reader were decoding it from ill-learnt Cyrillic. Yod Crewsy now said:

'Me teeth is slipping a bit.' Laughter. 'I can write em but I can't say em. Anyway, here's how it finishes:

> But the thin tuning-fork of one of the needs of men,
> The squat village letter-box, approached, awoke,
> Called all to order with its stump of red;

In a giant shudder, the monstrous organ then
Took shape and spoke.'

There was applause. Yod Crewsy said: 'Don't ask me what it means;
I only wrote it.' Laughter. 'No, serious like, I feel very humble. But
I put them poems together in this book just like to show. You
know, show that we do like think a bit and the kvadrats, or squares
which is what some of you squares here would like call yourselves,
can't have it all their own way.' Cheers.

Hogg stood frozen like an ice cream *monumento*. He had left,
when he had run away from that bitch in there, several manuscript poems in her Gloucester Road flat. They had been written;
later they had been written off. The holograph of *The Pet Beast*
had been among them. Unable to reconstitute them from
memory, he could not now be absolutely sure – But wait. A
painter friend of that bitch, his name Gideon Dalgleish, had
said something on some social occasion or other about driving
with a friend through green summer England and being over-
whelmed with its somehow, my dear, *obscene* greenness, a great
proliferating green carcinoma, terrifying because shapeless and
huge. And then the sudden patch of red from a letter-box
concentrated and tamed the green and gave it a comprehensible
form. Nature *needs* man, my dear. The words CURTAL
SONNET had flashed before his, Hogg's, Enderby's, eyes, and
the rhymes had lined up for inspection. And then – He stood
gaping at nothing, unable to move. He heard Yod Crewsy's voice
again, calling microphonically over loud cheers:

'Right. So much for the F.S.L.S. lot, or whatever it is. And I'd
like to say a artfelt *ta* to our mum here, who like encouraged me.
Now we're going to do our new disc, and not mime neither. I see
the lads is all ready up there. All they want is me.' Ecstasy.

Hogg painfully turned himself about. Then, as against a G
science-fictionally intensified twentyfold, he forced his legs to slide
forward towards the open door of the Wessex Saddleback. Jed Foot
was trembling. Across the smoky luncheon-room, now darkened
by drawn curtains, he saw, glorious in floodlighting, the Crewsy
Fixers ranged grinning on a little dais. Yod Crewsy held a flat guitar
with flex spouting from it. In front of each of the others was a

high-mounted sidedrum. They poised white sticks, grinning. Then they jumped into a hell of noise belched out fourfold by speakers set at the ceiling's corners.

> 'You can do that, *ja*, and do this. *Ja*.
> You can say that you won't go beyond a kiss. *Ja*.
> But where's it goin to get ya, where's
> It goin to get
> Ya (*ja*), babaaah?'

Where was she, that was the point! Where was she, so that he could go in there and expose her, the whole blasphemous crew of them, before high heaven, which did not exist? Hogg squinted through the dark and thought he saw that cruel feathered hat. Then, in that little group by the open door, there seemed to be violent action, noise, the smell of a sudden pungent fried breakfast. A couple of chambermaids screamed and clutched each other. The sidedrums on the dais rimshotted like mad. Yod Crewsy did a crazy drunken dance, feet uplifted as if walking through a shitten byre. His autonomous mouth did a high scream, while his eyes crossed in low comedy. The crowd clapped.

'Here yare,' panted Jed Foot, and he handed something to Hogg. Hogg automatically took it, a barman used to taking things. Too heavy for a brandy glass. Jed Foot hared off down the corridor.

'Lights! Lights!' called somebody, the king in *Hamlet*. 'He's shot, he's hurt!' Yod Crewsy was down, kicking. The dullest of the Crewsy Fixers still leered, singing inaudibly. But drums started to go over. Hogg was being started back from, John incredulous, the chambermaids pointing and screaming, a minor cook, like a harvest-caught rabbit, wondering whither to run, whimpering. Hogg looked down at his hand and saw a smoking gun in it. Shem Macnamara was yelling: 'Him! Stop him! I knew that voice! Sworn enemy of pop-art! Murderer!' John the Spaniard was quick, perhaps no stranger to such southern public violence. He yapped like a dog, most unspanishly, at Hogg: 'Out out out out out out!' It was like a Mr Holdenish nightmare of umpires. Hogg, with an instinct learnt from the few films he had seen, pointed the gun at Shem Macnamara, marvelling. Some of the guests still thought this part

of the show. Others called for a doctor. Hogg, gun in hand, ran.
He ran down the corridor to the service lift. The indicator said it
was on another floor, resting. He called it and it lazily said it was
coming. He kept the gun pointing. John was in everybody's way,
but some were thinking of coming for him. Vesta now would be
weeping over her favourite client, the impersonal and opportunist
camera-lights cracking. The lift arrived and Hogg entered, still
marvelling. Armed. Dangerous. The lift-door snapped off the sound
of running feet. Drunk, that was the trouble with them: all drunk.
Hogg stood dazed in a fancied suspension of all movement, while
the lighted floor-pointer counted down. He had pressed, for some
reason, the button marked B for basement. As low as you could
get. He landed on a stone corridor, full of men trundling garbage
bins. Useless to hope to hold off. It was a matter of running, if
he could, up a short dirty flight to a ground-level back entrance. He
remembered, near-dead with breathlessness, to drop the gun at the
top of the stairs. It clanked down and, the safety-catch still off,
somehow managed to fire itself at nothing. *El acaso inevitable.* With
that frail barricade. Would the frozen monument be melting now
up there, Yod Crewsy dissolving first? Men were coming to the
noise of firing. He was out. It was a staff car-park, very unglam-
orous. For time himself will bring. You in that high-powered car.
A taxi. London lay in autumn after-lunch gloom, car-horns
bellowing and yapping. Rushing on to it. Air, air. Hogg gasped for
it. 'Taxi,' he breathed, waving like mad, though feebly. Amazingly,
one stopped. 'Air,' he said. 'Air.'

'Airport?' The driver wore sinister dark glasses. 'Air terminal?
Cromwell Road?' Hogg's head sunk to his chest; the driver took
it for a nod. 'Right, gav. Hop in.' Hogg hopped in. Fell in, rather.

4

So they were trying to go west, Gloucester Road way, despite the
opposition (frivolous and treacherous) of contrary traffic and stulti-
fied red signals. There, he supposed, his days of misery had really
begun, in the flat of that woman. And now the unavoidable
happening was rushing him (well, hardly rushing) to the same

long street to make his escape from not merely Vesta's world but
Wapenshaw's as well. Well, they were the same world, they had to
be the same. They were not the poet's world. Did such a world
really exist? Where, anyway, did he think he was going to? He
had better make up his mind. He could not say, 'What planes do
you have, please?' Quite calm now, iced by his wrongs, he got his
five-pound notes out of their hiding-place. His passport rode in
hard protectiveness over his right pap. It was decidedly an ill wind.
About passports, he meant. He had nothing in the way of luggage,
which was a pity. Airlines, he thought, must be like hotels as far
as luggage was concerned. But you had to pay in advance, didn't
you? Still, there must be nothing to arouse suspicion. The newspapers would be cried around the streets shortly. Man answering
to this description. May be using an alias. Was he being followed?
He looked out of the rear window. There were plenty of vehicles
behind, but from none of them were hands and heads broadcasting
agitation. He would be all right, he was sure he would be all right.
He was innocent, wasn't he? But he hadn't behaved innocent.
Who would speak up for him? Nobody could. He had pointed
a loaded gun at Shem Macnamara. Besides, if that ghastly yob was
dead he was glad he was dead. He had desire and motive and
opportunity.

The taxi was now going up the ramp that led into the air
terminal, a stripped-looking and gaudy place like something from
a very big trade exhibition. He paid off the driver, giving a very
unmemorable tip. The driver looked at it with only moderate
sourness. Would he remember when he saw the evening papers?
Yus yus, I picked him ap ahtside the otel. Fought vere was something a bit fishy. Flyin orf somewhere he was. Hogg entered the
terminal. Where the hell was he going to go to? He suddenly
caught the voice of John the Spaniard, talking of his brother Billy
Gomez. In some bar or other, very exotic, knifing people. Where
was that now? Hogg had a confused image of the Moorish Empire:
dirty men in robes, kasbahs without modern sanitation, heartening
smells of things the sun had got at, muezzins, cockfights, shady
men in unshaven hiding, the waves slapping naughty naughty at
boats full of contraband goods. Hogg noticed a raincoated man
pretending to read an evening paper near an insurance-policy

machine. The news would not be in yet, but it wouldn't be long. There was a crowd of people having its luggage weighed. Hogg got in there. One married man was unpacking a suitcase on the floor, almost crying. His wife was angry.

'You should have read it proper. I leave them sort of things to you. Well, it's your stuff that'll have to stay behind, not mine.'

'How was I to know you couldn't take as much on a charter flight as on one of them ordinary uns?' He laid a polythene-wrapped suit, like a corpse, on the dirty floor. Hogg saw a yawning official at a desk. Above him stretched a title in neon Egyptian italic: PANMED AIRWAYS. Panmed. That would mean all over the Med or Mediterranean. He went up and said politely:

'A single to Morocco, please.' Morocco was, surely, round the Mediterranean or somewhere like that. Hogg saw the raincoated paper-reader looking at him. Lack of luggage, no coat over arm, a man obviously on the run.

'Eh?' The official stopped yawning. He was young and ginger with eyes, like a dog's, set very wide apart. 'Single? Oh, one person you mean.'

'That's right. Just me. Rather urgent, actually.' He shouldn't have said that. The young man said:

'You mean this air cruise? Is that what you mean? A last-minute decision, is that it? Couldn't stand it any longer? Had to get away?' It was as though he were rehearsing a report on the matter; he was also putting words into Hogg's mouth. Hogg said:

'That's right.' And then: 'I don't *have* to get away, of course. I just thought it would be a good idea, that's all.'

'Charlie!' called the young official. To Hogg he said: 'It looks as though you're going to be in luck. Somebody died at the last minute.'

Hogg showed shock at the notion of someone dying suddenly. The man called Charlie came over. He was thin and harassed, wore a worn suit, had PANMED in metal on his left lapel. 'They won't ever learn,' said Charlie. 'There's one couple there brought what looks like a cabin-trunk. They just don't seem able to *read*, some of them.'

'The point is,' said the young ginger man, 'that you've had this cancellation, and there's this gentleman here anxious to fill it.

Longing to get to the warmth, he is. Can't wait till the BEA flight this evening. That's about it, isn't it?' he said to Hogg. Hogg nodded very eagerly. Too eagerly, he then reflected.

Charlie surveyed Hogg all over. He didn't seem to care much for the barman's trousers. 'Well,' he said, 'I don't know really. It's a question of him being able to pay in cash.'

'I can pay in nothing else,' said Hogg with some pride. He pulled out a fistful in earnest. 'I just want to be taken to Morocco, that's all. I have,' he said, improvising rapidly, 'to get to my mother out there. She's ill, you see. Something she ate. I received a telegram just after lunch. Very urgent.' *Very* urgent: the type-setters would be setting up the type now; the C.I.D. would be watching the airports.

Charlie had a fair-sized wart on his left cheek. He fiddled with it as though it activated a telegraphic device. He waited. Hogg put his money back in his trouser-pocket. A message seemed to come through. Charlie said: 'Well, it all depends where in Morocco, doesn't it? And how fast you want to get there. We'll be in Seville late tonight, see, and not in Marrakesh till tomorrow dinner-time. This is an air-cruise, this is. If it's Tangier you want to get to, we shan't be there for another fortnight. We go round the Canaries a bit, you see.'

'Marrakesh would do very nicely,' said Hogg. 'What I mean is, that's where my mother is.'

'You won't get anybody else, Charlie,' said the young ginger official. 'That seat's going begging, all paid for by the bloke who snuffed it. He's got cash.' He spoke too openly; he seemed to know that Hogg was making a shady exit. 'The bus,' he looked at the big clock, 'leaves in ten minutes.'

'Shall we say fifty?' Charlie licked his lips; the young official picked up the gesture. 'In cash, like I said.'

'Done,' said Hogg. He lick-counted the money out. A good slice of his savings. Savings. The word struck, like a thin tuning-fork (he was glad Yod Crewsy was dead, if he *was* dead), a pertinent connotation. He put the money on the counter.

'Passport in order, sir?' said the ginger official. Hogg showed him. 'Luggage, sir?'

'Wait,' said Hogg. 'I've got it over there.' He pierced the waiting crowd. That unpacking man had finished unpacking. In the big suitcase lay only a pair of Bermuda shorts, some shaving gear, and two or three paperbacks of a low sort. The unpacked garments were on his arm. 'They said I could leave them in their office here,' he puffed. 'Collect them on the way back. Still, it's a bloody nuisance. I've practically only got what I stand up in.' Hogg said:

'Saw you were in a bit of trouble over weight.' He smiled at the couple as if they were going to do him a favour, which they were. 'That suitcase could go with mine, if you like. I'm taking practically nothing, you see.'

The couple looked at him with proper suspicion. They were decent fattish short people in late middle age, unused to kindness without a catch in it. The man groused: 'It means I'll have to shove it all in again.'

'That's right,' said Hogg. 'Shove it all in again.' The man, shaking his head, once more got down heavily on his knees.

'It's very kind, Mr er,' said the wife, grudgingly.

They never took their eyes off Hogg as he swung the reconstituted bag to the weighing. Charlie and the ginger official had seen nothing: they were busy doing a split on Hogg's money. The raincoated paper-reader, Hogg noticed, had gone. Perhaps to buy a later edition. Hogg was glad to be herded to the bus.

5

This Charlie seemed to be what they called a dragoman. He counted his charges on, and then, when they were on, counted them again. He frowned, as if the numbers did not tally. Hogg was seated next to a rather dowdy woman in early middle age, younger than himself, that was. She smiled at him as to a companion in adventure. She wore churchgoing clothes of sensible district-nurse-type hat and costume in a kind of underdone pie-crust colour. Her stockings, of which the knees just about showed, were of some kind of lisle material, opaque gunmetal. Hogg smiled back tentatively, and then warily surveyed the other members of the party. They were mostly unremarkable people subduedly thrilled at going off to exotic places. The men were already casting themselves for

parts, as if the trip were really going to be full of enforced priva-
tions and they had, somehow, to make their own entertainment.
One beef-necked publican-type was pointing out the sights on the
way to the airport and inventing bogus historical associations, like
'Queen Lizzy had a milk stout there'. There was cautious fencing
for the role of low comedian, and one man who, his teeth out,
could contort his face in a rubbery manner seemed likely to win.
There was a loud and serious man, a frequenter presumably of
public libraries, who was giving a preliminary account of the more
hurtful fauna of North Africa. Another man could reel off exchange
rates. Hogg's seat-companion smiled again at him, as if with pleasure
that everything was going to be so nice and cosy. Hogg closed his
eyes in feigned (but was it feigned?) weariness.

When they got to the airport the news was still unbroken.
Perhaps the management, on the instructions of the police, had
sealed everything off, and it was no good the Prime Minister
saying he had to get back to the House. Twenty minutes before
take-off. Hogg spent most of that time in one of the lavatories,
sitting gloomily on the seat. Could he do anything about disguising
himself? With teeth out he would be expected to compete for
the part of cruise comedian perhaps. Spectacles off? He tried that;
he could just about see. Rearrange hair-style? Too little hair really,
but he combed what he had down in a Roman emperor arrange-
ment. Walk with a limp? Easy enough, if he could remember to
keep on doing it. He heard ladylike intonations from a loudspeaker,
so he pulled the chain and went to join his party. The man with
the overweight luggage had suddenly woken up to the fact of
Hogg's kindness; he did not seem to notice any change in Hogg's
appearance. With bleary unfocused eyes, top denture out (a
compromise that a sudden feeling of nausea had forced upon him
on leaving the lavatory), and scant imperial coiffure, Hogg nodded
and nodded that that was really quite all right, only too glad to
oblige.

They all walked to the aircraft. Wind blew grit across the tarmac.
Farewell, English autumn. It did not seem to Hogg to be a very
elegant aircraft. There was a button missing from the stewardess's
uniform jacket, and she herself, though insipidly and blondly pretty,
had a look of vacancy that did not inspire confidence. Things

done on the cheap, that was about it. Hogg sat down next to a starboard window, taking his last look of England. Somebody sat next to him, a woman. She said, in a semi-cultured Lancashire accent:

'We seem destined, don't we?' It was the one who had sat next to him on the bus. Hogg grunted. The unavoidable happening. In the elastic-topped pocket on the back of the seat in front of him, Hogg sadly found reading-matter, very cheerful and highly coloured stuff. No need to worry if we go down into the sea. We have a fine record for air safety. Keep calm, the stewardess will tell you what to do. But who, wondered Hogg, would tell her? There were brochures about the ports of call on the air cruise.

'This is my first time,' said the woman next to Hogg. 'Is it yours?' Her teeth seemed to be all her own. She had taken off her hat. Her hair was prettily mousy.

'First time to do what?' said Hogg dourly.

'Oh, you know, go on one of these things. It's funny really, I suppose, but I know all about the moon yet I've never seen the Mountains of the Moon.'

'A stronger telescope,' said Hogg. He was leafing through a booklet, full of robes, skies of impossible blue, camels, palms, the wizened faces of professional Moorish beggars, which told him of the joys of Tangier.

'No, no, I mean the Mountains of the Moon in Africa.' She giggled.

Hogg heard the door of the aircraft slam. It did not slam properly. Charlie the dragoman, who now wore a little woolly highly coloured cap, helped the stewardess to give it a good hard slam, and then it seemed to stay shut. Engines and things began to fire and backfire or something. They were going to take off. Hogg felt safe for an instant, but then realized that there was no escape. They had things like Interpol and so on, or some such things. Spanish police, with teeth all bits of gold like John, waiting for him at Seville. But perhaps not, he thought with a little rising hope. Perhaps Spain would consider the murder of a pop-singer a very nugatory crime, which of course it was. Not really a crime at all if you took the larger view. Well then, landed in Spain, let him stay in Spain, *el señor inglés*. But how live there? With his little bit of money he could not, even in that notoriously cheap (because poverty-stricken) country, find a retreat or lavatory that would accommodate him long enough to coax, like a costive bowel, the art of verse back. The Muse had still made no real sign. There was a poem still to be completed. And, besides, there was terrible repression in Spain, a big dictator up there in the Escorial or wherever it was, directing phalanges of cruel bruisers (no, not bruisers; thin sadists, rather) with steel whips. No freedom of expression, poets suspect, foreign poets arrested and eventually handed over to Interpol. No, better to go to a country full of men on the run and smugglers and (so he had heard) artistic homosexuals, where English, language of international shadiness, was spoken and understood, and where at least he might hide (even out of doors; the nights were warm, weren't they?) and work out the future. One step at a time.

'You haven't fastened your safety-belt,' said the woman. Hogg grumbled, fumbling for the metal-tipped tongues of dirty webbing. The airfield, his last view of England, was speeding as a grey blur back into the past. Speed increased; they were getting off the ground. You in that high-powered car. Perhaps an old-fashioned image, really. Hogg leafed through the Tangier brochure absently, noticing little box advertisements for restaurants and bars. He frowned at one of these, wondering. It said:

AL-ROKLIF
English Spoken Berber Dances
Wide Range of Exotic Delights
A Good British Cup of Tea
'IN ALL THE ANTHOLOGIES!'

He wondered, he wondered, he wondered. Artistic, which included literary, homosexuals. The name, rationalized into mock-Arabic. The slogan. Well. He began to breathe hard. If they caught him, and he would surely know if they were going to catch him, he would not be punished gratuitously. There was something very just but highly punishable he would do before Interpol dragged him off in handcuffs. When you came to think of it, Tangier sounded like just the sort of place a man of Rawcliffe's type would end up in. Moorish catamites. Drinking himself to death. Drinking was too slow a process.

Hogg came to to find the woman gently unclicking his safety-belt for him. 'You were miles away,' she smiled. 'And we're miles up. Look.' Hogg, mumbling sour thanks, surveyed without much interest a lot of clouds lying below them. He had seen such things before, travelling to Rome on his honeymoon. He gave the clouds the tribute of a look of weary sophistication. It was the Romantic poets really who should have flown; Percy Shelley would have loved to see all this lot from this angle. How did that thing go now? He chewed a line or two to himself.

'Did you say something?' asked the woman.

'Poetry,' said Hogg. 'A bit of poetry. About clouds.' And, as if to make up for his neglect of her, kind and friendly as she was, he recited, in his woolly voice:

> 'I silently laugh at my own cenotaph,
>   And out of the caverns of rain,
> Like a child from the womb, like a ghost from the tomb,
>   I arise and unbuild it again.'

'Oh, I do love poetry,' this woman smiled over the engines. 'It was a toss-up whether I did literature or astronomy, you know. But it was the moon that won.'

'How do you mean,' asked Hogg carefully, 'it was the moon that won?'

'That's what I do,' she said. 'That's what I lecture in. The moon. Selenography, you know.'

'Selene,' said learned Hogg. 'A fusion of Artemis and Hecate.'

'Oh, I wouldn't know about that,' she said. 'Selenography is what it's called. I'd better introduce myself, I suppose. My name's Miranda Boland.'

Miranda: a wonder to her parents: poor woman, all alone as she was. 'Well,' said Hogg cautiously, 'my name –'

Charlie the dragoman suddenly boomed through a crackling speaker. 'My name,' he announced, 'is Mr Mercer.' No familiarity, then; he was no longer to be thought of as Charlie. 'My job,' he said, 'is to look after you on this cruise, show you around and so on.'

'Come wiz me to ze Kasbah,' said the rubbery man. He had made it, then. It was his début as resident comedian. 'Shut up, George,' his wife said, delightedly. Members of the party grinned and made their bottoms and shoulders more comfortable. The holiday was really beginning now.

'I hope you will enjoy this cruise,' crackled Mr Mercer. 'Lots of people do enjoy these cruises. They sometimes come again. And if there's anything you don't like about this cruise, tell me. Tell *me*. Don't bother to write a letter to Panmed. Let's have it out at once, man to man, or to woman should such be the case. But I think you'll like it. Anyway, I hope so. And so does Miss Kelly, your charming air-hostess, and Captain O'Shaughnessy up front. Now the first thing is that we can expect a bit of obstruction at Seville. It's this Gibraltar business, which you may have read about. The Spanish want it and we won't let it go. So they get a bit awkward when it comes to customs and immigration and so on. They try and delay us, which is not very friendly. Now it's quicker if I show your passports all in one lump, so I'm coming round to collect them now. And then Miss Kelly here will serve tea.'

Miranda Boland (Mrs? Miss?) opened a stuffed handbag to get her passport out. She had a lot of things in her bag: tubes of antibiotics and specifics against diarrhoea and the like. Also a little Spanish dictionary. That was to help her to have a good time. Also a small writing case. This put into Hogg's head an idea, perhaps a salvatory one. Hogg, without fear, produced his own passport.

'Miss Boland?' said Mr Mercer, coming round. Miss, then. 'Quite a nice photo, isn't it?' And then: 'Mr Enderby, is it?'

'That's right.' Mr Mercer examined a smirking portrait of an engaged man, occupation not yet certain at that time but given as *writer*, a couple of official Roman chops: in and then, more quickly, out again.

'And what do *you* do, Mr Enderby?' asked Miss Boland.

'I,' said Enderby, 'am a poet. I am Enderby the Poet.' The name meant nothing to this poetry-loving selenographer. The clouds below, Shelley's pals, were flushed with no special radiance. 'The Poet,' repeated Enderby, with rather less confidence. They pushed on towards the sun. Enderby's stomach quietly announced that soon, very soon, it was going to react to all that had happened. Delayed shock said that it would not be much longer delayed. Enderby sat tense in his seat, waiting for it as for an air-crash.

3

1

'Copernicus,' Miss Boland pointed. 'And then a bit to the west there's Eratosthenes. And then farther west still you get the Apennines.' Her face shone, as if she were (which in a sense she really was) a satellite of a satellite. Enderby looked very coldly at the moon which, for some reason to do with the clouds (Shelley's orbèd maiden and so on), he had expected to lie beneath them. But it was as high up as it usually was. 'And down there, south, is Anaxagoras. Just under the Mare Frigoris.'

'Very interesting,' said Enderby, not very interested. He had not himself ever made much use of the moon as a poetic property, but he still thought he had more claim on it than she had. She behaved very familiarly with it.

'And Plato, just above.'

'Why Plato?' They had had not only tea but also dinner, spilt around (hair fallen over her right eye and her tongue bitten in concentration) by that Miss Kelly. It had not been a very good dinner, but Enderby, to quieten his stomach, had wolfed his portion and part of (smilingly donated; she did not have a very big appetite) Miss Boland's. It had been three tepid fish fingers each, with some insufficiently warmed over crinkle-cut fresh frozen potato chips, also a sort of fish sauce served in a plastic doll's bucket with a lid hard to get off. This sauce had had a taste that, unexpectedly in view of its dolly-mixture pink and the dainty exiguity of even a double portion, was somehow like the clank of metal. And, very strangely or perhaps not strangely at all, the slab of dry *gâteau* that followed had a glutinous filling whose cold mutton fat gust clung to the palate as with small claws of rusty iron. Enderby had had to reinsert his top teeth before eating, doing this under cover of the need to cough vigorously and the bright pamphlet on Tangerine delights held to his left cheek. Now, after eating, he had to get both plates out, since they tasted very defiled and bits of cold burnt batter lodged beneath or above them, according to jaw. He should really get to the toilet to see about that, but, having first had doubts as to whether this aircraft possessed a toilet and then found these dispelled by the sight of the rubbery comedian called Mr Guthkelch coming back from it with theatrical relief, he felt then superstitiously that, once he left the cabin, even for two minutes, a stowaway newsboy might appear and distribute copies of a late edition with his photograph in it, and then they would, Mr Guthkelch suddenly very serious, truss him against the brutal arrest of the Seville police. So he stayed where he was. He would wait till Miss Boland had a little doze or they got to moonlit Seville. The moon was a very fine full one, and it burnt framed in the window to be tickled all over with classical names by Miss Boland.

'I don't know why Plato. That's what it's called, that's all. There's a lot of famous people commemorated all over the lunar surface. Archimedes, see, just above Plato, and Kepler, and right over there on the edge is Grimaldi.'

'The clown Grimaldi?'

'No, silly. The Grimaldi that wrote a book on the diffraction of light. A priest I believe he was. But,' she added, 'I often thought it might be nice if some *newer* names could be put up there.'

'There are a lot of new Russian ones at the back, aren't there?' said well-informed Enderby.

'Oh, you know what I mean. Who's interested in the Rabbi Levi and Endymion, whoever he was, any more? Names of great modern people. It's a daring idea, I know, and a lot of my colleagues have been, you know, aghast.'

'The trouble is,' said Enderby, 'that nobody knows who's really great till they've been a long time dead. The great ones, I mean. Dead, that is.' Mount Enderby. 'Like some of these Russian towns.

One minute they're one thing and the next another. Stalingrad, I mean. Now it's something else.'

'Volgograd.'

'Yes, and that's another. You'd be having pop-stars up there perhaps, and then in ten years' time everybody would be wondering who the hell they were.' Pop-stars. He shouldn't have mentioned that. He felt very and metallically sick. Then it passed. 'Sorry I said "hell",' he said.

'People who give pleasure to the world,' said Miss Boland. And then: 'There's a Hell on the moon, did you know that? A bit old-fashioned really, but that's true of a lot of lunar nomenclature, as I say.' And then: 'Of course, you being a poet wouldn't like pop-stars much, would you? I can quite see that. Very inferior art, you'd say. I know.'

Enderby wished he could get his teeth out and then back again. But he said quickly: 'No, no, no, I wouldn't say that. Some of them are very good, I'm sure. Please,' he begged, 'don't consider me an enemy of pop-art.'

'All right, all right,' she smiled, 'I won't. All these long-haired young singers. It's a matter of age, I suppose. I have a nephew and niece who are mad on that sort of thing. They call me a kvadrat.'

'Because I'm not, you see.'

'But I was able to say to them, you know, that this special idol of theirs seemed very unkvadrat, if that's the right expression, publishing this book of quite highbrow verse. Now that ought to change your opinion of pop-artists, if not of pop-art. I take it you saw the book? One of our junior English lecturers was quite gone on it.'

'I've got to get out,' said Enderby. She looked surprised. This was not, after all, a bus. 'If you'll excuse me –' It wasn't just a matter of teeth any more; he really had to go. A fat beaming woman was just coming away from it now. 'A matter of some urgency,' Enderby explained and prepared to go into further, plausible, details. But Miss Boland got up and let him out.

The stewardess, Miss Kelly, was sitting at the back with Mr Mercer. Mr Mercer still had his woolly cap on but he was sleeping with his mouth open. Miss Kelly seemed totally content with an expression and posture of sheer vacancy. Enderby nodded grimly at her and entered the toilet. Why hadn't he known these things – kvadrats and so on and that lout publishing a book of verse, and who blasted Vesta had got married to? He had read the *Daily Mirror* every day with positively adenoidal attention. Very little had got home, then: his rehabilitation had never had a hope of being perfect. He quietened his stomach via his bowels and, the while, rinsed his clogged teeth under the tap, and scrubbed them with the nailbrush. Then he reinserted them and, with hands gently folded on his bared lap, cried bitterly for a minute or two. Then he wiped his eyes and his bottom with the same pink paper and committed both lots of wrapped excreta to the slipstream, as he supposed it was called. He blinked at himself in the little mirror, very recognizable Hogg. If he had still had that beard which, in the intensive phase of personality change, he had been made to grow, he could be shaving it off now, having borrowed a razor from somebody, perhaps even Miss Boland, who must surely have one for leg-hair and so on in her crammed bag. Ha ha, you and the start of a holiday make me feel quite young again: I can't wait to divest myself of this fungus, ha ha. But that beard had had to go when he became a barman. So there was nothing between him and the urgently telegraphed photographs (straight from Holden's bloody secret-police dossier) now being handled by swarthy Interpol Spaniards. Nothing except the name. But damnable and treacherous Wapenshaw would already be talking away, baling out what were properly secrets of the confessional. And tomorrow morning copies of the *Daily Mirror*, which was notoriously on sale before other newspapers, as if unable to wait to regale egg-crackers with the horrors of the world, would be circulating among British holidaymakers on the Costa Brava or whatever it was called. There would be a stern portrait of Hogg on the front page, under a very insulting headline. On the back page would be great air disasters and bombs in Vietnam and avalanches and things. But on the front page would be the murderer Hogg. He did not, it seemed, read the *Daily Mirror* closely enough, but he had a sufficient appreciation of its editorial philosophy.

He re-entered the long dozing cabin with its little sprays of ceiling light blessing bald and dyed heads. Miss Boland seemed to be counting moon-craters with a puzzled finger: perhaps something new had got up there since her last going-over with a telescope. Enderby said with sudden fierceness to Miss Kelly:

'This woman in charge of pop-singers and so on. Who was it she married?'

Miss Kelly seemed unsurprised by the question. It seemed that pride in her ability to answer the question overcame such surprise as she ought properly to be showing. 'Vesta Wittgenstein? Oh, she married this man called Des Wittgenstein who ran the Fakers and the Lean Two, but now she runs them and a lot more besides. She'd been married before, to the racing-driver Pete Bainbridge, but he got himself killed. Very tragic, it was in all the papers. Then there was something about her marrying a middle-aged man and that did not bring her true happiness and it lasted less than a year, just imagine. But now she's found true happiness with Des Wittgenstein and they've both got pots of money. You ought to see her clothes. I was on an aircraft she flew on once, coming back from Rome. That's when she was very ill with this unhappiness, but she was still terribly smart.'

Enderby nodded a casual thank-you, as if for some pedestrian information about time of arrival. Miss Kelly smiled conventionally and went into a vacant relapse. Enderby thought he would now write a letter on some of Miss Boland's stationery, so he went back to his seat purposefully, like a man with something other to do than merely be flown to Seville. She welcomed him as if he had been a long time away and even said: 'Feeling all right now?'

'I've got to write,' said Enderby at once. 'A matter of some urgency.' He felt he had perhaps used those words before. 'If you could oblige me with the wherewithal.'

'A poem? How thrilling. What do you mean by the wherewithal? You want me to pay you for it? I will if you like. This is the first time anybody's ever said they'd write a poem for me.' Enderby looked sternly at her. She seemed to be teasing. It was possible she did not believe that he was a poet. Her eyes were, he noted with gloom, what might be termed merry.

'Paper is what I want,' he said. 'And an envelope, if you can spare it. Two envelopes,' he amended.

'Dear, dear, you do want a lot.' She took out her writing materials gaily. Enderby said:

'I'll write you a poem tonight. When we get there.'

'I'll hold you to that.'

Enderby took out his ballpoint and wrote to John the Spaniard: 'You know I didn't do it. Pass this note on to you-know-who. I shall be in you-know-where. Your brother. That fat dog place you mentioned. Keep in touch. Yours –' He didn't know how to sign himself. At last he wrote PUERCO. Then he took another piece of paper and addressed it from In The Air. He wrote: 'To Whomsoever It May Concern. It was not me who shot that pop-singer, as he is called. It was –' He was damned if he could remember the name. To Miss Boland he said once more: 'I've got to get out. I've forgotten something.' She let him out, mock-sighing and smiling. He kept paper and ballpoint in his hands. He went back to Miss Kelly, still in a trance of vacancy. Mr Mercer was lip-smacking, ready to surface. A monitor in his sleep had perhaps warned him that soon they would be starting to drop towards Seville. Enderby said:

'That one that used to be with Mrs Einstein's lot –'

'Mrs Wittgenstein.'

'That's right. The one that got out and became unsuccessful and goes round the clubs now.'

'Jed Foot, you mean.'

'That's it.' He wrote the name in standing. He might forget it again if he waited till he got back to his seat. Might spill it on the way. He nodded thanks and went back now, and Miss Boland, letting him in, said:

'You *are* a busy little bee.'

Enderby wrote: 'He handed me the gun and I took it without thinking. I panicked and ran. Pick him up and get him to confess. I am innocent.' Then he signed that abandoned pseudonym. He addressed one envelope to The Authorities and the other to Mr John Gomez, Piggy's Bar, Tyburn Towers Hotel, W.I. He licked and folded and arranged. Then he sighed. Finished. He could do no more. He thought he had better shut his eyes and get ready for Seville. That would stop Miss Boland teasing him further. Miss Boland, he noticed, was looking something up in her little Spanish dictionary. She was grinning. He didn't like that. It was too small a dictionary to have anything to grin at in it. He killed her grin with his eyelids.

2

Enderby slept, though without dreaming, as though the recent materials made available for dreams were far too shocking to be processed into fantasy. He was shaken awake by Miss Boland, who smiled on him and said, for some reason, 'Dirty.' He said:

'Eh?'

'We're there,' she said. 'Sunny Spain, though it's the middle of the night and it's been raining. The rain in Spain,' she giggled.

'What do you mean, dirty? Did I do something I shouldn't? In my sleep, that is?' He wondered what incontinent act might have overtaken him.

'That's what it says. Come on, we're to get out.' People were passing down the aisle, some yawning as after a boring sermon. Miss Boland smiled as if she were some relative of the vicar. 'Also,' she said over her shoulder, 'it says nasty and foul.' Enderby saw wet-gleaming tarmac under dim lamps. There was something he had to worry about. He said:

'What does?'

'Oh, come on.' She was getting her raincoat and overnight satchel from the rack. Enderby had nothing to get. Feeling naked, he said:

'I'll carry that if you like.' And then his fear smote him and his hand shook.

'That's sweet of you. Take it then.' He could hardly get his hand through the straps of the bag, but she didn't notice: she had arrived in non-sunny, not even moony, Spain. Mr Mercer seemed as nervous as Enderby himself; it was as though he had to introduce Seville like his wife and, perhaps being on the menopause, she might do something embarrassing. This was it, Enderby thought, this was it. He was cold and sober and ready and he would bluff it out to the end. He looked coldly and soberly on Miss Boland and decided that she must, in a manner, help him. He would laugh down the steps with her, linked, as if she were his wife. They were looking for a single desperate fugitive, not a laughing married man. But, as they smiled and Enderby nodded at Miss Kelly, standing at the aircraft exit, he saw that the stairway was very narrow and that he must go down unlinked. Miss Kelly beamed at everybody as if they had all just arrived at her party, which was being held in the cellar. Enderby heard Mr Guthkelch ahead, singing 'The Spaniard who blighted my life', doing his job.

'He shall die! He shall die! He shall die tiddly iddly eye tie tie eye tie tie tie!'

In very bad taste, Enderby thought. Stepping out into moist velvet warmth, he saw at the stair-bottom only Mr Mercer with an armful of passports chatting quite amiably, though in the loud and slow English needful when speaking to a foreigner, to a foreigner. It was a uniformed Spaniard in dark glasses. He had both hands in his trousers pockets and seemed to Enderby to be playing the solitaire game known as pocket billiards. He looked up at Miss Kelly, blowing up sparks from his cigarette at her like impotent signals of desire. He was not, Enderby was sure, from Interpol.

Miss Boland descended before him. As soon as he had reached damp tarmac, Enderby skipped up to her and took her arm. She seemed surprised but not displeased; she pressed Enderby's arm into her warm side. There seemed, and Enderby's knees liquefied in relief as he saw what there seemed, to be no raincoated men waiting anywhere for him on the passage over the tarmac to the airport building. There seemed to be only very lowly workmen, thin and in blue, leaning against walls, smoking vigorously, and eyeing the tourists with the hungry look of the very poor. The airport itself, despite its being very late at night, was busy. There was an aircraft with Arabic letters on it preparing to take off and there was one called IBERIA taxiing in. There were men in overalls pulling carts around and chugging about in little tractors. Enderby approved of all this bustle, especially the passenger-bustle that was evident in the building they now approached. He saw himself being chased and hiding behind people. But no, he was safe for the time being. Miss Boland said:

'There's no *luna*. That's what it's called, isn't it? *Luna*. Better than "moon". Lunar. Lunation. Endo-lunar. I thought the *luna* would be here to meet me. Never mind.'

'You've had plenty on the way,' said Enderby in a slightly chiding tone. 'You'll get plenty while you're here. On holiday, I mean. But I thought perhaps you'd want to get away from it.' A fellow-tourist walking near them gave Enderby a suspicious look. 'The *luna*, I mean,' Enderby said.

'You can't get away from it,' said Miss Boland. 'Not if you've given your whole life to it, as I have.' And she squeezed Enderby's arm with hers. She was very warm. 'Where did you learn Spanish?' she asked.

'I never did. I don't know any Spanish. Italian, yes, a bit. But not Spanish. They're similar, though.'

'You're very mysterious,' said Miss Boland mysteriously. 'You intrigue me rather. There seems to be a lot you're holding back. Why, you haven't even brought a raincoat. But I suppose that's your business, not mine. And no overnight bag of your own. You give me the impression of a man who had to get away in a hurry.'

'Oh, I had to,' palpitated Enderby. 'What I mean is, I'm a man of impulse. I think of a thing and then I do it.' She squeezed his arm again and said:

'You can call me Miranda if you like.'

'A very poetical name,' said Enderby in duty. He couldn't quite remember who wrote that poem. A big Catholic winy man in a cloak. 'The fleas that tease in the high Pyrenees,' he quoted. And then: 'Never more, Miranda, never more. Only the something whore.'

'Pardon?'

'And something something something at the door.' They had now entered the airport building. It was small, dark, and smelt faintly of men's urinals, specifically foreign ones, a garlic-scented effluent. There was a big photograph of General Franco, dressed as a civilian, a bald man with jowls and parvenu lifted eyebrows. There were also yellowing notices probably forbidding things. Mr Mercer was already there, having perhaps been given a lift on one of those tractors. All the cruise members clustered round him, as for protection. Enderby saw that his arm was still in Miss Boland's. He disengaged it by saying he had to post a letter.

'Mysterious again,' she said. 'You're no sooner here than you have to post a mysterious letter. Signed with a mysterious name.'

'What?' squawked Enderby.

'I'm sorry. I couldn't help seeing it. You left it on the seat. Do forgive me. It was with those brochures and things, and I picked them up to look at them and there was your letter. But it's no

good my pretending that I don't know your first name now, is it?
Or nickname it must be.'

'Oh, no.'

'It *must* be. I've never seen the name Puerco before.' She
pronounced it *Pure co*. 'And then, since it looked foreign, I looked
it up in my Spanish dictionary, and, lo and behold, there it was.
Meaning "dirty".'

'Actually,' Enderby improvised in delirium, 'it's an old border
name. Welsh border, I mean. My family came from near Shrewsbury.
That's a coincidence, that is, the Spanish business, I mean. Look,
I've *got* to post this letter. I'll be back.' As soon as he had clumsily
pushed his way through the crowd that was round woolly-capped
Mr Mercer, he realized he had behaved foolishly in being willing
to leave her if only for five minutes. She wouldn't believe that
story about Puerco being an old border name; she'd look it up
again in her Spanish dictionary and she'd find more than dirty and
filthy and so on. She was bound to. He hesitated at a door that
led on to a dismal wet garden, beyond it a kind of restaurant all
made of big dirty windows. He would have to get that dictionary
away from her, tear out the dangerous page or lose the whole
book. Or should he now, with his five-pound notes and anthology
of exotic *pourboires*, get out there into the great rainy windy penin-
sula, lose himself in cork-woods, become dried up like a raisin
tramping the hot white country roads? He thought not. A lean
poor man was standing by the door, opposing cigarette-sparks to
the dull damp night. It was possible, thought Enderby, that Spanish
John's hispaniolizing of his mother's maiden name represented a
historical phase of the word, long superseded. But if, of course, it
was the same as Italian and – Enderby said to this man:

'*Amigo.*' The man responded with a benison of sparks. Enderby
said: 'In *español. L'animal.* What's the *español* for it?' He snorted and
snuffed the air all around at chest-level as though rooting for truffles.
Then he saw that a man in smart uniform, just behind, was watching
with some interest. The lean poor man said: '*Entiendo. Un puerco.*'

That was it then, Enderby thought grimly. He stood wavering,
letter in hand. The thin poor man seemed to be awaiting further
charades from Enderby. The uniformed man frowned, very puzzled.
The thin poor one whinnied and said, '*Un caballo.*' Enderby said

'*Sí*' then tripped over the uniformed man's left boot as he went in again, letter unposted.

'My goodness, you were quick,' said Miss Boland.

'It's the language,' Enderby said. 'I don't know the language, as I said. Perhaps if I could borrow your little dictionary –'

'Right,' Mr Mercer was now saying. 'Everybody please stand round there where the baggage is.' They'd got it out pretty quickly, Enderby thought distractedly: no spirit of *mañana* here. 'As you know, they have customs here same as everywhere else –'

'Old Spanish customs,' cried Mr Guthkelch.

'– But only a few of you will have to open your bags –'

'As long as nobody has to drop 'em,' cried Mr Guthkelch, perhaps going too far.

'– It's a sample, you see, what you might call a sample checkup.'

'I don't suppose,' said Miss Boland to Enderby, 'that you've got anything so bourgeois as luggage, have you? I suppose you'll be sleeping in your shirt or in the altogether.' Her eyes glistened when she said that, as though excited by it. Enderby was disgusted; he said:

'You'll soon see whether I've got it or not. I'm no different from anybody else.' The man who had looked at him suspiciously on the way across the tarmac now did the same thing again. 'In the sense, that is,' expanded Enderby, 'of personal possessions and the like.'

'This is a bit like an identification parade, isn't it?' giggled Miss Boland. 'Very thrilling.' They were all there near the pile of luggage, and an official with a peaked cap did a caged-tiger walk up and down in front of this squad of pleasure-seekers, hands folded behind his back. Enderby saw who it was: that man out there who had frowned at his pig-snorting. The man now halted and faced them. He had jowls not unlike those of his Caudillo and even allelomorphs of those eyebrows; perhaps a lowly relative for whom the régime had had to find a job. He sternly pointed at people. He pointed at Enderby. Enderby at once looked round for the man with the overweight luggage. He found him and said:

'Where is it?'

'What? That? Why can't you show him your own?'

'Reasons,' Enderby said. 'Things nobody must see.'

'Thought there was a catch in it. Right liberty, I call it. Anyway, I've got nothing to fear.' And he showed where the supernumerary bag was. Enderby lugged it to the customs-counter. The official was already delicately rooting in a pair of very clean white cotton gloves. He was perfunctory about most passengers' luggage; with supposed Enderby's he was thorough. At the bottom of the bag he found, under that man's Bermuda shorts, the three garish paperbacks that had looked quite harmless in the London air terminal. Here, in a repressed and repressive Catholic country that discharged its extramarital lust in bullfights, they suddenly seemed to flare into the promise of outrageous obscenity. Miss Boland, though not of the luggage-opening elect, was nevertheless by Enderby's side. She saw; 'Dirty,' she said, grinning. The official held up the three books very nearly to the level of the portrait of the Caudillo, as if for his curse. Mr Guthkelch said: 'Who'll start the bidding?' The covers blared three allotropes of mindless generic blonde, in shock and undress. The official pronounced: '*Pornográficos.*' Everybody nodded, pleased that they could understand Spanish. And then straight at Enderby he snorted and gave back Enderby's own mime of snout-truffling, adding: '*Puerco.*'

'I see, I see,' said Miss Boland, quietly gratified, pressing into Enderby's flank. 'So that's how you pronounce it. And it means "pig" too. Stupid of me, I should have seen that. They know you here then. You *are* a dark horse. Pig, I mean, a dark pig.'

From one of the upheld books two flat square little packets dropped out. They fell on to the exposure of somebody's sensible white underwear. All the men at once knew what they were, but one elderly woman, evidently sheltered from the world, said: 'Sort of rings. What are they for then?' The man who could best tell her was heard groaning: those objects were obviously ferial, not marital, equipment. The official wiped one cotton-gloved hand against another, made an extravagant gesture of disgust and dismissal, and turned his back on the lot of them. '*Ipocritico,*' murmured Enderby. The official did not hear, or else the Spanish was different from the Italian.

'It pays to be straight,' the overweight man was whining. 'I've learned my lesson, that I have.' His wife looked out, dissociated from him but there would be hell tonight in a foreign bedroom, into wet dark Seville, Don Juan's town. 'Let me down, you have,' he said unreasonably to Enderby. Everybody else frowned, puzzled, not quick on the uptake. Even Miss Boland. Miss Boland took Enderby's arm, saying: 'Come on, Piggy.' A very liberalizing influence the moon, Enderby bitterly thought. Mr Mercer called them, in a fatigued voice, to the waiting bus.

3

An hour later, Enderby lay exhausted on his hotel bed. He had posted that letter in the box in the hotel lobby, having found pesetas in his little treasury of tips and been able to buy stamps from the moustached duenna yawning with dignity at the reception desk. None of the hotel staff, admittedly tired and proudly resentful of the late-arriving guests, seemed even minimally agitated by news of the death of a British pop-singer. So things were all right so far. But soon they would not be. A lot of course depended on the chief guardian of the true identity of Hogg, namely bloody Wapenshaw; much depended on the Hogg-photograph in tomorrow's newspapers; a little depended on Miss Boland's semantic investigations into the word *puerco*.

Soon, when he was less exhausted, he would go and see Miss Boland. She was on this floor of the hotel, which was called the Hotel Marruecos; she was just a couple of doors down. Soon. Enderby had had sent up a bottle of Fundador and a glass. He knew Fundador from Piggy's Sty: it was a kind of parody of Armagnac. He was drinking it now for his nerves. He lay on the bed, whose coverlet was the colour of boiled liver. The wallpaper was cochineal. There were no pictures on the walls. It was all very bare, and he had done nothing to mitigate that bareness. Nothing in the wardrobe, no suitcase on the luggage-stand at the bed's bottom. The window was open, and a hot wind had started blowing up, one which seemed to match the cochineal walls. This hot wind had scattered the clouds and disclosed what was now a Spanish moon, a Don Juan stage property. Miss Boland, in a sensible dressing-gown, would now be putting curlers in her hair, looking at the moon. *Luna*. Perhaps she would be checking the word in her handbag dictionary.

Painfully Enderby got up and went to the bathroom. He could hear, through the wall, in the adjoining bathroom, the man with overweight luggage being rebuked bitterly by his wife. Libidinous wretch. Condom-carrier. Thought he'd have a nasty sly go at the *señoritas* or *bintim*, did he? Words to that effect, anyway. Best years of her life slaving away for him. Enderby, sighing, micturated briefly, pulled the chain, and left his room buttoning, sighing. Leaving his room, he met Miss Boland coming to his room. Quite a coincidence, really.

'I've come,' she said, 'for my poem.' She looked rather like a woman who was coming to collect a poem, not a bit the lecturer in selenography. Her dressing-gown was far from sensible: it was diaphanous black, billowing in the hot wind from the window at the corridor's end, and under it was a peach-coloured nightdress. Her pretty mousy hair had been brushed; it crackled in the hot wind; a peach-coloured fillet was binding it. She had put on cochineal lipstick, matching the hot wind. Enderby gulped. Gulping, he bowed her in. He said:

'I haven't had time yet. To write a poem, that is. I've been unpacking, as you can see.'

'You've unpacked *everything*? Goodness. A bit pointless, isn't it? We're only here for the night. What's left of it, that is. Ah,' she said, billowing in the hot wind over to the window, 'you have the *luna* too. My *luna* and yours.'

'We must,' Enderby said reasonably, 'be on the same side of the corridor. The same view, you see.' And then: 'Have a drink.'

'Well,' she said, 'I don't usually. Especially at this hour of the morning. But I am on holiday after all, aren't I?'

'You most certainly are,' Enderby said gravely. 'I'll get a glass from the bathroom.' He went to get it. The row was still going on next door. Uncontrollable lust in middle age. Comic if it was not disgusting. Or something like that. He brought back the glass and found Miss Boland sitting on his bed. 'Mare Imbrium,' she was saying. 'Seleucus. Aristarchus.' He poured her a very healthy slug. He would make her drunk and have a hangover, and that would distract her tomorrow morning from *puerco* business. Soon he would go to her room and steal her dictionary. Everything was going to be all right.

'You've been thorough,' she said, taking the glass from him. 'You've even packed your suitcase away.'

'Oh yes,' he said. 'It's a sort of mania with me. Tidiness, that is.' Then he saw himself in the dressing-table mirror – unshaven since early this morning in London (he had written *Londra* on the envelope; was that right?) and with shirt very crumpled and trousers proclaiming cheapness and jacket thin at the elbows. He gave himself a grim smile full of teeth. They looked clean enough, anyway. He transferred the smile to Miss Boland. 'You poor man,' she said. 'You're lonely, aren't you? I could see that when you got the bus in London. Still, you've no need to be lonely now. Not for this holiday, anyhow.' She took a sip of the Fundador without grimacing. 'Hm. Fiery but nice.'

'*Mucho fuego*,' said Enderby. English man no *fuego*: he remembered that.

Miss Boland leaned back. She wore feathery slippers with heels. Leaning back, she kicked them off. Her feet were long and clean and the toes were unpainted. She closed her eyes, frowned, then said: 'Let me see if I can remember. *A cada puerco* something-or-other *su San Martin*. That means: every dog has his day. But it should be "every hog" really, shouldn't it? The dictionary says hog, not pig.'

Enderby sat down heavily on the other side of the bed. Then he looked with heavy apprehension at Miss Boland. She seemed to have lost about two stone and fifteen years since embarking at London. He tried to see himself imposing upon her a complex of subtle but vigorous amation which should have an effect of drowsy enslavement, rendering her, for instance, totally indifferent to tomorrow's news. Then he thought he had perhaps better get out of here and find his own way to North Africa: there must surely be something hopping over there at this hour. But no. Despite everything, he was safer in Mr Mercer's party – a supernumerary, fiddled in with a wink, no name on the manifest, waved through by officials who were waved back at by Mr Guthkelch. Moreover, Mr Mercer had returned everybody's passport, and Enderby's was snug once more in its inside pocket. He was not going to let it go again, unless, in final desperate abandonment of identity, to the fire of some Moorish kebab-vendor. He saw this man quite clearly, crying his kebabs against the sun, brown and lined and toothless, opposing his call to the muezzin's. That was the poetic imagination, that was.

'And,' Miss Boland was now saying, having helped herself to more Fundador, 'mother and dad used to take me and Charles, that was my brother, to see Uncle Herbert when he lived in Wellington – Wellington, Salop, I mean; why do they call it Salop? Oh, the Latin name I suppose – and we went up Bredon Hill several times –'

'The coloured counties,' Enderby said, doing an estimate of her for seduction purposes and realizing at the same time how purely academic such a notion was, 'and hear the larks on high. Young men hanging themselves and ending up in Shrewsbury jail. For love, as they call it.'

'How cynical you are. But I suppose I've every right to be cynical too, really. Toby his name was – a silly name for a man, isn't it? – and he said I had to choose between him and my career – I mean, more the name for a dog, isn't it, really? – and of course there was no question of me abandoning my vocation for the sake of anything he said he had to give. And he said something about a brainy wife being a bad wife and he wasn't going to have the moon lying in bed between us.'

'A bit of a poet,' said Enderby, feeling himself grow drowsy. The hot wind puppeteered the window-curtains and plastered Miss Boland's nightdress against her shin.

'A bit of a liar,' Miss Boland said. 'He lied about his father. His father wasn't a solicitor, only a solicitor's clerk. He lied about his rank in the Royal Corps of Signals. He lied about his car. It wasn't his, it was one he borrowed from a friend. Not that he had many friends. Men,' she said, 'tend to be liars. Look at you, for instance.'

'Me?' said Enderby.

'Saying you're a poet. Talking about your old Shropshire name.'

'Listen,' said Enderby. And he began to recite.

> 'Shrewsbury, Shrewsbury, rounded by river
> The envious Severn like a sleeping dog
> That wakes at whiles to snarl and slaver
> Or growls in its dream its snores of fog.'

'That's yours, is it?'

> 'Lover-haunted in the casual summer:
> A monstrous aphrodisiac,
> The sun excites in the noonday shimmer,
> When Jack is sweating, Joan on her back.'

'I was always taught that you can't make poetry with long words.'

> 'Sick and sinless in the anaemic winter:
> The nymphs have danced off the summer rout,
> The boats jog on the fraying painter,
> The School is hacking its statesmen out.'

'Oh, I see what you mean. Shrewsbury School. That's where Darwin went to, isn't it?'

> 'The pubs dispense their weak solution
> The unfructified waitresses bring their bills,
> While Darwin broods upon evolution,
> Under the pall of a night that chills –'

'Sorry, I shouldn't have interrupted.'

> '– But smooths out the acne of adolescence
> As the god appears in the fourteenth glass
> And the urgent promptings of tumescence
> Lead to the tumbled patch of grass.'

'A lot of sex in it, isn't there? Sorry, I won't interrupt again.'
'This is the last bloody stanza,' Enderby said sternly. 'Coming up now.

Time and the town go round like the river,
　　But Darwin thinks in a line that is straight.
A sort of selection goes on for ever,
　　But no new species originate.'

They were silent. Enderby felt a spurt of poet's pride, and then exhaustion. It had been a terrible day. Miss Boland was impressed. She said: 'Well, you *are* a poet, after all. If that *is* yours, that is.'

'Of course it's mine. Give me some from that bottle.' And she glugged some out for him gladly, handmaiden to a poet. 'That's from my early volume, *Fish and Heroes*. Which you haven't read. Which nobody's read. But, by God,' said Enderby, 'I'll show them all. I'm not finished yet, not by a long chalk.'

'That's right. Don't you think you'd be more comfortable with your shoes off? Don't bother – leave it to me.' Enderby closed his eyes. 'And your jacket too?' Enderby soon lay on one half of the bed in shirt and trousers; she had had his socks off too and also his tie, which was in the hotel colours of red, white, and blue. The hot wind was still there, but he felt cooler. She lay next to him. They had a cigarette apiece.

'Associations,' Enderby found himself saying. 'Mind you, everybody's done it, from that Spanish priest right up to Albert Camus, with Kierkegaard somewhere in the middle.'

'Who's Kierk-whatever-it-is?'

'This philosopher who made out it was really like God and the soul. Don Juan using women and God using man. Anyway, this is his town. And I was going to write a poetic drama about Don Juan who bribed women to pretend that he'd done it to them because really he couldn't do it, not with anybody. And then poetic drama went out of fashion.' His toenails, he decided, could really do with cutting. The big toenails, however, would have to be attacked with a chisel or something. Very hard. He had not changed all that much, after all. A bath, after all, was a tank for poetic drafts. He felt a new poem twitching inside him like a sneeze. A poem about a statue. He looked rather warmly on Miss Boland. *The final kiss and final* – if only he could get that one finished first.

'And who was this barber of Seville?'

'Oh, a Frenchman invented that one, and there's a French newspaper named after him. A sort of general factotum, getting things for people and so on.' Enderby nodded off.

'Wake up.' She was quite rough with him; that would be the Fundador. 'You could have a play in which this barber was really Don Juan, and he did horrible things with his razor. In revenge, you know.'

'What do you mean? What revenge?'

'I said nothing about revenge. You dropped off again. Wake up! I don't see why the moon couldn't be a proper *scientific* subject for a poem instead of what it is for most poets – you know, a sort of lamp, or a what-do-you-call-it aphrodisiac like the sun in your poem. Then you could have as many nice long words as you wanted. Apogee and perigee and the sidereal day and ectocraters and the ejecta hypothesis.'

'What did you say about ejectors?'

She hadn't heard him. Or perhaps he'd said nothing. 'And the months,' she was now saying. 'Synodic and nodical and sidereal and anomalistic. And isostasy. And grabens and horsts. And the lunar maria, not seas at all but huge plains of lava covered in dust. Your body is a horst and mine a graben, because horst is the opposite of graben. Come on, let's get out of here and wander the streets of Seville as we are, in our night clothes I mean. But your night clothes are the altogether, aren't they? Still, it's a lovely night though the moon's setting now. Feel that warm wind on your flesh?' That was not true about the moon setting. When they were walking down the *calle* outside the hotel, Enderby totally bare, his little bags aswing, the moon was full and huge and very near. It was so near that an odour came off it – like the odour of cachous from old evening bags, of yellowing dance-programmes, of fox-fur long lain in mothballs. Miss Boland said: 'Mare Tranquillitatis. Fracastorius. Hipparchus. Mare Nectaris.' She had brought the moon right down to the Seville housetops so that she could go burrowing into its maria. She disappeared temporarily into one of those, and then her head, its mousy hair become golden Berenice's and flying about, popped through the northern polar membrane. She seemed to be agitating this hollow moon from the inside, impelling it towards

Enderby. He ran from her and it down the *calle*, back into the
hotel. The old hall-porter yawned out of his *hidalgo* lantern jaws
at Enderby's twinkling nakedness. Enderby panted up the stairs,
once getting his toe caught in a carpet-hole, then cursing as a tack
lodged in his calloused left heel. He found his room blindly and
fell flat on the bed, desperate for air. There was not much coming
from the open window. What was coming in by that window was
the moon, much shrunken but evidently of considerable mass, for
the window-frame creaked, four unwilling tangents to the straining
globe, bits of lunar substance flaking off like plaster at the four
points of engagement. Miss Boland's head now protruded at a pole
which had become a navel, her hair still flying in fire. Enderby
was stuck to that bed. With one lunge she and the moon were on
him.

'No,' he grunted, waking up. 'No, you can't do that, it isn't right.'
But she and her heavy lunar body held him down. That left heel
was fluked by one of her toenails; the staircarpet-hole turned out
to be a minute gap between the fabric of her dressing-gown and
its lacy border. There was no real nakedness, then: only exposure,
things riding up and pulled down.

'Show me then, show me what's right. *You* do it.'

He rolled her off, so that she lay expectant on her back now
and with desperate agility he trampolined his buttocks away from
the punished mattress. This was springier than he had thought, for
he found himself on his feet looking sternly down at her. 'If,' he
said, 'you want that sort of a holiday there'll be plenty to provide
it. Gigolos and what-not. Little dark-skinned boys and so on. Why
pick on me?'

She started to whimper. 'I thought we were going to be friends.
You're unnatural, that's what you are.'

'I'm *not* unnatural. Just very very tired. It's been a terrible day.'

'Yes.' She wrapped her dressing-gown round her body and looked
up at him, hard but tearfully. 'Yes, I'm sure it has. There's something
not quite right about you. You've got things on your mind. You've
done something you shouldn't have done. You've got away in a
hurry from something or other, I can tell that.'

This wouldn't do at all. 'Darling,' creaked Enderby, holding out
his arms and advancing, smirking.

'You can't get round me that way.'

'Darling.' Enderby frowned now, but with his arms still out.

'Oh, take your non-pyjamas out of your non-suitcase and get to bed after your terrible terrible day. There's something very fishy about you,' said Miss Boland. And she started to get up from the bed.

Enderby advanced and pushed her back again somewhat roughly, saying: 'You're right. I *have* run away. From her. From that woman. I couldn't stand it any longer. I got out. Just like that. She was horrible to me.' A back cinder in Enderby's raked-out brain spurted up an instant to ask what was truth and niggle a bit about situation contexts and so on. Enderby deferred to it and made an emendation: 'I ran away.'

'What woman? Which woman?' Woman's curiosity had dried her tears.

'It was never really a marriage. Oh, let me get to bed. Make room there. I'm so desperately tired.'

'Tell me all about it first. I want to know what happened. Come on, wake up. Have some more of this brandy stuff here.'

'No no no no. Tell you in the morning.' He was flat on his back again, ready to drop off. Desperately.

'I want to know.' She jerked him roughly as he had pushed her. 'Whose fault was it? Why was it never really a marriage? Oh, *do come on.*'

'Hex,' said Enderby *in extremis.* And then he was merrily driving the rear car of the three, a red sports job, and arms waving jollily from the Mercedes in front. It was a long way to this roadhouse-type pub they were all going to, but they were all well tanked-up already though the men drove with steely concentration and insolent speed. The girls were awfully pretty and full of fun. Brenda had red hair and Lucy was dark and small and Bunty was pleasantly plump and wore a turquoise-coloured twin-set. Enderby had a college scarf flying from his neck and a pipe clenched in his strong white smiling teeth. 'You wait, Bunty old girl,' he gritted indistinctly. 'You'll get what's coming to you.' The girls yelled with mirth. Urged on by them hilariously, he fed ever greater speed with his highly-polished toecap to the growling road-eating red job, and he passed with ease the other two. Waves of mock rage and mock

contempt, laughter on the spring English wind. And so he got to
the pub first. It was a nice little pub with a bald smiling barman
presiding in a cocktail bar smelling of furniture polish. He wore a
white bum-freezer with claret lapels. Enderby ordered for everybody,
telling the barman, called Jack, to put a wiggle on so that the
drinks could be all lined up and waiting when the laggards arrived.
Bitter in tankards, gin and things, and advocaat for Bunty. 'That'll
make you bright-eyed and bushy-tailed, old girl,' winked Enderby.
And then the watery signal from within. As Frank and Nigel and
Betty and Ethel and the others roared into the bar, Enderby at
once had to say: 'Sorry all. Got to see a man about a dog.' Bunty
giggled: 'Wet your boots, you mean.' At once the urgency roared
in his bladder, drowning the roaring of his pals, but he did not
run to the gents: he walked confidently, though he had never been
in this pub before. But, seeing it at the end of the corridor, he
had to run. Damn, he would only just make it.

He would only just make it. He jumped out of bed and made
for the toilet, fumbling cursing for the light-switch. Pounding his
stream out, he grumbled at the prodigality of dreams, which could
go to all this trouble – characters, décor, and all, even an advertisement for a beer (Jason's Golden Fleece) which didn't exist – just
so that he would get out of bed and micturate in the proper place.
He pulled the chain, went back to bed, and saw, by the bathroom
light he had not bothered to put out, that there was a woman
lying in it. He remembered roughly who it was, that lunar woman
he'd been flying with (why flying?) and also that this was some
foreign town, and then the whole lot came back. He was somewhat
frightened that he wasn't as frightened as he should be.

'What, eh, who?' she said. And then: 'Oh. I must have dropped
off. Come on, get in. It's a bit chilly now.'

'What time is it?' Enderby wondered. His wrist-watch had
stopped, he noticed, squinting in the light from the bathroom.
Somewhere outside a big bell banged a single stroke. 'That's a lot
of help,' said Enderby. Funny, he hadn't noticed that bell before.
They must be near a cathedral or town hall or something. Seville,
that was where they were. Don Juan's town. A strange woman in
bed.

'So,' she said. 'Her name was Bunty, was it? And she let you down. Never mind, everybody gets let down sometime or other. I got let down by Toby. And that was a silly name, too.'

'We were in this car, you see. I was driving.'

'Come back to bed. *I* won't let you down. Come and cuddle up a bit. It's chilly. There aren't many clothes on the bed.'

It was quite pleasant cuddling up. *I've been so cold at night.* Who was it who had said that? That blasted Vesta, bloody evil woman. 'Bloody evil woman,' muttered Enderby.

'Yes, yes, but it's all over now. You're a bit wet.'

'Sorry,' Enderby said. 'Careless of me.' He wiped himself with the sheet. 'I wonder what the time is.'

'Why? Why are you so eager to know what the time is? Do you want to be up and about so soon? A night in Seville. We both ought to have something to remember about a night in Seville.'

'They lit the sun,' said Enderby, 'and then their day began.'

'What do you mean? Why did you say that?'

'It just came to me. Out of the blue.' It seemed as though rhymes were going to start lining up. Began, plan, man, scan, ban. But this other thing had to be done now. She was not a bit like that blasted Vesta, spare-fleshed in bed so that she could be elegant out of it. There was plenty to get hold of here. He saw one of his bar-customers leering, saying that. Very vulgar. Enderby started to summon up old memories of what to do (it had been a long time). The Don himself seemed to hover over the bed, picking his teeth for some reason, nodding, pointing. Moderately satisfied, he flew off on an insubstantial hell-horse and, not far from the hotel, waved a greeting with a doffed insolent feathered *sombrero* at a statue of a man.

'They hoisted up a statue of a man,' mumbled Enderby.

'Yes, yes, darling, I love you too.'

Enderby now gently, shyly, and with some blushing, began to insinuate, that is to say squashily attempt to insert, that is to say. A long time. And now. Quite pleasant, really. He paused after five. And again. Pentameters. And now came an ejaculation of words.

> What prodigies that eye of light revealed!
> What dusty parchment statutes they repealed,
> Pulling up blinds and lifting every

A sonnet, a sonnet, one for a new set of *Revolutionary Sonnets*, the first of which was the one that bloody Wapenshaw had raged at. The words began to flood. He drew the thing out, excited.

'Sorry,' he said. 'I've got to get this thing down. I've got to get some paper. A sonnet, that's what it is.' There was, he thought, a hanging bulby switch-thing over the bed-head. He felt for it, trembling. Seville's velvet night was jeered out by a sudden coming of light. She was incredulous. She lay there with her mouth open, shocked and staring. 'I'll just get it down on paper,' promised Enderby, 'and then back on the job again. What I mean is –' He was out of bed, searching. Barman's pencil in his jacket-pocket. Paper? Damn. He dragged open drawers, looking for that white lining-stuff. It was all old Spanish newspaper, bull-fighters or something. Damn.

She wailed from the bed. Enderby dashed into the bathroom, inspired, and came out swathed in toilet-paper. 'This will do fine,' he smiled. 'Shan't be long. Darling,' he added. Then he sat at the dressing-table, horridly undressed, and began to write.

> Pulling up blinds and lifting every ban.
> The galaxies revolving to their plan,
> They made the coin, the couch, the cortex yield
> Their keys

'You're hateful, you're disgusting. I've never in my whole life been so insulted. No wonder she –'

'Look,' said Enderby, without turning round, 'this is important. The gift's definitely come back, thank God. I knew it would. Just give me a couple of minutes. Then I'll be in there again.' In the bed, he meant, raising his eyes to the dressing-table mirror as to make them tell her, if she was in that mirror, precisely that. He saw her all right. He ought, he knew, to be shocked by what he saw, but there was no time for that now. Hell has no fury. Better not let other poems get in the way. Besides, that quotation was wrong, everybody always got it wrong.

> And in a garden, once a field,
> They hoisted up a statue of a man.

'Finished the octave,' he sang out. 'Shan't be long now.'

'You filthy thing. You sexless rotter.'

'Really. Such language.' Mirror, terror, error. Pity there was no true rhyme for *mirror*, except that bloody Sir Launcelot thing Tennyson had pinched from Autolycus. 'And you a seleno–what–ever–it–is.'

'You won't get away with this. You wait.' And, dressing-gown decently about her, she was out through that door to Enderby's mild surprise, and was gone, slamming it.

'Look here,' Enderby said feebly. And then the mirror, holding out its English name, told him to get on with the sestet.

4

The sestet. It was all right, he thought. He told the Spanish dawn he thought it was all right. Then he had a swig of Fundador. Not all that much left. She'd put her name into it, that one, Miss whoever-it-was, moon-woman. He told the sestet to his reflection like an elocutionist:

> 'Of man, rather. To most it seemed a mirror:
> They strained their necks with gazing in the air,
> Proud of those stony eyes unglazed by terror.
> Though marble is not glass, why should they care?
> There would be time for coughing up the error.
> Someone was bound to find his portrait there.'

And the meaning? It seemed pretty clear, really. This was what happened in a humanist society. The Garden of Eden (and that was in the other sonnet, the one that had rendered bloody Wapenshaw violent) was turned into a field where men built or fought or ploughed or something. They worshipped themselves for being so clever, but then they were all personified in an autocratic leader like this Franco up there in Madrid. Humanism always led to totalitarianism. Something like that, anyway.

Enderby was moderately pleased with the poem, but he was more pleased with the prospect of a bigger structure, a sequence.

Some years before he had published the volume called *Revolutionary Sonnets*. The book had contained other than sonnets, but the title had derived from that opening group of twenty, each of which had tried to encapsulate – exploiting the theme and counter-theme paradigm of the Petrarchan form – some phase of history in which a revolution had taken place. He felt now that it might be possible to wrest those twenty sonnets from that volume and, by adding twenty more, build, with the cooperation of the Muse, a sizeable sequence which would make a book on its own. A new title would be needed – something more imaginative than the old one, something like *Conch and Cortex* or something. So far he had these two sonnets – the Garden of Eden one and the new one about man building his own world outside the Garden. Somewhere at the back of his mind there pricked the memory of his having started and then abandoned, in a very rough state, another sonnet that, nicely worked up and carefully polished, would make a third. It was, he thought, really an anterior sonnet to these two, an image of the primal revolution in heaven – Satan revolting, that sort of thing. Lucifer, Adam, Adam's children. Those would make the first three. He felt that, with a certain amount of drunkenness followed by crapulous meditation, that sonnet could be teased back to life. He was pretty sure that the rhymes, at least, would come marching back, in U.S. Army soft-soled boots, if he left the gate open. Octave: Lucifer fed up with the dead order and unity of heaven. Wants action, so has to conceive idea of duality. Sestet: he dives, creates hell to oppose heaven. Enderby saw him diving. An eagle dropping from a mountain-top in sunlight. Out of Tennyson, that. The wrinkled sea beneath him crawls. Alls, balls, calls. Was that one of the sestet rhymes?

He felt excited. He toasted himself in the last of the Fundador. That bloody woman. But there was time for shame now and for the desire to make amends. He thought he better go now to her room and apologize. He saw that it was not perhaps really all that polite to get out of bed and so on with a woman in order to write down a poem. Especially on toilet-paper brought in like triumphal streamers. Women had their own peculiar notion of priorities, and this had to be respected. But he had no doubt that she would see his point if properly explained. Suppose, he might say, she had suddenly spotted a new lunar crater while so engaged, would she not herself have leapt up as he had done? And then he could read his sonnet to her. He wondered whether it was worth while to dress properly for his visit. The dawn was mounting and soon the hotel would stir with insolent waiters coming to bedrooms with most inadequate breakfasts. But she might, thoroughly mollified by the sonnet, bid him back to bed again, her bed now, to resume what had, so to speak, that is to say. He blushed. He would go, as a film Don Juan he had once seen had gone, in open-necked shirt and trousers.

He went out on to the corridor, his sonnet wrapped round his wrist and one end secured with his thumb. Her room was just down there, on the same side as his own. When they had all, with Mr Mercer leading and Mr Guthkelch crying: 'Keep in step there, you horrible lot', marched up together, he had definitely seen her allotted that room there. He went up to it now and stood before it, taking deep breaths, and trying out a plenidental smile. Then he grasped the door-handle and boldly entered. Dawn light, the curtains drawn back, a room much like his own though containing luggage. She was lying in bed, possibly asleep, possibly – for every woman was supposed to be able to tell at once when there was an intruder, something to do with the protection of honour – pretending to be asleep. Enderby coughed loudly and said:

'I came to tell you I'm sorry. I didn't mean it. It just came over me, as I said.'

She started awake at once, more surprised, it seemed, than angry. She had changed her nightdress to demure cotton, also the colour of her hair. It was the aircraft's stewardess. Miss Kelly was the name. Enderby frowned on her. She had no right – But perhaps he had entered the wrong room. She said:

'Did you want something? I'm not really supposed to be available to passengers, you know, except on the flight.'

'No, no,' frowned Enderby. 'Sorry. I was after that other woman. The moon one. Miss Boolan.'

'Miss Boland. Oh, I see. It's your wrist, is it? You've got that thing round your wrist. You've cut your wrist, is that it? All the first-aid stuff's on the aircraft. The hotel people might be able to help you.'

'Oh, no, no, no,' Enderby laughed now. 'This is a poem, not an improvised bandage. I had to get up and write this poem, you understand, and I fear I annoyed Miss Boland, as you say her name is. I was going to apologize to her and perhaps read out this poem as a kind of peace-offering, so to speak. It's what is known as a sonnet.'

'It's a bit early, isn't it?' She slid down into her bed again, leaving just her head and eyes showing. 'I mean, everybody's supposed to be still asleep.'

'Oh,' Enderby smiled kindly, 'it's not that sort of poem, you know. You're thinking of an aubade – a good-morning song. The Elizabethans were very fond of those. Hark hark the lark, and so on. When all the birds have matins said, and so forth. A sonnet is a poem in fourteen lines. For any occasion, I suppose.'

'I know what a sonnet is,' her voice said, muffled but sharp. 'There's a sonnet in that book by Yod Crewsy.'

Enderby stood paralysed, his own sonnet held forward like a knuckle-duster. 'Eh?' Thoughts fell in at a great distance and, in British tommies' clodhoppers, advanced steadily at a light infantry pace.

'You know. You were asking about pop-singers on the plane. Vesta Wittgenstein you were asking about too, remember. Yod Crewsy did this book of poems that won the prize. There's one in it he calls a sonnet. I couldn't make head nor tail of it really, but one of the BOAC ground-hostesses, educated you see, she said it was very clever.'

'Can you,' faltered Enderby, 'can you remember anything about it?' Like Macbeth, he began to see that it might be necessary to kill everybody

'Oh, it's so early. And,' she said, a girl slow on the uptake, sitting up again, things dawning on her, 'you shouldn't be in here really at this hour. Not at any hour you shouldn't. Nobody asked you to come in here. I'll call Captain O'Shaughnessy.' Her voice was growing louder.

'One line, one word,' begged Enderby. 'Just tell me what it was about.'

'You're not supposed to be in here. It's taking advantage of being a passenger. I'm not supposed to be rude to passengers. Oh, why don't you go?'

'About the devil and hell and so on? Was that it?'

'I've had enough. I'm going to call Captain O'Shaughnessy.'

'Oh, don't bother,' groaned Enderby. 'I'm just going. But it's liberty after liberty.'

'You're telling *me* it's taking a liberty.'

'First one thing and then another. If he's dead I'm glad he's dead. But there'll be other heads rolling, I can tell you that. Did it have something about an eagle in it? You know, dropping from a great height?'

Miss Kelly seemed to be taking a very deep breath, as though in preparation for shouting. Enderby went, nodding balefully, closing the door. In the circumstances, he did not much feel like calling on Miss Boland. Women were highly unpredictable creatures. No, that was stupid. You could predict them all right. He had thought he would never have to see blasted treacherous Vesta again, but he obviously had to confront her before he did her in. The future was filling itself up horribly. Things both monstrously necessary and sickeningly irrelevant. He wanted to get on with his poetry again.

4

1

Calm, calm. Enderby reflected that it was morning and he was up and there was nothing to prevent his engaging Seville in the doing of what had to be done. First, a question of pesetas. Unshaven, dirty-shirted, otherwise respectable, he asked the day-porter of the hotel, yawning to his duty, where sterling might be changed. He asked in Italian, which, thanks to the Roman Empire, the porter clearly understood. Enderby had some idea that it was forbidden by the British government, treacherously in league with foreign bankers (even Franco's fiscal thugs), to present naked pounds in any Continental place of official monetary transaction. They found you had more pound-notes on you than you ought, by law, to have, and then, by various uncompassionate channels, they reported you to the Chancellor of the Exchequer, an insincerely smiling man Enderby had once seen with a woman in Piggy's Sty. In Italy that time, on his brief and dummy honeymoon, it had been travellers' cheques, which were all right. The porter, in mime and basic Romance, told Enderby that there was a barber round the corner who gave a very good rate of exchange. Enderby felt a little ice cube of pleasure, soon to be pounced on and demolished by the hot water he was in. He needed a shave, anyway. A barber of Seville, eh? 'Figaro?' he asked, momentarily forgetting his actual, and other people's proleptic, trouble. Not Figaro, said the unliterary and literal porter. He was called Pepe.

The barber breathed hard on Enderby as he shaved him, a sour young man smelling of very fresh garlic. He seemed not unwilling to change fifty pounds of Enderby's money, and Enderby wondered if the suspiciously clean pesetas he got were genuine. The world was terrible really, full of cheating and shadiness, as much in low as in high places. He tested his pesetas in a dirty eating-den full of loud dialogue (the participants as far away from each other as possible: one man tooth-picking at the door, another hidden in the kitchen, for instance). Enderby asked for *ovos* which turned out to be *huevos*, and for *prosciutto*, not cognate with *jamón*. He was learning essential words: he would not starve. He changed a big note with no trouble, receiving back a fistful of small dirty rags. Then, on the counter, he saw a copy of a newspaper called *Diario Pueblo*.

How often had he, on the day of publication of a volume of his verse (or the day before, if publication day had been Monday), gone to the quality papers as to a condemned cell, his stomach sick and his legs pure angelica. Usually there was no review, poetry being left to accumulate in literary editors' offices until there was enough of it for one expert to do a single clean sweep in a grudging brief article, everybody – Enderby, poetesses, poetasters, Sir George Goodby – all fluffed up together. But once, surprisingly, there had been a prompt solus of condemnation, all for Enderby, in a very reputable paper. Since then, the smell of newsprint had always made him feel slightly giddy. The fear he felt now was strong enough, since it was to do with his appearance in a context of action, but it was mitigated somewhat by the fact of the newspaper's foreignness. It seemed a very badly put together newspaper, with a lot of news items boxed in thick black, as though they were all obituaries. '*Scusa*,' he said to the curled dark youth who took his money. And then he looked for news of himself.

He did not have far to look. It was on the front page. There was, thank God, no photograph, but there were frightful succinct words, as though from some sensational foreign novel. *Chocante. Horroroso*. Come, that was going too far. *Delante del Primer Ministro Británico*. They had to bring that in, make it political. *Banquete para celebrar* something or other. And then *Yod Crewsy, cuadrillero de los Fixers*. Was he dead, then? What was 'dead' – *morto*? No, Enderby concluded from both his Spanish pseudonym and his eggs, now repeating violently, it must be *muerto*. References to a *revólver*, very clear that, and to a *tiro* and – what the hell was this? – an *escopetazo*. And then it said: *La víctima, en grave estado, fué conducido al* some *hospital* or other, English name for it all messed up. Not *muerto* yet, then. Enderby was horrified at feeling cheated. All this upset for just *en grave estado*. Still, that might be pretty bad. Then it said something about *Scotland Yard buscando* something something *un camarero*. He knew what that was: Spanish John had once or twice been hailed by that title facetiously by men and women who had been to the Costa del Sol. John had always responded readily, gleaming in complaisant dentition, all of gold. And now it was he, Enderby, who was the *camarero*. He was wanted, the paper said, to *ayudar* the *policía* in their *investigación*. Well, he'd already helped, hadn't he? He'd sent them the name of the true attempted *matador*, or whatever it was. And now the newspaper gave Enderby's own abandoned other name, or a version of it. *Hagg*. That was hardly fair to that barely imaginable sweet woman.

Un camarero quien se llama Hagg. He now felt somewhat better, the eggs settling down, the reality of the thing confirmed, no bad dream. So he went out now, nodding politely to various walnut-skinned early-morning coffee-suckers, and looked on the *calle* for a general outfitter's shop. The cathedral bell banged once at him, as to announce that the fight was on. So he went and bought himself a drip-dry green *camisa*, a pair of cheap grey *pantalones*, and a very light *americana* or jacket of fawn moygashel. Also a tie or *corbata* of rather mouth-watering lime. He changed into these in a dark breadcrumby cubby-hole at the rear of the shop. He also bought a black Basque beret (ah, that took him back, back to the old gusty seaside days when he had fed the ungrateful gulls every perishing morning; happy days, before the horrible outside world's impinging, pressing, overpowering). Also a little overnight bag to put his Hogg clothes in. *Hagg*, indeed. He couldn't help laughing. Also a razor and blades. And a kind of superstructure of plain anti-sun lenses to clip on to his spectacles. Then he sat outside a café and drank Spanish gin and tonic while a shoeblack blacked his shoes. He counted what money he had left in sterling and pesetas. Not a lot, really, though the shoeblack seemed to think so: his hands performing busily away, he gave money-counting Enderby close attention, as if he were a conductor. And then Enderby saw her, Miss Boland, walking down the *calle* with arms full of little toys and dolls bought from street-vendors.

Of course, she had as much right to be here as he had, if not more. And so had various other members of the tour who were walking down this main street (the hotel just around the corner), probably newly released from breakfast. There was even Mr Guthkelch over there on the pavement opposite, full of gummy fun though inaudible because of the traffic. Enderby stood up, one foot still on the cleaner's box, and shyly waved at her with both arms. She recognized him, despite his new smartness, and looked grim. She seemed fifteen years older than last night, also very thin, as though wasting away. Her summer dress was suitable for the warm southern autumn, but very dowdy − a blue flowery sack with string defining her waist. Having given Enderby a filthy look, she was prepared to walk on, but Enderby cried:

'It was inspiration, that's what it was, inspiration. Can't you see that? That hadn't happened to me for years. And I came round to your room, but the door was locked, and I −'

'Don't shout,' she hissed. 'Don't shout at me. For that matter, don't speak to me. Do you understand? I don't want to see you again. Ever. I want to make that clear, here and now. I don't know you and I don't want to know you.' She prepared to move

on. Enderby put pesetas on the table, leaving their apportion-
ment to waiter and shoeblack, and then grabbed her arm. He
said:

'I know precisely how you must feel.' He found he had left his
overnight bag on the table, so he went back to get it. 'How you
must feel,' he panted, 'but just think,' panting to keep up with her
long strides. 'It was you who brought the gift back. You. The
excitement. I didn't dare lose that poem. It meant so much. It was
you. The poem was you.' He marvelled at himself. 'I knew you'd
understand.' She shook her body impatiently, as if to shake him,
Enderby, away, and a small clockwork goose, with articulated neck,
fell from her arm to the pavement. Enderby picked it up and the
beak came off. He panted worse than ever. He said: 'In my bag.
Put these things in my bag. See, I bought this bag this morning.
I got up early and bought things, including this bag. But I'll take
my things out, if you like, and you can use the bag for putting
your things in.'

She began to cry, still walking down the *calle*. A swarthy man
saw her tears and looked with distaste on Enderby. 'Oh, you're
horrible,' she said.

'I'll buy you another goose,' promised Enderby. 'Though it wasn't
my fault it broke,' he added, justly. 'Look, give me those dolls and
things and they can all go in my bag.'

She wanted to dry her eyes but couldn't, her arms being full of
toys. Who were they for? Perhaps a maternal lust had welled up in
her suddenly, thought Enderby with fear. Perhaps she was looking
ahead. Perhaps any man would do. He had read of such matters. She
was buying playthings for children yet unborn. Enderby said eagerly:

'I wanted to read you the poem, but I couldn't get in.' Then
he saw that that particular poem, with its tabloid history, would
not have done. He was slow in learning about women. Only a
love poem could placate her. Had he anything in stock? 'See,' he
said, 'look. There's a horse and carriage thing.' A *coche* was creaking
along, drawn by a glossy sugar-fed mare. 'We'll go for a drive in
that, and you can tell me how horrible I am.'

'Oh, leave me alone, go away.' But she wanted to wipe her
cheeks. The coachman, a lined, knowing, very old man, had stopped
in response to Enderby's eager look.

'Get in,' Enderby said, pushing her. A small tin tortoise prepared to dive from her arm. Enderby saved it and made it nest in his bag, along with the goose. Life was terrible, really. 'Go on, get in,' he said, more roughly. And then: 'I've told you I'm sorry. But you can't get in the way of a poem. Nobody can.' So then, sniffing, she got in. 'The way of a poem,' Enderby said, 'passes all human understanding.' The cathedral bell clanged a sort of amen. And so they were trotted off gently, and she was able to dry her eyes.

'It could have waited,' she said. She began to look plumper again; she was becoming near-mollified. They turned right down a narrow street of pleasant yellow houses with balconies, empty, at this hour, of coy serenaded señoritas.

'A kind of sprung rhythm,' said Enderby. He now thanked God, or *Dios* as He was here, that some crude lines from an apprentice poem came wriggling back. 'Listen.' He gave her them in counterpoint to jaunty bouncing crupper with its blue-ribboned tail:

> 'I sought scent, and found it in your hair;
> Looked for light, and it lodged in your eyes;
> So for sound: it held your breath dear;
> And I met movement in your ways.'

'I see what you mean.' She was quick to forgive, a bit too quick. She was thinking of her holiday; Enderby was primarily for holiday use. And on holiday my dear I met this poet. Really? A poet, just imagine. 'But even so.'

'That time will come again, often.' Oh no, it bloody well wouldn't. The ghost of Juan was in the sunlit streets approving his proposed desertion. 'Whereas the time for paying homage – to your beauty, that is –'

'Oh, you *are* a pig, aren't you?' She came up close to him. 'A dirty pig, a *puerco puerco*. Piggy.'

'Don't call me that.'

'Hog, then. Hoggy.' Enderby sweated. 'Perhaps,' she said, 'we could get off soon and have a drink. I'm terribly thirsty.'

'It's the crying that does it. A big thirst-maker is crying.' He remembered his stepmother jeering at him when she'd clouted his earhole and made him howl: *Go on, cry more and you'll pee less.* 'A loss of liquid, you see. It needs replacing.'

2

They had lunch at an open-air café place, and of course it had to be paella. She had read about this in some coloured supplement as being one of the glories of the Spanish cuisine, but Enderby considered that never in his life had he been served with anything so insolent. It was warm sticky rice pudding embedded with strips of latex and small gritty seashells. Before it they had cold tomato soup full of garlic. She giggled and said: 'It's a good thing we're both having garlic.' Enderby choked on that, but later choked harder on both a seashell and her saying: 'Oh, look, there's a little man selling newspapers. Do let's have a Spanish newspaper. I've got my little dictionary with me.' He choked so frightfully at the vendor that the vendor went off.

'Has something gone the wrong way? Have a drink of your nice wine.' It was *not* nice wine: it tasted of ink and alum and eels and catarrh. 'Oh, I did so want a newspaper.'

'Lies,' snarled Enderby. 'Spanish bloody lies. All propaganda and censorship. You're not to have one, do you hear?'

'Darling Hoggy. Quite the heavy husband, aren't you? Perhaps there was fault on both sides.'

'What do you mean?'

'Your wife.'

'Oh, her.' He sourly tongued wine-lees from his palate. 'She's got a lot to answer for. Plagiarism, apart from anything else.' As soon as he got to Morocco he would get hold of that book. Some effete expatriate writer would probably have it.

'Plagiarism?'

'Oh, never mind.' He had gone too far, or nearly had. 'I don't want to talk about it.'

'Perhaps she didn't like your poem-writing habits.' Miss Boland had had too much of this adenoidal wine-substitute. Enderby scowled at her. 'No poems tonight, hm?'

'That,' said Enderby, with a kind of reproving leer, 'I can promise.'

'Oh, good heavens, look at the time. There won't be any tonight at all if we don't get back to the hotel. The coach leaves at one-thirty.'

Enderby paid the bill, leaving no tip. It had been a horrible meal and it was a horrible place, full of eroded statues and stunted trees. She squeezed his arm, linking him, as he went to the pavement's edge to call at any vehicle that looked like a taxi. One taxi already had Miss Kelly and two uniformed men, pilot and copilot probably, in it. Miss Kelly clearly recognized Enderby but did not smile or wave. A damned silly girl. Enderby thought he would mention that business of the wrong room to Miss Boland, but then he decided not. The female temperament was a strange one.

At last a taxi took them to the Hotel Marruecos, where tour-members were already assembling at the entrance, luggage all about them. Miss Boland had to rush to her room to see about hers, not quite finished packing. Enderby saw another newspaper-seller hovering and gave him a five-peseta note to go away. Things would be all right, but for God's sake let things be hurried up. Mr Guthkelch had bought a pair of castanets and was fandangoing clumsily, clumsily clacking them. The man with the condoms in his luggage looked very tired, but his wife was erect, in rude health. Mr Mercer counted and recounted and stopped counting when Miss Boland appeared, flushed and panting, a porter bearing her bags. And then the coach came and then they were off.

The airport was full of gloomy British travellers from Gibraltar, and they were being punished for that by being made to wait a long time for customs clearance. So, anyway, their courier whined to Mr Mercer, whom he seemed to know as an old pal in the game. And then Mr Mercer's lot marched across the tarmac and Miss Boland, God be praised, was a little sleepy after the wine. There was Miss Kelly waiting to welcome them all aboard again, but she had no welcome for Enderby. Mr Mercer came round with immigration forms, and they took off. It was a lovely golden Spanish afternoon.

Courteously, Enderby gave Miss Boland the window-seat he had had on the first leg of the journey. She slept. Enderby slept. Enderby was awakened. A uniformed man, pilot or co-pilot, was bending over him. He was a thick man, not old, jowled with good living, hangoverishly bloodshot. 'Is your name,' he said, his rather hairy hand on Enderby's shoulder, 'Enderby?'

Enderby could do no more than feebly nod. So, then, radio messages were crackling all over the world's air. Wapenshaw had talked, killing in childish spite his own handiwork.

'I'm the pilot of this aircraft. You'll appreciate I have certain responsibilities.' O'Shaughnessy then, but it was not an Irish voice. Enderby said, voicelessly:

'I'll come quietly. But I didn't do it. I just took his gun without thinking.'

'Well, perhaps it might be better if you *did* think a bit, man of your age. She's my responsibility as a member of my crew. I won't have passengers taking advantage.'

'Oh, that. You mean that.' Enderby's relief was vented in a cough of laughter.

'It may be just a bit of a holiday lark to you, but this is our work. This is what we do for a living. We take our work seriously, but you don't help much with that sort of liberty-taking.'

'I took no liberty,' Enderby said with heat. 'I made a mistake. I went to the wrong room. The room I meant to go to was the room of this lady here.' He jerked his eyes and thumb at Miss Boland and saw she was awake.

'Make a habit of going to ladies' rooms, do you? Well, if it was a mistake you took long enough apologizing for your mistake. She said something about you spouting poetry about putting the devil in hell and whatnot. Now, I may be only an ignorant pilot, as you'd think me, I suppose, but I've read that thing about putting the devil in hell. The Cameron it's called.' There were many passengers straining to listen, but the engines were loud. But Captain O'Shaughnessy was becoming loud too.

'The Dee Cameron,' said Enderby. 'Look, she's been telling you lies.'

'We've never had any complaints before about passengers' behaviour. I don't want to be nasty, but it's my duty as pilot of this aircraft to give you fair warning. Any more of this interfering with Miss Kelly and I must ask you to leave the tour. I'm sorry, but there it is.'

'It's a tissue of lies,' said flushed Enderby. 'I demand an apology.'

'There it is. I take full responsibility. So no more messing about. Is that clear?'

'I'll give you messing about,' cried Enderby. 'If I could get off now I would. But I'm getting off at Marrakesh anyway. It's an insult and an injustice, that's what it is.' Captain O'Shaughnessy jerked a salute at Miss Boland and went back to his engines. 'That's what one's up against all the time,' said Enderby to Miss Boland. 'It makes me sick.'

'All the time,' said Miss Boland. 'It makes you sick.'

'That's right. It was the wrong room, as I said.'

'As you said. And now would you kindly sit somewhere else? Otherwise I shall scream. I shall scream and scream and scream. I shall scream and scream and scream and scream and scream.'

'Don't do that,' said Enderby, very concerned. 'Darling,' he added.

'How dare you. *How dare you.*' She pressed the little bell-push up above.

'What did you do that for?' asked Enderby.

'If you won't go you must be made to go. I'm defiled just by sitting next to you.' Miss Kelly, wisely, did not come to the summons. Mr Mercer came, sad and troubled in his woolly cap. 'You,' said Miss Boland. 'Make this man sit somewhere else. I didn't come on this tour to be insulted.'

'Look,' said Mr Mercer to Enderby. 'I didn't say anything about that other business. It's the captain's responsibility, not mine. But this sort of thing is something that I'm not supposed to let happen. I made a big mistake having you on this, I did that. Now will you be told?'

'If you won't do something,' said Miss Boland, 'I'll scream.'

'Don't worry,' said Enderby. 'I'll go. I'll go into that lavatory there.' He got up and took his bag and beret from the rack. There were toys still in the bag. Enderby gravely dropped them into Miss Boland's lap – tortoise, beakless goose, flamenco doll, cymbal-pawed clockwork brown bear. She at once became thin and evil and ready to throw these things at Enderby, crying:

'He's hateful. No woman is safe with him. Throw him out.' Many of the passengers looked on with interest, though not well able to understand, or even hear, what was proceeding. Behind, the condom overweight man and his wife sat stiffly, still not on

speaking terms. They refused to be interested in the Miss Boland–
Enderby trouble, though it was just in front of them, since showing
interest would have drawn them into a common area of attention,
which would have been rather like, or indeed might have led to,
being on speaking terms again. Enderby stood stony in the corridor,
swaying with the plane in a slight air turbulence (the Mountains
of the Moon perhaps, or something), waiting for instructions. To
the condom man's wife, who was in the outer seat, Mr Mercer
said:

'I wonder if you'd mind, Mrs er, changing places with this er.
It's only for a short while, really. We're not all that far from Marrakesh
now.'

'Men on holiday. Brings the beast out as you might call it. *I
know*. I have no objection if she there hasn't.' And, getting up, she
gave Enderby a murderous look which he considered unfair, since
he had, after all, been the instrument of disclosure of her husband's
beastliness, meaning the truth. As she sat down grunting next to
Miss Boland, Enderby saw that she had an English newspaper folded
to what looked like a simple crossword puzzle. She had a ballpoint,
but she did not seem to have filled anything in yet. He leaned
across her bosom to squint at the date and saw that, as far as he
could judge, it was yesterday's. That was all right, then. Before that
lot happened. And then he saw that it was the *Evening Standard*
and it was not all right. He said to this woman, leaning over more
deeply:

'Where did you get that? Give it me, quick. I must have it.
Something I've got to see.'

'Right,' said Mr Mercer. 'Go and sit down quietly behind next
to this lady's husband. We don't want any more trouble, do we now?'

'Cheek,' said the woman. 'It was left in the ladies at the airport
by one of them Gibraltar people. I've as much right to it as what
he has.'

'Oh, please go on now,' said Mr Mercer in distress. 'If you can't
hold it you shouldn't take it. A lot of this foreign stuff's stronger
than what many are used to.'

'*She* may be drunk,' said Enderby, shoulder-jerking towards Miss
Boland, 'but I'm not, thank you very much. All I want to see is
that paper. Something in it. A book review, very important. And

then I'll go to that lavatory and sit there quietly.' Seeing Miss Boland gasp in a lot of air to revile him further, he made a grab for the newspaper. The condom man's wife strengthened her hold.

'For God's sake,' said Mr Mercer, uncourierlike, 'let him see what he wants to see and then let's get him out of the way.'

'I want to find it myself,' said Enderby. 'I don't need her to show it me.'

'And who's *her* when she's at home?' said the woman. Miss Boland looked cunning and said:

'Let *me* see. There's something very fishy about all this. Running away from his wife, so he said.'

'Really? Told you, did he?'

'Let *me* see.' And Miss Boland, unhandily in the manner of all women with a newspaper, unfolded the *Evening Standard*, and the safe backwater of small ads and cartoons and crossword gave place, after a rustling tussle, to the horrid starkness of front page news. There it was, then. Enderby gulped it all in like ozone.

'Oh,' said the woman, 'I never seen that. Oh terrible, that, oh my word.'

'Yes,' said Miss Boland. 'Terrible.'

A screaming banner announced the shooting of Yod Crewsy. In hour of triumph. In Premier's presence. Waiter believed assailant. There was a large blurred photograph of Yod Crewsy with stretched gob or cakehole, but whether shot or just singing was not indicated. There was also a still photograph of the Prime Minister looking aghast, probably taken from stock. No picture, thank God, of waiter believed assailant. But Miss Boland was reading avidly on. Enderby had to now or never. He leaned over the condom man's wife and grabbed. The paper did not tear: he got the thing whole. He said:

'Very important review. Book page, book page,' rustling tremulously through. 'Oh, stupid of me. Wrong day for book page.' And then, as though an issue without the book page were an insult to the literate, he crumpled the *Evening Standard* into a ball.

'That's going too far,' said Mr Mercer.

'You mannerless thing,' said the woman. 'And that poor lad dead, too.'

'Not yet,' said Enderby unwisely. 'Not dead yet.'

'Hogg.' That was Miss Boland.

'Eh?' Enderby looked at her with bitter admiration. He had been right, then; he had known all along this would happen.

'Hogg. *Puerco*. That's why you're on the run.'

'She's mad,' Enderby told Mr Mercer. 'I'm going to the lavatory.' He began to unball the paper and smooth it out. She had seen the name Hogg; the only thing to do now was to insist that he was not Hogg. There was no point in hiding the fact that Hogg was wanted to assist in a police inquiry. If, that is, one were oneself not Hogg. And one was not, as one's passport clearly showed. Enderby nearly drew out his passport, but that would look too suspiciously eager to prove that he was not Hogg. A lot of people were not Hogg, and they did not have to keep presenting their passports to prove it.

'The police,' said Miss Boland. 'Send a radio message to the airport. He did it. That's why he's run away.'

'I don't have to put up with all this, do I?' said Enderby with a show of weariness.

'He said all the time that he hated pop-singers.'

'That's not true,' said Enderby. 'All I said was that you mustn't necessarily regard me as an enemy of pop-art.'

'Jealousy,' said Miss Boland. 'A bad poet jealous of a good one. And what was that you said just then about a gun? I'm quite sure I didn't dream it.' She seemed very calm now, glinting, though breathing heavily.

'I'll give you bad poet,' said Enderby, preparing to shout. 'If there's any good in that book of his, it's because it's been pinched from me. That bitch. Plagiarism. I hope he dies, because he deserves to die.'

'Look,' said Mr Mercer. 'We don't want any trouble, right? This is supposed to be for pleasure, this cruise is. Will you both stop shouting the odds? If there's anything to be seen to I'll see to it, right?'

'If you don't,' said Miss Boland, 'I will. I will in any case. He killed him, no doubt about it. He's as good as admitted it.'

'Who's a bitch?' said the condom wife, belatedly. 'Who was he saying was a bitch? Because if he was meaning me —'

'I'm going to the lavatory,' said Enderby. Mr Mercer did not attempt to stop him; indeed, he followed him. The crumpled *Evening*

Standard had somehow reached Miss Kelly. She was spelling all that front page out, reserving her reaction till she had taken everything in. Just by the lavatory door Mr Mercer said:

'What's going on with her down there? Is she potty or what?'

'A matter of sex,' Enderby said. 'I spurned her advances. I don't think it's decent the way she carries on, and me with my mother dying in Marrakesh.'

'Look,' said Mr Mercer without sympathy. 'You shouldn't rightly be on this plane at all, as you well know, and I'm bloody sorry I let you come on it. It was a bit of a fiddle, and I think I've learned my lesson now about that sort of thing. Now she's going on about you being a dangerous criminal, which sounds to me like a load of balls. You've not been killing anybody, have you?'

'I have enough on my hands,' said Enderby gravely, 'with a dying mother.'

'Right then. I'll get her calmed down and I'll tell her that I'm doing whatever has to be done. The police and that. The customers have got to be satisfied, that's laid down in the rules. Now it won't be long to Marrakesh now, so I'll tell you what I'll do with you. You nip off before everybody else, see, because I'll let you.'

'Thanks very much,' said Enderby.

'I'll keep them all back till you have time to get away. I don't want her on the job again, howling murder and upsetting the other mugs,' said Mr Mercer frankly. 'So you'll find three taxis laid on specially for the tour. They take one lot to the Hotel Maroc and then keep coming back for the rest. Well, you get into one and get the driver to drop you wherever it is you want to be dropped and then send him back to the airport, right? How far is it you have to go?'

'Near that place where Winston Churchill used to stay,' said Enderby with sudden inspiration.

'Not too far then, that isn't. And then,' said Mr Mercer, 'that'll be the end as far as you and me and everybody else is concerned. Got that?'

'That suits me well enough,' said Enderby.

'You'd better get in there, then. Look, she looks like getting up to start asking for immediate action. Summary execution and that.

You thrown out into the bleeding slipstream. You sure you done nothing wrong?'

'Me,' said Enderby, 'with a dying mother?'

'You don't look the type, anyway. Get in there. If anybody else wants to go I'll have to tell them to let it bake till we get to Marrakesh. I wish,' said Mr Mercer with large sincerity, 'I'd never bloody well set eyes on you.' Enderby bowed his head. 'Mysterious fascination for women, eh? Now get yourself locked in there.'

It was better in the lavatory, an interim of most delectable peace and quiet. All Enderby could hear was the engines except for a brief phase of shock and howling from Miss Kelly. She was, it seemed, sorry that Yod Crewsy had been shot. Then she appeared to have got over it.

3

Mint, mint, mint. It was too easy to think that, though the immigration official waved him through when he cried: '*Ma mère est mortellement malade,*' though the leading taxi opened up smartly for him when he mentioned *Monsieur Mercer*, he was destined for the butcher's block. The sun was about half way down the sky, but it was still up to Regulo Mark 4 and there was all this mint. The memory fumed in of his once trying out a small leg of fatty New Zealand in Mrs Meldrum's gas oven. It had emerged not well-cooked, and he had made a stew out of it. You could not really go wrong with a stew. There had been a lot of grease to skim off, though. The driver, a Moor as Enderby took him to be, was stewy in the armpits – no, more like a tin of Scotch Broth. But he was fumigating himself and his cab with a home-rolled cigarette that reeked of decent herbs, though possibly hallucinogenic. He also rolled his eyes. Soon, Enderby considered, the time must come for jettisoning his Enderby passport. Miss Boland would soon be uncovering aliases to the police. He could not be Hogg, he could not be Enderby. The nasty world outside had succeeded in taking pretty well everything away from him. Except his talent, except that.

A well-made road with trees, probably bougainvillea and

eucalyptus and things. And plenty of mint. Also people in turbans, caftans, nightgowns with stripes, and what-you-call-them djelabas. The driver drove with the automatism of a pony pulling a trap, though much faster, his being not to reason why Enderby had to reach the tour hotel before everyone else. It was time to tell him some other place to go. Enderby said:

'*Je veux aller à Tanger.*'

'*Demain?*'

'*Maintenant.*'

'*Impossible.*'

'*Regardez,*' Enderby said, 'I'm not going to that bloody hotel. *Une femme. Une question d'une femme. Il faut que j'évite une certaine femme.*'

With care the driver steered his cab round the next corner and stopped by the kerb. His hand-brake ground painfully. '*Une femme?*' It was a pleasant little residential avenue full of mint. But down it a bare-legged man in Sancho Panza hat and loose brown clouts urged a laden donkey. '*Tu veux une femme?*'

'Just the opposite,' said Enderby, frowning at the familiarity. '*J'essaie à éviter une femme, comme j'ai déjà dit.*'

'*Tu veux garçon?*'

'Let's get this straight,' cried Enderby. 'I want to get away. *Comment puis-je* get to bloody Tangier?'

The driver thought about that. '*Avion parti,*' he said. '*Chemin de fer* –' He shrugged. Then he said: 'You got money, Charlie?'

'I thought it would come to that,' said Enderby. He brought out his small bundle of old international tips. What was the currency here? There were a couple of notes with a bland capped and robed ruler on them, *Banque du Maroc,* and a lot of Arabic. What were these? Dirhams. He had, it seemed, ten dirhams. He didn't know how much they were worth. Still, resourceful Enderby. Ready cash for all emergencies of travel. The driver was quick to grab the ten dirhams. He pushed them, as if he were a woman, into his un-buttoned hair-whorled brown breast. Then he cheerfully started up his cab again. 'Where are we going?' Enderby wanted to know. The driver didn't answer; he just drove.

Enderby was past being uneasy, though. After all, what was he trying to do except borrow time against the inevitable? If Yod

Crewsy died, well then, he, his supposed murderer, could only be put in jail for a long period, the death penalty having kindly been abolished. And in jail poetry could be written. There would be ghastly stews, but he knew all about those. Great things had been written in jail – *Pilgrim's Progress, De Profundis*, even *Don Quixote*. Nothing to worry about there. Slops out. Here's your skilly, you horrible murderer, you. Snout-barons. What you in for, matey? I murdered a practitioner of foul and immoral art. You done a good job, then, you did. But, sheep for a lamb (all this mint, mint everywhere), he had things to do first. They had to catch him first, and it was up to him, rules of the game, to make things difficult. They drove down a great smooth highway, then turned right. It was all French colonialism, with decent official buildings, green lawns, palms. Little Moroccan girls were coming out of school, gaily shrieking, and some were sped off home to their mint tea, as Enderby supposed, in haughty squat automobiles. But soon the road changed its character. Instead of shooting cleanly along an artery, the cab began to engage a capillary that was pure, and dirty, Moorish.

'Where are we going?' asked Enderby again.

'*Djemaa el Fna*,' said the driver. This meant nothing to Enderby. They were now honking among fruit-barrows, donkey-whippers, brown and black vociferators in pointed hoods and barmcake turbans and even little woolly caps like Mr Mercer's. The faecal-coloured houses and windowless shops (loaves, strangled fowls, beads, egg-plants) bowed in towards each other at the top. Somebody wailed about Allah in the near distance. It was what was known as very picturesque, all laid on for Winston Churchill as amateur painter. Then, shouted at through gold or no teeth, the cab-flanks resonantly fisted, they drove into a great square which was full of robed people and very loud. There seemed to be native shows going on: Enderby glimpsed a fire-swallower and a man who let snakes crawl all over his person. Then, above the heads of the crowd, a small black boy went up into the air, wiggled his fingers from his ears, then sailed down again. Enderby did not really like any of this. The driver stopped and, with a vulgar thumb, pointed to where Enderby should go. It seemed to be a soft-drink stall, one of many set all about the square. He shooed Enderby out.

Enderby got out, bag on arm, groaning. The driver did an urgent and insolent turn, butting bare shins with deformed fenders and, cursed at by some but greeted toothily and, Enderby presumed, with ribaldry by others, probed the crammed barefoot alley whence he had come. He honked slowly among thudded drums and weak pipe-skirls, fowl-squawks and ass-brays, then was smothered by nightshirts and most animated robes, pushing his way back to a world where an airport, complete with waiting Miss Boland, might be possible. Enderby encountered blind men howling for baksheesh. He brutally ignored them and made his shoes pick their way among great splay brown feet towards this soft-drink stall that had been thumbed at him. He would have a soft drink, anyway. No harm in that. And that climbed hill of an act would show the next one. But just by the stall, newly disclosed by a small mob that came away chewing things, probably nasty, he saw a patriarch tending a small fire. A little boy, his head shaven as for ringworm, was threading rubbery gobs of what Enderby took to be goatmeat on to skewers. Enderby nodded in awed satisfaction. His imagination had not failed him, then. It was time to get rid of that passport.

He stood by the fire, the passport in his hands open, mumbling to himself the liturgy of its shards of autobiography. There were still so many blank pages of travelling Enderby to be filled, and they would not now be filled. He must appear, he thought, like some Zoroastrian missionary to these who skirted him warily in robes and yashmaks: murmuring a late afternoon office to the fire. And then, as he prepared to drop the well-bound document in, the act was, as by an Oriental miracle, arrested. A bony tanned wrist gripped his chubbier whiter one, pulled, saved. Enderby looked from wrist to shoulder, meekly surprised. Then up to face above that. A white man, though brown. Lined, crafty, the eyes blue but punished. The straight hair as though bleached.

'I was,' said Enderby with care, 'just getting rid of it. No further use, if you catch my meaning.'

'You cracked? You skirted? You got the big drop on? Grandmother of Jesus, I never seen.' The man was not old. His accent and vernacular were hard to place. It was a sort of British colonial accent. One hand still gripped Enderby's wrist; the other hand snatched the passport. The man then let go of Enderby and began to pant over the passport as if it were a small erotic book. 'Holy consecrated grandad of Christ Jesus Amen,' he said. 'And this is you too on it and the whole thing donk and not one little bit gritty. The genuine, and you ready to ash it up. If you don't want it, others as do. A right donk passy. Feel his uncle, O bastard daughters of Jerusalem.'

Enderby almost smiled, then felt cunning creeping along his arteries. 'I tried to sell it,' he said. 'But I could find no buyers. All I wanted was a trip to Tangier. No money, you see. Or not very much.'

'You better come over,' said the man. 'Ariff's got a swizer of that-there at the back.' And he led Enderby across to the very soft-drink stall that had been thumbed to him by that driver.

'Funny,' Enderby said. 'This man who brought me wanted me to wait there or something. I wondered what for.'

'Who? One of the cab-nogs? Ahmed, was it?'

'Don't know his name,' said Enderby. 'But I told him I had to get away.'

'You on the out, then? How did he know it was tonight? Some shitsack's been on the jabber.' He mumbled strange oaths to himself as he led Enderby over. The drink-stall was a square wooden structure covered in striped canvas. There was a counter with cloudy glasses and bottles of highly coloured liquids. There were oil-lamps, blind at the moment, since the sun had not yet gone down. A few Moors or Berbers or something were downing some sticky yellow horror. Behind the counter stood a lithe brown man in an undervest, snakes of veins embossed on his arms. Crinkled hair rayed out, as in shock, all over his bullet-head. 'Right,' said this British colonial man, 'swing us two bulgies of arry-arry.'

'Where do you come from?' asked Enderby. 'I can't quite place the accent. No offence,' he added hurriedly.

'None took. Name of Easy Walker. Call me Easy. Your name I know but I won't blart it. Never know who's flapping. Well now, you'll have heard of West Rothgar in New Sunderland. Fifty or so miles from the capital, boojie little rathole. Had to blow, see the great wide open. And that. And other things.' As if to symbolize the other things, he stretched his left mouth-corner, as also the left tendon of his neck, and held the pose tremulously. This, Enderby seemed to remember, was known as the ki-yike. Easy Walker then scratched his right ear with Enderby's passport and said: 'You sound to me like from back.' Enderby stared. Easy Walker snarled a full set in impatience. 'Great Dirty Mum,' he explained. 'How shall we extol thee?'

'I beg your pardon?'

'Who were born of thee,' danced Easy Walker. 'Here it is, then. Down the upbum or,' he said, in a finicking uncolonial accent, 'the superior arsehole.' There were on the counter two tumblers of what looked like oily water. Easy Walker seemed to wrap his lips round the glass-rim and, with a finger-thud on the glass-bottom, drive the substance down as though it were corned beef hard to prise from its container. He smacked in loving relish. Enderby tasted what tasted of aniseed, lubricator, meths, and the medicinal root his stepmother had called ikey-pikey. 'Similar,' Easy Walker told the barman. 'And now,' to Enderby, 'what's on? Why you on the out, brad?'

'You can't really say "similar" if it's the same again you want. "Similar" means something different. Oh, as for that,' Enderby recalled himself from pedantry that reminded him poignantly of those good seaside days among the decrepit, 'it's partly a matter of a woman.'

'Ark.' Easy Walker was not impressed.

'And,' Enderby bid further, 'the police are after me for suspected murder of a pop-star.'

'You do it?'

'Well,' said Enderby, 'I had the means and the motive. But I want to get to Tangier to see off an old enemy. Time is of the essence.'

This seemed reasonable to Easy Walker. He said: 'See that. Right right. Gobblers watching at the airport and on the shemmy. Clever bastard that cab-nog, then. Ahmed, must have been. Well,' he said, fanning Enderby with Enderby's passport, 'give me this and you can come on the lemon-pip by the long road. Fix you up in Tangey up the hill. No questions, get it? The gobblers leave it strictly on the old antonio. Wash me ends, though. Right up to you, brad. Never clapped mincers on you, get it?'

'Oh, yes,' Enderby said. 'Thank you very much. But,' he added, 'what are you on then, eh?'

'Well,' said Easy Walker, rolling his refilled tumbler. 'It's mostly Yank camps, junkies, had-no-lucks. See what I mean?'

'American troops in Morocco?' Enderby asked.

'Riddled,' said Easy Walker. 'All off the main, though. Forts, you could call them. Very hush. Moscow gold in Nigeria I mean Algeria. PX stuff – fridges mainly – for Casablanca and Tangey. That's why I've got this three-ton.'

'A lorry? Where?'

'Up the road. Never you mind.'

'But,' said Enderby with care, 'what are you doing here, then?'

'Well, that's the real soft centre,' Easy Walker said. 'See these niggers here? Not the Marockers, more brown they are than the others, the others being from more like *real* blackland.'

'The heart of darkness,' said Enderby.

'Call it what you like, brad. Berbers or Barbars. Barbar black shit, but no offence is what I tell them. They bring the stuff up with them for this here racketytoo.'

'What stuff? What is all this, anyway?'

'Everything,' said Easy Walker, with sudden lucidity, 'the heart of darkness could desire. Tales of Ali Baba and Sinbad the whatnot, and snake-charmers and all. Suffering arsehole of J. Collins, the sprids they get up to in this lot. Hear them drums?'

'Go on,' said Enderby.

Easy Walker did a mime of sucking in dangerous smoke and then staggered against the flimsy counter. The barman was lighting the lamps. 'Pounds and pounds of it, brad. I'm like telling you this because you won't gob. Daren't, more like, in your state of you-know-what. They grind up the seeds and nuts and it burns cold, real cold, like sucking ice-lollies. The Yank junks go bonko for it.'

'Drug addicts,' questioned Enderby, 'in army camps?'

'Drag too,' said Easy Walker calmly. 'Human like you and I, aren't they? Loving Aunt Flo of our bleeding Saviour, ain't you seen the world? What you on normal, brad? What you do?'

'I,' said Enderby, 'am a poet. I am Enderby the poet.'

'Poetry. You know the poetry of Arthur Sugden, called Ricker Sugden because he played on the old rickers?'

'I don't think so,' said Enderby.

'I know him all off. You can have the whole sewn-up boogong tonight on the road.'

'Thank you very much,' Enderby said. 'What time do we start?'

'Moon-up. Crounch first. You crounch with me. Little stoshny I got up this street of a thousand arseholes. Up above Hassan the hundred delights. Know what those are? Glycerine like toffees with popseeds, stickjaw that'll stick to your jaw, shishcakes and marhum. And I mean a thousand arseholes. Not my creed. Yours?'

'I don't like anything any more,' Enderby said. 'I just want to get on with the job.'

'Right, too. Ah, here comes the jalooty.' A sly black man came in. He grinned first then peered behind as he thought he feared he was being followed. He had a woolly cap on, a knee-length clout done up like a diaper, a stiff embroidered coat with food-stains on it. He carried a grey darned gunnysack. Easy Walker tucked away Enderby's passport in the breast-pocket of his shirt, then from the back-pocket of his long but creaseless canvas trousers he pulled out a wallet. 'This,' he told Enderby, 'is as it might be like my agent. Abu.' The black man responded to his name with a kind of salivation. 'Mazooma for pozzy, as my dad used to say. Died at Gallipoli, poor old reticule. It's my Aunt Polly as told me he used to say that. Never clapped mincers on him myself. Abu grabs what per cent he has a fish-hook on. Leave it to him.' To this Abu Easy Walker told out what appeared to Enderby to be no more than fifty dirhams. Then he took the gunnysack and shushed Abu off like a fly. 'Now then,' he said, his hand on Enderby's arm, leading him out of the flared and oil-lamped sinister gaiety of the evening, 'time for the old couscous. You like couscous?'

'Never had it,' said Enderby.

'The best one of Ricker Sugden's,' said Easy Walker, as they walked among baskets and moonfruit in the reek of lights, 'is The Song of the Dunnygasper. You not know that one, brad?'

'What,' asked Enderby, 'is a dunnygasper?' A youngish woman raised her yashmak and spat a fair gob among chicken-innards. Two children, one with no left leg, punched each other bitterly.

'A dunnygasper is a bert that cleans out a dunny. Now, the

pongalorum of a dunny is that bad that you'd lay out a yard in
full view if you drew it in in the way of normality. So he has to
like under water hold his zook shut then surface for a gasp. You
see that then?' An old man with a bashed-in turban tottered by,
crying some prayer to the enskied archangels of Islam. Easy Walker
started to recite:

> 'Gasping in the dunny in the dead of dark,
>> I dream of my boola-bush, sunning in the south,
> And the scriking of the ballbird and Mitcham's lark,
>> And bags of the sugarwasp, sweet in my mouth.'

'That's not bad,' said Enderby. 'Not much meaning, though.'
Meaning? Too much meaning in your poetry, Enderby. Archdevil
of the maceration of good art for pop-art. Kill, kill, kill. He could
be calm at soul, whatever justice said.

> 'For here in the city is the dalth of coves,
>> Their stuff and their slart and the fall of sin,
> The beerlout's spew where the nightmort roves
>> And the festered craw of the filth within.'

A moustached man, the veins of his head visible under a dark
nap, called hoarsely at Enderby and, with flapping hands, showed
small boys in little shirts lined up behind the lamp in his shop-
front. A woman squatted on a step and scooped with a wooden
spatula the scum from a seething pot on a pungent wood-fire.
   'That drink,' belched Enderby, 'whatever it was, was not a good
idea.'
   'Feel like a sack of tabbies when you've gooled up a pompey
of couscous.'
   Graaarch, went Enderby. Perfwhitt.

> 'God's own grass for this porrow in my tail,
>> Surrawa's lake for this puke and niff,
> Prettytit's chirp for the plonky's nipper's wail,
>> And the rawgreen growler under Bellarey's Cliff.'

'Rawcliffe,' growled green Enderby. 'It won't (errrrgh) be long now.'

Easy Walker stopped in his tracks. A beggar clawed at him and he cleaned the beggar off his shirt like tobacco ash. 'You say Rawcliffe, brad? Rawcliffe the jarvey you bid to chop?'

'Plagiarist, traitor (orrrph), enemy.'

'Runs a little beacho. Called the Acantilado something-or-the-next-thing. Not far from the Rif. Not there now, though. Very crookidy. Quacks pawing him all over on the Rock.'

'In Gibraltar? Rawcliffe? Ill?'

'Crookidy dook. He'll be back, though. Says if he's going to snuff he'll snuff in his own dung.'

'Rawcliffe,' said Enderby, 'is (orrrf ff) for me.'

'We're there,' said Easy Walker. 'Up that rickety ladder. Niff that juicy couscous. Yummiyum. Then we hit it. Moon's up, shufti.' Enderby saw it with bitterness. Miss Boland seemed to rage down from it.

'This jarvey Rawcliffe,' said Easy Walker, leading the way up the ladder, 'is some big kind of a jarvey. Big in films and that. You sure you know what you're on, brad?'

'I (arrrp) know,' said Enderby, following him up. A fresh beggar, wall-eyed, embraced his left leg passionately, shrieking for alms. Enderby kicked him off.

Part Two

1

Ali Fathi sat on the other bed and pared his footsoles with a table-knife honed to lethal sharpness on the window-sill. He was on the run from Alexandria, which he called Iskindiriyya, and was scornful of the Moors, whose language he considered debased. He himself spoke a sort of radio announcer's Arabic, full of assertive fishbone-in-the-throat noises and glottal checks that sounded like a disease. He was very thin, seemed to grow more and more teeth as time went on, and was always talking about food. '*Beed madruub*,' he said to Enderby now. He had a passion for eggs. '*Beeda masluugha*.' Enderby said, from his own bed:

'*Mumtaaz*.' He was learning, though not very quickly. It was hardly worth while to learn anything new. Soon, he saw, he must give up giving money to Wahab to buy the English newspapers that were sold on the Boulevard Pasteur. They were a terrible price, and money was fast running out. When the hell was Rawcliffe going to come back to be killed? He read once more the latest Yod Crewsy news. It could not be long now, they reckoned. Yod Crewsy was in a coma. Day and night vigils of weeping fans outside the hospital. Stones hurled at windows of No. 10 Downing Street. Probability of National Day of Prayer. Mass of Intercession at Westminster Cathedral. In Trafalgar Square protest songs, some of them concerned with the Vietnam war. Attempted suttee of desperate girls in a Comprehensive School.

'*Khanziir*.' That was not right, Ali Fathi being a Muslim, but Enderby himself would not have minded a nice plate of crisply grilled ham. His diet, and that of Ali Fathi and the other two men, Wahab and Souris, was very monotonous: soup of kitchen scraps and rice, boiled up by fat Napo in the snack-bar below, the odd

platter of fried sardines, bread of the day before yesterday. Enderby
was now sorry that he had exchanged his passport for a mere
jolting trip from Marrakesh to Tangier. He had discovered that
British passports fetched a very high price on the international
market. Why, this Ali Fathi here had looked at Enderby as if he
were mad when he had been told, in French, what small and
uncomfortable (as well as to him hazardous) service in lieu of
money Enderby had been willing to take in exchange for a valuable document. If he, Ali Fathi, had it he would not be here now.
He would be in Marseilles, pretending to be an Arabic-speaking
Englishman.

'*Beed maghli.*' He was back on eggs again. Well, that valuable
document, with its old identity razor-bladed and bleached out and
new substituted, was now at its charitable work in the world of
crime and shadiness. It was saving somebody from what was called
justice. It could not, nor could its former guardian (Her Majesty's
Government being the avowed owner, though it had not paid for
it) ask better than that. Enderby nodded several times. Encouraged,
Ali Fathi said:

'*Bataatis mahammara.*' That meant, Enderby knew now, potato
crisps. An inept term, soggy-sounding. It had been, Enderby admitted
to himself, a boring trip on the move under the moon (courtesy
of Miss treacherous bloody Boland), with Easy Walker reciting the
collected works of Arthur Sugden, called Ricker Sugden because
he had used, when composing his verses, to clash out the rhythm
with the castanetting bones once a percussive staple of nigger, christy
rather, minstrel shows. Easy Walker had given Enderby not only a
reprise of The Song of the Dunnygasper but also The Ballad of
Red Mick the Prancerprigger, The Shotgun Wedding of Tom
Dodge, Willie Maugham's Visit to Port Butters, My Pipe and Snout
and Teasycan, and other specimens of the demotic literature of an
apparently vigorous but certainly obscure British settlement.

'*Kurumba.*' Some vegetable or other, that. Cabbage, probably. And
then these American camps, off the main north-south motor route,
with torches flashing through the Moorish dark, a rustling in the
shadows and whispers as of love (money and goods changing hands),
the loading – Enderby cajoled to help – of refrigerators, huge cans
of butter, nitrited meatloaf, even military uniforms, all on to Easy

Walker's truck. And then more of Ricker Sugden – The Ditty of the Merry Poddyman, Wallop for Me Tomorrow Boys, Ma Willis's Knocking Shop (Knock Twice and Wink for Alice) – till the next call and, finally, what Easy Walker knew as Dear Old Tangey. Well, Easy Walker had at least found him what seemed a safe enough retreat off the Rue El Greco (many of the streets here were named for the great dead, as though Tangier were a figure of heaven) – no passports needed, no questions asked of guests or tolerated of casual visitors to bar below or brothel above, but, on the other hand, too much cash demanded in advance, too little to eat, the bedclothes never changed, not enough beds.

'*Shurbit tamaatim*,' watered Ali Fathi, still slicing thin shives, as of restaurant smoked salmon, from a footsole. At once, as though he had spoken of the source of gingili or benne oil, the doorhandle began to turn. He poised that knife at the ready. The door opened and Wahab came in. Smiling teeth popped and rattled as the two men embraced, full of loud throaty crooning greeting, yum yum yum and the voice clearing of phlegm from pharyngeal tracts. Enderby looked with distaste on this, not caring much for sex of any kind these days really, for himself or for anybody else. Ali Fathi hugged his friend, knife still clutched in a hand that knuckled his friend's vertebrae, all his teeth displayed in glee to Enderby. Enderby said coldly:

'*Le patron de l' Acantilado Verde, est-il revenu?*'

'*Pas encore*,' said Wahab's back. Wahab was a Moor, hence his mind was despised by Ali Fathi, but his body was apparently loved. He had fled from trouble in Tetuan and was lying low till things cooled. He spent much of the day trying to steal things. Now, as evening prepared to thud in, tally-hoed on by the punctual muezzin, he grinningly pushed Ali Fathi temporarily away, then took off his long striped nightshirt with hood attached. He was dressed underneath in blue jeans and khaki (probably American army) shirt. He had a marsupial bag knotted round his waist, and from this he produced his spoils, neither choice nor lavish, holding them up for Ali Fathi to admire. He was not a very good thief; it was evident that he was not on the run for thievery; perhaps he had merely spat on the King's picture. On the bed he placed, with a smile that was meant to be modest, a couple of gritty cakes of the kind

dumped with the coffee on outside cafe tables, also a single Seville.
Then he produced a small round tin labelled in English. Enderby
could read that it was tan boot-polish, but Ali Fathi seized it with
a kind of gastronome's croon, probably believing it to be a rare
(hence the exiguity of the tinned portion) pâté.

'*Pour les bottines,*' said Enderby helpfully. '*Ou pour les souliers. Pas
pour manger, vous comprenez.*' Soon Ali Fathi and Wahab saw that
this was so, and then they started a kind of married wrangle.
Enderby sighed. He hated these public homosexual carryings-on.
Shortly Ali Fathi would have Wahab down on the bed, and they
would perhaps indulge in the erotic refinement that they called
soixante-neuf, which reminded Enderby of the Pisces sign on newspaper horoscope pages. Or else there would be plain howling
sodomy. And to them Enderby was only a piece of insentient
furniture – the only piece indeed, save for the two beds, in the
whole room. Souris, the other man, would not come in till very
much later, often when Ali Fathi and Wahab were already in bed,
and then what took place took place, mercifully, in the dark. The
bed was not big enough for three of them, so there was a lot of
crying and writhing on the floor and, if a synchronized triple
crisis was reached, which happened occasionally, the window rattled
and the beds, one of them with tired but sleep-deprived Enderby
in it, shook from the legs up. Souris was not a murine man. He
was very gross and he sweated what looked like crude oil. He had
hurt somebody very badly on the outskirts of Casablanca – a
totally unwilled act, he swore frequently, an ineluctable side-issue
of a process designed mainly for pleasure. When the three of them
had completed their Laocoon performance, they would sometimes
(Enderby had seen this in the moonlight, Miss Boland also grimly
seeming to look down from the moon) shake hands, though not
heartily: it was like the end of a round in a wrestling bout, which
in a sense it was, though three were involved and there was no
purse. Once or twice, Souris had then tried to get into bed with
Enderby, but Enderby would have none of that. So Wahab, the
youngest, was often made to sleep in his robe on the floor, as
though it were the desert. He would sometimes cry out in his
uneasy sleep, seeming to roar like a camel. This was no life for
anyone.

'*Moi*,' said Enderby, pocketing the tan boot-polish, '*j'essayerai à le vendre ou, au moins, à l'échanger pour quelquechose de comestible.*'

'*Tu sors?*' said Ali Fathi, who already had Wahab round the neck.

Enderby did not like this familiarity. He nodded frowning. Yes, he was going out. The time had come to find out what was going on with respect to himself as regards the impending death of Yod Crewsy. For nobody back there in Scotland Yard seemed to be doing anything. There was the usual odd statement about investigations still proceeding, but most of the newspaper concentration now seemed to be on Yod Crewsy as a dying god, not one of the daily victims of common murderous assault. The butcher had become somehow shadowy and august, a predestined and impersonal agent of the dark forces, proud and silent in a Frazerian grove. But the police back there in England were brought up on Moriarty, not Frazer, and Enderby felt sure they were slyly about something. They might be grilling Jed Foot in under-river cellars. Or they might be here, raincoated, holding on to their hats in the Tangerine sea-wind. It was time to go to this Fat White Doggy Wog place and see if John the Spaniard had sent a letter to Enderby through his brother Billy Gomez, if Enderby had remembered the name right.

There were two other bedrooms on this floor, and these comprised the brothel part of the establishment, though, on busy nights, cubicles in the bar below were curtained off for the more urgent and perfunctory clients, and fat Napo's kitchen had once or twice been used, since it had a stout table for table-corner specialists. The room that Enderby shared with Ali Fathi, Wahab, and Souris had not, so far as Enderby knew, ever been desecrated by acts of a heterosexual nature, but it was understood that, normally in the late morning, an occasional sharp act of commercial pederasty might be consummated there, Enderby and Ali Fathi (who were not supposed to leave the premises, Napo apparently not trusting them not to be caught) going into the backyard with the scrawny hens, there to smoke a soothing marijuana fag or two, given to them by Napo as a little reward for temporarily and gratuitously leasing lodgings for which they had paid in advance.

Out now on the landing, which had a naked light-bulb and a portrait of the King of Morocco, Enderby saw disgustedly that one

of these other bedrooms had its door open. A couple of
laughing male friends, both of a Mediterranean complexion, were
preparing to engage houris – whose giggles agitated their yashmaks
– on adjacent beds. Enderby angrily slammed their door on them,
then went down the carpetless stair grumbling to himself. A scratchy
record of popular Egyptian music was playing in the bar – the
same theme over and over again in unison on a large and wasted
orchestra. Peering through a hole in the worn curtain of dirty
Muslim pink, Enderby saw Napo behind his counter. A man grosser
than Souris, he had modelled himself on the Winston Churchill
he had once, he alleged, seen painting in Marrakesh, but the baby-
scowl sat obscenely on a face bred by centuries of Maghreb
dishonesty. He was now arguing about the magical properties of
certain numbers with a customer Enderby could not see: something
to do with a lottery ticket.

Enderby went loudly to the lavatory by the kitchen, then tiptoed
through the kitchen to the back door. It was a blue evening but
rather gusty. In the little yard the hens had gone to roost in the
branches of a stunted tree that Enderby could not identify. They
laid on a quiet crooning protest chorus, all for Enderby, and their
feathers ruffled minimally in the wind. Enderby frowned up at the
moon, then climbed to the top of the low wall by means of an
empty Coca-Cola crate and a couple of broken-brick toe-holds.
He dropped easily, though panting, over the other side. It was an
alley he was in now, and this led to a street. The street went downhill
and led to other streets. If you kept going down all the time you
eventually came to the Avenue d'Espagne, which looked at the
plage. That dog place was down there, not far from the Hotel Rif.

It was very steep and not very well lighted. Enderby teetered
past a crumbling theatre called the Miguel de Cervantes then,
finding that the next turning seemed to take him some way uphill
again, tried a dark and leafy passage which went unequivocally
down. Here a little Moorish girl cried when she saw him, and a
number of house-dogs started to bark. But he went gamely on,
supporting himself by grasping at broken fences. Precipitous: that
was the word. At last he emerged from the barking dark, finding
himself on a street where a knot of Moorish boys in smart suits
called to him:

'You want boy, Charlie?'

'You very hot want nice beer.'

'For cough,' said Enderby, in no mood for foreign nonsense, and a boy riposted with:

'You fuck off too, English fuckpig.' Enderby didn't like that. He knew that this place had once belonged to the English, part of Charles II's Portuguese queen's dowry. It was not right that he should be addressed like that. But another boy cried:

'You fucking German. Kaput heilhitler.' And another:

'Fucking Yankee motherfucker. You stick chewing-gum up fucking ass.' That showed a certain ingenuity of invective. They were very rude boys, but their apparently indifferent despication of foreigners was perhaps a healthy sign, stirring in sympathy a limp G-string in his own nature. He nodded at them and, more kindly, said once more:

'For cough.' They seemed to recognize his change of tone, for they merely pronged two fingers each in his direction, one or two of them emitting a lip-fart. Then they started to playfight, yelping, among themselves. Enderby continued his descent, coming soon to a hotel-and-bar on his left called *Al-Djenina*. The forecourt had birdcages in it, the birds all tucked up for the night, and Enderby could distinctly see, through the long bar-window, middle-aged men drunk and embracing each other. Those would, he thought, be expatriate writers. He was, of course, one of those himself now, but he was indifferent to the duties and pleasures of sodality. He was on his own, waiting. He had written, though. He was working on things. The wind from the sea upheld him as he tottered to level ground. Here it was then: the Avenue d'Espagne, as they called it.

He turned left. A fezzed man outside a shop hailed him, showing rugs and saddles and firearms. Enderby gravely shook his head, saying truthfully: *'No tengo bastante dinero, hombre.'* He was becoming quite the linguist. A gormless-looking boy, thin and exhibiting diastemata in the shop-front lights, offered him English newspapers. This was different. Enderby drew out dirhams. He tried to control his heavy breathing as he looked for news. The wind breathed more heavily, seeming to leap on the paper from all four quarters, as though it was all the news Enderby could possibly want. Enderby took his paper into the doorway of the rug-and-saddle shop. The fezzed man said:

'You man like good gun. I see.' That was not a discreet thing to say, and Enderby looked sharply at him. 'Bang bang bang,' added the man, indicating his rusty Rif arsenal of Crimean rifles and stage-highwayman pistols. Enderby read. *All Hope Abandoned*, a headline said Dantesquely. The end was very near now, a few days off at most. He was in a coma. Where the hell then, Enderby wondered, had that bullet struck him? Police would be treating case as murder, the paper said. Redoubling efforts, acting on valuable information, Interpol on job, arrest expected very soon. The wind pushed, with a sudden whoosh, those words into Enderby's open mouth. Enderby pushed back and then looked at the date of the newspaper. Yesterday's. He might be dead already, his gob, money-coining but not golden, shut for ever. The shopkeeper now showed a real golden mouth, like Spanish John's (and, there again, how far was *he* to be trusted?), as he softly placed, on the newsprint Enderby held tautly at chin-level like a communion cloth, a specimen pistol for his inspection and admiration. Enderby started and let it drop in the doorway. One of its fittings clattered free and the shopman got ready to revile Enderby. '*No quiero*,' Enderby said. 'I said that before, bloody fool as you are.' And then he entered the wind, looking troubled at flickering lights on headlands. He didn't need his newspaper any more, so he threw it into the wind's bosom. The wind, like a woman, was clumsy with it.

The sea. *La belle mer.* Why had he never realized that that was the same as *la belle-mère*, which – with some kind of French irony – had been forced into meaning 'stepmother'? Well, he had come back to her for a brief time, belching and grousing over there, brewing strong green tea all day long, groaning in her bed at night. She had seen him taken off by a woman, and soon it would be by the police. Which was Rawcliffe's place? Street-lamps showed the Sun Trap, with a kosher inscription, and the Well Come. They were in the dark; people moved inland with the night, to fat belly-dancers and bottles of alum Valpierre. There it was: *El Acantilado Verde*, a tatty yellowish place. Rawcliffe had had, apparently, several little Tangerine bars and tea-shops. This would be his last.

Enderby mastered his breathing before entering the bar-restaurant that had a shagged dog sign swinging, with its lamp of low wattage, in the paper-ravaging wind. The crossword, pathetically unsolved, rode and span briefly on the air at Enderby's eye-level as he made for the closed door. There were deserted metal tables with chairs on top of them stretching along the pavement. From within came piano-music. He pushed the door open.

The piano was an upright, in tone tinny, scarred in appearance, on a platform made of old beer-crates, and the man who played seemed to be a North European. He played slow jazz with sad authority, sadly chewing his lips. He had suffered, his blank face said, but had now passed beyond suffering. An American, Enderby decided. All Americans, he thought, looking shyly round: it was to do with sitting postures of insolent relaxedness. There was a herbal smell on the air, an autumn smell. *Herbst* was the German for autumn, was it not? A poem, like the transient randiness felt when coming upon a gratuitous near-nude set in the pages of a magazine article one finds absorbing, twitched. These Americans would call it the fall. A fall of herbs, of grace, herb of grace. No, there were other things to think of and do, and he already had a poem on the forge. Still, he sniffed. Drugs, he tingled; something stronger than that harmless marijuana (Mary Jane, that meant: a mere kitchen-maid of narcotics) he had been given to smoke. A very thin young man in dark glasses mouthed and mouthed in a trance. A white-haired cropped man, also young, sat reading a thin, or slim, volume. 'Shit,' he kept judging. Nobody took any notice; nobody took any notice of Enderby. There was a man in the corner in a skin-tight costume as for ballet practice writing words shakily on a blackboard. *Braingoose*, he wrote, and, under it, *Rape of Lesion*. Enderby nodded with tiny approval. Literary exiles of a different sort. Which reminded him: that bloody book of that dying yob; here might they know? 'Shit,' said the white-haired man, turning a page, then laughed.

There seemed to be no waiter about. There was a wooden bar in the distant corner, its lower paint ruined by feet, and three barstools were empty before it. To get to it Enderby had to get past a dangerous-looking literary man who had arranged three tables about himself like an ambo. He had shears with which he seemed to be busy cutting strips out of newspaper-sheets, and he looked frowning at Enderby while he pasted some of these, apparently at random, on a pawed and sticky piece of foolscap. He looked like an undertaker, mortician rather; his suit was black and his spectacles had near-square black rims, like the frames of obituary notices in old volumes of *Punch*. Enderby approached diffidently, saying: 'Pardon me –' (good American touch there) '– but can anybody?'

'If,' said this man, 'you mean aleatoric, that only applies to the muzz you embed the datum in.' He sounded not unkind, but his voice was tired and lacked nuances totally.

'What I meant really was a drink, really.' But Enderby didn't want to seem impolite; besides, this man seemed engaged on a kind of literature, correcting the sheet as he started to now with a felt-tipped inkpencil; he was a sort of fellow-writer. 'But I think I see what you mean.'

'There,' said the man, and he mumbled what he had stuck and written down, something like: 'Balance of slow masturbate payments inquiries in opal spunk shapes notice of that question green ass penetration phantoms adjourn.' He shook his head. 'Rhythm all balled up, I guess.'

'I'm really looking,' Enderby said, 'for the waiter you have here. Gomez his name is, I believe.' A man came out, somewhat dandy-ishly tripping, from behind a curtain of plastic strips in various primary colours. He had a greenish shirt glazed with never having been, for quite a time anyway, taken off, and thin bare legs that were peppered with tiny holes, as with woodworm. His face was worn to the bone and his hair was filthy and elflocked. To the scissored man he said:

'He reckons he's through on the hot line now.'

'Any message?'

'Fly's writing it down. May I inquire whom you are?' he then said to Enderby.

'Something about Gomez, I guess,' said the mortician.

'Later.' The other dabbled his fingers in air as in water. 'He's off till *un poco mas tarde*.' The pianist was now working on some high-placed old-time discords, school of Scriabin. 'Crazy,' the dabbler said.

'I'll have a drink,' said Enderby, 'if I may.'

'British,' nodded the mortician. 'Guessed so. Goddamn town's lousy with British. Out here to write about tea with Miss Mitford, rose gardens in rectory closes, all that crap.'

'Not me.' Enderby made a noise which he at once realized was like what the cheaper novels called a gay laugh. He must be very ill-at-ease then. 'I'll have a Bloody Mary, if you have it, that is.' He clanked out a few dirhams. The tomato-juice would be nourishing; he needed nourishment.

'*Sangre de María*,' shrugged the filthy-shirted man, who seemed to own this place, going to behind the bar. Enderby went to climb a stool.

'Very baroque, that is,' he pronounced. 'They all call it that, I believe. They lack a knowledge of English history, naturally, the Spaniards, I mean, so they make a kind of Crashaw conceit out of it, though, of course, the Crashavian style derives, so they tell me, from Spanish models. Or that statue of St Teresa, I think it is, with the dart going through her. But this, of course, is the Virgin Mary, bleeding. A virgin, you see: blood. The same sort of thing, though. Professor Empson was very interested in that line of Crashaw – you know: "He'll have his teat ere long, a bloody one. The mother then must suck the son." Two lines, I mean. Baroque, anyway.' All who were not in a drug-trance looked at Enderby. He wondered why his nerves babbled like that; he must be careful; he would start blurting everything out if he wasn't. 'And your Gomez,' he said, 'is, I am credibly informed, something of an expert on Spanish poetry.'

'Gomez,' said the mortician, 'is an expert only on the involutions of his own rectum.'

The man with the blackboard shakily wrote *Comings in the Skull*. The white-haired reader said, very seriously:

'Now, this, I reckon, is *not* shit. Listen.' And he read out:

'Society of solitary children –
Stilyagi, provo, beat, mafada,
Nadaista, energumeno, mod and rocker –
Attend to the slovos of your psychedelic guides –
Swamis, yogins and yoginis,
Amerindian peyote chiefs, Zen roshis.

Proclaim inner space, jolting the soft machine
Out of its hypnosis conditioned by
The revealed intention of the Senders –'

'But,' said Enderby unwisely, dancing the bloody drink in his hand, smiling, 'we don't have mods and rockers any more.' He had read his *Daily Mirror*, after all, to some purpose. 'That's the danger, you see, of trying to make poetry out of the ephemeral. If you'll forgive me, that sounded to me very old-fashioned. Of course, it isn't really clear whether it *is* actually poetry. Back to the old days,' he smiled, 'of *vers libre*. There were a lot of tricks played by people, you know. Seed catalogues set out in stanzas. Oh, a lot of the *soi-distant avant-garde* were taken in.'

There were low growls of anger, including, it appeared, one from a man who was supposed to be in a trance. The white-haired reader seemed to calm himself through a technique of rhythmic shallow breathing. Then he said:

'All right, buster. Let's hear from you.'

'How? Me? You mean –?' They were all waiting.

'You know the whole shitting works,' went the mortician. 'You've not quit talking since you came in. Who asked you to come in, anyway?'

'It's a bar, isn't it?' said Enderby. 'Not private, I mean. Besides, there's this matter of Gomez.'

'The hell with Gomez. Crap out with your own.'

The atmosphere was hostile. The owner air-dabbled from behind the bar, sneering. The pianist was playing something deliberately silly in six-eight time. Enderby said:

'Well, I didn't really come prepared. But I'm working on something in the form of an Horatian ode. I've not got very far, only a couple of stanzas or so. I don't think you'd want to hear it.' He felt doubt itching like piles. All that stuff about swamis and inner space. A sonnet, yet. Horatian ode, yet. He was not very modern, perhaps. A critic had once written: 'Enderby's addiction to the sonnet-form proclaims that the 'thirties are his true home.' He did not like the young very much and he did not want to take drugs. He was supposed to have killed a quintessential voice of the new age. But that voice had not been above gabbling Enderby's own work and getting a fellowship of the Royal Society of Literature for it. Enderby now recited stoutly:

> 'The urgent temper of the laws,
> That clips proliferation's claws,
>   Shines from the eye that sees
>   A growth is a disease.
>
> Only the infant will admire
> The vulgar opulence of fire
>   To tyrannize the dumb
>   Patient continuum
>
> And, while the buds burst, hug and hold
> A cancer that must be controlled
>   And moulded till it fit
>   These forms not made for it.'

Out of a trance somebody farted. 'That last couplet,' Enderby said trembling, 'needs a bit of going over, I see that, but I think you'll get the general idea.' In confusion he swigged his Bloody Mary and presented the flecked glass (splash of some small slaughtered animal on a wind-screen) for another. When Enderby had been a boy he had gone to sleep on the upper deck of the last tram of the night and had awakened in the tramshed. Leaving in shame he had noticed uniformed men looking at him in the quiet wonder which was the proper tribute to an act of an imbecile. He seemed to be getting that same look now. He said: 'I stand for form and denseness. The seventeenth-century tradition modified. When is this man Gomez coming in?' The mortician resumed snipping and gumming, shaking his head, grinning like a clown. The white-headed cropped man hid his own grin in a new slim volume. The entranced offered the loudest criticism, great farts cometing through inner space. 'Well,' said Enderby, growing angry, 'what about that bloody act of plagiarism of bloody Yod Crewsy?'

A man came limping from behind the blackboard (which now had, very vulgar, *My cuntry is the yoniverse* scrawled on it) and said: 'I'll tell you about that, friend.' He was totally bald but luxuriantly

bearded and spoke in an accent Enderby had hitherto associated with
cowboy films on television. 'That was pure camp. Is, I guess. A new
frame of awareness. It's not the poems as such so much as how he
looks at them. Like you get these good pictures with shitty Victoriana
in them, a frame inside a frame. Man, it's called the Process.'

'I'd very much like to see −' Enderby's nausea was complicated.
And if that sonnet-draft was in there, the Satan one. And, whether
it was there or not, could he control himself, handling richly
rewarded flagrant sneering theft?

'You can learn any place,' said the bald bearded man. 'You'll find
it in the john library.' He pointed beyond the curtain of many-
coloured plastic strips with a finger that seemed half-eaten, a kindly
man really. 'And as for plagiarism, everything belongs to everybody.
Man, that's called the Lesson.' He returned to behind the blackboard,
limping. On the blackboard was now written *Vinegar strokes through
magnified sebacities*. Enderby went, his heart fainting, towards the
john. There was a dark passage, sibilant with the wind, and crunchy
rubbish underfoot. In a kind of alcove a man lay on a camp-bed
under a dull bulb, another man beside him with a notebook. The
supine man, on a drugged trip, sent reports up from the unconscious. Down there ghostly scissors were at work on newspapers
out of eternity. It was a lot of nonsense.

The lavatory was small and dirty, but there was a red light of
the kind used in electric log-fires. There were a lot of books, many
of them eaten by mould. Enderby sat heavily on the hollow seat
and disturbed the books with a paddling right hand, panting. That
sinful volume was not far from the top. The title was *Fixes*; there
was a bold leering portrait of the pseudo-author. The sixteenth
impression, Enderby noted with gloom. He noted too that many
of the poems were not his own; it was a case of multiple theft,
perhaps, unless bloody Vesta or that Wittgenstein man had written
some of them. Enderby found six unpublished poems by himself
and, a small mercy in a world of filth, not one of them was that
sonnet. There was, as Miss Kelly had said, a poem entitled 'Sonnet',
but that had twelve bad unrhyming lines and might well be something that Yod Crewsy himself had composed at his secondary
modern school. Enderby read it shuddering:

My mum plonks them on the table for Susie and Dad and I
Plonk plonk and dull clanks the sauce bottles
And Susie reads their names to herself
Her mouth is open but that is not for reading aloud
The fact is that her nose is stopped up like those sauce bottles are
Like OK and HP and A1 and FU and CK and O
I mean oh red red tomato
And I dream while the frying goes on and Dad has his mouth
   open too at the TV
How I would like catsup or ketchup splattering
All over the walls and it would be shaken from these open
   mouths
And it would be red enough but not taste of tomato

'God,' said Enderby to his shrinking bowels. 'God God God.' So they had come to this, had they? And his own finely wrought little works desecrated by contact. He dropped the book on the floor; it remained open, but a sharp draught from under the far from snugly fitting door pushed at the erect fan of its middle pages and disclosed a brief poem that Enderby, squinting in the dim red light, seemed thumped on the back into looking at. Something or somebody thumped him: an admonitory goblin that perhaps lived wetly in the lavatory cistern. He had not noticed this poem before, but, by God, he knew the poem. He felt a terrible excitement mounting. He grabbed the book with both hands.

Then the door opened. Enderby looked, expecting to see the wind, but it was a man. Excited though he was, he began to deliver a standard protest against invasion of privacy. The man waved it away and said: 'Gomez.'

'The fact that the door isn't locked is neither here nor there. All right then, I've finished anyway.' Something in the spread sound of his words seemed to tell him that he was smiling. He felt his mouth, surprised. It was the excitement, it was the first rehearsal of triumph. Because, by God, he had them now. By the short hairs, as they said. But was he sure, could he be sure? Yes, surely he was sure. Or was it just a memory of having foreseen it in print? He could check, he was bound to be able to check, even in this bloody heathen place. There might be some really cultivated man here among the expatriate scribblers.

'Gomez. Billy Gomez.' He was a bit rodent-like and, so Enderby twitched at once, might be dangerous. But in what context? Gomez finned out his paws in a kind of cartoon-mouse self-depreciation. He had a dirty white barman's jacket on but no tie. He seemed also to be wearing tennis-shoes.

'Ah.' That other structure of urgency was suddenly re-illuminated. Heavy as an ivied tower, it crashed the blackness, decollated, to the sound of brass, like something in *son et lumière*. '*Sí* Enderby said. '*Su hermano*. In London, that is. *Mi amigo*. Or colleague, shall I say. Has he sent anything for me?' That sonnet by Wordsworth, on the sonnet. Key becomes lute becomes trumpet. This book he now thrust into his side pocket. Load of filthy treachery becomes, quite improbably, sharp weapon of revenge.

'You come.' He led Enderby out of the lavatory down a passage that took them to stacked crates of empties and then to a garlicky kind of still-room, brightly lighted with one bare bulb. Enderby now saw Gomez very clearly. He had red hair. Could he possibly be the true brother of swarthy John? Gomez was a Goth or perhaps even a Visigoth: they had had them in Spain quite a lot, finishing off the Iberian part of the Roman Empire: they had had a bishop who translated bits of the Bible, but that was much later: coarse people but very vigorous and with a language quite as complicated as Latin: they were perhaps not less trustworthy than, say, the Moors. Still, Enderby was determined to be very careful.

In this still-room a small brown boy in a striped nightshirt was cutting bread. Gomez cuffed him without malice, then he took a piece of this bread, went over to a stove maculate with burnt fat, sloshed the bread in a pan of what looked like sardine-oil, folded it into a sandwich, and, drippingly, ate. He took in many aspects of Enderby with darting pale eyes. The boy, still cutting bread, as it were clicked his eyes into twin slots that held them blazing on to Enderby's left ear. Enderby, embarrassed, changed his position. The eyes stayed where they were. Drugs or something. Gomez said to Enderby:

'You say your name.' Enderby told him what he had been called in his regenerate, barman's capacity, but only in the Spanish version. Enderby said:

'He said he'd send a letter through you. *Una carta*. He promised. Have you got it?' Gomez nodded. 'Well,' said Enderby, 'how about handing it over, then, eh? Very urgent information.'

'Not here,' dripmunched Gomez. 'You say where you stay. I come with letter.'

'Ah,' Enderby said, with something like satisfaction. 'I see your little game.' He smiled, it seemed to him, and to his astonishment, brilliantly: it was that triumph pushing up. 'Perhaps it would be more convenient if we could go to your place and pick up the letter there. It would be quicker, wouldn't it?'

Gomez, who had eaten all his oiled bread and licked some fingers, now took an onion from a small sack. He looked at the boy, who still cut bread but whose eyes had now clicked back down to the operation, and seemed to relent of cuffing him, however unmaliciously. He stroked the boy's griskin, grinning. Spanish poetry, thought Enderby. This man was supposed to know all about it. Was a knowledge of poetry, even a nominal one, a sort of visa for entry into the small world of Enderby-betrayal? Gomez topped and tailed the onion with his teeth (*tunthus*, Enderby suddenly remembered for some reason, was the Gothic for tooth, but this man would know nothing of his ancestral language), then, having spat the tufts on to the floor, he tore off the onion's scarfskin and some of the subcutaneous flesh and started to crunch what was pearlily revealed. There was a faint spray of zest. It smelt delicious. Enderby knew he had to get out. Fast. Gomez said:

'Tonight I work. You say you where you live.'

The boy left off bread-cutting (who the hell would want all that bread, anyway?) and ran the knife-blade across his brown thumb. Enderby said:

'It doesn't matter, after all. Thanks for your help. Or not help, as the case may be. *Muchas gracias*, anyway.' And he got out of the room, clanking loose bottles on the floor of the dark corridor. Gomez called after him something ending with *hombre*. Enderby passed the man on the couch and in the next world and the amanuensis who sat by him. Then he breasted the plastic strips and blinked into the bar. There was a new man there, a Scot apparently, for he talked of 'a wee bit fixie'. The man at the blackboard had just finished writing *Hot kitchens of his ass*. Salami, Enderby thought

in his confusion, salami was made of donkeys. The whitecropped
man was reciting:

> 'Archangels blasting from inner space,
> Pertofran, Tryptizol, Majeptil,
> Parstelin and Librium.
> And a serenace for all his tangled strings.'

Romantic, thought Enderby distractedly, better than that other
stuff. Remembering that he had stolen a book from their john, he
clapped his hand in his pocket. A dithery young man in dark glasses
recoiled, pushing out his palms against the expected gunshot.
Enderby smiled at everybody, thinking that he had ample cause to
smile, even when carted off. But not yet, not just yet. He yearned
towards solitary confinement like a lavatory, but duty, like an *engaged*
sign, clicked its message. The mortician did not smile back. The
dithering young man had recovered: all a joke, his manic leer
seemed to say. Enderby held that book in, as if it might leap out.
Out, out. Into the windy Moroccan night.

It was a slow and panting climb, and Enderby had to keep
stopping suddenly, holding himself in shadow against whatever wall
offered, listening and watching to find out if he was being followed.
It was hard to tell. There were plenty of little Moorish boys about,
any one of whom could be that bread-cutting lad, but none seemed
furtive: indeed, one pissed frankly in the gutter (but that might be
his cunning) and another hailed a smartly dressed elderly Moor
who was going downhill, running after him then, crying unheeded
certain complicated wrongs. Enderby passed dirty coffee-shops and
then came to a hotly arguing group of what seemed beggars at a
street-corner. They had thin though strong bare legs under swad-
dling bands and ragged European jackets, and all were turbaned.
Enderby stood with them a space, peering as best he could between
their powerful gestures. Things seemed to be all right; there was
nobody following; he had given that treacherous Gomez the slip.
Two treacherous Gomezes. That bloody John in London was, after
all, the rotten bastard Enderby had always known him to be. Enderby,
filling his lungs first like a dog running to the door in order to
bark, turned left for a steeper hill. Halfway up was a very loud

cinema with what he took from posters to be an Egyptian film showing (an insincerely smiling hero like Colonel Nasser). He felt somehow protected by all that row, which was mostly the audience. A tooth-picking dark-suited young man by the pay-desk looked at Enderby. The manager probably. '*Alors, ça marche, hein?*' Enderby panted. If anybody asked that man if he had seen an Englishman going that way he would say no, only a Frenchman. Now he said nothing, merely looked, tooth-picking. Enderby climbed on.

When, dying and very wet, he came to the Rue El Greco, he realized he was not too sure what would be the right back wall. Fowls, stunted trees: they all probably had them round here. He should have chalked a sign: he was new to this business. He would have to risk going in the front way. After all, there would be a lot of customers at this hour and fat Napo would be too busy hitting the rotten ancient coffee-machine to notice. Enderby caught a sudden image of El Greco himself, transformed into his own Salvador, peering down in astigmatic woe at the deplorable street that bore his name. There were some very nasty-looking places called snack-bars, as well as upper windows from which small boys thrust their bottoms, either in invitation or contempt. You could also hear very raucous female laughter – wrong, wrong; should not Islam's daughters be demure? – from down dark passageways. An old man sat by deserted and boarded-up premises. Inside, Enderby saw with poetic insight, would be rats and the memories of foul practices, the last fleshly evidence of outrage being gnawed, gnawed; the man cried his wares of tiny toy camels with here and there a dromedary.

Enderby gave his sweated spectacles a good wipe with his tie before approaching *El Snack Bar Albricias*. By conceiving an image of fat Napo waiting for him on the doorstep, as a tyrannical father his precocious debauched son, he was able to forestall any such reality. Indeed, scratched Cairo music was coming out very loud, but not so loud as the noise of customers. Enderby peered before entering and was satisfied to see Napo fighting the coffee-machine before a thick and applauding bar-audience. '*Pardon,*' said a bulky fezzed would-be entrant to Enderby, Enderby being in the way. '*Avec plaisir,*' Enderby said, and was happy to use this man as a shield for his own ingress. To be on the safe side, he tried to make himself look Moorish, flattening his feet, imagining his nose bigger, widening his eyes behind their glasses. There were girls, giggling, yashmaks up like beavers, drinking the local bottled beer with real Moorish men. Enderby tut-tutted like one in whom the faith burned hot. Then he noticed something he had not seen before – little verse couplets hanging on the wall behind the bar. He had time to read one only before going to the lavatory before going upstairs. It said:

> *Si bebes para olvidar,*
> *Paga antes de empezar.*

That, thought Enderby, meant that if you drank to forget you'd better pay before you began. Drinking and forgetting, that was. Enderby felt a bit cold. Verse and treachery went together. He hadn't thought of it before, but Napo had, in the nature of things, to be a traitor. Fugitives had sooner or later to be kicked out from upstairs; no criminal could afford to stay for ever; the quickest way of getting rid of a guest who'd outstayed his welcome was to – But no, no. There had to be someone you could trust. Wasn't Napo, especially when a customer gave him a cigar, an admirer of Winston Churchill? But when you thought of political coat-turning and the guns pointing the wrong way at Singapore and some rumour of ultimate perfidy in the Straits of Gibraltar – No, no, no. Napo was all right. Well in with the police, too. Enderby felt colder.

2

He came to full wakefulness in the middle of the night, the Boland moon looking grimly in on him. He had gone to sleep early, so that his eyes could avoid a very complicated and laborious (with hand-spitting beforehand) bout of triple sodomy on the floor. He had had enough sleep, then, but his room-mates were hard at it, snoring, Wahab on his back, mouth open to the spiders, in his robe on the bare boards. But what really seemed to have jolted him awake was the Muse, pushing lines at him. It was a bit more of that Horatian Ode:

> And something something something can
> Take partners for a plonk pavane
> The blinded giant's staff
> Tracing a seismograph.

Accompanying this was a burbling of unhappy tomato-juice, together with, in the throat, a metallic suspicion that it had not been all that fresh. And then. And then. The derision of that bloody merry crowd (ha) in that place at what had seemed to him, Enderby, and still seemed very respectable verses. Was it then possible that art that was good for one time was not good for another, the laughter justified, himself out of date? There was a Canadian professor who had once been in Piggy's Sty with fawning hosts, going on burringly about new modes of communication and how words were all finished or something and everybody was too much bemused by Gutenberg and not wide enough awake to the revolution in electronics, whatever that was. And there were also these people who, by taking drugs, were vouchsafed visions of the noumenon, and this made them scornful of art that used merely phenomenal subject-matter. But what could you do about a noumenal medium, mused Enderby, putting his glasses on. The moon defined itself in sharper craters and ridges, as though the spectacles themselves were in the service of Miss Bloody Boland. And, while bloody came into things, that Bloody Mary was dancing about very obscenely inside, and that vodka had probably not been vodka at all but something merely sold as vodka. Enderby winced on a sour vague image of the noumenon behind the label. Diluted surgical spirit, home-made potato-fire, meths. He had better get up and go to the lavatory.

He was fully dressed, except for his shoes, which he now painfully put on. It seemed to him to be cold tonight, and he shivered. He also, despite the shattering evidence that had been granted him this evening, felt depressed. Was anything he could now do as a poet of any value to the world or God the ultimate noumenon? Graaarp, answered his stomach, like some new mode of communication. Behind the door on a nail was hanging the hooded nightshirt garment, djelaba or whatever they called it, that Souris, now snoring on top of Ali Fathi, wore when he essayed the streets.

Enderby took it and wrapped it round himself, but he saw that his shivering came from the expense of body-fuel in the service of the visceral bubbling that oppressed him. He went downstairs to the lavatory, hearing nothing from either brothel-dormitory, calm of brerrrrgh mind all aaaaarfph passion gockle spent.

But from below he heard quiet but somehow urgent talking, and he saw that a dim lamp, apt for furtive colloquy, was on. He tiptoed down, suppressing his inner noises by some obscure action of the epiglottis and diaphragm. When he got to the bottom of the stairs, he saw, from shadow, that Napo was with a couple of men in the pretentious uniform of the local police. These men, lean, moustached, mafia-swarthy, crafty-eyed, were each taking from Napo a glass of something gold and viscid in the lamplight. Alcohol, against the tenets of the faith, they ought to be had up for that, police and upholders of Islamic law as they were supposed to be. Enderby, flat against his dark wall, listened, but the language was Moghrabi Arabic. It was a serious discourse, though, evidently, and Napo's part in it sounded a bit breathy, even whining. Enderby listened for certain illuminative international or crassly onomatopoeic words, but the only word that was made much of was something sounding like *khogh*. It was, as Enderby's viscera quietly attested, parroting and nipping him like a parrot, a very visceral sound. *Khogh*, the viscera went. And then, somewhat louder, *Genggergy*. Enderby suddenly saw, and then he panicked.

The police and Napo had heard. Enderby saw, in addition to who *Khogh* was, opened mouths and wide eyes turned on to his patch of dark. He thought he heard a safety-catch clicking off. His first instinct was to run to the lavatory, but they would, he knew, soon have that door shot open. Still, his insides, like spoilt cats demanding milk as lava begins to engulf the town and the cats with it, complained and switched on a kind of small *avant-garde* chamber piece for muted brass. Enderby, like, with that gown on his shoulders, a student late for a lecture, ran through the kitchen, sufficiently lighted by Miss bloody Boland, and out into the yard. The roosting fowls crooned at him, and the stunted tree raised, like some outworn Maeterlinck property, a gnarled fist. He got over the wall with agility he marvelled at and then panted a second or two in the alleyway. They were after him all right, though they

seemed first to be, from a sudden meagre uprush of lunated feathers
and a squawked track of conventional gallinaceous protest, abusing
the fowls for letting him get away. Enderby ran a yard or two
downhill and tried a backdoor on the opposite side of the alley.
It was locked, so he padded, in frightful borborygms and breathlessness, to the next. This was open. He got in, finding himself
alone with a tethered white ruminating goat who surveyed Enderby
with no surprise, and closed the door, a very warped one, gently.
Very usefully, a dog next door made a deep chest-bay once only,
as though Enderby had entered a frame or two of his dream, and
this sparked off a small violent yapper farther up the hill and,
farther up again, what, very improbable, could only be a pet hyena.
Towards these noises, Enderby could tell, four feet were now, with
a sketch of urgency, proceeding. The voice of Napo, back at base,
made a brief speech with elements of controlled Churchillian
outrage in it, then turned into grumbling coughs going back to
the kitchen. Good. This would do very well.

Enderby was, in a sense, pleased that a new phase was beginning,
perhaps the last phase of the fugitive. It was all a question now of
how long Rawcliffe would be in rendering himself available for
death. And that was absurd, when one came to think of it, he,
Enderby, killing Rawcliffe. But, if one accepted that killing was a
legitimate and sempiternal human activity, authorized by the Bible,
was there any better motive than Enderby's own? The State made
no provisions for the punishment of the perversion of art; indeed,
it countenanced such perversion. God, whose name had so often
been invoked in the name of bad art, was, at bottom, a Philistine.
So it was up to him, Enderby, to strike a blow for art. Was he not
perhaps by some considered to have done so already? The popular
press might be against him, but surely some letters, suppressed by
editors, must have been written on his behalf? There might even
be a fund started by Earl Russell or somebody to provide cates
and art for him in prison and set him up on his distant release.
He was, he was convinced, not alone. His stomach felt easier.

Watched by the chewing goat, Enderby put the djelaba or
whatever it was on properly, so that, what with the hood, he became
a kind of capuchin. He had slept in his teeth as usual, fearing their
theft if he did not, but now he removed and stowed them.

Remembering the tin of shoe-polish in his pocket, he allowed his heart to leap in awe at the poetry which existence itself sometimes contrived: the fusion, or at least meaningful collocation, of disparates – as, for example, a tin of tan boot-polish and himself, Enderby. He removed his spectacles and bedded them with his teeth. Now he disposed his hood in the academic position, pushed up all available sleeves to near the elbow, got out the tin and his handkerchief, then began to dye himself, all that was likely to be visible, by dipping his handkerchief in the tin and thinly spreading the polish. He did not forget nape and ear-crevices. The smell of the stuff was not unpleasant – astringent, vaguely military. Why, there had been that man Lawrence, colonel and scholar, got up like this. He had been viciously debauched by Turks, but his country had honoured him. He too, like Enderby, had had to change his name. He had died in lowly circumstances, riding a motor-cycle.

What, when he had finished, he now looked like there was no means of finding out. In the moonlight his hands seemed of a richer colour than nature herself might allow, a richness that suggested dye, or perhaps thinly spread tan boot-polish. Still, it would serve, sleeves well down, hood well over. The goat, with the blessed indifference granted to animals, saw no difference between the two Enderbys. It took without gratitude the empty polish-tin and began to crunch it up roundly, its goatee wagging. Enderby took his leave, Ali bin Enderbi or some such name.

Whither? The Boland moon, asked, would not answer. His true place was that Kasbah, high up at the end of the town, where beggars slept at night in the doorways of shark shops, all Rif rifles from the iron-founding Midlands. But it was necessary that he stay near Rawcliffe's beach-place, not to let his quarry slip out of his tan-polished hands. It was not windy now, but it was not warm. Autumnal Morocco. He could doze, all hunched up, in the shadow of *El Acantilado Verde*. In the morning he could drink coffee and eat a piece of bread (there was a dirham or so still in his pocket) and then, an eye open for Rawcliffe, get down to begging. There was a lot of begging here: no shame in it. There were a couple of rich hotels near *El Acantilado Verde* – the Rif and the Miramar: good begging pitches.

He padded gently down the hill-alley, silently rehearsing the

Koranic name of God. Properly enunciated, it could serve for many things – disgust, gratitude, awe, admiration, pain. Enderby had heard the name several times a day in his hideout: he thought he could manage the gymnastics of its articulation. You had to try to swallow the tip of your tongue, growling, then pretend you had to give up the attempt because you had to expel a fragment of matter lodged in your glottis. Easy: *Allah*. He allahed quietly towards the sea under a frowning moon.

2

1

'Heart. He let himself get upset about something. Blowing his top. Ranting and raving. Carrying too much weight, of course. That's what comes of building up rugger-muscle in youth.'

'Where's he been sent?'

'That place of Otto Langsam's. Out in the wilds. Cut off from the great world. Not even a daily newspaper.'

'They say he was going on about some piece of poetry. Abusive. Lines written in a public lavatory. Obviously needed a rest. Good job they got him in time.'

'Oh, very good job. Look, *emshi emshi* or whatever it is. All right, take this. Now bugger off and buy yourself a shave.'

'*Allah*.'

President of the moon's waning. Enderby was not too cold at night. He slept uncertainly, however, in the lee provided by the suntrap arena of *El Acantilado Verde*, a sandyard for torso-bronzing with a couple of umbrella-topped tables. The seaward-looking gate as easily climbed over. Crouched in an angle, he would see at first light two walls made of bathers' changing-cubicles, a corner of the kitchen, the back door of the bar-restaurant. Mercifully, so far, there had been no night rain. Rawcliffe could bring the rain with him if he wished. Nobody seemed to be sleeping on the premises, and Enderby moved away at dawn. Dawn brought the diamond weather of a fine autumn. Skirring his fast-growing grey face-bristles with a tanned hand, Enderby would gum-suck his way to a small dirty shop off the esplanade, sticking out the other hand for alms ('*Allah*') if any untimely European were about, and then take breakfast of coffee-in-a-glass and a fatty Moorish pastry. He feigned mostly dumb, except for the holy name. A holy man perhaps, above dirt and toothlessness, once granted a vision of the ultimate garden (houris, nectar-sherbet, a crystal stream) and then struck speechless except for the author's signature.

Up the cobbled street tottered the saint-eyed donkeys, most cruelly panniered, driven by bare-legged Moors in clouts, ponchos, and immense straw sombreros. Biblical women with ancient hard eyes and no yashmaks carried hashish-dreaming fowls in upside-down bundles, scaly legs faggoted together. They climbed, in a whirl of wind-blown feathers, up to the dirty small hotels for long haggling on the pavement outside, then the leisurely *halal* slaughter, blood sluggishly rolling downhill, the chickens dying on a psych-edelic vision. And just along there was that treacherous White Doggy Wog place. Were its denizens right? Was it right that art should mirror chaos? What kind of art would it be proper for him to produce in his coming cell?

His brain, aloof from his begging hand, worked away at one poem or another. Was it perhaps a kind of holiness that gathered the disparate arbitrarily together, assuming that God or Allah – at the bottom of the mind's well, a toad with truth's jewel in its brow – could take care of the unifying pattern, that it was blas-phemy for the shaping human mind to impose one of his own? Shatter syntax also, and with it time and the relationships of space. That Canadian pundit had said something about the planet itself, earth, becoming, as perceived by a new medium which would be no more than heightened consciousness, a kind of work of art, so that every aspect would be relevant to every other aspect. Fish, spit, toe, antenna, cognac, spider, perspex, keyboard, grass, helmet. Helmeted in grass, the perspex spider spits with toed antenna, a noise like fish, the cognac keyboard. Too elegant that, too much like Mallarmé or somebody. Old-fashioned too, really. Surrealist.

'*Allah.*'

Up there the white huddled Medina on the hill, once watchful of the sea-invaders. Blood and buggery, the Koranic cry of teeth as the scimitar slashed. And now a pretty cram of stucco for the visiting painter. Donkeys, palms, the odd insolent Cadillac with a sneering wealthy young Moor in dark glasses. This bilious sea. There were not, thank Allah, many police about and, in any case, they did not greatly molest beggars.

'Give him something, George, go on. Poor old man.'

And the plebeian tourist, in open-necked shirt and double-breasted town suit, handed Enderby a tiny clank of centimes. His wife, growing a lobster colour that was vulgarly Blackpool, smiled in pity. Enderby bowed and allahed. It was really surprising what you could pick up on this game – handfuls of small tinkle that often added up to well over a dirham, filthy torn notes that the donors probably thought carried plague, absurd largesse of holiday drunks. He was eating, if not sleeping, well on it all. Arab bread with melon-and-ginger *confiture*, yummiyum couscous (better than Easy Walker's), fowl-hunks done with saffron, thin veal-shives in a caraway sauce – all at a quiet fly-buzzing incurious shop near the little Souk or Socco, one that had, moreover, a Western WC instead of a hazardous wog crouch-hole. He was also drinking a fair quantity of mint-tea, good for his stomach.

'*Pauvre petit bonhomme. Georges, donne-lui quelquechose.*'

It was a living. For occupation he had the working-out, though not on paper (there would be paper in prison), of a sonnet concerned with the relationship of the Age of Reason and the so-called Romantic Revival:

> Augustus on a guinea sat in state –
>> The sun no proper study but each shaft
>> Of filtered light a column: classic craft
> Abhorred the arc or arch. To circulate
> (Blood or ideas) meant pipes, and pipes were straight.
>> As loaves were gifts from Ceres when she laughed –

A difficult form, most exigent. Those drug-takers in the Doggy Wog place didn't have all that to worry about: no octaves and sestets in the free wide-open unconscious. A load of bloody rubbish, of course, but he couldn't quell his new self-doubt. As for reading, he would glance shyly at foreign papers left on outdoor café tables: there seemed to be nothing about Yod Crewsy.

And then, outside the Rif, he had heard these two men, talking loudly about someone who could only be Wapenshaw. The Turkish Delight commercial doorman was whistling a taxi to come over for them from the taxi-stand opposite the Miramar. And one of the two men, his belly pushed out to keep up his unbelted long shorts, had said to the other (both had spatulate scrubbed and shaven-looking fingers): 'Heart. He let himself get upset about something.' It was as they were climbing into their *petit taxi* or *taxi chico* that the other one, oldish but thin and strong like a surgical instrument, had said: 'Now bugger off and buy yourself a shave,' handing Enderby a fifty-centime piece.

'*Allah.*'

Retribution, justice: that was what it was. Serve Wapenshaw right. He had grinned and then seen his grin reflected in the glass door of the Rif, the back of a fat woman in black rompers making a temporary mirror-back. He had looked pretty horrible − a face without margins peering from the cave of the capuchin hood, toothless. He could not see his grey whiskers, but he felt them: skirr skirr. He grinned in horror.

At this moment another beggar, sturdy and genuine, had come up to remonstrate loudly. He had been crouched in the entrance to the hotel garage, but now, seeing the grin, he had risen, it seemed, in reproach of one not taking the business seriously enough. He was darker than Enderby, more of a Berber, and had plenty of teeth. He gnashed these in execration, starting to push Enderby in the chest. 'Take your hands off,' Enderby cried, and a visitor in a Palm Beach suit turned in surprise at the British accent. 'For cough,' Enderby added, preparing to push back. But careful, careful; respectable beggary only: the police might conceivably come. He saw then what the trouble was: pitch-queering. '*Iblis,*' he swore mildly at this colleague or rival. '*Shaitan. Afrit.*' He had learned these words from Ali Fathi. And then, the real beggar calling terms less theological after him, he began to cross the road rather briskly. Perhaps he ought, anyway, to haunt the beach more, specifically that segment

near *El Acantilado Verde*, even though so many people on it had
their clothes off and locked away, able with good conscience to
grin (more kindly than Enderby had grinned) and show empty
hands and armpits filled only, in the case of the men, with hair.

The restaurant part of Rawcliffe's establishment was glassed like
an observatory. The rare eaters sweated on to their food, brought
to them by an amiable-looking negroid boy in an apron and a
tarboosh. Windows were open, and Enderby would shyly squint
in, but Rawcliffe did not seem to be about yet. He would justify
the peering by shoving in a hand for alms, and, on the first day
of this new pitch, he had a squashy egg-and-salad sandwich plopped
on to his paw. Palms, alms. Was there a poem there? But he gained
also the odd bit of small change when customers – mostly German,
needing a substantial bever between meals – paid their bills.

These last two days had yielded a sufficiency, and the fine weather
held. Padding the sand, on which the sea, clever green child but
never clever at more than a child's level, had sculpted its own waves,
he breathed in salt, iodine, the sea's childish gift of an extra oxygen
molecule, and thought in quiet sadness of old days – bucket and
spade, feet screaming away from jellyfish, Sam Brownes of seaweed
and the imperial decoration of a starfish (belly thrust out like that
Wapenshaw-talking man, chest sloped to keep it on). And *El
Acantilado Verde* reminded him of later days by the sea, betrayed
and ruined by so many. '*Baksheesh*,' he suggested now to a mild
German-looking couple who, in heavy walking dress except for
bare feet, drank the wind, strolling. They shook their heads regretfully. 'German bastards,' Enderby said quietly to their well-fed backs.
The light was thicker, less heat was coming today from the piecrust
cloud. There might be rain soon.

Here was a family that looked British. The wife was thin as
from a long illness, the husband wore stern glasses, a boy and girl
undressed for water-play chased and tried to hit each other.

'Daft old Jennifer!'

'Silly stupid Godfrey! You've got all sand in your tummy-button!'

Enderby addressed the father, saying, with begging hand: '*Allah
allah. Baksheesh, effendi.*'

'Here,' said the man to his wife, 'is an example of what I mean.
You have a good look at him and what do you see? You see a

wog layabout in the prime of life. He ought to be able to do a decent day's work like I do.'

'*Allah,*' with less confidence.

'They should be made to work. If I had the running of this tinpot little dictatorship I'd make sure that they did.' He had a cheap-looking plastic-bodied camera dangling from a cord. His stare was bold and without humour.

'He's only a poor old man,' said his wife. She was, Enderby could tell, a woman much put upon; the children too would be insolent to her, asking *why* all the time.

'Old? He's not much older than what I am. Are you? Eh? Speak English, do you? Old.'

'No mash Ingrish,' Enderby said.

'Well, you should learn it, shouldn't you? Improve yourself. Go to night-classes and that. Learn something, anyway. This is the modern world, no room for people that won't work, unless, that is, they've been thrown out of it through no fault of their own. Don't understand a blind bit of what I'm saying, do you? Trade, eh? Learn a trade. If you want money, do something for it.'

'Come on, Jack,' said the wife. 'There's a man there keeps looking at our Godfrey.'

Enderby had not previously met a response to mendicancy as hard-hearted and utilitarian as this. He looked grimly at this man of the modern world: a trade union man, without doubt; perhaps a shop steward. He wore a dark suit with, concession to holiday, wings of open-necked shirt apparently ironed on to lapels. 'Trade,' Enderby said. 'I got trade.' The sky seemed to be getting darker.

'Oh, understand more than you let on you're able to, eh? Well, what trade have you got, then?'

'*Bulbul,*' Enderby said. But that might not be the right word. '*Je suis,*' he said, '*poète.*'

'Poet? You say poet?' The man's mouth had opened into a square of small derision. He took from a sidepocket a ten-centime piece. 'You say some poetry, then. Listen to this, Alice.'

'Oh, let him alone, Jack.'

It might have been the word *bulbul* that did it. Suddenly Enderby, in a kind of scorn, found himself reciting a mock *ruba'iy*. Would

those debauchees of the Doggy Wog laugh less at this than at his
Horatian ode?

> 'Kazwana ghishri fana kholamabu
> Bolloka wombon vurkelrada slabu,
> Ga farthouse wopwop yairgang offal flow
> Untera merb —'

A voice behind him said: 'Better, Enderby. Much better. Not quite
so obsessed with meaning as you used to be.' It was an eroded dysp-
noeal voice. Enderby turned in shock to see Rawcliffe being helped,
by two Moorish youths in new black trousers and white shirts, up
the three steps that led to the door of his bar-restaurant. Rawcliffe
paused at the top, waiting for the door to be opened. He panted
down ghastily at Enderby, his palsied grey head ashake. 'Thou art
translated,' he wavered, 'but not so much as thou thinkest. Full of
surprises, though. I'll concede so much.' The door opened, and its
glass panels mirrored momentarily the thickening sea-clouds. 'Gracias,'
Rawcliffe said to the two Moors and trembled from his trouser-pocket
a ten-dirham note for them. They hand-waved and grinned off. Then,
to Enderby: 'Come and drink with one about to die.'

'All right,' said the trade union man. 'You win. Take your ackers.'
But Enderby ignored him and followed, with his own shaking, the
broken frame of Rawcliffe from which an Edwardian suit bagged
and hung. About to die, death, dying. That man Easy Walker had
said something about his being crookidy dook. But was it rather
that Rawcliffe, out of the vatic residuum of a failed poet's career,
knew that he was going to be killed? Enderby then realized that
he'd done nothing, despite this long wait, about getting hold of a
weapon. God knew the shops had offered him enough. Not cut
out for murder perhaps really. Not really his trade.

2

Enderby climbed those three steps like a whole flight, shaking and
panting. When he entered the bar he found that Rawcliffe, helped
now by a dark and curly pudding of a young man, had not yet

arrived at the place he was groaning and yearning towards – a fireside-type chair at the end of the room, facing the main door, with the back door near it open for air. There was too much glass here altogether: it was to bake the summer customers and make them drink more. But now, in the expected pathetic fallacy, the sky was darkening fast, rain on its way. The bar-counter was to the right, facing the doorless entrance to the eating-conservatory. The pudding young man got behind the bar before starting to shoo Enderby out. Rawcliffe, now heavily sitting, said: '*Oqué, oqué, Manuel. Es un amigo.*'

'That's not,' Enderby said, 'quite what I'd call myself.' There was an aloof interested inner observer, he was concerned to be interested to note, noting all this as possible material for a future poem, including the notation of the interest. That was not right: it was that inner observer, also creator, that had primarily been wronged. 'The enemy,' Enderby said. 'Come to get you. You know what for.' The inner observer tut-tutted.

'I knew you'd give it up, Enderby,' Rawcliffe said. 'You did bloody well, really. All those years writing verse when, by rights, you should have flitted to the tatty Olympus of remembered potency.' He wavered all this like an ancient don pickled in the carbon dioxide of his college rooms. Then he coughed bitterly, cursing with little breath. Recovering, he gasped: 'Brandy, Manuel. Large.'

'Doctor he say –'

'Curse the bloody doctor and you and every bloody body. Who's master here, God blast you? Brandy. Very very large.' Manuel, his eyes on Rawcliffe, slopped much Cordon Bleu into a lemonade glass. 'Bring it over, Enderby. Have one yourself.'

'How did you know it was me?' Enderby asked, interest much too active.

'I can see through things. Poetic clairvoyance. Bring that brandy over.'

'I'm not here –'

'To be a bloody waiter. I know, I know. Bring it over just the same.' Enderby shambled to where Rawcliffe was and splashed the glass down on a small table by the chair. This table had a mass of personal trash on it, as, Enderby thought, in that poem by Coventry Patmore: to comfort his sad heart. A pile of old newspapers, a Woolworth watch, a couple of stones (ha) abraded by the beach, an empty bottle, no bluebells, cigarette packets. Beware of pity, however. Pity spareth many an evil thing. Rawcliffe took the glass and, in an aromatic brandy tempest, put it to his starved lips. Bleeding to death, Enderby saw; he was near the end of his blood. Pity causeth the forests to fail.

'Swine,' Enderby said as Rawcliffe drank. 'Filthy traitor and pervert.'

Rawcliffe surfaced from drinking. His face started to mottle. He looked up at Enderby from behind his Beetle goggles, his eyes bloodless like his mouth, and said: 'I grant the latter imputation, Enderby,' he said, 'if you call a search for pure love perversion.' As on cue, the negroid waiter in the tarboosh appeared from the kitchen, posed against the doorpost, and looked in a sort of loving horror at Rawcliffe. 'There, my black beauty,' cooed Rawcliffe's abraded larynx. 'Anybody noshing in there? *Quién está comiendo?*' His head twitched towards the dining-room.

'*Nadie.*'

'Shut up bloody shop, Manuel,' coughed Rawcliffe. 'We're closed till further notice. The bloody *baigneurs* and *baigneuses* – and a fat pustular lot they are, Enderby – can do key-business at the scullery door.' Manuel began to cry. 'Stop that,' said Rawcliffe with a ghost of sharpness. 'As for,' he turned back to Enderby, 'being a filthy traitor, I've done nothing to contravene the Official Secrets Act. The beastly stupid irony of sending you out here as a spy or whatever it is you are. That *maquillage* is ridiculous. It looks like boot-polish. Get it off, man. You'll find turps in the kitchen.'

'To me,' Enderby said. 'A traitor to me, bastard. You grew fat on the theft and travesty of my art.' Pity slayeth my nymphs. 'I mean metaphorically fat.'

'Of course you do, my dear Enderby.' Rawcliffe finished his brandy, tried to cough and couldn't. 'Better. A mere palliative, though. And that's why you got yourself up like that, eh? My brain's fuddled, such of it as has not yet been eaten away by this encroaching angel. I fail to see why you should dress up as whatever it is you're supposed to be in order to tell me I've grown metaphorically fat on your whatever it is.' He grew suddenly drowsy and then shook himself awake. 'Have you locked those bloody doors yet, Manuel?' he tried to shout.

'*Pronto, pronto.*'

'It's a bit of a long story.' Enderby saw no way out of seeming to make an excuse. 'I'm hiding from the police, you see. Interpol and so on.' He sat down on a stackable chair.

'Make yourself comfortable, my dear old Enderby. Help yourself to a drink. You look sunken and hungry. There's Antonio sleeping in his kitchen, a very passable past-master of short order cookery. We'll shout him awake and he will, singing his not altogether trustworthy Andalusian heart out, knock you up his own idiosyncratic version of a mixed grill.' He probed his throat for a cough but none came. 'Better. I feel better. It must be your presence, my dear old Enderby.'

'Murder,' Enderby said. 'Wanted for murder. Me, I mean.' He couldn't help a minimal smirk. The Woolworth watch ticked loudly. As in a last desperate gasp, the sun slashed the shelves of bottles behind the bar with fire and crystal, then retired. The clouds hunched closer. Bathers were running into Rawcliffe's arena, after keys and clothes. Manuel was there shouting at them, jangling keys. '*Cerrado. Fermé. Geschlossen.* Shut up bloody shop.'

'Like something from poor dear dead Tom Eliot,' said Rawcliffe. 'He always liked that little poem of mine. The one, you remember, that is in all the anthologies. And now the rain laying our dust. No more shelter in the colonnade and sun in the Hofgarten.' He seemed ready to snivel.

'Murder,' Enderby said, 'is what we were talking about. I mean me being wanted for murder.'

'Be absolute for life or death,' said Rawcliffe, fumbling a dirty handkerchief from one of the many pockets of his jacket-face. He gave the handkerchief to his mouth with both hands, coughed loosely, then showed Enderby a gout of blood. 'Better up than down, out than in. So, Enderby,' he said, folding in the blood like a ruby and stowing it with care, 'you've opted for the fantasy life. The defence of pretence. I can't say I blame you. The real world's pretty horrible when the gift goes. I should know, God help me.'

'It went but it came back. The gift, I mean. And now,' Enderby said, 'I shall write in prison.' He crossed one leg over the other, disclosing much of his European trousers, and, for some reason, felt like beaming at Rawcliffe. 'They don't have the death penalty any more,' he added.

Rawcliffe shook and shook. It was with anger, Enderby saw with surprise. 'Don't talk to me about the bloody death penalty,' Rawcliffe shook. 'Nature exacts her own punishments. I'm dying, Enderby, dying, and you burble away about writing verse in prison. It's not the dying I mind so much as the bloody indignity. My underpants filling with bloody cack, and the agony of pissing, and the smell. The smell, Enderby. Can you smell the smell?'

'I've got used to smells,' Enderby apologized, 'living as I've been doing. You don't smell any different,' he smelled, 'than that time in Rome. You bloody traitor,' he then said hotly. 'You stole my bloody poem and crucified it.'

'Yes yes yes yes.' Rawcliffe seemed to have grown tired again. 'I suppose the decay was always with me. Well, it won't be long now. And I shall infect neither earth nor air. Let the sea take me. The sea, Enderby, *thalassa, la belle mer*. Providence, in whatever guise, sent you, in whatever guise. Because, delightful though these boys could often be in my violent-enough-smelling, though really Indian summer, days, they can't altogether be trusted. With me gone, a mere parcel of organic sludge yumyumyummed away at by boring phagocytes, Enderby, the posthumous memory of my request will not move them to fulfil it. Oh, dear me, no. So that can be handed over to you with total confidence, a fellow-Englishman, a fellow-poet.' The boys could be heard in the kitchen, hearty Mediterranean lip-smacking, the rarer and more sophisticated ping of a fork on a plate, Moghrabi conversation, laughter escaping from munches. Not altogether to be trusted. The rain now came down, and Rawcliffe, as if pleased that a complicated experimental process were under way, nodded. Enderby suddenly realized that that was who he'd got his own nod from: Rawcliffe.

'Rawcliffe,' he said, 'bastard. I'm not here to do anything for you, bastard as you are. You've got to be killed. As a defiler of art and a bloody traitor.' He noticed that he still had one leg comfortably crossed over the other. He disposed himself more aggressively, hands tensely gripping knees, though still seated. That tan polish seemed to be sweating off, a bit streaky. He'd better do something about that before killing Rawcliffe.

'If you killed me,' Rawcliffe said, 'you'd be doing me a very large favour. There might be a small obituary in *The Times*. The triumph of that early poem might be recalled, the poem itself reproduced, who knows? As for a weapon, there's a till-protecting service revolver in that cupboard behind the bar. Or our steak-knives are pretty sharp. Or you could feed me, say, fifty sleeping-capsules, pellet by pellet. Oh, my dear Enderby, don't be a bloody bore. Let me expiate in nature's way, blast you.'

'That's not right,' Enderby started to mumble. 'Justice. What I mean is.' What he meant was that he'd been quite looking forward to a life sentence, a bit of peace and quiet, get on with his. 'I mean that if they're going to get me it'd better be for something real.' Then: 'I didn't mean that. What I meant to say was for a sheep as well as a lamb. Look, I will have a drink after all.'

'Better, Enderby, much better. There's a nice bottle of Strega behind the bar. Remember those brief sunny Strega-drinking days by the Tiber? Days of betrayal, you will say. Was I the only betrayer?' He sat up with sudden alertness. 'Do pass me that bottle of life-surrogate there, my dear Enderby. Cordon Bleu, a blue cordon to keep out that scrabbling crowd of clawers hungry for my blood. They must wait, must they not? We have things to see to, you and I, first.' Enderby went to the bar, handed shaking Rawcliffe his bottle, unwilling anyway to pour for the sod, then looked at all the other bottles, embarrassed for choice. 'Didn't go well, that marriage, did it, Enderby? Not cut out for marriage, not cut out for murder. Tell me all about that. No, wait. Dear Auntie Vesta. Married now to some sharp Levantine with very good suits. But she failed really, you know, failed despite everything. She'll never be in anybody's biography, poor bitch. You're a remarkable man, Enderby. It was in all the papers, you know, that marriage. There was a pop nuptial mass or something. Choreography round the altar, brought down-stage for the occasion. A lot of bloody ecumenical nonsense.'

'That,' grudgemumbled Enderby, 'is just what I said. Not in that connection. I mean in the other one. That priest, I mean. The day it happened.' Fundador. Not too bad a drink, despite that blasted moon woman. Rawcliffe clanked and clanked out his slug, then drank. Enderby, ashamed at his quieter coordination, did a real professional barman's pour of his own. 'What happened was this,' he said, before drinking. 'This yob got shot, Crewsy that is, was, and someone put the gun in my hand. I ran, you see. You'd have done the same.'

Rawcliffe frowned, made a shot at his lips with his glass, sprayed and dribbled cognac, sucked in a fair amount, gasped. 'Let's get all this straight, Enderby,' he gasped. 'I read the papers. I read nothing else. I've been hanging on to life, you know. The ephemeral, I mean, the sad, pretty, awful, tragic everyday, not the transcendencies of great art. I shall meet the eternal soon enough. I shall get my chamber music without the trouble of having to attend to profundities squeezed sweating from sheepgut. Or there will be nothing, like Sam Beckett. I read the papers – the pipe-smoking dogs, the topless weddings, the assassinations of pop-singers. Yod Crewsy I know all about. Dying, soon to die. Perhaps we shall die on the same day, he and I. That will be fitting, somehow. A barman shot him. I don't remember the name. Wait: something porcine.'

'Hogg,' said Enderby with impatience. 'Hogg, Hogg.' There was a young wall-eyed man in a dirty apron, the cook Antonio probably, standing by the kitchen door, picking his teeth with a quill and frowning puzzled at Enderby's get-up. 'Hogg.'

'That's it. So you read the papers too. A poetical name, that I did know. A very Jacobitical poet, that one. Charlie he's my darling. Wha the deil hae we goten for a King but a wee wee German lairdie. I like that weewee bit. He spoke out, Enderby. He didn't give a worsted-stocking damn.'

'Listen,' Enderby hissed, coming from behind the bar with his glass of Fundador. 'That was me. Hogg. That was my mother's name. They turned me into a barman, Wapenshaw and the rest of them. Yes, yes, they did. A useful citizen, they said, poet no longer. You didn't know, nobody knew. *That* was never in the papers.' Rawcliffe was all rigidity now, staring. 'But,' Enderby said, 'I got away. As Enderby. I'd got my passport. And then that bloody woman found out that Enderby and Hogg were the same. So I had to get rid of the passport. It's a long story really.' He drank some Fundador and tasted again that night of the bloody woman. Bloody women.

'It must be, it must be. But,' said Rawcliffe, 'it's a man called Hogg they were looking for.' Enderby borrowed Rawcliffe's rigidity, staring. 'Oh yes. Nothing about may be travelling under an alias. Ill-known minor poet who mysteriously disappeared, nothing like that. Nobody blew the gaff, my dear Enderby.'

'She must have done. Selenographer, she called herself. The police scouring Morocco. Me in hiding. And then there's John the Spaniard.'

'Yes yes yes.' Rawcliffe spoke soothingly. 'The world's full of traitors, isn't it? But tell me, Enderby, why did you shoot him?'

'He deserved to be shot. Plagiarism. A travesty of art. He stole my poems. The same as you.'

'Oh, for God's sake,' said Rawcliffe with emphatic weariness, 'get it over with. Shoot everybody. Shoot the whole damned treacherous world, then get behind bars and write your bloody self-pitying doggerel.'

'Doggerel,' Enderby sneered. 'You're a right bastard to talk about me writing doggerel.'

'Wait, though, wait. Didn't you say something about not having shot him at all? All about someone putting the smoking gun in your innocent paw? That figures, as the smoking gun films put it. Spaghetti Westerns. They had me writing those, Enderby. But I got out. I didn't do too badly out of L' Animal Binato. That was a bloody good idea of yours.' He shook himself back to the immediate topic. 'You're no killer, Enderby, be sure of that. You're not even the predestined victim. You wriggle out of the real striking of the blow by the operation of a time-warp or space-woof or something. You fall on your feet. You'll have to rename El Acantilado Verde, of course.'

'Eh?'

'Green cliff, raw cliff. You've got somebody on your side. Who? There you stand, absurd but vigorous. And Auntie Vesta is vanquished and poor Rawcliffe is dying. Is there anything more you want? Oh, yes. I shall dictate a letter to Scotland Yard – there's an old office Oliver in my bedroom behind the bar – and confess all. After all, Enderby, I could quite easily have done it. I even had an invitation. After all, I have been one of the great diluters, worthy to be asked. And I was in London, seeing the last of my hand-shaking consultants. Very grave he was. Prepare to meet thy God. My Goddess, rather. Yes yes yes, the mockers and diluters and travestists deserve to die.' Enderby frowned, unsure whether this was all drunkenness or the start of terminal delirium. Rawcliffe closed his eyes, his head lolled, his trouser-fly darkened, and then his crotch dripped. Enderby saw barman and waiter and cook all crammed in the kitchen doorway, open-mouthed.

'Get him to bed,' he ordered. 'Come on, jump to it.' Antonio crossed himself, quill still in his teeth. They did not exactly jump to it, but Manuel and the tarbooshed waiter grabbed each an oxter of Rawcliffe. Rawcliffe was dimly roaring. Enderby took the legs. He had done that before for Rawcliffe, he remembered. In Rome, honeymooning. Rawcliffe was lighter now than then. Antonio pointed where the bedroom was. The rain was easing a bit.

3

'You one of his *friends*, then?' asked the doctor. 'Didn't know he had any *British* ones.' He looked at Enderby with little favour, despite the restored teeth and shaved pinkness (that tan stuff had been hard to get off, the solvents painful), scant hair but washed and brushed, serious spectacles catching the pale after-rain Tangerine light. He was also wearing one of Rawcliffe's neo-Georgian suits, grey and hairy and not too tight in the armpits. The three boys, who were growing pimples and mannerisms as Enderby got to know them better (the tarbooshed waiter had also grown a name – Tetuani, after his home-town Tetuan), had been helpful with the restoration. They had even made up a sort of bed for him with the fireside-type chair and two or three stackable ones. It seemed to them to be a relief to have an Englishman around who was not dying.

'Not in that sense,' Enderby said sternly. 'A sort of friend, but not in the sense you mean.'

'What do you mean, in what sense I mean?' The doctor was an upright tall man in his hale sixties, with a lot of wavy silver hair; he looked like a military medical officer who, on the repatriation of a superior garrison, had elected to stay behind. Liked the place or something. But probably secrets of his own; shadiness. He was a bit too sharp with his 'What do you mean?'

'You know what I mean,' Enderby said, blushing. 'I'm finished with sex, anyway,' he babbled, ill at ease, unhappy with doctors. As if this declaration were a clue to identity, the doctor said:

'Seen you before somewhere, haven't I?'

'My picture in the papers perhaps. Or rather,' Enderby amended with haste, 'the picture of a man who looks very much like me, or so I'm told. A man called Hogg.'

'I wouldn't know. Never read the papers. A lot of lies mostly. As for that sex business, I'm not all that interested in what people do in that line so long as they don't come moaning to me about the consequences. This one,' he said, shouldering towards Rawcliffe, who lay feebly snorting under a blanket, 'has favoured the dirty and diseased. But you know that, of course, being his *friend*. *Nostalgie de la boue*, if you know what that means. But what he's dying of could happen to anybody. To you,' he said. 'To your maiden aunt in Chichester or wherever it is.'

'I haven't got —'

'He's riddled with it, no respecter of persons. All we can do is to ease the end. You can pay me for the hypodermic and the morphine now if you like. And for this and two previous consultations. Call me in again when you think he's gone. I'll have to sign the death certificate.'

'The body,' said Enderby. 'There's the question of —'

'He should have done what most of the British do out here. Fifty quid or thereabouts for a patch at St Andrew's. Burial service, resurrection and the life, the lot. Told me once he was a conscientious hedonist, though. Pleasure the end of life, that means. Very unwise, look where it's got him.'

'But you said it could happen to —'

'He'll have to be interred at Bubana. I daresay they'll say a few words over the grave. Somebody from the consulate usually turns up. Leave all that to you.'

'Look here —'

'I usually get paid in cash. Out of the till.' He marched ahead of Enderby into the bar and, nodding at Antonio and Manuel, who were playing Spanish Scrabble, helped himself to what looked like forty-five dirhams.

'ELLA.'

'ELLAS.'

'He says,' Enderby said, 'that he wants to be dropped into the sea. It's in writing, signed and witnessed. That he's to be dropped into the sea. Is there any law against that?'

'Damned irregular,' the doctor said, helping himself to a snifter of Bell's. 'The thing ought to be done properly. What must they think of the white man here, I often ask myself. Pederasty, if you know the term, and drunkenness. Also drugs and writing. You're new here so you wouldn't know half that goes on. Keep away from that stupidly-named Dog place across the road. Americans of the worst type. Still, *autres temps autres moeurs*. I need not, I hope, translate. I leave everything to you, his *friend*. Don't neglect to get me on the blower when the time comes.'

'Enby.' It was Rawcliffe, very feeble.

'You'd better go in and see what he wants. Don't excite him. He's in your hands now.'

'Look here –'

'DIOS.'

'ADIOS.'

'Little poem in itself, that, you could call it I suppose,' said the doctor. He smacked off the last of his Bell's. 'Still, I leave poetry to you and your kind. I must be off now.'

'What do you mean by –'

'Enby.' Rawcliffe had pumped up a few extra teaspoonfuls of painful air to strengthen his call. No compassion in his march, the doctor let himself out. 'Bgr you Emby. Comere.' Enderby went back into the sickroom. It was small but cool. Rawcliffe's bed was a double mattress laid on a worn Bokhara; thrown about all over the floor were local goatskins, of different degrees of off-whiteness; there were cheap ornaments from the bazaar – a hand of Fatma, a cobra which was really an iron spring – it throbbed and jumped and burred on the Moorish coffee table if you touched it, a Rif saddle, a hubble-bubble, scimitars, and daggers on the walls. One wall was all books in army cartridge-boxes disposed like shelf-units. Enderby had not yet had time to look through those books: there might conceivably be a copy of – The smell of dying Rawcliffe fought against an incense-burner and an aerosol lavender spray. Rawcliffe, naked under his blanket, said: 'Brandy. Vry lrge.'

'He said you're to have morphine,' Enderby said uneasily. 'Alcohol won't help the pain, he said.'

'Bgrim. Wanna talk. Bndy.' Enderby tried to harden his heart against him, traitor, traducer, diluter, sinner against literature. He went to get a new bottle of Cordon Bleu. Could Rawcliffe cope with a lemonade glass?

'CACA.'

'CACAO.'

There was a china feeding-cup next to the iron cobra. Enderby poured cognac in, sat on Rawcliffe's bed, and helped him to drink. Rawcliffe spluttered, coughed, tried to say *Christ*, but he got down what Enderby estimated to be about a bar quintuple. He had once, in Piggy's Sty, had to serve one of those to a Cabinet Minister: it had come to thirty shillings, taxpayers' money.

'Better, Enderby, much better. Taken that letter to the post, has he? Loiters on the way sometimes, wayward. Good fundamentally, though. A bottom of good sense. Dr Johnson or somebody said that, Enderby.'

'It was about a woman.'

'Woman, was it? Well, of course, that's more your line, isn't it? God God God God, the bloody pain. The thing to do is to try to see the bloody pain as working in something out there. The body is not me. No transubstan. But Christ Christ, there's a hot line to the brain. Snip the nerve-endings, is there a me still there when all have been snipped? Psychoneural paral paral parallelism ism. Very popular that, before the war. The new immortality.'

'There's this morphine here,' Enderby said.

'More your line. Two lines there, though, hot and cold. Sun and moon. Moon's no power over you, Enderby. Me, I sinned against the Muse, all woman, and she took her revenge. And now to be sacrificed to her. But she'll be partly cheated, Enderby. New moon coming up about now. But eastward there are tideless waters. Drop this exterior thing in the tideless waters, Enderby. More brandy.'

'Do you think you –'

'Yes, I do. Got to tell you. Give instructions.' Enderby poured

more cognac into the feeding-cup. Obscene, somehow, that festive
gold and heady vapour in bland invalid china. Rawcliffe sucked
more in avidly. 'There's a man called Walker, Enderby. Useful sort
of man, British colonial. His precise terry territory uncertain. He's
in Casablanca now. Get in touch with him, his phone number's
behind the bar. He knows how to get a small aircraft, borrows it
from Abdul Krim or somebody, bloody rogue whoever he is. Bloody
rogue. What was I saying? Tight, a bit, that's the trouble. Empty
stomach, that's the trouble.'

'I know this Walker. Easy Walker he calls himself.' And then:
'Can you eat anything? An egg or something?'

'It's not your job to keep me alive, is it, Enderby? What's the
bloody use of nutriment to me? Listen. The money's in this mattress.
For Christ's sake don't let anybody burn it. It's not that I don't
trust the banks. It's the buggers in the banks I don't trust, Enderby.
Tattle tattle tattle about how much he's got, then coming along
for a loan, then beat you up in a back-alley if they can't have it.
I know them all too well. You know them all too well. You know
Easy Walker. Always said you'd fall on your feet, Enderby. Get that
bloody Antonio in here.'

'What for?'

'Tell him to bring his guitar. Want to hear. To hear. In all the
anthol. He sings it.'

Enderby went out to the bar and said: '*Antonio, Señor Rawcliffe
quiere que tu, usted canta, cante,* subjunctive there somewhere, whatever
it is. *Su cancion, él dice.*' Antonio and Manuel both looked up from
a Scrabble board now nearly full of words, their eyes ready to brim.
Enderby went back to Rawcliffe. 'That letter to Scotland Yard,' he
said. 'It won't do any good. There must be a lot who send in letters
like that.' And where was he to go, where? He had reconciled
himself, hadn't he? But that was when it had seemed possible to
be able to murder Rawcliffe. Rawcliffe's eyes were closed. He had
started snorting again. His body writhed feebly. And then he started
violently awake.

'You've no bloody idea,' he said with slow seriousness, 'of the
bloody agony. You wouldn't think it possible. Don't leave it too
long, Enderby.'

'Morphine?'

'Brandy. Insult to the brain. Poor Dylan. Kill me with bloody kindness.' Enderby sighed, then recharged the feeding-cup. Antonio came in, trying his strings, crying. 'Sing, blast you,' said Rawcliffe, spluttering out cognac. The smell of it was fast overcoming his own. Antonio sat on the Rif saddle and twanged his thumb from E to e, sniffing his tears back. It was a well-worn guitar; Enderby could see the abrasions of fingers that, in Andalusian style, had drummed its body. Antonio gave out a thrummed major chord that, with the smell of cognac, seemed to affirm life (sun, zapateados, death in the afternoon). He wailed:

> *'Per ap sa yamna tuonti diri seyed,*
> *Per ap sayid beter go,*
> *Ji seyed. Mocionles jer ayis, jer jeyed,*
> *Seyin not yes, not no.'*

'In all the anthologies,' Rawcliffe cried, then coughed and coughed. Antonio did not go on. 'Put that, death, in your bloody pipe,' said Rawcliffe more weakly when the racking had subsided. '*Exegi monumentum.* And what of yours, Enderby?' He was so faint that Enderby had to drop his ear towards him. 'Better to be the one-poem man. But she left me then. Opened up heaven of creativity and then closed it. All right, Antonio. Later, later. *Muchas gracias.*' Antonio blew his nose on his cook's apron. 'Read me something of yours, Enderby. They're there, your slender volumes, somewhere. I bought your books at least. Least I could do. I am not all badness.'

'Well, really, this is hardly – What I mean is –'

'Something appropriate. Something to one about to die or one dead.'

Enderby felt grimly in his left jacket pocket. He had transferred that stolen horror thither. 'I can,' he said, 'without going to your shelves.' But there was here at last, and his heart began to climb as with muscular pseudopodia, the chance of checking. Auntie Vesta. He strode over Rawcliffe's hidden feet towards the wall of books. A lot of cheap nasty stuff there: *Bumboy, Mr Wigg's Fancy, Lashmaster.* He thought, from the shape and size, he saw a copy of his own *Fish and Heroes*, but it turned out to be a small collection of glossy photographs: men and boys complicatedly on the job, with idiot eyes. But here it was, that other volume, the one the critics had trounced: *The Circular Pavane*. He flicked and flicked through the pages. There weren't many. And then. 'Right,' he said. Rawcliffe's eyes were closed again but he could tell Enderby was smiling. He said:

'Glee, eh? The creator's glee? You've found something that recalls the actual ecstasy of its making. Don't exass exacerbate my agony. Read it.'

'Listen.' Enderby tried to be gruff, but his reading made the poem sound sneering, as though the emotions of the mature were being mocked by some clever green child:

'They thought they'd see it as parenthesis –
   Only the naked statement to remember,
Cleaving no logic in their sentences,
   Putting no feelers out to the waking dreamer –

So they might reassume untaken seats,
   Finish their coffee and their arguments,
From the familiar hooks redeem their hats
   And leave, with the complacency of friends.

But strand is locked with strand, like the weave of bread,
   And this is part of them and part of time –'

'Oh God God,' Rawcliffe suddenly cried. 'Ugly hell gape not come not Lucifer.' He began to babble. 'And if the eternal finds its figures in the temporal then they can find their inferno here.' He screamed and then collapsed, his head lolling, his tongue out, blood coming from his left nostril. Antonio's guitar clanged gently superposed fourths and my–dog–has–fleas as he put it down. He made the sign of the cross and prayed weeping. 'A shot, Enderby, for Christ's sake.' Enderby started: a test; see if he could really kill? 'A lot of shots.' He saw then and went over to the coffee-table and the syringe and the morphine ampoules in their box. He hoped he could cope. Those Doggy Wog people would be able to cope all right.

4

Rawcliffe did not stay under for long. There was a powerful life-urge there, despite everything. 'Brandy,' he said. 'I'll beat them all yet, Enderby.' Enderby filled the cup: the bottle was near its end. Rawcliffe sucked it all in like water. 'What news?' he asked. 'What irrelevancies are proceeding in the big world?'

'There's nothing as far as I can see,' Enderby said. 'But we've only got the Spanish paper, and I can't read Spanish very well.'

Enough, though. When Tetuani came back from posting that air-letter, he brought with him a copy of *España*, which Enderby took with him to a bar-table. Rawcliffe unconscious, though roaring terribly from deep in his cortex, Enderby sat with a large whisky, breathing the prophylactic of fresh air from an open window. '*Quiere comer?*' Antonio asked. Enderby shook his head: he couldn't eat anything just yet, not just yet, *gracias* all the same. He drank his drink and looked at the paper. It was better that he read what he was undoubtedly going to read not in English: he needed the cushioning of a foreign tongue, with all its associations of literature and tourism, despite his foreknowledge. Words had power of their own: *dead* would always be a horrible word. On the front page the Caudillo still howled for the Rock, and some Arab leader called vainly for the extermination of Israel. When, on the second page, he came to the headline YOD CREWSY MUERTO, his response was that of a printer who had set the type himself. The score was, say, 10-2, and you had to wait ten minutes, say, for the anti-climax of the final whistle. What it said under the headline was brief. It said, as far as Enderby could tell, that he had passed into a terminal coma after a moment of flickering his eyes open and that soon there were no further indications of cardiac activity. There would be a sort of lying in state somewhere and then a requiem mass at the Catholic Cathedral in London (they meant Westminster). Fr O'Malley would deliver the panegyric. Nothing about girls weeping, as over Osiris or Adonis or somebody. Nothing about Scotland Yard expecting immediate arrest.

'Nothing at all,' Enderby said.

What would Scotland Yard do about Rawcliffe's letter? Enderby had two-fingered it himself to Rawcliffe's dictation. It would do no good, Enderby had said, but Rawcliffe had insisted. Repentance, seeing the light, symbolic blow against anti-art. A guest (check guest-list) who had come with full cold-blooded intention of killing and then being arrested – dying of those encroaching claws, what had he to lose? – he had succumbed in reflex to panic and handed gun to an anonymous waiter. He was not sorry, oh no, far from it: so perish all art's enemies, including (but with him it was the fullest blackest knowledge: he knew what he did) himself. Rawcliffe's scrawl, two witnesses: Antonio Alarcón and Manuel Pardo Palma. Well, Enderby thought, it might resolve things one way or the other. It would welcome the police to one terminus or another. And your name, sir, *señor*? Enderby. Your passport, please, *por favor*. Well, a slight problem there, officer. Whispered consultation, sergeant calling inspector over, comparing photograph with. All right, Hogg then. I recognized the true murderer and pursued him. Doing the job of the police for them, really, in best fictional tradition. I say no more. All right, arrest me then. Obviously I say no more. No warning necessary.

He was indifferent, really. All he wanted was a small room and a table to write verse on and freedom from the necessity to earn a living. But there remained self-doubt. Was the Muse so generous now only because she was dispensing rubbish? The future, perhaps, lay with those Doggy Wog people. He didn't really know; he wanted to be told, shown. But was he being reserved for something? Why did not everybody know that Hogg was Enderby? Why had that moon-bitch been silent? If John the Spaniard had blown the gaff, why was Tangier not milling with Interpol, demanding to see all foreign passports, combing? What force had struck down Wapenshaw, if it was Wapenshaw they'd been talking about, and rendered him dumb?

Enderby wondered now, sitting on the Rif saddle, keeping away from the putridity, whether he should ask Rawcliffe (meaning the still not foundered intelligence in the penthouse above the demolition squads), as a dying man who had nothing to gain by mendacity, what he thought of his, Enderby's, work and (what he really meant) whether he should go on with it. But heaving and groaning Rawcliffe gave him an answer without being asked, without speaking. Go on with anything so long as you're alive; nothing matters except staying alive. Enderby could see that now, but had not always thought so. Rawcliffe said:

'Get on to Walker. It's going to be *it* soon, Enderby. Never mind what he asks. Money money money. All money these days. Fortunately it's stuffed in here, mine I mean, by my feet. No danger, Enderby, of ultimate incontinence fouling it. Clean money, most. The dirty part did not really harm my country. Hashish a harmless enough drug. More brandy.'

'I'll have to get a new bottle.'

'Get it then, blast you. What are those bloody boys doing?'

'The siesta.'

'Something in the Bible about that. What, could ye not watch with me one hour? This night, before the cock crow.' Rawcliffe took breath, rattling, and went feebly cocorico. Then he coughed and coughed. Blood bubbled from both nostrils and some trickled from his right mouth-corner. 'Good Christ,' he panted, 'I won't have this. Bewrayed, beshitten. Die in one's own bloody dung.' He tried to shift his body away from the new foulness but rolled back on to it. 'I'm getting up,' he said. 'I'm going to die on my feet. Help me, blast you, Enderby.'

'You can't, you mustn't, you —'

'Best to be shot, knifed, standing.' He threw his blanket off. He was naked except for a safety-pinned towel like a baby's diaper. 'I insist, Enderby, you bastard. I'll drink my terminal liquor in a bar, like a man. My viaticum, you swine.' He started, cursing, to get up. Enderby had to help, no way out of it. He went further than he'd gone for anybody. He pulled off Rawcliffe's diaper and wiped him clean with the clean part of it. He forgave his stepmother everything. There was a bathrobe on a nail behind the door. He put his arm round bare shivering Rawcliffe and shuffle-danced him towards it. 'Better, Enderby, better,' as he was clothed in gay yellow and blue. 'Take me to the bar. Wake those bloody boys. They must be my crutch.'

Pushing Rawcliffe before him, Enderby yelled. Antonio peered out from the kitchen first, startled, naked as Rawcliffe had been. He went back in to get the others, himself yelling. Rawcliffe tried to yell but collapsed into coughing. He collapsed against the bar-counter, coughing, trying to curse. Soon Antonio and Manuel were

holding him up, an arm each about him, in dirty white shirts;
Manuel's trousers were already black. 'Now, Enderby,' Rawcliffe
gasped at last. 'You say you've been a bloody barman. Mix me
something. A cocktail called *Muerte*. Stop that blasted snivelling,
you two.' Tetuani, tarboosh on, came out, frightened.

And I will, thought Enderby. 'Leave it to me,' he said, adding,
in desperate facetiousness, 'sir.' He took a large beer glass and
slopped brandy in, then white rum, gin, whisky, vodka. The bottles
flashed in the fair afternoon light. It was like celebrating
something.

'No need for ice,' Rawcliffe gasped. 'Get that, maybe, soon. That
thing in bloody Shakespeare. Measure for measure, eh? Altogether
fitting. Thrilling regions of ribbed ice. Top it, Enderby, with something spumous. Asti, memories of Rome. Add, for old times sake,
a dollop of Strega. Strega, a witch. Witchbitch. That bloody man
in Mallorca, Enderby, says the day of the moon goddess is done.
The sun goddess takes over.' Enderby found a bottle of Asti on the
shelf, very warm, favoured of the sun. He cracked its neck against
the counter-edge. 'Good, Enderby.' There was a fine gush. The
stench of Rawcliffe was now well overlaid with powerful yea-saying
aromas. But, admired Enderby, those boys' stomachs were strong.
He gave the full spuming glass to both Rawcliffe's claws. 'A toast,'
Rawcliffe said. 'What shall it be, eh? *La sacra poesía?* The sun goddess?
The survival of the spirit? to the,' he began to droop, 'impending
dissolution,' to snivel; the strong-handed boys began to snivel with
him, 'of this, of this –' Enderby became stern: he didn't like this
snivelling. He cried:

'Ah, shut up. Get that bloody drink down and shut up.' It was
strong fatherly talk; the medicine was wholesome; had not he,
Enderby, once dared death, though dragged gurgling back? 'Get
on with it, Rawcliffe. Bloody traitor.'

'Good, Enderby, good, good. No false compassion there.
Excellent.' Rawcliffe braced himself, pumped air into his lungs like
a parody of a dog's panting, then took his medicine. It spilled and
rilled, the *mousse* got up his nose, he coughed some back into the
glass, but he went gamely on to the dregs. Antonio put the flecked
glass down for him. Rawcliffe gasped and gasped. 'Put. That. On.
The.' He coughed, like payment, a coin of bloody sputum on to

the counter. 'I mean. *Muerte*. The. Ult. Ult. Ultmte. Cktl.' He yearned towards his chair, feebly turning. The boys took him over, only his bare toes touching the floor. Rawcliffe collapsed next to his chair-side table, full of toys. Coventry Patmore. 'Lil slp now.' He at once began to snore. The boys put his feet up on the stackable. Enderby thought he had better now telephone Casablanca.

5

It was growing dark when Rawcliffe surfaced for the last time. Enderby had sent the boys out, sick of the hand-wringing and snivelling. He sat at the other side of Rawcliffe's chair, smoking the local cigarettes that were called *Sporl*, not drinking. The thought of drink made him shudder. When Rawcliffe surfaced, it was with an accession — that condemned man's supper — of clarity and calm. He said:

'Who's that there?'

'Me. Enderby.'

'Ah yes, Enderby. Know your poetry well. Stole one of your ideas once, a bloody good one. No regrets. Now I give you something in return. My last poem. It came to me in sleep. Listen.' He cleared his throat like an elocutionist and intoned slowly but with vigour:

> 'The benison of lights and the
> Hides of asses and the
> Milk of the tide's churns.
> She should not have
> Rejected me like any copulative
> Of the commonalty.

Too much light, Enderby. Turn one of those lights off.'

There were no lights on. 'I've done that,' Enderby said.

'Good. Now where was I? Ah, I know. Listen.

> At length I heard a ragged noise and mirth
> Of thieves and murderers. There I him espied,
> Who straight, *Your suit is granted*, said and died.'

'That,' Enderby said, 'is George Herbert.'

Rawcliffe suddenly began to rage. 'It's not it's not it's not you fucking swine. It's me. Me.' In the dusk his head rolled. Quietly, 'Your suit is granted,' he said, and died. With the conventional accompaniment of rattle and postlude of rictus and liquidity.

3

1

'And,' Easy Walker cried above the engine, 'real donk dirt-bibles. Got a jarvey, brad, all towsermouth for that variety of how's-your-Auntie-Doris-and-little-Nora-and-the-twins. So we'll march on markers when this lot's dooby-dooed.'

The physical assumption of Rawcliffe. His body, in clean pyjamas and wrapped in a Union Jack that Manuel had bought for a few dirhams in, of all places, the Big Fat White Doggy Wog, sat next to Easy Walker in what Enderby took to be the co-pilot's seat. At least a kind of half-eaten steering-wheel or joystick in front of Rawcliffe twitched and turned in sympathy with Easy Walker's. And also dead Rawcliffe had his share of very lively dials and meters and emergency instructions, exclamation-pointed. His arms were pinioned beneath the flag, and he was corded at neck, waist, thighs, and ankles. No danger of his, its, flailing around if ithe came back to life.

'You sure he's footed the old garbage-can proper?' Easy Walker had asked while they had been bundling him in. 'Because there's been cases. There's this case now, brad. Tell you after. Maybe you minced it all masterman.'

Enderby sat behind Rawcliffe, an empty seat next to him. It was a small but neat aircraft, American-made, though there was a spelling mistake, Enderby noted, in one of the instructions on the instrument-panel: *jetison*. That did not make him doubt the

airworthiness of the craft, for it was always a matter of every man
to his own trade. This one of piloting seemed as much a trade of
Easy Walker's as any of the others he professed. He had cried
conversationally above the engine even as, tearing down the runway,
he brought the speed up to air-speed:

'A real donk passy too, there'll be there. Left the whole bimbang
kadoozer to you then, has he, brad?'

'There's the question of,' Enderby had shouted. 'That one of
mine, I mean.'

'Welcome to Bird County,' Easy Walker had yelled as the craft
nosed into the old-gold Moroccan air. The late afternoon sky to
themselves, except for rare gulls and, far to port, a migrant exalta-
tion of brownish birds that, after a rest on the top of Gibraltar,
were crossing the Straits for their African wintering. No Air
Maroc flight till very much later. Below on the cabochon-cut
Mediterranean very few boats, though what looked like a rich
man's yacht gleamed to starboard. It was still the sun's time. The
moon, thin last night, was not watching over Rawcliffe's ascension
into heaven. Fattened, she would draw at him vainly from the
deep, gnawed by fishes, his flag defiled. Over the aircraft wireless
strange English crackled from Tangier control tower. Easy Walker
ignored it. Aft lay Ceuta.

'There was one,' he yelled without effort, 'Ricker Sugden did
for like his booze brad when he kicked. Do too for this jarvey, I
reckon.' He recited, drowning the engine:

> 'Dragged from his doings in the roar of youth,
>   Snipped like the stem of a caldicot flower,
>   Snarled time's up ere he'd quaffed his hour,
> Tossed to the tearing of the dour dog's tooth.'

'That's not quite right for Rawcliffe,' Enderby shouted. It wasn't
either. The right one was in all the anthologies, but Enderby's
calling of it would never prevail against this of Ricker Sugden's. It
was the right one only because it was the only one.

> 'Bye, my brad, let the bright booze pour
>   That is suds of stars in the Milky Way,

And its door swing open all the joylit day
And the heavenlord landlord cry you time no more.'

'Not one of his best,' called Enderby, but he was not heard. Not
obscure enough, too much meaning. Poor Rawcliffe. Traitor
Rawcliffe rather, but he had paid. Your suit is granted. What suit?
To be granted a cell, smallest unit of life. Enderby feebly tried to
give out to sea, sky, and Easy Walker that last stanza ('His salts have
long drained into alien soil'), and then saw how inappropriate it
really was. His soil would drain soon into alien salt. There was
nothing for Rawcliffe. But it was something to rest in bones, rags
of flag fluttering, at the sea's bottom between two continents. It
was a kind of poem. Easy Walker cried:

'Nowsy wowsy. You right for the shove, brad?' Enderby nodded,
forgetting that Easy Walker's eyes were ahead and there was no
driving mirror. The corpse of Rawcliffe had lolled to rest against
the perspex of the starboard door. Enderby roughly pushed it so
that it began to topple gracefully against Easy Walker. 'Watch it,
watch it, brad.' Leaning over, Enderby turned the door-handle,
panting. It was rather stiff. Suddenly it opened and swung, and the
huge roaring air without seemed to pull at him, but he dug his
nails into Rawcliffe's seat-back. 'Nowsy wowsy powsy.' Easy Walker
made the craft list hard to starboard. There was a torrent of frozen
air rushing in up diagonally now. Enderby clawed at the corpse
through its flag-shroud, heaving it out, but, falling to the air, it
seemed to be merely buoyed up by it. 'Blast you, Rawcliffe,' went
Enderby for the last time. 'Righty right,' Easy Walker sang, and he
kicked out at a dead shin. Then he listed farther. Enderby pounded
and pushed. As it were reluctantly, Rawcliffe's body launched itself
into this quite inferior region of the sky, lower, surely, than Parnassus.
'Got him, brad,' meaning space had. The tricolour, crude in this
sapphire and turquoise ambience, span slowly down. 'Gone.' Without
sound, and with lips parted only as for a cigarette, the sea took
him. Here lies one whose name was *not* writ in water, he had once
said in his cups.

It was hard to get that door, which had swung open to its limit,
back in place. But Easy Walker lurched violently to port and the
door hurtled in and, on a lurch that brought them both lying on

their sides as at a Roman supper, it slammed to. Then he righted the
craft and, widely circling in the air, its nose sniffed round towards
home. Home: what else could you call it? Green Africa ahead, then
the geometry of the little airport, then a sudden urgent love for the
runway. A three-point landing of the kind called insolently skilled,
a taxiing towards Easy Walker's waiting Volkswagen.

'Talking about passports,' Enderby said as they sped through the
brown country outside town, 'I'd like that back if you've still got
it. I let it go too soon.'

'Not poss, brad. Swallowed up, that, in the great dirty passy-hungry
what-does-your-dad-do. Have this, though, your need being greater
than. Dead jarveys help the living from their heart of darkness. Still.
A pig of a pity.'

'What I mean is,' said Enderby. 'I'm entitled to an official identity
of some sort.' But was he? And, if so, why? He might yet be taken
somewhere, but he had no intention of making a move of his own.
And, anyway, did bearing a name matter? Rawcliffe would be glad
to be called anything or nothing if he could be alive again.

'There was the time I got this passy just as the jarvey as todded
it seemed like as to take off. But he came to, yes he did, when it
was already swapping fumblers. Well, you're all right, I'd say, with
this Rawcliffe jarvey. He won't come up, no, not never no more.
Different from this jarvey back in Great Dirty Mum.'

When they arrived back at *El Acantilado Verde*, Rawcliffe's other
verbal monument, Easy Walker was eager to see what shady treasures
there might be to buy cheap and sell dear. The three boys sat, in
clean white, at a table by the bar-counter, playing some game
which involved the linking of little fingers. They had difficulty in
composing their faces to a funeral look. 'All finished,' Enderby said.
'*Finito.*' But there must be a better Spanish word than that.
Consommado? It sounded soupish. '*Consummatum,*' he said, pushing
down to the roots.

'March on markers,' said Easy Walker. He was very deft. The
amount of pornography he uncovered was shocking. It was mostly
in the cartridge-box book-shelves, though previously – because of
the austerity of the binding – unsuspected by Enderby. 'Here,' said
Easy Walker, 'is some right donk flag for such as takes a swizzle to
it,' showing Enderby Victorian steel-engravings of bloody wounds,

lovingly detailed, and knobbed whips and knotted thongs. 'And there's them shoving up the old kazerzy with it, very painful for my shekels and sherbet. And here,' Easy Walker said, shock on his unshockable, 'is what I would not have if it was my own Aunt Ada as did it, brad. Cause there's limitations to all bozzles, has to be, stands.' In his hands trembled a leather-bound folio of what, to squinting Enderby, seemed at first to be illustrations to the Bible. But they were very perverted illustrations, and there was one that made Enderby feel sick. 'I mean,' Easy Walker said, slamming the book shut, 'that was bad enough in itself without making it worse and dirty sexual.' It was the first time Enderby had heard him use plain language. 'Making a mock of it like that jarvey I said. When a jarvey snuffs it's not up to him to come back, up-your-piping and that. All right for him in here,' he bowed his head, 'because he was what he was and no up-my-tickle. But this jarvey like I said. And there was like that saucepan-lid, Lazarus his all-the-same. And crucifixions too in this one, very dirty. Very clear that came off.'

'What?' said Enderby. 'Who?' Time himself will bring you in his high-powered car. And supposing the car doesn't go on to pick someone else up but, instead, goes back to the garage. Things as they were before, or as near as you could get them. He would not be surprised, he would not be surprised at anything. 'You mean,' said Enderby, 'Yod Crewsy. You mean he's not dead after all.'

Easy Walker nodded and nodded. 'Laid out, brad, in some arsee plum-and-apple in the Smoke. Then all them teens brooping round, going sniff sniff. Turn-the-handles lighted all about him in his best whistle. And his three brads keeping double-scotch, two at his toots and one behind his uncle. Then he flicks open and says "Where am I?" Got it this morning on the talkbox, in the near-and-far, coming here.'

Enderby nodded and nodded. Bitch. Blasphemous bitch. Very clever. Easily done, bribed doctors or not even that. Genuine error. Clinical death and real death. And now sermons about miracles and popsters flocking to give thanks. Our Thammuz, Adonis, Christ for that matter. 'And,' Enderby said, 'I suppose there was one sly pseudo-mourner, come to see, his only chance, his handiwork, lurking in the shadows of the chapel, and, when this body rose from the dead, he screamed. Screamed that the times have been that, when the brains were out, the man would die, and there an end, but now they rise again, this is more strange than such a murder is.'

Easy Walker shook his head, baffled. 'Don't get that at all, brad. Forked me on the cobbles and no rare-with-Worcester. Have to mince the papers when they come out, not out yet, not with that, pennywise.'

Enderby shook his head, not baffled. 'No more papers. Bugger the outside world,' he said violently. 'If not that way, some other. I'll hear about it, only a question of waiting. No resurrection for Rawcliffe, not of any kind. They'll crumple his letter up at Scotland Yard, another crank.'

'I'll ghoul these off now,' Easy Walker said, 'dirt-bibles.' He showed new shock on the realization that his slang had, for once, slung at the gold and pierced it. Enderby then had an intuition that he was going to throw off what must be a home-stitched patchwork of patois and, strayed sheep or remittance-man, speak a true language that was far more middle-class than his, Enderby's. 'It's all dirt and cheating,' he said, and only on the last word (*cheadn*) did the innominate colonial really sound out. He seemed for an instant as feeble as in a plonk hangover. Enderby nodded. He said kindly:

'Come back tomorrow or the next day for the rest of the stuff. Except for what I want, that is. Any heterosexual pornography I'll keep. I've finished with women.'

'Finish with them.' It was clear and bitter. And then: 'What's all them there sling-your-hooks there, brad?' He headed at a set of cartridge-boxes set aside, special.

'Those,' said Enderby, 'are all the anthologies.'

When Easy Walker had left, Enderby ripped open Rawcliffe's mattress with a tarnished curved dagger. There were bundles of dirty notes, high and low in denomination: about, he reckoned, fifteen thousand dirhams. He would buy a new mattress tomorrow; tonight he would make a dog's bed of rugs and cushions. Then he went thoughtfully to examine Rawcliffe's bath and lavatory, rather well-appointed; for the customers there was only a stark, though regularly sluiced, W C off the dining-conservatory. Then he went to the bar. All three boys looked at him in expectation, a composition, as for early Picasso, of coffee-mug handlers: Antonio sipped wide-eyed; Tetuani warmed both dark brown hands on the mug's belly; Manuel, finished drinking, swung his gently, handle on little finger. 'No,' Enderby said firmly. 'I sleep alone. *Yo duermo solo.*' They nodded with degrees of vigour: they had merely wanted to know. Manuel said:

'Open up bloody shop?'

'*Mañana.*'

'*Quiere café?*' asked Antonio.

Enderby did not resist his yearnings towards a resumption of chronic self-imposed dyspepsia. He had convinced himself that he could be healthy enough if he wanted to be. 'Make,' he said slowly, 'very strong tea. *Muy fuerte.* Not tea-bags but spoonfuls of the real stuff. *Comprendido?* Tinned milk. *Leche condensada.*' And later he would eat – What? Something stepmotherly gross – a corned beef stew with bacon added to make floating flowers of grease, a grumbling huddle of boiled spuds, pickled onions. He nodded with relaxed kindness, then went for his first for a hell of a long time leisurely session in the lavatory.

2

'What I say is,' said the oldest of the men, his skin of broken veins and capillaries like an enlargement of a microscopic picture of motor oil, 'there couldn't have been any conspiracy. They choose crack shots. A political assassination is, in our country at least, a rather serious undertaking.'

'It's altogether possible,' said a dried ancient, goitrous thyroid colloidally distended, eyes popping, voice hoarse, 'that it was the act of a private entrepreneur. More enthusiasm than skill. They should never have got rid of National Service.'

'Well, that's just what I said, isn't it?'

'Implied, if you will. Hardly said.'

'He too,' said a brisk barking small ex-major, the youngest, about seventy-five, 'might have been resurrected. Wouldn't put anything past them. An everlasting premier.'

'Or he was just a liar.' This was a dithering man with twittering toothless mouth. 'Jealousy of the bug for the flea. Shot at him.

Failed to kill. Now he tries to make himself a political hero. What do you think, Rawcliffe?'

'I really have no opinion on the matter,' said Enderby. He sat in the fireside-type chair, the table in front of him, paper and ballpoint on the table, not a line added to the lines already there:

> As loaves were gifts from Ceres when she laughed,
>   Thyrsis was Jack, but Crousseau on a raft
> Sought Johnjack's rational island –

The sun was weakish, what Tangier called winter inching up. The bottles behind the bar caught that meagre light as if to store anew what was already long stored. Manuel measured out whisky for the old men, retired here for the warmth and fancied cheapness. Manuel was cheerful and honest, to be trusted with the till. Honesty was a Tangerine luxury, to be enjoyed. There were bright pin-up calendars, promising, after the mild though windy winter, torrid abandon renewed, golden flesh, the heart-breaking wagging cruppers of the bikinied young over the golden beaches. And there were plaques advertising Byrrh, Rivoli, Royal Anjou, Carlier, a British beer called Golden Fleece. The Coca-Cola ice-box had been freshly polished by Tetuani. Marie Brizard's name was on the water-jugs, Picon's on the ashtrays. Antonio sang, preparing *tapas* in the kitchen. 'Both politicians and pop-singers,' Enderby said, 'are boils on the bottom of the communal body.' The oldest elder went aaaaargh. He liked that. Writer fellow this Rawcliffe. The apt phrase.

Enderby was not pushing on with the sonnet, nor with the letter he still had to write. The question was, he was thinking, how he was to address her. When he wrote. If he wrote. Dear Vesta: never. Dear Mrs – He'd forgotten her new name. (The address was easy: the publisher of this filthy volume.) An abusive salutation, that would be letting himself down. He had written to his own publisher, for he thought he might need him, them, again. Tiny royalties had accrued: they had been keeping them for him (£5.7.9.); they were glad, they said, to know where he was at last. As for this business of plagiarism, that was his affair, since he owned copyright. They themselves were not willing to take action, since they were in the bidding for the resurrected Yod Crewsy's next book – a brief prose volume, they understood, humorous, inspirational, even religious. And they enclosed a personal letter, still in its envelope, only recently arrived at the office. Enderby had frowned over the handwriting, female. You and your female hadmirers. With a thudding heart he had opened it up.

Dear Piggy or Hoggy or Dirty (for I don't know what else to call you, do I?),

I was sorry about things and still am. And now this is the only way I can get in touch with you. Because I got it out of that silly girl on the plane that it was all really a mistake and you *had* gone to the wrong room without meaning to do what that silly captain of the plane thought (you know what I'm talking about, don't you?). They choose too many of these air-hostesses for their looks, though hers weren't much to write home about really, and not their intelligence, and that silly captain was a bit too quick to draw conclusions, and I certainly shan't fly with them again, that courier with the stupid woolly cap on was also very rude, I thought. The number of wrongs that seem to have been done you! I was stupid too, wasn't I, thinking you could have anything to do with that shooting, it must have been my inflamed holiday imagination. I've been thinking about you a lot and am sure you must have been thinking very bad thoughts about me. But could you blame me really? I mean, you were a bit mysterious, no luggage and all. What I *had* to do to try and make amends was to get some of your poems from the library – very difficult, the library had to send off for them – and I found some of them rather obscure and others very sad. Very modern, of course. I can't make up my mind yet about whether I really like them – that sounds ungrateful, doesn't it, but I do like to think of myself as an Honest Person, but one of our junior English lecturers – did I tell you about him? Harold Pritchard, he's trying to get a little book of criticism published – was quite gone on them. He said there were curious resemblances to the poems of Yod Crewsy (the more I think of this whole scandalous business the more convinced I am it was a big publicity stunt, and in the presence of the Prime Minister as well, and that makes me think less of *him*). Then Harold found the same poem in both books, and that gave him an unholy thrill, he loves anything like a literary scandal. There was no doubt, he said, who stole from whom. So he's written a letter to the Times Literary Supplement and thinks the sparks will fly.

Where are you, dear Piggy? I wish I could make proper amends. Looking back I see that, despite everything, that Seville night was really romantic – love and your sudden inspiration and my dear moon and even your mistake when, bless you, you were looking for me. Write to me and accept my love if you will and forgive me.

Your
Miranda.

Sitting here on this quiet weekday, the train from royal Rabat just going by on the single-tracked line that separated the Spanish Avenue from the beach cafes, the inkpaint congealing in his ballpoint, the harmless winter approaching, he thought that, despite the luck that had been granted (*said, and died*), the autumn should, for the sake of justice, flame out with a last act of vengeance. But he could not write the letter and, the letter unwritten, the poem would never flood into the estuary of its sestet. What did he really want from her? His money back? No, this place made enough, even in winter. Her humiliation, her smartness wrecked once more but by more devastating waters than the rain of Castel whatever-it-was, the snivelling, the running eye-shadow, the smooth face collapsed into that of a weary crone? No, not that either. Rawcliffe had taught him pity, that maketh the forests to fail.

'It will die down,' said the goitrous old man,' 'and new sensations will come up. That new shiftless generation must be fed with fresh novelties.' He took some Wilson's snuff, then hawked, carked, and shivered with the dour pleasure of it.

'Not a religious man,' said the snapping ex-major. 'But when I see a central tenet of my father's faith – he held it, poor devil, through all his suffering – when I see that, I say, turned to a trick or gimmick or whatever the fashionable word is, then I wonder. I wonder what new blasphemy they can devise.' He shuddered his whisky down in one.

'No morals,' said the twittering man. 'No loyalty. They will turn on their friends as if they were enemies. It was at a private party that this youth with the gun boasted in his cups. Isn't that so, Rawcliffe?'

'I don't really know,' said Enderby. 'I don't read the papers.'

'Very wise too,' said the senior elder. 'Stay away from that world. Get on with your job, whatever it is.'

'Sam Foote,' said the goitrous old man. 'A ridiculous name. Probably made up.'

'Samuel Foote,' said Enderby, 'was an eighteenth-century actor and playwright. He was also an agent for small beer. *And they all fell to playing the game of catch as catch can, till the gunpowder ran out at the heels of their boots.*'

There was a silence. 'They did, eh?' said the senior. 'Well, suppose I'd better be thinking about getting home for lunch. Takes me longer and longer. Walking, that is.'

'He wrote that,' said Enderby. 'It was a test-piece. This other man said that he could recite anything hearing it once only.'

'On my way too,' said the ex-major. 'Bit of a blow on the prom.'

The door opened and a girl came in, very tanned. She wore, as for high summer, a simple green frock well above her knees, deepcut at her young bosom, her golden arms totally bare. She carried a beach-bag. She smiled shyly and went up to Manuel at the bar. 'I understand,' she said, 'that I can hire a changing-cubicle or whatever it's called.' Her voice was low in pitch, the accent classless. Susannah among the elders, Enderby thought. The ex-major said quietly:

'Susannah among the elders.' Enderby could see them feeling old, impotent, lust too tired within to rage at so many opportunities lost, the time gone, perhaps death to be their next season. And himself? He got up and said to the girl:

'Well, you *can* actually, but –' She looked at him from green eyes sprinkled, like a *sireh* quid, with gold. They were set apart but not too much: enough for beauty, perhaps honesty; not enough for the panic mindless world of the animals. Hair? Enderby at once, to his surprise, thought of the flower called montbretia. 'What I mean is that, surely, it's getting a bit cold now. This time of the year I mean.'

'I don't feel the cold. A cold sea doesn't frighten me.' As in an allegory or *Punch* title-page, the aged trundled off – winter or war or industrial depression or an all-round bad year – from the presence of youth as peace, spring, a change of government. They creaked and groaned, snorted, limped, winced at arteriosclerotic calf-ache, went. One or two waved tiredly at Enderby from beyond the closed glass door, a safe distance. 'Could I have one then? For a couple of days. Do I pay in advance?'

'No, no, no need – Certainly. *Un llave*, Manuel.'

'*Numero ocho*,' Manuel smiled.

They all – Tetuani clearing the old men's whisky-glasses, Antonio at the kitchen door, Manuel from the arena with its furled umbrellas, Enderby turned in his chair – watched her prancing seawards over the deserted sand, in scanty crimson, her hair loose. Enderby turned back in rage to his table. He took paper and wrote fiercely: 'You bitch, you know you ruined my life. You also stole my verse to give to that blasphemous false commercial Lazarus of yours. Well, you won't get away with it. One of the stolen poems had already been published in one of my volumes. I'm going to sue, you're all going to suffer.' And then he could see Vesta standing there, cool, smart in spotless dacron, unperturbed, saying that *she* wouldn't suffer, only that mouthing creature of hers, and he was going to be abandoned anyway, past his peak, the time for the chaotopoeic groups coming, or the duo called Lyserge and Diethyl, or Big D and the Cube and the Hawk and the Blue Acid. Or worse. Enderby took another sheet of paper and wrote:

> Smell and fearful and incorrigible knackers
> With the crouched pole under
> And strings of his inner testes strewn
> Over curried pancreas and where the
> Hollowed afternoon vomits
> Semen of ennui and

And and and. Send it round, signed, to the bloody Doggy Wog, showing that I can beat them at their own game if I want to, but the game isn't worth the, in Walkerian locution, turn-the-handle. And, *amigo* with the onion, I know what's in the *carta* you wanted to bring round to my lodgings where my razor and antisolar spectacle clip-on and few dirty handkerchiefs have been long snapped up by those who had not that night yet been betrayed to the police by fat Napo. *Khogh*. It was some word of their language, no deformed proper name from another. And the letter surely says that he saw who did it, *hombre*, and told Scotland Yard as much. A curious and perhaps suspicious lack of treachery from treacherous Spain. Enderby felt ungratefully gloomy. All was set for writing and yet he could not write. Draft after unfinished draft. Gloomily he read through his sonnet octave again.

Augustus on a guinea sat in state. This is the eighteenth century, the Augustan age, and that guinea is a reduction of the sun. *The sun no proper study*. Exactly, the real sun being God and that urban life essentially a product of reason, which the sun melts. And no more sun-kings, only Hanoverians. *But each shaft of filtered light a column*. Meaning that you can't really do without the sun, which gives life, so filter it through smoked glass, using its energy to erect neo-classic structures in architecture or literature (well, *The Rambler*, say or *The Spectator*, and there's a nuance in 'shaft' suggesting wit). *Classic craft abhorred the arc or arch*. Yes, and those ships sailed a known world, unfloodable by a rational God, and the *arc-en-ciel* covenant is rejected. Something like that. *To circulate (blood or ideas) meant pipes, and pipes were straight*. Clear enough. You need the roundness of the guinea only so that it can roll along the straight streets or something of commercial enterprise. The round bores of the pipes are not seen on the surface, the pipes in essence being means of linking points by the shortest or most syllogistical way. And, to return to that pipe business, remember that pipes were smoked in coffee-houses and that news and ideas circulated there. And that craft business ties up with Lloyd's coffee-house. *As loaves were gifts from Ceres when she laughed, Thyrsis was Jack*. A bit fill-in for rhyme's sake, but, rejecting the sun, you reject life and can only accept it in stylized mythological or eclogue forms. But Jack leads us to Jean-Jacques. *Crousseau on a raft sought Johnjack's rational island* – the pivot coming with the volta. Defoe started it off: overcome Nature with reason. But the hearer will just hear *Crusoe*. Jack is dignified to John, glorification of common, or natural, man. Then make Nature reason and you start to topple into reason's antithesis, you become romantic. Why? A very awkward job, the continuation.

'Lovely.' She had come running in, wet. She wrung a hank of hair, wetting the floor. Fat drops broke on her gold limbs. Her high-arched foot left Man Friday spoors. Seeing her round jigging nates, Enderby could have died with regret and rage. 'Like a fool I brought everything except a towel. Could you possibly –' She smiled, her chin dripping as from a crunching of grapes.

'Just a minute.' He puffed to his bedroom and brought out a bath-towel, not yet, if ever to be, used by him, and also the gaudy robe, not greatly stained, that Rawcliffe had died in. He put it round her shoulders. Clear gold skin without a blemish and a flue of ridiculous delicacy. She rubbed her hair dry with vigour, smiling her thanks. Manuel hovered smiling. She smiled back. Enderby tried to smile.

'Could I,' she smiled, 'have a drink? Something a bit astringent. Let me see –' The bottles smiled. No, they bloody well didn't: Enderby was not going to have that. 'A whisky sour.'

'Weeskee –?'

'I'll do it,' said Enderby. 'Fetch some white of egg. *Clara de huevo.*' Manuel ran into the kitchen. She rubbed herself all over in, with dead Rawcliffe's brilliant robe. 'A difficult art,' blabbed Enderby, 'making a whisky sour.' That sounded like boasting. 'Americans are very fond of them.' An egg cracked loudly off. She rubbed and rubbed. Enderby got behind the bar and looked for the plastic lemon that contained lemon-juice. Manuel, having brought a tea-cup with egg-white in it and some minute embedded triangles of shell, watched her rub instead of his master mix. 'There,' said Enderby, quite soon.

She took it and sipped. 'Hm. Is nobody else drinking?'

'About time,' Enderby said, 'I had my preprandial, if that's the right word.' He seemed to himself to simper, pouring out straight Scotch.

'Do I pay now or do you give me a bill afterwards? And can I get lunch here, talking about preprandials?'

'Oh,' said Enderby, 'have this one on me. It's a kind of custom here, the first drink of a new customer on the house.' And 'Oh, yes. You can have steak and salad or something like that. Or spaghetti with something or other. Anything you like, really. Within reason, that is.' Reason. That brought him back to that bloody poem. To his shock, he saw her bending over his table, looking openly at his papers.

'Hm,' she said, having sipped again. 'You've certainly got it in for this person, bitch rather.'

'That,' went flustered Enderby, coming round from the counter, 'is of no consequence. I'm not sending it. It was just an idea, that's all. Really,' he said, 'you shouldn't, you know. Private.' But it was your privates you were only too ready to expose, wasn't that so, when you – He felt a kind of tepid pleasure promising warmth, not outrage at all. She sat down in his fireside-type chair. She started reading his octave frowning a little. A curiously tutorial aura seemed to be forming. Enderby went to sit down on one of the stackable chairs near his table.

'Bring it closer,' she said. 'What's all this about?'

'Well,' babbled Enderby, 'it's a sonnet, very strict. It's an attempt, really, to tie up the Age of Reason with the French Revolution. Or on another level, the rational and the romantic can be regarded as aspects of each other, if you see what I mean.' Sitting, he moved towards her without getting up, as though this were an invalid chair. 'What I have to do is to show that romantic curves are made out of classical straightness. Do you see what I mean?' And then, gloomily, to himself: Probably not. She was young. She had perhaps mourned Yod Crewsy's death, gone to some open-air evangelical meeting on his resurrection.

She closed her eyes tight. 'Keep a triplet pattern in your sestet,' she said. 'A breath between your cdc and your dcd. How will classical pillars become Gothic arches? The sun will melt them, I suppose. And then you ought to have the guillotine. A very rational machine – sorry about the rhyme, but it's rhymes you're after, isn't it?'

'What,' Enderby asked gravely, 'would you like for lunch? There's Antonio, you see, waiting there ready to cook it.' Antonio stood at the kitchen door, trying to smile while chewing something. She nodded, not smiling but puckered charmingly, thoughtful. Guillotine, machine, seen, scene.

'What are you going to eat?' she asked. 'I'll eat what you eat. Not fish, though. I can't stand fish.'

'Well,' Enderby mumbled, 'I don't normally till – We close for the siesta, you see, and then I usually have –'

'I hate eating on my own. Besides, we've got to work this thing out. Is it something with meat in it?'

'Well,' Enderby said, 'I have a sort of stew going most of the time. Beef and potatoes and turnips and things. I don't know whether you'd like it, really.'

'With pickled onions,' she said. 'And Worcestershire sauce, plenty of it. I like gross things sometimes.' Enderby blushed. 'I like to come down to earth sometimes.'

'Here with your family?' She didn't answer. Monied, probably. 'Where are you staying? The Rif? The El Greco?'

'Oh, vaguely. It's right up the hill. Now, then. Try it.'

'Eh?' And, while Tetuani set places in the conservatory, he tried it.

> Sought Johnjack's rational island, loath to wait
> Till the sun, slighted, took revenge so that
> The pillars nodded, melted, and were seen
> As Gothic shadows where a goddess sat –

'Volta not strong enough. The rhyme-words are far too weak. That *that* is shocking.'

Then, over the thick stew, grossly over-sauced, with pickled onions crunched whole on the side and a bottle of thick red eely alumy local wine, they, he rather, literally sweated over the rest of the sestet.

> For, after all, that rational machine
> Imposed on all men by the technocrat
> Was patented by Dr Guillotine.

'This is terrible,' she said. 'Such bloody clumsiness.' She breathed on him (though a young lady should not eat, because of the known redolence of onions, onions) onions. 'I'd like a bit of cheese now,' she crunched. 'Have you any Black Diamond cheddar? Not too fresh, if that's possible. I like it a bit hard.'

'Would you also like,' asked Enderby humbly, 'some very strong tea? We do a very good line in that.'

'It must be really strong, though. I'm glad there's something you do a very good line in. These lines are a bloody disgrace. And you call yourself a poet.'

'I didn't – I never –' But she smiled when she said it.

3

Enderby dreamt about her that night. It was a nightmare really. She was playing the piano in her scanty green dress for a gang of near-closing-time pot-swinging male singers. But it was not a pub so much as a long dark gymnasium. On top of the piano lay a yawning black dog, and Enderby, knowing it was evil, tried to warn her against it, but she and the singers only laughed. At last, though, he dragged her out protesting into the winter night (but she did not seem to feel the cold) of a grimy Northern industrial town. They had to get away quickly, by bus or tram or cab, or the dog would be out after her. He rushed her, still protesting, to a main road, and he stopped, with no difficulty, a southbound truck. She began to think the adventure funny and she made jokes to the driver. But she did not see that the driver was the dog. Enderby had to open the truck cabin door while the vehicle was in motion and get her on to the road again to thumb a lift. Again it was the dog. And again. The new drivers were always the old dog and, moreover, though they barked they were southbound, they would almost at once turn left and left again, taking her passengers back north. Finally Enderby lost her and found himself in a town very much like Tangiers, though in a summer too scorching for North Africa. He had a room but it was at the top of a high stair. Entering, he met with no surprise this girl and her mother, an older Miss Boland. His heart pounded, he was pale, they kindly gave him a glass of water. But then, though there was no wind, the shutters of the window began to vibrate, and he heard a distant rather silly voice that somehow resembled his own. 'I'm coming,' it said. The girl screamed now, saying that it was the dog. But he swam up through leagues of ocean, gasping for air. Then he awoke.

He had foul dyspepsia, and, switching on the bedside lamp, he took ten Bisodol tablets. But the word *love*, he noticed, was in his mouth in the form of a remotish pickled-onion aftertaste, and he resented that. The moon was dim. Some Moorish drunks quarrelled in the distance and, more distant, real dogs started a chain of barking. He was not having it, it was all over. He drank from a bottle of Vittel, went brarrgh (and she had done that too, just once and with no excuse-me), then padded in his pyjama top to the bathroom. The striplight above the mirror suddenly granted him a grousing image of The Poet. He sat down on the lavatory seat and, a big heterosexual pornographic volume on his knees as a writing-board, he tried to get the dream into a poem, see what it was all about. It was a slow job.

> At the end of the dark hall he found his love
> > Who, flushed and gay,
> > > Pounded with walking hand and flying fingers
> > > The grinning stained teeth for a wassail of singers
> > That drooped around, while on the lid above
> > > The dog unnoticed, waiting, lolling lay.

She had been unwilling to give her name, saying it was not relevant. She had gone off about three o'clock, back in green, swinging her towelless beach-bag, giving no clue where she was going. Manuel, out later to pick up the cigarette order, said he had seen her coming out of the Doggy Wog. Enderby was jealous about that: was she helping those filthy drug-takers with their filthy drugged verses? Who was she, what did she want? Was she an anonymous agent of the British Arts Council, sent out to help with culture in, in Blake's phrase, minute particulars?

> He noticed, cried, dragged her away from laughter.
> > Lifts on the frantic road
> > > From loaded lorries helpful to seek safe south
> > > Slyly sidestreeted north. Each driver's mouth,
> > Answering her silly jokes, he gasped at after
> > > The cabin-door slammed shut: the dogteeth showed.

She had better stop being a dream of boyhood, for it was all too late. He had reached haven, hadn't he? He would not be in the bar tomorrow morning (this morning really); he would be out taking a walk.

> At last, weary, out of the hot noon's humming,
> > Mounting his own stair

> It was no surprise to find a mother and daughter,
> The daughter she. Hospitable, she gave him water.
> Windless, the shutters shook.

This was all messed up. The story wouldn't run to another stanza, and this stanza was going to be too long. And the rhythm was atrocious.

> A quiet voice said: 'I'm coming.'
> 'Oh God God it's the dog,' screamed the daughter,
> But he, up the miles of leaden water,
> Frantically beat for air.

A good discussion about that with somebody, over whisky or stepmother's tea: that was what was needful. The realization suddenly shocked him. Had not the poet to be alone? He converted that into bowel language and noised it grimly in the still night, clenching the appropriate muscles, but the noise was hollow.

And so she was there again in the lemony Tangerine sunlight of nearwinter, this time bringing her towel. The old men, perhaps frightened of the gunpowder running out of the heels of their boots, had stayed away, but there were other customers. Two youngish film-men, in Morocco to choose locations that might serve for Arizona, kept going *ja* at each other and greedily scoffing Antonio's *tapas* – fat black olives; hot fried liver on bread; Spanish salad of onion, tomato, vinegar, chopped peppers. An Englishman in fluent but very English Spanish, expressed to Manuel his love of baseball, a game he had followed passionately when he lived three miles outside Havana. A quiet man, perhaps a Russian, sat at the corner of the counter, steadily and to no effect downing Spanish gin.

'Not worth writing,' she said, 'a poem like that.' She had changed back into a crimson dress even briefer than the green one. The baseball *aficionado*, greying vapidly handsome, kept giving her frank glances, but she did not seem to notice. 'You yourself may be moved by it,' she said, 'because of the emotional impact of the dream itself. But it's dreary old sex images, isn't it, no more. The dog, I mean. North for tumescence. And you're trying to protect me from yourself, or yourself from me – both silly.' Enderby looked at her bitterly, desirable and businesslike as she was. He said:

'That *love* in the first line. I'm sorry about that. I don't mean it, of course. It was just in the dream.'

'All right, we're scrapping it anyway.' And she crumpled the work of three hours of darkness and threw it on the floor. Tetuani gladly picked it up and bore it off to nest with other garbage. 'I think,' she said, 'we'll go for a walk. There's another sonnet we have to work out, isn't there?'

'Another?'

'One you mentioned yesterday. About the Revolt of the Angels or something.'

'I'm not sure that I –' He frowned. She punched him vigorously on the arm, saying:

'Oh, don't dither so. We haven't much time.' She led him out of the bar, stronger than she looked, and the customers, all of whom were new, assumed that Enderby was an old customer who had had enough.

'Look,' Enderby said, when they stood on the esplanade, 'I don't understand anything about this at all. Who are you? What right have you? Not,' he added, 'that I don't appreciate – But really, when you come to consider it –'

The wind whipped rather coldly, but she felt no cold, arms akimbo in her ridiculously brief dress. 'You do waste time, don't you? Now how does it begin?'

They walked in the direction of the Medina, and he managed to hit some of it into the wind. It was as though she were telling him to get it all up, better up than down.

> Sick of the sycophantic singing, sick
> Of every afternoon's compulsory games –

Sturdy palms set all along the sea-front, the fronds stirred by that wind. The donkeys with loaded panniers, an odd sneering camel.

'That's the general idea, isn't it? Heaven as a minor public school. Did you go to a minor public school?'

'I went,' said Enderby, 'to a Catholic day-school.'

It was Friday, and the devout were shuffling to mosque. The

imam or bilal or whatever he was was gargling over a loudspeaker. Brown men, of Rif or Berber stock, followed the voice, looking at her legs, though, with bright-eyed, frank but hopeless desire. 'It's a lot of superstitious nonsense,' she said. 'Don't, whatever the temptation, go back to it. Use it as mythology, pluck it bare of images, but don't ever believe in it again. Take the cash in hand and waive the rest.'

'An indifferent poet, Fitzgerald.' Enderby loved her for saying what she had said.

'Very well, let's have something better.'

> Sick of the little cliques of county names,
> The timebomb in his brain began to tick –

Luncheon in a little restaurant crammed with camp military gear not too far from the Hotel El Greco. It was run by two men in love with each other, one American, the other English. A handsome Moorish boy who waited on seemed himself in love with the Englishman, who was flaxen, bronzed, petulant, and given to shouting at the cook. The Moor was not adept at hiding emotion: his big lower lip trembled and his eyes swam. Enderby and she had a thin dull goulash which she said loudly was bloody terrible. The English lover tossed his head and affricated petulantly against his alveolum, then turned up the music – a sexy cocksure American voice singing, against a Mahlerian orchestra, thin dull café society songs of the thirties. She prepared to shout that the bloody noise must be turned off: it was interfering with their rhythm. Enderby said:

'Don't, please. I've got to live in this town.'

'Yes,' she said, her green eyes, their gold very much metal, hard on him. 'You lack courage. You've been softened by somebody or something. You're frightened of the young and the experimental and the way-out and the black dog. When Shelley said what he said about poets being the unacknowledged legislators of the world, he wasn't really using fancy language. It's only by the exact use of words that people can begin to understand themselves. Poetry isn't a silly little hobby to be practised in the smallest room of the house.'

He blushed. 'What can I do?'

She sighed. 'Get all these old things out of your system first. Then push on.'

> Beating out number. As arithmetic,
>> As short division not divided aims,
> Resentment flared. But then, carved out in flames,
> He read: *That flower is not for you to pick.*

'It's time,' she said, 'you started work on a long poem.'

'I tried that once. That bastard stole it and vulgarized it. But,' and he looked downhill, seaward, 'he's paid. Wrapped in a Union Jack, being gently gnawed.'

'You can get something here. This is a junction. Deucalion's flood and Noah's. Africa and Europe. Christianity and Islam. Past and future. The black and the white. Two rocks looking across at each other. The Straits may have a submarine tunnel. But it was Mallarmé who said that poetry is made with words, not ideas.'

'How do you know all this? You're so *young.*'

She spat out breath very nastily. 'There you go again. More interested in the false divisions than the true ones. Come on, let's have that sestet.'

The sestet ended in a drinking-shop not far from the Souk or Socco, over glasses of warmish pastis. Drab long robes, hoods, ponchos, assbeaters, loud gargling Moghrabi, nose-picking children who used the other hand to beg. Sympathetic, Enderby gave them little coins.

> Therefore he picked it. All things thawed to action,
>> Sound, colour. A shrill electric bell
> Summoned the guard. He gathered up his faction,
>> Poised on the brink, thought and created hell
> Light shimmered in miraculous refraction
>> As, like a bloody thunderbolt, he fell.

'That *bloody*,' Enderby said. 'It's meant really to express grudging admiration. But that only works if the reader knows I've taken the line from Tennyson's poem about the eagle.'

'To hell with the reader. Good. That needs a lot of going over, of course, but you can do that at leisure. When I'm gone, I mean. Now we'd better take a look at that Horatian Ode thing. Can we have dinner at your place?'

'I'd like to take you *out* to dinner,' Enderby said. And, 'When you're gone, you said. When are you going?'

'I'm flying off tomorrow evening. About six.'

Enderby gulped. 'It's been a short stay. You can get a very good dinner at a place called the *Parade*. I could get a taxi and pick you up about —'

'Still curious, aren't you? Bit of a change for you, isn't it, this curiosity about people? You've never cared much for people, have you? From what you've told me, anyway. Your father let you down by marrying your stepmother, and your mother let you down by dying too young. And these others you've mentioned, men and women.'

'My father was all right,' Enderby said. 'I never had anything against him.' He frowned, though ungrudgingly.

'Many years ago,' she said, 'you published a little volume at your own expense. Inevitably it was very badly printed. You had a poem in it called "Independence Day".'

'I'm damned if I remember.'

'A rather bad poem. It started:

> Anciently the man who showed
> Hate to his father with the sword
> Was bundled up in a coarse sack
> With a frantic ape to tear his back
> And the squawking talk of a parrot to mock
> Time's terror of air-and-light's lack
> Black
> And the creeping torpor of a snake.'

'I can't possibly have written that,' went Enderby, worried now. 'I could never possibly have written anything as bad as that.'

'No?' she said. 'Listen.

> Then he was swirled into the sea.
> But that was all balls and talk.

Nowadays we have changed all that,
Into a cleaner light to walk
And wipe that mire off on the mat.
So when I knew his end was near
My mind was freer
And snapped its thumb and finger then
At the irrelevance of birth,
And I had a better right to the earth
And knew myself more of a man,
Shedding the last squamour of the old skin.'

'That's somebody else,' said Enderby urgently. 'Honestly, it's not me.'

'And you love your mother because you never knew her. For all you know she might have been your stepmother.'

'It's different now,' pleaded Enderby. 'I forgive my stepmother, I forgive her everything.'

'That's very generous of you. And who do you love?'

'I was just coming to that,' said Enderby with approaching banners of wretchedness. 'What I wanted to say was —'

'All right, all right. Don't pick me up in a taxi. You can't anyway, because you don't know where I am. *I'll* pick *you* up about eight. Now go home and work on your bloody Horatian Ode. No, leave me here. I go in a different direction.' She seemed needlessly irritable, and Enderby, having once, though briefly, lived with a woman, wondered if it was possibly — She was old enough, wasn't she, to have —

'Gin and hot water,' he suggested kindly, 'are said to work wonders.' But she didn't seem to hear. She seemed to have switched off Enderby like a television image, looking blankly at him as if he had become a blank screen. A very strange girl altogether. But he thought that, having got the better of the moon, he could perhaps this time live with his fear.

4

She was smartly dressed for the evening in bronze stockings and a brief, but not too brief, gold dress, a gold stole round her tanned shoulders, her hair up at the back. On her left wrist she had a gold chain from which miniscule figurines depended. It was a restaurant of subdued lights, and Enderby could not see what the figures were or meant. She was perfumed, and the perfume suggested something baked – a delicate but aphrodisiacal soufflé seasoned with rare liqueurs. Enderby was wearing one of Rawcliffe's Edwardian suits – it did not fit too badly – and even Rawcliffe's gold watch and chain. One thing Enderby did not like about this place was that the mortician *collage* man from the Doggy Wog was in it and was obviously a respected and regular customer. He sat at a table opposite and was eating with his fingers a brace of roast game birds. He had greeted this girl with a growl of familiarity but now, picking the meat from the backbone, he kept his eyes sternly on her. He did not apparently remember Enderby. She had returned his greeting with an American air-hostess's 'Hi'.

Tonight she was not going to have greasy stew and pickled onions and stepmother's tea. She read the menu intently, as though it contained a Nabokovian cryptogram, and ordered a young hare of the kind called a capuchin, marinated in *marc*, stuffed with its own and some pig's liver as well as breadcrumbs, truffles, and a little preserved turkey-meat, and served with sauce full of red wine and double cream. Before it she had a small helping of jellied boar. Enderby, confused, said he would have sheep's tongue *en papillotes*, whatever they were, that was. And, after dry martinis which she sent back as neither dry nor cold enough, they had champagne – Bollinger '53. She said it was not very exciting, but it seemed to be the best they had, so they put, at her demand, another bottle on ice while they were drinking this one. Enderby uneasily saw signs of a deliberate intention to get tight. Soon, clanking down her fork, she said:

'A fancied superiority to women. Despise their brains so pretend to despise their bodies as well. Just because you can't have their bodies.'

'I beg your pardon?'

'Juvenilia. One of your.' She belched gently. 'Juvenilia.'

'Juvenilia? But I never published any of my juvenilia.' Several bar-customers were interested in the repeated word: a gland injection, a sexual posture, a synthetic holiday resort. She began to recite with mocking intensity:

'They fear and hate
the Donne and Dante in him, this
cold
gift to turn heat to a flame, a kiss
to the gate
of a mons-
ter's labyrinth. They hold
and anchor a thin thread –'

'Not so loud,' went Enderby with quiet force, blushing. The
mortician was looking sardonic over a large dish of blood-coloured
ice cream.

'– the tennis party, the parish dance:
stale pus out of dead
pores.'

Someone at the bar, unseen in the dimness, applauded. 'I didn't
write that,' said Enderby. 'You're getting me mixed up with somebody else.'

'Am I? Am I? I suppose that's possible. There's so much minor
poetry about.'

'What do you mean – minor?'

She downed a long draught of Bollinger, as though the recitation
had made her thirsty, belched with no excuse-me, and said: 'There
was that other nasty little thing about meeting a girl at a dance, wasn't
there? Juvenilia, again.' Or a disease perhaps, one of those gruesomely
pleasant-sounding ones like salmonella. She took more champagne
and, with world-weary tone and over-sharp articulation, recited:

'Semitic violins by the wailing wall
Gnash their threnody
For the buried jungle, the tangle of lianas –'

'I think,' Enderby said sternly, 'that I have some right to know –'

'Or say that was before, in the first flush,
And say that now

> A handful of coins, image and milled edge worn,
> Is spilled abroad to determine
> Our trade of emotions.'

'I mean, apart from how you know all that, and I don't believe it's mine anyway –'

> 'On this background are imposed
> Urges, whose precise nature it is difficult to define:
> Shells shaped by forgotten surges.'

'I'm not having any more of this,' and Enderby grasped her thin wrist firmly. She shook herself free with little effort and said:

'Too rich for you, is it?' She sniffed at his half-eaten sheep's tongue *en papillotes*. 'A lot of things are too rich for you, aren't they? Never mind, mumsy will ook after him den. Let me finish.' Enderby, very wretched, let her.

> 'One understands so little, having no words
> To body forth thoughts, no axe
> To reach flagged soil, no drills
> To pierce to living wells. It would tax
> My energies overmuch now to garner you
> Out of worn coins, worn shells.'

She took another bumper of fuming wine, belched like an elfin trumpet of triumph, then waved smiling across to the mortician. He said:

'That's telling him.'

'You're being bloody unfair,' said Enderby loudly and to the mortician, more loudly, 'You keep your nose out of this, sod.' The mortician looked at Enderby with very small interest and went on eating ice cream.

'Big untrue postures,' she delivered. 'Pretence. You can't make major poetry out of pretence.'

'I tell you,' said Enderby, 'it was my stepmother's fault, but that's all over now. Pretence, you say,' he added cunningly, 'but very memorable pretence. Not,' he super-added, 'that I wrote that. I'm sure I didn't.' He was pretty sure, anyway.

'I can remember anything,' she said smugly. 'It's a gift.' Then she went *phew*. 'God, it's warm in here.' And she pulled her stole off roughly, showing her glowing young shoulders.

'It's not really warm, you know,' said Enderby. And, hopefully: 'Perhaps it's all that champagne. Perhaps you're not feeling too well.'

'I feel fine,' she said. 'It's the sun within me. I'm a beaker full of the warm south. Nice tension of opposites there: cooled a long age in the deep-delvèd earth.' She had drunk most of the first bottle and was now doing very well with the second. 'I won't pretend that you wrote that, because you didn't. Poor boy. But his name was *not* writ in water.' Enderby felt chilled when he heard that. 'Posterity,' she then said. 'The poet addresses posterity. And what is posterity? Schoolmarms with snotty kids trailing round the monuments. The poet's tea-mug with an ingrained ring of tannin-stain. The poet's love-letters. The poet's falling hair, trapped in brush-bristles rarely washed. The poet's little failings – well-hidden, but not for ever. And the kids are bored, and their texts are covered with thumb-marks and dirty little marginalia. They've read the poems, oh yes. They're posterity. Do you never think of posterity?'

Enderby looked warily at her. 'Well, like everybody else –'

'Minor poets hope that posterity will turn them into major ones. A great man, my dear, who suffered the critics' sneers and the public's neglect. Halitosic breathing over your corpse. Reverent treading through the poet's cottage, fingering the pots and pans.'

Enderby started. 'That's brought back a dream. I think it was a dream. The pots and pans fell, and I woke.'

'Oh, come on, let's finish this champagne and go. I can't eat any more of this muck. Creamed leveret's bones, ugh. Let's go and swim.'

'At this hour? And it's very cold, the sea I mean. And besides –'

'You don't swim, I know. You're preparing your body for honoured corpsedom. You don't do anything with it. All right, you can watch *me* swim.' She filled both their flutes and downed hers, re-filled and downed again.

'What I meant to say was – It's a bit difficult, I know, but –' He called for the bill. '*Cuento, por favor*,' Quite the little Tangerine, he was thinking. Settling here for corpsedom. No, not that. He had his work, hadn't he? And there was this other matter, and he'd better blurt it out now before the bill came. 'I know,' he said stiffly but urgently, 'there's a great disparity of age. But if you could see your way – I mean, we get on all right together. I would leave it to you to decide on the precise nature of the relationship. I ask nothing.' The bill came: another flame-haired Goth of a Spanish waiter, flashing a gold tunthus. It was a lot of dirhams. Enderby counted out note after note after note, all from Rawcliffe's mattress.

'You only ask *me*,' she said. The champagne was done, and she upturned the bottle to hold it like a thyrsus. 'Come on, I'm burning.'

The mortician growled something about that being okay then. She smiled and nodded. 'What do you do over there?' asked Enderby jealously. 'You go over there. The dog place, I mean. I know you do.'

'I go to a lot of places. I'm a beezy leetle girl. The world's bigger than you could ever imagine.'

The doorman whistled a *petit taxi* or *taxi chico*. It was a windy night in a hilly street, no more. But a dirty old Moor shuffled to them to offer a small parcel of marijuana for five dirhams. 'Shit,' she said. 'Dilutions for the tourists. All teased out of fag-ends collected from the gutters.' She gave the old man a brief mouthful of what sounded like fluent Arabic. He seemed shocked. Enderby was past being surprised. In the taxi he said:

'What do you say then? The precise nature of the relationship –'

'You leave to me. Right. I heard you the first time.' They rolled seawards. The driver, a moustached thin Moor with a skullcap, kept turning round to have a look at her. She banged him on the shoulder, saying: 'Keep your fucking eyes on the road.' And to Enderby: 'All I want at the moment is my swim. I don't want avowals and the precise nature of the relationship.' She was silent then, and Enderby thought it prudent also to be silent. They came to near the gate, only the single track to cross, which opened on to the beach steps and the – But *El Acantilado Verde* had been painted out and the new name as yet only lightly stencilled. Manuel had a brother who did that sort of thing.

The bar looked grim and functional under the plain lights. 'Come in here,' Enderby invited, leading her to his own room. There were table-lamps, shaded in warm colours, that all came on

together when he clicked the switch by the door. Many of
Rawcliffe's Moorish curiosa were still around, but there was now
a lot of naked shelf-space to be clothed. But with what? He didn't
read much. Perhaps he ought to read more, keep in touch with
the posterity of which she, all said and done, was very nearly a
member. Read about media and the opening up of the psyche
with drugs. All sorts of things. Enderby had bought a bedspread
of camel-hair, its design undistinguished, as well as new sheets and
a new mattress. There was still something raffish, riffish, Rawcliffesque
about the bed on the floor, in the middle of the floor. Enderby
had not yet sufficiently breathed on things.

'Hm,' she said. 'How about calling that cookboy of yours to see
about some coffee? I'd like some coffee afterwards.'

'Oh, he's not here. They all sleep out. *Yo*.' Enderby said, with
painful roguery, '*duermo solo*.' And then: 'Of course, you can't swim,
can you? You forgot, I forgot. You've nothing to swim in.' He
smiled.

'That's right,' she said. 'Nothing. I shall swim in nothing.' And,
before Enderby could say anything, she darted over to his book-
shelves and picked on a gilt-edged folio.

'That,' said Enderby, 'isn't mine. It was left by him. Don't look at
it, please.' Fool, he should have thought. 'And don't swim with nothing
on. It's too cold, there are laws against it, the police will come along,
this is a Muslim country, very strict about indecency.'

'Indecency,' she said, looking through the volume. 'Yes. Dear
dear dear. That seems more painful than pleasurable.'

'Please don't.' He meant two things. He felt he wanted to wring
his hands. But she dropped the book on the floor and then started
to take her dress off. 'I'll make coffee myself,' he said, 'and there's
some rather good cognac. Please don't.'

'Good, we'll have that afterwards.' And she kicked off her spiky
shoes and began to peel down her stockings, sitting on Enderby's
bedside chair to do it more easily. And then. He gulped, wondering
whether to turn his back, but that somehow, after that book, might
seem hypocritical. Bold Enderby, unmoved, watching. But:

'Go in as you are, by all means, but −' But going in as she was
meant going in very nearly as she wanted to go in. And now
entirely. Oh God. Enderby saw her totally naked, all gold, with no

shocking leprous bands where they might, beach decency being observed, be expected to be. He just stood there, a butler called in by her eccentric ladyship. She looked him hard, though soft, in the eyes. He gnashed his teeth at her ghastly young beauty, all revealed. She said:

'Time enough.' Huskily. Then she lay on the camel-hair, eyes not leaving his, and said: 'Love. You meant to say love. Come on, take me, darling. I'm yours, all yours. When I give I give. You know that.' He did know it. And she held out gold blades of arms, gold foil gleaming in her oxters. And gold below on the mount. 'You said,' she said, 'I must decide on the precise nature of the relationship. Well, I'm deciding. Darling, darling. Come on.'

'No,' gasped Enderby. 'You know I can't. That isn't what I meant.'

'Just like Mr Prufrock. Darling, darling, you can do anything you like. Come, don't keep me waiting.'

'It won't do,' said Enderby, dying. He saw himself there with her, puffing in his slack whiteness. 'I'm sorry I said what I said.'

She suddenly drew her knees up to her chin, embracing her shins, and laughed, not unkindly. 'Minor poet,' she said. 'We know now where we stand, don't we? Never mind. Be thankful for what you've got. Don't ask too much, that's all.' And she leapt from the bed, brushing his hand with the smoothness of her gold flank, just for a fraction of time, as she ran past him to the door, out of the door, out of the building, out of the arena, towards the sea.

Enderby sat on the bed, blood forming patterns in his eyes. His heart growled as it thumped. Off to the bloody sea, where Rawcliffe was. But no. Rawcliffe was in the Mediterranean, east of here. She was out in the fringes of the Atlantic, a bigger sea. One sometimes forgot that it was the Atlantic here, the Atlantic and Africa and all the big stuff. Minor poet in Africa, facing the Atlantic. There would undoubtedly be phosphorescence all round her as she plunged farther into the Atlantic.

5

She didn't come in the following morning, and he didn't expect her. Yet there had been no good-bye, not yet. She had high-heeled into the kitchen, glowing, clothed, even perfumed (yet smelling somehow, to his fancy, of drowned poets) to see him watching the bubbling coffee as if it were an alchemical experiment. And she hadn't liked the coffee: too weak, too minor-poetic. Well, he had never been good at coffee. Tea, now, was altogether a different matter. Anyway, she had to fly, so much to see to before really flying. And then, lightly and without satire, a kiss on each cheek for him, as at the award of some *prix* for minor poetry. And off.

Tossing in his bed, he had wondered about minor poets. There was T. E. Brown, three legs of Man, who had said: 'O blackbird, what a boy you are, how you do go it,' and giving to British gardens pot or plastic godwottery. And Leigh Hunt, whom Jenny had kissed. And the woman who'd seen Faunus in Flush, later married to a poet deemed major. *Minor Poets of the Twentieth Century* (OUP, 84s), with a couple or three of his well separated, because of the alphabetical order, from that one of Rawcliffe. But once they had thought *Aurora Leigh* the greatest thing since Shakespeare, and Hopkins to be just jesuitical hysteria. It all depended on posterity. One kiss, two kisses. And he saw that her name didn't matter.

He sighed, but not hopelessly. He had gone back to the Horatian Ode this morning, in a rather crowded bar.

> So will the flux of time and fire,
> The process and the pain, expire,
> And history can bow
> To one eternal now.

He had to get behind the counter, expert, Hogg of the Sty (When you say gin, Piggy knows you mean Yeoman Warder. False smile flashing over the shaker in some glossy advertisement), to mix a Manhattan for a dour Kansan who believed the drink was named for the university town in his own state. And a young but archaic what-what haw-haw Englishman, doggy scarf in his open shirt, had brought in two girls, one of them called Bunty, and said that nobody in this town knew how to mix a hangman's blood. But he, Enderby, Hogg, knew, and the man was discomfited. Three old men had been in, the fourth, the one with skin like microscope slides, not being too well, confined to his room. Doubt if he'll see another spring. Won the Bisley shoot in, let me see, when was it? MC and bar, but never talked about it much.

What was emerging, Enderby saw, was a long poem based on the characters in *Hamlet*. The Horatian Ode was for the King, type of the absolute ruler who would seal a timeless Denmark off from the flux of history. An epithalamium for him and Gertrude, the passion of the mature. He'd written a good deal of that in Gloucester Road, when Vesta went off to work for the day, bitch.

> The greenstick snaps, the slender goldenrod
> Here cannot probe or enter. Thin spring winds
> Freeze blue lovers in unprotected hollows, but
> Summer chimes heavy bells and flesh is fed
> Where fruit bursts, the ground is crawling with berries.

Something like that. It would come back to him in time. A long soliloquy for Hamlet. Marsyas, was he, he Enderby, risking a minor poet's flaying? Never mind. On with bloody job is best way, *hombre*.

She came in when he was ready for his stew, followed by tea and siesta. She was dressed rather demurely, not unlike Miss Boland, beige suit, skirt to her knees, stockings of a gunmetal colour, shoes sensible and well-polished. There were blue rings, half-rings really, under her eyes. She wore a hat like a Victorian sailor's. She said:

'I've got a cab waiting outside.' Meaning over the sand, up the steps, across the railway line and pavement, by the kerb with a palm strongly clashing above. The wind was high. 'You're not to worry too much about anything,' she said. 'Do what you can do. Don't try and tame dogs or enter a world of visions and no syntax.' This was very sybilline talk.

'I'm doing a long poem based on the characters in *Hamlet*. I don't quite know yet what the overall theme is, but I daresay it'll come out in time. Could I make you a cup of tea? Antonio's got the day off. He's gone to see a man in Rabat.'

'Good. No, thanks. I'll be back to visit you. Next year perhaps. I suppose I should have come before, but I have so much to do.' Enderby was aware now that there was no point in asking further questions: taking your degree in English, are you; doing a thesis

on contemporary poetry, is that it? These things didn't apply, no
more than curiosity, which he no longer felt, about her identity
or origin or age. All things to all poets, but to this poet perhaps
less than to some others. No envy. Posterity would sort things out.
But, of course, posterity was only those snotnosed schoolkids.

'I'm grateful,' he said, though, out of habit, grudgingly. 'You
know I am.'

'You can't be blamed,' she said, 'if you've opted to live without
love. Something went wrong early. Your juvenilia days.' Enderby
frowned slightly. 'Look,' she said, 'I really must rush now. I only
came to say good-bye. But not good-bye really,' grimacing at her
watch. Enderby stood up, wincing a bit. A spasm in the right calf,
altogether appropriate to middle age. 'So,' she said, and she walked
the three paces up to him and gave him one brief kiss on the lips.
His share, his quota, what he was worth. Her mouth was very
warm. *The final kiss and final* – As if she knew, she gave him the
referent, leaving the words to him, very briefly grasping his writing
fingers, pressing them. Her gloves were beige, of some kind of soft
and expensive skin. *Tight pressure of hands.* That was it then, the
poem finished. But the whole thing was a lie (opted to live without
love), though it would not be a lie to anybody who could use it,
somebody young and in love, saying an enforced good-bye to the
beloved. Poets, even minor ones, donated the right words, and the
small pride might swallow the large envy.

'Right, then,' she said. They went together to the door, almost
with the formality of distinguished customer and bowing *patron*.
He watched her climb up to her taxi, feeling a spasm of hopeless
rage, briefer than a borborygm, at the last sight of her neatly moving
buttocks. But he had no right to that feeling, so the feeling quickly
modulated, as a nettle-sting modulates to warmth (the bare-legged
legionaries had kept themselves warm in British winters by lashing
themselves with nettles: might there not be a poem there?), to
something which had, as one of its upper partials, that very pride.
She waved before getting in, and then called something that sounded
a bit like *all the anthologies, anyway*, but a passing coach, full of
sightseers collected from the Rif, roared at it. The gear ground, *for
time himself will bring*, but this was only a decrepit Moroccan taxi.
The wind blew hard. She was gone; like a hypodermic injection

it was all over. He wondered if it might not be a pious duty to find out more about Rawcliffe's slender and thwarted *oeuvre*, edit, reprint at expense of mattress. There might be odd things, juvenilia even, concealed about the place, perhaps even in these tomes of pornography. But no, best keep away. He had enough work of his own to do, the duty of at least being better than T. E. Brown or Henley or Leigh Hunt or Sir George Goodby or Shem Macnamara. Whatever the future was going to be about, things ought to be all right, namely not too good, with enough scope for guilt, creation's true dynamo. It would be polite to reply to Miss Boland's letter, perhaps. If she proposed visiting him he could, if he wished, always put her off. He would go in now to his gross stew and stewed tea, then sleep for a while. The C major of this life. Was Browning minor? He turned to face the Atlantic but, going brrrrrr, was glad to be able to hurry in to escape from it.

6

This, children, is Morocco. Does it not give you a thrill, seeing what you have all heard or read about so often? Pashas and the Beni-Quarain and camels. Mulai Hafid and Abd-el-Kadir. The light-coloured Sherifians, who claim descent from the Prophet. Palmetto and sandarach and argan and tizra. You say it does *not* give you a thrill, Sandra? Well, child, you were never strong on imagination, were you? And I do not wish to hear of these silly giggly whispers about what *does* give you a thrill. Some of you girls have very few thoughts in your heads. Yes, I mean you too, Andrea. And, Geoffrey, because that elderly Berber is picking his nose you need not feel impelled to do the same. Lions, Bertrand? Lions are much farther south. Leopards here, bears, hyenas, and wild pigs. Bustard, partridge, and water-fowl. Dromedaries and dashing Barbary horses.

This is Tangier, which, you may not know this, once actually belonged to the British. Part of the dowry of Catherine of Braganza, Portuguese queen of a merry monarch. A pleasant enough town, no longer very distinguished, with some deplorable specimens of architecture. The beach is deserted. This is not the tourist season and, besides, it is the hour of the siesta. The beach cafés are garish, the paint peeling on many, but some of their names are rather charming. The Winston Churchill, the Sun Trap, the Cuppa, the Well Come. Those Hebrew letters there mean *kosher* (it is three consonants, the Semitic languages not greatly favouring the alphabeticization of vowels. Yes, Donald, Arabic too is a Semitic language and is vowel-shy. Why then do not the Jews and Arabs, aware of a common origin in speech and alphabetic method as well as genes, taboos, and mythology, get on better together? There, child, you have the eternal mystery of brotherhood. As Blake might have said, Let me hate him, or let me be his brother. But a good question, Donald, and thank you for asking it) which means, of food, not forbidden by religion. A holiday, you see, condones no relaxations of fundamental covenants. Stop grinning, Andrea. I shall lose my temper in a minute.

That one there is having its name repainted. You can see what it will be, in tasteful ultramarine. *La Belle Mer.* Very pretty. Some Frenchman probably, offering a most delicate cuisine, but now neatly sleeping. Listen, you can hear them sleep. Zrrrzzz. Ghraaaaaakh. Ong. Sleep possesses so many of the better sort, and it is sleep that sustains our visitation, to be fractured and fantasticated on waking, perhaps even totally forgotten.

Why are we here? A fair question, Pamela. What has all this to do with literature? I am very glad you asked that. Well, let me say this. Here you have expatriates of Northern stock, interwoven with the Moors and Berbers and Spanish. Many of them have fled their native lands to escape the rigour of the law. Yes, alas, crimes. Expropriation of funds, common theft, sexual inversion. I thought you would ask that, Sandra. That term *sexual* effects, in your case, an almost voltaic connection. The term means nothing more than philoprogenitive urges deflected into channels that possess no generative significance. What's all that when it's at home? I expected that remark from you, ignorant girl. I shall ignore it. Ignoration is the only rational response to ignorance. Think that one over, you over-developed little flesh-pot.

And among the exiles from the North are artists, musicians, writers. They have sinned, but they have talent. Desperately they exercise their talent here, dreaming of bitter ale and meadowsweet but cut off for ever, yes for ever, from the Piccadilly flyover and the Hyde Park State Museum and the Communal Beerhall on Hammersmith Broadway. Those are the British. The Americans weep too nightly into their highballs for the happy shopping evenings in the Dupermarket, the drive-in color stereo-video, the nuclear throb of the fully automated roadglobe. But they practise their arts. It is writers mostly. Up that hill lives a man who has already produced twenty-five volumes of autobiography: he tears at each instant of his pre-exilic past as though it were a prawn. Another man, on the Calle Larache, eats into his unconscious heart and mounts the regurgitated fragments on fragments of old news-paper. Another man again writes sneering satire, in sub-Popean couplets, on an England already dead. They are small artists, all. Here there is a *rue* Beethoven, also an *avenida* Leonardo da Vinci, a *plaza* de Sade. But no artist here will have a square or thorough-fare named for him. They are nothing.

And yet think what, on three sides, surrounds them, though the fierce Atlantic will give a right orchestration to the muscularity of what, to the sun's own surprise, has sprung out of sunbaked Africa and Iberia. The glory of the Lusiad (George, you will please not yawn) and the stoic bravery and heartbreak of the Cid, and the myth of Juan and the chronicle of the gaunter Don on the gaunt horse. Clash of guitars up there and the drumroll of hammering heels in the dance, and down there the fever of native timpani. And, east, the tales told of the cruel Sultan Shahriyar, and the delicate verse-traceries of Omar this and Abdul that (all right, Benedict, there is no need to snigger: Islamic poetry is not my subject) and Sayid the other thing.

Yawwwwww. Ogre. Uuuuuugh.

The pain of their awakening, not all of them alone, to the coming of the Tangerine evening. All right, we all know that a tangerine is a small orange, much flattened at the poles. Very funny, Geoffrey. But perhaps now you will consider why it is called what it is called. The calligraphic neons will glow − *fa* and *kaf* and *kaf* and *nun* and *tok* − and the shops resume their oil-lit trades. Ladies in yashmaks and caftans will stroll the *rues* or *calles*, and the boys will jeer and giggle at the few male tourists and point at their younger brothers as if they were carcases of tender lamb. And the writers will groan at their words of the forenoon and despair.

So away! Our camels sniff the evening and are glad. A quotation, if you *must* know, Benedict. Let us leave them, for men must be left to, each, the dreeing of his own weird. A man must contrive such happiness as he can. So must we all. So must we all, Geoffrey and Benedict and George and Donald and Andrea and Pamela and that horried Sandra and – Oh, get into line there. We take off, into the Atlantic wind. The moon, sickle of Islam, has risen. The planets Marikh and Zuhrah and Zuhal shine. The stars, in American issue army boots, slide silently to their allotted posts. And the words slide into the slots ordained by syntax and glitter, as with atmospheric dust, with those impurities which we call meaning. Away, children! Leave them to it.

> Until the final glacier grips
> Each island, with its dream of ships

And and and and. Keep on. It will come out right, given time and application. You can, when depressed, pluck your own sweet bay or *laurus nobilis*. It grows here. Nobody will pluck it for you. The aromatic leaves are useful in cookery, and you can cure your sick cat with the berries.

Appendix

Some Uncollected Early Poems by F. X. Enderby

The poems that follow have not, for some reason, appeared in any of the published volumes of Enderby's verse, and the last poem has not previously been published at all. The poems beginning 'Anciently the man who showed . . .', 'They fear and hate the Donne and Dante in him . . .', and 'Semitic violins by the wailing wall . . .', allegedly from Enderby's juvenile productions, cannot be traced either in published or manuscript form. It may be of interest to note, however, that the catalogue of the ill-fated Gorgon Press, which specialized in verse printed at the author's own expense, lists a volume by one A. Rawcliffe – *Balls and Talk*: Poems 1936. No copies of this volume have as yet come to light.

A.B.

September 1938

There arose those winning life between two wars,
Born out of one, doomed food for the other,
Floodroars ever in the ears.

Slothlovers hardly, hardly fighters:
Resentment spent against stone, long beaten out of
Minds resigned to the new:
Useless to queue for respirators.

Besides, what worse chaos to come back to.
Home, limbs heavy with mud and work, to sleep
To sweep out a house days deep in dirt.

Knowing finally man would limbs loin face
Efface utterly, leaving in his place
Engines rusting to world's end, heirs to warfare
Fonctionnant d'une manière automatique.

Summer 1940

Summer swamps the land, the sun imprisons us,
The pen slithers in the examinee's fingers,
And colliding lips of lovers slide on sweat
When, blind, they inherit their tactile world.

Spectacles mist, handveins show blue, the urge to undress
Breeds passion in unexpected places. Barrage balloons
Soar silver in silver ether. Lying on grass,
We watch them, docile monsters, unwind to the zenith.

Drops of that flood out of France, with mud and work
Stained, loll in the trams, drinking their cigarettes,
Their presence defiling the flannels and summer frocks,
The hunters to hound our safety, spoil the summer.

Spring in Camp 1941

War becomes time, and long logic
On buried premises; spring supervenes
With the circle as badge which, pun and profundity,
Vast, appears line and logical,
But, small, shows travel returning.
Circle is circle, proves nothing, makes nothing,
Swallows up process and end in no argument,
Brings new picture of old time.
Here in barracks is intake of birds,
The sun holds early his orderly room,
The pale company clerk is uneasy
As spring brings odour of other springs.
The truckdriver sings, free of the road,

The load of winter and war becomes
Embarrassing as a younger self.
Words disintegrate; war is words.

The Excursion

The blue of summer morning begs
The country journey to be made,
The sun that gilds the breakfast eggs
Illuminates the marmalade.

A cheque is smiling on the desk.
Remembered smells upon the lane
Breed hunger for the picaresque
To blood the buried springs again.

Here is the pub and here the church
And there our thirty miles of sun,
The river and the rod and the perch,
The noonday drinking just begun.

Let beer beneath the neighbour trees
Swill all that afternoon away,
And onions, crisp to sullen cheese,
Yield the sharp succulence of today.

Today remembers breaking out
The fire that burned the hayfield black.
An army that was grey with drought
Shows to my stick its fossil track.

Returning evening rose on rose
Or pomegranate rouge and ripe;
The lamp upon the pavement throws
The ectoplasm of my pipe.

Eden

History was not just what you learned that scorching day
Of ink and wood and sweat in the classroom, when mention
Of the Duke of Burgundy lost you in a voluptuous dream
Of thirst and Christmas, but that day was part of history.

There were other times, misunderstood by the family,
When you, at fifteen, on your summer evening bed
Believed there were ancient towns you might anciently visit.
There might be a neglected platform on some terminus

And a ticket bought when the clock was off its guard.
Oh, who can dismember the past? The boy on the friendly bed
Lay on the unpossessed mother, the bosom of history,
And is gathered to her at last. And tears I suppose

Still thirst for that reeking unwashed pillow,
That bed ingrained with all the dirt of the past,
The mess and lice and stupidity of the Golden Age,
But a mother and loving, ultimate Eden.

One looks for Eden in history, best left unvisited,
For the primal sin is always a present sin,
The thin hand held in the river which can never
Clean off the blood, and so remains bloodless.

And this very moment, this very word will be Eden,
As that boy was already, or is already, in Eden,
While the delicate filthy hand dabbles and dabbles
But leaves the river clean, heartbreakingly clean.

The Clockwork Testament
or: Enderby's End

To Burt Lancaster
('. . . *deserves to live, deserves to live.*')

1

The first thing he saw on waking was his lower denture on the floor, its groove encrusted with dried Dentisement, or it might be Orastik, Mouthficks, Gripdent, or Bite (called *Bait* in Tangier, where he could be said to have a sort of permanent, that is to say, if you could talk of permanency these days in anything, so to speak, address), the fully teethed in my audience will hardly conceive of the variety of denture adhesives on the market. His tongue, at once sprung into life horribly with no prelude of decent morning slug-gishness, probed the lower gum briskly and found a diminution of yesterday's soreness. Then it settled into the neutral schwa position to await further directives. So. The denture, incrustations picked loose, laved, recharged with goo of Firmchew – family size with N E W wintergreen flavour – could be jammed in without serious twinge. As well, since today students must be met and talked at.

He lay, naked for the central heat, on his belly. If the bed, which was circular in shape, were a clock, then he was registering twenty of two, as Americans put it, meaning twenty to two. If, that was, his upper part were the hour hand. If, that was, twelve o'clock was where the bed touched the wall. The Great Bed of York of English legend had been round also, though much bigger, the radius being the length of a sleeper – say six feet. How many pairs of dirty (read Rabelaisian, rollicking) feet meeting at the center (re)? Circumference 2 pi r, was it? It didn't seem big enough somehow. But all the big things of European legend were smaller than you had been brought up to imagine. American scholars sorted that sort of thing out for you. Anybody could eat whole mediaeval sheep, being no bigger than rabbit. Suits of armor (our) would accommodate twelve-year-old American girl. Not enough vitamins in roystering rollicking diet. Hell was originally a rubbish-dump outside Jerusalem.

He lay naked also on a fast-drying nocturnal ejaculation, wonderful for man of your age, Enderby. What had the dream been that had conduced to wetness? Being driven in a closed car, muffled to the ears, in black spectacles, funereal sombrero, very pimply guffawing lout driving. Driven into slum street where twelve-year-old girls, Puerto Rican mostly, were playing with a ball. Wait, no, two balls, naturally. The girls jeered, showed themselves knickerless, provoked. He, Enderby, had to go on sitting in black and back of car while guffawing driver got out and ministered very rapidly to them all, their number of course changing all the time. *Finnegans Wake*, ladies and gentlemen, is false to the arithmetic of true dreams, number in that book being an immutable rigidity while, as we know, it is a mutable fluidity in our regular dreaming experience. There are seven biscuits, which you call er cookies, on a plate. You take away, say, two and three remain. Or, of course, they could be what *you* call biscuits and we, I think, muffins. Principle is the same. I question that, said a sneering Christ of a student. Professor Enderby, asked a what Enderby took to be Polack, Nordic anyway, lacking eyelashes, please clarify your precise threshold of credibility.

This driver lout got through the lot, standing, with quick canine thrusts. Then Enderby was granted discharge and the entire scene, as in some story by that blind Argentinian he had been urged to read by somebody eager and halitotic in the Faculty Lounge, collapsed.

The bed he lay on, twenty of two, squinting down at his watch also on the floor, ten of eight of a New York February morning, was circular because of some philosophy of the regular tenant of the apartment, now on sabbatical and working on Thelma Garstang (1798–1842, bad poetess beaten to death by drunken husband, alleged anyway) in British Museum. The traditional quadrangular bed was male tyranny, or something. This regular tenant was, as well as being an academic, a woman novelist who wrote not very popular novels in which the male characters ended up being castrated. Then, it was implied, or so Enderby understood, not having read any of them, only having been told about them, they became considerate lovers eager for cunnilingus with their castratrices, but they were sneered at for being impotent. Well, he unimpotent Enderby, temporary professor, would do nothing about cleaning that sperm-stain from her circular mattress, ridiculous idea, must have cost a fortune.

Enderby had slept, as now he always did, with his upper denture in. It was a sort of response to the castrating aura of the apartment. He had also found it necessary to be ready for the telephone to ring at all hours, an edentulous chumble getting responses of *Pardon me?* if the call were a polite one, but if it were insulting or obscene or both, provoking derision. Most of the Serious Calls came from what was known as the Coast and were for his landlady. She was connected with some religiolesbic movement there and she had neglected to send a circular letter about her sabbatical. The insults and obscenities were usually meant for Enderby. He had written a very unwise article for a magazine, in which he said that he thought little of black literature because it tended to tendentiousness and that the Amerindians had shown no evidence of talent for anything except scalping and very inferior folkcraft. One of his callers, who had once termed him a toothless cocksucker (that toothlessness had been right, anyway, at that time anyway), was always threatening to bring a tomahawk to 91st Street and Columbus Avenue, which was where Enderby lodged. Also students would ring anonymously at deliberately awkward hours to revile him for his various faults – chauvinism, or some such thing; ignorance of literary figures important to the young; failure to see merit in their own free verse and gutter vocabulary. They would revile him also in class, of course, but not so freely as on the telephone. Everybody felt naked these days without the mediacy of a mode of mechanical communication.

Eight of eight. The telephone rang. Enderby decided to give it the honour of full dentition, so he jammed in the encrusted lower denture. Try it out. Gum still sorish. But, of course, that was the hardened Gripdent or whatever it was. He had them all.

'Professor Enderby?'

'Speaking.'

'You don't know me, but this is just to inform you that both my husband and I consider that your film is filth.'

'It's not my film. I only wrote the –'

'You have a lot to answer for, my husband says. Don't you think there's enough juvenile crime on our streets without filth like yours abetting it?'

'But it's not filth and it's not my —'

'Obscene filth. Let me inform you that my husband is six feet three and broad in proportion —'

'Is he a Red Indian?'

'That's just the sort of cheap insult I would expect from a man capable of —'

'If you're going to send him round here, with or without tomahawk —'

She had put down the receiver. What he had been going to say was that there was twenty-four-hour armed protection in the apartment lobby as well as many closed-circuit television screens. This, however, would not help him if the enemies were within the block itself. That he had enemies in the block he knew — a gat-toothed black writer and his wife; a single woman with dogs who had objected to his mentioning in his magazine article the abundance of cockroaches in this part of Manhattan as though it were a shameful family secret; a couple of fattish electronic guitarists who had smelt his loathing as they had gone up together once in the elevator. And there might also be others affronted by the film just this moment referred to.

Flashback. Into the bar-restaurant run by Enderby, exiled poet, in Tangier, film-men had one day come. Kasbah location work or something of the kind. One of the film-men, who had seemed and indeed proved to be big in his field, an American director considered for the brilliance of his visual intention quite as good as any director in Europe, said something about wanting to make, because of the visual possibilities, a shipwreck film. Enderby, behind bar and hence free to join in conversation without any imputation of insolence, having also British accent, said something about *The Wreck of the Deutschland*.

'Too many Kraut Kaput movies lately. Last days of Hitler, Joe Krankenhaus already working on Goebbels, then there was Visconti.'

'A ship,' said Enderby, 'called the *Deutschland*. Hopkins wrote it.'

'Al Hopkins?'

'G.M.,' Enderby said, adding, 'S.J.'

'Never heard of him. Why does he want all those initials?'

'Five Franciscan nuns,' Enderby said, 'exiled from Germany because of the Falk Laws. "On Saturday sailed from Bremen, American-outward-bound, take settler with seaman, tell men with women, two hundred souls in the round . . ."'

'He knows it all, by God. When?'

'1875. December 7th.'

'Nuns,' mused the famed director. 'What were these laws?'

'"Rhine refused them. Thames would ruin them,"' Enderby said. '"Surf, snow, river, and earth,"' he said, '"Gnashed."'

'Totalitarian intolerance,' the director's assistant and friend said. 'Nuns beaten up in the streets. Habits torn off. Best done in flashback. The storm symbolic as well as real. What happens at the end?' he asked Enderby keenly.

'They all get wrecked in the Goodwin Sands. The Kentish Knock, to be precise. And then there's this final prayer. "Let him easter in us, be a dayspring to the dimness of us, be a crimson-cresseted east . . ."'

'In movies,' the director said kindly, as to a child, 'you don't want too many words. You see that? It's what we call a visual medium. Two more double scatches on the racks.'

'I know all about that,' Enderby said with heat, pouring whisky sightlessly for these two men. 'When they did my *Pet Beast* it became nothing but visual clichés. In Rome it was. Cinecittà. The bastard. But he's dead now.'

'Who's dead?'

'Rawcliffe,' Enderby said. 'He used to own this place.' The two men stared at him. 'What I mean is,' Enderby said, 'that there was this film. Movie, you'd call it, ridiculous word. In Italian, *L'Animal Binato*. That was *Son of the Beast from Outer Space*. In English that is,' he explained.

'But that,' the director said, 'was a small masterpiece. Alberto Formica, dead now poor bastard, well ahead of his time. The clichés were deliberate, it summed up a whole era. So.' He looked at Enderby with new interest. 'What did you say your name was? Rawcliffe? I always thought Rawcliffe was dead.'

'Enderby,' Enderby said. 'Enderby the poet.'

'You did the script, you say?' the assistant and friend said.

'I wrote *The Pet Beast*.'

'Why,' the director said, taking out a visiting card from among embossed instruments of international credit, 'don't you write us a letter, the shipwreck story I mean, setting it all out?'

Enderby smiled knowingly, a poet but up to their little tricks. 'I give you a film script for nothing?' he said. 'I've heard of this letter business before.' The card read *Melvin Schaumwein, Chisel Productions.* 'If I do you a script I shall want paying for it.'

'How much?' said Mr Schaumwein.

Enderby smiled. 'A lot,' he said. The money part of his brain grew suddenly delirious, lifelong abstainer fed with sudden gin. He trembled as with the prospect of sexual outrage. 'A thousand dollars,' he said. They stared at him. 'There,' he said. And then: 'Somewhere in that region anyway. I'm not what you'd call a greedy man.'

'We might manage five hundred,' Schaumwein's assistant-friend said. 'On delivery, of course. Provided that it's what might be termed satisfactory.'

'Seven hundred and fifty,' Enderby said. 'I'm not what you'd call a greedy man.'

'It's not an original,' Mr Schaumwein said. 'You mentioned some guy called Hopkins that wrote the book. Who is he, where is he, who do I see about the rights?'

'Hopkins,' Enderby said, 'died in 1889. His poems were published in 1918. *The Wreck of the Deutschland* is out of copyright.'

'I think,' Mr Schaumwein said carefully, 'we'll have two more scatches on the racks.'

What, after Mr Schaumwein had gone back to the Kasbah and then presumably home to Chisel Productions, was to surprise Enderby was that the project was to be taken seriously presumably. For a letter came from the friend-assistant, name revealed as Martin Droeshout (familiar vaguely to Enderby in some vague picture connection or other), confirming that, for $750.00, Enderby would deliver a treatment for a film tentatively entitled *The Wreck of the Deutschland*, based on a story by Hopkins, which story their researchers had not been able to bring to light despite prolonged research, had Enderby got the name right, but it didn't matter as subject was in public domain. Enderby presumed that the word *treatment* was another word for *shooting script* (a lot of film-men had been to his bar at one time or another, so the latter term was familiar to him). He had even looked at the shooting script of a film in which a heavy though not explicit sexual sequence had actually been shot, at midnight with spotlights and a humming generator truck, on the beach just near to his beach café-restaurant, *La Belle Mer.* So, while his boys snored or writhed sexually with each other during the siesta, he got down to typewriter-pecking out his cinematization of a great poem, delighting in such curt visual directives as VLS, CU, and so on, though not always clearly understanding what they meant.

1. Exterior   Night
(*Lightning lashes a rod on top of a church.*)
PRIEST'S VOICE: Yes. Yes. Yes.

2. Interior   Night   A Church
(*Thunder rolls. A priest on his knees at the altar looks up, sweating. It is Fr Hopkins, S. J.*)
FR HOPKINS, S. J.:

> Thou hearest me truer than tongue confess
> Thy terror, O Christ, O God.

3. Exterior   Night   A Starlit Sky
(*The camera pans slowly across lovely-asunder starlight.*)

4. Exterior   Night   The Grounds of a Theological Seminary
(*Father Hopkins, S. J., looks up ecstatically at all the firefolk sitting in the air and then kisses his hand at them.*)

5. Exterior   Sunset The Dappled-with-Damson West
(*Father Hopkins, S. J., kisses his hand at it.*)

6. Interior   Day   A Refectory
(*The scene begins with a CU of Irish stew being placed on a table by an*

*illgirt scullion. Then the camera pulls back to show priests talking
vigorously.)*

PRIEST #1: These Falk Laws in Germany are abominable and totally
   sinful.

PRIEST #2: I hear that a group of Franciscan nuns are sailing to America
   next Saturday.

   (The voice of Father Hopkins, S.J. is heard from another part of the table.)

HOPKINS (OS):

> Glory be to God for dappled things,
> For skies of couple-colour as a brinded cow . . .

(The priests look at each other.)

7. The Same   Two Shot

*(Father Hopkins is talking earnestly to a very beautiful fellow-priest who
listens attentively.)*

HOPKINS: Since, though he is under the world's splendour and wonder,
   his mystery must be instressed, stressed . . .

FELLOW-PRIEST: I quite understand.

   *(The camera pans rapidly back to the other two priests, who look at each
   other.)*

PRIEST #1: *(sotto voce)* Jesus Christ.

It worried Enderby a little, as he proceeded with his film version
of the first part of the poem, that Hopkins should appear to be a
bit cracked. There was also a problem in forcing a relevance between
the first part and the second. Enderby, serving one morning abstract-
edly sloe gin to two customers, hit on a solution. 'Sacrifice,' he
said suddenly. The customers took their sloe gins away to a far
table. The idea being that Hopkins wanted to be Christ but that
the tall nun, Gertrude, kindly became Christ for him, and that her
sort of crucifixion on the Kentish Knock (sounded, he thought
gloomily, like some rural sexual aberration) might conceivably be
thought of as helping to bring our King back, oh, upon English
souls.

12. Exterior   Day   CU   A Sloe

(We see a lush-kept plush-capped sloe in a white well-kept priestly hand.)

13. CU Father Hopkins S.J.
(*Hopkins, in very large close-up, mouths the sloe to flesh-burst. He shudders.*)

14. Exterior   Day   Calvary
(*Christ is being nailed to the cross. Roman soldiers jeer.*)

15. Resume 13
(*Hopkins, still shuddering, looks down at the bitten sloe. The camera tracks on to it into CU. It dissolves into:*)

16. Interior   Day   A Church
(*The hands of a priest hold up the host, which looks a bit like the sloe. It is, of course, Fr Hopkins, S. J., saying mass.*)

17. The Same   CU
(*In CU, Father Hopkins murmurs ecstatically.*)
HOPKINS: (*ecstatically*) Be adored among men, God, three-numbered form. Wring thy rebel, dogged in den, man's malice, with wrecking and storm.

18. Exterior   Day   A Stormy Sea
(*The* Deutschland, *American-outward-bound. Death on drum, and storms bugle his fame.*)

The second part was easier, mostly a business of copying out Hopkins's own what might be thought of as prophetic camera-directions:

45. Exterior   Day   The Sea
(*Wiry and white-fiery and whirlwind-swivelled snow spins to the widow-making unchilding unfathering deeps.*)

And so on. When it was finished it made, Enderby thought, a very nice little script. It could be seen also as the tribute of one poet to another. People would see the film and then go and read the poem. They would see the poem as superior art to the film. He sent the script off to Mr Schaumwein at Chisel Productions. He eventually received a brief letter from Martin Droeshout saying that a lot of it was very flowery, but that was put down to Enderby's being a poet, which claim of Enderby had been substantiated by researchers. However, they were going ahead, updating so as to make Germany Nazi, and making the nun Gertrude a former love of Father Hopkins, both of them coming to realization that it was God they really loved but they would keep in touch. This meant re-write men, as Enderby would realize, but Enderby's name would appear among the credits.

Enderby's name did indeed eventually appear among the credits: *Developed out of an idea of.* Also he was invited to London to see a preview of *The Wreck of the Deutschland* (they couldn't think of a better title, any of them; there wasn't a better title). He was pretty shocked by a lot of it, especially the flashbacks and it was nearly all flashbacks, the only present-tense reality being the *Deutschland* on its way to be ground to bits on the Kentish Knock (which, somebody else at the preview said, to ecstatic laughter, sounded a little like a rural sexual aberration). For instance, Hopkins, who had been given quite arbitrarily the new name Tom, eventually Father Tom, was Irish, and the tall nun was played by a Swede, though that was really all right. These two had a great pink sexual encounter, but before either of them took vows, so that, Enderby supposed, was all right too. There were some over-explicit scenes of the nuns being violated by teenage storm-troopers. The tall nun Gertrude herself tore off her Franciscan habit to make bandages during the storm scenes, so that her end, in a posture of crucifixion on the Kentish Knock, was as near-nude as that of her Master. There was also an ambiguous moment when, storms bugling, though somewhat subdued, Death's fame in the background, she cried orgasmatically: 'Oh Christ, Christ, come quickly' – Hopkins's own words, so one could hardly complain. On the whole, not a bad film, with Hopkins getting two secondsworth of solo credit: *Based on the story by.* As was to be expected, it got a very restrictive showing rating, nobody under eighteen. 'Things have come to a pretty pass,' said Mr Schaumwein in a television interview, 'when a religious film is no longer regarded as good family viewing.'

So there it was then, except for complaints from the reactionary and puritanical, though not, as far as Enderby could tell, from

Hopkins's fellow-Jesuits. *The Month*, which had originally refused the poem itself, made amends by finding the film adult and serious. 'Mr Schaumwein very sensibly has eschewed the temptation to translate Hopkins's confused grammar and neologistic tortuosities into corresponding visual obscurities.' Enderby's association, however small, with a great demotic medium led to his being considered worthy by the University of Manhattan of being invited to come as a visiting professor for an academic year. The man who sent the invitation, the Chairman of the English Department, Alvin Kosciusko, said that Enderby's poems were not unknown there in the United States. Whatever anybody thought of them, there was no doubt that they were genuine Creative Writing. Enderby was therefore cordially invited to come and pass on some of his Creative Writing skill to Creative Writing students. His penchant for old-fashioned and traditional forms might act as a useful corrective to the cult of free form which, though still rightly flourishing, had led to some excesses. One postgraduate student had received a prize for a poem that turned out to be a passage from a vice-presidential speech copied out in reverse and then seasoned with mandatory obscenities. He had protested that it was as much Creative Writing as any of the shit that had been awarded prizes in previous years. Anyway, the whole business of giving prizes was reactionary. Subsidies were what was required.

2

Naked as the day he was born though much hairier, Enderby prepared himself breakfast. One of the things he approved of about New York – a city otherwise dirty, rude, violent, and full of foreigners and mad people – was the wide variety of dyspeptic foods on sale in the supermarkets. In his view, if you did not get dyspepsia while or after eating, you had been cheated of essential nourishment. As for dealing with the dyspepsia, he had never in his life seen so

many palliatives for it available – Stums and Windkill and Eupep
and (magnificent proleptic onomatopoesis, the work of some high-
paid Madison Avenue genius, sincerely admired by Enderby) Aaaarp.
And so on. But the best of all he had discovered in a small shop
specializing in Oriental medicines (sent thither by a Chinese waiter)
– a powerful black viscidity that oozed sinisterly from a tube to
bring wind up from Tartarean depths. When he went to buy it,
the shopkeeper would, in his earthy Chinese manner, designate it
with a remarkable phonic mime of the substance at work. Better
than Aaaarp but not easily representable in any conventional
alphabet. Enderby would nod kindly, pay, take, bid good day, go.

Enderby had become, so far as use of the culinary resources of
the kitchen (at night the cockroaches' playground) were concerned,
one hundred per cent Americanized. He would whip up a thick
milk shake in the mixer, thaw then burn frozen waffles in the
toaster, make soggy leopardine pancakes with Aunt Jemima's buck-
wheat pancake mixture (Aunt Jemima herself was on the packet,
a comely Negress rejoicing in her bandanna'd servitude), fry
Pepperidge Farm fat little sausages. His nakedness would be fat-
splashed, but the fat easily washed off, unlike with clothes. And he
would make tea, though not altogether in the American manner
– five bags in a pint mug with ALABAMA gilded on it, boiling water,
a long stewing, very sweet condensed milk added. He would eat
his breakfast with HP steak sauce on one side of the plate, maple
syrup on the other. The Americans went in for synchronic sweet
and savoury, a sign of their salvation, unlike the timid Latin races.
He would end his meal with a healthy slice of Sara Lee orange
cream cake, drink another pint of tea, then, after his black Chinese
draught, be alertly ready for work. A mansized breakfast, as they
said. There was never need for much lunch – some canned corned
beef hash with a couple of fried eggs, say, and a pint of tea. A slice
of banana cake. And then, this being America, a cup of coffee.

Heartburn was slow in coming this morning, which made Enderby,
stickler for routine, uneasy. He noted also with rueful pride that,
despite the emission of the night, he was bearing before him as he
left the kitchen, where he had eaten as well as cooked, a sizeable
horizontal ithyphallus lazily swinging towards the vertical. Something
to do perhaps with excessive protein intake. He took it to a dirty

towel in the bathroom, called those Puerto Rican bitches back from that dream, then gave it them all. The street was littered with them. The pimpled lout, astonished and fearful, ran round the corner. This meant that Enderby would have to drive the car away himself. He at once sold it for a trifling sum to a grey-haired black man who shuffled out of an open doorway, evening newspaper in his hand, and made his getaway, naked, on foot. Then dyspepsia struck, he took his black drops, released a savoury gale from as far down as the very caecum, and was ready for work, his own work, not the pseudo-work he would have to do in the afternoon with pseudo-students. For that he must shave, dress, wash, probably in that order. Take the subway, as they called it. Brave mean streets full of black and brown menace.

Enderby, still naked, sat at his landlady's desk in the bedroom. It was a small apartment, there was no study. He supposed he was lucky to have gotten (very American touch there: *gotten*) an apartment at all at the rent he was able, the salary not being overlarge, to pay. His landlady, a rabid ideological man-hater, had addressed one letter to him from her digs in Bayswater, confirming that he pay the black woman Priscilla to come and clean for him every Saturday, thus maintaining a continuity of her services useful for when his landlady should return to New York. Enderby was not sure what sex she thought he, Enderby, had, since there was a reference to not trying to flush sanitary pads down the toilet. The title *professor*, which she rightly addressed him by, was common, as the old grammars would put it. Perhaps she had read his poems and found a rich femininity in them; perhaps some kind man in the English Department had represented Enderby as an ageing but progressive spinster to her when she sought to let her apartment. Anyway, he had answered the letter promptly on his own portable typewriter, signing with a delicate hand, assuring her that sanitary pads would go out with the garbage and that Priscilla was being promptly paid and not over-worked (lazy black bitch, thought Enderby, but evidently illiterate and not likely to blow the sex gaff in letter or transatlantic cable). So there it was. On the other hand, his landlady might learn in London from librarians or in communications from members of the Californian religio-lesbic sorority that Enderby was really a (*sounded suspiciously like the voice of an MCP to me, toothless too, a TMCP, what little game are you playing, dear?*). But it was probably too late for her to do anything

about it now. Couldn't evict him on grounds of his sex. The United
Nations, conveniently here in New York, would, through an appropriate department, have something very sharp to say about that. So
there it was, then. Enderby got down to work.

Back in Morocco, as previously in England, Enderby was used to
working in the toilet, piling up drafts and even fair copies in the
never-used bath. Here it would not do, since the bath-taps dripped
and the toilet-seat was (probably by some previous Jewish-mother
tenant who wished to discourage solitary pleasures among her
menfolk) subtly notched. It was ungrateful to the bottom. Neither
was there a writing table low enough. Nor would Priscilla understand.
This eccentric country was great on conformity. Enderby now wrote
at the desk that had produced so many androphobic mistress pieces.
What he was writing was a long poem about St Augustine and
Pelagius, trying to sort out for himself and a couple of score readers
the whole worrying business of predestination and free will. He read
through what he had so far written, scratching and grunting, naked,
a horrible White Owl cigar in his mouth.

> He came out of the misty island, Morgan,
> Man of the sea, demure in monk's sackcloth,
> Taking the long way to Rome, expecting –
> Expecting what? Oh, holiness quintessentialized,
> Holiness whole, the wholesome wholemeal of,
> Holiness as meat and drink and air, in the
> Chaste thrusts of marital love holiness, and
> Sanctitas sanctitas even snaking up from
> Cloacae and sewers, sanctitas the effluvium
> From his Holiness's arsehole.

Perhaps that was going a bit too far. Enderby poised a ball-point,
dove, retracted. No, it was the right touch really. Let the *arsehole*
stay. Americans preferred *asshole* for some reason. This then very
British. But why not? Pelagius was British. Keep *arsehole* in.

> On the long road
> Trudging, dust, birdsong, dirty villages,
> Stops on the way at monasteries (weeviled bread,

Eisel wine), always this thought: *Sanctitas.*
What dost seek in Rome, brother? The home
Of holiness, to lodge awhile in the
Sanctuary of sanctity, my brothers, for here
Peter died, seeing before he died
The pagan world inverted to sanctitas, and
The very flagged soil is rich with the bonemeal
Of the martyrs. And the brothers would
Look at each other, each thinking, some saying:
Here cometh one that only islands breed.
What can flourish in that Ultima Thule save
Holiness, a bare garment for the wind to
Sing through? And not Favonius either but
Sour Boreas from the pole. Not the grape,
Not garlic not the olive, not the strong sun
Tickling the manhood in a man, be he
Monk or friar or dean or
Burly bishop, big ballocks swinging like twin censers.
Only holiness. God help him, God bless him for
We look upon British innocence.
And the British innocent, hurtful of no man,
Fond of dogs, a cat-stroker,
Trudged on south – vine, olive, garlic,
Brown tits jogging while brown feet
Danced in the grapepress and the
Baaark ballifoll gorstafick

That last was inner Enderby demanding the stool. He took his
poem with him thither, frowning, sat reading.

Monstrous aphrodisiac danced in the heavens
Prrrrrrp faaaark
Wheep
Till at length he came to the outer suburbs and
Fell on his knees *O sancta urbs sancta sancta*
Meaning sancta suburbs and
Plomp

422   THE COMPLETE ENDERBY

Enderby wiped himself with slow care and marched back, frowning, reading. As he reached the telephone on the bed table the telephone rang, so that he was able to pick it up at once, thus disconcerting the voice on the other end, which had not expected such promptitude.

'Oh. Mr Enderby?' It was a woman's voice, being higher than a man's. American female voices lacked feminine timbre as known in the south of vine and garlic, were just higher because of accident of larynx being smaller.

'Professor Enderby speaking.'

'Oh, hi. This is the Sperr Lansing Show. We wondered if you –'

'What? Who? What is this?'

'The Sperr Lansing Show. A talk show. Television. *The* talk show. Channel Fif –'

'Ah, I see,' Enderby said, with British heartiness. 'I've seen it, I think. She left it here, you see. Extra on the rent.'

'Who? What?'

'Oh, I see what you mean. Yes. A television. She's a great one for her rights. Ah yes, I've seen it a few times. A sort of thin man with a fat jackal. Both leer a good deal, but one supposes they have to.'

'No, no, you have the wrong show there, professor.' The title now seemed pretentious, also absurd, as when someone in a film is addressed as *professor*. 'What you mean is the Cannon Dickson Show. That's mostly show business personalities. The Sperr Lansing Show is, well, *different*.'

'I didn't really mean to insist, ha ha,' Enderby said, 'on the title of professor. Fancy dress, you know. A lot of nonsense really. And I really must apologize for . . .' He was going to say *for being naked*: it was all this damned visual stuff. 'For my innocence. I mean my ignorance.'

'I guess I ought to introduce myself – we've already been talking for such a long time. I'm Midge Tauchnitz.'

'Enderby,' Enderby said. 'Sorry, that was . . . So, eh? "The strong spur, live and lancing like the blowpipe flame." I suppose that's where he got it from.'

'Pardon me?'

'Anyway, thank you for calling.'

'No, it doesn't go out live. Nothing these days goes out live.'

'I promise to watch it at the earliest opportunity. Thank you very much for suggesting . . .'

'No, no, we want you to appear on it. We record at seven so you'd have to be here about six.'

'Why?' Enderby said in honest surprise. 'For God's sake why?'

'Oh, makeup and so on. It's on West 46th Street, between Fifth and . . .'

'No, no, no. Why me?'

'Pardon me?'

'Me.'

'Oh.' The voice became teasing and girlish. 'Oh, come now, professor, that's playing it too cool. It's the movie. *The Deutschland.*'

'Ah. But I only wrote the – I mean, it was only my idea. That's what it says, anyway. Why don't you ask one of the others, the ones who really made it?'

'Well,' she said candidly. 'We tried to get hold of Bob Ponte, the script-writer but he's in Honolulu writing a script, and Mr Schaumwein is in Rome, and Millennium suggested we get on to you. So I phoned the university and they gave us your –'

'Hopkins,' Enderby said, in gloomy play. 'Did you try Hopkins?'

'No luck there either. Nobody knows where he is.'

'In the eschatological sense, I should think it's pretty certain that –'

'Pardon me?'

'But in the other it's no wonder. 1844 to 89,' he twinkled.

'Oh, I'll write that down. But it doesn't sound like a New York number –'

'No no no no no. A little joke. He's dead, you see.'

'Gee, I'm sorry, I didn't know. But you're okay? I mean, you'll be there?'

'If you really want me. But I still don't see –'

'You don't? You don't read the newspapers?'

'Never. And again never. A load of frivolity and lies. They've been attacking it, have they?'

'No. Some boys have been attacking some nuns. In Manhattanville. I'm shocked you didn't know. I assumed –'

'Nuns are always being attacked. Their purity is an affront to
the dirty world.'

'Remember that. Remember to say that. But the point is that
they said they wouldn't have done it if they hadn't seen the movie.
That's why we're —'

'I see. I see. Always blame art, eh? Not original sin but art. I'll
have my say, never fear.'

'You have the address?'

'You ignore art as so much unnecessary garbage or you blame
it for your own crimes. That's the way of it. I'll get the bastards,
all of them. I'm not having this sort of nonsense, do you hear?'
There was silence at the other end. 'You never take art for what
it is – beauty, ultimate meaning, form for its own sake, self-subsisting,
oh no. It's always got to be either sneered at or attacked as evil.
I'll have my bloody say. What's the name of the show again?' But
she had rung off, silly bitch.

Enderby went snorting back to his poem. The stupid bastards.

But wherever he went in Rome, it was always the same –
Sin sin sin, no sanctity, the whole unholy
Grammar of sin, syntax, accidence, sin's
Entire lexicon set before him, sin.
Peacocks in the streets, gold dribbled over
In dark rooms, vomiting after
Banquets of ostrich bowels stuffed with saffron,
Minced pikeflesh and pounded larkbrain,
Served with a sauce headily fetid, and pocula
Of wine mixed with adder's blood to promote
Lust lust and again.
Pederasty, podorasty, sodomy, bestiality,
Degrees of family ripped apart like
Bodices in the unholy dance. And he said,
And Morgan said, whom the scholarly called Pelagius:
Why do ye this, my brothers and sisters?
Are ye not saved by Christ, are ye not
Sanctified by his sacrifice, oh why why why?
(Being British and innocent) and

What was the name of that show again? Art blamed as always. Art was neutral, neither teaching nor provoking, a static shimmer, he would tell the bastards. What was it again? And then he thought about this present poem (a draft of course, very much a draft) and wondered: *is it perhaps not didactic?* But how about *The Wreck of the Deutschland?* Hopkins was always having a go at the English, and the Welsh too, for not rushing to be converted back (the marvellous milk was Walsingham Way, once) to Catholicism. But somehow Hopkins was of the devil's party without knowing it (better remember not to say that on this Live Lancing Show, that was the name, something like it anyway), people were stupid, picked you up literally on that sort of thing. It was a kind of paganism with him: lush-kept plush-capped sloe, indeed, with God tacked on. The our-king-back-oh-upon-English-souls stuff was merely structural, something to bring the poem to an end. But how about this?

No, he decided. He was not preaching. Who the hell was he to preach? Out of the Church at sixteen, never been to mass in forty years. This was merely an imaginative inquiry into free will and predestination. Somewhat comforted, he read on, scratching, the White Owl, self-doused, re-lighted, hooting out foul smoke.

> They said to him cheerfully, looking up
> From picking a peahen bone or kissing the
> Nipple or nates of son, daughter, sister,
> Brother, aunt, ewe, teg: Why, stranger,
> Hast not heard the good news? That Christ
> Took away the burden of our sins on his
> Back broad to bear, and as we are saved
> Through him it matters little what we do?
> Since we are saved once for all, our being
> Saved will not be impaired or cancelled by
> Our present pleasures (which we propose to
> Renew tomorrow after a suitable and well-needed
> Rest). Alleluia alleluia to the Lord for he has
> Led us to two paradises, one to come and the other
> Here and now. Alleluia. And they fell to again,
> To nipple or nates or fish baked with datemince,
> Alleluia. And Morgan cried to the sky:

How long O Lord wilt thou permit these
Transgressions against thy holiness?
Strike them strike them as thou once didst
The salty cities of the plain, as through
Phinehas the son of Eleazar the son of Aaron
Thou didst strike down the traitor Zimri
And his foul whore of the Moabite temples Cozbi.
Strike strike. But the Lord did nothing.

Here came the difficulties. This whole business of free will and
predestination and original sin had to be done very dramatically.
And yet there had to be a bit of sermonizing. How the hell?
Enderby, who was not at present wearing his spectacles (ridiculous
when one was otherwise naked, anyway he only needed them for
distance really), gazing vaguely about the bedroom for an answer
found none forthcoming. The bookshelves of his landlady sternly
turned the backs, spines rather, of their contents towards him: not
our business, we are concerned with the *real* issues of life, meaning
women down-trodden by men, the economic oppression of the
blacks, counter-culture, coming revolt, Reich, Fanon, third world.
Then Enderby, squinting, could hardly believe what he saw. At the
bedroom door a woman, girl, female anyway. Covering his genitals
with his poem he said:

'What the devil? Who let you? Get out.'

'But I have an appointment with you at ten. It's ten after now. It
was arranged. I'll wait in the – Unless – I mean, I didn't expect –'

She had not yet gone. Enderby, pumping vigorously at White
Owl as if it would thus make him an enveloping cloud, turned
his back to her, covered his bottom with his poem, then found his
dressing-gown (Rawcliffe's really, bequeathed to him with his other
effects) on a chair behind a rattan settee and near to the air-
conditioner. He clothed himself in it. She was still there and talking.

'I mean, I don't mind if you don't –'

'I do mind,' Enderby said. And he flapped towards her on bare
feet but in his gown. 'What is all this anyway?'

'For *Jesus*.'

'For *who*, for Christ's sake?' He was close to her now and saw
that she was a nice little thing he supposed she could be called,

with nicely sculpted little tits under a black sweater stained with, as he supposed, coke and pepsi and hamburger fat (*good food* was what these poor kids needed), long American legs in patched worker's pants. Strange how one never bothered to take in the face here in America, the face didn't matter except on films, one never remembered the face, and all the voices were the same. And then: 'They shouldn't have let you in, you know, just like that. You're supposed to be screened or something, and then they ring me up and ask me if it's all right.'

'But he knows me, the man downstairs. He knows I'm one of your students.'

'Oh, are you?' said Enderby. 'I didn't quite – Yes,' peering at her, 'I suppose you could be. We'd better go into the sitting-room or whatever they call it.' And he pushed past her into the corridor to lead the way.

The room where he was supposed to *live*, that is, watch television, play protest songs on his landlady's record-player, look out of the window down on the street at acts of violence, was furnished mostly with barbaric nonsense – drums and shields and spears and very ill-woven garish rugs – and you were supposed to sit on *pouffes*. Enderby waved this girl to a *pouffe* with one hand and with the other indicated the television set, saying, puffing out White Owl smoke, 'I'm to be on that thing there.'

'Oh.'

'The Blowpipe Show or something. Can't think of the name offhand. What did you say your name was?'

'Oh, *you know*. Lydia Tietjens.' And, as he sat on a neighbouring *pouffe*, she gave him a playful push, as at his rather nice eccentric foreign silliness.

'Ah yes, of course. Ford Madox Ford. Met him once. He had terrible halitosis, you know. Stood in his way. The Establishment rejected him. And it was because he'd had the guts to fight and get gassed, while the rest of the bastards stayed at home. I say, you're not recording that, are you?' For, he now saw, she had a small Japanese cassette machine and was holding it towards him, rather like a sideswoman with offertory-box.

'Just getting a level.' And then, after some whirring and clicking, Enderby heard an unfamiliar voice say: *rest of the bastards stayed at home I say you're not rec.*

THE COMPLETE ENDERBY

'What did you say it was for?'

'For *Jesus*. Our magazine. Women for Jesus. *You know*.'

'Why just women for Jesus? I thought anyone could join.' And Enderby looked with fascination at the xeroxed thing she brought out of what looked like a British respirator haversack – *their* magazine, typewritten, as he could see from the last page, with no margin justifying, and the front page just showing the name JESUS and a crude portrait of a beardless though plentifully haired messiah.

'But that's not him.'

'Right. Not *him*. What proof is there that it was a *him*?'

Enderby breathed hard a few times and said: 'Would you like what we English call elevenses? Cakes and tea and things? I could cook you a steak if you liked. Or, wait, I have some stew left over from yesterday. It wouldn't take a minute to heat it up.' That was the trouble with all of them, poor kids. Half-starved, seeing visions, poisoned with cokes and hamburgers.

3

'Do you believe in God?' she asked, a steak sandwich in one paw and the cassette thing in the other.

'Is that tea strong enough for you?' Enderby asked. 'It doesn't look potable to me. One bag indeed. Gnat piss,' he added. And then: 'Oh, God. Well, believing is neither here nor there, you know. I believe in God and so what? I don't believe in God and so what again? It doesn't affect his own position, does it?'

'Why do you say *his*?' she hissed.

'Her, then. It. Doesn't matter really. A matter of tradition and convention and so on. Needs a new pronoun. Let's invent one, unique, just for himherit. Ah, that's it, then. Nominative *heshit*. Accusative *himrit*. Genitive *hiserits*.'

'But you're still putting the masculine first. The *heshit* bit's all right, though. Appropriate.'

'I don't mind what goes first,' Enderby said. 'Would you like something by Sara Lee? Please yourself then. All right. *Shehit. Herimit. Herisits*. It doesn't affect herisits position whether I believe or not.'

'But what happens when you die?'

'You're finished with,' Enderby said promptly. 'Done for. And even if you weren't – well, you die then, gasp your last, then you're sort of wandering, free of your body. You wander around and then you come into contact with a sort of big thing. What is this big thing? God, if you like. What's it, or shehit, like? I would say,' Enderby said thoughtfully, 'like a big symphony, the page of the score of infinite length, the number of instruments infinite but all bound into one big unity. This big symphony plays itself for ever and ever. And who listens to it? It listens to itself. Enjoys itself for ever and ever and ever. It doesn't give a bugger whether you hear it or not.'

'Like masturbation.'

'I thought it would come to that. I thought you'd have to bring sex into it sooner or later. Anyway, a kind of infinite Ninth Symphony. God as Eternal Beauty. God as Truth? Nonsense. God as Goodness. That means shehit has to be in some sort of ethical relationship with beings that are notGod. But God is removed, cut off, self-subsistent, not giving a damn.'

'But that's horrible. I couldn't live with a God like that.'

'You don't have to. Anyway, what have you or anybody else got to do with it? God doesn't have to be what people want shehit to be. I'm fed up with God,' Enderby said, 'so let's get on to something else.' And at once he got up painfully and noisily to find the whisky bottle, this being about the time for. 'I haven't got any glasses,' he said. 'Not clean ones, anyway. You'll have to have it from the bottle.'

'I don't want any.' She didn't want her tea either. Quite right: gnat piss. Enderby got down again. 'If there's no life after death,' she said, 'why does it matter about doing good in this world? I mean, if there's no reward or punishment in the next.'

'That's terrible,' Enderby sneered. 'Doing things because of what you're bloody well going to get out of it.' He took some whisky and did a conventional shudder. It raged briefly through the inner streets and then was transmuted into benevolent warmth in the citadel. Enderby smiled on the girl kindly and offered the bottle. She took it, raised it like a trumpet to the heavens, sucked in a millilitre or so. 'And, while we're at it,' he said, 'let's decide what we mean by good.'

'You decide. It's you who are being interviewed.'

'Well, there are some stupid bastards who can't understand how the commandant of a Nazi concentration camp could go home after torturing Jews all day and then weep tears of joy at a Schubert symphony on the radio. They say: here's a man dedicated to evil capable of enjoying the good. But what the imbecilic sods don't realize is that there are two kinds of good – one is neutral, outside ethics, purely aesthetic. You get it in music or in a sunset if you like that sort of thing or in a grilled steak or in an apple. If God's good, if God exists that is, God's probably good in that way. As I said.' He sipped from the bottle she had handed back. 'Before.'

'Or sex. Sex is as good whether – I mean, you don't have to be in what they used to call a state of grace to enjoy it.'

'That's good,' Enderby said warmly. 'That's right. Though you're still going on about sex. You mean lesbian sex, of course, in your case. Not that I have anything against it, naturally, except that I'm not permitted to experience it. The world's getting narrower all the time. All little sects doing what they call their own thing.'

'Why do you keep showing your balls all the time?' she said boldly. 'Don't you have underpants or anything?'

Enderby flushed very deeply all over. 'I had no intention,' he said. 'I can assure you. What I mean is, I'll put something on. I was not trying to provoke – I apologize,' he said, going off back to the bedroom. He came out again wearing nondescript trousers, something from an old suit, and a not overclean striped shirt. Also slippers. He said. 'There.' The hypocritical little bitch had been at the bottle in his brief absence. He could tell that from her slight slur. She said:

'Evil.'

'Who? Oh, evil.' And he sat down again. 'Evil is the destructive urge. Not to be confused with mere wrong. Wrong is what the government doesn't like. Sometimes a thing can be wrong and evil at the same time – murder, for instance. But then it can be right to murder. Like you people going round killing the Vietnamese and so on. Evil called right.'

'It wasn't right. Nobody said it was right.'

'The government did. Get this straight. Right and wrong are fluid and interchangeable. What's right one day can be wrong the next. And vice versa. It's right to like the Chinese now. Before you started playing ping pong with them it was wrong. A lot of evil nonsense. What you kids need is some good food (there you are, see: good in non-ethical sense) and an idea of what good and evil are about.'

'Well, go on, tell us.'

'Nobody,' said Enderby, having taken a swig, 'has any clear idea about good. Oh, giving money to the poor perhaps. Helping old ladies across the street. That sort of thing. Evil's different. Everybody knows evil. Brought up to it, you see. Original sin.'

'I don't believe in original sin.' She was taking the bottle quite manfully now. 'We're free.'

Enderby looked on her bitterly, also sweating. It was really too hot to wear anything indoors. Damned unchangeable central heating, controlled by some cold sadist somewhere in the basement. Bitterly because she'd hit on the damned problem that he had to present in the poem. She ought to go away now and let him get on with it. Still, his duty. One of his students. He was being paid. Those brown bastards in whose hands he had left *La Belle Mer* would be shovelling it all from till to pocket. Bad year we had, señor. Had to near shut up bloody shop. He said carefully:

'Well, yes. Freeish. *Wir sind ein wenig frei.* Wagner wrote that. Gave it to Hans Sachs in *Die Meistersinger.*' And then: 'No, to hell with it. Wholly free. Totally free to choose between good and evil. The other things don't matter − I mean free to drink a quart of whisky without vomiting and so on. Free to touch one's forehead with one's foot. And so forth.'

'I can do that,' she said. The latter. Doing it. That was the whisky, God help the ill-nourished child.

'But,' Enderby said, ignoring the acrobatics. She didn't seem to be bothering to use her cassette thing any more. Never mind. 'But we're disposed to do evil rather than good. History is the record of that. Given the choice, we're inclined to do the bad thing. That's all it means. We have to make a strong effort to do the good thing.'

'Examples of evil,' she said.

'Oh,' said Enderby. 'Killing for the sake of doing it. Torturing for pleasure – it always is that, though, isn't it? Defacing a work of art. Farting during a performance of a late Beethoven quartet. That must be evil because it's not wrong. I mean, there's no law against it.'

'We believe,' she said, sitting up seriously, checking the cassette machine and holding it out, 'that a time will come when evil will be no more. She'll come again, and that will be the end of evil.'

'Who's *she*?'

'Jesus, of course.'

Enderby breathed deeply several times. 'Look,' he said. 'If you get rid of evil you get rid of choice. You've got to have things to choose between, and that means good *and* evil. If you don't choose, you're not human any more. You're something else. Or you're dead.'

'You're sweating just terribly,' she said. 'There's no need to wear all that. Don't you have swimming trunks?'

'I don't swim,' Enderby said.

'It *is* hot,' she said. And she began to remove her coke-and-hamburger-stained sweater. Enderby gulped and gulped. He said:

'This is, you must admit, somewhat irregular. I mean, the professor and student relationship and all that sort of thing.'

'You exhibited yourself. That's somewhat irregular too.' By now she had taken off the sweater. She was, he supposed, decently dressed by beach standards, but there was a curious erotic difference between the two kinds of top worn. This was austere enough – no frills or representations of black hands feeling for the nipples. Still, it was *undress*. Beach dress was not that. He said:

'An interesting question when you come to think of it. If somebody's lying naked on the beach it's not erotic. Naked on the bed is different. Even more different on the floor.'

'The first one's functional,' she said. 'Like for a surgical operation. Nakedness is only erotic when it's obviously not for anything else.'

'You're quite a clever girl,' Enderby said. 'What kind of marks have I been giving you?'

'Two Cs. But I couldn't do the sestina. Very old-fashioned. And the other one was free verse. But you said it was really hexameters.'

'People often go into hexameters when they try to write free verse,' Enderby said. 'Walt Whitman, for instance.'

'I have to get As. I just have to.' And then: 'It *is* hot.'

'Would you like some ice in that? I can get you some ice.'

'Have you a cold coke?'

'There you go again, with your bloody cokes and seven ups and so on. It's uncivilized,' Enderby raged. 'I'll get you some ice.' He went into the kitchen and looked at it gloomily. It *was* a bit dirty, really, the sink piled high. He didn't know how to use the washing-up machine. He crunched out ice-cubes by pulling a lever. Ice-cubes went tumbling into dirty water and old fat. He cleaned them on a dishrag. Then he put them into the GEORGIA tea mug and took them in. He gulped. He said: 'That's going too far, you know.' Topless waitresses, topless students. And then: 'I forgot to wash a glass for you. Scatch on the racks,' he added, desperately facetious. He went back to the kitchen and at once the kitchen telephone rang.

'Enderby?' It was an English voice, male.

'Professor Enderby, yes.'

'Well, you're really in the shit now, aren't you, old boy?'

'Look, did you put her up to this? Who are you, anyway?'

'Ah, something going on there too, eh? This is Jim Bister from Washington. I saw you in Tangier, remember. Surrounded by all those bitsy booful brown boys.'

'Are you tight?'

'Not more than usual, old boy. Look, seriously. I was asked by my editor to get you to say something about this nun business.'

'What nun business? What editor? Who are you, anyway?' He was perhaps going too far in asking that last question again, but he objected to this assumption that British expatriates in America ought to be matey with each other, saying *in the shit* and so forth at the drop of a hat.

'I've said who I am. I thought you'd remember. I suppose you were half-pissed that time in Tangier. My newspaper is the *Evening Banner*, London if you've forgotten, what with your brandy and pederasty, and my editor wants to know what you –'

'What did you say then about pederasty? I thought I caught something about pederasty. Because if I did, by Jesus I'll be down there in Washington and I'll –'

'I didn't. Couldn't pronounce it even if I knew it. It's about this nun business in Ashton-under-Lyne, if you know where that is.'

'You've got that wrong. It's here.'

'No, that's a different one, old man. This one in Ashton-under-Lyne — that's in the North of England, Lancashire, in case you don't know — is manslaughter. Nunslaughter. Maybe murder. Haven't you heard?'

'What the hell's it to do with me anyway? Look, I distinctly heard you say pederasty —'

'Oh, balls to pederasty. Be serious for once. These kids who did it said they'd seen your film, the *Deutschland* thing. So now everybody's having a go at that. And one of the kids —'

'It's not mine, do you hear, and in any case no work of art has ever yet been responsible for —'

'Ah, call it a work of art, do you? That's interesting. And you'd call the book they made it from a work of art too, would you? Because one of the kids said he'd read the book as well as seen the film and it might have been the book that put the idea into his head. Any comments?'

'It's not a book, it's a poem. And I don't believe that it would be possible for a poem to — In any case, I think he's lying.'

'They've been reading it out in court. I've got some bits here. May have got a bit garbled over the telex, of course. Anyway, there's this: "From life's dawn it is drawn down, Abel is Cain's brother and breasts they have sucked the same." Apparently that started him dreaming at night. And there's something about "the gnarls of the nails in thee, niche of the lance, his lovescape crucified." Very showy type of writing, I must say. They're talking about the danger to susceptible young minds and banning it from the Ashton-under-Lyne bookshops.'

'I shouldn't imagine there's one bloody copy there. This is bloody ridiculous, of course. They're talking of banning the collected poems of a great English poet? A Jesuit priest, as well? God bloody almighty, they must all be out of their fucking minds.'

'There's this nun dead, anyhow. What are you going to do about it?'

'Me? I'm not going to do anything. Ask the buggers who made the film. They'll say what I say — once you start admitting that a work of art can cause people to start committing crimes, then you're lost. Nothing's safe. Not even Shakespeare. Not even the

Bible. Though the Bible's a lot of bloodthirsty balderdash that ought to be kept out of people's hands.'

'Can I quote you, old man?'

'You can do what the hell you like. Pederasty, indeed. I've got a naked girl in here now. Does that sound like pederasty, you stupid insulting bastard?' And he rang off, snorting. He went back, snorting, to his whisky and *pouffe*. The girl was not there. 'Where are you?' he cried, 'you and your bloody Jesus-was-a-woman nonsense. Do you know what they've done now? Do you know what they're trying to do to one of the greatest mystical poets that English poetry has ever known? Where are you?'

She was in his bedroom, he found to no surprise, lying on the circular bed, though still with her worker's pants on. 'Shall I take these off?' she said. Enderby, whisky bottle in hand, sat down heavily on a rattan chair not too far from the bed and looked at her, jaw dropped. He said:

'Why?'

'To lay me. That's what you want, isn't it? You don't get much of a chance, do you, you being old and ugly and kind of fat. Well, anyway, you can if you want.'

'Is this,' asked Enderby carefully, 'how you work for this bloody blasphemous Jesus of yours?'

'I've got to have an A.'

Enderby started to cry noisily. The girl, startled, got off the bed. She went out. Enderby continued crying, interrupting the spasm only to swig at the bottle. He heard her, presumably now sweatered again and clutching her cassette nonsense that was partially stuffed with his woolly voice, leaving the apartment swiftly on sneakered feet. Then she threw in her face, as it were, for him to look at now that her body had gone – a lost face with drowned hair of no particular colour, green eyes set wide apart like an animal's, a cheeseparing nose, a wide American mouth that was a false promise of generosity, the face of a girl who wanted an A. Enderby went on weeping and, while it went on, was presented intellectually with several bloody good reasons for weeping: his own decay, the daily nightmare of many parcels (too many cigarette-lighters that wouldn't work, too many old bills, unanswered letters, empty gin-bottles, single socks, physical organs, hairs in the nose and ears),

everyone's desperate longing for a final refrigerated simplicity. He
saw very clearly the creature that was weeping – a kind of Blake
sylph, a desperately innocent observer buried under the burden of
extension, in which dyspepsia and sore gums were hardly distinguishable from past sins and follies, the great bloody muckheap of
multiplicity (make that the name of the conurbation in which I
live) from which he wanted to escape but couldn't. I've got to
have an A. The sheer horrible innocence of it. Who the hell didn't
feel he'd got to have an A?

It was still only eleven-thirty. He went to the bathroom and,
mixing shaving-cream with tears not yet dried, he shaved. He
shaved bloodily and, in the manner of ageing men, left patches of
stubble here and there. Then he shambled over to the desk and
conjured Saint Augustine.

> He strode in out of Africa, wearing a
> Tattered royal robe of orchard moonlight
> Smelling of stolen apples but otherwise
> Ready to scorch, a punishing sun, saying:
> Where is this man of the northern sea, let me
> Chide him, let me do more if
> His heresy merits it, what is his heresy?
> And a hand-rubbing priest, olive-skinned,
> Garlic-breathed, looked up at the
> Great African solar face to whine:
> If it please you, the heresy is evidently a
> Heresy but there is as yet no name for it.
> And Augustine said: All things must have a name
> Otherwise, Proteus-like, they slither and slide
> From the grasp. A thing does not
> Exist until it has a name. Name it
> After this sea-man, call it after
> Pelagius. And lo the heresy existed.

What could be written some time, Enderby suddenly thought, was
a saga of a man's teeth – the Odontiad. The idea came to him
because of this image of the African bishop and saint and chider,
whose thirty-two wholesome and gleaming teeth he clearly saw,

flashing like two ivory blades (an upper teeth and a lower teeth) as he gnashed out condemnatory silver Latin. The Odontiad, a poetic record of dental decay in thirty-two books. The idea excited him so much that he felt an untimely and certainly unearned gust of hunger. He sharply down-sir-downed his growling stomach and went on with his work.

> Pelagius appeared, north-pale, cool as one of
> Britain's summers, to say, in British Latin:
> Christ redeemed us from the general sin, from
> The Adamic inheritance, the sour apple
> Stuck in the throat (and underneath his solar
> Hide Augustine blushed). And thus, my lord,
> Man was set free, no longer bounden
> In sin's bond. He is free to choose
> To sin or not to sin, he is in no wise
> Predisposed, it is all a matter of
> Human choice. And by his own effort, yea,
> His own effort only, not some matter of God's
> Grace arbitrarily and capriciously
> Bestowed, he may reach heaven, he may indeed
> Make his heaven. He is free to do so.
> Do you deny his freedom? Do you deny
> That God's incredible benison was to
> Make man free, if he wished, to offend him?
> That no greater love is conceivable
> Than to let the creature free to hate
> The creator and come to love the hard way
> But always (mark this mark this) by his own
> Will by his own free will?
> Cool Britain thus spoke, a land where indeed a
> Man groans not for the grace of rain, where
> He can sow and reap, a green land, where
> The God of unpredictable Africa is
> A strange God

It was no use. He ached with hunger. He went rumbling to the kitchen and looked at his untidy store cupboards. Soon he sat down to a new-rinsed dish of yesterday's stew reheated (chuck-steak, onions, carrots, spuds, well-spiced with Lea and Perrin's and a generous drop or so of chili sauce) while there sang on the stove in deep though tepid fat a whole bag of ready-cut crinkled potato pieces and, in another pan, slices of spongy canned meat called Mensch or Munch or something. The kettle was on for tea.

To his surprise, Enderby felt, while sitting calm, relaxed, and in mildly pleasant anticipation of good things to come, a sudden spasm that was not quite dyspepsia. An obscene pain struck in the breast-bone then climbed with some difficulty into the left clavicle and, from there, cascaded like a handful of heavy money down the left upper arm. He was appalled, outraged, what had he done to deserve – He caught an image of Henry James's face for some reason, similarly appalled though in a manner somehow patrician. Then nausea, sweating, and very cruel pain took over entirely. What the hell did one do now? The dish of half-eaten stew did not tell him, except not to finish it. What was that about the something-or-other distinguished thing? Ah yes, death. He was going to die. That was what it was.

He staggered moaning and cursing about the unfairness to the living-room (dying-room?). Death. It was very important to know what he was dying of. Was this what was called a heart attack? He sat on a comfortless chair and saw pain dripping on to the floor from his forehead. His shirt was soaked. It was so bloody hot. Breathing was very difficult. He tried to stop breathing, but his body, ill as it was, was not going to have that. Forced to take in a sharp lungful, he found the pain receding. Not death then. Not yet. A warning only. There was a statutory number of heart attacks before the ultimate, was there not? What he was being warned against he did not know. Smoking? Masturbation? Poetry?

He smelt smoke. Ah, was that also a symptom, a dysfunctioning of the olfactory system or something? But no, it was the damned food he had left sizzling. He tottered back into the kitchen and turned everything off. Didn't feel much like eating now.

4

Enderby left the apartment building itself with great caution, as though death, having promised some time to present himself in one form, might (with a dirtiness more appropriate to life) now present himself in another. Enderby was well wrapped against what he took to be the February cold. He had looked from his twelfth-floor window to see fur caps as if this were Moscow, though also sun and wind-scoured sidewalks. Liverish weather, then. He was dressed in his old beret, woollen gloves, and a kind of sculpted Edwardian overcoat bequeathed by his old enemy Rawcliffe. Rawcliffe was long-dead. He had died bloodily, fecally, messily, and now, to quote his own poem, practically his only own poem, his salts drained into alien soil. He had got death over with, then. He was, in a sense, lucky.

Perhaps posthumous life was better than the real thing. Oh God yes, I remember Enderby, what a man. Eater, drinker, wencher, and such foreign adventures. You could go on living without all the trouble of still being alive. Your character got blurred and mingled with those of other dead men, wittier, handsomer, themselves more vital now that they were dead. And there was one's work, good or bad but still a death-cheater. *Aere perennius*, and it was no vain boast even for the lousiest sonneteer that the Muse had ever farted on to. It wasn't death that was the trouble, of course, it was dying.

Enderby also carried, or was part carried by, a very special stick or cane. It was a swordstick, also formerly Rawcliffe's property. Enderby had gathered that it was illegal to go around with it in America, a concealed weapon, but that was the worst bloody hypocrisy he had ever met in this hypocritical country where everybody had a gun. He had not had cause to use the sword part of the stick, but it was a comfort to have in the foul streets that, like pustular bandages, wrapped the running sore of his university around. For corruption of the best was always the worst, lilies that fester, etc. What had been a centre of incorrupt learning was now a whorehouse of progressive intellectual abdication. The kids had to have what they wanted, this being a so-called democracy: courses in soul-cookery, whatever that was, and petromusicology, that being teenage garbage now treated as an art, and the history of black slavery, and innumerable branches of a subject called sociology. The past was spat upon and the future was ready to be spat upon too, since this would quickly enough turn itself into the past.

The elevator depressed Enderby to a vestibule with telescreens on the wall, each channel showing something different but always people unbent on violence or breaking-in, it being too early in the day and probably too cold. A Puerto Rican named Sancho sat, in the uniform designed by Ms Schwarz of the block police committee, nursing a sub-machine-gun. He greeted Enderby in Puerto Rican and Enderby responded in Tangerine. The point was: where was the capital of Spanish these days? Certainly not Madrid. And of English? Certainly not London. Enderby, British poet. That was exact but somehow ludicrous. Wordsworth, British poet. That was ludicrous in a different way. When Wordsworth wrote of a British shepherd, as he did somewhere, he meant a remote shadowy Celt. Enderby went out into the cold and walked carefully, leaning on his swordstick, towards Broadway. This afternoon he had two classes and he wondered if he was up to either of them. The first was really a formal lecture in which, heretically, he taught, told, gave out information. It was minor Elizabethan dramatists, a subject none of the regular English department was willing – or, so far as he could tell, qualified – to teach. This afternoon he was dealing with –

At the corner of 91st Street and Broadway he paused, appalled. He had forgotten. But it was as if he had never known. There was a blank in that part of his brain which was concerned with minor, or for that matter, major Elizabethan drama. Was this a consequence of that brief heart attack? He had no notes, scorned to use them. Nobody cared, anyway. It was something to get an A with. He walked into Broadway and towards the 96th Street subway entrance, conjuring minor Elizabethans desperately – men who all looked alike and died young, black-bearded ruffians with ruffs and earrings.

He would have to get a book on – But there was no time. Wait. It was coming back. Dekker, Greene, Peele, Nashe. The Christian names had gone, but never mind. The plays they had written? *The Shoemaker's Holiday, Old Fortunatus, The Honest Whore*. Which one of those syphilitic scoundrels had written those, and what the hell were they about? Enderby could feel his heart preparing to stop beating, and this could not, obviously, be allowed. The other class he had was all right – Creative Writing – and he had some of the ghastly poems they had written in his inside jacket pocket. But this first one – Relax, relax. It was a question of not trying too hard, not getting uptight, keeping your cool, as they said – very vague terms.

Reaching the subway entrance, moving as ever cautiously among muttering or insolent or palpably drugged people whom it was best to think of as being there mainly to demonstrate the range of the pigmentation spectrum, he observed, with gloom, shock, pride, shame, horror, amusement, and kindred emotions, that *The Wreck of the Deutschland* was now showing at the Symphony movie house. The 96th Street subway entrance he had arrived at was actually at the corner of 93rd Street. To see the advertising material of the film better, he walked, with his stick's aid, towards the matrical or perhaps seniorsororal entrance, and was able to take in a known gaudy poster showing a near-naked nun facing, with carmined lips opened in orgasm, the rash-smart sloggering brine. Meanwhile, in one inset tableau, thugs wearing swastikas prepared to violate five of the coifèd sisterhood, Gertrude, lily, conspicuous by her tallness among them, and, in another, Father Tom Hopkins S.J. desperately prayed, apparently having just got out of the bath to do so. Enderby felt his heart prepare, in the manner rather of a stomach, to react to all this, so he escaped into the dirty hell of the subway. A tall Negro with a poncho and a cowboy hat was just coming up, and he said no good to Enderby.

Hell, Enderby was thinking as he sat in one of the IRT coaches going uptownwards. Because we were too intellectual and clever and humanistic to believe in a hell didn't mean that a hell couldn't exist. If there were a God, he could easily be a God who relieved himself of the almost intolerable love he felt for the major part of his creation (on such planets, say, as Turulura 15a and Baa'rdnok and Juriat) by torturing for ever the inhabitants of 111/9 Tellus 1706defg. A touch of pepper sauce, his palate entitled to it. Or perhaps an experiment to see how much handing out of torture he himself could tolerate. He had, after all, a kind of duty to his own infinitely variable supersensorium. Hamlet was right, naturally. Troubles the will and makes us rather. This little uptown ride, especially when the train stopped long and inexplicably between stations, was a fair miniature simulacrum of the ultimate misery – potential black and brown devils ready to rob, slice, and rape; the names of the devils blowpainted on bulkheads and seats, though never on advertisements (sacred scriptures of the infernal law) – JESUS 69, SATAN 127, REDBALL IS BACK.

Coming out of the subway, walking through the disfigured streets full of decayed and disaffected and dogmerds, he felt a sudden and inappropriate accession of wellbeing. It was as though that lunchtime spasm had cleared away black humours inaccessible to the Chinese black draught. Everything came back about minor Elizabethan drama, though in the form of a great cinema poster with a brooding Shakespeare in the middle. But the supporting cast was set neatly about: George Peele, carrying a copy of *The Old Wives' Tale* and singing in a fumetto about chopcherry chopcherry ripe within; poor cirrhotic Robert Greene conjuring Friars Bacon and Bungay; Tom Brightness-falls-from-the-air Nashe; others, including Dekker eating a pancake. That was all right, then. But wait – who were those other others? Anthony Munday, yes yes, a bad playbotcher but he certainly existed. Plowman? A play called *A Priest in a Whorehouse*? Deverish? *England's Might or The Triumphs of Gloriana*?

Treading through rack of crumpled protest handouts, dessicated leaves, beercans, admitted with reluctance by a black armed policeman, he made his familiar way to the officially desecrated chapel which now held partitioned classrooms. Heart thumping, though fairly healthily, he entered his own (he was no more than five minutes late) to find his twenty or so students waiting. There were Chinese, skullcapped Hebrews, a girl from the Coast who piquantly combined black and Japanese, a beerfat Irishman with red thatch, an exquisite Latin nymph, a cunning knowall of the Kickapoo nation. He stood looking vaguely at them all. They lounged and ate snacks and drank from cans and smoked pot and looked back at him. He didn't know whether to sit or not at the table on which someone had chalked ASSFUCK. A little indisposed today, ladies and gentlemen. But no, he would doggedly stand. He stood. That bright Elizabethan poster swiftly evanesced. He gaped. All was blank except for imagination, which was a scurrying colony of termites. He said:

'Today, ladies and gentlemen, continuing our necessarily super-ficial survey of the minor Elizabethan dramatists —'

The door opened and a boy and a girl, wan and breathless from swift fumbling in the corridor, entered, buttoning. They sat, looking up at him, panting.

'We come to —' But who the hell did we come to? They waited, he waited. He went to the blackboard and wiped off some elemen-tary English grammar. The chalk in his grip trembled, broke in two. He wrote to his astonishment the name GERVASE WHITELADY. He added, in greater surprise and fear, the dates 1559–1591. He turned shaking to see that many of the students were taking the data down on bits of paper. He was committed now: this bloody man, not yet brought into existence, had to have existed. 'Gervase Whitelady,' he said, matter-of-factly, almost with a smear of the boredom proper to mention of a name nauseatingly well-known among scholars. 'Not a great name — a name, indeed, that some of you have probably never even heard of —' But the Kickapoo knowall had heard of it all right: he nodded with superior vigour. '— But we cannot afford to neglect his achievement, such as it was. Whitelady was the second son of Giles Whitelady, a scrivener. The family had settled in Pease Pottage, not far from the seaside town we now call Brighton, and were supporters of the Moabite persua-sion of crypto-reformed Christianity as far back as the time of Wyclif.' He looked at them all, incurious lot of young bastards. 'Any questions?' There were no questions. 'Very well, then.' The Kickapoo shot up a hand. 'Yes?'

'Is Whitelady the one who collaborated with — what was the name of the guy now — Fenprick? You know, they did this comedy together what the hell was the name of it?'

A very cunning young redskin sod, ought to be kept on his reservation. Enderby was not going to have this. 'Are you quite sure you mean Fenprick, er, er . . .'

'Running Deer is the name, professor. It might have been Fencock. A lot of these British names sound crazy.'

Enderby looked long on him. 'The dates of Richard Fenpick,' he said – 'note that it is *pick* not *prick*, by the way, er, er –' Running Deer, indeed. He must sometime look through the admission cards they were supposed to hand in. 'His dates are 1574–1619. He could hardly have collaborated with er . . .' He checked the name from the board. 'Er, Whitelady unless he had been a sort of infant prodigy, and I can assure you he was er not.' He now felt a hunger to say more about this Fenpick, whose career and even physical lineaments were being presented most lucidly to a wing of his brain which, he was sure, had been newly erected between the heart attack and now. 'What,' he said with large energy and confidence, 'we most certainly do know about er Fenpick is his instrumentality in bringing the Essex rebellion to a happy conclusion.' To his shock the hand of a girl who had just come in with that oversexed lout there, still panting, shot up. She cried:

'Happy for whom?'

'For er everybody concerned,' Enderby er affirmed. 'It had happened before in history, English naturally, as Whatsisname's own er conveniently or inconveniently dramatized.'

'Inconvenient for whom?'

'For er those concerned.'

'What she means is,' said the redthatched beerswollen Irish student, 'that the movie was on last night. The Late Late Date-with-the-Great Show. What Bette Davis called it was *Richard Two*.'

'*Elizabeth and Essex*,' the buttoned girl said. 'It failed and she had his head cut off but she cried because it's a Cruel Necessity.'

'What Professor Enderby was trying to say,' the Kickapoo said, 'was that the record is all a lie. There was really a King Robert the First on the British throne, disguised as the Queen.' Enderby looked bitterly at him, saying:

'Are you trying to take the – *Are you having a go?*'

'Pardon me?'

'The vital statistics,' a young Talmudist said, pencil poised at the ready. 'This Whitelady.'

'Who? Ah, yes.'

'The works.'

'The works,' Enderby said, with refocillated energy. 'Ah, yes. One long poem on a classical theme, the love of er Hostus for Primula. The title, I mean the hero and heroine are eponymous.' He clearly saw a first edition of the damned poem with titlepage a horrid mixture of typefaces, fat illdrawn nymphs on it, a round chop which said Bibliotheca Somethingorother. 'Specimen lines,' he continued boldly:

> 'Then as the moon engilds the Thalian fields
> The nymph her er knotted maidenhead thus yields,
> In joy the howlets owl it to the night,
> In joy fair Cynthia augments her light,
> The bubbling conies in their warrens er move
> And simulate the transports of their love.'

'But that's beautiful,' said the beautiful Latin nymph, unfat, unilldrawn, unknotted.

'Crap,' the Talmudist offered. 'The transports of *whose* love?'

'Theirs, of course,' Enderby said. 'Primavera and the er her lover.'

'There were six plays,' the Kickapoo said, 'if I remember correctly.'

'Seven,' Enderby said, 'if you count the one long attributed to er Sidebottom –'

'Crazy British names.'

'But now pretty firmly established as mainly the work of er the man we're dealing with, with an act and a half by an unknown hand.'

'How can they tell?'

'Computer work,' Enderby said vaguely. 'Cybernetic wonders in Texas or some such place.' He saw now fairly clearly that he would have to be for the chop. Or no, no, I quit. This was intolerable.

'What plays?' the Chinese next to the Talmudist said, a small round cheerful boy, perhaps an assistant cook in his spare time or main time if this were his spare time.

'Yes,' with fine briskness. 'Take these down. *What do you lack, fair mistress?* A comedy, done by the Earl of Leicester's Men, 1588. *The Tragedy of Canicula*, Earl of Sussex's Men, the same year. A year later came *The History of Lambert Simnel*, performed at court for the Shrovetide Revels. And then there was, let me see —'

'Where can we get hold of them?' the Melanonipponese said crossly. 'I mean, there's not much point in just having the titles.'

'Impossible,' prompt Enderby said. 'Long out of print. It's only important for your purpose that you know that Longbottom that is to say Whitelady actually existed —'

'But how do we know he did?' There were two very obdurate strains in this mixed Coast girl.

'Records,' Enderby said. 'Look it all up in the appropriate books. Use your library, that's what it's for. One cannot exaggerate the importance of er his contribution to the medium, as an influence that is, the influence of his rhythm is quite apparent in the earlier plays of er —'

'Mangold Smotherwild,' the Kickapoo said, no longer sneeringly outside the creative process but almost sweatily in the middle of it. Enderby saw that he could always say that he had been trying out a new subject called Creative Literary History. They might even write articles about it: *The Use of the Fictive Alternative World in the Teaching of Literature*. Somebody called out: 'Specimen.'

'No trouble at all,' Enderby said. 'In the first scene of *Give you good den good my masters* you have a soliloquy by a minor character named Retchpork. It goes, as I remember, something like this:

> So the world ticks, aye, like to a tocking clock
> On th'wall of naked else infinitude,
> Am I am hither come to lend an ear
> To manners, modes and bawdries of this town
> In hope to school myself in knavery.
> Aye, 'tis a knavish world wherein the whore
> And bawd and pickpurse, he of the quatertrey,
> The coneycatcher, prigger, jack o' the trumps
> Do profit mightily while the studious lamp
> Affords but little glimmer to the starved
> And studious partisan of learning's lore.
> Therefore, I say, am I come hither, aye,
> To be enrolled in knavish roguery.
> But soft, who's this? Aye, marry, by my troth,

> A subject apt for working on. Good den,
> My master, prithee what o'clock hast thou,
> *You* I would say, and *have* not *hast*, forgive
> Such rustical familiarity
> From one unlearn'd in all the lore polite
> Of streets, piazzas and the panoply
> Of populous cities –

Something like that, anyway,' Enderby said. 'I could go on if you wished. But it's all a bit dull.'

'If it's all a bit dull,' the Irish one said, 'why do we have to have it?'

'I thought you said he was influential,' somebody else complained.

'Well, he was. Dully influential,' the Kickapoo said.

'Dead at thirty-two,' Enderby said, having checked with the blackboard data. 'Dead in a duel or perhaps of the French pox or of a surfeit of pickled herrings and onions in vinegar with crushed peppercorns and sour ale, or, of course, of the plague. It was a pretty bad year for the plague, I think, 1591.' He saw Whitelady peering beseechingly at him, a white face from the shades, begging for a good epitaph. 'He was nothing,' Enderby said brutally, the face flinching as though from blows, 'so you can forget about him. One of the unknown poets who never properly mastered their craft, spurned by the Muse.' The whole luggage of Elizabethan drama was now, unfantasticated by fictional additions, neatly stacked before him. He knew what was in it and what wasn't. This Whitelady wasn't there. And yet, as the mowing face and haunted eyes, watching his, showed, in a sense he was. 'The important thing,' Enderby pronounced, 'is to get yourself born. You're entitled to that. But you're not entitled to life. Because if you were entitled to life, then the life would have to be quantified. How many years? Seventy? Sixty? Shakespeare was dead at fifty-two. Keats was dead at twenty-six. Thomas Chatterton at seventeen. How much do you think you're entitled to, you?' he asked the Kickapoo.

'As much as I can get.'

'And that's a good answer,' Enderby said, meaning it, meaning it more than they, in their present stage of growth, could possibly mean it. He suddenly felt a tearful love and compassion for these poor orphans, manipulated by brutal statesmen and the makers of tooth-eroding sweet poisonous drinks and (his face blotted temporarily out that of anguished Whitelady) the bearded Southern colonel who made it a virtue to lick chickenfat off your fingers. Schmalz and Chutzpah. The names swam in, as from the Book of Deuteronomy. Who were they? Lawyers? He said: 'Life is sensation, which includes thought, and the sensation of having sensation, which ought to take care of all your stupid worries about identity. Christ, Whitelady has identity. But what he doesn't have and what he never had is the sensation of having sensations. Better and cleverer people than we are can be invented.' He saw how wrong he was about *aere perennius*. 'But what can't be invented is,' he said, directly addressing the couple who had come in late, 'what you two were doing outside in the corridor.'

The boy grew very red but the girl smirked.

'The touch of the skin of a young girl's breast. A lush-capped plush-kept sloe —'

'You got that the wrong way round,' the Kickapoo said.

'Yes yes,' Enderby said, tired. And then, in utter depression, he saw who Whitelady was. He winked at him with his right eye and Whitelady simultaneously winked back with his left.

5

After the lesson on Whitelady (lose sensation, he kept thinking, and I become a fictional character) Enderby walked with care, aware of a sensation of lightness in his left breast as though his heart (not the real one, but the one of non-clinical traditional lore) had been removed. So sensation could lie, so whither did that lead you? His feet led him through a half-hearted student demonstration against or for the dismissal of somebody, a brave girl stripping in protest, giving blue breasts to the February post-meridian chill, to the long low building which was the English Department.

Outside the office he shared with Assistant Professor Zeitgeist or some such name, there were black girl students evidently waiting for Professor Zeitgeist and beguiling their wait with loud manic music on a transistor radio. Enderby mildly said:

'Do switch that thing off, please. I have some work to do.'

'Well, you goan work some place else, man.'

'This is, after all, my office,' Enderby smiled, feeling palpitations drumming up. 'This is, after all, the English Department of a university.' And then: 'Shut that bloody thing off.'

'You goan fuck yoself, man.'

'You ain't nuttin but shiiit, man.'

Abdication. What did one do now – slap the black bitches? Remember the long servitude of their people and bow humbly? One of them was doing a little rutting on-the-spot dance to the noise. Enderby slapped the black bitch on the puss. No, he did not. He durst not. It would be on the front pages tomorrow. There would be a row in the United Nations. He would be knifed by the men they slept with. He said, smiling, rage boiling up to inner excoriation: 'Abdication of authority. Is that expression in your primer of Black English?'

'Pip pip old boy,' said the non-jigging one with very fair mock-British intonation. 'And all that sort of rot, man.'

'You go fuck yo own ass, man. You aint nuttin but shiiiiit.'

Enderby had another weapon, not much used by him these days. He gathered all available wind and vented it from a square mouth.

Rarkberfvrishtkrahnbrrryburlgrong.

The effort nearly killed him. He staggered into his office, saw mail on his desk, took it and staggered out. The black girls, very ineptly, tried to give, in glee, his noise back to him. But their sense of body rhythm prevailed, turning it to oral tomtom music. The radio took four seconds off from discoursing on garbage of one sort to advertise garbage of another – male voice in terminal orgasm yelling sweet sweet sweet O Pan piercing sweet. Enderby went into the little lounge, empty save for shouting notices and a bearded man who looked knowingly at him. He opened his letters, chiefly injunctions to join things (BIOFEEDBACK BRETHREN GERONTOPHILIACS ANONYMOUS ROCK FOR CHRIST OUR SATAN THE THANATOLOGY

MONTHLY), coming at length to a newspaper clipping sent, apparently out of enmity, by his publisher in London. It was from the *Daily Window* and was one of the regular hardhitting noholdsbarred nononsense manofthepeople responsibilityofagreatnationalorgan addresses to the reader written by a staffman named Belvedere Fellows, whose jowled fierce picture led, like a brave overage platoon officer, the heavy type of his heading. Enderby read: SINK THE DEUTSCHLAND! Enderby read:

My readers know I am a man that faces facts. My readers know that I will sit through any amount of filthy film rubbish in order to report back fairly and squarely to my readers about the dangers their children face in a medium that increasingly, in the name of the so-called Permissive Society, is giving itself over to nudity, sex, obscenity, and pornography.

Well, I went to see *The Wreck of the Deutschland* and confess that I had to rush to the rails long before the end. I was scuppered. Here all decent standards have finally gone Kaput. Here is the old heave-ho with a vengeance.

But enough has been said already about the appalling scenes of Nazi rape and the blasphemous nudity. We know the culprits: their ears are deafened to the appeals of decency by the crackle of the banknotes they are now so busily counting. There are certain quiet scoundrels whose names do not reach the public eye with the same tawdry glamour. Behind the film image lies the idea, lies the writer, skulking behind the cigarette smoke and whisky in his ivory tower.

I say now that they must take their share of the blame. I have not read the book which the film is based on, nor would I want to. I noted grimly however that there were no copies the other day in my local library. My readers will be horrified however to learn that he is a Roman Catholic priest. This what the liberalism of that great and good man Pope John has been perverted into.

I call now, equivocally and pragmatically, for a closer eye to be kept on the filth that increasingly these days masquerades as literature and even as poetry. The vocation of poet has traditionally been permitted to excuse too much – the lechery of Dylan

Thomas and the drunken bravoing of Brendan Behan as well as the aesthetic perversions of Oscar Wilde. Is the final excuse now to be sought in the so-called priestly vocation? Perhaps Father Enderby of the Society of Jesus would like to reply. I have no doubt he would find an attentive congregation.

Enderby looked up. The bearded man was still looking knowingly at him. He said something. Enderby said: 'I beg your pardon?'

'I said: how are things in Jolly Old?'

Enderby could think of absolutely no reply. The two looked at each other fixedly for a long time, and the bearded man's jaw dropped progressively as if he were silently demonstrating an escalier of front vowels. Then Enderby sighed, got up and went out to seek his Creative Writing class. Like a homer he tapped his way with his swordstick through the dirty cold and student-knots to a building named for the inventor of a variety of canned soups, Warhall or somebody. On the second floor, to which he clomb with slow care, he found them, all ten, in a hot room with a long disfigured conference table. The Tietjens girl was there, drowned and sweatered. She had apparently told them everything, for they looked strangely at him. He sat down at the top or bottom of the table and pulled their work out of his inside pocket. He saw that he had given Ms Tietjens a D, so he ball-pointed it into a rather arty A. The rest shall remain as they are. Then he tapped his lower denture with the pen, plastic to plastic: tck tck, tcktck tck, TCK. He looked at his students, a mostly very untidy lot. They looked at him, lounging, smoking, taking afternoon beverages. He said:

'The question of sartorial approach is relevant, I think. When John Keats had difficulty with a poem he would wash and put on a clean shirt. The stiff collar and bow tie and tails of the concert-goer induce a tense attitude appropriate to the hearing of complex music. The British colonial officer would dress for dinner, even in the jungle, to encourage self-discipline. There is no essential virtue in comfort. To be relaxed is good if it is part of a process of systole and diastole. Relaxation comes between phases of tenseness. Art is essentially tense. The trouble with your er art is that it is not tense.'

They all looked at him, not tense. Many of their names he still refused to take seriously – Chuck Szymanowski, for instance. His sole black man was called Lloyd Utterage, a very reasonable name. This man was very ugly, which was a pity and which Enderby deeply regretted, but he had very beautiful clothes, mostly of hot-coloured blanketing materials, topped with a cannibal-style wire-wool hairshock. He was very tense, and this too Enderby naturally approved. But he was full of hate, and that was a bore. 'I will not,' Enderby said, turning to him, 'read out all your poem, which may be described as a sort of litany of anatomic vilification. Two stanzas will perhaps suffice.' And he read them with detached primness:

> 'It will be your balls next, whitey,
> A loving snipping of the scrotum
> With rather rusty nail-scissors,
> And they tumble out then to be
> Crunched underfoot crunch crunch.

> It will be your prick next, whitey,
> A loving chopping segmentally
> With an already bloodstained meat hatchet,
> And it will lie with the dog-turds
> To be squashed squash squash.

One point,' he said. 'If the prick is to be chopped in segments it will not resemble a dog-turd. The writing of er verse does not excuse you from considerations of er . . .'

'He says it will lie *with* the dog-turds,' Ms Tietjens said. 'He doesn't say it will look like one.'

'Yes yes, Sylvia, but —'

'Lydia.'

'Of course, thinking of Ford. Sorry. But you see, the word *it* suggests that it's still a unity, not a number of chopped bits of er penis. Do you see my point?'

'Yeah,' Lloyd Utterage said, 'but it's not a point worth seeing. The point is the hate.'

'The poetry is in the pity,' said Enderby. 'Wilfred Owen. He was wrong, of course. It was the other way round. As I was saying, a unity and rather resembling a dog-turd. So the image is of this er prick indistinguishable from –'

'Like Lloyd said,' said a very spotty Jewish boy named Arnold Something, his hair too cannibalistically arranged, 'it's the hate that it's about. Poetry is made out of emotions,' he pronounced.

'Oh no,' Enderby said. 'Oh very much no. Oh very very very much no and no again. Poetry is made out of words.'

'It's the hate,' Lloyd Utterage said. 'It's the expression of the black experience.'

'Now,' Enderby said, 'we will try a little experiment. I take it that this term *whitey* is racialist and full of opprobrium and so on. Suppose now we substitute for it the word er *nigger* –' There was a general gasp of disbelief. 'I mean, if, as you said, the point is the hate, then the hate can best be expressed – and, indeed, in poetry *must* be expressed – as an emotion available to the generality of mankind. So instead of either *whitey* or *nigger* you could have, er, *bohunk* or, say, *kike*. But *kike* probably wouldn't do . . .'

'You're telling me it wouldn't do,' Chuck Szymanowski said.

'Since the end-words are disyllabic or, er, yes trisyllabic but never monosyllabic. A matter of structure,' Enderby said. 'So listen. *It will be your balls next, nigger*, etc etc. *It will be your prick next, nigger*, and so on. Now it is the structure that interests me. It's not, of course, a very subtle or interesting structure, as er Lloyd here would be the first to admit, but it is the structure that has the vitality, not all this nonsense about hate and so on. I mean, imagine a period when this kind of race hate stupidity is all over, and yet the poem – *aere perennius*, you know – still by some accident survives. Well, it would be taken as a somewhat primitive but still quite engaging essay in vilification in terms of an anatomical catalogue, the structure objectifying and, as it were, cooling the hate. Comic too on the personal level, '*It will be your balls next*, er *Crassus* or say *Lycidas*. Rather Catullan. You see.' He smiled at them. Now they were really learning something.

'You think,' Lloyd Utterage panted, 'you're going to get away with that, man?'

'Away with what?' Enderby asked in honest and rather hurt surprise.

'Look,' Ms Tietjens said kindly, 'he's British. He doesn't understand the ethnic agony.'

'That's rather a good phrase,' Enderby said. 'It doesn't mean anything, of course. Like saying *potato agony*. Oh I don't know, though. The meanings of imaginative language are not the same as those of the defilers of language. Your president, for instance. The black leaders. Lesbian power, if such a thing exists . . .'

'He understands it,' said Lloyd Utterage. 'His people started it. Nigger-whippers despite their haw-haw-haw old top.'

'Now that's interesting,' Enderby said. 'You see how the whipping image immediately begat in your imagination the image of a top? You have the makings of a word-man. You'll be a poet some day when you've got over all this nonsense.' Then he began to repeat *nigger-whipper* swiftly and quietly like a tongue-twister. 'Prosodic analysis,' he said. 'Do any of you know anything about that? A British linguistic movement, I believe, so it may not have er gotten to you. *Nigger* and *whipper*, you see, have two vowels in common. Now note the opposition of the consonants: a rich nasal against a voiceless semi-vowel, a voiced stop against a voiceless. Suppose you tried *nigger-killer*. Not so effective. Why not? The g doesn't oppose well to the l. They're both voiced, you see, and so —'

'Maaaaaan,' drawled Lloyd Utterage, leaning back in simulated ease, smiling crocodilewise. 'You play you little games with youself. All this shit about words. Closing your eyes to what's going on in the big big world.'

Enderby got angry. 'Don't call me *maaaaaan*,' he said. 'I've got a bloody name and I've got a bloody handle to it. And don't hand me any of that *shiiit*, to use your own term, about the importance of cutting the white man's balls off. All that's going to save your immortal soul, *maaaaaan*, if you have one, is words. Words words words, you bastard,' he crescendoed, perhaps going too far.

'I don't think you should have said that,' said a mousy girl called Ms Crooker or Kruger. 'Bastard, I mean.'

'Does he have the monopoly of abuse?' Enderby asked in heat. 'It's he who's doing the playing about, anyway, with his bloody castration fantasies. He wouldn't have the guts to cut the balls off a pig. Or he might have. If it were a very little pig and ten big fellow melanoids held it down for him. I say,' he then said, 'that's good. *Fellow melanoids*.'

'I'm getting out of here,' Lloyd Utterage said, rising.

'Oh no you're not,' Enderby cried. 'You're going to stay and suffer just like I am. Bloody cowardice.'

'There's no engagement,' Lloyd Utterage said. 'There's no common area of understanding.' But he sat down again.

'Oh yes there is,' Enderby said. 'I understand that you want to cut a white man's genital apparatus off. Well, come and try. But you'll get this sword in your black guts first.' And he drew an inch or so of steel.

'You shouldn't have said black guts,' Ms Flugel or Crookback said. It was as though she were Enderby's guide to polite New York usage.

'Well,' Enderby said, 'they *are* black. Is he going to deny that now?'

'I never denied anything, man.'

Suddenly the cannibal-haired kike or Jew, Arnold Something, began to laugh in a very high pitch. This started some of the others off: a bespectacled big sloppy student with a sloppy viking moustache, for instance, began to neigh. Lloyd Utterage sulked, as did Enderby. But then Enderby, trying, which was after all his job here, to be helpful, said, 'Greek *hystera*, meaning the womb. This shows, and this might possibly bring er here, our friend I mean, and myself into a common area of understanding, that etymology can get in the way of scientific progress, since Sigmund Freud's opponents in Vienna used etymology to confute his contention that hysteria, as now and here to be witnessed, could be found in the male as well as the female.' Little of this could be heard over the noise. At length it subsided, and the sloppy viking whose name was, Enderby thought and would now check from the papers before him and yes indeed it was, Sig Hamsun, said:

'And now how's about look at *my* crap.'

That very nearly made the cannibal Jew Arnold begin again, but he was rebuked ironically by Lloyd Utterage, who said: 'This serious, man, yeah serious, didn't you know it was serious? Yeah serious, as you very well know.'

Hamsun's crap, Enderby now saw again, looking through it, was in no way sternly Nordic. To match its excretor it was rather sloppy and fungoid. Enderby recited it grimly however:

'And as the Manhattan dawn came up

> Over the skyline we still lay
> In each other's arms. Then you
> Came awake and the Manhattan dawn
> Was binocularly presented in your
> Blue eyes and in your pink nipples
> Monostomatic heaven . . .'

'What does that word mean?' a Ms Hermsprong asked. 'Mono something.'

'It means,' Enderby said, 'that he had only one mouth.'

'Well, we all know he only has one mouth. Like everybody else.'

'Yes,' Enderby said, 'but she had two nipples, you see. The point is, I think, that he would have liked to have two mouths, you see. One for each nipple.'

'No,' Hamsun said. 'One mouth was enough.' He leered.

'Permit me,' Enderby said coldly, 'to tell you what your poem means. Such as it is.'

'I wrote it, right?'

'You could just about say that, I suppose. It means fundamentally – which means this is the irreducible minimum of meaning – play between unitary and binary, that is to say: 1 dawn, 2 eyes, 2 nipples, 1 mouth. There's also colour play, of course: pink dawn in blue sky, two pink dawns in two blue eyes, two pink nipples, one pink mouth (also two pink lips), one blue heaven in pink nipples and pink mouth. You see? Well then, now we come to the autobiographical element or, if you like, the personal content. It's a childhood reminiscence. The woman in it is your mother. You're greedy for her breasts, you want two mouths. Why should there be two of everything else, even the manifestly single city and single dawn, and only one sucking mouth? There.' He sat back in post-exegetical triumph that the twin simmering murder in Lloyd Utterage's eyes did something to qualify. Ms Tietjens said, in counter-triumph:

'If you want to know the truth, it was me.'

'You mean you wrote it? You mean he stole it? You mean –'

'I mean I'm the woman in the poem, complete with two nipples. As you can vouch for.'

'Look,' Enderby said.

'He wrote it about me.'

'What I mean is that I didn't bloody well ask to see them. Here, by the way, is *your* poem back. With an A on it. And a lousy poem it is, if I may say so. Coming into my apartment,' he told the class, 'and stripping off. Something to do with Jesus Christ being a woman. And you,' he accused, 'pretending to be lesbian.'

'I never said I was that. You make too many false assumptions.'

'Look,' Enderby said in great weariness and with crackling energy. 'All of you. A poem isn't important because of the biographical truth of the content.'

'Look,' countersaid the sloppy Nordic, 'it was one way of keeping her there, can't you see that? She's there in that fucking poem for ever. Complete with pink nipples.'

'I'm not a thing to be kept,' Ms Tietjens said hotly. 'Can't you see that attitude makes some of us go the way we do?'

'The point is,' Enderby said, 'that there are certain terrible urgencies.' Lloyd Utterage guffaw-sneered in a way that Enderby could only think of as *niggerish*. It was in the act of the formulation of the term that he realized with great exactitude the impossibility of his position. There was no communication; he was too old-fashioned; he had always been too old-fashioned. 'The urgencies are not political or racial or social. They're, so to speak, semantic. Only the poetical inquiry can discover what language really is. And all you're doing is letting yourselves be ensnared into the irrelevancies of the slogan on the one hand and sanctified sensation on the other.' So. Identity? Unimportant. Sensation? Unimportant. What the hell was left? 'The urgent task is the task of conservation. To hold the complex totality of linguistic meaning within a shape you can isolate from the dirty world.'

'The complex *what*?' Ms Hermsprong asked. The rest of them looked at him as if he were, which he probably was, mad.

'Never mind,' Enderby said. 'You can't fight. You'll never prevail against the big bastards of computerized organizations that are kindly letting you enjoy the illusion of freedom. The people who write poems, even bad ones, are not the people who are going to rule. Sooner or later you're all going to go to jail. You have to learn to be alone, no sex, not even any books. All you'll have is language, the great conserver, and poetry, the great isolate shaper. Stock your

minds with language, for Christ's sake. Learn how to write what's
memorable. No, not write, compose in your head. The time will
come when you won't even be allowed a stub of pencil and the
back of an envelope.' He paused, looking down. He looked up at
their pity and wonder and the black man's hatred. 'Try,' he said
lamely, 'heroic couplets.'

The cannibal Arnold said: 'How long will you be staying?'

Enderby grinned citrously. 'Not much longer, I suppose. I'm not
doing any good, am I?' Nobody said anything. Hamsun did a slow
and not ungraceful shrug. Chuck Szymanowski said:

'You're defeatist. You're anti-life. You're not helping any. The time
will come later for all this artsy shmartsy crap. But it's not now.'

'If it's not now,' Enderby said, 'it's not ever.' He didn't trouble
to get angry at the designation of high and neutral art as crap.
'You can't split life into diachronic segments.' He would write a
letter of resignation when he got back to the apartment. No, he
wouldn't even do that. Today was what? Friday the twenty-sixth.
There would be a salary cheque for him on Monday. Grab that
and go. He was, by God, after all, despite everything, free. Ms
Cooper or Krugman said, kindly it seemed:

'What's your idea of a good poem?'

'Well,' Enderby said. 'Perhaps this:

> Queen and huntress, chaste and fair,
> Now the sun is gone to sleep,
> Seated in thy silver chair,
> State in wonted manner keep.
> Hesperus entreats thy light,
> Goddess excellently bright . . .'

'Jesus,' Lloyd Utterage said with awe. 'Playing your little games,
man.' And then, blood mixed somewhere down there in his larynx:
'You bastard. You misleading reactionary *evil* bastard.'

Enderby saw, in gloomy clarity, going back to 96th Street on the IRT, that the area of freedom was very small. *Ein wenig frei* was about right. He was not free, for instance, not to be messily beaten up by the black gang Lloyd Utterage had, in sincere and breathy confidence with much African vowel-lengthening, promised to unleash on him during the weekend. He was not free not to feel excruciating stabs in his calves, something probably to do with the silting up of the arteries, which had now come upon him as he embraced the metal monkey-pole in the IRT train, all the seats having been taken by young black and brown thugs just out of school, who should by rights be forced to stand up for their elders. But he was free to leave America. A matter of booking on a plane to Madrid and then another to Tangier. Being free in this area, however, he decided not to make use of his freedom. Which meant he would not be free not to be messily beaten up etc etc. Which meant he was *choosing* to be messily . . . etc. They would bruise and rend his body, but there would be a thin clear as it were refrigerated self deep within, unbruisable and unrendable and, as it were, free. Augustine of Hippo, whom he now saw blanketed and shockhaired like Lloyd Utterage, was waiting for him back in the apartment to sort out other aspects of freedom for him. But, wait . . . he had to appear on a television talk-show some time this evening, didn't he? He must not forget that, he must keep track of the time. *Ein wenig frei* to speak out for Gerard Manley Hopkins, sufferer, mystic, artist, pre-Freudian.

As he let himself into the apartment, he was aware of the ghost of the cardiac attack, if that was what it was, earlier; not shooting but already shot, a sort of bruised line of trajectory. It was obvious that he was intended to be doing some urgent thinking about death. He gloomed at the mess of the kitchen, lusting for a pint of strong tea and a wedge of some creature of Sara Lee. He gave way to the lust defiantly, grumbling round the sitting-room while the water boiled, searching for his ALABAMA mug. He found it eventually, full of warmish water that had once been ice. Soon he was able to sit on a *pouffe*, gorging sponge and orange cream out of one fist, the other holding the handle of the mug of mahogany tea like a weapon against Death, what time he looked at a children's cartoon programme on television. It was all talking animals in reds, blues, and yellows, but you could see the chained wit and liberalism of the creators escaping from odd holes in the fabric: that legalistic pig there was surely the vice-president? Might it be possible to get the story of Augustine and Pelagius across in cartoon-form?

Back in the study-bedroom with his draft, he saw how bad it was and how much work on it lay ahead. And yet he was supposed to start thinking of death. It was the leaving of things unfinished that was so intolerable. It was all very well for Jesus Christ, not himself a writer though no mean orator, to talk about thinking not of the morrow. If you'd started a long poem you had to think of the bloody morrow. You could better cope with the feckless Nazarene philosophy if you were like those scrounging dope-takers who littered the city. Sufficient unto the day is the evil thereof, as also the dope thereof.

Augustine said: If the Almighty is also Allknowing,
He knows the precise number of hairs that will fall to the floor
From your next barbering, which may also be your last.
He knows the number of drops of lentil soup
That will fall on your robe from your careless spooning
On August 5th, 425. He knows every sin
As yet uncommitted, can measure its purulence
On a precise scale of micropeccatins, a micropeccatin
Being, one might fancifully suppose,
The smallest unit of sinfulness. He knows
And knew when the very concept of man itched within him
The precise date of your dispatch, the precise
Allotment of paradisal or infernal space

Awaiting you. Would you diminish the Allknowing
By making man free? This is heresy.
But that God is merciful as well as allknowing
Has been long revealed: he is not himself bound
To fulfil foreknowledge. He scatters grace
Liberally and arbitrarily, so all men may hope,
Even you, man of the northern seas, may hope.
But Pelagius replied: Mercy is the word, mercy.
And a greater word is love. Out of his love
He makes man free to accept or reject him.
He could foreknow but refuses to foreknow
Any, even the most trivial, human act until
The act has been enacted, and then he knows.
So men are free, are touched by God's own freedom.
Christ with his blood washed out original sin,
So we are in no wise predisposed to sin
More than to do good: we are free, free,
Free to build our salvation. Halleluiah.
But the man of Hippo, with an African blast,
Blasted this man of the cool north . . .

No no no, Enderby said to himself. It could not be done. This
was not poetry. You could not make poetry out of raw doctrine.
You had to find symbols, and he had no symbols. The poem could
not be written. He was free. The paper chains rustled off. He
stuffed them into the waste-basket. Free. Free to start writing the
Odontiad. Hence bound to start writing the *Odontiad*. Hence not
free.

He sighed bitterly and went to the bathroom to start tarting
himself up for the television show. Clean and bleeding, he put on
garments bequeathed to him by Rawcliffe and stood, at length, to
review himself at length in the long wall-mirror near the bedroom
door. Seedy Edwardian, recaller of dead glories, finale of Elgar's
First Symphony belting out Massive Hope for the Future. There
was an empire in those days, and it was assumed that the centre
of the English language was London. Wealthy Americans were still
humble provincials. Ichabod. He put on the sculpted overcoat and
his beret and, swordstick pathetic in his feeble gripe, went out.

The subway had not yet erupted into violent nocturnal life. His fellow-passengers on the downtown express to Times Square were as dimly ruminant as he, perhaps recalling dimly the glories of other departed empires, Ottoman, Austro-Hungarian, Pharaonic. But one black youth in a rutilant combat jacket saw drug-induced empires within; under the *pax alucinatoria* the rhomboid and spiral became one. Enderby looked again at the torn-off corner of the abandoned poem on which he had written *Live Lancing Show 46th Street or somewhere like that*. He had time, also two ten-dollar bills in his pocket. He would go to the Blue Bar of the Algonquin Hotel, a once very literary place, and have a quiet gin or so. He felt all right. The black tea and Sara Lee were worrying the heart combat troops: why was not the rutilant enemy scared?

He got out quite briskly at Times Square and walked down West 44th Street. In the lobby of the Algonquin there were, he saw, British periodicals on sale. He bought *The Times* and leafed through it standing. In a remote corner of it, he saw, a member of parliament was pleading for a special royal commission to clean up the Old Testament. Dangers even in great classics, provocation to idle and affluent youth etc. In the Blue Bar there were some conspiratorial and lecherous customers at tables, but seated on a bar-stool was a rather loud man whose voice Enderby seemed to recognize. Good God, it was Father Hopkins himself. No, the man who played him in the film. What was his name now?

'So I said to him *up yours*, that's what I said.'

'That's it, Mr O'Donnell.'

Coemgen (pronounced Kevin) O'Donnell, that was the man. Enderby had met him briefly at a little party after the London preview, when he had been affably drunk. No coincidence that he was here now: the Algonquin took in actors as much as writers. Sitting at a stool two empty stools away from O'Donnell, Enderby asked politely for a pink gin. O'Donnell, hunched to the counter, heard the voice, swivelled gracelessly and said:

'You British?'

'Well, yes,' Enderby said. 'British-born but, like yourself I presume, living in exile. Look, we've already met.'

'Never seen you before in my life.' The voice was wholly

American. 'Lots of guys like you, seen me on the movies, assume acquaintanceshhh. Ip. You British?'

'Well, yes. British-born but, like yourself I presume, living in . . .'

'You said all that crap already, buster. All I asked was a straight queschhh. Okay, you're British. Needn't keep on about it. No need to eggs hhhibit the flag tattooed on your ass. And all that sort of. What? What?'

'The film,' Enderby said. 'The movie. *The Wreck of the Deutschland.*'

'I was in it. That was my movie.' He thrust his empty tumbler rudely towards the bartender. He was most unpriestlike in his dress, glistening cranberry suit, violet shirt, shoes that Enderby took to be Gucci. The face was a rugged cornerboy's, apt for some slum baseball-with-the-kids Maynooth type priest, but hardly for the delicate intellectual unconscious pederast ah-my-dear Hopkins.

'The point is,' Enderby said, 'that I too was in it in a sense. It was my idea. My name was among the credits. Enderby,' he added, to no applause. 'Enderby,' to not even recognition. Coemgen O'Donnell said:

'Yeah. I guess it had to be somebody's idea. Everything is kind of built on the idea of some unknown guy. You seen the figures in this week's *Variety*? Sex and violence, always the answer. But the guy that wrote the book was not like the guy I played in the movie. No, sir. The original Father Hopkins was a fag.'

'A priest a fag?' the bartender said. 'You don't say.'

'There are priest's fags,' O'Donnell said. 'Known several. Have it off with the altar boys. But in the movie he's normal. Has it off with a nun.' He nodded gravely at Enderby and said: 'You British?'

'Listen,' Enderby said, 'Gerard Manley Hopkins was not a homosexual. At least not consciously. Certainly not actively. Sublimation into the love of Christ perhaps. A theory, no more. A possibility. Of no religious or literary interest, of course. A love of male beauty. *The Bugler's First Communion* and *The Loss of the Eurydice* and *Harry Ploughman*. Admiration for it. "Every inch a tar. Of the best we boast our sailors are." "Hard as hurdle arms with a broth of goldish flue." What's wrong with that, for Christ's sake?'

'Broth of goldfish my ass,' O'Donnell said. 'Has that guy from the front office come yet?' he asked the bartender.

'He'll come in here, Mr O'Donnell. He'll know where you are. If I was you, sir, I'd make that one the last. Until after the show, that is.'

'Show?' Enderby said. 'Are you by any chance on the −' He consulted the tear-off from his pocket. 'Live Lancing Show?'

'Hey, that's good. Sperr would like that. Not that it's live, old boy, old boy. Nothing's live, not any more.' And then: 'You British?'

'I've said already that I −'

'You a fag? Okay okay. That's not what I was going to ask. What I was going to ask was − What was I going to ask?' he asked the bartender.

'Search me, Mr O'Donnell.'

'I know. Something about a bugle-boy. What was that about a bugugle-boy?'

'*The Bugler's First Communion?*'

'That's it, I guess. Now this proves that he was a fag. You British? Yeah yeah, asked that already. That means you know the town of Oxford, where the college is, right? It was my father.'

'*What?*'

'Got that balled-up, I guess. Big army barracks there. Cow cow cow something.'

'Cowley?'

'Right, you'd know that, being British. Another scatch on the −'

'Sorry, Mr O'Donnell. You yourself give me strict instructions when you started.'

'Okay okay, gotta be with old Can Dix. Sending a limousine.'

'Who? What?'

'Sending a car round. This talk-show.'

'I,' Enderby said, 'am on the other one, the Spurling one. What,' he said with apprehension, 'are you going to tell them?'

'Listen, old boy old boy, not finished, had I, right? Right. It was my mother's father. British, with an Irish mother. Sent him off to be good Catholic. Right? One hell of a row, father was Protestant.'

'Yes,' Enderby said. '"Born, he tells me, of Irish/Mother to an English sire (he/Shares their best gifts surely, fall how things will)."'

'Not finished, had I, right?'

'Sorry.'

'No need to be sorry. Never regret anything, my what the hell do you call it slogan, right? Went over to Ireland with my mother's father's mother, he was my mother's father, you see that?'

'Right.'

'Married Irish, the British all got smothered up. Well, that was his story.'

'What was his story?'

'Had him down there in the what do you call it presbyt presbyt, his red pants off of him and gave him, you know, the stick. Met him again in Dublin when he was some sort of professor, reminded him of it. Made him very sick. Very sick already.'

'Oh God,' Enderby said.

O now well work that sealing sacred ointment!
O for now charms, arms, what bans off bad
    And love locks ever in a lad!
Let me though see no more of him, and not disappointment
Those sweet hopes quell whose least me quickenings lift . . .

'I can't believe it,' Enderby said. 'I won't.' He had intimations of a renewal of quasi-lethal pains ready to shoot from chest to clavicle to arm. No, he wouldn't have it. He frightened the promise away with a quick draught of gin. 'So,' he said. 'You're going to tell them all about it?'

'Not that,' O'Donnell said. 'Crack a few gags about nuns. I was with this dame in a taxi and she was a nun. She'd have nun of this and nun of that.'

'What a filthy unspeakable world,' Enderby said. 'What defilement, what horror.'

'You can say that again. Ah, Josh. It is Josh? Sure it's Josh. How are things, Josh? How's the kids and the missus? The old trouble-and-strife our British friend here would say.' His Cockney was tolerable. 'A cap of Rosy Lee and dahn wiv yer rahnd the ahzes.'

'Getting married next month,' this Josh said unelatedly. He looked Armenian to Enderby, hairy and with an ovine profile.

'Is that right, is that really right, well I sure am happy for you, Josh. Our friend here,' O'Donnell said, 'has been talking about our movie, *Kraut Soup*.' He stood up and appeared not merely sober but actually as though he had just downed a gill of vinegar. He was, after all, an actor. Could you then believe anything he said or did? But how did he know about the barracks at Cowley? 'What defilement, what horror,' he said, in exactly Enderby's accent and intonation.

'Is that right?' Josh said. 'We'd best be on our way, Mr O'Donnell. There may be a fight with the autograph hounds.'

'Say that story isn't true,' Enderby begged. 'It *can't* be true.'

'My granddaddy swore it was true. He always remembered the name. We had a Mrs Hopkins who cleaned for us. He had nothing against priests, he said. He was a real believer all his life.'

Though this child's drift/Seems by a divíne doom chánnelled, nor do I cry/Disaster there . . .

'The car's waiting, Mr O'Donnell.'

'And he saw it wasn't real sexual excitement. Not like he'd seen in the barracks. It was all tied up with – Well, his hands were shaking with the joy of it, you know.' Low-latched in leaf-light housel his too huge godhead. *Too huge*, my dear. 'Come on, Josh, let's go. He was only a kid but he saw that.' He nodded very soberly. 'So I had to do the part, I guess.' O'Donnell waved extravagantly to the bartender and guccied out, shepherded by Josh. Enderby had another pink gin, feeling pretty numb. What did it matter, anyway? It was the poetry that counted. I am gall, I am heartburn, God's most deep decree/Bitter would have me taste. And no bloody wonder.

The ways leading to the television place on 46th Street were warming up nicely with the threat of violence. Violence in itself is not bad, ladies and gentlemen. In a poem you would be entitled to exploit the fortuitous connotations – violins, viols, violets. We need violence sometimes. I feel very violent now. Beware of barbarism, violence for its own sake. It was a little old theatre encrusted with high-voltage light-bulbs. There was a crowd lining up outside, waiting to be the studio audience. They would see themselves waving to themselves tomorrow night, the past waving to the future. The young toughs in control wore uniform blazers, rutilant with a monogram SL, and they would not at first let him in by the stagedoor: you line up with the rest, buster. But then his British accent convinced them that he must be one of the performers. They let him in.

7

PARTIAL TRANSCRIPT OF SPERR LANSING SHOW B/3/57. RECORDED BUT NOT USED. RESERVE 2 (AUSTRALIAN TOUR) PUT OUT AS LAST MINUTE SUBSTITUTE.

SPERR: Thank you thank you (*no response to applause killer*) thank you thank you well this is what Id call a real dose of the (*laughter and applause*) I didnt say that I didnt say no I didnt. Seriously though (*laughter*) the rise in prices. I went to a new barber yesterday and before I even sat down he said thatll be one dollar fifty (*laughter*). Thats cheap I told him for a haircut (*laughter*). That he said is for the estimate (*laughter and applause*). Seriously though (*laughter*) the way they speak English in New York (*laughter*). I saw two men at Kennedy Airport the other day and one said to the other When are you leaving. The other said I am leaving in the Bronx (*laughter and applause*). I have a new tailor did I tell you or should I say I HAD a new tailor (*L*). I took the suit back and said this doesnt fit. Sure it doesnt fit he said. Youre not wearing it right (*L*). You have to stick out your left hip and your right shoulder and bend that knee a bit (*L and A*). Then it fits nice (*L*). So I did as he said (*visual. L and A*) and was walking along 46th Street when two doctors came by and I heard one say to the other Look at that poor feller a terrible case of deformity (*L*). Right says the other. The suit fits nice though (*L and prolonged A*). Seriously though clients and customers anybody here tonight from Minneapolis and St Paul (*A and jeers*). I thought not (*L*). That means I cant say I went out with a girl from up there (*L*). She was called the tail of two cities (*prolonged L and A. Sperr shouts over*). Be right back. A great guest list tonight folks desirable Ermine Elderley Jake Summers Prof (*Premature start commercial break*).

SPERR: So if you want to stay slim and feel overfed girls try it. My
first guest tonight is a famous British poet at present visiting
professor at . . . University of Manhattan. Weve asked him to
come and say something about a movie that was all his idea and
is at present causing a riot in the movie houses of the civilized
world. Ladies and gentlemen – Professor Fox Enderby. (*Applause
card applause. Visual unrehearsed guest trips on wire. A and L*).

SPERR: Must say we all admire the suit Professor Enderby (*A*). A
bit of Oldy England (*A*).

ENDERBY: (*Unintelligible*) right name.

SPERR: Oh I see just the initials. Pardon me. Well an O is a zero
right. And a zeros nothing right. So its just an F and an X. With
nothing between. Like I said. FOX. (*prolonged A*).

ENDERBY: (*Unintell*).

SPERR: Are you married, professor? (*headshake no*) Do you have
children? (*L*)

ENDERBY: A wise child knows his own (*?*)

SPERR: What I want to say is do you would you like children of
yours to see a movie like Wreck of the Deutschland.

ENDERBY: Anybody can see what the hell they like for all I care.
Anybodys children. Cluding (*?*) yours.

SPERR: I have a daughter of six. (*A*) You wouldnt object to her
seeing a movie of nuns being er (*prolonged A*).

ENDERBY: Not the point. The point is to have a world in which
nuns are not. Then it wouldnt be in films. Then thered be no
danger of your daughter. Besides its adults only.

SPERR: Maybe. But there are disturbing reports of the young seeing
the film and then committing atrocities (*A*).

ENDERBY: What the hell are they clapping for. Because of the
atrocities. Would your six year old daughter go round raping
nuns.

SPERR: No but shed be disturbed and maybe wake up crying with
nightmares. (*A*) We like to protect our children professor (*very
prol. A*).

ENDERBY: And wheres it got (*?*) you protecting them. More juvenile
violence in America than anywhere else in the world. Not that
I object to violence (*audience protest*). You cant change things
without violence. You baggers (*?*) were violence when you broke

away from us in 1776. Not blaming you for that of course. You
wanted to do it and were term into do it (*??*). You were wrong
of course. Might still be a bit of law and order if you were still
colonial territory. Not ready for self gov (*audience protest and
some A*).

SPERR: Your attitude ties up with your dress professor (*prol. A*). I
understand then that youre very patriotic. But youre not living
in Britain are you.

ENDERBY: Cant stand the bloody place. Americanized. The past is the
only place worth living in. Imaginary past. Lets get back to what
we were talking about before you introduced irreverences (*?*).

SPERR: You did it not me (*A*).

ENDERBY: People always blame art literature drama for their own
evil. Or other peoples. Art only imitates life. Evils already there.
Original sin. Curious thing about America is that it was founded
by people who believed original sin and also priesty nation (*???*)
but then you had to watch for signs of gods grace and this was
in commercial success making your own way building heaven
on earth and so on this led to American plagiarism (*?*).

SPERR: What words that professor.

ENDERBY: A British monkey called Morgan in Greek Plage us
(*??????*) taught no national pensity (*?*) to evil. Errorsy (*?*). Evils
in everybody. Desire to kill rape destroy mindless violence . . .

SPERR: I thought you said you liked violence (*prol A*).

ENDERBY: Never said that you silly bagger (*?*). Never said mindless
MINDLESS violets. Constructive different.

SPERR: Oh I see sorry. Take a break now. Be right back. Dont go
away (*prol A. MUSIC POMP CIRCUS DANCE (?*)). (*Commercial break*)

SPERR: Oh there you are. Hi. My next guest is also a professor
youve met often on the show. Expert on human behaviour and
author of many books such as er The Human Engine Waits will
you please welcome back professor of psychology Stations of
the Cross university Ribblesdale NY Man Balaglas. (*Applause
card applause. Prof Balaglas*)

SPERR: Well hi. Its been quite some time professor.

ENDERBY: What did you say it was called.

BALAGLAS: What.

ENDERBY: This university where youre at. I didnt quite catch the.

BALAGLAS: Stations of the Cross.

ENDERBY: Catholic.

BALAGLAS: Theres Protestant there too. Jews. Fifth Day Adventists. What youd call ecommunionicle (?).

SPERR: And do you like violence too professor (*A and some L*).

ENDERBY: I never said I like the bloody thing. Mindless I said.

BALAGLAS: Most emphatic no. The great scourge of our age and one of the most urgent of our needs is to laminate (?) it and that is what my own department along with others in other universities regards as research priority. (*Pause then some A*).

ENDERBY: Youll never get rid of it. Original sin.

BALAGLAS: I would there most emphatic disagree an urgent problem we have to make our cities places where people can walk at night without getting mugged and raped and killed all the time (*A*).

ENDERBY: (*Unintell*) all the time.

SPERR: And how can this be done professor.

BALAGLAS: Positive rain forcemeat (?). Instructive urge is not killed (kwelled?) by prison or punishment. Brainwashing that is to say negative through fear of pain already tried but is fundamentally inhuman (*e?*). We must so condition human mind that reward is expected for doing good not the other way about.

ENDERBY: What other way about.

SPERR: Like he said professor. Psychology.

ENDERBY: A lot of simple (sinful?) bloody nonsense. You take the filament of human choice out of ethnical decisions. Men should be free to choose good. But theres no choice if theres only good. Stands to region there has to be evil as well.

BALAGLAS: I emphatic disagree. What does inhabited or unconditioned human choice go for. For too much rape and mugging (*A*).

ENDERBY: In other words original sin. Which leads us to the stations of the cross.

BALAGLAS: Pardon me.

ENDERBY: Youre not Christian then.

BALAGLAS: An irreverent question. Were all in this together (*A*).

SPERR: You think its possible then professor that people can be made to be good by er positive er.

BALAGLAS: Right. Its happening already. Volunteers in our prisons.

Also in our universities. Stations of the Cross is proud of its volunteer record.

SPERR: Well thats just (*interrup by loud A*).

ENDERBY: What you mean is that the community is more important than the individual.

BALAGLAS: Pardon me.

ENDERBY: Stop saying bloody pardon me all the time. What I said was that you think human beings should give up freedom to choose so that the community can be free of violence (*A*).

BALAGLAS: Right. Youve said it loud and clear professor. Bloody clear if I may borrow your own er locomotion (*???*). The individual has to sacrifice his freedom to some extent for the benefit of his fellow citizens. (*Prolong A*).

ENDERBY: Well I think its bloody monsters (?). Human beings are defined by freedom of choice. Once you have them doing what theyre told is good just because theyre going to get a lump of sugar instead of a kick up the ahss(*?!*) then ethnics no longer exists. The State could tell them it was good to go off and mug and rape and kill some other nation. Thats what its been doing. Look at your bloody war in . . .

SPERR: Well be right back after this important message. Dont go away folks. Be right b (*prem start comm break*) (*Music. Band on camera. Audience shots*)

SPERR: This is the Sperr Lansing Show. Be right back after this station break. (*Station Break*)

SPERR: Were talking with two professors Professor Balaglas psychologist and Professor er Endivy British poet. Professor Balaglas . . .

BALAGLAS: Call me Man. (*Pause then A*) Representative Man. (*P then A*)

EENDERBY: Whats that short for. I knew you weren't a bloody Christian.

SPERR: Do you believe professor that movies and books and er art can influence young people to violence rape mugging and so on (*A*).

BALAGLAS: There is I would consider ample proof that the impressionable and not merely those in the younger age groups can be incited to antisocial behaviour by the artistic representation of er antisocial acts. There was the instance in the township of

Inversnaid NY not too far from Ribblesdale where as you know I am at present on the faculty of the university there of the young man who killed his uncle and said that seeing Sir Laurence Oliviers movie of Hamlet had influenced him to perform the crime.

ENDERBY: How old was he. I asked how old was.

BALAGLAS: About thirty. And very unbalanced.

ENDERBY: And had his uncle just married his mother (L). His mother. Not his uncles mother (L).

BALAGLAS: I dont recollect as much. It was just the killing of his uncle as in this movie. And also if I recollect rightly that also comes in the play on which the movie was based.

ENDERBY: Shakespeare.

SPERR: Thats right. And would you believe in the restricting of the viewing of professor.

ENDERBY: Of course not. Bloody ridiculous idea.

SPERR: I meant the other professor professor (L and A).

BALAGLAS: Well as we are committed to control of the violentment (?) and as works of art and movies and the like are part of it then for the sake of society there must be control. There are too many dirty books and movies and also violent ones (A).

ENDERBY: This is bloody teetotal Aryan (??) talk. You mean that kids wouldnt be allowed to see or read Hamlet because they might go and kill their uncles. Ive never in my life heard such bloody stupid actionary (?) talk. Why by Christ man

BALAGLAS: Thas right Man thats my name (L and A). Call me Man by all means but cut out the blasph (very loud A).

ENDERBY: But bagger (?) it man you idiot I mean that would mean that nobody could read anything not even Alice in Windowland (?) because it says Off with his Head and the Wizard of Oz because of the wicked witch is

BALAGLAS: I do not know what standards of etiquette prevail in your part of the world Professor Elderley but I do most strenously object to being called idiot (very loud A).

SPERR: And at that opportune moment we take a break. Stay with us folks. (A).

(Commercial Break)

SPERR: Professor Balaglas made an interesting slip of the tongue folks which weve just been discussing during the break.

ENDERBY: I still say he was trying to be bloody insulting. A man cant help his age.

SPERR: Right. Because if a girls name was ever improper that is to say not appropriate to what she is then the name of my next guest must be. Beautiful charming talented and above all YOUNG star of such movies as The Leaden Echo Mortal Beauty Rockfire and just about to be released Manshape here she is folks Ermine Elderley. (*Very loud and sustained applause also male whistles as she comes on kisses Sperr and Prof Balaglas not Prof Enderby sits down*)

SPERR: Wow (*L and A*).

ENDERBY: I see so youre Elderley. I thought he was trying to take the (*unintell* piece? pass?)

ERMINE: Sure I am. How young do you like em (*L and A*).

ENDERBY: What I meant was (*not heard under L and A*)

SPERR: Ermine if I may call you Ermine.

ERMINE: Just buy it for me sweetie (*L and A*). I apologize. You always have done before baby (*L and A*). Called me it I mean (*L and A*).

SPERR: How would you like to be raped (*very sust L with a lot of visual L L and again L*). I meant in a movie of course. Seriously (*L*).

ERMINE: Seriously yes. If I was playing that sort of part okay but I don't think I would oh I might if there was a kind of you know moral lesson and the guy gets his comeuppance after or before he really gets under way his teeth knocked out that sort of thing not shooting shootings too good. But I wouldnt have it if I was playing a nun like in this German movie. Thats irreligious.

ENDERBY: Look Im not trying to defend it. What she calls this German movie. As a matter of fact its not allowed to be shown in Germany.

SPERR: No Deutschland for Deutschland right (*L*).

ENDERBY: I have to make this clear dont I.

ERMINE: You should know brother (*L*).

ENDERBY: The film is very different from the poem.

SPERR: What poem is that.

ENDERBY: Why the poem its based on.

ERMINE: You mean no rape in the poem (L). Well what do they do in the poem pluck daffodils (L).

Enderby, sweating hard under the lights and the awareness of his unpopularity, looked at this hard woman who exhibited great sternly supported breasts to the very periphery of the areola and was dressed in a kind of succulent rutilant taffeta. The name, he was thinking: as artificial as the huge aureate wig. He said:

'I grant its cleverness. The name, I mean. I should imagine your real name is something like let me see Irma Polansky. No, wait, Edelmann, something like that.' She looked very hard back at him.

'Do you read much poetry, professor?' Sperr Lansing asked.

'Well, I guess I hardly have the time these days.' This Professor Balaglas flashed glasses in the lights. He had the soft face of a boy devoted to his mother and wore a hideous spotted bowtie. 'What with working on the problems that this kind of movie under present discussion gives rise to.' There was laughter. The audience was full of mouths, always as it were at the ready, lips parted in potential ecstasy. 'I have a collection of rock records like everybody else, of course. It's the job of poets to get close to the people. We shall be able to use poets in the new dispensation,' he promised. 'Rhymes are of considerable value in hypnopaedia or sleep-teaching. A great deal of the so-called poetry they write these days . . .'

'Who writes?' Enderby asked.

'I don't mean you, professor. I never read anything you wrote. You may be very clear and straightforward for all I know.' Laughter. 'I mean, you've been using very clear and straightforward language to me tonight.' Very great laughter.

'The point I was trying to make,' Enderby said. 'About her name, that is.' He shoulderjerked towards the star, 'There you see the poetic process exemplified in a small way. Ermine, suggesting opulence, wealth, softness, luxury. Elderley, the piquancy of contrast with her evident near-youth, no longer *very* young, of course, but it happens to everybody, and the denotation of the name. The small *frisson* of gerontophilia.'

Sperr Lansing did not seem to be greatly enjoying his job. He was a man adept at appearing to be on top of everything, ready with quip and *oeillade*, but the eyes now had become as glassy as those of a hung hare. 'Get on top of whom?' he tried, and then saw he was being betrayed into unbecoming lowness. There was, rightly, no audience laugh.

Miss Elderley cunningly got in with 'I used to know a poem about the wreck of something.' There were relieved sniggers.

'The Hesperus perhaps,' Professor Isinglass (?) brightly said.

'Naw, this went "The boy stood on the burning deck . . ."'

A thing exquisitely coarse shot up from Enderby's schooldays. It was neat, too. Dirty verse depended upon an almost Augustan neatness. '"The boy stood in the witness-box,"' he recited, '"Picking his nose like fury —"' There were loud cries of hey hey and Lansing picked up a packet of Shagbag or something from among the various commercial artefacts stowed behind the ashtray-and-water-bottle table. 'I think,' he cried, 'it's time we heard another important message. Girls,' he counter-recited, 'is your fried chicken greasy?'

'— "Little blocks, And aimed it at the jury."'

'Because if you want it to be crisp and dry as the bone within, here's how to do it.' There were at once waving fat studio major-domos running around, and the monitor screens began to show hideous greasy fried chicken, oleic, aureate.

'All right all right,' Sperr Lansing was saying, 'it's going to be Jake Summers next. Look,' he said to Enderby, 'keep it clean, willya.'

'I was only trying to keep it vulgar,' Enderby said. 'It's evidently a vulgar sort of show.'

'It wasn't till you got on to it, buster,' Miss Elderley began.

'Well, damn it,' Enderby said, 'the amount of tit you're showing, if you don't mind my saying so, is hardly conducive to the main-tenance of a high standard of intellectual discourse.'

'You leave my bosoms out of this —'

'There's only *one* bosom. A bosom is a dual entity.'

'I object to him using that word about me. I've met these bastards before —'

'I object to being called a bastard —'

'Either sex maniacs or fags —'

Sperr Lansing composed his face to beatific calm and told the camera and the audience: 'Welcome back, folks. Now here's the man who pays for a moon shot with every Broadway success he writes.

Somebody once said that there were only two men of the theatre, Jake Speare and Jake Summers. Well, here's one of them.'

Underneath the applause and the shambling on of a small near-bald clerkly man in spectacles and sweatshirt, Enderby said to Miss Elderley:

'I suppose you wouldn't call that vulgar. Eh? Jakes Peare, indeed. And I'll tell you another thing – I won't be called a bloody fag.'

'I didn't say that. I said the British are either fags or sex maniacs. Keep it quiet, willya.'

For Sperr Lansing was now praising this Summers man lavishly to his face. '– Five hundred and forty-five performances is what I have written down here. To what do you attribute –'

Summers was wearily modest. 'Write well, I guess. Keep it clean, I guess. When they do it, they do it offstage.' Applause and laughter. 'No, yah. Let them hear about sex and violence, I guess, not see it.' (*A and L.*) 'Talking about poetry,' he said, 'I used to write it. Then I meet this guy on his yacht and he says give it up, there's nothing in it.' Applause.

Enderby saw the tortured ecstatic face of Father Hopkins on top of the bugler and went mad. 'Filth,' he said, 'filth and vulgarity.'

'Aw, can it willya,' Miss Elderley said. Professor Glass said:

'It is not my place, not here and now that is, to proffer any diagnosis of er Professor Endlessly's perpetual er manic state of excitation. Facts must be faced, though. The world has changed. England is no longer the centre of a world empire. The English language has found its finest er flowering in what he called a colonial territory.'

'Attaboy,' Miss Elderley said. 'Wow.'

'Be fair, I guess,' Summers said. 'Those boys with guitars.'

'He feels his manhood threatened,' Professor Elderglass went on. 'Note how his dress proclaims an, er, long dead national virility. He thinks man is being abolished. His kind of man.'

'Bankside,' Summers said. Everybody roared.

'Yes, the character or homunculus in your play. Man *qua* man. Man in his humanity. Man as Thou not It. Man as a person not a thing. These are not very helpful expressions, but they supply a clue. What is being abolished is autonomous man, the inner man, the homunculus, the possessing demon, the man defended by the literatures of freedom and dignity.'

'That's it, you bastard,' Enderby said, 'you've summed it all up.'

'His abolition has been long overdue. He has been constructed from our ignorance, and as our understanding increases, the very stuff of which he is composed vanishes. Science does not de-humanize man, it de-homunculizes him, and it must do so if it is to prevent the abolition of the human species. Hamlet, in the play I have already mentioned, by your fellow-playwright, Mr Summers, said of man 'How like a god.' Pavlov said 'How like a dog.' But that was a step forward. Man is much more than a dog, but like a dog he is within range of a scientific analysis.'

'Look,' shouted Enderby over the applause, 'I won't have it, see. We're free and we're free to take our punishment. Like Hopkins. I suppose you'd watch him doing it with your bloody neat little bowtie on and say how like a dog. Well, he's been punished enough with this bloody film or movie as you'd call it, bloody childish. That's his hell. He was gall, he was heartburn.'

'He should have taken Windkill,' Jake Summers said and got roars. Enderby was very nearly sidetracked.

'Leave the commercials to me, Jake,' Lansing said, delighted. 'And talking about commercials it's time we took another −'

'Oh no it bloody well isn't,' Enderby shouted. 'You can keep your bloody homunculus, for that's all he is −'

'Pardon me, it's you who believe in the homunculus −'

'Man was always violent and always sinful and always will be.'

'And now he's got to change.'

'He won't change, not unless he becomes something else. Can't you see that that's where the drama of life is, the high purple, the tragic −'

'Oh my,' Jake Summers sighed histrionically and was at once loudly rewarded. 'No time for comedy,' he added and then was not clearly understood.

'The evolution of a culture,' Professor Lookingglass said, 'is a gigantic exercise in self-control. It is often said that a scientific view of man leads to wounded vanity, a sense of hopelessness, and nostalgia −'

'Nostalgia means homesickness,' Enderby cried. 'And we're all homesick. Homesick for sin and colour and drunkenness −'

'Ah, so that's what it is,' Miss Elderley said. 'You're stoned.'

'Homesick for the past.' Enderby could feel himself ready to weep. But then fire possessed him just as Sperr Lansing said, 'And now we let our sponsor get a word in –' Enderby stood and declaimed:

> 'For how to the heart's cheering
> The down-dugged ground-hugged grey
> Hovers off, the jay-blue heavens appearing
> Of pied and peeled May!'

'Fellers,' Sperr Lansing said, 'do you ever feel, you know, not up to it?' He held in his hands a product called, apparently, Mansex. 'Well, just watch this.' Then he turned on Enderby, as did everybody, including the sweating studio major-domos. The band, which appeared to have a whole Wagnerian brass section as well as innumerable saxophones and a drummer in charge sitting high on a throne, gave out very piercingly and thuddingly.

> 'Blue-beating and hoary-glow height; or night, still higher,
> With belled fire and the moth-soft Milky Way,
> What by your measure is the heaven of desire,
> The treasure never eyesight got, nor was ever guessed what for
> the hearing?

SPERR: Well I don't think it can. Youd better get on to Harry right away.

ENDERBY: Fucking home uncle us (????) indeed. Ill give you fucking home uncle us (?????). Degradation of humanity. No, but it was not these the jading and jar of the cart (?) times tasking it is fathers (?) that asking for ease of the sodden with its sorrowing hart (art?) not danger electrical horror then further it finds the appealing of the passion is tenderer (?) in prayer apart other I gather in measure her minds burden in winds (????????)

8

'And I'll tell you another thing,' said the man in the bar. 'Your Queen of England. She owns half of Manhattan.'

'That's a lie,' Enderby said. 'Not that I give a bugger either way.'

It was a small dark and dirty bar not far from the television theatre whence Enderby had been not exactly ejected but as it were ushered with some measure of acrimony. The programme that had been recorded could not, it was felt, go out. The audience had been told too and had been angry until told that they were going to do it all over again but without Enderby.

'What's the matter with you then?' this man asked. 'You not patriotic?' He had a face round and shiny as an apple but somehow unwholesome, as though a worm was burrowing within. 'Your Winston Churchill was a great man, wasn't he? He wanted to fight the commies.'

'He was half American,' Enderby said, then sipped at his sweetish whisky sour.

'Ain't nothing wrong with that. You trying to say there's something wrong with that?'

'After six years of fighting the bloody Germans,' Enderby said, 'we were supposed to spend another six or sixty years fighting the bloody Russians. And he always had these big cigars when the rest of us couldn't get a single solitary fag.'

'What's that about fags?'

'Cigarettes,' Enderby explained. 'While you've a lucifer to light your fag, smile, boys, that's the style.'

'My mother was German. That makes me half German. You trying to say there's something wrong with that?' And then: 'You one of these religious guys? What's that you was saying about Lucifer?'

'The light-bringer. Hence a match. For lighting a fag.'

'I'd set a light to them. I'd burn the bastards. It's fags that pretends the downfall. The Sin of Sodom. You ever read that book?'

'I don't think so.'

'Jack,' this man called to the bartender, 'do you have that book?'

'Gave it back to Shorty.'

'There,' the man said. 'But there's plenty around. Where you going now?'

'No more money,' Enderby said. 'Just one subway token.'

'Right. And your Queen of England owns half the real estate in Queens. That's why they call it Queens, I guess.'

Enderby walked slowly, not too displeased, towards the Times Square subway hellmouth. He had told the bastards anyway. Not apparently as many as he had expected to tell, but these matters could not always be approached quantitatively. He passed a great lighted pancake house and hungered as he did. No, watch diet, live. A whining vast black came out at him and whined for a coin. Enderby was able sincerely to say that he had no money, only a subway token. Well gimme that mane. I kin sell that for thirty cents. But how do I get home? That ain't ma problem mane. Enderby shook his head compassionately. Two other blacks and a white man, dispossessed or alienated, had made a little street band for their own apparent pleasure: guitar, flageolet, tambourine. Music of the people. Was that a possible approach?

> An ole Sain Gus he said yo born in sin
> Cos when Eve ate de apple she let de serpent in

He shook his head sadly and went down below, wondering not for the first time whether it was really necessary to be so punctilious about setting the turnstile working with a token in the slot, since so many black and brown youths merely used, without official protest, the exit gate as an entrance. There were a lot of noisy ethnic people, as they were stupidly called, around, but Enderby did not fear. Nor was it just a matter of his being illegally armed. It was a matter of being *integer vitae* and also of having committed himself to a world in which pure and simple aggression was to be accepted as part of the human fabric. Die with Beethoven's Ninth howling and crashing away or live in a safe world of silly clockwork music?

He got into a train, thinking, and then realized his mistake. This was not the uptown express to 96th Street but the uptown local. Never mind. He was interested to see that, among the few passengers, all harmless, there was a nun. She was a nun of a kind not to be seen in backward Europe or North Africa, since she wore the new reformed habit, fruit of ill-thought-out Catholic liberalism. There had been a nun in a class he had taught the previous semester, though it had been a long time before he realized it, since she wore a striped sailor sweater and bell-bottomed trousers. When he discovered her name was Sister Agnes, he had wondered if she were part of some religious mission to seawomen. But then she left the class, being apparently put off by Enderby's occasional blasphemies. This nun on the train was dressed in a short skirt that revealed veal-to-the-heel legs in what looked like lisle stockings, a modest tippet, a rather heavy pectoral cross, and the wimple of her order. She had a round shining Irish face with a dab of lipstick. Of the world and yet not of it. She had a Bloomingdale's shopping-bag on her lap. She smiled at some small inner vision, perhaps of the kettle on the hob singing peace into her breast, a doorstep spiced veal sandwich waiting for her supper. Enderby looked kindly at her.

The two brown louts who got on, quickening Enderby's heart, spoke not Spanish but Portuguese. Brazilians, a new spice for the ethnic stew, plenty of Indian blood there. Enderby at once feared for the nun, but she seemed protected either by her reformed uniform or their own superstition. They leered instead towards a blonde lay girl reading some thick college tome, probably on what was called sociology, further up the car. CRISTO 99. JISM 292. They wore long flared pants with goldish studs stretching on the outer seams from waist to instep. Their jackets were of a bolero type, blazoned with symbols of destruction and death: thunderbolt, rawhead, fasces, unionjack, swastika. One of them wore a *Gott Mit Uns* belt. They stood, two brown left hands gently frotting the metal monkey-pole. They spoke to each other. Enderby hungrily hearkened.

> *'E conta o que ele fez com ela e tem fotografia e tudo.'*
> *'Um velho lélé da cuca.'*

They were apparently talking about literature. At the next stop they grinned at everybody, leered at the girl with the tome, mock-genuflected at the nun, then got off. '*Boa noite*,' Enderby said, having once had a regular drunk from Oporto in his Tangier bar, one much given in his cups to protesting the deuterocaroline dowry. Now there was a kind of quiet general exhalation. At the next stop but one three nice WASP boys, as Enderby took them to be, got on. In the eyes of two of them was the very green of the ocean between Plymouth and Plymouth Rock. The other had warm tea-hued pupils. They were chubby-faced and wore toggled dufflejackets. Their hair belonged to some middle crinal zone between aseptic nord and latinindian jetwalled lousehouse. Without words and almost with the seriousness of asylum nurses they at once set upon an unsavoury-looking matron who began to cry out Mediterranean vocables of distress. Staggering but laughing, they had her staggering upright, held from the back by the tea-eyed one, while her skirt was yanked up to disclose sensible thick navy blue knickers. One drew nail-scissors and began delicately to slice at them. Oh my God, Enderby prayed. Gerontal violation. The nun, who had lapsed back into her dream of supper, was quicker than Enderby. She staggered on to them, the train jolting much, hitting with her Bloomingdale's bag. Delighted, the nail-scissored one turned on her, while the knicker-ripping was completed by hand by the others. Enderby was, in the desperate resigned second before his own intervention, interested to see the reading girl go on reading and even turn a page, while an old man slept uneasily and two black boys chewed and watched as if this were television. Enderby tottered to the train's rocking, was now there with his stick. How much better to be out of it, the kettle on the hob, a spiced veal sandwich. Delighted, the nail-scissored one turned on him, dropping his nun to the deck to pray or something. And yet God has not said a word, nor they either. Yet noises were coming out, even out of Enderby, such as yaaark and grerrr and gheee.

'Scrot,' one of them said. 'Balzac.' Educated then. You did not educate people out of aggression, great liberal fallacy that. The one with scissors was trying to stab at Enderby's crotch. The other two had left the matron to moan and stagger and were grinning at the prospect of doing in an old man. Enderby lunged out at random with his stick and, as he had expected, it was at once grasped by, strangely, two left hands Enderby pulled back. The sword emerged, half then wholly naked. They had not expected this. It flashed Elizabethanly in the swaying train, hard to keep upright, they all had legs bowed to it like sailors. Whitelady looked down amazed at Enderby from an EMPLOY A VETERAN advertisement. LOPEZ 95 MARLOWE 93 BONNY SWEET ROBIN 1601. Enderby at once pinked one of them in the throat and red spurted. 'Glory be to God,' the nun prayed, getting up from the deck. Spot-of-blood-and-foam dapple Bloom lights the orchard apple. Enderby tried a more ambitious thrust in some belly or other. It hit a belt. He tried underarm pricking on one who raised a fist wrapped round an object dull and hard. He drew out a sword-tip on which red rode and danced. And thicket and thorp are merry With silver-surfèd cherry. The train danced clumsily to its next stop. There was a lot of loud language now: fuckabastardyafuckingpiggetyafuckingballs. One of the boys, the throat-pinked one who now gave out blood like a pelican, led the way out. Enderby thrust towards his backside and then felt pity. Enough was enough. He lunged half-heartedly instead at the one who had not yet received gladial attention. Ow ouch. Nothing really: plenty of flesh there: a fleshy-bottomed race. They were all out now, the oxterpierced one bleeding quite nastily, all crying bitterly and fiercely fuckfuckassbastardcuntingfuckbastard-fuckingpig and so on. The door closed and their faces were execrating holes out there on the platform. The human condition. No art without aggression. Then they were execrating briefly out of the past into the future. Enderby, winded and dangerously palpitant, picked up his hollow stick from the deck, not without falling on his face first. He found his seat and, with great difficulty, threaded the trembling bloody metal back in. The matron sat very still, handbag on lap, blue at the lips, seeing visions that made her cry out. The reading girl turned another page. The old man slept uneasily. The two black boys, seated tailorwise, made fencing gestures wow sssh zheeeph and so on at each other. The nun, still standing, said:

'That's a terrible weapon you have there.'

'Look,' Enderby panted, 'that was my stop. I've gone past my bloody stop.'

'You can ride back from the next one.'

'But I've no money.' And then: 'Are you all right now? Is she all right now?' They were all all right now except for the shock.

'You can get on without a token,' the nun said. 'A lot of them do it.' And then: 'You shouldn't be carrying a thing like that around with you. It's against the law.'

'Entitled self-protection. Bugger the law.'

'Are you an Englishman?' Nodnod. 'I thought so from your way of swearing. Are you a Protestant?' Shakeshake. 'I said to myself you had a Catholic face.'

'Aren't you,' Enderby said, 'frightened? Travelling like this. A lot of thugs and rapists and.'

'I trust in Almighty God.'

'He wasn't all that bloody quick in. Coming to your. Help.'

'Are you all right now? You look very pale.'

'Heart,' Enderby said. 'Heart.'

'I'll say a decade of the rosary for you.'

'You have your supper first. A nice veal sandwich. A cup of.'

'What a strange thing to say. I can't stand veal.'

Enderby got shakily off at the next stop but would not take a free ride back to 96th Street. Timorousness? No, he did not think it was that. It was rather something to do with vital integrity, not lowering oneself, wearing a suit evocative of an age of decency when gentlemen thrashed niggers but paid their bills. So he walked as far as the Symphony movie house and thought it might be a good plan to sit there, resting in the dark, judging once more, if he had the strength, certain ethical aspects of *The Wreck of the Deutschland*, and then go home calmly and starving to bed. But, of course, approaching the pay-box, he realized once more he had no money. He said, to the bored chewing black bespectacled girl behind the grille:

'Look, I just want to go in for a minute. I was involved in the making of this er movie, you see. Something I have to check. Business not pleasure.' She did not seem to care. She waved him towards the cavern of the antechamber, see man in charge, man. But there was no one around who cared much. It was past the hour for anyone to care much. Enderby entered tempestuous darkness: the breakers were rolling on the beam of the Deutschland with ruinous shock. And canvas and compass, the whorl and the wheel idle for ever to waft her or wind her with, these she endured. There did not seem to be, now he could see better, many audients taking it all in. An old man slept uneasily. Some blacks chortled inexplicably at the sight of one stirring from the rigging to save the wild womankind below, with a rope's end round the man, handy and brave. Some fine swooping camerawork showed him being pitched to his death at a blow, for all his dreadnought breast and braids of thew. Cut to night roaring, with the heart-break hearing a heart-broke rabble, the woman's wailing, the crying of child without check. Then a lioness arose breasting the babble. Gertrude, lily, Franciscan robe already rent, spoke of courage, God. Then came the flashback – Deutschland, double a desperate name. Beautifully contrived colour-contrasts: black uniforms, white nunflesh, red yelling gob, blood, a patch of yellow convent-garden daffodils crushed under the blackbooted foot. Hitler appeared briefly, roaring something (beast of the waste wood) to black approbation in the audience.

Away in the loveable west, on a pastoral forehead of Wales, Father Tom Hopkins S.J. seemed mystically or ESPishly aware of something terrible going on out there somewhere. Putting down his breviary, he dreamed back to boy-and-girl love. A student in Germany, Gertrude not yet coifed, passion amid *Vogelgesang* in Schwarzwald. Rather touching, really, but far too naked. Song of Hitlerjugend marching in the distance. Bad times coming for us all. Ja ja, Tom. It all seemed pretty harmless, Enderby thought. It aroused desire to see off the Nazis, no more, but that had already been done, Enderby vaguely assisting. And so he left. He walked down chill blowing Broadway as far as 91st Street, then crossed towards Columbus Avenue.

At this point it happened again. Pain was pumped rapidly into his chest and he stopped breathing. The surplus of pain over-flowed into his left shoulder and went rattling down the arm to the elbow. At the same time both legs went suddenly dead and the tough metalled stick was not enough to sustain him. He went over gently on to the sidewalk and lay, writhing, trying to deal with the pain and the inability to breathe like a pair of messages that both had to be answered at once. Pain passed and breath

shot in with the hiss of an airtight can being opened. But still
he lay, now feeling the cold. A few people passed by, naturally
ignoring him, some junky, a man knifed, dangerous to be involved.
And they were right, of course, in a world that thought the
worst of involvement. Why did you help him, mister? Got scared,
did you? Let's see what you got in your pockets. What's this? A
stomach tablet? That's a laaaugh. Soon he was able to get up.
Blood and a kind of healthy pain were flowing into his legs. He
felt all right, even gently elated. After all, he knew now where
he stood. There was no need to plan anything long, that *Odontiad*,
for instance. A loosening artistic obligation. There was only the
obligation of setting things in order. He might live a long time
yet, but time would be doled out to him in very small denomi-
nations, like pocket-money. On the other hand, there was no
need to work at living a long time. He had not done too badly.
He was fifty-six, already had done four years better than
Shakespeare. As for poor Gervase Whitelady. Kindly he suddenly
decided to allow Whitelady to live till 1637, which meant he
could benefit from the critical acumen of Ben Jonson.

He got to the apartment block without difficulty. Mr Audley,
the black guard, sat in his chair in the warmth of the foyer,
while the many telescreens showed dull programmes: people
muffled up hurrying round the corner, the basement empty, the
main porch newly free of entering Enderby. They nodded at
each other, Enderby was allowed in, he took the elevator to his
floor, he entered his apartment. Thanked, so to speak, be Almighty
God. He drew his bloody sword and executed a courtly flourish
with it at the mess in the kitchen. Then he cleaned off the
blood with a dishrag. His stomach, crassly ignoring the day's
circulatory warnings, growled at him, knowing it was in the
kitchen, messy or not.

There was an episode, Enderby remembered, in Galsworthy's
terrible Forsyte or Forsyth epic, in which some old scoundrel of
the dynasty faced ruin and determined to kill himself like a
gentleman by eating a damn good dinner. In full fig, by George.
By George, they had got him an oyster. By George, he had forgotten
to put his teeth in, and here was a brace of mutton chops
grilled to a turn. A rather repulsive story, but it did not debar

Galsworthy from getting the Order of Merit and the Nobel Prize. Enderby had never got or gotten anything, not even the Heinemann Award for Poetry, but he did not give a bugger. He did not now propose to eat himself to death, in a subforsytian manner befitting his station, but rather just not to give a bugger. To take a fairly substantial supper with, since time might be short, a few unwonted luxuries added. Such as that French chocolate ice cream that was ironhard in the deep freeze. And that small tin of pâté mixed in the great culminatory stew he envisaged after, for tidiness's sake, finishing off his Sara Lee collection and eating the potato pieces and spongemeat that waited for a second chance, nestling ready in their fat. And to get through the mixed pickles and Major Grey's chutney. He had always hated waste.

9

Enderby's supper was interrupted by two telephone calls. During the stew course (two cans of corned beef, frozen onion-rings, canned carrots, a large Chunky turkey soup, pâté, a dollop of whisky, Lea and Perrin's, pickled cauliflowers, the remains of the sponge-meat, and the crinkle-cut potato-bits) Ms Tietjens sobbed to him briefly without preamble: I'm sick, I tell ya, I'm all knotted up inside, I'm sick, sick, there's something gone wrong with me, I tell ya; and Lloyd Utterage confirmed the impending fulfilment of his threat, so that Enderby was constrained to tell him to come along and welcome, black bastard, and have an already bloody sword stuck into his black guts. Enderby placidly ended his meal with the French ice cream (brought to near melting in a saucepan over a brisk flame) with raspberry jam spread liberally over, spooning the treat in on rich tea biscuits he ate as he spooned. Then he had some strong tea (six Lipton's bags in the pint ALABAMA mug) and lighted up a White Owl. He felt pretty good, as they said in American fiction, though distended. All he needed now, as again they would say in American fiction, and he laughed at the conceit, was a woman.

A woman came while he was making himself more tea. He was surprised to hear the doorbell ring with no anterior warning on the intercommunication system from the black guard below. Every visitor was supposed to be screened, frisked, reported to the intended visited before actually appearing. The woman at the door was young and very attractive in a reactionary way, being dressed in a bourgeois grey costume with a sort of nutria or coypu or something coat swinging open over it. She wore over decently arranged chastaigne hair a little pillbox hat of the same fur. She was carrying a handful of slim volumes. She said:

'Mr Enderby?'

'Or Professor, according to the nature of. How did you get here? You're not supposed just to come up, you know, without a premonition.'

'A what?'

'A forewarning from the gunman.'

'Oh. Well, I said it was a late visit from one of your students and that you were expecting me. It *is* all right, isn't it?'

'Are you one of my students?' Enderby asked. 'I don't seem to —'

'I am in a sense. I've studied your work. I'm Dr Greaving.'

'Doctor?'

'From Goldengrove College.'

'Oh very well then, perhaps you'd better. That is to say.' And he motioned courtlily that she should enter. She entered, sniffing. 'Just been cooking,' Enderby said. 'My supper, that is to say. Can I perhaps offer?'

In the sitting-room there was a small table. Dr Greaving put down her books on it and at once sat on the straightbacked uncomfortable chair nearby.

'Whisky or something like that?'

'Water.' Now in, she had become vaguely hostile. She looked up thinly at him.

'Oh, very well. Water.' And Enderby went to get it. He let the faucet run but the stream did not noticeably cool. He brought back some warmish water and put the glass down with care next to the slim volumes. He saw they were of his own work. British editions, American not existing. 'Oh,' he said. 'How did you manage to get hold of those?'

'Paid for them. Ordered them through a Canadian bookseller. When I was in Montreal.' Enderby now noticed that she had taken out of her handbag a small automatic pistol, a lady killer.

'Oh,' he said. 'Now perhaps you'll understand why they're so keen down below on checking visitors and so on. Why have you brought that? It seems, to say the least, unnecessary.' He marvelled at himself saying this. (Cinna the poet: tear him for his bad verses?)

'You deserve,' she said, 'to be punished. Incidentally, my name is *not* Doctor Greaving. But what I said about being a student of your work is true.'

'Are you Canadian?' Enderby asked.

'You seem to be a big man for irrelevancies. One thing you're a big man in.' She drank some water, keeping her eyes on him. The eyes were of a kind of triple sec colour. 'You'd better bring a chair.'

'There's one in the kitchen,' Enderby said with relief. 'I'll just go and –'

'Oh no. No dashing into the kitchen to telephone. If you tried that anyway I'd come and shoot you in the back. Get that chair over there.' It was not really a chair. It was a sort of very frail Indian-style coffee-table. Enderby said:

'It's really a sort of very frail. It belongs to my landlady. I might . . .' He was really, to his surprise, quite enjoying this. It seemed quite certain to him now that he was not going to die of cancer of the lung.

'Bring it. Sit on it.' He did. He sat on its edge, pity to damage so frail a thing, horrible though he had always thought it. He said:

'Now what I can do for you, Miss er?'

'I'm not,' she said, 'going to tolerate any more of this persecution. And it's Mrs, as you perfectly well know. Not that I'm living with him any more, but that's another irrelevance. I'm not going to have you,' she said, 'getting into my brain.'

Enderby gaped. 'How?' he said. 'What?'

'I know them by heart,' she said, 'a great number of them. Well, I don't want it any more. I want to be free. I want to get on with my own things, can't you see that, you bastard?' She pointed the little gun very steadily at Enderby.

'I don't understand,' Enderby said. 'You've read my things, you say. That's what they're for, to be read. But there's no er compulsion to read them, you know.'

'There's a lot of things there's no compulsion for. Like going to the movies to see a movie that turns out to be corruptive. But then you're corrupted, just the same. You never know in advance.' As this seemed to her ears apparently, as certainly to his, to be a piece of neutral or even friendly expository talk, she added sharply, with a gun gesture, 'You bastard.'

'Well, what do you want me to do?' Enderby asked. 'Unwrite the damned things?' And then, this just striking him, 'You're mad, you know, you must be. Sane readers of my poems don't –'

'That's what they all say. That's what *he* said, till I stopped him.'

'How did you stop him?' Enderby asked, fascinated.

'Another irrelevance. Don't you bastards ever think of your responsibility?'

'To our art,' Enderby said. 'Oh my God,' he added in quite impersonal distress, 'do you mean there's to be no more art? Aye, by Saint Anne,' he added, seeing that *mad* was a very difficult term to define, 'and ginger shall be hot in the –'

'There you go again. Decent people suffer and you sit on your fat ass talking about *art*.'

'That's just low abuse,' he frowned. 'Besides, I don't think you could call this really sitting.' She had, he could see, beneath the peel of the mad hate, a sweet face, a Catholic face, ruined, God help the girl, ruined. 'No, no,' he said in haste. 'Relevance is what is called for. I see that.' And then: 'Look. If you shoot me, it won't make any difference, will it? It won't destroy the words I wrote.' And then: 'What intrigues me, if that doesn't sound too irrelevant a term, is how you got to know them in the first place. My poems, I mean. I mean, not many people do. And here you are, young as I see, also beautiful if I may say that without sounding frivolous or irrelevant, knowing them. If you do know them, that is, of course, I mean,' he ended cunningly.

'Oh, I know them all right,' she cried scornfully. 'I see lines set up at eyelevel in the subway. There's one in fifteen-foot-high Gothic letters just by the Port Authority. They get sort of stitched into that Times Square news ticker thing.'

'Interesting,' Enderby said.

'There you go,' she gun-pointed. '*Interesting*. So tied up in yourself and your so-called work you're just *interested*. *Interested* in how it happened, and all that crap about youth and beauty and the other irrelevancies.'

'They're not irrelevant,' Enderby said sharply. 'I won't have that. Beauty and youth are the only things worth having. Dust hath closed Helen's eye. And they go. And here you are, saying they don't matter. Silly bitch,' he attempted, not sure whether that would pull the trigger.

'That bastard introduced me to them, if you must know,' she said, not listening. 'It started off when we were on our honeymoon and it was in the morning and he giggled and said The marriage contract was designed in spite of what the notaries think to be by only one pen signed and that is mine and full of ink. But he didn't, oh no, just giggled.'

'A mere *jeu d'esprit*,' Enderby mumbled regretfully, remembering his own honeymoon when he didn't either, just giggled.

'That's how that bastard started me off. Anything to make me suffer, bastard as he was.'

'That doesn't sound like a North American idiom,' Enderby said in wonder. 'That's more the way they speak where I come from.'

'Yes. Possession, isn't it? Takeover. *Bastard.*'

'Well, blame him, not me. I mean, damn it, it could have been William Shakespeare, couldn't it? Or Robert Bridges, bloody fool, not worthy of him. *And thy loved legacy, Gerard, hath lain Coy in my breast.* Bloody evil idiot. Or Geoffrey Grigson.'

'Shakespeare's dead,' she said reasonably. 'So may the other two be, whoever they are. But you're alive. You're here. I've waited a long time for this.'

'How did you know I was here?'

'Irrelevant irrelevant. It was announced, if you must know, after a talk-show this evening that you were going to be on tomorrow night.'

'Recorded it too early. Take too much for granted. I'm not. It's all been changed now.'

'And I called them and they said you wouldn't be on and they'd never have you on. But they gave me your address.'

'The swine. They're not supposed to. Address a private thing. Sheer bloody vindictiveness.' He fumed briefly. She smiled thinly in scorn and said:

'Self self self. Self and art. You bastard.'

'Oh,' Enderby said, 'get the bloody shooting over with. We've all got to die sometime. You too. They'll send you to the chair, or whatever barbarity they have now. I don't believe in capital punishment. I cancelled this long poem about Pelagius. I won't write the Odontiad. I've nothing on hand. Come on, get it over.'

'Oh no. Oh no. Oh no. What you're going to do is grovel. And after that I may or I may not –'

'May not what?'

'You're not going to have a nice easy martyrdom. I know men. You'll be glad to grovel.'

'Grovel grovel grovel,' Enderby growled like a tom-turkey. 'Artists are expected to grovel, aren't they? While the charlatans and the plagiarists and the corrupters and the defilers and the politicians have their arseholes licked. What do you want me to do – *eat* the bloody things? I've just had supper, remember. And,' cunningly, 'you won't want to turn me into Jesus Christ, will you?'

'Blasphemous bastard.'

'And, moreover, if I may say so, I don't see how you're going to *make* me grovel. Your only alternative is to use that bloody thing there. Well, I don't mind dying.'

'Of course you don't. Enderby flopped over his slim volumes, blood coming out of his mouth. Not that that would ever get into books. I'd make sure of that. There are no martyrs these days. Except blacks.'

'All right, then. I'm going to get up now, this bloody table's uncomfortable anyway, and walk into that kitchen there, and get the block guard on the blower, tell him to bring the cops along.' *Cops* was the only possible word, a *thriller* word. Okay buster you call the cops.

She kept shaking her head all the time. 'Glad to grovel, glad to. I've seen it before. With him. I have six rounds in here. I'm a good shot, my father taught me, my father, worth ten of you, you bastard. I can nip at bits of you. Nip nip nip. Make you deaf. Make you noseless. Give you a fucking anatomical excuse for being sexless.'

'Where did you get that idea from? Who taught you that? Who's been talking –'

'Irrelevant.'

'Look,' Enderby said, wondering whether, to be on the safe side, to make a good act of contrition or not. 'I'm getting up.' He got up. 'That's better. And I'm going to go, as I said I would, to –'

'You won't make it, friend. Your anklebone will be shattered.'

He realized bitterly that he did not want his anklebone shattered. Good clean death, yes. Altogether different, by George. 'Well, then,' he said. And then: 'They'll come up, in. Pistol-shots. Break the door down.'

'Do you honestly believe that, you innocent bastard of an idiot? This is not safe little England. Do you honestly think that anyone would care?' She shook her head at his lack of cisatlantic sophistication. 'Listen, idiot. Listen, bastard.'

Enderby listened. Of course, yes. You got used to it in time. In time it was just a decoration of the silence. Silence in a baroque frame. I say, that's good, I could use that. He heard the whining of police cars and the scream of ambulances. And then, from the west, bang bang. 'Yes, of course.'

'But,' she said, 'we'll make sure, won't we? Go over there and turn on the TV. Turn it on *loud*. Keep going round the dial till I tell you to stop.' Enderby moved with nonchalance, but only to sit down on a *pouffe*. Much much better. He said, with nonchalance:

'You do it. Play Russian roulette with it. That's Nabokov,' he said in haste, 'not me. *Pale Fire*,' he clarified.

'Bastard,' she said. But she got up and walked towards him, pointing her little gun. It was a nice little weapon from the look of it. She had delightful legs, Enderby saw regretfully, and seemed to be wearing stockings, not those pantee-hose abominations. Suspenders, what they called garters here, and then knickers. He was surprised to find himself, under the thick hot Edwardian trousers, responding solidly to the very terms. Camiknicks. Beyond his *pouffe*, she moved sidelong to the television set. She then switched on and turned the dial click click click with her left hand, looking towards Enderby and pointing her weapon. Enderby sat on his *pouffe* calmly, hands about his knees. She had been drawn now into a harmless area of entertainment. It was sound she was choosing, she would be in charge of the visual part. A new kind of art really, pop and audience participation and so on, gestures of creative impotence. There was a swift diachronic kaleidoscope of images and a quite interesting synthetic statement: That's it I guess its quality for you and for your so send fifteen dollars only its Butch you love isn't it I guess so emphatic denial issued by. Then she came to a palpable war-film and, eyes uninterested still, turned up the noise of bombardment. Enderby said:

'That's much too loud. The neighbours will complain.'

'What?' She hadn't heard him. 'Now,' coming towards him, pointing. Enderby could see, in black and white, brave GIs in foxholes. Then grenades were thrown lavishly by the undersized enemy. 'Take your clothes off.'

'What?'

'Everything off. I want to see you in your horrible potbellied hairy filthy nakedness.'

'How do you know it's . . .' And then: 'Why?'

'Degradation. The first phase.'

'No. Ow.' She had fired the little gun but it had not hit Enderby. It had merely whisted past him at very nearly ear-level. He saw her there, a kind of numinous blue smoke before her, and smelt what seemed rather appetizing smoked bacon. And thus he faced the breakfast of his death. He turned his head to see that the spine of a large illustrated volume on his landlady's shelves now looked disfigured. It was called *Woman's Bondage*. He had dipped into it once, a very humourless book, not about sex after all. She had timed the firing very felicitously, as though she knew the war-film by heart. A village had gone up very loudly into the air. But now there was a love-scene between a GI and a woman in a nurse's uniform, her hair crisp in a wartime style.

'Go on. Take them off.'

Enderby was wearing neither jacket nor tie. It was, of course, very hot. He was, God knew, often enough naked in here, but he was damned if he was going to be told to be naked.

'Go on. Now.' And she prepared to aim.

'It is, after all, quite . . . I mean, I meant to do this anyway. I normally do, you see. But I'm doing it because I want to. Do you understand that?'

'Go on.'

Enderby took off his waistcoat and then his shirt. He smelt his axillary fear very clearly.

'Go on.'

'Oh dear,' Enderby said with mock humorous exasperation. 'You are a hard little taskmistress.'

'I've not even started yet. Go on.'

In socks and underpants Enderby said: 'Will that do?'

'Argh. Disgusting.'

'Well, if I'm disgusting why do you want to.'

'Go on. To the horrible disgusting limit.'

'No. Ow.'

There was an ugly violet glass vase on the mantelpiece. She hit it very neatly as thunderous strafing was resumed on the screen. But at once a commercial break broke in. In unnatural high colour a smirking naked-shouldered woman made love to her slowly floating hair. Weave a circle round him, girls. No, not that. They wouldn't have the bloody sense. Sighing, Enderby stripped down to the limit. His phallus too palpably announced its interest in that camiknick business. He was, as they had so often told him in critical reviews, very much a belated man of the thirties. Sonnet-form and so on. The television screen homed in on fried chicken. Enderby hid the thing with his hands.

'Disgusting.'

'Well, it was your idea, not mine.'

'Now,' she ordered. 'You're going to piss on your own poems.'

'I'm going to what?'

'Urinate. Micturate. Squirt your own filthy water on your own filthy poems. *Go on.*'

'They're not filthy. They're clean. What stupid fucking irony. All the genuinely filthy pseudo-art and not-art that's about, and you pick on honest and clean and craftsmanlike endeavour –'

The weapon (in thrillerish locution: Enderby saw the word in botched print at the very moment of firing) spoke again. That frail Indian-type table thing proved itself very frail, tumbling over as though fist-hit in aesthetic viciousness. Enderby's phallus rose a few more notches. He said: 'That's three. That means only three left.'

'It's enough. Next time I promise it's going to be some of that ugly filthy fat hairy blubbery bloated . . .' She spoke out of smoke.

Enderby took up the top book with his right hand, his left hand still serving pudeur. It was *Fish and Heroes*, he saw tenderly. He couldn't open it one-handed, so he turned his bottom towards her and gave both hands to leafing the few but thickish leaves. By God what a genius he had then.

> *Wachet auf!* A fretful dunghill cock
> Flinted the noisy beacons through the shires.
> A martin's nest clogged the cathedral clock.
> Still, it was morning. Birds could not be liars . . .

And what would Luther have done in these circumstances? He was a great one for farting and shitting, but only on the Fiend. Piss on the Bible, Luther. Unthinkable. But then (O my God, poem there to be written. Meaning to have to live?) he might have thought: only a copy, the Book subsists above the single copy, I must live, spread the Word, the mature man gives in occasionally to the foolish, evil, mad. Luther lifted up his great skirts, disclosing a fierce red thursday, and pissed vigorously on a mere mess of Gothic print. Here stand I, I can in no wise do otherwise. Enderby said loudly:

'No!'

'I can see what you're looking at,' she said. 'That sonnet about the Reformation.' She knew the bloody book so well, it seemed such a pity. The television film showed a whining GI, cap tucked in epaulette, whining: 'Can't we talk this thing over, Mary?'

'Oh, all right then,' Enderby said wearily. And he turned his nozzle, with some slight muscular effort, on to the page. 'See,' he said. 'I'm doing my best. But nothing will come. It stands to reason nothing will come. *Stand*, blast you, is the operative word.'

And then, Luther throwing, but it was an inkpot, they showed you the inkstained wall in Wittenburg, Enderby threw the book, which fluttered vogelwise, towards her. Instinctively she shot at it. He had known, somehow, she would. He strode, heavily naked, balls aswing, weapon pointing, through the smoke and the echo of noise. And yet God has not said a word. She aimed straight at him, saying, 'If you think you're going to be a fucking martyr for art –'

'Said that already,' Enderby said, and he grasped her wrist at the very instant of her firing vaguely at the ceiling. The noise and smell were surely excessive. He had that damned gun now, a dainty hot little engine. She clawed at his buttocks as he went to the window partly open for the heat. Threw the bloody thing out. 'There,' he said. Luther, he remembered for some reason, had married a nun. Christ's lily and beast of the waste wood. This girl now beat at him with teeny fists. Enderby had had a good supper. He saw the two of them in the little mirror above a bookshelf devoted to psychology deeply Jewish and anguished. He had his glasses on, he observed, would not indeed have been able to observe otherwise, otherwise, of course, naked. He gave her a push somewhere around the midriff. She ended up crying on a *pouffe*.

'Bastard bastard.'

Enderby took off his glasses and placed them carefully on top of the television set which, well into the noise of impending victory, he clicked off. 'You and your bloody guns,' he said. 'Get you into a bloody mediaeval monastery full of great ballocky monks, that would teach you. Flabby, indeed. Blubber, for Christ's sake. Silenus, Falstaff.' This was for his own benefit. 'Think of those, blast you.' His heart seemed to be pumping away very healthily. Noise of impending victory. Not with a whimper but . . . 'Blaming me, indeed. Blaming poor dead Hopkins. As though I held the nuns down for them.'

'Go away. Get away from me.'

'I live here,' Enderby said. 'Sort of.' And then he pulled, two-handed, at the hems. Cry, clutching heaven by the. That was just to get a rhyme with *Thames*. Rhine refused them Thames would ruin them. Francis Thompson a far inferior poet. Hopkins appeared an instant, open-mouthed, clearly seen moaning at another's sin, though in the dark of the confessional. 'You did it,' Enderby said. 'So fagged, so fashed, indeed. Get away for a bit, can't you?' Hopkins became a pale daguerrotype, then was washed completely out. The skirt was elasticated at the waist and pulled down with little difficulty. In joy, Enderby saw the tops of stockings, suspenders, peach knickers.

'You filthy fucking –'

'Oh, this is all too American,' Enderby said. 'Sex and violence. What angel of regeneration sent you here?' For there was no question of mumbling and begging now. *Enderbius triumphans, exultans.*

10

This third heart attack, if that was what it had really been, did not seem to be really all that bad – a mere sketch to remind him of its shape. But he knew its shape intimately already, that of a Spenglerian parabola. Yet another interpretation seemed, as he sat in the toilet and excreted as quietly as he could, there being a guest in the apartment, possible, though he was fain to reject it. An inner hand showing in delicate deadly gesture the impending chop or noose. He was glad in a way that she had taken possession of the circular bed, no room for him, since bed was a place where people frequently died, sometimes in their sleep. She lay naked on her back, telling, say ten-twenty with her arms and seven-thirty with her legs, her delicate snoring indicating that it was a fine February night and all was well. She had left her home in Poughkeepsie, it appeared, and was obviously welcome to stay here with Enderby so long as she did not go out to buy another gun. She at least knew his work. Anyway, there was no question of thinking in terms of a nice long future. These heart attacks had been as good to Enderby as a *like* and *you know* harangue from one of his students. But he did not really want the chop to come tonight and in his sleep. He fancied doing some more vigorous death-dodging in the light. There was this to be said for New York: it was not dull.

Wiped and having flushed, Enderby went out to the kitchen to

make tea. There would be a hell of a row tomorrow, today that
was, when that dusky bitch Priscilla came to do the chores (How
come an educated man like you live in such Gadarene filth? She
was, after all, a Bible scholar); but there always was a hell of a row.
This time there would probably be something about fornication
and Cozbi as well as dirt. Enderby ate pensively a little cold left-
over stew while he waited for the water to boil: quite delicious,
really. He seemed to have lost a fair amount of protein in the last
few hours, perhaps cholesterol too. When the tea had sufficiently
brewed or drawn (five bags only; not overtempt providence) and
had been sharply sweetened and embrowned, he took it into the
living-room. He piled *pouffe* on *pouffe* to make himself comfortable
in order to watch for the dawn to come up. He switched on the
television set, which gave him a silly film apt for these small hours.
It was a college musical of the thirties (*How come that such a scholar/
Can put up with such a squalor?/Just gimme hafe a dollar/And I'll make
it spick and span, man.* There was a coincidence!) but it was made
piquant with girls in peach-looking camiknicks with metallic
hairdos. Enderby did some random leafing through the slim volumes
she had brought for him to defile. God, what a genius, etc. The
film, with interludes of advertising suspiciously cheap albums of
popular music, went harmlessly on while he sipped his tea and
browsed.

> You went that way as you always said you would,
> Contending over the cheerful cups that good
> Was in the here-and-now, in, in fact, the cheerful
> Cups and not in some remotish sphere full
> Of twangling saints, the-pie-in-the-sky-when-you-die
> Of Engels as much as angels, whereupon I . . .

He could not well remember having written that. Besides, the type
was blurring. He saw without surprise that the film had changed
to one, in very good colour too, about Augustine and Pelagius.
Thank God. The thing had been at last artistically dealt with. No
need after all for him to worry about finding an appropriate poetic
form.

35. (Say) Exterior   Day   A Road

(A man is vigorously whipping his donkey, which brays in great pain. His wife comes along to tell him to desist.)

WIFE: Desist, desist. The poor creature meant no harm, Fabricius.

MAN: Farted in my face, didn't it? A great noseful of foul air.

  (he continues beating)

WIFE: Foul, you say? She eats only sweet grass and fresh-smelling herbs, while you – you guzzle sour horsemeat and get drunk on cheap wine.

MAN: Oh, I do, do I? Take that, you slut.

  (he beats her till she bleeds)

36. The Same   Two Shot

(Pelagius and Obtrincius are watching. The noise and the cries are pitiable.)

OBTRINCIUS: What think you of that, O man of the northern seas? Evil, yes? It comes of the primal fetor of Adam which imbrues the world.

PELAGIUS: Ah no, my dear friend. Adam's sin was his own sin. It was not inherited by the generality of mankind.

OBTRINCIUS: But this is surely foul heresy! Why was Christ crucified except to pay, in Godflesh whose value is incomputable, for the Adamic sin we all carry? Have a care, my friend. There may be a bishop about listening.

PELAGIUS: Ah no, he came to show us the way. To teach us love. *Be ye perfect*, he said. He taught us that we are perfectible. That what you call evil is no more than ignorance of the way. Hi, you, my friend.

37. Resume 35

(The man Fabricius has now turned to his son who, having apparently intervened to save his mother from the vicious blows, is bloody and bowed. The mother weeps bloodily. The ass looks on, sore but impassive, also bloody.)

MAN *(temporarily desisting)*: Huh? You address me, sir?

38. Resume 36

PELAGIUS *(cheerfully)*: Yes, my good man and brother in Christ.

  (He moves out of the shot and into:)

THE CLOCKWORK TESTAMENT 501

39. Two Shot: Man and Pelagius

PELAGIUS: Ah, my poor friend, you have much to learn. Sweet reason has temporarily deserted you. Take breath and then blow out your anger with it. It is a mere ghost, a phantasm, totally insubstantial.

MAN: You use fine words, sir. But try using sweet reason to stop a donkey farting in your nose.

PELAGIUS: You should keep your nose away from the, er, animal's posterior. Sweet reason must surely tell you that.

MAN: Oh, well, mayhap you're right, sir. Anger wastes time and uses up energy. Come, wife. Come, son. I will be reasonable, God forgive me.

(*Sketching a blessing, Pelagius moves out of shot*)

Sweet reason, my ass.

40. Exterior   Day Rome: A Scene of Unbridled Revelry

(*LS of a sort of carnival. Instruments of the fifth century* AD *are blaring and thumping, while unbridled revellers frisk about, kissing and drinking and lifting kirtles.*)

41. The Same   Group Shot

(*A group of gorgers are greasily fingering smoking haunches and swine-shanks, stuffing it in, occasionally vomiting it out.*)

PELAGIUS (OS): My friends!

(*They all look, in the same direction, open mouths exhibiting half-chewed greasy protein.*)

42. Their Pov: Pelagius

(*He stands with pilgrim's staff, looking with calm sorrow.*)

PELAGIUS: Does not reason tell you that such excess is unreasonable?

It coarsens the soul and harms the body.

(*Noise of lavish vomiting*)

There, you see what I mean.

43. Pelagius's Pov

(*The gorgers look somewhat abashed, but a bold fat bald one speaks up baldly and boldly.*)

FAT GORGER: We cannot help it, man of God, whoever you are, a stranger by your manner of speech. The seven deadly sins, of which gluttony, as thou mayhap knowest, is one, are the seven worms in the apple we ate at the great original feast which still goes on, and of which Adam and Eve are the host and the hostess.

ANOTHER GORGER (*much thinner, as with a worm, or even seven, inside him*): Aye, he speaketh truly, monk, whoever thou art. We are born into sin through none of our willing, and has not Christ atoned for our sins, past, future, and to come?

44. Resume 42

PELAGIUS (*very loudly*): No He Has Not.

45. A Group of Fornicators

(*Mitred bishops, bearded, venerable, lusty, look up from clipping their well-favoured whores. They look at each other, frown.*)

46. Interior   Night   The House of Flaccus

(*The bishop Augustine sits at the end of dinner with his friend Flaccus, a public administrator. There are other guests, including Bishop Tarminius – one of the bishops who frowned in Scene 45.*)

FLACCUS (*while a slave proffers a dish*): Perhaps an apple, my lord bishop?

AUGUSTINE (*shuddering*): Ah no, Flaccus my friend. If you only knew what part apples have played in my life . . .

TARMINIUS: And one apple in the life of all mankind.

AUGUSTINE (*looking at him for an instant, then nodding gravely*): Yes, Tarminius, very true. But oh, the moonwashed apples of wonder in the neighbour orchard. I did not steal the apples because I needed them. Indeed, my father's apples were far better, sweeter, rosier. I stole them because I wished to steal. To sin. It was my sin I loved, God help me.

FLACCUS: Aye, it is in all of us. Baptism is but a token of extinguishing the fire . . .

AUGUSTINE: Burning burning burning burning . . .

FLACCUS: But Christ paid, atoned, still makes the impact of our daily sin on the godhead less acute.

AUGUSTINE: Beware of theology, Flaccus. These deep matters have driven mad many a young brain.

TARMINIUS: You speak very true, Augustine. There is a man from Britain in our midst – didst know that?

AUGUSTINE: There are many from Britain in our midst – that misty northern island where the damp clogs men's brains. They are harmless enough. They blink in our southern light. They go down with the sun. (*laughter*)

TARMINIUS: I refer to one, Augustine, who seems not to be harmless, whose gaze is very steady, who is impervious to sunstroke. His name is Pelagius.

FLACCUS (*frowning*): Pelagius? That is not a British name.

TARMINIUS: His true name is Morgan which, in their tongue, means man of the sea. Pelagius, in Greek, means exactly the –

AUGUSTINE (*testily*): Yes yes, Tarminius. I think we all know what it means. Hm. I have heard a little about this man – a wandering friar, is he not? He has been exhorting the people to be kind to their wives and asses and warning of the dangers of gluttony. Also, I understand –

(*He looks sternly at Tarminius, who looks sheepish rather than shepherdish*) Fornication. I see no harm in such simple homiletic teaching. A puritanical lot, our brothers of the north.

TARMINIUS: But, Augustine, he is doing more. He is denying Original Sin, the redemptive virtues of God's grace, even, it would seem, our salvation in Christ. He seems to be saying that man does not need help from heaven. That man can better himself by his own efforts alone. That the City of God can be realized as the City of Man.

AUGUSTINE (*astounded*): But – this – is – heresy! Oh my God – the poor lost British soul . . .

(*There is a sudden spurt of flame which ruddies the scene. All look to its source. The camera whip-pans to the spit, where flames are fierce. A toothless scullion grins, touching a forelock in apology.*)

SCULLION: Sorry, my lords, sir, gentlemen. A bit of fat in the fire.

47. Group Shot
(*Augustine, Tarminius, Flaccus look very grim.*)
AUGUSTINE: Fat in the fire, indeed.

48. Interior   Day   A Hovel
(*Pelagius is talking gently and wisely to a group of poor men, artisans, layabouts, who listen attentively. A pretty girl named Atricia sits at his feet and looks up in worship.*)

PELAGIUS: In my land the weather is always gentle, rather misty, never lacking rain. The earth is fertile, and by our own efforts we are able to bring forth fair crops. The sheep munch good fat grass. There are no devilish droughts, there is no searing sun. It is no land for praying in panic – not like the arid Africa of our friend the Bishop Augustine.

ATRICIA: Oh, how I should love to see it. Could one be happy there without fear, without constant fear?

PELAGIUS: Fear of what, my dear child?

ATRICIA: Fear of having to suffer for one's happiness?

PELAGIUS: Ah yes, Atricia. In Britain we have no vision of hellfire, nor do we need to invoke heaven to make life's torments bearable. It is a gentle easy land, it is a kind of heaven in itself.

A LAYABOUT: But you said something about making a heaven there. And now you say it is a heaven already.

PELAGIUS: A *kind* of heaven I said, friend. We have many advantages. But we are not so foolish as to think we are living in the garden of Eden. No, our paradise is still to be built – a paradise of fair cities, of beauty and reason. We are free to cooperate with our neighbours, which is another way of saying *to be good*. No sense of inherited sin holds us in hopeless sloth.

ATRICIA: I can see it now – that misty island of romance. Oh, I should so love to breathe its air, smell its soil . . .

PELAGIUS: And why should you not, my dear? What the heart of man conceives may ever be realized. I was just saying the other day –

(*There is a noise of entering feet. They all look up. They are obscured somewhat by the gross shadow of those entering.*)

A VOICE (OS): Is your name Pelagius?

PELAGIUS: Why, yes –

49. Pelagius's Pov

(*Two gross authoritative men in imperial uniform stand in the way of the sunlight. They look sternly at the assembly.*)

FIRST MAN: You are to come with us. At once.

50. Pelagius and Atricia

(*She clings to him in fear. He comforts her with a patting hand.*)

PELAGIUS (*smiling*): You appear to be men of authority. It would be useless for me to ask why or where.

51. Two Shot
(*The two authoritative men look at him in burly contempt.*)
SECOND MAN: Quite quite useless.

52. Interior   Day   A Convocation of Bishops
(*Augustine speaks while the camera pans along a line of grave bishops. Pelagius is out of shot.*)
AUGUSTINE: Quite quite useless to deny that you have been spreading heresy.

53. The Same   Pelagius
(*Pelagius is sitting on a kind of creepystool, humble and tranquil during his episcopal investigation.*)
PELAGIUS: I do not deny that I have been spreading gospel, but that it is heresy I do most emphatically deny.

54. Group Shot
(*A number of beetlebrowed bishops beetle at him.*)
AUGUSTINE (OS): Heresy! heresy! *heresy!*

55. Resume 52
(*Augustine strides up and down the line of bishops. His mitre frequently goes awry with the passon of his utterance, but he straightens it ever and anon.*)
AUGUSTINE: Yes, sir. You deny that man was born in evil and lives in evil. That he needs God's grace before he may be good. The very cornerstone of our faith is *original sin.* That is doctrine.

56. Resume 54
(*The bishops nod vigorously.*)
BISHOPS: Originalsinriginalsinrignlsn.

57. Pelagius
(*He gets up lithely from his creepystool.*)
PELAGIUS: Man is neither good nor evil. Man is rational.

58. Augustine

(In CU the writhing mouth, richbearded, of Augustine sneers.)

AUGUSTINE: *Rational.*

59. Exterior   Day   A Scene of Riot

(The Goths have arrived and are busily at their work of destruction. They pillage, burn, kill in sport, rape. A statue of Jesus Christ goes tumbling and breaking, pulverizing itself on harmless screaming citizens. The Goths, laughing, nail an old man to a cross. Some come out of a church, bearing a holy chalice. One micturates into it. Then a pretty girl is made to drink ugh of the ugh.)

60. Exterior   Nightfall   A Windy Hill

(Augustine and Pelagius stand together on the hill, looking grimly down.)

AUGUSTINE: Rational, eh, my son?

PELAGIUS *(hardly perturbed)*: It is the growing pains of history. Man will learn, man *must* learn, man *wants* to learn.

AUGUSTINE: Ah, you and your British innocence . . .

61. Their Pov

(A view of the burning city. Cheers and dirty songs. Screams.)

AUGUSTINE (OS): Evil evil evil – the whole of history is written in blood. There is, believe me, much much more blood to come. Evil is only beginning to manifest itself in the history of our Christian west. Man is bad bad bad, and is damned for his badness, unless God, in his infinite mercy, grants him grace. And God foresees all, foresees the evil, foredamns, forepunishes.

62. Resume 60

(Augustine takes Pelagius by the shoulders and shakes him. But Pelagius gently and humorously removes the shaking hands. He laughs.)

PELAGIUS: Man is free. Free to choose. Unforedained to go either to heaven or to hell, despite the Almighty's allforeknowingness. Free free *free*.

63. The Burning City

(A vicious scene of mixed rape and torture and cannibalism. The song of a drunk is heard.)

DRUNK (OS) *(singing)*:

Free free free
We be free to be free . . .

64. Group Shot
(*The drunk, surrounded by dead-drunks and genuine corpses, spills pilfered wine, singing.*)
DRUNK:

> Free to be scotfree,
> But
> Not free to be not free,
> Free free fr

(*There is a tremendous earthquake. A tear in the shape of a Spenglerian tragic parabola lightnings across the screen.*)

AND NOW THIS IMPORTANT WORD FROM
OUR SPONSOR

FRSHNBKKKKGGGGRHNKSPLURTSCHGROGGLEWOK

11

This, children, is New York. A vicious but beautiful city, totally representative of the human condition or, for any embryonic existentialists among you, *la condition humaine*. What's that when it's at home, you vulgarly ask, Felicia? You will find out, God help you, soon enough, child. It is named New York in honour of the Duke of York who became King James II of Great Britain, a foolish and bigoted monarch who tried to reimpose Catholicism on a happily Protestant nation and, as was inevitable, ignominiously failed. No, Adrian, this is no longer a British city: it is part of a great free complex or federation of states that are welded together under a most unBritish constitution: rational, frenchified, certainly republican. They revolted against the British king to whom they had once owed allegiance and tribute. No, Charles, that was a *Protestant* king and also bigoted and foolish. Let us swoop a little lower: How beautiful those exalted towers in the Manhattan dawn now we have descended to clear air under the enveloping blanket, Wilfrid. The jagged teeth of a monostomatic monster? One way of looking at it, Edwina.

We are here, under the aegis of Educational Time Trips, Inc., to seek out our poet. This is a great city for poets, though there are few like ours. We swim aerially over the island a little way, north of the midtown area, nearer to the Hudson than to the East River. He is round here somewhere. Yes, Morgana, we will have to *peek* a little. Through the dawn windows of 91st Street, as they call it (a rational city, a *numerical* city). Avert your eyes, Felicia; what they are doing is entirely their own affair. Here, dear dear, a young man is murdering his bedmate in postcoital tristity. Those two middleaged men are actually *dancing*: it would seem somewhat early for that. A tired girl eats an insubstantial breakfast at a kitchen table. A man in undress and blue spectacles peers at the obituary page of the New York Times. Look at the squalor of the bedroom of that scholarly-seeming youth, cans and bottles and untidy stacks of an obviously filthy periodical. Here another murder, there a robbery, and now – the contortions in the name of pleasure, God help us.

That is interesting, that round bed. Do you see the round bed, Felicia, Andrea? Very unusual, round bed. And on the round bed a skeletal lady sleeps alone, telling (if that tangent touches at twelve) the right time. Astonishing! Eight-ten, if her lower limbs are the hour-hand. But here. And now. Look look. We have found him! Gather round, children, and see. Mr Enderby, temporary professor as we are told he is in this fashed fag-end of his days, asleep naked in a nest of *pouffes*. Ugly, hairy, fat; ah yes, he always was. The television set, to which he is not listening, discourses the morning news, which is all bad. He seems, dear dear, to have been somewhat incontinent in his sleep. Gracious, the weaknesses of the great!

And now – a little surprise for you. A black woman, key in hand, of pious face but ugly gait, waddles in, sees him, is disgusted, holds up her key in pious deprecation of his besmirched nudity. But, soft. She goes closer, looks closer, touches. She holds up both her hands in expression of a quite different emotion, runs out of the room with open mouth, strange words emanating therefrom. So we now know, and it is a sort of satisfaction, for *nunc dimittis* is the sweetest of canticles. Remember us in the roads, the heaven-haven of the Reward. Let him easter in us, be a dayspring to the dimness of us, be a crimson-cresseted east. No, hardly that, I go too far perhaps. Is there anything of his own that will serve? Yes, Edmund?

> The work ends when the work ends,
> Not before, and rarely after.
> And that explains, my foes and friends,
> This spiteful burst of ribald laughter.

Stop giggling, will you, all of you? You are both foolish and too clever for words, Edmund, with your stupid and irreverent and *meaningless* doggerel improvisation. You will all smile on the other sides of your faces when I get you back to civilization. All right, all right, I am aware that I involuntarily rhymed. Come on, out of it. Another instalment of the human condition is beginning. Out of it: *he* is well out of it, you say, Andrea? But no: he is in it, we are all always in it. Do not think that anyone can escape it merely by . . . I will not utter the word: it is quite irrelevant. Out of it, indeed; he is not out of it at all.

Rome, July 1973.

Enderby's Dark Lady
or: No End to Enderby

Composed to placate kind readers of
The Clockwork Testament, or Enderby's End,
who objected to my casually killing my hero

A Prefatory Note

Enderby first got into my head in early 1959, when I was a colonial civil servant working in the Sultanate of Brunei, North Borneo. One day, delirious with sandfly fever, I opened the door of the bathroom in my bungalow and was not altogether surprised to see a middle-aged man seated on the toilet writing what appeared to be poetry. The febrile vision lasted less than a second, but the impossible personage stayed with me and demanded the writing of a novel about him. I wrote half this novel in 1960, a year in which the medical authorities had condemned me to death with an inoperable cerebral tumour. It did not appear that there would be time to write the second part of the novel, so I published the first part as a whole book under the title of *Inside Mr Enderby*. To the chagrin of the doctors, who did not like their prognosis to be proved false, I lived and was able, in 1967, to write the second part of the novel, under the title of *Enderby Outside*. A few years later Enderby demanded that he be killed off in a novella entitled *The Clockwork Testament*. I duly murdered him with a heart attack. Now, in this new brief novel, he is alive again. It seems that fictional characters, though they sometimes may have to die, are curiously immune to death. Is Don Quixote dead or alive? Is Hamlet? Is Little Nell? Enderby's demand to be resurrected has come inconveniently, for I am engaged on a longish novel about Nero and St Paul.

A decent respect to people's notions of plausibility demands that I try to explain why Enderby, having died of a heart attack in New York about ten years ago, should be alive three years later in the state of Indiana. (And why Indiana, a part of the United States I do not know very well?) I think we have to look at it this way: all fictional events are hypotheses, and the condition of Enderby's going to live in New York would be that he should die there. If the hypothesis is unfulfilled, he does not have to die. Enderby was condemned to visit the United States, there to suffer, and there was a choice between his going to Manhattan to teach Creative Writing and his being employed to write the libretto for a ridiculous musical about Shakespeare in a fictitious theatre in Indianapolis. He took the second course, which involved his staying alive to risk a suicidal identification (himself with the Bard) but to come through unscathed. He will, of course, eventually die, but only because his creator will die. On the other hand, being a fictional character, he cannot die.

Enderby's name comes from two sources – the remote and uninhabitable Antarctic territory called Enderby Land, and a poem about a shipwreck by Jean Ingelow in which church bells clang out a tune called 'The Brides of Enderby'. His poems are, inevitably, written by myself, but only myself in disguise as Enderby. A reviewer in *Punch* said, of the first novel or half-novel, 'It would be helpful if Mr Burgess could indicate somewhere whether these poems are meant to be good or bad,' a fine instance of critical paralysis. T.S. Eliot liked at least three of the poems, but posterity is beginning to find his taste unsure, especially since he too, like Enderby, became the librettist for a Broadway musical. I have no opinion about either Enderby's poems or Enderby himself. I do not know whether I like or dislike him; I only know that, for me, he exists. I fear that he may probably go on existing.

A.B.

Lugano, November 1983

1

Will and Testament

When Ben Jonson was let out of jail he went straight to William Shakespeare's lodgings in Silver Street and said: 'Let us drink.'

'Ben,' Will cried. 'Your ears are untrimmed and your nose whole. The shearers were held off, then. I'm glad to see you well.'

'But thirsty. Let us go and drink.'

'We can drink here and shall. Malmsey? Sherrisack? Or shall I send out for ale? Ben Ben Ben, have a care. Next time the shearer may be the ultimate trimmer, the sconce-chopper as they call him.'

'I've a mind to drink in a tavern. Let us go.'

'As you will, this being a sort of great day for you. How was it in jail? Are Marston and Chapman there yet?'

'There still and like to stay. After all, the offending line was of their making. As for the jail – stink, maggots, rats, lepers, pocky chancres. But there was a man I will tell you of while we drink.'

'You swore to me the line was your line, the best line in the whole of *Westward Ho* as you would have it. How does it go now? "The Scotch –" It begins with "The Scotch –".'

'*Eastward Ho* is the title. You look as ever the wrong way. Back when the rest of us look forward. It is this: "The Scotch are good friends to England, but only when they are out of it." Well, indeed I wrote it, but it seemed politic to father it on the other two. Under oath, aye, but a poet could not live did he not perjure.'

They went down the stairs and past the workshop of the tiremaker Mountjoy, Will's landlord. Mountjoy was scolding, in Frenchified English, the apprentice Belott.

'Immortal,' Will said. 'He can never say that I did not make him immortal. But no gratitude there.'

'How immortal?'

'I have him in *Harry Five* as the herald.'

'He taught you the dirty French for the same?'

'He put right the grammar. I knew the dirt already.' Out in Silver Street, which the sun had promoted to gold, they saw beggars, limbless soldiers, drunken sailors, whores, dead cats, ordinary decent citizens in stuff gowns, a kilted Highlander with a flask of usque-baugh in place of a sporran. A ballad singer with few teeth sang:

> 'For bonny sweet Robin was all my joy,
>   And Robin came oft to my bed.
> But Robin did wrong, so to end his song
>   The headsman did chop off his head.'

'An old one,' Ben said. 'And still I cannot hear it without a shudder.'

'It seems older than it is. A great deal has happened in the interim. Poor Robin.'

'That was your name for him? You called him Robin to his face?'

'He was Robin to my lord of Southampton, and my lord of Southampton was ever Harry to me. So it was always out-upon-titles. But, he was ever saying, when he was become King Robert the First of England there would be no familiarity then. Would it had been so, sometimes I think, though bloodless, bloodless.'

'Treason, man, careful.'

'What will you do, report me to Gobbo Cecil? "An't please you, good my lord, there is this low playmaker that doth say how the Essex rebellion should have succeeded." He'll say, "Aye aye, and maybe he's in the right of it." He's no love for slobbering Jamie with his bishops and buggery and drinking tobacco is an unco foul sin to the body, laddie, and doth inflame the lung, if thou lovest tobacco then lovest thou not thy king.'

Ben sighed. 'I know how it is. I say too many Scotchmen about and I am flung in jail. You could tell the king to his face that he's a – I say no more, you see that sour man in black there? Following us, is he? Nay, he turned off. You could skite in his majesty's mouth and he'd say, "Aye, I do dearly love a guid witty jest, laddie, will ye be raised to a Knicht o' the Garrrterrr?" Some men are born jail meat. Others – Here, round here. At the bottom of this lane. Go tipatoe, 'tis all slime underfoot. Careful, careful.'

'The Swan with Two Necks.' Will read the warped sign with a fastidious nose-wrinkle. 'This is not a tavern I mind ever to have visited before.'

'It is quiet,' Ben said, leading the way into noise, stench, striding over a vomit pool, between knots of swarthy men with daggers. 'We can talk in peace and quiet.' They sat on a settle before a rickety much-punished table whereon fat flies fed amply from greasy orts and a sauce-smear unwiped. A girl with warty bosom well on show showed black teeth and took an order for wine. 'Red wine,' Ben said. 'Of your best. Blood-red, red as the blood of our blessed Saviour.' Some villains turned to look with surly interest. A man with an eyepatch nodded as in friendly threat at Ben. '*Buenos dias, señor,*' Ben said.

'For God's sake, Ben, what manner of place is this?'

'A good place, though something filthy. Good fellows all, though but rogues to look on. Now let me speak. A great change is come into my life.'

The wine arrived. Will poured. 'Change? You have fallen in love with some pocked tib of the Clink and think her to be a disguised angel?'

'Ah, no. By heaven, this is good wine, red, aye, red as the blood that is decanted daily on the blessed holy altars of the one true faith.'

'For Christ's sake, Ben.'

'Aye, for Christ's sake, you say truly. What I do I do for Christ's dear sake. Let me tell you, my dear friend, what befell. In this noisome stinking rathole behold the word of the Lord came to me.'

'Oh Jesus the word of the.'

'Aye, a good old priest of the true faith, aye, though carning his bread as a dancing-master, thrown into jail for debt, spake to me loving words and told where the truth doth lie. It was by way of being in the manner somewhat of a revelation.' Ben drank fiercely and then said: 'Good wine. *Enim calix sanguinis.* Drink a salute to my holy happiness.'

'Keep your voice well down, man,' Will said, his voice well down. 'See how they all listen.'

'They may listen and be glad. I have friends, have I not? Have

I not friends here?' he called to the drinkers. '*Amigos*?' There was no response save for a man hawking, though all looked still.

'I am getting out of here,' Will said.

'Aye, ever the prudent. Well, there is another word for prudent and you know it well. A plague on all cowards. Why should I not speak aloud my joy in being restored to the one true holy bosom? Is not the Queen's self of the blessed company? I tell you, the day is at hand when we may take the holy body in sunlight before the eyes of all men, not skulking in a dark hole. Hallelujah.'

'You know the danger, fool,' Will said, sweating. 'There was an expectation of tolerance, but it is not fulfilled. The bishops will see it is not. Let us be out of here.'

'With this blessed red wine unfinished? With this blood of the grape crimson as the blood of.'

'I am going.' Will drained the sour stuff and turned down his cup with a clank.

'Well, well, very well, I have told my story. Now, thanks be to God, my true story doth begin.' Ben drank straight from the jug, beastlily, emerging spluttering. He wiped his mouth with the dirty back of his hand and nodded in a friendly manner at the company. 'Give you good day, all. And God's blessing be ever on your comings and goings and eke your staying where you are.'

'Come, idiot.'

They left. Ben said, 'Aye, aye, we will see how the spirit works. Is anyone following?'

'None. None yet. Do you wish someone to follow?'

'I say no more of it now, Ben Jonson his conversion. Except that you may speak of it to your friends and colleagues and all you will. I care not. I dare all for the lord Jesus. I owe him a death.'

'That is mine. I wrote that.'

'You did? It is all one. There is a tale they tell of you, do you know that?'

'What tale? Where?'

'Jack Marston told me. It is of Master Shakespeare dead and ascending to heaven's gate and demanding admittance. St Peter says: We have too many landlords here, we need poets to sweeten long eternity. Well, says Master Shakespeare, I am well known to be a poet. Prove it, says St Peter. I am of poor memory, says Master

S, and can remember no line I wrote. Well then, says heaven's warder, extemporize somewhat. At that moment within the gates and all visible from the threshold little bow-legged Tom Kyd goes by, a poetic martyr, with his fingers cruelly broke by the late Queen's Commissioners. A bow-legged one, says the saint. Extemporize on him. Whereupon, firequick, Master S comes out with:

> 'How now, what manner of man is this
> That beareth his balls in parenthesis?'

'Whereupon St Peter sighs and says: We have no room for landlords.'

'Not funny,' Will said. And then: 'So they talk of me as dead already, do they?'

'Not dead. Shall we say retired. Your sun setteth. Westward Ho is your cry.' Ben looked behind him to see two daggered ruffians following. He said in some small excitement: 'Leave me here. Take your leave, aye. I think there are two coming who will show me where I may hear mass Sundays and saint-days. The blessing of Mother Church on you, Will.'

'No, no, I want no such blessing.'

It was some week or so later that Ben Jonson sat at dinner with new friends, the room being an upper one in Eastcheap. There was Bob Catesby at the head of the table, very fierce and sober, and a swarthy one that had been in that low tavern that time they called Guy though his true name was Guido, somewhat drunk on Spanish wine, and there were Rob Winter, little big-eyed Bates, Kit Wright, Tom Winter brother of Rob, and also Frank Tresham who kept wetting a dry lip and looking shifty. Catesby said to Ben:

'You are wide open, Master Jonson. Your days are numbered.'

'By whom?' Ben said. 'If you mean that I blab of the brotherhood, by God you are mistaken.'

'You have not done that, no, you have been prudent enough there. If you had not been so, Guy here – a soldier, remember, who will cut off ten heads before his breakfast – Guy, I say, would have had you, by God. No, I mean imprudent in that you talk too much of the Godless King and the runagate Queen, who will show her bosom and legs to all and go to mass hiccuping with the drink. I mean treasonable talk. I believe you are destined for a martyr's crown.'

'No,' Ben said. 'I want not that. I will not force apart the jaws of heaven for my precocious entering. Heaven may open in its own good time without my prompting. There is wine for the drinking yet and wenches for the fondling. Nay, no martyrdom.'

'Speak out the scheme, Rob,' Catesby said to Tom Winter's brother. 'You are he that must hold it in his memory. You are our living parchment.'

'Well, then,' Rob Winter said, looking at Ben, 'it is this. It is to do with the new session of the parliament. All will be there – King, Queen, Prince Henry, nobles, judges, knights, esquires and all, all for the forging of new acts and laws to put down the true faith. They will be blown up.'

'They will be – ?' Ben asked carefully.

'Blown up. We are to place twenty barrels of gunpowder in the cellar beneath with faggots on top. Set but flame to the faggots and there will be a greater blowing up than has ever before been seen in the long tale of tyranny and human suppression.'

'Blown up,' Catesby said after a pause, as to make sure Ben properly understood.

'The Queen,' Ben said, 'is of the true faith. Is it right she too should be blown up?'

'You are always ready to talk of her Godlessness,' Catesby said. 'Well, she will be punished. Alternatively, she will be a martyr. Destiny puts forth a choice.'

'However you gloss it,' Ben said, 'she will be blown up.'

'Everybody will be blown up,' Tom Winter said, pausing in the picking of his teeth. They had eaten of a roast ham, each mouthful full of teeth-hugging fibres. 'Everybody.'

'And then there will be a new era of love for the true faith?' Ben asked.

'We will think of that after the blowing up,' Catesby said. 'Certainly there will be a many problems, but sufficient to the day as the Gospel saith. First the blowing up.'

'And the choice of the one to whom shall be given the glory

of setting flame to the faggots for the blowing up,' Kit Wright said. They all now looked at Ben.

'He too will be blown up?' Ben asked.

'There is every likelihood that he will be blown up,' Catesby said. 'But he will at once be endued with a crown of martyrdom. You, Master Jonson, are wide open.' They all continued to look at Ben. Ben said:

'How first are you to convey the barrels to the cellar?'

'It is a wine cellar,' Rob Winter said. 'The barrels will be brought on a vintner's dray. What have you there, the guards will ask. Wine, will come the answer. Wine, as hath been ordered. It is all very simple.'

'And the faggots?'

'The faggots will be in another barrel, dry and ready for the laying on. And he that is to do the brave deed will go as guard in a borrowed livery. Bearing a torch.'

'In broad daylight?' Ben asked.

'He will say he has orders to search the cellar for possible treasonous men lurking. It is all very simple.'

Francis Tresham now spoke. 'I am against it,' he said. 'It is a plot of some cruelty. Also of some injustice. The Queen, true, is a foreigner and doth not matter. But there are enow good Catholic Englishmen in hiding among those of the parliament. We are blowing up our own.'

'Martyrs' crowns,' Ben said. 'Think not of it.'

'You will do the deed?' Catesby said, leaning closer to Ben and, indeed, discharging a blast of hammy garlic onto him.

'I will think on it,' Ben said. 'Your reasons are of a fairly persuadent order. I will go home now and start to think on it.'

'Guy here will go home with you,' Catesby said, 'and help you think on it.'

'No, he will not,' Ben said. 'I want none breathing on me while I think. I go into this in full *libero arbitrio*. I cannot be made to do it.'

'That is true,' Catesby said. 'Except by the promptings of your own destiny, Master Jonson. I see the martyr's crown hovering above you.' He looked somewhat fiercely at Tresham. 'Frank,' he said, 'you waver. It is strange you waver when you were loudest once in saying perdition to the betrayer of the faith of his own royal mother. There are measures may be taken to discourage waverers.' He looked at dark Guido and then back at pale Tresham.

'I am no waverer. I ask only that we right our souls on this matter of the killing of Catholics along with Protestants. It is a matter of theology I would ask that we concern ourselves withal.'

'Theology,' little Bates now said. 'There is enow of theology at the Godless court, holy Jamie and his atheistical bishops. Out on theology. Let us have the true faith back and God's enemies blown up. I drink to you,' he said, 'Master Jonson,' and drank.

'I too drink to me,' Ben said, and drank likewise. He wiped his loose lips and wrung his beard and said, looking at the company severally, 'Now I go home. To pray. For blessing and eke for guidance.'

'Guido will go with you for guidance through the perilous streets,' Catesby said.

'I go alone. I am in no peril.'

'Guy will be your guide.'

Ben, with Guido Fawkes at his flank, was some way advanced through the warren of stinks and drunkenness and stinking drunken bravoes that led to his lodgings when, to keep up his courage, he began to sing:

> 'Here will we sit upon the rocks
> And see the shepherds feed their flocks
> By shallow rivers to whose falls
> Melodious birds sing madrigals.'

At the song Fawkes clicked his fingers and said:

'Spy.'

'I cry your mercy, what was that?'

'Spy, I said. I think you to be a manner of spy.'

Ben ceased walking or rolling and looked at him fair and straight beneath the moon. 'You are drunk, man. You know not what you say.'

'Spy. I asked myself long who it was you put me in mind of, and he too was a poet and spy. He cried his sodomitical atheism to the streets, and none did him harm. I conclude he was under protection. His name was Kit Marlowe. That was a song of his you were singing but now. Spy.'

'Marlowe,' Ben said soberly. 'He was all our fathers, though he was slain young, God help him. You flatter me more than you know. But I am no spy.' They heard as it were antiphonal singing, though more drunk than sober, approach.

> 'Sit we amid the ewes and tegs
> Where pastors custodise their gregs
> And cantant avians do vie
> With fluminous sonority.'

'O Jesus,' Ben prayed. 'Jack Marston.'

It was Marston, true, drunk, true, but able to see, mainly from the bulk, who stood in his path. 'Jonson, cheat, rogue, liar, ingrate, thief too. I am out now, see, and have learned all. Graaagh.' The sound was of blood rising in the throat.

'You speak too plain to be true Marston. Where be your inkhorn nonsensicalities? Thief, you say. No man says thief to Jonson. Any more,' he added to Fawkes, 'than he says spy.'

'Thief I say again. You said that you would pay me when Henslowe paid you, that Henslowe had not paid you, therefore you could not pay me. But Henslowe has paid you, has, thief. I was with him this night, I saw his account book. Draw, thief.' He drew himself, though staggering.

'If it is but six shilling and threepence you want, let us have no talk of drawing. Come to my lodgings and you shall have a little on account. I will not have that *thief,* Jack. I am a man of probity and of religion.'

'Of that we hear too,' Marston cried. 'The lactifluous nipples of the Christine genetrix and the viniform sanguinity of the eucharistic abomination. Draw.'

'Very well.' Ben sighed and unsheathed his short dagger. 'I have killed, Jack,' he said, 'and my adversary was sober. I killed Gab Spencer, remember, and he too said *thief.*' Ben now saw the reflection of flames in a bottle-paned window. Torches lurching round the corner of Cow Lane. Four men with swords and cudgels, the watch. With relief he lunged towards Marston. Lunging, he saw

Fawkes flee. Wanted no trouble, right too, right for his filthy cause. Marston thrust, tottered, fell. Ben sheathed his dagger and leapt onto Marston's back, took his ears like ewer handles and began to crack his nose into the dirt of the cobbles. Then the watch was on him.

It was four of the morning when Will received the message to go at once to the Marshalsea. A boy hammered at the door below and Will went to his window, Mountjoy in his nightshirt also appearing, a minute later, at his.

'Mester Shakepaw?'

'Approximately. What, boy?'

'Mester Jonson in the jail do want ye naow vis minik.'

'He wants money?'

'I fink not sao. E gyve me manny, a ole groat, see ere.'

'Go away, garsoon,' Mountjoy cried harshly, 'discommoding the voisinage so. We desire no parlying of prisons in this quartier. It is a quartier respectable.'

'I'll come,' Will sighed. 'I'll come now.'

Few were sleeping in the Marshalsea. There was a kind of growling merriness, with drink, cursing, fumbling at plackets, gaming, a richer though darker version of the dayworld of the free. There was even a one-eyed man selling hot possets. Will listened, sipping, to Ben's story. 'The names,' Ben said, 'take down the names.'

'I can remember well enough of the names.'

'You cannot. You are poor at remembering. You cannot remember even your own lines. Take your tablet, take down the names. And then to Cecil.'

'Now?'

'Now, yes. Easy enough for you. You're a groom of the bedchamber, a sort of royal officer.'

'This is no jape?'

'This is by no manner of means a jape, God help us. Go. I am, thank God, safe enough here. Cecil will understand all that, why I wish to be shut away. I am safe enough here till he has them.'

'I will write them down, then.'

'Do, quick. Then go.'

'So,' Will said. 'Kit is truly your master. Though look where his spying got him. A reckoning in a little room. Keep off it, Ben. Playwork is duller and pays less well. But it is safer.'

'Go now. He will be up. He does a day's work before breakfast.'

Will sat, in groom's livery, too long in the anteroom. He had spoken of his business to secretaries of progressively ascending status, and none would come alive to the urgency of it. One had even said: 'If you would speak of plots for new plays, then must you go to the Lord Chamberlain. Here be grave matters in hand.'

'You will be at no graver work than the scotching of this that I tell you of.' Weary, three hours gone by, Will took to sketching of a drinking song he had been asked for by Beaumont, something for a comedy to be called *Have at You Now Pretty Rogue* or some such nonsense:

> Red wine it is the soldier's blood
> And if it be both old and good
> So take a rouse
> And let's carouse
> And

Strange, he had been infected by Ben's feigned unreformed eucharisticism. No, it was tother way around. Blood turned to wine, not wine to. His head was spinning with lack of sleep, he needed much sleep these days, past his best, looking westward. He began to calculate his fortune in real estate, but that led him to things needful to be done in Stratford. The load of stone still encumbering the grounds of New Place and neither paid for yet by the Council nor taken away. His brother Gilbert had written of some odd useful acres he might – He was shaken to here and now by the top secretary, who said:

'You are to come in. And quickly, rouse. My lord speaks of urgency.'

'He was not very urgent in speaking of it.'

'Come your ways.'

Robert Cecil, Earl of Salisbury, big-headed and dwarf-bodied, stood with his hunchback turned to the great seacoal fire. Papers, papers everywhere. He said:

'I am glad, albeit it be brief, to make acquaintance of the man. The plays I know. Your *Amblet* was fine comedy. What is this story?'

Will told him. 'And Master Jonson fears for his life now. He deserves, if I may say this, my lord, very well of you.'

Cecil picked up a letter from his desk. 'This has but now come to me. You know of a certain Francis Tresham Esquire?'

'His name is, I think, on the list I gave.'

'He has a brother-in-law, Lord Monteagle. Lord Monteagle has sent me a letter from this Tresham, and it saith nought but this: "They shall receive a terrible blow this parliament, and yet they shall not see who hurts them. The danger is past as soon as you have burnt this letter." As you see, it was not burnt, nor will it be. I am conveying it at once to His Majesty. So what you bring from Master Jonson conjoined with this does but confirm what the King will say he knew all along, that he hath enemies.' Cecil smiled very thinly. 'Moreover, it would seem that his dreams are often charged with what may be termed a *memoria familiaris*. Blowing up comes much into them. His father, the Lord Darnley, was, as you will know, blown skyhigh at Kirk-o-Fields in Scotland while his royal mother was dancing at some rout or other. So, I thank you for this your loyal work —'

'A tragedy, good my lord.'

'It might well have been so.'

'No, no, my play, which some call *Hamlet*.'

'Was it so? I remember laughing. Now I will remember the intention was tragic. And remember too to have Master Jonson out of the jail where he languisheth as soon as the conspirators be apprehended.' Cecil gave his hand, very crusty with rings, to Will. Will was not sure whether he was meant to kiss it. But he shook it sturdily and left.

When Ben Jonson was let out of jail he went straight to William Shakespeare's lodgings in Silver Street and said:

'Let us drink.'

'Ben,' Will said, 'if you mean we are to go again to this low papist tavern full of vomit —'

'Nay, show sense, man, that was but show. That was part of the part I played and played well. I am as good a son of the English Church as any that was fried under Bloody Mary, and I will prove it Sunday by drinking the whole chalice off before all the world. I say let us drink. I say also let us eat, it being near noon. I have good King's gold here.' He made jangle the little purse at his waist or no-waist. Clink clank. 'We will eat roach pie and flawns at the Mermaid.'

Ben told it all over the fishbones and pasty fragments. 'Of course,' he said, 'the King will have it that he foreknew all. Let them, says he, get in theirrr Godless butts of gunpowderrr and I myself, laddies, will marrrch thither with guarrrd and witness to prrrove it was no tale. So he did, and so he says that he has singlehanded saved the rrrealm. Will you come to the hanging?'

'I will not.'

'Squeamish as ever. Twelve men swinging aloft in the sun and enow guts and blood and hearts ripped out to feed the King's kennels a whole day. There is a little book to come,' he coughed modestly.

'I thought you were waiting to print all your plays, such as they be, in one great book called Ben Jonson's *Works*, mad notion. Or is it epigrams and corky expatiations all in Greco-Latin?'

'I will let pass your pleasantries. This little book will have no name of author below the title, though all shall know from the mastery whose it is. The title is to be *A Discourse of the Manner of the Discovery of the Late Intended Treason.*'

'That is too long.'

'Have a care, man. It is the King's own. And it is to be spread abroad that the King's self had the writing of it but was too royally modest to set his name thereto. It is a terrible false world.'

Will now quoted from something he was writing. 'We have seen the best of our time. Machinations, hollowness, treachery, and all ruinous disorders follow us disquietly to our graves.'

'You sound as though you cite somewhat from some new kennel of misery you are hammering together unhandily.'

'A tragedy, aye. About a king that insists on divine right and knee-killing deference and fulsome fawning and will not have the plain truth. He is cast out into the cold and goes mad and dies.'

'A care, Will, a care.'

'It is for the court.'

'O Jesus, O blood of Christ not really present on the altar. You will be hanged and quartered like any Guy Fawkes.'

'I care not. We have seen the best of our time.'

When Christmas came to court, Lear, done by Dick Burbage, ranted and tore his beard, and Queen Anne slept or woke and pouted at what seemed most unseasonable for Yule, a time of drunken showing of one's legs in some pretty wanton masque, while James drank steadily and chewed kickshawses offered by a succession of lords on bended knee. After the play he ranted. The Grooms of the Royal Bedchamber were there, in livery after their acting, yawning, Will among them, hound-weary, half-listening.

'Therrre ye see, my lorrrds and ladies and guid laddies a'', what befalleth a king that trusts too much in human naturrre. It is the trrragedy of ane that insisteth not enough on his divine rrricht. He lets gang the rrrule o's rrrealm tae ithers. Weel, thank God though I hae drrrunken sons I hae nae ambitious dochters of yon stamp. Aye aye aye.' Then he suddenly shouted: 'Kingship, kingship, kingship,' so that many of the drowsy started full awake. 'I was but rrreading in the Geneva Bible this day, aye, and find therrre mickle to offend, aye. Much flouting I find of the divinity of kingship in the saucy marrrgins therrreof. Aye, I was in the rrricht of it, the divine rrricht I may say, to hae thrrrown oot of the rrrealm a buik nae matterrr hoo holy that hath been defiled by the pens of Godless rrrepublicans, aye. It is verrry parrrtial in its notes and glosses, verrry untrrrue, seditious, and savourrring tae much of dangerrrous and traitorrrous conceits. When, my lorrrd arrrchbishop, shall we see our ither, our new, our Godly?'

'They are hard at work, your grace,' said the Archbishop of Canterbury, huge archiepiscopal rings of weariness under his eyes. 'All fifty-four translators, all six companies. Andrewes and Harding and Lively report well of the progress of the holy work and say but four years more will see it sail gloriously all pennants flying into port.'

'So Harrrding looks lively and Lively labourrrs harrrd, eh, eh?' There was loud and immediate laughter that went on long while the King beamed around and said: 'Aye aye aye.'

Will could see that his majesty was looking in vain for a pun that should bring Lancelot Andrewes, head of the Westminster translating groups, into his fancy. Without premeditation, Will came out, in a firm all too audible actor's voice, with:

'Each Bible scholar, so the ungodly say,
Works *lively hard Eng*lishing for no pay
The royal Bible, aye, *and rewes* the day
When such an unholy labour came his way.'

There was a terrible silence into which the King waded rather than leapt. He said:

'And wha micht ye be, laddie? Wait noo, I ken, I ken, ye are he that wrrrit the play of this nicht, are ye not?'

'Aye, William Shakespearrre, yourr majesty,' Will said, hearing with horror an effortless parody of the royal accent.

'Ye maun wrrrite it doon, you saucy blasphemous irrreverrrent and impairrrtinent lump o' clairrrty doggerrrel, that all may see, laddie.'

'I have forgot it already, your royal majesty,' Will said, hearing in horror the faint traces of the sobbing Danish intonations of the Queen.

'Aye.' It was clear that James did not know well what to do. Will had often met this situation when being unpremeditatedly pert to the great. He now willed the King out of his problem. *Be sick, great greatness.* 'Aye, ye and yourr saucy rrrhymes.' He looked green and began to heave. It was, indeed, the usual end of a court soirée. Some writer of music for the virginal, Tomkins or somebody, had spoken of producing a tiny sequence consisting of the King's Rouse, the King's Vomiting, the King's Rest. 'I maun gang,' the King said, very green. 'I mind ye, laddie, I'll mind yourr sauciness.' Then, on the arms of two simpering earls, he was led away to the Harington water closet, invention of the late Queen's godson, Britain's contribution to the civilization of Europe.

'By Christ,' Burbage said, 'you get away with murder.'

'What Ben Jonson says. Thank God our revels now are ended, aye.'

When, much much time later, Ben Jonson was let out of jail he went straight to William Shakespeare's lodgings in Silver Street and said:

'Let us drink.'

'Ben,' Will cried. 'Your ears are untrimmed and your nose whole. I'm glad to see you well.'

'But thirsty.'

'Drink water then. It seems to me that less and less of wine makes in you more and more of oppugnancy. If this drunken watch-beating continues it will be a matter of one day's holiday between longer and longer lingerings in the Clink.'

'The Marshalsea. Listen. It was a strange time. I worked on the Bible.'

'What?' They went down the stairs, past Mountjoy scolding his daughter Marie for loving the apprentice Belott, into the street, demoted to lead by the dull day. There were more drunk about than usual, belike because of the dull day. 'The Bible, this I know, has already been worked on, nay worked out. They are at the great final stage of the galleys. And it is Harding and Lively and Andrewes, not you, that had the making of it. You are a man of some small reasonable talent, Ben, but you are no man of God. It is work for men of God that gratuitously or necessarily know Greek and Latin and Hebrew.'

'I know all those tongues,' Ben said. 'I can Hebrew you as well as any clipped rabbi. It is, indeed, the work that comes before the final launching that has made lively my days in the stinking rathole of the Marshalsea. For, since I am a poet, they brought to me the poesy of the Bible. Meaning Job and the Psalms and the like. You are a poet, they said. Tickle our sober accuracy into poetic life. So I dip quill in horn and correct the galleys to a diviner beauty.'

'Who brought the galleys and said all this to you?' Will said with some jealousy.

'Some man of the Westminster company – Bodkin or Pipkin or some such name. No whit abashed at the prospect of seeing God's work buffed and polished in a foul and pestilential prison. The apostles, he said, were in prison before being variously crucified.'

'That will not be your fate. Whatever your fate is, it will not be that. That is the fate of the godly.' And then, before they entered the Dog Tavern, 'Is it you only of all our secular versifiers that are bidden trim the sails of the galleys?'

'Oh, there is Chapman, also Jack Donne – not properly secular, there is talk of his taking holy orders this year. Marston's name was mentioned but I was quick there. If, I said, you want a Bible that beginneth with *In the initialities of the mondial entities the Omnicompetent fabricated the celestial and terrene quiddities*, then have Jack Marston by all means. There were others mentioned, smaller men.'

'Was I,' Will asked, 'mentioned?'

They sat down not far from Beaumont and Fletcher with their one doxy who, being born under the sign of Libra, was fain to bestow kisses and clips equally on both. When the jug of canary came Ben was able to have his laugh out.

'Why do you laugh? What is risible in me or others or elsewhere?'

'There were special orders that you should not be brought in. No Latin or Greek nor Hebrew – that was brushed aside as of small moment. But the King has a long memory and himself said that he would not hae that quick laddie that was perrrt with his imperrrtinencies.'

'How do you know this?'

'There is some foolish rhyme fathered on you about the King sticking his lively harding andrew up the translators to make them come quicker and threatening to cut off their old and new testicles if they did not. It could not be you, it is too corky and bad even for you. But I will be kind. You shall not be out in the cold like the foolish virgins. I, Ben-oni, the Benjamin that Jacobus loveth, though he cannot keep me out of jail, I am ready to deliver sundry psalms into your palms.'

'Is there money in it?'

'Honour, glory, perhaps an eternal crown.'

'I am done with all writing,' Will said, 'even for money. I grow old, I grow old. I am forty-six this year. I will retire to Stratford and hunt hares and foxes.'

'You would rather be hunted with them. And you have said this too often before of being done with writing. You will go and stay a week and then be back here thirsting to write some new nonsense. I know you.'

'You *poets*,' Will said, 'may keep your Bible. You may stuff your old and new testes up your apocrypha.'

'There speaketh sour envy. Well, we will keep it and be glad. For the day may come, some thousand years hence, when even the *Works* of Ben Jonson will be read little, but the bright eyes of Ben Jonson will flash out here and there in a breathtaking felicity of phrase from the green Eden of God's own book that may never die.'

'You may stick your holofernes up your methuselah.'

'Master Shakespeare,' said Frank Beaumont timidly, 'there is a matter we would talk of, to wit a collaboration betwixt you and us here.'

'She hath enough to do fumbling two let alone three.'

'I mean with Jack here and myself. A comedy called *Out on You Mistress Minx* which must be ready for rehearsing some two days from now and not yet started though the money taken. You are quick, sir, as is known. A night of work with Jack and me as amanuenses and it can be done. We can pay a shilling. It is safe here in a little bag in Kitty here her bosom.'

'I have done with writing,' Will said proudly. 'I go to tend my country estates. All you *poets* may stick your zimris up your cozbis.'

'Well bethought and *à propos* and *a proposito*. We were held up in our playwork by the need to work on the Song of Songs that is Solomon's for Dekker that hath an ague. Kitty here gave us a good phrase. Love, she said, is better than wine. Is not that a good phrase?'

'She carries two fair-sized flagons on her, I see. If by love she means comfort more than intoxication, then she is not right.'

'*Comfort me with flagons*,' Beaumont said to Fletcher. '*Flagons* is better than *apples*. Make a note.'

'You may all,' Will said, getting up, 'comfort your deuteronomies with your right index leviticus. I go now.'

'It is jealousy,' Ben said when he had gone. 'He has no part in the holy work.'

Will rode to Stratford nevertheless with three or four psalms in galley proof in his saddlebag, a gift from Ben Jonson. He was to see what he could do with them; to Ben they seemed not to offer matter for further poeticization. But for Will there would be much non-writing work in Stratford, save for the engrossing of signatures. The hundred and twenty acres bought from the

Coombes which Gilbert was managing ill: these must be worked well. Gardeners needed for gardens and orchards. The tithes in Old Stratford and Welcombe and Bishopston. He, Will, was now a lay rector, a front-pew gentleman. Thomas Greene, the town clerk, together with his bitch of a wife and the two beefy squallers named Grayston and Hamnet, Gray and Ham, should be out of New Place by now, the lease up on Lady Day, 1610, this year. Forty-six years of age. Four and six make ten. One of the psalms in his saddlebag was number 46.

New Place, when he got there, was bright as a rubbed angel, Anne his wife and Judith his daughter yet unmarried having nought much to do save buff and sweep and pick up hairs from the floor. The mulberry tree was doing well. Anne was fifty-four now and looked it. Ben was right: his home was a place for dreaming of going back to; he would be back in London before the month was up, nothing more certain. On his second day home a murmuration of blacksuited Puritans infested his living room. Anne gave them ale and seedcake. They had a session of disnoding a knotty dull point of scripture, something to do with Elijah or some other hairy unwiped prophet. When they came out of the living room to find Will poking for wood-worm at a timber in the hall, they sourly nodded at him as if to begrudge his being in his own house. The following day they came again for a prayer meeting. He spoke mildly to Anne about this black or Brownist intrusion.

'While I am here,' he said, 'I will not have it. Tell them that, tell them I will not have it.'

'They are godly,' she said, 'and a blessing on the house.'

'I can do without their blessing. Besides, their aliger faces show no warmth of blessing.'

'They know what you are.'

'I am a gentleman with an escutcheon. I am, moreover, one of the King's servants. I am, I do not deny, also a player and a playmaker, but that was the step to being a gentleman. Will they begrudge me my ambition?'

'Plays are ungodly, as is known. They will have no plays in this town. Nor will it avail you aught to flaunt your king's livery in their faces. They know that kings are mortal men and subject to the will of the Lord.'

'Genevan saints, are they? Holy republicans? What do they say of Gunpowder Plot?'

'They said that it showed at least a king might be punished for his sins by an action of the people, though to put down the Scarlet Woman of Rome is no sin and the voice of a papist is no part of the voice of the people.'

'God help us, Christ give us all patience.'

'You blaspheme, you see, you are in need of the power of prayer.'

'I am in need of nothing, woman, save a quiet life after a feverish one. I would have some seedcake with my ale.'

'There is no crumb left and there has been no time for baking.'

'If you must give up your hussif's duties in the name of dubious godliness, at least there is an idle daughter who could set to and bake.'

'Judith hath a green melancholy on her. It is a sad life for the girl. None asks for her hand.'

'Ah, they cannot stomach to have a player as a father-in-law. Well, at least Jack Hall takes me as I am. Jack is a poor physician but a good son-in-law and husband and father. Susannah, thank God, has done well.'

Susannah came next afternoon, with her husband Dr Hall and little two-year-old Elizabeth. Will played happily with the child and sang, in a cracked baritone, 'Where the Bee Sucks'. Anne said with suspicion:

'Is that from a play?'

'Not yet. The play that it is to be in is not yet writ, but it will be, fear not.'

'I fear not anything,' Anne said, 'save the Lord's displeasure.' She called to Judith to bring in ale and seedcake. Seeing married Susannah and the child now drowsy on her lap, Judith let out a howl of frustration and left. Anne said:

'It is the father's office to seek a husband for a daughter. Judith is ripe and over-ripe.'

'So ripeness is not after all all,' Will sighed. 'I will go seek in the taverns and hedgerows, crying *Who will wed a player's brat?*' He turned to Jack Hall, whose lips were pursed, and said, 'Will you come stroll a little in the garden?'

Jack said, after a strolling silence, 'Your book has been read here, you may know that.'

'What book?'

'The book that is called *Sonnets*.'

'But God, man, that is old stuff, it came out all of a year ago, and I have disclaimed the book, I did not publish it, it is pirate work. What do they say that read it, not that I care, does it confirm them in their conviction of Black Will Shakebag's damnation?'

'It is a book of things that a man might do in London,' Jack Hall said gloomily. 'It is pity that Dick Field brought home a copy.'

'Ah, poor corrupted Stratford. So you too join the headwaggers?'

'There is such a thing as propriety. Dick Field has been long a London man like yourself, father-in-law, but he has ever shown propriety. He hath printed foul stuff enow in his trade of printing, but he hath not the filthy ink of printed scandal sticking to him. You will, I trust, forgive the observation of one who is, besides your daughter's husband, a professional man and also your physical adviser.'

'Dick Field is a man tied to a cold craft, not one like me who has had to make himself a motley to the view and unload his naked soul to the world.' Then he said, 'What has being my physical adviser to do with the book that is called *Sonnets*?'

'I have wondered at times about your cough and your premature baldness. Now I read records of licentiousness in that book.'

'You mean,' groaned Will, then gasped, then growled, then cried aloud, 'I have the French pox, the disease of that pretty shepherd Syphilis of Fracastorius of Verona his poem? Oh, this drinks deep, this drinks the cup and all. And what thinks your sainted mother-in-law?'

'She knows nought of it. The book has been kept from her and from her friends the brethren. The bridge of the nose,' he said, squinting, 'seems soft in the cartilage. That is an infallible sign. Do keep your voice low. It will crack if you shout out so and not easily be mended.'

Will howled like a hound and strode into the house to his study, passing his womenfolk on the way. He growled at them, even at gooing little Elizabeth. In his study he took from a drawer the galleys of the psalms that Ben had given him. He took them, waving in the draught of his passage, to shake like little banners

at his family, crying, 'These, you see these? The King's new Bible
that is not to appear until next year, given to me in part, along
with my brethren the other poets of London, that the language
be strengthened and enriched. You think me godless and a libertine
but it is to me, me, me, not the black crows of Puritans that daily
infest this house and shall not infest it more that the task of
improving the word of the Lord is given. You see,' he said to Anne,
'you see, see?'

'A new Bible,' she said. 'It is all too like what one may expect
of unreligious London, where the holy Geneva Bible is not good
enough for them. That it is the King's Bible renders it no whit
more holy. Nay, less from what we hear. Even kings are subject to
the law.'

'The King,' Will cried, 'is my master and bathed in the chrism
of the Lord God. Generous and good and holy.' Then he stopped,
seeing he had gone too far. 'The King hath his faults,' he now said.
Yes, indeed: ingratitude to Ben and himself; pederasty; immoderate
appetite; cowardice, but half the man the old Queen had been.
'But still,' he said, and then: 'All men have their faults, myself
included. But I deserve better of the world and of this little world,
and, by God, I will have my eternal reward.'

'That,' said Anne, 'is the foul sin of presumption.' Jack Hall was
now back with them, listening to his father-in-law rave, grow quiet,
rave again: infallible symptoms.

'My name I mean, my name. My son, poor little Hamnet, dead.
And the name Shakespeare dishonoured in its own town and soon
to die out along with the poor parchments that put innocent words
in the mouths of players.' Jack Hall shook his head slightly: self-pity
too perhaps a symptom. 'Wait,' Will cried. 'Do not leave. I, your
king, lord of this disaffected small commonweal, do order you to
wait. Wait.' And he sailed back to the study, galley pennants flying,
and took the forty-sixth psalm out of the bundle. He sat to it,
calling 'Wait wait' as he dipped quill in ink and counted. Forty-six
words from the beginning, then. It would do, the change improved
not marred. He crossed out the word and put another large in the
margin. He then, ignoring the cry or cadence *Selah* at the bottom,
counted forty-six words from the end, felt awe at the miracle that
this forty-sixth word too could be changed for the better, or

certainly not for the worse, by the neat mark of deletion and the new word writ clear and large in the margin. 'Wait,' he cried. Then he was there to show them.

Anne's jaw dropped as in death. Susannah, whose sight was dim, squinnied at the thing he had done. Jack Hall said, 'This is also a –,' and then kept his peace.

'You see, you see? To do this I have the right. I am not without right, do you see? Now another thing. On Sunday I will read this out in the church, aye, in Trinity Church during matins will I, and eke at evensong if I am minded to do it. For I am a lay rector. Not without right. And I have a voice that will fill the church to the rafters, not the piping nose-song of your scrawny unlay rector, do you hear me? *Non sanz droict*, which is the Shakespeare motto, and the name too shall prevail as long as the word of the Lord. Now, mistress,' he said to Anne, 'I would have supper served, and quickly.' Then he strode out to stand beneath his mulberry tree, granting her no time to rail.

On Sunday morning he stood, every inch a Christian gentleman in his neat London finery, on the altar steps of Trinity Church. Family, neighbours, the scowling brethren, shopkeepers, nosepicking children filled the pews. His voice, the voice of an actor, rose clear and strong:

'This Sunday you are to hear not the Lesson appointed for the day but the word of the Lord God in a form you do not know. Next year you will know it, for it is His Majesty King James's new Bible. But now you have this for the first time on any stage, I would say any altar. The word of the Lord. The forty-sixth psalm of King David.' He read from the galley expressively, an actor, clear, loud, without strain, so that all attended as they were in a playhouse and not in the house of God:

> 'God is our refuge and strength; a very present helpe
> in trouble. Therefore will not we feare, though the earth
> be removed: and though the mountaines be carried
> into the midst of the sea. Though the waters thereof
SHAKE/ > roare and be troubled, though the mountaines ~~tremble~~
> with the swelling thereof. Selah.
> There is a river, the streames whereof shall make glad

the citie of God: the holy place of the Tabernacles of
the most High. God is in the midst of her: she shal
not be mooved; God shall helpe her, and that right
early. The heathen raged, the kingdomes were mooved:
he uttered his voyce, the earth melted. The Lord of
hosts is with us; the God of Jacob is our refuge. Selah.
Come, behold the workes of the Lord, what desolations
hee hath made in the earth. He maketh warres to cease
unto the end of the earth: hee breaketh the bow, and
SPEARE/ cutteth the ~~sword~~ in sunder, he burneth the chariot in
the fire. Be stil, and know that I am God: I will bee
exalted among the heathen, I will be exalted in the
earth. The Lord of hosts is with us; the God of Jacob
is our refuge. Selah.'

He ceased, looked fearlessly on them all, then stepped down, with
an actor's grace, to return to his pew. One man at the back, forgetting where he was, began to applaud but was quickly hushed.
Before Will arrived at his seat, Judith said to her mother:

'I wonder that God has not struck him down.'

'Wait,' Anne said grimly. 'The Lord does things in his own good
time. Fear not, the Lord will repay.' Will sat down next to her.
Then, having looked on her and Judith and Susannah and Jack
Hall and Mrs Hart his sister with a peculiar lingering hardness, he
knelt and prayed. He prayed long and with evident sincerity, so
that his wife grew tight-mouthed with suspicion. Then he got up,
looking much refreshed, sat down and waited till the dull long
sermon was finished. Then he said very clearly to Anne and, indeed,
to any on the pew that would hear:

'I am minded to turn papist.'

'God forgive you. Keep your voice down. This is not place nor
time for atheistical japes.'

'I will turn papist.' He tasted the term gently then gently spat it
out: *tpt*. 'I will not say that. It is a word of contempt. More, it puts
overmuch emphasis on the Pope of Rome. It is the faith that matters.'

'Be quiet,' she said in quiet fury. The service was continuing,
and eyes were on Will, ears striving to pick up his words.

'Catholic,' he said. Then he said no more. She remained

tightlipped. He did not speak of the matter again in the two days more he remained in Stratford.

When Ben Jonson was let out of jail he went straight to William Shakespeare's lodgings in Silver Street. Before he could say aught of going out to drink, Will said:

'I have writ this new play. It is called *November the Fifth*, but Burbage will doubtless change the title as he always does. It is based on Gunpowder Plot.'

Ben sat down carefully on a delicate French chair. 'It is based on —'

'Gunpowder Plot. There is a king that is a fool and an ingrate. He believes that God exists but to confirm the holiness of his kingship. Conspirators led by a poet seek to destroy him for his blasphemy.'

'A *poet*?'

'I had you much in my mind there. Not a very good poet and most apt for meddling in state matters. His name is Vitellius. Here is one of his speeches. Listen.'

'No,' Ben said. 'Let me read instead.' He looked at the fair copy that was also the first draft and read to himself:

> Conserve agst ye putrifyinge feende
> The fathe yt fedde oure fathers, quite put doune
> His incarnacioun in thes worst of tymes,
> Casting hys hedde discoronate to ye dogges.

Then he said: 'They will not let you. This will be construed as present treason.'

'I am sick of it all,' Will said. 'The black bastards of Puritans in Stratford that will have nothing but grimness, and a church that is the lapdog of a slobbering king and no king. My father died quietly in the old faith, I will die more noisily in it.'

'Have you spoke of this yet to any?'

'To my lord Cecil, aye, and he said he needed no more spies aping to be papists to dig out popish plots. I have said it to many, but none will take it that I mean what I say. It is part of the peril of being a player, that all one says is thought to be but acting.'

Ben said, 'The great work is now in page proof. They expect it to be out in the new year.'

'What is all this to do with what I said?'

'The forty-sixth psalm has *shake* and *speare* in it.'

'That is not possible. None would have it, this I knew. It would be seen as bombastic and overweening.'

'Tillotson, one of those charged with the overseeing of our emendations, said that the two words came nearer to the original than what they formerly had.'

'That is not possible.'

'He had never, I could see,' and Ben smiled sweetly, 'heard of the name Shakespeare.'

'Let us,' said Will, 'go and drink.'

2

ZARF.

Enderby came fighting awake with the word halfway down his nose. With too an unexpected and certainly premature homesickness for La Belle Mer in Tangiers, expressed in thirst for tea made with six Lipton sachets in the mug with the blazon CHICAGO — MY KIND OF TOWN. His men, Antonio, Manuel and the lad from Tetuan called Tetuani blowing on boiling lemon tea in glasses inserted in handled metal zarfs or zarfim. Windy Tangerine morning.

The mug had been given him by a Jewish visitor to Tangiers, citizen of that city full of wind, who claimed acquaintanceship with a Jewish novelist called Bellow, name appropriate to a windy city. Enderby did not read novels. Even less did he practise the craft of prose fiction, but he had published much earlier in the year a short or shortish story. This was in response to a Canadian university magazine's begging for free contributions, preferably money but prose acceptable. He had submitted a fantasy about Shakespeare's free contribution to the King James Bible. That was why he was on this aircraft now. They rode over an endless bed of dirty whipped cream. High above the wind.

He had had the fantasy in mind ever since the sneering response to his *Collected Poems* in the British literary press. Shakespeare must have suffered the same kind of self-pity, doubt as to validity of vocation and all the rest of it, reading sneers from MAs Oxon. and Cantab. in duodecimo summations of the proto-Elizabethan literary achievement, the greatness of Munday, Tibbs, Gough, Welkinshaw and other swollen poetasters, bellowsed by bribed or sincerely stupid criticasters. But Shakespeare could comfort himself by stroking his coat of arms and thinking on the swelling of his acres and bags of malt stored up against the next eagerly awaited famine. He, Enderby, could not in honesty find a germane comfort in his proprietorship of a Tangerine beach restaurant with changing rooms for pustular bathers.

In the aircraft a film was proceeding. It was, to Enderby, a silent film, for he had no headset as it had been called. He had been unwilling to pay 3 dollars 50 for the hire of the apparatus. In front and behind and to his left fellow passengers were undergoing each the private experience of hearing shouts and screams and the roar of flames as people were burned alive in an aircraft. It was a very indiscreet sort of film.

He would, he had said a month ago, addressing himself to a bloody shave, write no more verse. There was nothing else to write about. Yet here he was being commissioned to write not only verse but mock Tudor dialogue. A musical play on the career of William Shakespeare to celebrate, for the commission was inevitably American, the second American centennial conjoined with the three hundred and sixtieth anniversary of Shakespeare's death. It was not immediately clear what connection there could be between the death of a poet and the birth of a sort of nation, and Enderby puzzled fuzzily, as the burning aircraft struck the sea and presumably sizzled, about the arithmology of the conjunction. 360. It was well known that Thomas Jefferson, Augustan voice of liberty, had possessed 360 slaves. With 360 degrees a wheel came full circle. With two centuries you came full circle twice. It was all a lot of nonsense.

The film ended with certain people wet but rescued and then an endless rolling list of the film's perpetrators. Plastic blinds were pushed up and the cabin's ports let in sick light. All that dirty whipped cream. The man next to Enderby removed his headset and said:

'It was about this aircraft catching fire.'

'So I gathered,' Enderby said. 'A visual experience really.'

'I guess you could say that.' He was middle-aged, overfed, and his face flaunted peeling shards of scarfskin from, Enderby divined, exposure to the Spanish sun. The plane came from Madrid. 'Guess,' he said, doing it with thickish fingers, 'I'd better adjust my watch to Chicago time.'

'My sort of town,' Enderby said.

'Is that right?'

'No, it's on this mug I have. For tea, that is.'

'Is that right?'

If he could have tea now, *real* tea, not the gnatpiss they prepared in that sort of galley there, he would have it with seven sachets, not six. As you got older you required your tea stronger, that was laid down somewhere. Enderby was getting old.

Not too old though, by George or by God, probably the same person, for some new small adventure. The world of the theatre or theater, by Godgeorge. America, by Gorge. He had gone, on receiving the letter, to his private quarters to look up Indiana in *Everyman's Encyclopaedia*, an oldish edition but, if the place at all existed, it would probably be there. It seemed at first not only there but very big and exotic, but it was India he was looking at. Indiana was, he found, just under India House, demolished 1861. N. central state of the USA, generally known as the Hoosier State. 91 per cent of total area farmland. Iron, glass, carriages, railroad cars, woollens, etc. Climate remarkably equable. Leading cities Indianapolis, Fort Wayne, South Bend, Evansville, Gary. Terrebasse not mentioned. The theatre in Terrebasse was called the Peter Brook Theater. He looked up in another volume Brook, Peter, but found no information. Some local villainous benefactor requiring memorialization perhaps. He said to the man next to him, hands on lap, watch adjusted:

'Hoosier.'

'Pardon me?'

'The Hoosier State.'

'That's what they call Indiana.'

'Why?'

'If you're from Indiana you're a Hoosier.'

No help there. He did not much like the sound of it. It sounded like the kind of jeer which might well greet, in a territory nearly all farms, a sensible stage presentation of the main facts of the life of a major poet.

The man reimposed his headset, get his money's worth, and turned a little black dial on his seat arm. 'Foog,' he said with disgust.

'Pardon me?', this being apparently the right mode of request for repetition or elucidation.

'This guy says they're going to play a foog.'

'Fugue,' Enderby said with energy. 'Tyranny of the verse line. They say there's no rhyme for fugue. But in song there is. Another fugue, oh, please no, Hugo. You can rhyme anything in a song. In Massachusetts ah took the pledge. Each glass ah chew sets mah teeth on edge.'

'That's it, I guess,' the man said; not listening, turning the black knob to, Enderby supposed, something infugal.

Enderby took from the inside pocket of his decent though oldish clerical grey suit the letter from Ms Grace Hope, a name he could not believe. Hollywood agent mixed up for some shady reason with play promotion. Understood from Toronto office Enderby only man who could do it. On strength of Toronto published work called *Will and Testament*. Enderby occasionally feared that the letter, having been maliciously typed in disappearing ink, might emerge from that pocket a folded blank. Fare and expenses recoverable, but must pay them himself first. Artistic director, Angus Toplady, was, he being a director, to direct. Long creative discussions required, meaning everybody wanted to be called creator nowadays. Consequence of death of God or something. Music to come from pencil of Mike Silversmith, valued client of Ms Hope. It was all there, though stained with strong tea and fried eggyolk and hamfat, breakfast reading. Frank Merely, London associate at World Creation in Soho Square, arrange contract. Enderby doubted the reality of all these names.

Well, the place would continue languidly to run in his absence. A home, after all, for Antonio, Manuel and Tetuani. They were good boys really, despite their kif and buggery, as honest as could be reasonably expected in a Moroccan ambience. A sufficiency of farinaceous meals in the kitchen, a doss down wherever it was convenient to lay the night's mattresses, the odd sly nip, though *haram* for Tetuani, from the bottles behind the bar. With their master away they would all sleep on his floorbed, covered with sheepskins. On his return they would still be there tiredly sweeping and frying, though reporting no profit with triumphant teeth, since no profit was better than a loss.

A beefy voice announced through static an impending descent to O'Hare Airport. There Enderby must find an aircraft that would take him to Indiana. There he was to be picked up by some minion of Toplady, who was possibly a debased descendant of the author of *Rock of Ages*, and be driven to a Holiday Inn, though not for a holiday. Having seen on Spanish television a film with Bing Crosby about the pioneering of this hotel chain, Enderby had an image of a large shack of decayed wood with snow swirling about it. But this was autumn, or the fall, and, the weather of Indiana being equable, there would probably be no snow.

A silly asthenic corn queen came round collecting headsets. The neighbour of Enderby gave his up and then turned to Enderby as if, he relieved of the responsibility of using it, the two of them could settle to an urgent colloquy necessarily deferred. 'This your first visit?' he said.

'To where?'

'To the States.'

'Well, yes, though not, I assure you, for lack of previous invitations. I should have gone to New York to become a professor for a time. A consequence of *The Wreck of the Deutschland*, *you know. It was a question of one or the other. So I chose this. More creative than Creative Writing, if you see what I mean.'

'Is that right?'

'More or less. A blasphemous cinematic adaptation of a great mystical poem, and I was involved, though in a way unwittingly. I didn't intend it should turn out the way it did.'

'Is that right?'

'Very much so.' Enderby had not been speaking English for a long time. It struck him that he was speaking it now as from a book. He must do something about making it more colloquial. 'Putting

*See *The Clockwork Testament*.

the boot in,' he said. 'The Nazis shagging coifed nuns. Violence and violation. Too much of that around.'

'You can say that again.'

'Too much of that around.'

This man did not, as might be expected from even an enforced companionship of several hours, assist Enderby on his entrance to a strange land. He was quick to get away with no valediction. Enderby was on his own. O'Hare Airport seemed very large. The immigration officials seemed to let everyone in, even Americans, very grudgingly and only after looking up every name in a big book like a variorum edition of something. But Enderby was eventually permitted to have his luggage examined with great thoroughness. The examiner of luggage was a hard man in outdoor middle age.

'What's this?'

'A kind of denture adhesive or tooth glue. A Spanish product. For affixing dentures to the gums or, in the case of the upper prosthesis, to the hard palate.'

'What?'

Enderby was roughly prevented from demonstrating. The stomach tablets came under closer scrutiny. The customs officer took samples of each in little vials.

'For dyspepsia,' Enderby said, and demonstrated the sonic aspects of the condition.

'You mean you got a bad stomach?'

'Only after eating. The food on the plane was bloody awful. They warm everything up, as you know.'

'Why,' the officer asked with great earnestness, 'are you entering the United States?'

'To work in what you people call a theater.'

'You an actor?'

'I am a poet. I am Enderby the poet.'

'*What?*'

'If you want proof,' Enderby said, coldly pointing to his messed up shirts, 'there are my poems.'

The officer picked up the book with the tips of his fingers. He opened it. 'Don't make much sense to me,' he said.

'Every man to his trade. What you're doing with people's luggage doesn't make much sense to, ah, myself. So there we are.'

'Listen, fella,' the man said quietly but rudely, 'I got my job to do, right?'

'And I mine.'

'There might be narcotics in those things you got there for your stomach, right?'

'Not right. I never touch them. Seen too much of the effects. But I thought we were talking about poetry.' The people behind Enderby were looking at their watches and muttering for Chrissake, as in an American novel. Enderby was growlingly let go. He walked long and in some pain through several miles of airport building. Twinges in the left calf, cholesterol buildup. There were a lot of irritable people, also shops and restaurants. He saw many copies of his own mug on sale. When he came to the place where it said INDIANAPOLIS he was exhausted. He would have given anything for a mug, CHICAGO MY KIND OF or not, of very strong tea. He compromised with a couple or so capsules of Estomag, chewing them vigorously. An eager shifty thin little man in jeans and a dirty singlet came up to him and said: 'Hi.' He had a shock of wirewool hair but was not Hamitic. Nor Japhetic either. 'Mike Silversmith,' he said.

'How did you know it was. Recognition, I mean.'

'You opened that bag to take out that stuff that's all round your mouth. There's a book in it with your name on.'

This was not the kind of assumption that Enderby liked. People with names like Gomez or Krumpacker could conceivably be comforting their journeys with the *Collected Poems*. Conceivably, only just. Enderby wiped his mouth with his hand. 'The composer,' he said.

'Right.' He sat without invitation next to Enderby. 'I got these cassettes in my bag here already. They'll knock you. "To be or not to be in love with you". Then there's "Tomorrow and Tomorrow"'

'And Tomorrow,' added Enderby. 'It's three times. But it's me who's doing the words.' Colloquial was coming nicely back to him. Anger was paying its first visit. He had thought it might be like this.

'You and Shakespeare,' Silversmith said. '"To be or not to be in love with you". You take it from there. But you hear the tune first.'

'How about the words I've written already and which, presumably, you've seen. Already,' he added.

'Never get in the charts with them.'

They were summoned aboard by a man in a powder blue blazer.

'What,' asked Enderby with care, 'kind of an orchestra do you propose?' A black child clinging to its necessarily black mother's hand looked up at him. They were shuffling aboard. Silversmith was in front of Enderby. 'Viols,' proposed Enderby, 'recorders, cornetts, tabors. Authenticity.'

But Silversmith was addressing the imbecilic stewardess as honey. He knew her, he had come this way before. Or perhaps not. Enderby was obliged to sit next to Silversmith and then to put on a headset attached to a Japanese cassette recorder which Silversmith eagerly took from a scuffed bag. 'Listen,' Silversmith said. Enderby heard a voice, Silversmith's from the sound of it, scrannelling perverted words from *Hamlet* while a guitar thrummed chords.

> 'To be or not to be
> In love with you,
> To spend my entire life
> Hand in glove with you.'

Then the voice, having no more words, lahed and booped on to the end, which was the same as the beginning. Enderby carefully fastened his seatbelt. He as carefully freed his ears of the noise and the foam rubber. Silversmith said:

'You take it from there, right?'

'Wrong,' Enderby said. 'If you think I'm going to permit William Shakespeare to sing inanities like that —'

'What's that word?'

'Inanities. It's a desecration.'

Silversmith sighed. 'I can see,' he said, 'it's going to be like I told Gus Toplady it was going to be. You got too many long words in that thing you sent him. You got to consider the public.'

'I've got to consider Shakespeare.'

'Ah, Jesus,' Silversmith said.

'After all,' Enderby said, 'we were all warned.'

'Warned about what?'

'About disturbing his bones. There's a curse waiting.'

'Yeah, sure,' Silversmith said, and he pretended to go to sleep. The aircraft started to bear them to Indianapolis.

3

'More of a prologue or induction really,' Enderby said.

'In what?' somebody crossly asked.

'Come, come,' Enderby said in an unwisely schoolmasterly tone. 'You all remember your *Taming of the Shrew.*'

This resident company, lounging in deplorable rags in a kind of classroom complete with blackboard, did not seem to like being instructed in the terminology of drama by a man in a decent, though old, clerical grey suit. Their director was not dressed like that. He was too old, though, for the coûture and coiffure he affected. Dirty grey sculpted sideburns. Silk shirt of black covered with sharpnosed Greek heroes in gold in postures of harmless aggression. Grey chest hairs and dangling medallions. Chinos stained at the crotch. Bare feet in fawn suede cowboy boots. Enderby felt he himself was there as for the reading of a will, which in a sense he was.

The people not there were the people who should have been there. But Shakespeare was to be played by a film actor who was the husband of Ms Grace Hope, and he was making a film. The dark lady who was to play the Dark Lady was completing a nightclub engagement. *Hamlet* without the prince, Enderby had quipped. Gus Toplady had morosely replied that he had tried it in Minneapolis at the Tyrone Guthrie but it had not really worked. Hamlet off stage all the time, Rosencrantz and Guildenstern eavesdropping on inaudible soliloquy. What's he say now? He say he not know whether he live or die but he use too many big words. Toplady had done a nude *Macbeth* somewhere. He appeared to have little confidence in Enderby. Enderby reciprocated with all his heartburn.

'Shakespeare,' Enderby said, 'is dying. His ageing wife and two daughters sit by his bed, the wife audibly jingling two pennies. These are to put on his eyes when he shall finally close them.'

'Why?' asked a girl whom Enderby knew to be Toplady's mistress.

'The custom in those days. These are not what ah you would call pennies. Not cents I mean. Big pennies. English ones.'

'Okay,' Toplady said without compassion. 'He's dying. Forget the pennies.'

'You can't,' Enderby said. 'Shakespeare says: "Ah, I hear you jingling your pennies to put on my eyes. Do not fret, wife. I shall not keep you waiting long." Then, though it's still April, he hears the song of boys and girls bringing in the May. They sing the ah following:

> 'Bringing the maypole home,
> Bringing the maypole home,
> Bringing the maypole home,
> Bringing the maypole home.'

'A deathless lyric,' Toplady said.

'There's more to it than that,' Enderby said, red. 'It goes on:

> 'Custom has blessed this strange festivity,
> Licensing every gross proclivity,
> Here's the year's nativity,
> Here is life, let's live it.
> To sin it is no sin
> When spring is coming in.'

He looked round for a positive response, but there was none, except of vague incredulity. He pushed on sturdily:

'In his dying delirium he sees the mayers prancing about the deathchamber, his younger self and Anne Hathaway among them. He says: "Thus it began. She overbore me in a wood. Needed a husband, even though one ten years younger. Susannah there born but six months after the marriage." Himself dying and his surrounding family fade into blackness, and the younger Shakespeare, whom we will call Will for brevity, is sitting in a chair nursing his son Hamnet.'

'What happens to the singing and dancing?' asked somebody.

'That is ah sung and danced off. But this is another May and Will hears the song in the distance. He hugs his little son and sings to him as follows:

> 'Little son,
> When I look at thee
> I am filled with won-
> Der such wonder should be.
> Part of me yet no part of me,
> Wholly good yet the wood of my tree.
> If I could
> I would live to see
> Fulfilled in me
> The man that I can never be,
> Born to property,
> Richly clad retainers about thee.
> Hawk on hand,
> You survey your land,
> Your acres shining in the summer's gold
> And I behold
> The glory of a name
> Restored to fame
> It had of old.
> Little son,
> If these things should be
> And I die before they are granted to thee,
> Think of me as he who carved them
> From the wood
> For the wood of my tree.'

There was a silence. Toplady said to Silversmith, who lay on the floor: 'Mike?' Silversmith pronounced:

'I say what I said already.' Toplady said with cold eyes to Enderby: 'Go on. But cut out the lyrics.'

'But the whole of this ah induction is done practically entirely in song.'

'Go on.'

'Well,' Enderby said, 'Will goes to the window and looks up at the clear night sky. He sees, but we do not see, Cassiopeia's Chair, a constellation in the shape of an inverted W, the initial of his name. He sings to it.'

'Ah Jesus,' said Silversmith from the floor.

'He sings to it as follows:

'My name in the sky
Burning for ever,
Fame fixed by fate
Never to die.
At least
I feast on that dream,
The gleam of gold, my fortunes mounting high.
To render my deed
More than pure fancy,
On lonely roads I must proceed,
My one companion a dream,
A seemly vision only I espy!
My name in the sky.

'But then his wife Anne appears and sings a contrary song which combines in counterpoint with Will's:

'Will o' the wisp,
A foolish fire,
Leads fools to fall
In mud and mire.
Better by far
The fire at home,
Smoke in the rafter,
Lamb's wool and laughter –'

'What,' Toplady's mistress asked, 'does lamb's wool have to do with it?'

'Lamb's wool,' Enderby authoritatively defined, 'was an Elizabethan drink for cold weather, consisting of heated ale mixed with the pounded pulp of roasted crab apples, which fragments

floated in the ale like the wool of lambs in a high wind. Seasoned
with nutmeg, cinnamon, ginger and cloves. Highly fortifying.'

'You'd have to have a programme note,' said a bearded youth,
'or some guy standing there to stop the song and explain it.'

'Push on,' Toplady said in the tone of one who leads a toiling
party through a high wind.

'Anne finishes the song:

> 'Will o' the wisp,
> Do not desire
> To follow fame,
> That foolish fire.
> Better by far
> The fire at home,
> Fresh dawn on waking
> And fresh bread baking.
> A will o' the wisp
> Should not aspire
> To be a star.'

'Mike?'

'Like I said already.'

'But,' pleaded Enderby, 'they both hear approaching song. It is
the company of players known as the Queen's Men. They have
been playing in Stratford and are now leaving it, with their property
carts and clopping horses. The troupe sings:

> 'The Queen's Men,
> The Queen's Men,
> Not beer-and-bread-and-beans men
> But fine men,
> Wine men,
> Music-while-we-dine men.
> The Queen's Men,
> The Queen's Men,
> Of-more-than-ample-means men,
> Are off now,
> Doff, bow,

We will come again,
The Queeeeeeen's Men.'

Enderby prolonged the long vowel in a gesture of song: 'Hearing
it, Will says: "By God, I will go with them. I will become a player
and eke write plays —"'

'Why does he go eek?' a fat frizzy girl in crimson asked.

'Eke means also,' learned Enderby said. 'Cognate with German
auch. But he can say also if that is what is, ah, desired.'

'That is, ah, desired,' the girl said.

'He says to his little son: "I will be back with fine gifts for
Hamnet. And eke Susannah and Judith. And eke their mother." Or,
if that is still desired, also. Anne sings her Will o' the Wisp song
and Will his Cassiopeia song again, and both are in counterpoint
to the song of the Queen's Men. The scene ends. The curtain goes
up almost at once on Elizabethan London in the full flush of
victory over the Spaniards. A song is sung which begins with a
kind of ah fart —'

'Your first job,' Toplady said, 'was to find out about the stage.
This stage has no curtains. Go and look at it sometime. No curtains.'

'Except for someone,' Silversmith said obscurely from the floor.

'A sort of er fart,' Enderby went on, 'like this:

'Prrrrrrrp
We ha' done for the Don,
Clawed off his breeches
And rent every stitch he's
Had on —'

'Right,' Toplady said to the company, 'you can see a lot of work
has to be done yet, and our friend here says that this is only what
he calls an induction —'

'Shakespeare too,' Enderby cut in. 'You all know your *Taming
of the.*'

'Watch noticeboard for next reading call. Okay,' dismissively. To
Enderby he said: 'You and me and Mike have to talk. In ten minutes
in my office.'

'You,' Enderby said, 'do not appear to like the project.'

'I like any project that has a fart in hell's chance of working.
This project we've got to do. There's money gone into it from
Mrs Schoenbaum. She wants it and to Mrs Schoenbaum you don't
say no. But we don't do the project the way you see the project
or think you see it.' He breathed on Enderby and exuded a memory
of breakfast blueberry pancakes. 'Ten minutes in my office.' Both
he and Enderby had to leave by the same door, but it was if they
were to exit by opposed wings. Silversmith remained on the floor.
Enderby said harshly to him:

> 'Good friend for Jesus' sake forbear
> To dig the dust enclosed here.
> Blest be the man who spares these stones
> But curst be he who moves my bones.'

'That too,' Silversmith said, 'is a shitty lyric.' Enderby was
constrained, though silently, to agree with him. He then lost himself
in the bowels of the theater among shut cabin doors, fat heating
pipes, growling engines. A big place, he concluded, having passed
twice the same boilersuited men playing cards. At length he found
himself in the wings of a stage and he timidly ventured onto the
stage itself which, true, had no curtains and jutted far into an
auditorium far too large for the town of Terrebasse but not for
playgoers from the state capital, which was near. Less shyly, he
moved downstage in the dusk mitigated by a working light and
tried certain lines:

'By God, I will follow them to London and make my fortune
there, acting plays and eke writing them.' Terrible. A man who now
appeared in the wings with a hamburger seemed to think so too,
for he clapped faintly.

Enderby went down to the auditorium and through it, uphill,
to doors which led to a wide corridor. Then there were stairs and
he came to the administrative area, where girls and grown women
were typing. He was somewhat late. Toplady glowered from his
open office. Silversmith was already lying on the floor. Toplady's
office was full of framed posters of his triumphs in high colour
and fancy lettering. Toplady drank coffee from a paper cup and so,
with some loss of the substance, did Silversmith. No coffee was

offered to Enderby but a chair was. Toplady sat behind his desk.
He said:

'What's the story?'

'The story, yes. Shakespeare, or Will as we may call him for
brevity's sake, said that already, sorry, leaves wife and children in
Stratford and goes to London. He sees how the Londoners like
violent sports like bearbaiting and beheadings at Tyburn, so he
writes the most violent play ever written. I see you presumably
know it, Mr Ladysmith, since a poster there says you once directed
it. Not a good play. In fact,' he said daringly, 'a lousy one.'

'Go on.'

'This leads him to the *Henry VI* plays and the friendship of the
Earl of Southampton and at least acquaintanceship with the Earl
of Essex, who wants to be king of England. Then there is *Richard
III*, which leads him to the Dark Lady. She sees the play and falls
for Burbage who plays the lead, and wants him to come to her
bed with the announcement at the door that Richard III is here.
But Will gets there first and is at his work when the announcement comes and says tell him William the Conqueror comes before
Richard III.'

The anecdote made Enderby smile but the two others remained
gloomily watching. He continued:

'The Earl of Southampton takes the Dark Lady away from him
and he falls into depression and whoring and drinking. You could
have a song about that,' he suggested.

'Depression, whoring and drinking,' Silversmith sang from the
floor.

'And then comes the news that his son Hamnet is very sick.
He rushes to Stratford to find his boy dead and being buried. But
he becomes a gentleman. Too late, too late, alas. This,' Enderby saw
fit now to explain, 'is a play about guilt.'

'Go on.'

'End of first act. Second act Will is involved in Essex rebellion
through putting on *Richard II*, which appears to justify usurpation.
He sees Essex beheaded and fears he will be beheaded himself.
But the Queen tells him to stay out of the big world of politics.
He is a little man, she says. He goes home to Stratford and looks
after his land and sues everybody in the manner of a country

gentleman. Then he dies. A brief outline only.' Silence. 'It could be expanded.' Silence. 'A lot of things happen really. Marlowe, Ben Jonson. Sex and murder.' Silence. 'No limit to dramatic possibilities. Gentlemen,' he added.

'You know what this is really about?' Toplady eventually said.

'Of course he could have syphilis, if that would help at all. He probably did have. Marvellous description of symptoms in *Timon of Athens*. Read it sometime. Nose dropping off, voice getting hoarse and so on. Everybody had syphilis in those days. America's gift to Europe. All the world's a tertiary stage, he might have said. I don't know why I'm telling you all this.'

'What I said,' Toplady said more loudly though untruthfully, 'is that this play is about its two stars.'

Enderby coldly answered his cold stare. 'You mean,' he said, 'like the *Guide Michelin*?' He had no confidence whatsoever in Toplady.

'I mean,' Toplady said, 'Pete Oldfellow and April Elgar. They're the stars. You'd better believe it. You can't put April on for a single scene and then shovel her off like dogshit. Once she's there she's there. You see that?'

'I don't,' Enderby said, 'think I know the lady. The name, of course. Elgar's great name. But I thought the family had died out. Worcestershire, as you know.'

'April is black,' reproved the voice from the floor. 'April is only Worcester in the sauce sense. April is the hottest property. April is tabasco.' Enderby listened with unwilling approval. This was pure poetry.

'April Elgar,' Toplady explained, 'is a great singing star. You don't seem to realize what's on here. We take this show to Broadway by way of here and Toronto and Boston. It could run for ever.'

'Why,' Enderby asked, with seeming irrelevance, 'did you pick on me?'

'Had to pick on somebody,' Toplady said. 'We didn't want one of these professors. Mrs Schoenbaum has to be convinced she's getting what she asked for. Meaning Shakespeare. Now get this first act ready. Shakespeare comes from Stratford bringing his kid with him.'

'Hamnet? But he didn't. Hamnet stayed with his mother.'

'You may,' Toplady said, 'think I'm an ignorant bastard, but I know what I don't know. More important, I know what *you* don't know. What you don't know is what really happened. Okay, who's to say he didn't bring his kid with him? He brings his kid with him but he protects him from the dirty world. He puts this dirty world on the stage. The Dark Lady comes into his life. He neglects his kid and his kid dies – plague, mugging, falls from a scaffold, gets roughed by a mad horse, gang rape, anything will do. So, right, you can have your guilt and remorse or whatever the hell it is.' He scooped the gift towards Enderby with a Toledo dagger Enderby assumed was used as a paper-knife. 'She leaves him for this other guy, the Earl of Southampton or Sussex. She's got ambitions, right?'

'Essex. But look here –'

'Who cares what sex, right, but she's back in Act Two. In Act Two Shakespeare wants his son back so he turns him into Hamlet, and Shakespeare plays the Ghost.'

'You got that from –'

'Never mind where I got it. The rebellion's because she wants to be queen. She only gets to be queen in Shakespeare's dream. She becomes Cleopatra. When he's sick and losing his teeth and getting old, she drops him. But she's really his mooz.'

'His what?'

'His inspiration. Fella, you have enough to be getting on with. But remember we don't have all that much time.'

'Right,' came, unurgently, from the floor.

'My title,' Enderby said. With great reluctance he had to admit to a faint admiration for Toplady. Horribly blasphemous and obscene though it was, he seemed to know what he wanted.

'Your title is out. Who wants to see a musical called *Whoever Hath Thy Will*? There's a lot round here can't say *th*. I thought of *Goats and Monkeys*. You know where that comes from.' He nodded up at a poster advertising his production of *Othello*, in which everybody in the blown-up photograph of turmoil on Cyprus seemed, except for Othello, who, in his general's uniform, looked like Patton, to be black. 'That's our working title, anyway. Something else may turn up. There's a room and a typewriter along there. You'd best get moving.'

Enderby humbly obeyed, or at least got out of there. Silversmith said: 'Your first lyric is the Tomorrow and Tomorrow one. Get it finished today.'

4

In the dark bar of the Holiday Inn, whisky sour before him, Enderby wrote a lyric:

> Give the people what they wish:
> Something trite and tawdry,
> Balladry and bawdry –
> Give the people what they wish.
> Give the groundlings what they crave:
> Bombast and unreason,
> Dog and bitch in season,
> Prophecies of treason
> Rising from the grave.
> Pillaging and ravishing and burning,
> Royal heads and maidenheads
> Presented on a dish,
> In a pie.
> Let them eat their stinking fish –
> What they find delicious
> Soon will seem pernicious.
> When the time's propitious
> That diet will cloy,
> They will come to enjoy
> What I wish
> What I wish
> What Iiiiiiiiiiiiiii
> Wish.

Let that bloody Silverlady or Topsmith try that one, see what his rhythmical sense was like. Enderby began to sketch the dialogue that followed. He preferred to work here than in the room they had given him. Too many people kept looking in to see how he was getting on. The mistress of Silvertop came twice to giggle. She was a thin long girl with red hair who was to play Queen Elizabeth. Enderby had set his scene in a brothel. Will in the dark with a spot on him while singing. Lights come up to disclose whores in undress. Henslowe with his account book. He frowns on Will and waves him away.

'State your requirements to the madam. She will be down anon.'

'No no no. It is you I want. Or him there, your son-in-law. Master Alleyn, that is.' For Ned Alleyn has appeared, putting his doublet on.

'I know you, I think,' Henslowe says. 'You owe me fourpence.'

'I owe nothing, not to any man. Forgive my seeking you here. I have a play.'

'Ah, sweet Jesus, will they never give up?'

'Listen. You may have it for nothing if it runs not more than three afternoons.'

'A prodigy,' Alleyn says. 'He owes no money and he gives things away.'

'Listen. I'll be brief. The scene is Rome. A barbarian empress is captured by the Romans but allowed her liberty. Hating the Romans nevertheless, she urges her sons to ravish a noble matron.'

'Why?' Alleyn asks.

'A sort of revenge. Listen. The sons kill the matron's husband, then ravish her on her husband's dead body, which serves in manner of a bloody mattress. Then, that the wretched woman may not tell, they cut out her tongue.'

'Go on. To hear costs nothing.'

'That she may not write the names of her ravishers, they cut off her hands as well.'

'Dirty stuff,' says Henslowe. 'Go on.'

'But she takes a stick between her two stumps and then scratches her ravishers' names on the earth. Then her father avenges her.'

'Ah' from both.

'He kills the sons and he grinds up their bones to a flour.

With this he makes a coffin of pastry. The filling is the cooked flesh of the two sons.'

'Indigestible,' says Alleyn. 'Let me see your script.'

'More indigestible than Tyburn hangings and quarterings? Then he invites the mother to a cannibalistic feast. There is also a black villain that gets the Gothic empress with child – a black child.'

'"He cuts their throats – He kills her – He stabs the empress – He stabs Titus – He stabs Saturninus –".' Alleyn riffles through.

'And the Moor, a sort of black Machiavelli, he is buried up to his waist and left to starve.'

'Delectable,' says Alleyn, and he declaims:

> 'Ah, why should wrath be mute and fury dumb?
> I am no baby, I, that with base prayers
> I should repent the evils I have done.
> Ten thousand worse than ever yet I did
> Would I perform, if I might have my will.
> If one good deed in all my life I did,
> I do repent it from my very soul.'

So then the lights go out on that side of the stage, and on the other side the lights go up, those same final words of Aaron the Moor sounding again through the theatre, electronic blessing, as a ballet of stabbers and ravishers and poisoners prances to a music of screams and groans. Boys carrying publicity posters – HENRY VI I II & III – RICHARD III – thread through the dancers while Will, downstage centre, repeats his song. He makes way for Alleyn as Richard Crookback, who delivers a bloody speech. Lights go up on previously darkened segment to show the Dark Lady with her duenna, rich brown flesh and diamonds and crimson brocade, watching and listening intently. A note is passed to Alleyn as he exits. All this might do very well. Enderby stopped scribbling on his yellow legal pad. If they could get somebody to do better let them bloody well get on with it. He raised his empty glass to himself and also to the shortskirted blonde matron who was waiting on. He deserved another of those.

He had, he had to confess, given in to those two in some measure. The travelstained Warwickshire yokel, snotnosed son held by the hand, gawking in a London street. Growling bear led off to its baiting. A severed head or two gawking back at Will from gatespikes. Bosom-showing wenches. Hucksters. A bit like a dirtied-up opening for *Dick Whittington*. And then Will sings to Hamnet:

> Tomorrow and tomorrow and tomorrow –
> That makes three.
> The first tomorrow is for me.
> The second tomorrow – we.
> The third tomorrow – thee.
> I start with my poetic fame,
> I then restore the family name,
> And last of all I see
> Thee –
> Sir Hamnet, Lord Hamnet
> The day after the day after tomorrow.
> I pledge that these things shall be.

Terrible, but the music was terrible. Henslowe follows his growling bear. Will follows Henslowe. Good idea: Hamnet, left outside the brothel, finds his way in, seeing lust and bosoms. The beginning of his corruption. Two first scenes there in, as they said, the bag. The company could start rehearsing.

Enderby looked at his watch. Time to ask somebody at the front desk to seek him a taxi. He had to go to dinner at Mrs Schoenbaum's. Toplady, thank God, would not be there: there was a play on and he had to give his troupe confidence by glaring at them from the wings. The play was some libellous nonsense about the Salvation Army by a dead German named Brecht. Silversmith had taken a flying, literally, visit to New York to superintend what he called the pressing of an album, old-fashioned phrase recalling the crushing to death of flowers in young ladies' commonplace books.

He got a taxi with small difficulty. 1102 Sycamore Street. What's that number again, mister? The driver, a white man with Silversmith wire-wool hair, seemed to be, as they said here, stoned. He growled all the time like Henslowe's bear. 1102. Ain't never heard of that number. I can assure you it does exist. What's that you say, mister, and so on. There were no sycamores. Sumachs, rather, and a kind of hornbeam or *carpinus betulus*. The driver seemed dissatisfied with his tip. He looked at his ensilvered palm as though Enderby had spat into it.

Enderby was let in by a muttering black man in a white jacket. Mrs Schoenbaum was there in the hallway to greet him. 'Mr Elderly? We are so honoured,' honored, really. Enderby shyly took in riches. Daubs on the walls which must be what were known as rich men's impressionists, cost millions. He knew that Mr Schoenbaum was dead from making money. Mrs Schoenbaum was clearly enjoying her widowhood. She wore a kind of harem dress of silk trousers and brocaded sort of cutdown caftan. Her silver hair was frozen into a photographed stormtossed effect, clicked into sempiternal tempestuousness on a Wuthering Heights of the American imagination. Her eyelids were gold-dusted and her lips white-lacquered. Her nose looked as though its natural butt had been surgically cut off. She took Enderby by the hand and led him into a salon with more daubs discreetly lighted. Enderby tottered and then recovered on bearskins laid on pine overpolished. 'Whoops,' Mrs Schoenbaum said, holding on to his hand. 'I'm sure,' she said, 'you know nobody here.' That was true. An evidently hired youth playing cocktail tripe on the Bechstein in a far corner sent over to Enderby a vulgar conspiratorial look. Enderby was introduced to two overweight men who got up from a couch as long as a barge with some difficulty. A middle-aged woman laden with beads did not, quite rightly, get up, but she fixed Enderby with eyes of hate. One overweight man was from the University of Indianapolis. The other seemed to be a lawyer or something shady of that kind. Enderby did not catch the names. 'Mrs Allegramente,' or something, said Mrs Schoenbaum, 'has promised to demonstrate her powers for us after dinner.' This Mrs Allegramente said, as Enderby boarded the couch and accepted a whisky with ice from the muttering black:

'When are you British going to quit Northern Ireland?'

'Which British do you mean?' Enderby asked with care.

'You colonizing British who are holding that poor country in a vice of disgusting tyranny.'

'Nothing to do with me. Ask Henry VIII and the Tudor founders of the Protestant plantation,' he jocularly added.

'I have already. A fat disgusting man with his mouth full of chicken bones.'

Mad. Good, he knew where he stood, lay rather. He too would have difficulty in getting up. The lawyer said:

'You just come over now then?'

'Well, yes. From Tangiers, where I live. I have ah severed connections with my country. Not its language, of course, nor its literature.'

'Mr Elderly,' Mrs Schoenbaum said, 'is a distinguished writer. He is doing this thing for us here. The life of Shakespeare set to music.'

'I guess so,' the lawyer said. He accepted more whisky. He and the black flunky grunted at each other. The distant pianist struck up a version of 'Greensleeves'. He knew what was wanted.

'Henry VIII himself wrote that,' Enderby blurted. 'A musician as well as a ah distinguished tyrant. Some of the words are obscene.'

'That figures,' Mrs Allegramente said. The academic said:

'Mrs Schoenbaum has done a lot for William Shakespeare.' He gave out the full name as though Mrs Schoenbaum had, for good reasons perhaps of an ethical nature, ignored the rest of the family. But Mrs Schoenbaum at once discountenanced that supposition by saying:

'Well, like I always said, Irwin, that's only natural. I am,' she told Enderby, 'related to the Shakespeares. By marriage, of course.' Enderby nodded. These American women were very straightforward people, quick to disclose their madness. The men were a little slower. These here would, after a few more whiskies, give out their madness with a circumspection proper to the professions they practised. 'Not, that is, through Mr Schoenbaum, of course, whose family was from Germany, but through the Quineys.'

'Thomas Quiney,' prompt Enderby said. 'He married Judith Shakespeare on 10 February 1616. Shakespeare had only a couple of months of life left after that. The shock did his health no good. A low tavernkeeper already convicted of fornication. The tavern he kept was called the Cage, an appropriate name considering the poor girl's virtually incarcerated condition. A barmaid. Now the place is a place that sells hamburgers.'

'Is that so,' said rather than asked the lawyer. Mrs Schoenbaum seemed unabashed by the details. She said:

'The Quineys emigrated to America and married into the Greenwoods, which is my family.'

'Under the Grünbaum tree,' unwisely quoted Enderby, 'who loves to lie with me.'

'Well, Greenwood was not always the name, as you so er quickly devised. But I got back to the baum bit with my late husband.'

'A lovely man,' obituarized the lawyer.

'He called me Queenie,' Mrs Schoenbaum said, 'when he found out that's how Quiney was sometimes pronounced. He spent much time and money, Mr Elderly, on my geneography. He was deeply interested. But my real name is Laura.'

'And my real name,' Enderby said, 'is Enderby. Not Elderly.'

'We're all getting on a little,' said the academic called Irwin, 'except for our lovely hostess. And, of course, for Mrs Allegramente.' The young man at the piano called across the room over his rolling chords the word shit. Mrs Schoenbaum said:

'There's no call for that language, Philip. My son,' she confided to Enderby. 'He is very unsociable.'

'He has a considerable social gift,' Enderby said. 'He er manages that superb instrument with great panache and er vivacity.'

'Do you have children, sir?' the lawyer asked in an accusatory manner. His thick eyebrows, Enderby now noticed, had been given, perhaps by art, a devilish upsweep at the outer edges. He had several chins.

'I think not,' Enderby said. 'Paternity, however, is said to be a legal fiction.'

'Surely, surely,' Mrs Schoenbaum seemed to soothe. 'And are they properly looking after you at the place where you are staying?'

'It is the Holiday Inn,' Enderby said. 'I cannot get tea. It's as bad as France with this dipping of bags into tepid water. I asked for one of their big coffee jugs to be filled with boiling water and for seven sachets to be steeped in it. They considered this to be British eccentricity.'

Mrs Allegramente, responding to the signal British, said: 'You better quit Northern Ireland right now if you know what's good for you. I can read the signs.'

'She has great gifts,' Mrs Schoenbaum said, 'as we shall see demonstrated after.'

'What they did,' Enderby continued, 'was to put *three* sachets in a jug which already contained what they call coffee. The manager was not helpful. So I bought my own apparatus.'

'You did, eh?' said the academic with uncalled-for animation. 'You went out and bought the wherewithal and now make tea of the required strength in your own room?'

'I most certainly did and do. A kind of kettle and a big mug. Condensed milk. A box of sachets from a store called CHEEP CHEEP with the recorded song of a canary playing all the time.'

'Is that so? Is that really so?' The academic's pisshued eyes glowed with interest. 'It's in the private sector that the major events of human life occur. Ah,' he said, 'here is Lucille.'

'My daughter,' Mrs Schoenbaum said. A girl with jeans and a tee-shirt came in saying hi to everyone. The tee-shirt had Shakespeare as bigfisted flying Superman on it with the legend WILL POWER. 'She is a dropout.'

Enderby assumed that the term, combining knockout and cough-drop, was a slangy tribute to beauty not at once apparent. 'She certainly is,' he said. She advertised the lipoid virtues of what he had heard called junkfood, presumably food for junkies, whom, living in Tangiers, he knew all about. A girl greasy as though basted. He was glad when she said she had to split. She had things to do with her friends, to whom too she would say hi. She took her big worn blue arse away. She collided with the black servant who came in to say they could all eat if they wanted. Mrs Schoenbaum told him that Philip would not be eating with them, an aspect of his unsociability. The black man could give Philip a sandwich and a coke. The black man seemed to demur and said things unintelligible but certainly rebellious in tone. Everybody helped each other to get out of the couch barge. Enderby slithered on wool and high polish. The black man cackled.

The dining room was like a great tomb with votive flowers and candles. Enderby could not see into its corners but he observed over his head an untenanted minstrels' gallery. There were high-lighted what he took to be Cézannes, bad paintings of apples and bottles. 'Paella,' Mrs Schoenbaum announced, pronouncing the double clear L as a single dark one. 'In honour of our guest who lives where it is part of the kwee zeen.'

'Never see it in Tangiers,' Enderby said. 'Couscous country.'

'Is that so,' the lawyer said. The dish that the black man grousingly put on the table was all shells and bits of rubber and soggy rice. There was chlorinated water but no wine. You were supposed to bring your highball in with you. Enderby had finished his. He had been placed next to Mrs Allegramente. She now started again on the theme of suffering Ulster. Enderby was fed up. He said:

'Get this straight. I was brought up an English Catholic. I've no time for those bloody Orangemen there. They say an Orangeman's dinner consists of roast spuds, boiled spuds, chips and croquettes.'

'Is that so.'

'Pudgy bastards who discharge their carbohydrated energy in gross tribalism. No time for the sods. So hand the place over to the IRA for all I care. But it's no business of the Yanks.'

Mrs Schoenbaum was a polite hostess. She ignored her British guest's snarl and said: 'I hear great things of our project. I understand that things are going really well.'

'Conflicts,' Enderby said, and spat a bit of shell onto his fork end. 'They will all be resolved. This was your idea, or so I'm credibly informed.'

'It was the idea,' Mrs Schoenbaum said, 'of the Bard himself. Ask Mrs Allegramente.' Enderby choked. 'He spoke from the Happy House and said he was delighted that America had achieved two hundred years of free nationhood. He wished to be associated in song and dance with our celebrations.' Enderby looked darkly, in the dark, at Mrs Allegramente, who looked, though chewing something unchewable, darkly back. 'After dinner we shall tune in to him again. It's a great privilege,' said Mrs Schoenbaum.

'He will not speak to the sceptical,' Mrs Allegramente said.

'What,' Enderby asked, 'is this Happy House you spoke of?'

'The mansion of the blessed,' Mrs Schoenbaum said. 'He is with his fellow writers. He sent greetings from John Steinbeck, who would not speak for himself.'

'I met Steinbeck,' Enderby said, 'when he was given, unjustly I thought and still think, the Nobel, oh I don't know though when you consider some of these dago scribblers who get it, think it was an unjust bestowal. There was a party for him given by Heinemann in London. I asked him what he was going to do with the prize money and he said: *Fuck off.* Before he could apologize, the academic said:

'Don't apologize. *Oratio recta.* Such a response I find deeply interesting. The private sector of a man's life.'

'This was in public,' Enderby said. 'I apologize for what he said,' he said to Mrs Schoenbaum. Mrs Schoenbaum, who evidently heard worse from her children, inclined queenlily. 'I trust,' he said with swimming brain, 'the er bard keeps his language clean.'

'He will not speak to sceptics,' Mrs Allegramente said.

'What kind of sceptics do you have in mind? People who believe his works were written by the gonorrheal Earl of Rutland?'

'People who do not believe in the open line to the beyond,' she said. 'I don't think there's any use proceeding tonight,' she told her hostess, who moaned in distress:

'Oh, Mrs Allegramente.'

'You must flout the sceptic,' the academic said. 'You do not preach to the converted.'

'I don't like,' Enderby said, seeing in gloom a big cake like an Edwardian lady's hat swim from darkness to light and hearing coffee cups arattle, 'the assumption that I don't believe. I am, after all, a poet. There are more things, et cetera. Horatio,' he added to the lawyer. 'My stepmother,' he prepared to say.

'Perhaps you would prefer tea,' Mrs Schoenbaum said. Enderby heard a black whine from the darkness.

'No, no, no. I shall have tea when I get back to my room. Along with the Late Late Show.'

'The Late,' the academic, 'Late,' tasting every word, 'Show,' said. It was clear he had never heard of it. 'That is an amusing locution.'

'It's on television every night,' Enderby informed him. 'An ancient ah movie interspersed with commercials for cutprice ah discs.' He accepted a plate of white and bloody goo. The lawyer now began to disclose his madness. He said:

'Don't knock free enterprise. Free enterprise made this country what it is.'

'I'm not ah er knocking anything –'

'We don't need smartass, pardon me Laura, Europeans coming over here to knock American institootions. This next year we have our bicentennial.'

'As I am certainly well aware. My heartiest felicitations.'

'We don't need smartass sarcasm, pardon me Laura and Mrs Allegramente, from smartass knockers of American traditions. We celebrate two centuries of American knowhow. Also liberty of conscience and expression.'

'I most heartfeltly congratulate you.'

'Don't give us that. There's a tone of voice that grates on me, pardon me Laura. We're your one bastion against the communist takeover. So don't knock.'

'I certainly will not,' Enderby promised.

'There you are again,' the lawyer cried. 'It's the tone of voice.'

'I can't help my bloody tone of voice,' Enderby countered with truculence. 'I can't help being a bloody Englishman.'

'Who,' said Mrs Allegramente, 'is oppressing the Irish.'

'Ah, hell,' Enderby said. He would have said more, but at that moment the son Philip lurched in, probably stoned. He clearly reserved articulacy to his pianoplaying, for what he said, though long and partially structured, made no sense. But his mother understood him, for she said:

'I've no intention of marrying him, do you hear me, Philip? I've no intention of dishonouring your dear father's memory.' Enderby nodded at this apparent Hamlet situation. He did not however understand why this Philip, his gaunt stoned face encandled and dramatically shadowed, should look menacingly at him, Enderby. 'He takes you for someone else, Mr Elderly,' the mother explained. 'Tell him that you are not who he thinks you are.'

'I am not,' Enderby said loudly, 'who he thinks I am.' And then, in Duchess of Malfi tones, 'I am Enderby, not Elderly. I am Enderby the poet.'

This quietened the son down somewhat. He grabbed himself a hunk of the carved goo from the table centre and left noisily ingesting it. 'Good boy, good boy,' the academic said in relief.

'I think I'd better go now,' Enderby said, getting up.

'Oh no, oh no,' Mrs Schoenbaum cried in new distress. 'Mrs Allegramente has to convince you.'

'I'm already convinced,' Enderby said. 'There is a Happy House far far away.'

'*Not* far away,' Mrs Schoenbaum cried. 'Let's start, Mrs Allegramente.'

'Nothing will come through. Too much British scepticism around.'

'Let's have him telling us to get out of Northern Ireland,' Enderby suggested nastily.

'You see?' Mrs Allegramente said to Mrs Schoenbaum.

'Be good,' pleaded Mrs Schoenbaum. 'Promise to be good, Mr Elderly.' And she got up. Enderby muttered something about Mrs Allegramente's better being good, but this was not heard in the chairleg skirring. He followed his hostess and the others out. Their hostess led them to a small chamber off the hallway. The son was to be heard back at his piano, playing a single monodic line, one hand evidently busy with his goo. The black servant in the white coat nodded balefully at everybody, not specifically Enderby. He too seemed stoned. The small chamber was brilliantly lighted. There was a round table in the middle, four chairs of a dining order, a kind of throne for, presumed Enderby, Mrs Allegramente. 'No chicanery,' the academic said to Enderby. 'All above board. I have participated in previous sessions.'

'Is that so?' Enderby said. 'What is your ah specialization?'

'Pardon me?'

'You do what?'

'I run a course in theosophy. Saul Bellow is visiting us at the moment. He is deeply interested.'

'My kind of town.'

'Pardon me?'

'Be seated, all,' Mrs Schoenbaum invited. 'You will have the small lamp, Mrs Allegramente?' There was such a lamp on the table, a bulb of low wattage with a parchment shade. Enderby asked the theosophist in a low tone:

'Is that human skin?'

'Pardon me?' But Mrs Allegramente was already on her throne, breathing from the diaphragm. Look at the bloody man filling himself up with air. That had been said of AE, George Russell, prototheosophist, in sceptical Dublin. High on a throne like this, ready to speak of the maharishivantatattarara or some such bloody thing. Mrs Schoenbaum, very eager, turned out the bright main light. Shadows, shadows and shadows. She put Enderby as far away as possible from Mrs Allegramente or whatever her bloody name was. She said:

'We all join hands.'

So Enderby had the dry bones of the academic on his left and the soft supermarket turkey breast of the paw of his hostess to the right.

'We may have to wait quite a while,' Mrs Schoenbaum whispered to Enderby after quite a while of waiting. Enderby nodded that he understood, quite a while, feeling, with a sensation of faint horripilation, that it was colder than it ought to be. Mrs Allegramente encouragingly groaned. Enderby realized he had neglected to micturate for several hours. His bladder, encouraged by the cold and not giving a damn whether or not it was astral, happily, like a dog, pawed its owner for walkies. Mrs Allegramente went: 'Oooooooh.' There was a sound in the room like the tearing of paper. Enderby did not like this. His bladder importuned. Mrs Allegramente said:

'Is there anybody there?'

There was a more irritable papertearing noise and then, after a minute or so, a hell of a knock on the wall behind Mrs Allegramente.

'One knock yes, two knocks no?'

There was another hell of a knock, though as it were structured like a monosyllable.

'Is that William Shakespeare?'

'I'm getting out of here,' Enderby said, hearing the wall banged in a sort of proud affirmation.

'Shhhh,' went panting Mrs Schoenbaum. Mrs Allegramente asked:

'Have you a message for anyone?'

There was no reply. 'Bloody nonsense,' Enderby muttered. And then he heard knocking on the underside of the table itself. There were four swift knocks, then a pause. There were six swift knocks and a longer pause. There were four swift knocks, then a pause. There were six swift knocks and a longer pause. There were four swift knocks, then a pause. There were six swift knocks and then silence. The damned table all the time tried to leap, but the spirit fist was not strong enough to raise it. 'Oh Jesus,' Enderby muttered. Mrs Allegramente could be heard breathing with decent, or

non-spirit-raising, shallowness. 'No more?' Mrs Schoenbaum dared
to ask. They all broke hands. Mrs Schoenbaum went to flood the
room with decent brightness.

'It had the feel of a somewhat enigmatic message,' the academic
said as they all rose. Enderby said:

'Pardon me. I'm afraid I have to −' The lawyer grimly pointed.

Enderby found a small and overdainty lavatory off the hallway.
He pounded his load out furiously. Enigmatic message his arse. His
arse, thus invoked, spoke. 46 46 46. If that wasn't bible-amending
Shakespeare, who the hell was it? Enderby did not like any of this
one little bit. He wiped his penis on a handy face towel. Poor sod,
proud of his contribution to the King James psalms. And now these
New English Bible bastards had cheated him of his major triumph.
Enderby pulled a lever which flushed the bowl, and, while it flushed
still, left. Mrs Allegramente was waiting for him outside the door.
She said:

'The message couldn't be clearer. It was QUIT ULSTER QUIT
ULSTER QUIT ULSTER. Even you must have gotten the message.'

'Oh hell,' Enderby said, zipping up his not wholly zipped fly, 'it
could have been KEEP ULSTER or KILL ULSTER or EGGS BOILED or
BEER BLOATS or anything. But it was him all right. And you don't
know why, do you, eh?' He wagged a finger at her. 'Leave him
alone is my advice. Don't meddle. Good friend for Jesus' sake
forbear, remember that.' Aaaaaargh. That was his stomach abetting.
'I'm getting out of here,' he said. And to Mrs Schoenbaum, who
now hovered: 'I'd better telephone for a taxi.'

'Irving here,' Mrs Schoenbaum said, 'will drive you. It's on his
way.' The lawyer beamed unexpectedly and said with overmuch
cordiality:

'Well, sure, delighted.' This seemed to mean to Enderby that he
would be dumped somewhere, having first been pistol-whipped,
in the heart of flat Indiana. Enderby said:

'Thanks, but I don't want to cause trouble. A taxi will be fine.'
He felt, obscurely, that he was involved in the causing of a deeper
trouble than any there yet realized or, with such cultural equipment
as they possessed, could ever realize.

5

The coming of April Elgar was harbingered by Enderby's coming onto the top sheet of his Holiday Inn bed. So, at least, he was to surmise. The lavish ejaculation was unwonted. It woke him at the useless hour of 4 a.m. Remarkable in man of your age, Enderby. He had not been dreaming of anything very specific. Later he was to see this as confirmation of the power of a woman he had not even seen and knew to be, which was pretty far away, in Miami, Florida. But she was having her bags packed for Terrebasse, Indiana, or rather for the Sheraton Hotel in Indianapolis, she being above Holiday Inns. And she was shooting out powerful erotic rays.

Holiday Inn bedrooms always had two beds, a thoughtful provision. Before getting into the so far untouched dry one, Enderby tugged the wet sheet free of its anchorage and then wondered what to do with it. Leave it to dry naturally and it would dry crinkled, announcing to the world of gossipy chambermaids the poverty of Enderby's sexual life. So he soaked the defiled patch in hot water and stretched it over a flat matt heat source. Then, naked as he was, he put on his glasses to examine himself with some care. There was no prevision in this: it was the marginal response to a marginally erotic situation, to wit an unpurposed seminal discharge. But there was also the matter of a long bathroom mirror. In Tangiers he had only a round shaving glass. Here you were cordially invited to look at yourself all over, no extra charge. He looked with interest at a naked man with spectacles on and no teeth in. This latter deficiency he fumblingly rectified. Better, but how much better?

There was fat there, but it was not slugwhite fat. He had got brown in Tangiers. Occasionally he climbed to the roof of La Belle Mer to sun himself. The sun was there and might as well be used. Bronzedness had a flattening effect: the Enderby that looked with interest and even faint approval out of the mirror was a less three-dimensional Enderby than the one he had occasionally seen before in the old days, that was to say, in other bathrooms. The encroaching baldness he did not approve. There were one or two members of the troupe who wore cowboy hats all the time, and one who wore a kind of Balaclava helmet of leather with earflaps. But they all had ample uncombed hair beneath. There was a shop near to the hotel with toupees in it. There was also, in Enderby's suitcase, a flat tout's cap with a peak that went back a long way and whose provenance was now very vague. The cook Arry he had known so long ago? Cut out a art shairped croutong with a art cootter. For piling on damson jelly as an accompaniment to joogged air. Enderby removed his spectacles and dug the cap out. Naked, he squinted at himself with the cap on. Anything went down all right in this mad America.

Enderby turned up at the theater next morning but one in the tout's cap and an overcoat of faded plum. He removed the overcoat to reveal blue linen trousers, an open yellow shirt with crimson foulard and a seagreen cardigan. He wore no spectacles. He could see enough, and some things he did not wish to see – the face of Toplady in full definition, for instance. He had to read a new scene to Toplady. There was no music in it really, so Silversmith did not have to be there. Before Will's sexual triumph following *Richard III* it had been decided to bring in brief homosexuality, espionage, violence and frightful death, in other words Christopher Marlowe. This was to scare Will and make him pack his and Hamnet's traps and ride back to Stratford, but then the Earl of Southampton was to appear and tell him not to. That would lead to Dark Lady and Southampton taking her from Will and her getting mixed up with the revolutionary party led by Essex. Toplady sat behind his desk apparently wondering at Enderby's new appearance while Enderby read aloud. First, though, Enderby sort of sang.

> 'There will we sit upon the rocks
> And see the shepherds feed their flocks
> By shallow rivers, to whose falls
> Melodious birds sing madrigals.'

'Oh, good that, you must admit,' says Marlowe. 'Will Shakespeare here could not do as well.'

'Give me time.'

'Give us all time,' says Frizer.

'Amen,' says Skeres. 'But for some the time is ordained to be short.'

'Ah,' says Marlowe, 'very mystical and occult.'

'All may be clarified in time,' says Poley. 'Though not, of course, to everyone. You have worn a good cloak, Kit.'

'From the best tailor,' says Marlowe.

'I mean,' says Poley, 'the figurative cloak of your pretty songs about shepherds, and your loud brawling stageplays and your even louder atheism that the Privy Council chooses to ignore.'

'Ignore?' says Marlowe. 'I have been up before the Privy Council but recently. A matter of some blasphemous papers found in Tom Kyd's rooms. You know Tom Kyd, Will?'

'He wrote one good play,' says Will. '*The Spanish Tragedy*.'

The three men titter, and Will wonders why. Skeres says:

'That is not too apt. Much depends on what happens in the last scene. It is too soon to talk of the Spanish tragedy.'

'Come, come,' says Frizer, 'this is intended to be a merry meeting. Give me the lute and I will sing you a song, though not about passionate shepherds.' He takes the lute that Marlowe has been absently plucking and sings:

> 'As you came from the holy land of Walsingham,
> Met you not my true love by the way as you came?'

'Ah,' says Poley, 'he knows the name Walsingham. It was, after all, his master's. His ears pricked like a dog's.'

'Sir Francis Walsingham,' says Skeres. 'Dead these two years, but once head of Her Majesty's Secret Service. He recruited you, Kit.'

'Sing him more,' says Poley, so Frizer sings:

> 'I sing of a spy, of a spy sing I,
> That under the cloak of tobacco smoke
> And drink and boys and blasphemous noise
> Had sharp enough eyes for other spies.

'Meaning that he was, or is, a counter-spy, matching the Counter-Reformation.'

'Will,' says Marlowe, frightened, 'go and call in those men. The Privy Council men we told to wait in the garden.' Will tries to get up, quick enough on the uptake, but finds Skeres' drawn sword at his chest. Skeres says:

'Nay, stay, we beg you, Mr Shakejelly. Play stuff, Kit,' he says to Marlowe, 'apt for the stage but not for real life.'

'I admit,' says Marlowe, 'real life has more surprises. I had no idea my three friends were creatures of King Philip of Spain.'

'You still have no idea, Kit,' says Frizer. 'You have no idea who we are working for, or, if thou wishest, *para quien nosotros estamos trabajando*. Why, we may also be working for Her Majesty's Secret Service, and that organization may deem it desirable to be rid of unreliability.'

'Look,' says Poley, his eyes stern on Will, 'this one here. Must he not too −?'

'He is not quite a gentleman,' says Skeres. 'He carries no sword. He may freely report what he is about to see. The judgement of God on an atheistical roarer.' They all have their swords drawn. Will remains rigid in his seat. Frizer says:

'Draw your dagger, Kit. Let us have some little argument about the honour of a wench or who shall pay the reckoning.' He lunges at Marlowe. Marlowe draws his dagger. Frizer laughs, keeping at a sword's length's distance. He says:

'Ah, Mr Shakeshoes, are you not now in the great world? Did you not dream of all the glory of this London life when you wiped your snotty country nose on your sleeve?'

'Tell them, Will,' says Marlowe. 'Tell them what you have seen.'

'He may tell them,' says Poley. 'He shall corroborate all.' So all three now have their swords out, but they clatter them to the floor. 'Strike, Kit,' says Poley, 'strike, you passionate shepherd.' Marlowe holds his dagger indecisively. 'Now,' says Poley. All three seize Marlowe's dagger hand and drive the dagger into his frontal lobes. Marlowe screams. Will is petrified.

'I still think,' says Skeres, 'we should dispatch this one too. A quarrel of drunken poets.'

'No, no,' says Frizer. 'It is a little man. Leave him.' And Will runs away.

Enderby looked up at the blur of Toplady, pleased. He could not tell from his look whether Toplady was pleased or not, but he took it that he was not, since he never was.

'Well,' Toplady began, and got no further. For his door flew open and in swam or sailed or flew April Elgar, saying:

'Hi.'

'Sweetie, marshmallow pie, angelcake' and so on went Toplady, half-rising and making a cold sketch of embracing her in hungry arms. Enderby not merely got up to give her his chair but retreated to the wall. 'This,' Toplady said with dramatic lack of enthusiasm, 'is er,' meaning Enderby.

'Hi.'

Enderby stood openmouthed underneath a poster for *Mother Courage*. He had never seen anything or body like this woman before. In Tangiers, true, he had presided, as owner of a perch of sunning ground windtrapped, over comely enough bodies and acceptable enough, if usually chronically dissatisfied, faces above them or, if they were lying down, at one end or other of them. These had been all white, meaning unwholesomely rich in greens and blues and carmines, and very pallid to begin with, earning slow increments of honey and ultimate toffee as the sun slowly chewed them. The women of darker hue he had been unable to judge of, since they showed only ankles under robes and kohled eyes over yashmaks. He had never really had standards for the assessing of black American beauty. This April Elgar was a revelation to his awed eyes, and would be even more so when he got his glasses on. She glowed in deep content with her Blue Mountain glow and exact sculpted line of feature. Quadroon? Octoroon? Blasphemous terms, obsolete musical instruments squeaking in accompaniment to a celestial choir. Denoting cold-blooded blood apportionments apt only for damnable race laws. Doubloon was more like it: hot gold, also cool. The divine sinuous body was skirted in cinnamon, ensilked shins and ankles and feet shod frivolously on frail plinths that were really artful engineering made Enderby groan with their frightful perfection. She had had pasted upon her a matching jumper of fairy chain metal. Her delicate breasts appeared unsupported. The hair, obligatorily raven, flowed a satin river, to whose blackness all blacks were chalk, scrawling their own reproach.

She sat, well pleased with herself, by God, and no wonder, by Christ. She said, in a voice of cassia honey or an Elgarian string section:

'Has that fucking fag schlepped his ass here yet?'

'Don't be like that, Ape,' whined Toplady. 'You like Pete, you know you'll be great together.'

'What did you call her then?' cried Enderby in outrage. 'Did you call her what I think you called her?' She turned and looked Enderby up and down, as to appraise his fag properties, if any, and said:

'Ape he said, short for April, that's my name, honey.'

'Well, I won't have it,' Enderby cried. 'It's a bloody disgrace. To have so exquisite a name apocopized into the libellously simian. And you too with your bloody *Goats and Monkeys*,' he told Toplady loudly.

'Wow,' she said, 'you better write that down big so I can frame it and stick it on my wall. Good for the lip muscles. What's this,' she then said, 'about goats and monkeys?' She took a gold étui from her Bayeux tapestry bag. Enderby shook for his lighter and shook out a flame as she gave a white tube to her lips. She held his hand steady with long cool brown fingers. Toplady said:

'Our title. Right out of *Othello*. I knew you'd like it.'

'I get it. I'm the monkey and that screaming fag is the goat. Or is it the other way round? It's a lousy title. And in future you can quit calling me Ape.'

'Not dignified enough for its ah protagonist,' Enderby said. 'I think now that *Will* might be better. Will the name and the drive, sexual and social, you know, and even the final testament with the second best bed. With an exclamation point possibly. *Will!* Or two, if you like – *Will!!*'

'*Dark Lady*,' she said. She'd done some homework, then.

'With respect,' Enderby said, 'there's a play by Bernard Shaw called *The Dark Lady of the Sonnets*. Of course, she's not really dark in your exquisite and overwhelming manner. Darkhaired only. Well, eyes too. My mistress' eyes are nothing like the sun. How about,' inspired, '*A Dark Lady's Will*?'

'When do I start work?' she asked Toplady.

'Reading after lunch. I booked a table at the Escoffier. Silversmith
will be back with some great songs day after tomorrow.'

'That fag,' she said. Enderby liked all this very much. But, of
course, he, being British, had to be the final repository of faghood.
'Lousy British fag,' she would tell Toplady over luncheon, to which,
Enderby did not have to be told, Enderby was not invited. She
now ignored Enderby till she had finished her fag, which she had
handled elegantly but on which she had drunk deep, discussing
with hard impersonality the while various contractual rights which
Toplady said could be clarified when the wife, Ms Grace Hope,
of the screaming fag Oldfellow arrived with the screaming fag
along with the other fag, screaming or not, Silversmith. Enderby
was quick to wrest the exhausted lipsticked butt from her and
grind it out in the concave plinth of some trophy, elongated
humanoid, which stood on Toplady's desk. She stood and smoothed
herself down laterally and said now to Enderby:

'What was that shit about exquisite apocalypse of the something
something?'

'*Not* shit,' Enderby reproved. 'I don't wish to hear that word in
your connection. It harms your beauty and elegance.'

'My my,' she said, with an oeillade meant to be comic. 'Okay,
Gus, we go and all that sort of nonsense.'

'A fair warning,' stern Enderby said. She glided out and Toplady
looked acidly on Enderby as he followed. Enderby lighted himself
a Robert Burns cigar and coughed in a sort of delirium round
the office. Her perfume, a complication of something expensively
distilled in the town of Grasse and her own salt animal emanation,
rode over the foul reek of non-tobacco ingredients. Enderby went
out, past the girl and women typists, and took the stairs down to
the greenroom, where he gave himself lunch from the vending
machine – yoghurt with boysenberries and coffee that went on
wasting itself on the sugar-encrusted grill beneath. A dirty business.
Later he went to the sort of classroom where, floor today unen-
cumbered by the fag Silversmith, the troupe would assemble for
the reading of Act One entire. He would have to read Will again.
Soon he must surrender his lines to this screaming fag Oldfellow.
It struck him with horror now that he must – The incongruity.
God, they would laugh their heads off.

She was late, stardom's privilege. Toplady, being with her, also had to be late. Enderby filled in some of the waiting time by telling the lounging troupe about the kind of English they had, properly, to employ in their roles. 'Remember,' he said, 'the *Mayflower.*'

'We ain't old enough, man,' said a black boy Enderby had not seen before. What the hell part was he to play? Henslowe? Sir Walter Raleigh?

'I mean, remember that the *Mayflower* brought over to America a kind of English very close to what Shakespeare and his ah contemporaries spoke. Do not attempt Sir John Gielgud accents, even if you know how. Speak the tongue of Boston, Massachusetts. It will be good enough.' He nodded kindly at them, who looked fuzzily, he being spectacleless, but unkindly back. Then April Elgar entered, followed by Toplady, and she looked at the men as if they were all fags, and at the others, which they were, frowsty frumpish sluts. She said, seated:

'Me.'

'I beg your pardon?' Enderby said.

'Me, me. Take it from where I come in, okay?'

'I,' Enderby apologetically said, 'have to read Will. Shakespeare, that is.'

'Okay. You wrote it. What page?' There was a fluttering of already soiled typescripts.

'Your name is Lucy,' Enderby said. 'There is a room with a pair of virginals in it.'

'A pair of who?'

'A musical instrument,' Enderby explained. 'Like a harpsichord. The Dark Lady plays it well. It says so in the Sonnets.'

'Well, this Dark Lady don't play nothing. Except a little stud poker.' Then she said very woodenly: 'Who are you, sir? Who sent you? You take a liberty, sir.'

'You summoned Richard the Third to your house,' Will Enderby said. 'You set your sights too low, madam. You should have asked for Richard the Third's creator.'

A pudgy ginger girl as duenna said, very woodenly: 'I knew he was not the man. Shall I have him thrown out, madam?'

Enderspeare said: 'The person of William Shakespeare is not

handled by kitchen ruffians. I come as a gentleman to pay my respects to a lady. Get you gone, woman, and learn your place.'

'Very well, Marion. I will hear his message,' went April Elgar. 'Stay close and listen for my bell. Now, sir.'

'Your beauty,' Shakeserby said earnestly, 'deserves better than the homage of a mere player. You need a poet. A poet is what I am.'

'You are very forward, sir.'

'Come, none of this. I glory in your beauty. I have here a sonnet.'

'You have writ a sonnet? For me?'

'I have writ them for only one man – my near friend whom I love with all my heart, the Earl of Southampton.'

'So,' said April Elgar as herself, which was no different from as Lucy, speaking to Toplady, 'he's faggy.'

'Not at all,' said non Will Enderby stoutly. 'He was omnifutuant. It was the way things were then.'

'Yeah, faggy.'

'Read,' commanded Toplady. Willerby read:

'But for one woman I have this:'

'So he takes out his shlong?'

'A sonnet. A sonnet. He takes out a sonnet. Shakespeare didn't write this sonnet. I did.' Enderby enWilled himself again. 'Hear, madam.

> 'All other beauty's light I lightly rate.
>   My love is as my love is, for the dark.
> In night enthroned, I ask no better state
>   Than thus to range, nor seek a guiding spark –'

'It is forward, to write of love so. You are very impertinent. I'll say he is.'

'I wrote this long ago to another lady, one I saw only in dreams. Now I see reality in your true and rich midnight darkness. I have always been seeking one such as you – goddess, genius, poetic pharos.'

'Poetic what?'

'Pharos, pharos. Greek for a lighthouse.'

'Okay, why can't he say lighthouse. Then it says that I play.'

'Where did you learn so delicate a touch? Surely not in your own country,' said Shakesby.

'I left my own country as a small child. I was torn away as a slave. I was brought up by a family in Bristol. It was a holy work to them to bring light to what they called the heathen. But then they freed me and made me into the lady you see, and when the father died he left me money.'

'Sing,' said Enderwill. 'A song in exchange for my sonnet.'

'Ah Jesus. You mean this?' And she minced out the words like a Moody and Sankey hymn:

'What doth it mean, to love?
It is to plumb the seas and scale the skies.
It is to wear the day away with sighs
Or mount the moon above.
Thus doth it mean, to love,
So wouldst thou seek the truth of this to prove,
And love?'

The entire troupe smirked at that. April Elgar gaped incredulous. 'It is,' Enderby stoutly said, 'in the Elizabethan manner. The sort of thing you'd sing to the virginals.'

'Sweetie,' she said, and then, in a kind of slave whine, 'ah doan want none of dem lil old virginals, whatever de shit dey are. Dey doan fit mah personality no way no how.'

'I've warned you before,' Enderby cried, 'about that sort of language. There's too much of this *shit*,' he told the whole troupe, 'going on. She there,' jerking his shoulder towards her, 'blasphemes against her exquisite beauty by bemerding her speech in that manner. For Christ's sake cut out the *shit* and let's be serious.' And he blazed his way back into the role, crying like a threat: 'You sing prettily, madam? Can you dance as well?'

'Some dances I can dance,' April Elgar said, first grinning and then not. 'The pavane – the galliard –'

'Canst,' Shenderspeare said, with a cunning change to the familiar mode, 'dance the Beginning of the World?'

'I know not such a dance.'

'I,' Spearesby said, 'will show thee.' And he beamed in embarrassment as pure Enderby.

'Well,' she said, in her proper person, 'we're waiting.'

'Oh, that. Well – he takes her in his arms and covers her with kisses. He imposes his will upon her, pun intended, he strips her of her taffeta elegance and carries her over to a gorgeous daybed. He untrusses himself and dances the dance called the Beginning of the World. A nice conceit,' he explained. 'The Elizabethans saw the sexual act in cosmic terms. It began with an image of creation and ended with death. To die meant to experience the ah orgasm.'

For the first time the assembled company responded to words of Enderby with something approaching attention and even respect. It evidently surprised some of the younger ones to learn that people who had been dead a thousand or a hundred years, same thing, knew about copulation and even had expressive figurative speech to decorate it in or with. 'Beginnin o the World,' the black lad said, drawing out *World* into something unglobular. 'I like that, man.' Before or after that night's Brecht nonsense some of them would be trying it out for the sake of the nomenclature. Baby, ah just died. Then a man in overalls entered to say that the Holiday Inn was on fire.

6

What had happened, so Enderby was to learn later, was that a disaffected busboy or bellhop, mandatorily stoned, had filled a familysize Coca-Cola bottle with gasoline siphoned from the hotel manager's car, glugged this inflammable out in the empty third-floor bedroom two doors away from Enderby's own and then enflamed it. He had then got the hell out with a cashbox containing something under a hundred dollars, there not being much cash around these days of credit cards. When Enderby got by taxi to the hotel he found a fire engine there, summoned from Indianapolis, with the firemen pumping not water but a grey chemical substance over all available surfaces. Not much of a fire, but the third floor had been evacuated. Enderby found his suitcase, fortunately closed, covered with grey dust and his decent clerical grey suit suited in a deeper grey. His tea mug and kettle were no longer around, but the rest of his stuff rested, along with other defiled luggage, by a pillar in the defiled foyer. He should by rights demand compensation for defilement but contented himself with getting the hell out, not paying his bill, and asking the taxi driver who had brought him hither and was staying to share in the excitement to take him and his defilements to the Sheraton Hotel in Indianapolis.

The driver insisted first on showing him the town he was to dwell in for a space, or it may have been a matter of his not knowing where the Sheraton Hotel was and hoping to find it by dint of cruising the entire city around. Central Park, Monument Place, radiating Massachusetts, Indiana, Virginia and Kentucky Avenues. State Capitol, Court House, Board of Trade building, Central College of Physicians and Surgeons, Blind and Deaf and Dumb Asylums. At length he said, with no hint of triumph, 'Well, here it is.' And there it was. Enderby expected sympathy from the reception clerk for his refugee condition and the state of his baggage but got none. But he was permitted to submit his suit for dry cleaning.

Lying on his bed, smoking a Robert Burns, he noted that he had been carrying all this while, and in spite of more immediate emotions and preoccupations, an inflated shlong, as she called it, and all because of her. Then he wondered about the fire and dismissed a superstitious supposition. Then he remembered that she was staying in this same hotel: he had heard a girl in the big open secretarial area of the theater's offices confirming her reservation on the telephone. Then he lusted for strong tea and raged in frustration. He would have to go out and resupply himself. He went down, overcoated though without his tout cap, and found a kettle and mug in a kind of hardware store off Kentucky Avenue and, in a supermarket entitled rather soberly EATGOOD, bought brown sugar lumps, canned milk and a box of two hundred tea sachets of unstated provenance, also a brand of toothglue he had not previously met called Champ. And then there was a new variety of stomach tablet named Whoosh. Rather exciting, really, all this consumerism. Fairly pleased, he took his purchases back to the hotel. In the lobby he saw Ms April Elgar. She was being silently admired, and no bloody wonder, by God. She was also flipping through mail that had arrived for her, frowning crossly at it. Enderby went straight up to her and said:

'Not much of a fire, really. But, as you see, I have been evacuated. I have the pleasure or honour of, both I suppose. As you observe.'

She did not at first seem to know who he was, a matter of his not wearing the tout cap, but his fag British accent presumably rang the bell of recognition that rang. 'Hi,' she said.

'A few essential purchases,' excusing the brown bags under his arm.

'I guess so,' distractedly. And then: 'You and me have to rap.'

'Rap?' Oh Christ, more spiritualist nonsense. 'I should be delighted to er.'

'Okay, the bar.' She swayed her way ahead to it. Enderby removed his overcoat but found it necessary to hold it folded on his lap. The linen trousers were thin. An insincerely cheerful matron dressed like a whore took their orders: whisky sours for both.

'More sweet than sour,' Enderby remarked. 'Something of a misnomer.'

'You always talk like that?' she said. 'All these words.'

'Well,' Enderby said, 'the British have no real slang on the American pattern, I mean not one diffused throughout the entire social system, if you see what I mean. Also, I am a poet, Enderby the poet. Also, I live alone and speak little English these days. It's becoming, from the spoken angle, something of a foreign language for me.'

'What do you mean, live alone?'

'In Tangiers, with these three boys.'

'Jesus, so you're another of these screaming fags.'

'No, no, far from it, although you will, of course, naturally assume that all the British are fags. That's because your American fags tend to speak with a British accent. A bit illogical, really. Cart before the horse, sort of. I am unimpeachably heterosexual.' And, by atavistic instinct, he confirmed the testimony by slapping his crotch smartly. 'Too many fags around,' he added. 'Especially in the theatre.'

'You can say that again.'

'Too many fags a —'

'And dykes too. Listen. This is my show, right?'

'Well,' Enderby said with care, 'it's supposed to be Shakespeare's really. And let's get this straight about this er fag element in his life. He had an affair with the Earl of Southampton, no doubt about that, but it didn't express his true nature, which was passionately heterosexual. He had to climb through the pretence of ah faggishness. Not uncommon at that time. Their sexuality was so intense that it expressed itself in many forms. But in the sense that the Dark Lady is not only a woman but also a kind of destructive and creative goddess at one and the same time, and even perhaps a disease, well, yes, it is, to some extent your show.'

'So the opening number is me, a production number. I'll put the shake in Shakespeare, I'll put the spear in too. Establish,' she said, much in Enderby's manner, 'priorities.'

'Where did you get that from?' Enderby asked with some admiration. 'That's rather witty.'

'Just thought of it. Sharp as a pistol, brought up in Bristol. The white man's knavery sold me in slavery. Hey,' she hailed the serving matron. 'Two more of those.'

'Thou art,' Enderby said, 'as wise as thou art beautiful.'

'Oh, come on.'

'Quotation from. Titania says that to Bottom. But,' Enderby said with some urgency, 'the beauty is real enough, God knows. I say this with total objectivity. Your beauty is overwhelming, of a kind rarely seen. But this, of course, you must know.'

'Yah,' she said, 'I know it. My beauty is my bread,' she added with mock solemnity. 'Talent, too, baby, I got talent.'

'That,' Enderby said, 'I still have to see.'

'You better believe it. Right. That fag Silverass is on his way and you gotta have words to give him. Songs, baby. So I want you to steer your pinko ass into that elevator and get up to your room and start writing.'

'Gladly,' Enderby said. 'After dinner. I thought,' he thought for the first time, 'we might have dinner together.'

'That's nice, that's real nice. Like in old movies. Not tonight, baby, some other time.'

'You,' Enderby said, 'have already arranged to dine with some other ah guy. I see.'

'No, you don't see.' She sipped at her fresh whisky sour and
Enderby at his. The tumescence was terrible. 'You see nothing. Ah
has mah prahvit lahf.'

'At least,' Enderby said, 'you've stopped saying *shit* all the time.
That's a word I've heard Americans use even at table. They don't
take in the referent of the word. It's become just a neutral
expletive.'

'Okay, no shit.' And then a great handsome man of her own
colour, though much darker, bore down on their table. She rose
in shrill ecstasy and they fondly embraced. Baby honey-bunch and
then an unintelligible duet in what Enderby took to be Black
English. He drained his whisky sour unnoticed and unintroduced
and stole off with his coat and packages. His shlong settled to
neutrality. Black bitch and so on. Christ, jealousy, a dark wine long
untasted. He hadn't come all this way to be jealous. He would
leave it to her, bitch, to sign for the whisky sours.

But up in his room, strengthened by mahogany tea, he got out
his yellow legal pad and started to scribble to her will. Lyrics, seeing
her in a richly crimson silk farthingale belting them out, brown
bosom fully exposed in the Tudor manner to proclaim, like the
Queen herself, putative virginity. This vision was physically very
painful. He had to cart the engorged shlong three times into the
bathroom and, on a face towel monogrammed with a fanciful S,
fiercely discharge his heat. He saw himself fierce in the lighted
mirror doing it and nodded fiercely at the fierce reflection. Then,
less fierce, indeed encalmed, he went down to dinner and ordered
a beefsteak and a half bottle of some ruby Californian muck, both
restorative, indeed freshly inflaming. The waiter, a frail Viennese
PhD immigrant, seemed to ask him what dressing he would take
with his salad. No dressing because no salad. Green stuff was not
good for you. April Elgar and her co-coloured fancy man were
not there. Swiving like rattlesnakes some place. He, Enderby, willed
himself not to care, finishing his french frieds with his fingers,
ordering apple pie with ice cream on it. Then he belched his way
back up to make tea.

> The white man's knavery
> Sold me in slavery

To an unsavoury
Household.
I slept in an attic all
Foully rheumatical,
Bedbugged and cobwebbed
And mouseholed.
I slaved like the slave I was,
Ripe for the grave I was,
But I was brave, I was
Ready
For my master's remorse and my
Freedom of course and my
Carriage and horse and my
Monetary source
Safe and steady.
Now see me here in London,
Ready for revenge –
All England will be undone
From Carlisle to Stonehenge
On the dayyyyyyyy
I get my wayyyyyy.

But here, by God, was corruption. You cease to celebrate the greatest poet in the world's history and ennoble nothing but lust of one kind or another. Goats and monkeys. Toplady was, after all, no fool.

I'll screw some sex into Essex,
I'll scourge Walter Raleigh's raw hide.
I'll make Francis Drake
Chase a duck on a lake
And eat Francis Bacon fried.
I'll inject the shakes into Shakespeare
And stick in the spear as well,
Wrench out Queen Bess's
Carroty tresses
And make her bald as a bell.
Right under your gaze

> I'm going to raise
> Elizabethan hell.

Enderby groaned, but not now with lust, that foul fundamental whose harmonics were admiration, awe and even the most dangerous word in the language. He had been drawn into the celebration of America, not Shakespeare. What voice from the dead had condoned the travesty to come? Robert Greene, perhaps, putting on the tame tiger's hide in his cunning. One in the eye for Shakescene. Enderby got blearily off his bed (lyricizing was bloody hard work) and dug his contract out of the dusty suitcase. He should have read the small print before signing. Sold into slavery, by God. Suable if he reneged. Best to embrace one's enforced corruption. He started to write one more song before sleep.

> To be or not to be
> Smitten by you
> Bitten by you
> Teased as a ball of wool is teased by a kitten by you:
> That is the question
> Which harms my digestion

Marry, *à propos*. He swallowed six Whoosh tablets with chlorinated water and got ready for troubled slumber.

The next day Enderby left them all to it. Let the bastards get on with it. He tried to work in the hotel lounge, but perpetual sedative music got in the way of his rhythms. He went to see the bell bald manager about it, but the manager did not easily comprehend his complaint. Anaesthetization of the ear or something. Offwhite noise. He returned to his room to find the bed yet unmade, but he was used to unmade beds. He stuck the DO NOT DISTURB notice up outside and made himself more tea. Fed up, fucked up and far from home. He dragged Ben Jonson grumbling from his long sleep and made him sing:

> Ale and Anacreon,
> Beer and Boethius,
> Sack and Sophocles, these

> Please my heart
> More than the farting littleness,
> Borborygmic brittleness,
> Jokes and japes
> Of the apes and jackanapes
> One sees
> Courting the great
> At court, on estate –
> Fleas!

He foreheard the bemerding response to that and crumpled the yellow legal paper up. Yet he needed Ben Jonson to sneak in a few extra blank verse lines to make the revival of *Richard II* relevant to the Essex rebellion which immediately followed and thus have poor Will bemerded. Keep out of the great world, sirrah, stick to your word games. I, your Queen, tell you so. Lucky for you your head rolleth not like his, that runagate traitorous earl, on Tower Hill. Get you gone from my royal sight. Will was turning out to be a very bemerdable character. Then he wrote lines to April Elgar:

> Edwardian brass, O enigmatic kingdom,
> Apostolic musicmaker, nobilmente
> Clashes the green roots, outyells returning swifts
> Derides the cuckoocall. I cannot go on I
> Cannot go on
> Cannot
> Enderby

He folded them into a Sheraton envelope, scrawled her name on, went downstairs overcoated, told the reception clerk to put it into her box. Surely surely. Then he went out to get drunk. He settled at length into a low bar behind the Board of Trade building. An old man whined to the bartender, who consoled him surely surely. Enderby ordered Scotch uniced and beer to pursue it. Workmen came in in hard hats. They heard Enderby's accent on his third ordering of the same again and derided his Britishry with what what and all that sort of rot jolly good eh old chap. They seemed to have watched a fair quantity of old films on television. Enderby grinned at them, unoffended. Then one man said that the Queen of England was a whore. Enderby grinned at him, unoffended. Then, Orpheus with his lute, he came out with:

'Four score and seven years ago our fathers brought forth on this continent a new nation, conceived in liberty, and dedicated to the proposition that all men are created equal. Now we are engaged in a great civil war, testing whether that nation, or any nation so conceived and so dedicated, can long endure. We are met on a great battlefield of that war —' Then he took a drink. The workmen looked solemn, as in church: Lincoln's speech was a powerful cantrip. They bought Enderby the same again. He was told that it was only kidding about the Queen of England being a whore. He said: 'Her circumstances hardly allow it. Of course, your President Kennedy was a whoremaster or lecher, but that sort of thing is expected in a male leader. A double standard, you know.' Somebody put a dime or quarter into the jukebox hidden in the corner in deep shadow. It illuminated itself and thumped and twanged. Unformed male voices pitched high excreted nonsense with bad rhymes. Kennedy, he was told, slept with Marilyn Monroe. Now they were conveniently dead, both assassinated by the FBI, and were screwing away in heaven. No such place as heaven. It's got to be heaven if you're screwing Marilyn Monroe, you better believe it. Then the disc changed and Enderby heard a known voice:

'Give the world a kiss
Although it rates a kick
Get in double quick
And give the world a kiss'

'Ah God,' he said. There, said somebody, is another one that screws. All dinges screw, they got no morality. She's here right now in Indianapolis, screwing. Screw a dog, screw a beer bottle, bottom end. 'Oh God,' moaned Enderby.

'There may be roars
But there are roses
A fiddle and a flute
There may be wars

But underneath your nose is
Juicy fruit still unpolluted'

Juicy fruit, I'll say. Give the world a fuck, I'll say. Enderby had
to get out. You tell the Queen of England from me, fella, she ain't
no whore. Enderby was surprised to find it dark without, street
lamps on, hail spinning lazily down. He had been there longer
than he thought. He wove his way back to the Sheraton. He carried
his key in his pocket, always forgot the number. He made several
stabs at the wrong door, somebody yelled, muffled, 'Who's there?',
then found his own, 360. That number meant something, he couldn't
for the moment think what. He fell inside, doffed and threw at
the television set his overcoat, then fell on the bed.

He was awakened by knocking. He got up with considerable
difficulty and groaned his way to the bathroom door. It was not
at that that the knocking was proceeding. He opened another door
and blinked painfully. She, paper in hand, dispossession notice. She
wore scarlet tailored slacks and matching jumper, heavy beaten
bronze earrings, scarfed montage of European cathedrals about her
throat. Enderby's heart thumped from drink. He bowed her shakily
in. She sat down on the one chair with arms and looked at him.
He said:

'I heard you singing. In some low place. Not you personally, of
course. I must take something. Heartburn. If you'll excuse me.' He
went to the bathroom for Whoosh and water. He came back with
a foul headache. He sat on the edge of the bed. 'That in your
hand,' he said. 'I see what it is now. Doesn't make much sense.
Nominal fantasy. Had to go out. Drank a little. My apologies.'

'What gives with you?' she said. 'I've never met any dude quite
like you.'

'Double agony,' Enderby said. 'I adore Shakespeare. I adore you.
Somebody has to be betrayed. You'll swallow him. You're swallowing
me. Old as I am. Ugly. Unworthy. You try that on for size,' he said
with bitter jocosity.

'You mean you want to get laid?'

'That's right,' cried Enderby, head cracking, 'bring it down to
animality. Things aren't as easy as that. Shakespeare didn't want just
to get laid, as you put it. She was stitched into his senses, made

his soul drunk. He cured himself, but only through his art. He had to lose his only son first. Oh yes, sex came into it, with all its connotations, universal, cosmic, yin and yang, ultimate sex. You don't get over it by screwing, as those men said.'

'Which men said?'

'The men in the pub, bar. They said the Queen of England was a whore. You can't complain if they said the same about you. Bloody animality. Then we come to the most dangerous word in the language, and you know what it is. A declaration of faith with little hope and not much bloody charity. Why aren't you with that bloody man you were with last night?'

'What? Who? Oh, him. That was Ben Jonson, my brother, and don't call him bloody. He plays piano with Mitch Frobisher's combo. Ah, the greeneyed dingus. And so you get paralytic.' Not a just word, he considered, looking down at his tremor. He said:

'Jonson with an aitch, I suppose. Without would be going too far. Although there's an aitch in Westminster Abbey. And where does the Elgar come in?'

'He was a British composer. I always liked that what I used to call when I was a kid Pompous Circus Dance of his.'

'He wrote a bloody sight more than that,' Enderby said. 'Edwardian hubris and neurosis, an incredible combination. And I suppose the April is really June.'

'Not far out. May Johnson, brought up Baptist. If they want to fantasize over the April Elgar image, okay, let them. That's what it's there for, I guess.'

'Funny,' Enderby said, 'girls are called after spring, only men after summer. Augustus, I was thinking of. But of course that's the cart before the horse again. Forgive me.'

'Like that thing in Kant, I guess. Noumenon and phenomenon. May Johnson is the dingus an sich.'

Enderby gaped. But, of course, everybody in this country got educated at the State U, a kind of superior high school. Then they forgot their bit of education in order to make money. Very sound, really. And then they could paralyse their interlocutors with Kant when they didn't expect it. 'I'm parched,' he said. 'I have to make very strong tea. Will you join me? But I only have this one mug.

I'll buy another tomorrow in case you. You can use this one first and I can swill it after.'

'Real English genlmn. But it's dinnertime. Wipe that white stuff off of your mouth and drink three glasses of water. Then I take you up on us having dinner together, okay?'

'I couldn't eat a thing.'

'Then watch you lil friend eat.'

The three glasses of water prescribed renewed the heartburn ferociously, but a couple of powerful martinis at table put him right: the headache merely hovered over like the awareness of a decorated ceiling. He felt he could tackle red meat. He looked with tolerant disapproval at April Elgar's cottage cheese and salad with thousand islands dressing. His tumescence did its best to find its aetiology in the Aprilian and Elgarian and leave May Johnson alone. How bloody beautiful she was, each functional eating gesture a shorter lyric. Men at other tables kept sneaking glances of envy at him. No one could say: that ugly old bastard is her father. And sick desire at her. Their wives ignored him and knifed her with bitter hate. Enderby monologuized, awaiting his red meat. 'Salads dry up my saliva. Green things have something unnatural about them. The most dangerous word in the language, as I said. Onanism is a logical safeguard, you know, a device of protection of the deeper emotion. Nobody wants to lust after people: images are what are required. Though love is a bloody nuisance. Helen's beauty in a brow of Egypt. Funny he should say that disparagingly. He felt differently when he got to Cleopatra.'

April Elgar picked on that along with a forkful of salad. She said: 'Right. Cleopatra. Think of Cleopatra and you won't go far wrong. Stick an asp on my left tit if you like at the end, but it's me they got to remember. A blaze of gold, you see that?'

'Don't use that word,' Enderby groaned.

'Which one?'

'That one.'

'Tit? Sorry, old boy, old boy. Bosom. Breast. Knocker.'

'Oh my God.'

'We'll beat the bastards, you and me. May sheow, eold felleow.'

7

Enderby sat in one of the many toilets of the Peter Brook Theater
reading a paperback volume of what were known as Science Fiction
Stories. He sat long partly because of a costiveness that seven
Gringe tablets had so far done nothing to ease. Perhaps, after all,
salads were healthful. Too much protein and starch. For breakfast
he had eaten pancakes and maple syrup and sausages on the side.
He had brought his own steaming mug of tea down with him, an
eccentricity now accepted by the Sheraton. Must do something
about diet. Must not reject little paper cup of coleslaw issued with
lunchtime sandwich. Spinach munched from can like marine character in old cartoons with ridiculously overdeveloped forearms. He
sat long sequestered also partly because there was such a hell of a
row proceeding at rehearsal. Clash of characters, egos really. That
fag Pete Oldfellow and the divine April Elgar were creating, with
claws distended and genuine hurled spittle, more compelling drama
than any dramaturge could contrive. God was still, after all, so
Enderby ungrudgingly conceded, the best of the dramatic poets,
though shapeless and uneconomical. A bit like Charles Dickens.
God was good on the physical and emotional sides and a great
one for hate. He generously spilled his own hate into his dearest
creation. That's why you had to have Jesus Christ, who unrealistic-
ally overstressed the love part. But God hated him too and sponged
him out one Friday afternoon. The play now enacted on the dimlit
stage was God's play, though God had to leave it to people to
provide an ending.

Enderby read about people travelling to imaginary galaxies. God,
if he would only grow arms and learn how to write, could do this
sort of thing much better. The monsters on the planetoid Anatrakia
were very anthropomorphically conceived. There seemed to be a
lot of this sort of thing around, alternative universes ten a penny,

and the young actor who had lent him this volume for a quiet lavatorial read boasted of possessing over four hundred science fiction paperbacks. Ought to have volumes of Shakespeare, really, Sophocles, Racine, Ben Jonson, others, but didn't. Didn't take his paid art seriously. Dick Corcoran from Manticore, near Toronto, Ontario, playing Essex and understudying the fag Oldfellow, who was making a very peevish job of Shakespeare.

Enderby read a story about the inhabitants of Garagogoki, the capital city of Berkibark on the planet Urkurk, who gave birth to little machines of no apparent purpose but produced babies in flesh factories. If the parents, or purlerguts as they were called (a term roughly meaning beneficiaries), did not discover the purpose of their machine within four orgs, a measurement of time relating to the periodic explosion of a renewable sun called Maha, the machine, which grew steadily to a monstrous size, Molochlike devoured them. The hero and heroine of the story, named Arg and Gogogoch respectively, tried to smash their machine at birth, but this resulted only in fissiparous replication of the monster. Enderby was deeply absorbed in this implausible narrative when a voice above his head said:

'Mr Enderby is urgently wanted on the telephone.'

No escape. There were loudspeakers everywhere. He discounted the allegation of urgency and wiped himself, alas, drily. There was nothing urgent for him, at least not on the telephone. He had managed to get through to Tangiers yesterday and, except for the explosion of the frying machine in the kitchen and a fire quickly doused, everything seemed to be all right there. *Muy bien. Adios.* Enderby took his time getting to the telephone in the main office and there heard a woman's voice say to his earhole:

'Mr Elderly? Laura Schoenbaum.'

'We must really, you know, get this business of the name properly sorted out. I am Enderby. Enderby the poet.'

'Oh, so glad you're there. Mrs Allegramente didn't want me to but I'm doing it just the same. Nobody else could say what it meant, but I'm sure you can.'

'Another tabletapping session, eh? A lot of nonsense. Somebody pretending to be William Shakespeare, eh? There's a lot of malice going on back there, ought to have something better to do with their time, eternity that is. What was —'

'Well, yes, it was the Bard himself from the Happy House and he just made the same sound three times. Through Mrs Allegramente's mouth of course, which was wide open, she was in a trance.'

'What was this sound?'

'Well, it sounds kind of silly – kha, kha, kha, just like that. And then a pause, and then the same again. And then another pause, and then the –'

'Kha, kha, kha?' asked Enderby. Girls looked up from their typing. 'Or was it more ha, ha, ha, though with a very strong aspiration?'

'You could say that, I guess, yes.'

'Hha, hha, hha, then,' Enderby said. 'Fairly clear, I should think. There's a sonnet beginning with the line. "The expense of spirit in a waste of shame", and it warns about the dangers of lust. The sin of animality. Then comes the line that begins "Had, having and in quest to have", and there's no doubt that he's mocking the noise of lustful panting. Dog and bitch on heat. Men too. Women also perhaps.' Typing had not been resumed. 'So he's reminding some-body not to get caught up in the toils of unconsidering sensuality. Hha, hha, hha, eh? Of course, it may not be Shakespeare at all. Just somebody who's read him.'

'There was nobody there it would apply to, Mr Elderly.'

'You can never be sure,' Enderby said darkly. 'Hha, hha, hha.'

'Well, thank you, I hope everything's going all right there.'

'Everything's going just fine,' Enderby said, as he heard the screams of April Elgar and Pete Oldfellow approaching the secre-tarial area and Toplady's office. 'Hha, hha, hha,' he said in valediction. And he put down the handset.

God, how bloody beautiful she was in a rage. Her raging elon-gated sunset of a rehearsal suit, a onepiece jersey jumpthing, turned her into a flame with teeth. Enderby's heart melted. Behind her, glum and nailbiting, was Toplady. They were going to have it all out in a kind of privacy. Oldfellow whined, but he had neither her vocabulary, suprasegmental tropes of remote jungle origin, nor her numinosity. He was a man of about Enderby's size with a nose that would not get in the way in kissing sequences, mean blue eyes and a pouting mouthful of porcelain crowns. With him was his wife, Ms Grace Hope, a thin woman in a ginger trouser suit and an extravagant fair wig. To her Enderby abruptly addressed himself, saying:

'A question of money. There are two hotels requesting nay demanding payment. My own resources are not ah unlimited. I invoke the terms of my contract.'

'Later,' Ms Grace Hope said. 'At the moment the show itself is in jeopardy.'

'Not through any fault of mine,' Enderby said. 'I've done everything required. Totally accommodating.'

'A smidgen too accommodating,' Oldfellow said. 'My part's been slashed to fucking ribbons.' And his head with its mean blue eyes tocked to April Elgar and ticked back to Enderby. Enderby said:

'I'll thank you not to use that word in ah her presence. Nor, for that matter, in the presence of ah her.' Meaning Ms Grace Hope, his wife. 'Questions of propriety.'

'Don't give me that kind of shit,' Oldfellow said. 'I know what's been going on around here.'

'In,' Toplady said with weary bitterness, his nailgnawed right thumb showing in where.

'What precisely,' asked Enderby of Oldfellow, 'are you suggesting?'

'Oh, for Christ's sake,' Toplady said, entering his office first.

'Myself also?' Enderby asked.

'Yeah, yourself also.'

'Why,' Enderby asked Toplady, when they were seated, 'are you called Angus?'

'I don't see what the shit that's got to do with anything.'

'What I mean is, the Scottish blood, if any, is not made manifest in any – Well, a certain directness of utterance, though usually coarse and improper, an apparent passion for whisky: that bottle on your desk is now empty but was full yesterday –'

'I get this for lagniappe,' Toplady told everybody.

'They were going to call him Agnes,' April Elgar said, 'but when they got a closer look –'

'Stop it, stop it, stop it,' Oldfellow screamed.

'Right,' Ms Grace Hope said, a very hardfaced woman. 'We keep our tempers, right? And we talk about the script. A musical's changed while it's in flight, we know that, but there've been too many changes behind Pete's back with no consultation. He's the star, right? He plays William Shakespeare, right? He gets the script and he says okay, lousily written but that can be put right later, and then when he gets here –'

'Who,' Enderby said, 'says that it's lousily written?'

'You may know Shakespeare,' Oldfellow said, 'but you don't know the theater. There's a difference.'

'You don't know the *theater*, either,' Enderby said. 'You're what is known as a film star.'

'Oh, for Christ's sake,' Ms Grace Hope said, a sudden winter sun shaft firing a faint lanugo Enderby had not before noticed, so that her face seemed to bristle, 'let's stick to the point. This is supposed to be a musical about Shakespeare.'

'Which it is,' Toplady said. 'It's also about the Dark Lady.'

'It's about the Dark Lady,' April Elgar said very sweetly. 'It's also about Shakespeare.'

'You see?' Ms Grace Hope told a poster.

'Well,' Enderby mumbled, 'the concept was bound to change. The talents of Miss ah Elgar here have to be employed. The emphasis is on the power of certain ah dark forces on the life of the poet. I admit there was no such emphasis before. The emphasis now seems to me to be a just one.'

'Thanks, kid,' April Elgar said.

'Practicalities,' Ms Grace Hope said. 'We want certain things restored that got cut out behind our backs.'

'This plurality,' Enderby said. 'Do you speak as ah Mr Oldfellow's wife or as his agent or as ah what?'

'I,' she told Enderby, 'am taking this show to Broadway. There's money being put into this show on certain strict understandings.'

'I assumed,' Enderby said, 'that Mrs ah Schoenbaum –'

'That applies here. It doesn't apply when the show takes off from this theater.'

'What she means,' April Elgar said, 'is that she's producing a musical to show that the great overpaid Pete Oldfellow is more than just a pretty face.'

'Listen who's talking about overpaid,' Oldfellow hotly said. 'I do this fucking thing for peanuts and she –'

'I will not,' Enderby cried, 'have this continual debasement of language.'

'Ah Jesus,' Toplady went.

'All that's needed,' Ms Grace Hope said, 'is cooperation, right?'

'Okay, tell that fag of a husband of yours to cooperate, okay?'

'I will not be called a fag by this black bitch.'

'Ah, I knew we'd get that sooner or later. Okay, maybe this black bitch better schlepp her black ass off home.'

'He didn't mean that,' Enderby said. 'And you didn't mean that about his being a fag.'

'Didn't I just, brother.'

'She calls everybody a fag,' Enderby explained. 'She calls me a fag too, but I don't object.'

'Baby,' April Elgar said, 'you may be an uptight ofay milk-toast limey bastard, but you ain't no fag.'

'Thank you,' Enderby said gravely. Pete Oldfellow said in heat:

'She's got him by the balls, she's made him pussydrunk, she eats him for dinner.' Toplady cried:

'We've got less than one month before opening. This can't go on.'

'Well, try a smaller size, baby,' April Elgar said.

'I'll say one thing,' Enderby suddenly said with weight. 'This thing is not entirely in our hands. There are too many messages coming through. Not very coherent perhaps, but we're being warned, I think, not to play ducks and drakes with the dead. I'm no more superstitious than the next person, but there have been various signs.' They all looked at him. Ms Grace Hope said:

'What do you mean – signs?'

'Mrs Schoenbaum has these seances, superstitious nonsense, of course, but there seems to be somebody out there, watching. A fire at the Holiday Inn. My fryer back in Tangiers exploded.'

'You're crazy,' Oldfellow said without conviction.

'"Good friend,"' Enderby said,' "for Jesus' sake forbear –"'

'Jesus,' went Toplady anticlimactically.

'A thought, that's all. We're trying to celebrate, in a popular and rather ah American form, altogether appropriate considering the double nature of the celebration, the human side of a great poet. That human side must not be traduced. The dead seem to have their own way of responding to the law of libel. If anybody's going to be made to suffer, it's going to be me. A fellow poet.

Letting the side down. You,' he said sternly to Oldfellow, 'had better watch out. You're acting Shakespeare like a kind of cowboy. And with what I take to be a Milwaukee accent. Shakespeare's not going to like that.'

'You're crazy, that's for sure,' Oldfellow said, now with conviction. 'And I come from Cedar Rapids, Iowa.'

'Listen,' Toplady hissed at Enderby, 'I'm director, okay? And I'll decide who does what and how. You just give what you're asked for, okay? That's laid down in your contract.'

'It's also laid down in my contract that I get some money.'

'Give him some money, for Christ's sake,' Toplady said to Ms Grace Hope. Ms Grace Hope at once gave him some money out of a big canvas bag covered with widowed letters of the alphabet in various typefaces. Enderby thanked her courteously. 'Okay,' Toplady said, 'next call's at two. Entire company. Act One.'

'That fag,' April Elgar, 'that plays piano. I want him out on his fat ass.'

'Mike Silversmith always has him,' Toplady patiently explained. 'Mike Silversmith needs him.'

'I don't need him, brother. And I don't have him.'

'Silversmith,' Enderby pronounced, 'is musically analphabetic. His sense of prosody is rudimentary. This fag, Coppola I gather his name is, is at the moment necessary. He can notate music.'

'Who,' Toplady said viciously, 'is running this show?'

Enderby bowed to everybody and then took his urgent engorgement and the image of April Elgar off to another toilet. Then, having finished the implausible story about the planet Urkurk, he went off to have a beef sandwich with coleslaw, which latter he ate.

That afternoon, from a lonely seat in the dark auditorium, he watched Act One unroll. The Induction was back in. Then Elizabethan London was primarily April Elgar and a dumpy woman choreographer. Oldfellow gawped at London, gumchewing kid as dumb Hamnet holding his dad's paw, and gave it slow hayseed (Cedar Rapids, he had said) greeting. He had prerecorded his songs, cheating but permitted in a star who had never sung before, and to the thumping of a live piano by the bald but hairy Coppola opened and shut a soundless gob. April Elgar did not warble

Enderby's little Elizabethan pastiche about love; instead she belted out gamier words, though still by him, Enderby:

> 'Love, you say love, you say love?
> All you're talking about
> Is fleshly philandering,
> Goosing and gandering,
> Peacock and peahen stalking about,
> Squawking about
> Love,
> He-goat, she-goat, mare and stallion,
> Blowsy trull, poxy rapscallion.
> You'd better know that my golden galleon
> Is not for your climbing aboard
> Of'

And so on. And it was not right. She was shaking her divine black ass to it. She was black America, which was better than Cedar Rapids, but she was not Elizabethan London. Nor, God help him, were his own rhythms. And another thing: what right had he, Enderby, to assume that Shakespeare had fallen for a genuine negress (inadmissible term nowadays, he had been told)? A dark lady was not necessarily a black lady. A chill fell on Enderby. He had been corrupted in advance, he had *wanted* a black lady, and nobody had questioned his assumption. Another thing: the dialogue was being steadily corrupted to modern American colloquial. Pete Oldfellow now said, in his Shakespeare persona: 'Okay, then, let's forget it.' Enderby yelled:

'No!'

Toplady, who sat in the centre aisle at a table with a light trained on his script and notes, looked round from over black-framed reading glasses at the source of the agonized cry, then he counteryelled:

'Out!'

'Are you talking to me?' a quieter Enderby said, while the cast looked down.

'Yeah, talking to you. And what I said was.'

'I know what you said. Am I to sit here and hear that bloody traduction and make no bloody protest? I said no and I mean bloody no. And if you haven't the sense of historical propriety to say bloody no too then you're a.'

'You want to be *thrown* out? You're barred from rehearsals, get that? When I want you I'll let you know, right? Now get your ass out of here.'

'Bugger you,' Enderby said doubtfully and getting up. 'The whole thing's a bloody travesty. I'm getting out. I'm also going home. Bugger the contract.' And he climbed panting up the deeply raked aisle. When he got outside into the dusking concourse or whatever they called it he breathed deeply and angrily. Also impotently. He had no return ticket nor money for one. He had, in the toilet, counted Ms Grace Hope's meagre handout. He had neither publisher nor literary agent in New York. He had no source of money to get him to what he called home. He lighted himself a White Owl, better than Robert Burns though not much, he had been recommended to try Muriel but he had once known a girl called Muriel, and he looked through the great window at the dusking carpark. Snow spun on blacktops and, tautomorphically, white tops. Gonna be a white Christmas, they said. He turned to snort smoke at the double door whence he had exited and puff disdain at what lay within. Then the doors opened to show April Elgar running on long legs out. Ah God, that damnable beauty, crystalline and coral concern, body like flame, arms like lesser flames towards him. Then she had him embraced, and he, White Owl awkward in gripe, had to embrace back, then throwing White Owl to hoot out disregarded smoke on oatmeal carpeting. Recover it later.

'Honey, honey,' she said, 'we'll beat the bastards, you'll see.' Then she raised her lips (only a little way necessary) and kissed, with surely histrionic though instinctually histrionic sincerity, him, Enderby. Who dithered. Who trembled kneewise. Who groaned. Who said with little breath:

'You shouldn't. You know. Changes world. Forces me to. Avowals. Most dangerous word in the.'

'I'm with you, baby. Screaming fags. Just thought I'd let you, you know, like know. Ow.' That was Enderby's embrace unwillingly pressing the air out of her. But a sturdy tumescence more appropriate to her image than to her pressed reality thrust them, in the first phase of its arc, apart like some instrument, a truncheon say, of moral order. One of her sharp metal heels transfixed Enderby's White Owl and it ceased, though not for that reason, to smoke. Enderby, seeing it, said:

'Ought to. Give it up. No breath, you see. Don't make me. Avowals.'

'That bastard Topass insulted you, kid, and I've come to take you back in there. You got your rights. He's gonna pologize.'

'I don't,' Enderby said, volume of SF at groin, 'want his bloody apologies. I wouldn't go in there again if I was dragged. I'd be on the next plane if I had the money. I'll lock myself into that bloody cell with the electric typewriter, obscene thing purring at you all the time, and I'll do what has to be done. Then I'll get paid and I'll bugger off. Forgive my bad language.'

'You coming back in there with me.'

'No, I'm not. And there's another thing. The whole damned enterprise is becoming farcical. Quite apart from Oldfellow's stupidity and incompetence. I mean, there's no sense of the past in it. I mean, what with jazzing things up and you, forgive me, wagging your divine ah buttocks.'

'Divine buttocks. I got to remember that. I'm singing the songs, right, saying the words, right, acting this Dark Lady, right? It's that fag Oldass that's fucking it up, right?'

Enderby sighed profoundly. 'It's as if there's no sense of the past here in America.'

'Well, who wants the past? Like the cigarette commercial says, we've come a loooong way, baby. This past you talking about is a bad bad time. You ask my mother. You coming back in there?'

'No,' Enderby said. 'I need tea.'

8

So, in the second act, Essex and Southampton come to see Will and tell him to organize a revival of *Richard II*, signal of rebellion. I cannot, my lords, it will be taken as treasonous. Is not the sale of the book of the play banned by the Privy Council? Thou hast thy responsibilities, Will. Did I not give thee a thousand pounds that thou mightest purchase a player's share in thy bedraggled and mouthing acting company? (True. Enderby had inserted that truth in the first act.) Aye, my lord, and did you not steal from me her I was besotted with to become your own mistress? Come, Will, thou knowest that she but used thee as a rung on a ladder of advancement. She is now our Boadicea. Oh, what bloody nonsense. A song for the rebels:

> Who'll fight for Essex,
> Our uncrowned king?
> From Anglia to Wessex
> Let affirmation ring.

Oh no oh no no no. He, Enderby, was encircled by discouragement, and when, as from her with the divine black ass and the other attributes of magnetism, he was granted encouragement it was in the direction of the further bemerding of poor Will, more, the whole of his spacious age. So the rebellion failed and the dissident earls were confronted by Toplady's silly mistress, who had to be thought of as Gloriana. You, sir, I confine to jail since you were but a foolish follower of this ingrate that knew not what he did. Mayhap my successor, a man of royal lineage whose nomination must be kept secret for fear of such as my almost late lord here, will release you at his royal pleasure. But this, this, this foul viper and toad of the commonweal, this flouter, this sneerer, this

minor satan in trunk hose and foolish smirk, shall to Tower Hill
and his condign end. Aye, his head shall roll with the smirk wiped
off by death's tersive napkin and no more shall be heard of him.
Where now is this black and evil tigress in a woman's hide that I
hear of? Let her be brought before me that I may look on her
and consider best of whether she shall live or die. So April Elgar
swings her divine black farthingaled ass into the royal presence,
and one in decaying ginger pallor looks on the fabled gold of
Afric. Oh Jesus Christ, this never happened and it never could have
happened.

Enderby nevertheless heard in his head all too clearly, dealt by
an evil muse, a conflatrix of the spirits of bemerded Will's poetaster
enemies, chirpy words in the tones of Mistress Lucy Negro, played
by April Elgar. Madam, queen you may be, but it is of a blanched
and bleached kingdom unblessed by the sun, a nearly quondam
queendom leprous, decayed, weakly tyrannical. Know you not
where the future lies? Look westward, sister/ from this derelict/
island, a blister/ soon to be pricked. I speak for the future, madam,
Cleopatran New Rome, I speak of black power,/ that's what we'll
get;/ although I lack power,/ I'll get it yet.

The response to all this of the spirit of Shakespeare was not
reported from Mrs Schoenbaum's residence, since she was spending
a week or so in Miami, but small and as it were distracted punishments dogged Enderby's residence at the Sheraton. He got himself
stuck in the elevator, between floors too; he fell heavily in the
bath, a proof that, anyway, baths were dangerous; plugging in his
kettle to make tea, he somehow managed to fuse all the lights of
that floor; he slipped on a patch of ice in the forecourt of the
hotel; he was served a decayed shirred egg. He was glad to get
back to the Holiday Inn in Terrebasse. Shakespeare's spirit, having
many preoccupations, probably mainly to do with the price of
formerly Shakespeare land in Stratford's environs, would not find
him there again, not being concerned to listen in to Ms Grace
Hope telling him, Enderby, that the budget for a writer had to be
kept low, stars costing so much, the Holiday Inn was where he had
been put in the first place and that was where he should stay.
Question of taxi fares also from Indianapolis to the theater. In
Terrebasse he could slither on the brief ice between place of work

and of repose. Well, it was just as well. Corruption because of proximity of, most dangerous word in language. Oldfellow too much around in bar and dining room too, when Ms Grace Hope had returned to California, betraying faggishness, a genuine attribute, not just conventional smear from April Elgar, by pawing his understudy, primarily Essex, Dick Corcoran the SF man. Get the bloody job finished, get air fare, get home.

'You not been around much,' she said to him one day when they met by chance, indeed coming simultaneously out of neighbouring toilet doors in the Peter Brook Theater. Enderby eyed her bitterly, trying to look like disguised Rosalind in some ridiculous black trendy production of *As You Like It*, that was to say in peaked corduroy cap and patched boilersuit, but breathing very quintessence of elegance and glamour. He also looked guiltily on her, since he had decided to get rid of her at the end of the first act. He could not go on with this ahistorical nonsense. Christ, they were dealing with real and documented situations. Toplady and she could do what the hell they wished, but he would not be a party to their falsifyings. 'Where,' she said, 'you go for Thanksgiving?'

'Thanksgiving?' he said. 'Oh, yes. Of course, that's why they served turkey and pumpkin pie, ridiculous washy stuff. I'd nothing,' he said, suddenly sorry for himself, 'to be thankful for, really. Besides, they were a hell of a long time achieving a reasonable harvest. The Pilgrim Fathers, that is. Good theologians but bad farmers. No, I just stayed where I was.'

'Where you going for Christmas.'

'Same thing, I suppose. Turkey and. Perhaps they don't serve pumpkin pie at Christmas.'

'Christmas,' she said, 'you're coming home with me.'

Enderby took that in very slowly. 'Home?' he said.

'Not my apartment in New York. Home where my momma is. And the kids. In Chapel Hill, North Carolina.'

'Kids? Which kids?'

'*My* kids. Bobby and Nelson. Five and seven. My momma looks after them.'

'And who,' dithered Enderby, 'is their father?'

'Their daddy done go away,' she slavesingsonged. 'I tell him to get the hell out. He was prime meatjuice, baby, but he done hit the bottle and was a real no good mean nigger. Now he's in a black stud agency for white women some place.'

'In what,' Enderby asked, 'capacity do I? That is to say.'

'Momma,' she said, 'don't hold with poets and showbiz people and all that crap. She's a gooood woman. Reads the bible all day. You got to come to momma's house that I bought for her out of my sinful showbiz success as an Englishman spreading the word of the Lord, kind of a smalltown Billy Graham, dig, I worked all this out in mah lil what ah calls mah mahnd, you got to be called Reverend. You'll be okay, momma cooks real good.'

Enderby had read in some magazine of soulfood, strange name, as though the soul resided in the lowliest of animal organs, intestines, hog's bellylinings, spleens. Perhaps it did, black wisdom. Also mustard greens.

'And,' she said, 'she makes tea good and strong in a quart brown pot, ladling it in by the shovel. She drinks it all day when the kids are at school, reading her bible. You better bone up on your bible, Reverend, don't want to be caught out.'

Enderby warmed at once to the quart brown pot. 'That goes with the name Johnson,' he said. 'Dr Samuel Johnson, great tea drinker. Boswell said he must have had exceptionally strong nerves.'

'How did you know that,' she asked, surprised, in a straight, or American straight, voice, 'about Boswell? My great grandpappy was called Boswell Johnson.'

'Some learned and facetious slaveowner,' Enderby said, catching with no pleasure an image of elephanthided men called Cudge whining under Simon Legree whips in the cottonfields, what time old massa in the parlour read with mild interest a great record of the conversation of the English Enlightenment. And then: 'Alas, I have no money. I can't afford the fare.'

'I pay, baby. Ah is a rich lil gal.'

'Well, then, yes, thank you, it's a great honour and you're very very generous.' Then he began to weep, he did not know why. The voice of Toplady sounded over loudspeakers, its very tones giving him a partial reason why, calling the company together. 'Sorry,' Enderby sniffed, 'ridiculous, I know. Emotional lability. Creative tension, something. Again thank you.'

She laid on him hands intended for comfort but provocative of a ferocious glandular gear change and said: 'Something's going on in there, I know. Life's not easy, kid. We'll talk again, okay.' And she darted off, showing a cunningly placed patch, affluent mockery of the Third World to which her colour entitled her to belong, but Abe Fourscore had changed all that, on her divine posterior. Enderby returned to his little room and switched on the electric typewriter, which sang gently to him of the need to work and not waste current. He relented somewhat (there was always this danger, adjacent toilet doors or a jaunty 'Hi' in the greenroom) and did not wipe her wholly out of Act Two, no confrontation of queens but mention of her part as evil genius of uprising, and then she was to languish in some jail or other or be thrown onto the ragheaps of Clerkenwell, no more be heard of Mistress Lucy Negro except as pocked whore. But then.

Then there was *Hamlet,* Will as ghost misnaming prince as Hamnet, sick for many reasons (death of son and end of Shakespeare line; his lordly friend Southampton in prison; the loss of a rare mistress, brightness falls from the air or hair) and sent off to Stratford to be made whole. And in marital embraces with ginger Anne (it had been decided, and no bad idea, to combine the parts of queen and Mistress Shakespeare) he dreams of Afric gold, Egypt being in Africa. And so Cleopatra. But who was he, Enderby, to adapt a great tragedy to the limited talents, New World phonemes and intonations and slangy lapses, cecity towards the past, Pyrrhonism and so on of this weak cry of players? A straight blank verse Cleopatra, and she could not do it. Dumbshow to music (not Silversmith's, better to drag in some genuine musician from Indiana University, a Moog man who, forced to write tonalities wholly atmospheric, would produce the diluted romanticism that was his true, if suppressed, idiom?)? Enderby lighted a White Owl. Let Rome in Tiber melt, and the wide arch/ Of the rang'd empire fall! The world well lost for love, and did the world include art and, for that matter, William Shakespeare?

> Let's have one other gaudy night,
> Let's have one other bawdy night
> And fright the white owls away.
> Come, captains, drink beneath the stars

Until the wine peeps through your scars,
Drink till the dawning of the day!

For some reason that needed a black voice, altogether male and fully ballsed, but it had to be the fag Oldfellow transformed in vision to a Will with a chest like twin kettledrums. And for her?

God knew, she was Cleopatrician enough as they boarded the plane for Chicago, she in plain moulded emerald dress with seagreen cloak that had flared in the wind as they left the taxi, he in cap and old overcoat, blinking without glasses. At Chicago they got on an aircraft bound for Raleigh, named for the father of smoking. Smoking, she said:

'Now, honey, you can talk.'

'What about?'

'You know what about, kid.'

Enderby sighed like furnace. 'You mustn't,' he said, 'consider me to be a sexless recluse advancing into grey middle age. I live alone after a brief failed marriage. Unconsummated, indeed. She was a woman of great chic and skill and ambition, and she wanted to be married to a poet. Then she became well known as a manager of pop groups and similar abominations.'

She looked at him wideeyed, new angle on him. 'Who?'

'A certain Vesta Bainbridge who became a certain Vesta Wittgenstein.'

'Oh Jesus, her I knew. She wanted to manage me one time. She was a bitch, one hundred per cent and no discount.'

'Well, there you are then. The muse was very angry about it and went away. I couldn't write. I attempted suicide. Then I was rehabilitated, as they put it. Then she came back.'

'Who came back? La Wittgenstein?'

'No, the muse.' Enderby looked very gravely at the smoking goddess beside him, a meanly framed vista of American bad weather beyond her. 'Personification, if you like. Writing poetry isn't like adding up figures. There's a force outside that gets inside and starts dictating. Easier to call it the muse. Her, I mean. She can be very jealous. She's gone for good now, I think. So much and no more is granted to a poet. I've published my *Collected Poems*, to no applause. What I do in that bloody theatre or theater is nothing. Pure craft. Not so pure either. I hope I'm not boring you.'

'No, honey. You just keep straight on.'

'My feelings towards ah your divine self, then. With a woman a man has to effect a dichotomy. You know the word?'

'Oh, come on.'

'Sorry, you keep assuming this Topsy act, the slangy front to the world, the virtues of deprivation and so on. What I mean is. Well, it was you who mentioned the noumenon and the phenomenon aspect of things. I take your image to bed with me and devour it growling. Need, you know, the filling up of the wells. Disgusting but ineluctable. A private indeed privy matter. But behind that is you, and yet not behind that, because your body is no mask. And if I say love —' The aircraft responded to that dangerous word by meeting clear air turbulence. '— I mean, what the hell can you do with love except cleanse yourself of it by debasing the image to a lust object? I mean, what do I say, I, an ugly ageing man whose skin was never washed in the sun's glory, running a beach restaurant in Morocco, all all alone? Marry me, prove that marriage can work, companionship and all the rest of it, let the love derived from total knowledge rub off onto the image and make it no longer an object of concupiscence, do I say that? Of course not. I suppose,' he said heavily, 'I wish to invoke a special relationship, impossible of course.'

'Yeah yeah yeah. Quite a speech.'

'And what,' Enderby asked, 'do you do about love? If I may ask.'

'I tried it. Now I have my career. Not simple then, is it? You don't just want to get laid.'

'Getting laid,' he said, 'solves no problems. Love is a bloody nuisance.' CAT agreed. 'And we have the business of this damned musical play to make matters worse. Because you're not Cleopatra. Divine, beautiful, heartstopping, a miracle of flesh and bone and air and fire but not Cleopatra. You see that?'

'Yeah, baby,' sighing like smaller furnace, 'I know. I'm me. But I'm being paid to be me. Me singing songs and — what was the expression you used? Wagging my divine buttocks, yeah.'

'And that fag Oldfellow as you rightly call him is not Shakespeare or Antony either. And I'm stuck in this thing, mired in it, and I can't get out. Look, that damned thing's on fire.'

'Port engine? Yeah, it does that sometimes. How's about my songs?'

'It's still on fire. No, it's gone out now. No, it's started again. Saw me getting on this plane, giving me warning. Leave his dust alone. It's gone out now. No, it's not. Yes, it has.'

'Songs.'

'One song. You can be Cleopatra in a kind of dumbshow, Will's vision. Then he gets drunk with Ben Jonson —'

'You're crazy.'

'Not your brother, the other one. He dies of a sweating fit, and he sees you for one last time in his delirium. Love of his life. Inspiration. The future. Nature. Sex. Libido. The dark unconscious.' Enderby kept his eyes warily on that port engine. It did not reflare. 'The trouble is the words. The trouble is that that bastard fag Silversmith doesn't understand prosody. The trouble is going to be the music. One song. Summing it all up.'

'To be or not to be,' she said. 'Pure what's the word ontology.' Enderby looked at her with some awe. 'To be or not to be, what is it you want of me, what am I to you except the one thing true that fades, evades, lives in the shades or a world unborn shorn of reality, no actuality, a dream, a gleam of gold unmined you'll never find.' Enderby wished now heartily to embrace her: what she was improvising complete with tune was, God knew, terrible enough but it would get the whole damn burden cleared off his shoulders, the godless task finished. But they now had to fasten seatbelts and prepare for landing. A lot of cold flat green. 'I did some Creative Writing at Chapel Hill,' she explained. When they were standing in the aisle to get out, following and followed by blacks and rednecks, none of any great beauty or distinction, he did attempt a tentative embrace. She was a slim girl, not much to get hold of. 'Hey, hey,' she said.

She drove them both expertly in a hired Avis Studebaker or something down what seemed to be dirt roads and then a highway towards the town of Chapel Hill, where also was the first of the United States state universities. Enderby did not know what to expect of her momma's house. No log cabin, certainly, redolent of chitterlings. It turned out to be a nice little detached dwelling in pink brick with a flower garden, just behind a hotel called the Carolina Inn. There was an aged black hoeing.

'Hi, Uncle Joe.'

He dropped his hoe in a clump of dead morning glories or something and went 'Wha howya hawa wah haha yeah' or something, chuckling his grey black head off. Then he came to the car to start taking bags out of the boot, trunk they said here, making to Enderby a similar speech, not however chuckling.'Hi ah,' Enderby offered, straightening his tie, which, he knew, was royal blue with gold spots. And then he followed her up steps and into a nice little hallway smelling of aerosol magnolias. And then.

Well, he lay awake that night of Christmas Eve digesting his welcome, expressed best in many mugs of mahogany tea, also a homecooked meatloaf. Her momma a welcoming woman with grey curls, old, she the divine one a product of ageing loins, in a royal blue sack of a gown with gold spots, her body gross with the enforced farinacity of long deprivation. Lemme looka you Reverend, with sharp old eyes blurred by a milky meniscus. You faaaaar from home for de birt o de Lord Jesus, and so on. An upright piano and on it photographs of family large, dispersed, done bad to by whites, Ben and little May grinning at making grade, the father long dead in bogey accident on railroad. The kids, Bobby and Nelson, televisiongawpers like other kids, showing no enthusiasm at sight of festive square packages from Indianapolis. You take dem walkin Reverend while me and ma daughter has lil talk. So Enderby had to walk the main street of Chapel Hill, empty of college students because the vacation was on, with a little black kid in either hand. This was not something he had foreseen. The kids rolled eyes of suspicion up at him but also demanded Cokes and ice cream sodas. They also demanded to be taken to one of the town's two cinemas, where a Swedish travesty of *Fanny Hill* was being shown. No kids allowed, he told them. He walked them back very wearily and at first could not find the house, nor could they, but at length saw the gardener wrenching up plantains and growling some ancient song of bondage. He and the kids had a brief colloquy that Enderby could not understand, and then the three of them went in. April Elgar had turned into May Johnson, in sloppy dressing gown and old mules, hair disarrayed and a daughterly whine. Enderby one of the family then.

He lay in the bedroom that had been intended, it seemed, for Ben the son, who had however Christmas engagements but

telephoned from somewhere to his mother, who said you just do
dat son and we be thinkin of you and lovin you just de same. After
the meatloaf and collard greens and a Sara Lea creature, strong tea
but no alcohol, Mrs Johnson opened up her bible, put on spectacles
and looked over the top of them at Enderby. Enderby felt fear: he
was going to be tested. But all she said was what your favourite
psalm Reverend, and he was able to answer Psalm 46 and even
quote some of it at her, so that she nodded and checked and said
dat right Reverend. And then she said: what you goana preach
about tomorrow Reverend and that made him spill his tea on his
tie. She had him there in the corner of the combined living and
dining room at the cleared table, while May Johnson had her arms
about the two kids on the biscuit-coloured settee, watching Bing
Crosby and Fred Astaire in *Holiday Inn*. 'The meaning of the
Nativity,' Enderby said, and she nodded and quoted about de census
to be taken ob all de world in de time ob Caesar Augustus.

Well, he lay there. Mrs Johnson lay in the room next to his, her
daughter in the room beyond, and the two kids on a two-tiered
bunk in the room beyond that. This was neither the time nor the
place to entertain lewd thoughts about April Elgar, so he lay there
partly illumined by a sodium street lamp working out tomorrow's
sermon. Of course, this had been inevitable and he, or that blasted
divine girl there, ought to have foreseen it. Distinguished visiting
inevitably Baptist preacher all the way from England. It was not
to give a sermon to Baptist blacks that he had come all the way
from Morocco. He ought really to try to convert them to his own
brand of apostate Catholicism, but perhaps Christmas was hardly
a discreet season for that. Soon, a Holiday Inn face towel stuffed
inside the crotch of his faded striped pyjamas in case of accidents,
he slept. He slept remarkably well, and was wakened in southern
winter sunlight by a small black boy bashing him on the shoulder
and offering him a mug, no inscription on it, of very strong hot
tea. The other black boy was with him, and then May Johnson
herself came in in dressing gown and worn mules to wish him a
merry Christmas and even to hand him a small gaudily wrapped
gift. She also kissed him on the lips, her lips being warm from
sleep and also greaseless, while the two kids looked solemnly on.
Fortunately he had slept with his teeth in. He said, unwrapping:

'Oh my God, you shouldn't, I didn't get anything for. Oh my God, oh just what I wanted.' It was not really, being a miniature calculator to be worn on the wrist with a dusky screen that showed time playing the game of numerical transformation, squarish figures becoming other figures with the minimum of dim-lit metamorphosis. The day, and all the days to follow till the end of the world, were presented to Enderby as a linear process, not the fall-rise cycle of the poet. As for calculating, what had he to calculate? He looked at her, sitting on the bed edge, with humble gratitude, saying: 'It was a problem of. Well, you see, I had to pay the hotel bill.'

'You gave me a poem,' she said.

He could not now very well upbraid her for getting him into this Reverend situation. He offered his tea mug to her but she shook her head. Enderby slurped. The voice of Mrs Johnson below called them to breakfast. The kids, jostling each other for precedence, ran. She remained seated, lovely though not, the deglamorized daughter, mythical. 'Strange,' Enderby said. 'Here we both are, in a clinal situation so to speak, a bed context I mean, the Greek word means to lean or repose I suppose, hence bed, hence clinic by the way, and this has nothing to do with my feverish imaginings. Domestic, I mean. I weep at the impossibility of it all.'

'Momma has breakfast ready. Eggs. Ham. Hominy grits.'

'I'll write you a proper poem,' Enderby said. 'You'll see. I weep at the.'

'Yeah, yeah, impossibility of it all. Say, there's a good title for a song, Cole Porterish. The impossibility of it all, the sheer futility of it all. You must work on that.'

'Even bad art,' Enderby solemnly said, half-empty mug in paws, 'is made out of elemental cries for help.' But she had gone.

Mrs Johnson sang crackily a song about the itty bitty baby born in Baithlaihaim as she served breakfast. Here was he, Enderby the all too white man, Bradcaster pink mitigated by Tangerine bronze, at home, dusky Morocco a mere station in its direction, in a black household. He could see himself for ever here, drinking ever stronger tea and reading the Book of Deuteronomy with Mrs Johnson, cracking the kids' woolly heads when they were fretful, waiting for the daughter-Female Friend-goddess-impossible she to be deglamorized on a flying visit. After breakfast of two fried eggs and ham and a sort of white porridge (get dem greeerts down, dey'll do you gud), he shaved, dressed in Christmas clerical (all metaphors in time become reality) grey, then trembled. God knew what he could do about this bloody sermon. Leave it to chance, muse, Holy Ghost? Cynicism. Compoundedly dangerous American visit. Surely the God of the black Baptists could not be less vindictive than dead Will?

They were driven by May Johnson down the main boulevard of Chapel Hill, Enderby at back flanked by kids. Both ladies were demurely hatted and gloved. They arrived at a whiteboard building of simple pseudocolonial charm between a Howard Johnson restaurant that looked much more like a church, spire and all, and a garage where hammering artisans defied Christmas. The chapel had its own carpark, and this was already full of Plymouths and Oldsmobiles. There were a lot of women waiting to go in, all blackly radiant in the mild sun, and black respectable men in decent suits. Big treble event this, evidently: Christmas, big singing star back in hometown, foreign Reverend: Mrs Johnson had clearly been busy on the telephone. A genuine or right Reverend, named on the outside board as Dr R. F. Grigson, greeted Enderby with warm black hands and secular gusto. A big man took Enderby on one side and handed him his card: Condor Life. You travellin a lot, Reverend, your dearest and nearest in need of first class protection, we have lil talk after service. Then they went into a plain place of worship with a dais, a lectern, and an electronic organ. The worshippers, gleamingly teethed and boldly coloured, were stained glass enough.

It was not at all like the Catholic masses of Enderby's youth, dyspeptic Maynooth leprechauns peevish about last week's collections, or the anaemic evensongs of his brief curative Anglicanism, with fine if archaic Jacobean prose apologetically delivered by cricketing rectors and very well-made hymns bleated by conservativeclubcakebaking etiolated housewives with herb gardens. They went in a lot for extravagant joy here, also a healthy concern with sin. They cried yeah, that right and we hearin you. May Johnson, as he ought to have expected, sang what was called a gospel song to a jazzy accompaniment from a young buck whose grin mimicked his two electronic manuals, while the congregation clapped in rhythm:

> And when I get to heaven where I belong
> It gonna be Christmas all eternity long.

They smiled on him with encouragement and expectation when he was called upon. He stifflegged it to the lectern and surveyed them all sickly, fine bright open godly black sods as they were, no, not sods, decent people really. May Johnson expected the best from him, he could see that. Not let her down. He had given, when in the army, lectures on the British Way and Purpose, now very remote entities and never easily definable even then. He had delivered a disastrous speech when receiving the Goodby gold medal for poetry, which, along with the meagre cheque that went with it, he had at once given back. He had always found it difficult to be insincere and that perhaps was why he had not got on in the world. He was worried now about the danger of sincerity breaking in. He was not worried about either articulacy or audibility. They would hear him all right. He said:

'My name is Enderby.' They all smiled at the quaintness of his accent. 'Enderby the poet,' he unwisely continued. They did not now all smile. 'So they call me sometimes in my own country, because I have endeavoured to praise the good of life and deplore its evil, and do other things as well, in the medium of verse. There is nothing wrong with being a poet, so long as one's poetry is not obscene or Godless or ill composed. King David, as you all know from your psalms, was a poet, and King Solomon, he er –' – he was not sure whether son or father, like a character in *Ulysses* – 'was also a poet, as you know from the Song of Songs that is his. A poet can be a witness for the divine posterior, that is to say truth, and he can thus be a martyr, which means witness in Greek.' The Reverend Grigson went amen at that. 'Now tomorrow is the feastday of St Stephen, who was battered to death with stones because he was a Christian, and you know who ordered the battering – Saul, who later had a sort of epileptic fit on the road to Damascus and was changed into St Paul.' To some in the congregation, including Mrs Johnson, this seemed to be news. Enderby had already lost his connection. Poets. Martyrs. 'William Shakespeare, a great martyr or witness for the truth, put himself into Psalm 46 – look it up after your Christmas dinner or even before – forty-sixth word from the beginning, forty-sixth word from the end, if you omit the flourish *Selah*.' Some of the older and ignorant, who presumably believed that the King James version was the direct word of God, no nonsense about having to go through the Hebrew first, showed wideeyed shock. 'Do not be afraid of poets,' Enderby cried bitterly, 'since they are often God's instruments, though they can also be the devil's as well, though not usually at the same time if it can be avoided.' Then: 'Martyrs, I said, and I say again martyrs. Your people have been martyrs, witnesses to the devilry and Godlessness of racial oppression. You think of the white man as the enemy, but I ask you to remember that white men have suffered, if you can accept the Jews as white, women too. My own people suffered in England in the times of the Godless Tudors, a sort of gingerhaired people from the principality of Wales, not of the race of the fish, mammal really, that swallowed Jonah, if you can believe that, a whale's throat being somewhat narrow.' They all looked at him in wonder, no cries of dat right and I hearin ya. 'My family stuck to God's truth as taught by the Church of Rome, and, by Christ, we suffered for it. Later, of course,' he added speedily, 'we became Baptist, another true faith battered by the forces of oppression. Oppression,' he then cried, 'intolerance, hatred – ah, by God, do we know them? By God we do, and will go on knowing them. Today, as some of you will know, we celebrate the birth of Jesus Christ in a filthy stable. He was on the side of intolerance, saying I come to bring not peace but a sword, and on the side of hatred, as of the Pharisees and of even your own father and mother if they got in the way of the truth and the light. Christians have been oppressors throughout the history of the faith, as you know, for it was at least nominal Christians who oppressed your people during the dark days of slavery. Christians oppressing Jews as well as blacks as well as Muslims, for the most part teetotal pederastic people, and of course the other way round, although neither Jews nor blacks have had much opportunity to be oppressive, except in Israel and Africa. Still, everything comes to those that wait. Some call slavery and oppression modes of cultural transmission, meaning that if you had not been enslaved and oppressed you would still be worshipping stocks and stones and sucking jujus in the heart of darkness, well, not quite, most of you coming from West Africa, an explanation of your natural artistry, don't bother to try to learn Swahili, that is an East Coast *lingua franca*. Therefore I ask you to move forward,' he said, 'forward to an age in which none of these things will happen, except in the Godless media, of which the damnable stage is one, and try to get on with the job, whatever it happens to be, insurance or singing or bongo drumming, and let us try to make a little money for our children and our children's children and, if the hideous future which has not yet come about but, by heaven, will come about will permit it, even our children's children's children, yea, unto seventy times seven. Not that I personally, so far as I know, I was briefly stationed in Catania in World War Two, have children of any colour whatsoever. Today is the feast of the holiest of all the children and, by God, let us not forget it. *In nomine Patris et Filii et Spiritus Sancti,*' making the sign of the cross, '*Amen.*' Then he got down.

9

They were sitting together on the flight back up north, so she had been retransformed into April Elgar, and very lovely and mythical with it. Her hair, newly straightened, was all ink and health. She was else fresh Blue Mountain coffee mixed with the morning's milk, scarlet too, dress and liprouge and fingernails and, as Enderby knew though scarlet leather hid them, toenails as well.

'That's what she said,' she said, 'when you weren't there, in the john or some place.'

'In the er yes,' Enderby corroborated. 'Never ask me to be insincere again. God won't attack, anyway. He could see through the confusion. A great one for sorting out chaos. In London on a hoarding I saw DEVLIN THE BIG NAME IN DEMOLITION. I misread that Devlin, naturally. It's the other up in Indiana we have to watch. Shakespeare, that is.'

'It's not Indiaaaaahna, it's Indianna, like in bananna.'

'Banahna,' Enderby corrected. 'That thing with jam and sliced bananas and custard your ah momma made was very good, took me back to my infancy. The turkey was good too, very crisp on the outside. But strong tea is her real, appropriate when you come to think of it, forte. She said I ought to stay on and help look after the kids and have some real good home cooking. She seemed to think I was not very well. A consequence of.'

'They're charitable people,' she said, 'and don't you forget it. My momma told everybody you been working too hard and got the word of the Lord all balled up. That's charity.'

'*Caritas*,' Enderby said. 'Well, she's welcome to come to Tangiers. Kids as well. Do them good, they can learn Moghrabi Arabic and be black Muslims or something. No, they can't, being Baptist, I see that. You too,' he then said. 'You'll knock them ah cold.' He then saw her very clearly lying naked in the sun and felt his flesh respond terribly. But she wouldn't lie in the sun, brown enough already. He spread *Time* magazine over his crotch. She said:

'That's in Africa some place, right?'

'North. The kingdom of Morocco. Not what they call Black Africa. This unitary concept you get over here from some of those woolhaired louts is a load of ah nonsense. Africa's very big, you know. So big that nobody can swallow it. They huddle into tribes in self-protection from it, you know. Anyway, we're all exiles. You and I, anyway. As for colour, that's only like furniture. A green chair or an orange one, it's for putting your fundament on. If white's no good it's because it has the wrong connotations. Leprosy, slugs, and all the rest of it. It's not real white anyway. If you think I like being white you're wrong. I see myself white writhing over your divine brownness. An abomination. I beg your pardon. Shouldn't have ah externalized that vision. Better off as we are,' he added vaguely.

'How do you mean – as we are?'

'I love you,' Enderby said boldly. 'I shall love you till the day I die. There,' he added unnecessarily, 'I've said it. Demand nothing. Totally disinterested. Perhaps,' he superadded, 'I can start writing poems again. Love poems. From a distance. Me white in Africa, you black here. Not really black, of course. A damnable politicoracial abstraction. There,' he finished.

She sighed out cigarette smoke. 'Brother,' she then said, 'you sure are one large pain in the ass.'

'Unfair. Disinterested. Ask nothing. If you wish, I apologize for that ah declaration. We're coming into Chicago now, my kind of town, sorry, that's back in Tangiers. Then back on the job, forget what I said. Partners in crime only. It is a bloody crime too. The things we're doing to Shakespeare. Then I pack your divine image among my dirty shirts and go. Love poems.'

'Pain,' she varied, as they prepared to get out, 'in the divine fundament.'

'What God showed to Moses,' Enderby said, following her down the aisle. 'I've often wondered why. God with a bottom. Some very profound significance.'

When they had marched a mile or so, to the accompaniment of ubiquitous Vivaldi, nice change from pop, pop of its day when you came to think of it, to the area whence the aircraft for Indianapolis took off, Enderby at once sat down and chewed a couple of Pepts. Silversmith was there, with two other men. 'Hi,' he offered. He effected laconic introductions. 'Len Bodiman, orchestrator. Pip Wesel, MD.' Bodiman carried a heavy canvas bag which presumably contained what would be called the score. His glasses, in heavy black mourning frames, were too big for him, and he kept them on by variously grimacing. He was a big soft man in a kind of Churchillian sirensuit. Enderby said:

'What kind of orchestra? Shawms, recorders, viols da gamba, sackbuts? Authentic, I mean?' It was this Pip Wesel who replied. Enderby assumed that Silversmith's rude terming of him as Mentally Deficient was either a joke or a tribute to his creative madness in whatever field he wandered, scenic artistry perhaps, but the young man, who was chihuahua-hairless, was full of uncoordinated gestures and he now bleated several times. He said:

'We've been hearing about you. Mike here said that's what you'd say. You want madrigals too? Hey nonny nonny and all that shit?'

Enderby felt his neck getting thicker. 'Don't,' he threatened, 'use that word in the presence of this lady here.' April Elgar was standing somewhat apart, and Enderby saw himself, with bitter regret, as physically not very disjunct from these three ugly leerers. White and unbalanced, paunchy and full of tics. He pulled in his own belly since he could not push in theirs. He had a vision of April Elgar writhing on a bed with a black man of comparable beauty. He nodded with desperate regret and satisfaction. April Elgar said:

'Save your breath, kid. He's crammed with that er commodity.' She had learned something from him, Enderby, then. Wesel said:

'Okay okay, colleagues, right? Working together, right? Peace and love and all that shit, right?'

'There you go again,' Enderby said. 'And what precisely is your ah role in this enterprise?'

'MD,' Wesel said.

'That's frank, or perhaps facetious, but what is it precisely that you do?'

'He wags the stick,' Bodiman said. 'He's the stickwagger.' And then, to April Elgar, 'You got rhythm yet, Ape?'

'Don't,' Enderby began, 'call –'

'One of the big black fallacies,' Bodiman continued. 'Rhythm as the inborn inheritance of the jungle.'

'I got more rhythm in my ass,' April Elgar said unwisely, 'than you got in your whole fat sluggy ofay corpse, brother. I can see we going to get along just fine.'

'Shakespeare at work,' Enderby pronounced. 'Sowing dissension. It's the curse he prophesied. Moving his bones.' But nobody listened. They had been told through a loudspeaker to get on the aircraft, but Bodiman found the opportunity to say:

'In your ass, right,' and she:

'What's that supposed to mean?'

'He's not referring,' Wesel said, 'to your singing, if that's what it's called.' And then he skipped ahead, bleating. If Enderby had had the money, he would have limped back through the crowds and Vivaldi to the international segment of O'Hare, there to purchase a homeward ticket and get, as they said here, the hell out. But he was chained. On the aircraft, next to an April Elgar who brooded and drank whisky sours in excess, by some dispensation, of the number allowed by the paternalistic airline, he gloomily regarded his new digital watch, faintly fascinated by the onward march of the square figures which turned one into the other with insolent ease, a kind of numerical paranomasia. Then he switched the instrument to a calculator and added up large sums.

He was adding up even larger sums on his bed later that day, having eaten hamburger steak with fried eggs, drunk lager that tasted of onions and water, taken Pepts and Windkill, then sadly onanized. He should rightly have done so to the stimulus of April Elgar's present, but it was not aromatic of her as a shoe or stocking would have been. The present was really an unwilled invitation to accept a very dull future in which one second was the same as another, as symbolized by the minimal metamorphosis from number to number, in which the achievement of a minute and later an hour was, so muted was the change, nothing for the instrument to crow over. The sums he added were, though large, small enough for him to check by simple arithmetic. The instrument told, it seemed, no lies and might be trusted with huge multiplications and even square roots. Then there was a knocking at his door. It was April Elgar in plastic rainhood and raincoat. It was hard to tell whether her face had been irrigated by rain or was being irrigated by tears. She said:

'I've moved in here. I can't stand the bastards.'

'You mean,' Enderby asked, 'in *here*?'

'Not in here, stoopid. In the hotel. Just down the corridor.' And then she sat on the nearer bed, that on which Enderby, in shirt, trousers and socks, had been lying calculating, and wept. Enderby sat next to her. He said:

'Take those things off. The outer ones, I mean. Then tell me why. Crying, that is. Not that there's any reason why you should. Explain, I mean. We all ought to be crying all the bloody time.' She needed, Enderby could see, comfort, so he put his arms about her. So, in his arms and in plastic rainwear, she sobbed. He patted the plastic rainwear, going 'There, there.' And then: 'Insulted you, did they, those white bastards? And then there's coming away from home and leaving your mother and your kids, a known loving ambience, and meeting sneering swine making uncalled-for references to your private life I took them to be, believe me, I don't believe any of it, I know you, it's the snarl the jealous world delivers to talent and beauty, there, there.' He nearly added, unthinking, his stepmother's cantrip: *Cry more and you'll pee less*. She stopped crying very suddenly, wiped her eyes and face vigorously on Enderby's shirt, then said, as all women were supposed to say, according to Enderby's reading, in such circumstances:

'I must look terrible.'

'Not at all. Young, defenceless, and, of course, very beautiful. Now take that stupid rain thing off. Have you eaten anything?'

'Yeah, I ate dinner, and those bastards were in the dining room kind of jeering, and then I went back up and was taking a shower, and I said the hell with it, I'm going to where my *friend* is, so I got my bags taken down and I put on my raincoat and. If I take it off,' she suddenly began to giggle, 'you'll see the real me, kid. Divine fundament and all.'

'You mean,' Enderby gulped, 'straight out of the bath, shower I mean, ridiculous unclean American custom, and and.' His body stiffened except for one member, which couched morbidly flaccid. 'I see.' He added, obscurely: 'The casting of the die.' He superadded: 'You mean you *would*?'

'You talked about loving me till you die, kid.'

'It's not the same,' Enderby said, much perturbed. 'Perhaps I've been too dualistic, too Platonic. I mean, there are too many difficulties involved. Aesthetic, for instance. Beauty and the beast. Not that I'm ungrateful. But love, love, that's something different from taking that thing off. Please understand.'

'I see.' Standing, she put her hands in the raincoat pockets. 'I got in one of my bags in the room down along there what they called publicity pictures. Tits and ass and teeth and legs in gunmetal stockings and frothy lingerie. The kind of thing pimply kids fire their wad at. You know what I mean?'

'Yes,' Enderby said unhappily. 'Pulling their wires, or monkeys. Bashing the bishop. Alas, yes.'

'That the me you want, brother?'

'If,' Enderby said hangdog and noticing a hole in his sock where an uncut craggy nail protruded, 'I were worthy. Young, black perhaps or browner than I am. All I can do is love humbly and cherish dreams.'

'Yah, wet ones.'

'It's been a long time. I am what I am. But I mean what I say about love.'

'Yeah, and you don't have to prove it. I'm not God, Baptist or Catholic. But, brother, I forbid the worship of images. Think about it. I got to go and unpack. We got an early call tomorrow. First band rehearsal.'

'I'll see you,' Enderby said with relief, 'at breakfast.'

'Yeah, early morning nourishment. Wadfiring must take a lot out of you.' Then she left.

10

'The signification in British, that is to say traditional, English is altogether −'

'There will have to be an emergency meeting of the −'

'Too late now. We open tomorrow.'

And so there had been a howling and scratching limping progression towards the moment of the first dress rehearsal, Enderby sometimes peering in at the screaming and shouting from one of the top doors of the auditorium, but Toplady always seeming to know he was doing this and turning to yell 'Out!' So Enderby had stood a short while outside, Lazarus at the feast of punching and hairtearing, listening to music which, whatever it was, was not Elizabethan. Instrumentalists who did not seem to care much for music except as a union-protected livelihood had been scraped in from all over flat Indiana, and these had demanded coffeebreaks at the very instant when, after several hours of paid unscraping and unblowing, they were bidden play. There had been disdainful dim men around copying band parts, but only after bitter sessions of negotiation with the head of the local part-copying union, who himself copied no parts.

'*Arse* is one thing, *ass* quite another.'

'That first word is a British perversion of that second one.'

'Ah, bloody nonsense.'

Enderby had been both surprised and fearful that he had no

longer, save for one small thing, been called in to make emendations or compose new verses. Everybody had appeared resigned
to the way things were, not knowing how to make them better,
or worse, and sensibly doubting that Enderby knew either. So the
second act had the Essex rebellion, the Dark Lady shoved into a
dark jail, the Bard collapsing with various kinds of distress as the
Ghost in *Hamlet*, which and whom (Hamlet) he kept, in bereaved
father's guilt, calling *Hamnet* and Hamnet, his going home to
Stratford to be nagged to death by Anne, but not before conjuring
the Dark Lady as Cleopatra and seeing, about his deathbed, visions
of her wagging her divine farthingaled ass to that early mocking
ditty about love.

'New England puritanism would not admit the real word. Bugger
it, man, look at Chaucer – *ers. Ass* is a euphemism.'

'The title will have to be changed. There will have to be an
emergency –'

So that was it and there it was. Pay me and let me get the hell
out. But Ms Grace Hope, who had previously disgrudged odd thin
sheaves of greenbacks, had buggered off back to the Coast, first
having quarrelled violently, in public too, with her husband the
fag Oldfellow, who had been carrying on overblatantly with his
understudy Dick Corcoran, the Earl of Essex. Enderby had brought
his overdue hotel bill to the concourse of wildly but silently clacking
typewriters to have something done about it and been sent, by
circuitous stairways, to a little Viennese Kantian sequestered in a
cellar, a refugee from Hitler's *Anschluss*, who would discourse
charmingly on the metaphysics of money but would pay not one
red cent out. Enderby had been, was, fed up.

'Believe you me, you will make yourselves bloody laughing-
stocks. The title comes from –'

'Not even William Shakespeare is immune from censure. We
have here a quorum, I think –'

'Some of them drunk.'

'That is uncalled for –'

He had assuaged his misery and boredom by raging around the
small office, uncleaned, unvisited, that had long before been
allotted to him, switching on the typewriter and mostly ignoring
its invitatory hum, thus vindictively wasting the Peter Brook

Theater's electricity, but also occasionally adding a pecked line to a formless poem he was allowing to accumulate, its theme Caesar (he, Enderby, unlaureled) and Cleopatra (she who these days uttered mostly a distracted *Hi* at him. Her dresser had arrived from New York, an Iras or Charmian of gross mammyish aspect who slept in the room next to Enderby's and laughed in her sleep).

> Nor will this quadrate marble crush
> Juice from the olive stone,
> No slave philosopher enmesh
> In marriage stone and moon.
> By narrow moongate let me in,
> Eased by the olive's gush.

He had had his chance, he could not deny it, but he had not wanted the chance, had he? Shakespeare would have understood, she not, never, either Dark Lady. Musing thus, he received a cold note ordering him to perform what seemed to be a final scriptorial office, namely to compose a kind of national anthem for Elizabethan England. He rattled off:

The babe's first breath
Is: Elizabeth.
The soldier's death
Is for Elizabeth.
Hail Gloriana, keep England our home
Safe from her enemies: Scotland and Ireland and France and
    Spain and Muscovy and the Holy Roman Empire and, it
    goes totally without saying, Rome.

Delivering it in an envelope (let them bloody well process that into something singable, the bastards) to the secretarial concourse, he had seen for the first time the presswet posters. ACTOR ON HIS ASS. Clever in a way. It could not be, though it was now being, considered obscene, since it was a citation from *Hamlet*, but its implication was totally vulgar. On a notice board he had read that the final dress rehearsal would be in the nature of a free performance for the schoolkids of Indianapolis and environs, three in the

afternoon of 6 January, Twelfth Night if anyone was interested, and
that in the evening there would be an obligatory party at the
mansion of Mrs Schoenbaum. That party was in progress now.
Enderby was having it out about the title with one of the board
of governors of the theater trust, a hardware magnate named, it
seemed, Humrig, retired and now, apparently, a full-time churchwarden. He drank teetotal punch, which few others there did.
Enderby said:

'Anyway, it's not my responsibility − either the title or your own
wretched squeamishness. *Ass* is *asinus*, a donkey.'

'You wrote the ah play.'

'I wrote something. Whether that something is still there I
can't say. I did not go to the dress rehearsal, though I heard lots
of ill-behaved schoolchildren. They seemed to enjoy it. On their
level.'

Enderby turned his back on Mr Humrig and went to the
improvised bar, which the mad son Philip and the grey black
retainer were running together. 'Gin,' Enderby ordered. The mad
son Philip whispered:

'I got this stuff spiked.'

'I beg your pardon?'

'Smell it.' A jug of murky orange liquid was raised to Enderby's
nose and he got a whiff of surgical spirit.

'That,' Enderby said, 'could be dangerous.'

'Shit to them. That guy there plays piano like shit.'

He meant the haired *répétiteur* Coppola, who was crashing out
what sounded like an atonal cancan, to which Toplady's ginger
mistress and another girl pranced with raised skirts. 'Gin,' Enderby
insisted. He observed April Elgar in a blazing scarlet directoire,
from the look of it, nightdress talking earnestly to the black lad of
the company, Sir Walter Raleigh for all Enderby knew, who counted
points off on his fingers. Toplady sat glumly with talking elders on
or in the deep couch. Enderby heard something about renewal of
contract, probably nonrenewal. Toplady was perhaps for the chop
for some reason, probably unconnected primarily with the ass
business. Mrs Allegramente came up to Enderby and said:

'Leave the Irish alone.'

'Only too glad,' Enderby said, 'to leave the murderous bastards alone. It's not my concern anyway. If you're so concerned get over to Belfast and have your kneecaps converted to Quaker Oats.'

Mrs Schoenbaum did not seem happy about her party. She stood at an end of the room with the lawyer Elvin or Alvin or something, clad in black silk pyjamas with a gold caftan over, her hair, as previously, glued to a snapshot wuthering. She seemed ready for a cardiac arrest when two genuine Elizabethans entered, late and tanked up elsewhere – William Shakespeare and the Earl of Essex, both bearded, wigged, ruffed, jerkined, slashtrunked, hosed. Enderby too had a profound tremor until William Shakespeare spoke in the accent of Cedar Rapids, Iowa. He cried:

'Greetings to ye all, let the nutbrown ale floweth, or, marry and egad, the iciclebythewalled martini.' He noticed Enderby and added: 'And all that sort of heynonnino shit.' Enderby growled:

'Learn your Elizabethan grammar before you start mocking it. The accusative of *ye* is *you*. And a profound heynonnino to you, fleerer and bad actor.'

'Do not,' said Humrig the churchwarden, 'use language of that sort in the presence of Mrs Schoenbaum.'

'Shit,' said the mad son Philip. 'Shit shit shit.'

'Philip,' his mother said, '*please*.'

'I wanna play the piano,' Philip said, 'and that guy there hogs it.'

'Welcome,' haired Coppola said, banging three Scriabinesque cacophonies and getting up with a low bow and an arm stretched in proffer. Philip drooled his way over and began to play something manic and unrecognizable. He cried:

'Dance! Dance!' Some obeyed. Enderby asked the grey black for more gin. Oldfellow Shakespeare was on to him now, saying:

'And what the fuck do you know about acting?'

'Enough to know that you're as much like Shakespeare as my arse or ass. And,' he added, 'your breath smells horrible.' It did too. Perhaps that was the origin of sodomy: avoiding partner's halitosis. Enderby got away and over to a corner where Mrs Schoenbaum's daughter was leasing her bedroom for half an hour for five dollars. Toplady and the conferrers got up with difficulty from the deep boat of a couch. Toplady cried:

'Stop that row for a minute.'

'Okay.' Oldfellow had followed Enderby. 'You try it, buster, that's all, you just try it.'

'I speak English anyway,' Enderby said, 'and I know the lines.'

The hands of Philip had been forcibly removed from the piano keys. Toplady cried: 'A few words, friends. You've worked hard. We've all worked hard. Some not so hard as others, but let that pass. Tomorrow we open. Or rather tomorrow *you* open. My contract as Artistic Director of the Peter Brook Theater was due to end in March. By mutual agreement it ends as of now. Certain elements do not like the way I have been doing things. There's a feeling that I should have concentrated on ordure like *Abie's Irish Rose* or *A Tree Grows in Brooklyn*. I have not made the Peter Brook Theater a centre of entertainment. It is wrong apparently to take the drama seriously. Until my successor has been chosen things will be in the incapable hands of my sleeping assistant director Jed Tilbury. Bless some of you and fuck others. I go.' He went. Some watched him go, others turned to look at this Jed Tilbury, who was the black lad enumerating points, though now no longer, to April Elgar. He cried:

'Hey, man –'

'De party over, I guess,' said the grey black retainer. 'An a gud ting too,' in the manner of Mr Woodhouse.

'More gin,' Enderby said. 'And then call me a taxi.'

'You call you own taxi, man. I don't call no taxis for no one no how.'

Toplady's mistress was meanwhile looking for her left shoe and calling: 'Gus, Gus, wait for me, Gus.' The shoe found, she stopped on her way out to fix hatefilled eyes on Enderby. 'It's you,' she said. 'You brought bad luck, you bastard.'

'Not me, kid or baby or whatever it is,' Enderby said heavily. 'Somebody bigger than me. Leave well alone is what I say. And don't call me bastard.'

'Bastard,' she said and was off, crying 'Gus.' Enderby said to the grey black:

'You're a servant. Call me a taxi. But first more gin.'

'You not call me servant, man. I ain't no servant.'

Mrs Allegramente was now there, saying: 'Is he giving trouble, Edwin? Is he being racist?'

'You keep out of this,' Enderby said. And then: 'Ah, please yourself. Protestant Ulster for ever. God bless King Henry the Eighth.' Before going to the hallway to call himself a taxi, he went over to April Elgar and the black now revealed as Jed Tilbury. To him he said: 'Congratulations are probably in order.' To her: 'I'm going back to the hotel. Will you come?'

'Why?' she said with a new pertness.

'Because the party seems to be over and it was a terrible party anyhow and we stay at the same hotel and I'm calling a –'

'Jed'll take me home,' she said.

From the tail of his right eye Enderby saw Dick Corcoran as Earl of Essex swill thirstily from an orange juice jug. Very sensible, do him good, all those vitamins. 'Right,' Enderby said. And then: 'A queer sort of time we've had when you come to think about it. Meddling with Shakespeare. All right on the night, though. As they say.' He saw now, coming in too late, Bodiman, Pip Wesel and Silversmith, all drunk and leering. The grey black retainer or hired man or whatever he was supposed to be called let out a great wail of distress. 'If,' Enderby said, 'those three start insulting you, let me know.'

'Certainly,' she said. 'I'll call your room and you can come back and hit them or something.' She spoke, for some reason, rather like the actress Bette Davis. Enderby knew now that it was far too late to start trying to learn about women. He sighed and said:

'That girl who left just then, the one who plays Queen Elizabeth I gather, says it's all my fault, whatever she means by *all*. Ah well, I suppose I must go and say good night to our hostess.'

'Don't be like that,' Jed Tilbury said. 'Nothing to be depressed about, man. Ain't the end of the world.' He showed many teeth, all his own, and added: 'Just what it's not.' It was only when a taxi arrived that Enderby realized what he might mean. Ah just died, baby. Well, let them get on with it. The taxi driver was prepared for a long literary conversation with Enderby. He was a young Canadian, down here visiting for the Christmas vacation, then back to Yorke University outside Toronto to resume work on his thesis, to be entitled 'Future in the Past'. About science fiction.

'Been reading some of it,' Enderby said tiredly.

'Only viable literary form we have,' said the Canadian. 'What did you say your name was?'

'Why are you driving a taxi?' Enderby said instead of replying.

'It's my brother-in-law's cab. He went bowling. Did I imagine it or were there two guys at that place dressed up like Shakespeare?'

'You didn't imagine it.'

'And what did you say your name was?'

'Enderby,' Enderby said. 'The poet,' with small hope of being known as such, not that it mattered.

'Right. I thought that was the name. And then when I saw these two guys it kind of rang a bell. Read that thing of yours if you're the guy that wrote it. It was in the *Koksoak*, hell of a name. About Shakespeare. What you ought to write is sort of SF Shakespeare, know what I mean? About some Martian landing in Elizabethan England and meeting Shakespeare and putting The Power on him. See what I mean?'

'It's the name of a Canadian lake, I think. *Not* pronounced Cock Soak. Yes yes, I see what you mean. Here we are, I think.'

'Yeah.' Meaning the Holiday Inn in Terrebasse. 'It's an idea anyhow. Although there's this theory that it's us are the Martians. We landed on this planet in prehistoric times and killed off the earthmen. We knew that Mars was dying, see, and saw the fertility of the earth through powerful instruments. Then the earth's lack of oxygen stunted our brains and we had to start all over again. Four dollars fifty.'

Enderby had a nightmare and woke from it, impertinently engorged, at something after four. He dreamed that he was forced to act the role of Shakespeare in *Actor on His Ass* because both leading man and understudy had walked out and there was nobody else who knew the lines. No question of cancelling the performance, too much investment involved, backers insisted that show go on. Enderby as Shakespeare went on stage and opened mouth but no words came out. The audience jeered and somebody threw a missile like a miniature moon. It hit his head and cracked open and covered him with olive oil. The audience roared. Enderby awoke sweating. Thank God it was only a dream, nightmare rather.

11

'I mean, damn it, look at me,' Enderby cried supererogatorily, for that was precisely what they were doing. The cast, with two notable exceptions and a nailbiting Jed Tilbury in charge, his colour today like that of a very old elephant, sat around in the greenroom, looking at Enderby. The coffee machine needed repair, and it growled within like a stomach and infrequently, into a plastic yellow bucket, gushed slop. 'Why can't somebody else do it, for Christ's sake?'

'Tomorrow night, okay,' Jed Tilbury said. 'Floyd learning the lines and Shep learning the other lines.' He meant a long youth in a lumberjack outfit with a yellow coxcomb and another, older, in jeans and a Monte Carlo Grand Prix tee-shirt. 'But there's tonight, man, and it's the opening and you got this British voice and you wrote the goddamned thing. And you'll have a wig and a beard – and, Jesus, you got Ape here to push you through it, and Oldfellow's songs are taped, and, Jesus, you got to do it, man.' Enderby looked at the sweating youth, not so blackly cocky as he had been, a lot on the poor bastard's plate. 'And it's Ape's show, we know that, she push you through.'

'Yes,' Enderby said, with some bitterness. '*Ape*.' April Elgar sat there in a mauve track or jump suit looking rested, as though after some great black night of black amation, her own kind, right. Baby, ah just died. 'Goats and monkeys. Actor on his ass. Shakespeare reduced to the animalistic was bad enough. Now Shakespeare's reduced to me. Besides, I don't belong to the appropriate union.'

'Ah, fuck that,' somebody said.

'You're a poet,' April Elgar said without warmth. 'You got that in common.'

'I fear,' Enderby said, 'I fear – You lot are actors, and that means you're superstitious. That fag Oldfellow would have made Shakespeare just vulgar. I'd make him absurd. I can't do it.'

'Oh Jesus God.' Jed Tilbury's black emotional lability began to show. 'I got this job to do, can't you see that, man? I got to put this show on now Gus Toplady has slung. I got a career to think of, man.' He began to cry. As Enderby had half-expected, April Elgar did a there there patting act and even kissed his limp hand. Call of the blood, fellow melanoid in distress. Just died. One of the girls from the secretarial concourse came pertly in to announce:

'Pete Oldfellow's still blacked out with concussion. Dick Corcoran has this broken arm they've set and cuts and bruises. And he's charged with drunk driving and damaging public property. A mailbox it was. That was the Illinois police on the line.'

'Orange juice,' Enderby said. 'I should have warned him. I didn't think, blast it.'

'What in the hell did they think they were doing?' Jed Tilbury cried. 'Wearing those goddamn costumes too?'

'They might have been in drag,' somebody said. 'Fart in gales or whatever they're called.'

'And the car,' the girl said, 'is a writeoff. Lucky to be alive, the police say.'

'No sense,' Jed Tilbury said with sad weight, 'of professional responsibility.'

'And,' said the girl, 'we have to tell the press and the radio and the TV. About cancellation.'

'Yeah,' bowed Jed Tilbury said, 'we gonna cancel.'

'Lifelong love and devotion,' April Elgar said obscurely, though not, in a second or so, to Enderby. 'Let's see some of that. We don't cancel. Stick your ass on the line. You going to do it.'

'Oh God oh God,' Enderby moaned. 'What have I to lose? The ultimate tomfoolery.'

'You just pretend,' she said, 'that you're acting a Baptist minister. The words are different, that's all.' Most frowned, not understanding.

Jed Tilbury showed both relief and the concern of immediate problems. 'We got to do a run through,' he said. 'Start now.'

'No rehearsals,' Enderby said. 'I know my own lines.'

'Yeah, but there been some changes —'

'About which I was not consulted. And I was barred from your bloody rehearsals. The joke, the man who wrote the bloody thing, that's all. Not one of you spoke up.'

'That's not true,' April Elgar said. 'It doesn't matter, but that's not true.'

'All right, thanks. So I get up on that stage as William Shakespeare, and you'd better all pray hard that the man himself doesn't punch through the bloody shoddy thing from the shades. Perhaps you'd better arrange a quick seance with Mrs Allegramente, if that's her real name, stupid bitch always going on about the sufferings of Northern Ireland, knows sod all about it. Get the enigmatic voice of the Bard on the hot line. Bugger everything and everybody.' He got stiffly up, the minor poet daring to be Shakespeare, Marsyas who was flayed for his temerity, and then hurried stiffly out to the nearest toilet. There he was urgently drained like a sump. Awaiting him outside was April Elgar. She said:

'You'll be all right. Just be yourself. If they laugh, okay they laugh. I don't think they going to laugh. You care for Shakespeare, that's got to come out.'

'That's the bloody trouble.' And then: 'What did you do last night?'

'No business of yours, sonny.'

'Tell me.'

'No, I don't tell you. You want to be jealous, okay you be jealous. Then you don't have to act jealous tonight. It's pretty hard to act jealous.' And then: 'You got no claim on me.'

'Love,' Enderby said heavily. 'Love, love. No, no claim, you're right. Love. I'm going off now to get drunk.'

'You better not.'

'*You've* no claim on *me*. I do what I want. What time do I have to report for duty?'

'You and me,' she said, 'are going to eat lunch, right. A couple martinis, okay. Then we go through the script. Then you have a little sleep. Then we come back here together. We give 'em all hell, you and me. Cabbages, sheep's heads, you got to despise them. Okay?'

Enderby sat in what had been, and might be again (emerging from blackout was the news), Pete Oldfellow's dressing room. He felt absolutely stone cold and indifferent as Pete Oldfellow's dresser, a retired minor actor new to the job, breathed Southern Comfort onto him. He sat and saw himself in a mirror framed with hot bulbs. Wig, beard secured with strong spirit gum. The Burbage portrait stared grimly back, though without earrings. Codpiece, hose, shirt, jerkin, ruff. Outside in the corridor there was scurrying and he could almost smell the sweat of nerves, as in a stable. A calm voice over a loudspeaker said: 'Fifteen minutes.' The dresser said: 'Your teeth okay? That bottom set looks kind of wobbly to me.' Enderby realized that he had left his tubes of toothglue back in his hotel bathroom. He gnashed at the mirror. They'd hold. The door opened and April Elgar came in in scarlet silk, *café au lait* bosom achingly on show. Her ink hair flashed with stage gems. She held out an envelope.

'Give 'em hell,' she said. 'My momma sent this. Enclosed, just for you. She sends her warm affection, happy in the Lord. We got a full house, baby. Don't open it now.' Enderby propped the letter against a Max Factor makeup outfit. 'There he goes.' They heard the faint voice of Jed Tilbury addressing the audience, apologizing for absence unavoidable of Pete Oldfellow and begging indulgence, part of William Shakespeare being taken at short notice by play's author the distinguished British. The audience's angry response did not come through. Soon, however, the farting of trombones and thuds of drums did. Overture and beginners. 'Luck,' she said and was off.

'You wanna a drop of this?' the dresser asked, bringing from a cupboard a fluted bottle of Southern Comfort. He was an undistinguished man on whom rested impertinently the distinguished though raddled mask of the late John Barrymore. Enderby could reply only with a headshake. He had no saliva and the mechanism of speech had totally to be remastered. He looked down with difficulty at sturdy legs in gooseturd hose. From these the power of locomotion had entirely departed. The feet just about worked still, however, and on these he slid towards the door. The door opened and Jed Tilbury, dressed presumably for Aaron the Moor, nodded at him. Enderby nodded back and said:

'Aaargh.'

Enderby was pushed by men in stagehand undress into total

blackness. From his right an orchestra boomed and screeched to its final chord or what passed for one. Farther right there was meagre and dutiful applause. Enderby saw below the young bald Pip Wesel dimly lighted wagging a stick with a glowworm stuck to its end at dimly lighted music stands. There was a faint response to the stick and Enderby heard sung faintly from ubiquitous loud-speakers words he had himself composed:

> 'Bringing the maypole home
> Bringing the maypole home
> Bringing the maypole home
> Bringing the maypole home'

He now saw a woman in a kind of nightgown rocking a kind of cradle. That would be Anne Shakespeare, née Hathaway. He saw her more clearly as dimmers undimmed. He presumed he had to have a colloquy with her. To his surprise he found he could walk. He walked towards her. She was downstage in a pool of pink light. He spoke words:

'Aye, they're bringing the maypole home. You remember?' He saw there was a kind of casement standing on little wheels, unsupported by a wall. He went to this object to pretend to look out of it. 'A night spent in the woods, cider and cold meat and hot lechery. You overbore me as Venus overbore Adonis. I was cozened, caught, caged in a loveless marriage. I have a mind to go.' These words, so far as he could remember, were not in the script. It seemed to him that he was probably improvising them. 'Aye, a mind to leave you.' He blinked at the cradle-rocking Anne, who was not being played by the mistress of Toplady. There were coughs and rustles from the audience. Enderby spoke out more boldly. 'I have my destiny to fulfil, my star to follow.' He peered through nonexistent glass and saw nothing. 'More than my star – my constellation – she is bright this night. Cassiopeia is roaring lionlike in the heavens – an inverted W signifying my name. Will and Will in overplus. My name in the sky.'

From nowhere and everywhere the voice of the fag Oldfellow began to bleat:

> 'My name in the sky
> Burning for ever
> Fame fixed by fate
> Never to die
> At least I feast on that dream
> The gleam of gold, my fortunes mounting high'

At the third line Enderby realized that he was supposed to mouth those words, so he did. But it offended him that his voice should have become the voice of that now blacked out or just emerging from blackout fag. He strode quite sturdily downstage to the very edge of the apron and addressed the audience:

'A mask, a copy, a travesty. The poet turned into a motley to the view. You have heard of the *A-Effekt*? Alienation. I am not Shakespeare, he is not Shakespeare. We mock, we defy, we admit absurdities. You and you and you must all be punished.' He had heard those lines before somewhere. Yes, Eliot, *Murder in the.* 'Beware.' He strode back upstage. The song ended, to no applause. Male voices off began to sing.

> 'The Queen's Men
> The Queen's Men
> Not bread-and-beer-and-beans men
> But fine men
> Wine men
> Music-while-we-dine men'

'By God,' Enderby cried, 'the players are leaving. I will leave with them. They return to London, I spoke to Dick Tarleton in the inn but today. By God, if they will have me I will be one of them.' Anne ceased her cradlerocking and began to sing:

> 'Will o' the wisp, do not desire
> To follow fame, that foolish fire'

Enderby again confided in the audience: 'A lot of nonsense. This ginger-haired bednag, having nagged me to screaming, having scraped my loins dry, now tries the craft of quasi-melodic seduction. Listen to that voice. Would you be seduced by it?' And then, with great confidence, he strode off. There was applause which drowned the last lines of the song. He had, by God, got them.

In the wings he collapsed and was offered Southern Comfort and smelling salts, which they called smelling sauce. The thin girl who played Anne was on to him, ready to tear off his well-glued beard. 'You bastard,' she cried. 'You fucked up my song.' She was dragged away by ready shirtsleeved muscles. The wings were suddenly cluttered by mock-Elizabethans. Flats were wheeled in and off. Full stage lights screamed. The orchestra blared. And then there she was, divine farthingaled ass awag, down centre:

> 'The white man's knavery
> Sold me in slavery
> To an unsavoury'

Enderby was on his feet again looking down at a small boy dressed like a miniature Elizabethan adult. This boy proffered a sticky hand which Enderby vaguely shook. 'No,' the boy said in a profound if juvenile Midwestern accent, 'you gotta hold on to it.' Of course, Hamnet his son. A property hand handed to Enderby a vague brown bundle. 'That's your grip,' he said.

Enderby and the lad toddled on and looked about them. London peopled mainly with prostitutes, some of them sitting sprawled, all bosom and legs anachronistically exposed, outside a door unupheld by a building. Enderby took the boy downstage and addressed the audience: 'The title, incidentally, must not be misunderstood. *Ass* means a donkey. This child is meant to be Shakespeare's son Hamnet. His accent, you will notice, is unauthentic. Speak, child.'

The boy said: 'Is this London, dad?'

'Yes, my boy, this is a London apparently peopled by tibs, trulls and holy mutton. And do not call me dad. Dad is a term used only for an illegitimate father. In other words, only a bastard may use it. You, whatever you are, are not a bastard. Your mother and I were married in Trinity Church, Stratford. Ah, I wonder if that is Philip Henslowe.' Some members of the audience seemed to consider all this funny. Enderby went up to an actor who was frowning over a daybook and addressed him. 'You are Master Henslowe? In charge of the Rose Playhouse on the Bankside? I have a play for you.'

'Ah, Jesus, will they never give up?'

It went rather well, Enderby thought, except that the small lad insisted on holding on to his hand while he was trying to gesture. He was forced to say: 'Go in there, Hamnet my boy, and play with the pretty ladies.' And he banged the boy's bottom thither. One way of getting him off. Unfortunately he collided with Ned Alleyn coming out, buttoning.

There was a kind of ballet with people carrying posters on sticks: TITUS ANDRONICUS; HENRY VI PART ONE; HENRY VI PART TWO — Finally there came RICHARD III. All Enderby had to do was to stand and watch and leave the work to others. But he had not to forget to note ostentatiously the passing of a message from April Elgar through her duenna to Dick Burbage. He was dragged off by a mass of exiters only to be pushed on later to find himself alone with the Dark Lady. He gulped. There was a frilled and tasselled daybed upstage. Downstage she sat combing her hair in an Elizabethan negligée. This was to be a love scene.

'Who are you, sir?'

'Madam, I noted at the play you did tender a message to Master Dick Burbage. You bade him come meet you here but be announced for discretion as Richard the Third. But, madam, I am the creator, with a little help from the historians, of that reprehensible hump-back. I am William Shakespeare, madam.' Enderby glanced timidly up at the flies, whose lord might launch flyshit, at the enskied bard's request, to punish the Marsyas temerity of that identification. Then he said: 'Will you not like better a visit from a king maker than from a mere king?'

'What do you want of me, sir?'

'To see closer your beauty,' Enderby proclaimed, 'and to,' declaimed, 'admire it.' He heard a donnish querulousness in his tones and subdued it with a not too proper gruffness. 'It is a special and translunary loveliness not much seen, alack, in our pale and shivering clime that enthroned Sol disdains to visit. A sore lack, alack. But how do we define beauty? As that special property in woman, and in man too for such as are so given, that ah generates love. Seeing your beauty, I love it. And must I not love the possessor of that beauty? Ah, madam, I long to take you in mine arms. Love, aye, love, love. Love.'

That was her cue for song, but Pip Wesel the MD was slow to pick it up. Only when Enderby growled the word once more, frowning at the orchestra and, while his hand was in, the audience too, did the jazzy chords of exordium thump. She sang. Enderby blinked at her, still and watching. That lower denture, damn it, felt loose. He wondered whether he should go downstage and talk to the audience in good A-Effekt manner, explain that in point of biographical fact what they were now observing, except for the song, probably truly happened, but, in fact or true truth, she played on the virginals, so called because, and there was a sonnet about it, though Shakespeare got the meaning of the term jacks wrong. But then the song ended, and he beamed as she got her due meed of applause. No doubt about it, she swung both voice and d.v.a. to remarkable effect. He forgot his line, beaming. She fed it to him.

'Do I sing to your satisfaction, sirrah?'

He could see the spit of her sibilants in the spot beam. He shook his head and said: 'Not sirrah, no. That's by way of insult. Sir will do nicely. Aye, madam, you sing prettily. Can you dance as well?'

'I can dance the galliard and the high lavolta and eke the heels-in-the-air.'

'I thank you for that eke, more expressive than also, however much it may be taken for a mouse stirring.' By God, now it was coming. 'Can you dance the dance called the Beginning of the World?'

'Nay, sir, I know it not.'

'Then, madam, I will teach you.' And he, kicking out the Enderby as unworthy and becoming solely, though with a loose lower denture, Shakespeare, advanced upon her, upstage as she already was and near to that daybed. He clipped her in Shakespeare's arms and did buss her rouged lips. His or Shakespeare's heart beat hard and hot. Had having and in quest to have. All was justified; this was, by God, no more than aesthetic duty. He had her on that daybed and lay upon her. *For Christ's sake* her occluded mouth tried to utter. He mouthed juicily the smooth brown of her wholly exposed shoulders and then, obeying Shakespeare's own Venus, Anne Hathaway really, strayed lower where the. *By God, madam, I have thee, I love, I love.* He was aware of the sturdy filling of his codpiece, really inside now, Mercutio, Benvolio, the codpieced lot of them. Then he heard a voice saying:

'Madam, Richard the Third is here.'

He tried to get his line out but could not. There were certain necessities that obliterated the obligations of art. Nay, more – was it not said that if a man made love on a railway line with an express train fast approaching he must say to himself that the driver had brakes and he not? Enderby was brakeless. But his panting succuba thrust him away and called:

'Tell him William the Conqueror came before –'

Then a whistle shrilled. That was the express coming. Bugger it, it had brakes, had it not? But it sounded like a police whistle. The watch had caught him at it, towsing in public, hale him before the Puritan magistrates for foul fornication. But the man who, to Enderby's surprise and Shakespeare's disgust, had just walked on the stage was in the costume of the twentieth century, that was to say a drab raincoat. He blew, as he had evidently blown before, his whistle, and then he addressed the audience. Enderby could not clearly hear what he said; he disdained the forward tone projection of the actor, though he said something about the actors' union. He pointed at Enderby, or Shakespeare, apparently to indicate that here was a foul fault and a sinful wight, to wit a non union member. Performance discontinued. Union regulation. Enderby, still clipping April Elgar, though looking towards the little expostulator with open mouth, now leapt off her and strode down, aware dimly of intercrucial wetness, to the edge of the apron and tried to push the man off. The man, who wore glasses that were filled with stage light, hit back. Enderby cried to the audience:

'I'm not acting now so this bastard here has no right to shove at me like that. Can you imagine such a monstrosity occurring at a stage performance in Shakespeare's own day? Shakespeare looks down from the heavens in disgust. Union rules, quotha. Devices of protection have become devices for dealing the death of the drama. Only one performance ever failed to reach its conclusion in Shakespeare's time, and that was in the Globe playhouse in 1613 when *Henry VIII* was being for the first time presented and the thatch caught fire.' From nowhere, though it might have been the flies, the word *fire* was, with a howl, repeated. The house lights came swiftly up. Enderby now saw, very rawly revealed, real seated people ready to unseat themselves, a lot of them, uneasily looking for the source of the cry or the source of the referent of the cry. *Fire.* 'Stay where you are, damn it,' Enderby yelled, as people began to panic their way into the aisles. 'There's no fire, I just said fire, that's all.' *Fire* came again. There was already the beginning of a dangerous pushing out, that woman there looked as if she expected to be trampled. 'Come back,' Enderby called, 'blast it. Back, you stupid buggers.' And, to the gawping orchestra, 'Play, damn it.' Shakespeare on the *Titanic.* They began to play, though not all the same thing. The audience, which had seen on films audiences tumbling out from fires, ready to trample, tumbled out none the less, ready to trample. Bloody Americans, no discipline, too prone to panic.

'My last number,' April Elgar called to Pip Wesel. She got a lumpish four bars in and began:

> 'Love, you say love.
> What you talking about
> Is filthy philandering,
> Goosing and gandering –'

Some of the audience turned, some even considered reoccupying their seats. Most left. A man lay in an aisle, not dead. A woman whimpered, looking for probably a child or a handbag or something. Enderby said:

'A pity. It wasn't going too badly.'

'Yeah,' April Elgar said, 'not too badly. Ah, let's go.' The stage was filling with stagehands and members of cast. *No fucking fire*, someone said. Enderby saw the union man in hot colloquy with Jed Tilbury. He pushed the union man in the small of the back with his, or Shakespeare's, nief. The man counted things, probably rules, off on his fingers.

'Some of this?' the fag Oldfellow's dresser suggested, proffering the fluted bottle. Enderby nodded: some of that. April Elgar nodded too. 'I only got the one glass,' the dresser said. Enderby now saw that he was wearing, had been all the time, the computer wristwatch she had given him for Christmas. He said:

'Never noticed. Nobody noticed. God curse everybody. First man to wear a wristwatch was Blaise Pascal. After Shakespeare's time. Stupid bugger that I am. Uncyclical future. Time a straight line. *Domine non sum dignus. Domina* too, for that matter. Got to get away. The shame of it all. The bastards owe me money. Where are the bastards?'

'That,' she said, pointing. She was pointing at the letter she had herself delivered. 'Better open it. Felt to me like more than a letter.'

Enderby sliced the envelope open with what had recently been Shakespeare's right index finger. Dollar bills, each of a hundred. Five in all. He frowned, puzzled. He read the note. It was from Dr R. F. Grigson and addressed Enderby as Dear Brother. Distressed to see how service in the Lord's name had brought to a stage of nervous breakdown, not uncommon in the vocation of pastor. Perhaps a brief vocation (crossed out and vacation substituted) might help to restore to health and renewed vigour in the preaching of the Word. The congregation had been glad to help. The widow's mite even. No mighty sum but still. God's blessings and much sympathy and affection. Enderby showed her the letter. She had already seen the money. 'Now,' she said, 'you better go home. I said they were good people.'

'I wonder,' wondered Enderby, 'how much he minded. I wonder if he'll have an air crash waiting for me. Or skyjackers or whatever they're called.'

'Everything going to be all right. He liked people to act, right? He was an actor first, right? Here everything going to be all right because of the publicity. One thing won't get in the newspapers, though. A man having to pretend to be William Shakespeare before he can dance the Beginning of the World. You sure are one great big pain in the ass,' she said.

'I have this poem to write,' Enderby said, having tasted with little relish the sweet fire of Southern Comfort. What he needed was a mug of tea, my kind of, with seven bags. 'You gave me something to write about.'

'Yeah, that was all it was for. Giving you something to write about. Brother, I been used for a lot of things in my life, but never before to give a guy something to write about.'

'Well,' Enderby said stoutly, 'poetry has to go on. Nobody wants it, but we have to have it. There's something else I have to write first, though. A little story. *Leave Well Alone* or *Leave Will Alone*, some such title. About Shakespeare. If he'll allow it.'

'You wanna get that stuff off?' the dresser asked. Meaning the beard and the wig and the 5 and 9. Shakespeare looked at Enderby from the mirror and coldly nodded.

12

The Muse

The hands of Swenson ranged over the five manuals of the instrument console and, in cross rhythm, his feet danced on the pedals. He was a very old man, waxed over with the veneer of rejuvenation chemicals. Very wise, with a century of experience behind him, he yet looked much of an age with Paley, the twenty-five-year-old literary historian by his side. Paley grinned nervously when Swenson said:

'It won't be quite what you think. It can't be absolutely identical. You may get shocks when you least expect them. I remember taking Wheeler that time, you know. Poor devil, he thought it was going to be the fourteenth century he knew from his books. But it was a very different fourteenth century. Thatched cottages and churches and manors and so on, and lovely cathedrals. But there were polycephalic monsters running the feudal system, with tentacles too. Speaking the most exquisite Norman French, he said.'

'How long was he there?'

'He was sending signals through within three days. But he had to wait a year, poor devil, before we could get him out. He was in a dungeon, you know. They got suspicious of his Middle English or something. White-haired and gibbering when we got him aboard. His jailors had been a sort of tripodic ectoplasm.'

'That wasn't in System B303, though, was it?'

'Obviously not.' The old man came out in Swenson's snappishness. 'It was a couple of years ago. A couple of years ago System B303, or at least the K2 part of it, was enjoying the doubtful benefits of proto-Elizabethan rule. As it still is.'

'Sorry. Stupid of me.'

'Some of you young men,' Swenson said, going over to the bank of monitor screens, 'expect too much of Time. You expect historical Time to be as plastic as the other kinds. Because the microchronic and macrochronic flows can be played with, you consider you ought to be able to do the same thing with –'

'Sorry, sorry, *sorry*. I just wasn't thinking.' With so much else on his mind, was it surprising that he should be temporarily ungeared to the dull realities of clockwork time, solar time?

'That's the trouble with you young – Ah,' said Swenson with satisfaction, 'that was a beautiful changeover.' With the smoothness of the tongue gliding from one phonemic area to another, the temporal path had become a spatial one. The uncountable megamiles between Earth and System B303 had been no more to their ship than, say, a two-way transatlantic flipover. And now, in reach of this other Earth – so dizzyingly far away that it was the same as their own, though at an earlier stage of history – the substance vedmum had slid them, as from one dream to another, into a world where solid objects might exist that were so alien as to be familiar, fulfilling the bow-bent laws of the cosmos. Swenson, who had been brought up on the interchangeability of time and space, could yet never cease to marvel at the miracle of the almost yawning casualness with which the *nacheinander* turned into the *nebeneinander* (there was no doubt, the old German words caught it best). So far the monitor screens showed nothing, but tape began to whir out from the crystalline corignon machine in the dead centre of the control turret – coldly accurate information about the solar system they were now entering. Swenson read it off, nodding, a Nordic spruce of a man glimmering with chemical youth. Paley looked at him, leaning against the parferate bulkhead, envying the tallness, the knotty strength. But, he thought, Swenson could never disguise himself as an inhabitant of a less well-nourished era. He, Paley, small and dark as one of those far distant Silurians of the dawn of Britain, could creep into the proto-Elizabethan England they would soon be approaching and never be remarked as an alien.

'Amazing how insignificant the variants are,' Swenson said. 'How finite the cosmos is, how shamefully incapable of formal renewals —'

'Oh, come,' Paley smiled.

'When you consider what the old musicians could do with a mere twelve notes —'

'The human mind,' Paley said, 'is straight. Thought travels to infinity. The cosmos is curved.'

Swenson turned away from the billowing mounds of tape, saw that the five-manual console was flicking lights smoothly and happily, then went over to an instrument panel whose levers called for muscle, for the blacksmith rather than the organist. 'Starboard,' he said. '15.8. Now we play with gravities.' He pulled hard. The monitor screen showed band after band of turquoise light, moving steadily upwards. 'This, I think, should be —' He twirled a couple of corrective dials on a shoulder-high panel about the levers. 'Now,' he said. 'Free fall.'

'So,' Paley said, 'we're being pulled by —'

'Exactly.' And then: 'I trust the situation has been presented to you in its perilous entirety. The dangers, you know, are considerable.'

'Scholarship,' Paley smiled patiently. 'My reputation.'

'Reputation,' Swenson snorted. Then, looking towards the monitors, he said: 'Ah. Something coming through.'

Mist, cloudswirl, a solid shape peeping intermittently out of vapour porridge. Paley came over to look. 'It's the Earth,' he said in wonder.

'It's *their* Earth.'

'The same as ours. America, Africa —'

'The configuration's slightly different, see, down there at the southern tip of —'

'Madagascar's a good deal smaller. And, see, no Falklands.'

'The cloud's come over again.' Paley looked and looked. It was unbelievable.

'Think,' Swenson said kindly, 'how many absolutely incomputable systems there have to be before you can see the pattern of creation starting all over again. This seems wonderful to you because you just can't conceive how many myriads upon myriads of other worlds are *not* like our own.'

'And the stars,' Paley said, a thought striking him. 'I mean, the stars they can actually see from there, from their London, say – are they the same stars as ours?'

Swenson shrugged at that. 'Roughly,' he said. 'There's a rough kinship. But,' he explained, 'we don't properly know yet. Yours is only the tenth or eleventh trip, remember. To be exact about it all, you're the first to go to B303 England. What is it, when all's said and done, but the past? Why go to the past when you can go to the future?' His nostrils widened with complacency. 'G91,' he said. 'I've done that trip a few times. It's pleasant to know one can look forward to another thirty years of life. I saw it there, quite clearly, a little plaque set up in Rostron Place: *To the memory of G. F. Swenson, 1963–2094.*'

'We have to check up on history,' Paley said, mumbling a little. His own quest seemed piddling: all this machinery, organization, expertise in the service of a rather mean inquiry. 'I have to know whether William Shakespeare really wrote those plays.'

Swenson, as Paley expected, snorted. 'A nice sort of thing to want to find out,' he said. 'He's been dead six hundred and fifty years, is it, and you want to prove that there's nothing to celebrate. Not,' he added, 'that that sort of thing is much in my line. I've never had much time for poetry. Aaaah.' He interposed his own head between Paley's and the screen, peering. The pages of the atlas had been turned; now Europe alone swam towards them. 'Now,' Swenson said, 'I must set the exactest course of all.' He worked at dials, frowning but humming happily, then beetled at Paley, saying: 'Oughtn't you to be getting ready?'

Paley blushed that, with so huge a swathe of the cosmos spent in near idleness, he should have to rush things as they approached their port. He took off his single boilersuit of a garment and drew from the locker his Elizabethan fancy dress. Shirt, trunks, codpiece, doublet, feathered French hat, slashed shoes – clothes of synthetic cloth that was an exact simulacrum of old-time weaving, the shoes of good leather handmade. And then there was the scrip with its false bottom: hidden therein was a tiny two-way signaller. Not that, if he got into difficulties, it would be of much use: Swenson was (and these were strict orders) to come back for him in a year's time. The signaller was to show where he was and that he was still there, a guest of the past, really a stowaway. Swenson had to move on yet farther into timespace: Professor Shimmins had to be picked up in FH78, Dr Guan Moh Chan in G210, Paley collected on the way back. Paley tested the signaller, then checked the open and honest contents of his scrip: chief among these was a collection of the works of William Shakespeare. The plays had been copied from a facsimile of the First Folio in fairly accurate Elizabethan script; the paper too was an acid-free imitation of the coarse stuff Elizabethan dramatists had been said to use. For the rest, Paley had powdered prophylactics in little bags and, most important, gold – angels firenew, the odd portague, écus.

'Well,' Swenson said with the faintest tinge of excitement, 'England, here we come.' Paley looked down on familiar river shapes – Tees, Humber, Thames. He gulped, running through his drill swiftly. 'Countdown starts now,' Swenson said. A syntheglott in the port bulkhead began ticking off cold seconds from 300. 'I'd better say goodbye then,' Paley gulped, opening the trap in the deck which led to the tiny jetpowered very-much-one-man aircraft. 'You should come down in the Thames estuary,' Swenson said. '*Au revoir*, not goodbye. I hope you prove whatever it is you want to prove.' 200–199–198. Paley went down, settled himself in the seat, checked the simple controls. Waiting took, it seemed, an age. He smiled wryly, seeing himself, an Elizabethan, with his hands on the controls of a twenty-third century miniature jet aircraft. 60–59–58. He checked his Elizabethan vowels. He went over his fictitious provenance: a young man from Norwich with stage ambitions ('I have writ a play and a goodly one'). The syntheglott, booming here in the small cabin, counted to its limit. 4–3–2–1.

Zero. Paley zeroed out of the mothership, suddenly calm, then elated. It was moonlight, the green countryside slept. The river was a glory of silver. His course had been preset by Swenson; the control available to him was limited, but he came down smoothly on the water. What he had to do now was ease himself to the shore. The little engine purred as he steered in moonlight. The river was broad here, so that he seemed to be in a world all water and sky. The moon was odd, bigger than it should by rights have been, with straight markings like fabled Martian canals. The shore neared – it was all trees, sedge, thicket; there was no sign of habitation, not even of another craft. What would another craft have thought, sighting him? He had no fears about that: with its wings folded, the little airboat looked, from a distance, like some nondescript barge, so well had it been camouflaged. And now, to be safe, he had to hide it, cover it with elmboughs and sedge greenery. But first, before disembarking, he must set the time-switch that would, when he was safe ashore, render the metal of the fuselage high-charged, lethally repellent of all would-be boarders. It was a pity, but there it was. It would switch off automatically in a year's time, in twelve months to a day. Meanwhile, what myths, what madness would the curious examiner, the chance finder generate, tales uncredited by sophisticated London.

Launched on his night's walk upriver, Paley found the going easy enough. The moon lighted fieldpaths, stiles. Here and there a small farmhouse slept. Once he thought he heard a distant whistled tune. Once he thought he heard a distant town clock strike. He had no idea of the month or day or time of the night, but he guessed that it was late spring and some three hours or so off dawn. The year 1595 was certain, according to Swenson. Time functioned here as on true Earth, and two years before Swenson had taken a man to Muscovy, where they computed according to the Christian calendar, and the year had been 1593. That man had never come back, eaten by bears or something. Paley, walking, found the air gave good rich breathing, but from time to time he was made uneasy by the unfamiliar configurations of the heavens. There was Cassiopeia's Chair, Shakespeare's first name's drunken initial, but there were constellations he had not seen before. Could the stars, as the Elizabethans themselves believed, modify history? Could this Elizabethan London, because it looked up at stars unknown on true Earth, be identical with that other one which was known only from books? Well, he would soon know.

London did not burst upon him, a monster of grey stone and black and white wood. It came upon him gradually and gently,

houses set in fields and amid trees, the cool suburbs of the wealthy.
And then, a muffled trumpet under the sinking moon, the Tower
and its sleeping ravens. Then came the crammed crooked houses,
all at rest. Paley breathed in the smell of this late spring London,
and he did not like what he smelled. It was a complex of old
rags and fat and dirt, but it was also a smell he knew from a time
when he had flipped over to Borneo and timidly touched the
periphery of the jungle: it was, somehow, a jungle smell. As if to
corroborate this, a howl arose in the distance, but it was a dog's
howl. Dogs, dogges, man's best friend, here in outer space; dog
howling to dog across the inconceivable vastness of the cosmos.
And then came a human voice and the sound of boots on cobbles.
'Four of the clock and a fine morning.' He instinctively flattened
himself in an alleyway, crucified against the dampish wall. The time
for his disclosure was not yet. He tasted the vowel sounds of the
bellman's call – nearer to the English of Dublin than of his own
London. 'Fowr vth cluck.' And then, knowing the hour at last and
automatically feeling for a stopped wristwatch that was not there,
he wondered what he should do till day started. Here were no
hotels with clerks on allnight duty. He tugged at his dark beard (a
three months' growth) and then decided that, as the sooner he
started on his scholar's quest the better, he would walk to Shoreditch
where the Theatre was. Outside the City's boundaries, where the
play-hating City Council could not reach, it was at this time, so
history said, a new and handsome structure. A scholar's zest, the
itch to know, came over him and made him forget the cold morning
wind that was rising. His knowledge of the London of his own
day gave him little help in the orientation of the streets. He walked
north – the Minories, Houndsditch, Bishopsgate – and, as he walked,
he retched once or twice involuntarily at the stench from the
kennel. There was a bigger, richer, filthier, obscener smell beyond
this, and this he thought must come from Fleet Ditch. He dug
into his scrip and produced a pinch of powder; this he placed on
his tongue to quieten his stomach.

Not a mouse stirring as he walked, and there, under rolling
cloud all besilvered, he saw it, the Theatre, with something like
disappointment. It was mean wood rising above a wooden paling,
its roof shaggily thatched. Things were always smaller and more

ordinary than one expected. He wondered if it might be possible to enter. There seemed to be no protective night watchman. Before approaching the entrance (a door for an outside privy rather than a gate to the temple of the Muses) he took in the whole moonlit scene, the mean houses, the cobbles, the astonishing and unexpected greenery all about. And then he saw his first living creatures.

Not a mouse stirring, had he thought? But those creatures with long tails were surely rats, a trio of them nibbling at some dump of rubbish not far from the way into the Theatre. He went warily nearer, and the rats at once scampered off, each filament of whisker clear in the light. They were rats as he knew rats – though he had seen them only in cages in the laboratories of his university – with mean bright eyes and thick meaty tails. But then he saw what they had been eating.

Dragged out from the mound of trash was a human forearm. In some ways Paley was not unprepared for this. He had soaked in images of traitor heads stuck up on Temple Bar, bodies washed by three tides and left to rot on Thames shore, limbs hacked off at Tyburn and carelessly left for the scavenging. Kites, of course, kites. But now the kites would all be roosting. Clinically, his stomach calm from its medicine, he examined the raw gnawed thing. There was not much flesh off it yet: the feast had been interrupted at its very beginning. On the wrist, though, was a torn and pulpy patch which made Paley frown – something anatomically familiar but, surely, not referrable to a normal human arm. It occurred to him for just a second that this was rather like an eye-socket, the eye wrenched out but the soft bed left, still not completely ravaged. And then he smiled that away, though it was difficult to smile.

He turned his back on the poor human remnant and made straight for the entrance door. To his surprise it was not locked. It creaked as he opened it, a sort of harsh voice of welcome to this world of 1595 and its strange familiarity. There it was – tamped earth for the groundlings to tamp down yet further; the side boxes; the jutting apron; the study uncurtained; the tarrass; the tower with its flagstaff. He breathed deeply, reverently. This was the Theatre. And then –

'Arrr, catched y'at it!' Paley's heart seemed about to leap from his mouth like a badly fitting denture. He turned to meet his first

Elizabethan. Thank God, he looked normal enough, though filthy. He was in clumsy boots, gooseturd-coloured hose, and a rancid jerkin. He tottered somewhat as though drunk, and, as he came closer to peer into Paley's face, Paley caught a frightful blast of ale breath. The man's eyes were glazed and he sniffed deeply and long at Paley as though trying to place him by scent. Intoxicated, unfocused, thought Paley with contempt, and as for having the nerve to sniff . . . Paley spoke up, watching his words with care:

'I am a gentleman from Norwich, but newly arrived. Stand some way off, fellow. Know you not your betters when you see them?'

'I know not thee, nor why tha should be here at dead night.' But he stood away. Paley glowed with small triumph, the triumph of one who has, say, spoken home-learnt Russian for the first time in Moscow and has found himself perfectly understood. He said:

'Thee? *Thee*? I will not be thee-and-thou'd so, fellow. I would speak with Master Burbage, though mayhap I am somewhat early for't.'

'The young un or th'old?'

'Either. I have writ plays and fain would show them about.'

The watchman sniffed at Paley again. 'Genlmn you may be, but you smell not like a Christian. Nor do you keep Christian hours.'

'As I say, I am but newly arrived.'

'I see not your horse. Nor your traveller's cloak.'

'They are – I ha'left 'em at mine inn.'

The watchman muttered. 'And yet he saith he is but newly arrived. Go to.' Then he chuckled and, at the same time, delicately advanced his right hand towards Paley as though about to bless him. 'I know what 'tis,' he said, chuckling. ''Tis some naughtiness, th'hast trysted ringading with some wench, nay, some wife rather, nor has she belled out the morn.' Paley could make little of this. 'Come,' the man said, 'chill make for 'ee an th'hast the needful.' Paley looked blank. 'An tha wants beddn,' the man said more loudly. Paley caught that, he caught also the meaning of the open palm and wiggling fingers. Gold. He felt in his scrip and produced an angel. The man's jaw dropped as he took it. 'Sir,' he said, hat-touching.

'Truth to tell,' Paley said, 'I am shut out of mine inn, late returning from a visit and not able to make mine host hear with e'en the loudest knocking.'

'Arrr,' and the watchman put his finger by his nose, then scratched his cheek with the angel, finally, before stowing it in a little purse at his girdle, passing it a few times in front of his chest. 'With me, sir, come.'

He waddled speedily out, Paley following him with pulse fast abeat. 'Where go we then?' he asked. He received no answer. The moon was almost down and there were the first intimations of early summer dawn. Paley shivered in the wind; he wished he had brought a cloak with him instead of the mere intention of buying one here. If it was really a bed he was to be taken to, he was glad. An hour or so's sleep in the warmth of blankets and never mind whether or not there would be fleas. On the streets nobody was astir, though Paley thought he heard a distant cats' concert − a painful courtship, just as on true Earth. Paley followed the watchman down a narrow lane off Bishopsgate, dark and stinking. The effects of the medicine had worn off; he felt his gorge rise as before. But the stink, his nose noticed, was subtly different from what it had been: it was, he thought in a kind of small madness, somehow swirling, redistributing its elements as though capable of autonomous action. He did not like this. Looking up at the paling stars he felt sure they too had done a sly job of refiguration, forming fresh patterns like a sand tray on top of a thumped piano.

'Here 'tis,' the watchman said, arriving at a door and knocking without further ado. 'Croshabels,' he winked. But the eyelid winked on nothing but glazed emptiness. He knocked again, and Paley said:

''Tis no matter. It is late, or early, to drag folk from their beds.' A young cock crowed near, brokenly, a prentice cock.

'Never one nor t'other. 'Tis in the way of a body's trade, aye.' Before he could knock again, the door opened. A cross and sleepy-looking woman appeared. She wore a filthy nightgown and, from its bosom, what seemed like an arum lily peered out. She thrust it back in irritably. She was an old Elizabethan woman, greyhaired, about thirty. She cried:

'Ah?'

'One for one. A genlman, he saith.' He took his angel from its nest and held it up. She raised a candle the better to see. The arum lily peeped out again. All smiles now, she curtseyed Paley in. Paley said:

"'Tis but a matter of a bed, madam.' The other two laughed at that 'madam'. 'A long and wearisome journey from Norwich,' he added. She gave a deeper curtsey, more mocking than before, and said, in a sort of croak:

'A bed it shall be and no pallet nor the floor neither. For the gentleman from Norwich where the cows eat porridge.' The watchman grinned. He was blind, Paley was sure he was blind. On his right thumb something winked richly. The door closed on him, and Paley and the madam were together in the rancid hallway.

'Follow, follow,' she said, and she creaked first up the stairs. The shadows her candle cast were not deep; from the east grey was filling the world. On the wall of the stairwell were framed pictures. One was a crude woodcut showing a martyr hanging from a tree, a fire burning under him. Out of the smiling mouth words ballooned: AND YETTE I SAY THAT MOGRADON GIUETH LYFE. Another picture showed a king with a crown, orb and sceptre and a third eye set in his forehead. 'What king is that?' asked Paley. She turned to look at him in some amazement. 'Ye know naught in Norwich,' she said. 'God rest ye and keep ye all.' Paley asked no further questions and kept his wonder to himself at another picture they passed: 'Q. Horat. Flaccus' it said, but the portrait was of a turbaned Arab.

The madam knocked loudly on a door at the top of the stairs. 'Bess, Bess,' she cried. 'Here's gold, lass. A cleanly and a pretty man withal.' She turned to smile with black teeth at Paley. 'Anon will she come. She must deck herself like unto a bride.' From the bosom of her nightgown the lily again poked out and Paley thought he saw a blinking eye enfolded in its head. He began to feel the tremors of a very special sort of fear, not a terror of the unknown so much as of the known. He had rendered his flying boat invulnerable; this world could not touch it. Supposing it was possible that this world was in some manner rendered invulnerable by a different process. A voice in his head seemed to say, with great clarity: 'Not with impunity may one disturb the.' And then the door opened and the girl called Bess appeared, smiling professionally. The madam said, smiling also:

'There then, as pretty a mutton slice as was e'er sauced o'er.' And she held out her hand for money. Confused, Paley dipped into his scrip and pulled out a dull-gleaming handful. He told one coin into her hand and she still waited. He told another, then another. 'We ha' wine,' she said. 'Wouldst?' Paley thanked her: no wine. The grey hair on her head grew erect. She mockcurtseyed off.

Paley followed Bess into the bedchamber, on his guard now. The ceiling bent like a pulse; 'Piggesnie,' Bess croaked, pulling her single garment down from her bosom. The breasts swung and the nipples ogled him. They were, as he had expected, eyes. He nodded in something like satisfaction. There was, of course, no question of going to bed now. 'Honeycake,' gurgled Bess, and the breast-eyes rolled, the long black lashes swept up and down coquettishly. Paley clutched his scrip tightlier to him. If this distortion – likely, as far as he could judge – were to grow progressively worse – if this scrambling of sense data were a regular barrier against intrusion, why was there not more information about it on Earth? Other time-travellers had ventured forth and come back unharmed and laden with sensible records. Wait, though: had they? How did one know? There was Swenson's mention of Wheeler, jailed in the Middle Ages by chunks of tripodic ectoplasm. 'White-haired and gibbering when we got him aboard.' Swenson's own words. How about Swenson's own vision of the future – a plaque showing his own birth and death dates? Perhaps the future did not object to intrusion from the past, since it was made of the same substance. But (Paley shook his head as though he were drunk, beating back sense into it) it was not a question of past and future, it was a matter of other worlds existing *now*. The now-past was completed, the now-future was completed. Perhaps that plaque in Rostron Place, Brighton, showing Swenson's death some thirty years off, perhaps that was an illusion, a device to engender satisfaction rather than fear but still to discourage interference with the pattern. 'My time is short,' Paley said suddenly, using urgent twenty-third-century phonemes, not Elizabethan ones. 'I will give you gold if you will take me to the house of Master Shakespeare.'

'Maister –?'

'Shairkspeyr.'

Bess, her ears growing larger, stared at Paley with a growing montage of film battle scenes playing away on the wall behind her. 'Th'art not that kind. Women tha likes. That see I in tha face.'

'This is urgent. This is business. Quick. He lives, I think, in Bishopsgate.' He could find out something before the epistemological enemies took over. And then what? Try to live. Keep sane with signals in some quiet spot till a year was past. Signal Swenson, receive his reassurances in reply; perhaps – who knew? – hear from far time-space that he was to be taken home before the scheduled date, instructions from Earth, arrangements changed –

'Thou knowest,' Paley said, 'what man I mean. Master Shakespeare the player at the Theatre.'

'Aye aye.' The voice was thickening fast. Paley said to himself: It is up to me to take in what I wish to take in; this girl has no eyes on her breasts, that mouth new-formed under her chin is not really there. Thus checked, the hallucinations wobbled and were pushed back temporarily. But their strength was great. Bess pulled on a simple smock over her nakedness, took a worn cloak from a closet. 'Gorled maintwise,' she said. Paley pushed like mad; the words unscrambled. 'Give me money now,' she said. He gave her a portague.

They tiptoed downstairs. Paley tried to look steadily at the pictures in the stairwell, but there was no time to force them into telling of the truth. The stairs caught him off his guard and changed to a primitive escalator. He whipped them back to trembling stairhood. Bess, he was sure, would melt into some monster capable of turning his heart to stone if he let her. Quick. He held the point-of-day in the sky by a great effort. There were a few people in the street. He durst not look on them. 'It is far?' he asked. Cocks crowed, many and near, mature cocks.

'Not far.' But nothing could be far from anything in this crammed and toppling London. Paley strained to keep his sanity. Sweat dripped from his forehead and a drop caught on the scrip which he hugged to himself like a stomachache. He examined the drop as he walked, stumbling often on the cobbles. A drop of salty water from his pores. Was it of this alien world or of his own? If he cut off his hair and left it lying, if he dunged in that foul jakes there from which a three-headed woman now appeared, would this B303

London reject it, as a human body will reject a grafted kidney? Was it perhaps not a matter of natural law but of some God of the system, a God against Whom, the devil on one's side, one could prevail? Was it God's club rules he was pushing against, not some deeper inbuilt necessity? Anyway, he pushed, and Elizabethan London, in its silver dawn, steadied, rocked, steadied, held. But the strain was terrific.

'Here, sir.' She had brought him to a mean door which warned Paley that it was going to turn into water and flow down the cobbles did he not hold its form fast. 'Money,' she said. But Paley had given enough. He scowled and shook his head. She held out a fist which turned into a winking bearded man's face, threatening with chattering mouth. He raised his own hand, flat, to slap her. She ran off, whimpering, and he turned the raised hand to a fist that knocked. His knock was slow to be answered. He wondered how much longer he could maintain this desperate holding of the world in position. If he slept, what would happen? Would it all dissolve and leave him howling in cold space when he awoke?

'Aye, what is't, then?' It was a misshapen ugly man with a row of bright blinking eyes across his chest, a chest left bare by his buttonless shirt. It was not, it could not be, William Shakespeare. Paley said, wondering at his own ability to enunciate the sounds with such exact care:

'Oi ud see Maister Shairkespeyr.' He was surlily shown in, a shoulder-thrust indicating which door he must knock at. This, this, then, at last. It. Paley's heart martelled desperately against his breast-bone. He knocked. The door was firm oak, threatening no liquefaction.

'Aye?' A light voice, a pleasant voice, no early morning displeasure in it. Paley gulped and opened the door and went in. Bewildered, he looked about him. A bedchamber, the clothes on the bed in disorder, a table with papers on it, a chair, morning light framed by the tight-shut casement. He went over to the papers; he read the top sheet ('. . . giue it to him lest he rayse al helle again with his fractuousness'), wondering if perhaps there was a room adjoining whence came that voice. Then he heard that voice again, behind him:

''Tis not seemly to read a gentleman's private papers lacking his

permission.' Paley spun round to see, dancing in the air, a reproduction of the Droeshout portrait of Shakespeare, square in a frame,
the lips moving but the eyes unanimated. Paley tried to call but
could not. The talking woodcut advanced on him – 'Rude, mannerless, or art thou some Privy Council spy?' – and then the straight
sides of the frame bulged and bulged, the woodcut features dissolved,
and a circle of black lines and spaces tried to grow into a solid
body. Paley could do nothing; his paralysis would not even permit
him to shut his eyes. The solid body became an animal shape,
indescribably gross and ugly – some spiked sea-urchin, very large,
nodding and smiling with horrible intelligence. Paley forced it into
becoming a more nearly human shape. His heart sank in depression
totally untinged by fear to see standing before him a fictional
character called 'William Shakespeare', an actor acting the part.
Why could he not get in touch with the *Ding an sich*, the Kantian
noumenon? But that was the trouble – the thing-in-itself was
changed by the observer into whatsoever phenomenon the catego-
ries of time and space and sense imposed. He took courage and
said:

'What plays have you writ to date?'

Shakespeare looked surprised. 'Who asks this?'

Paley said: 'What I say you will hardly believe. I come from
another world that knows and reveres the name of Shakespeare. I
come, for safety's sake, in disguise as a man from Norwich who
seeks his fortune in the theatre and has brought plays of his own.
I believe that there was, or is, an actor named William Shakespeare.
That Shakespeare wrote the plays that carry his name – this is a
thing I must prove.'

'So,' said Shakespeare, tending to melt into a blob of tallow badly
sculpted into the likeness of Shakespeare, 'you speak of what I will
hardly believe. For my part, I will believe anything. You will be a
sort of ghost from this other world you speak of. By rights, you
should have dissolved at cockcrow.'

'My time may be as short as a ghost's. What plays do you claim
to have written up to this moment?' Paley spoke the English of
his own day. Though the figure before him shifted and softened,
tugged towards other shapes, the eyes changed little, shrewd and
intelligent eyes, modern. Paley noticed now a small fireplace, in

which a meagre newlit fire struggled to live. The hands of Shakespeare moved to their warming through the easy process of elongation of the arms. The voice said:

'Claim? *Heliogabalus. A Word to Fright a Whoremaster. The Sad Reign of Harold First and Last. The Devil in Dulwich.* Oh, many and many more.'

'Please.' Paley was distressed. Was this truth or teasing, truth or teasing of this man or of his own mind, a mind desperate to control the sense data and make them make sense? On the table there, the mass of papers. 'Show me,' he said. 'Show me somewhat,' he pleaded.

'Show me your credentials,' Shakespeare said, 'if we are to talk of showing. Nay,' and he advanced merrily towards Paley, 'I will see for myself.' The eyes were very bright now and shot with oddly sinister flecks. 'A pretty boy,' Shakespeare said. 'Not so pretty as some, as one, I would say, but apt for a brief tumble of a summer's morning before the day warms.'

'Nay,' Paley protested, 'nay,' backing and feeling the archaism to be strangely frivolous, 'touch me not.' The advancing figure became horribly ugly, the neck swelled, eyes glinted on the hairy backs of the approaching hands. The face grew an elephantine proboscis, wreathing, feeling; two or three suckers sprouted from its end and blindly waved towards Paley. Paley dropped his scrip the better to struggle. The words of this monster were thick, they turned into grunts and lallings. Pushed into the corner near the table, Paley saw a sheet of paper much blotted ('Never blotted a line,' did they say?):

I have bin struggling striuing seeking how I may compair
This jailhouse prison? where I liue unto the earth world
And that and for because

The scholar was still alive in Paley, the questing spirit clear while the body fought off those huge hands, each ten-fingered. The scholar cried:

'*Richard II?* You are writing *Richard II?*'

It seemed to him, literary history's Claude Bernard, that he should risk all to get that message through to Swenson, that *Richard II* was, in 1595, being written by William Shakespeare. He suddenly dipped to the floor, grabbed his scrip and began to tap through the lining at the key of the transmitter. Shakespeare seemed taken by surprise by this sudden cessation of resistance; he put out forks of hands that grasped nothing. Paley, blind with sweat, panting hard, tapped: 'UNDOUBTED PROOF THAT.' Then the door opened.

'I did hear noise.' It was the misshapen ugly man with eyes across his bare chest, uglier now, his shape changing constantly though abruptly, as though set upon by silent and invisible hammers. 'He did come to attack tha?'

'Not for money, Tomkin. He hath gold enow of's own. See.' The scrip, set down so hurriedly, had spilt out gold onto the floor. Paley had not noticed; he should have transferred that gold to his −

'Aye, gold.' The creature called Tomkin gazed on it greedily. 'The others that came so brought not gold.'

'Take the gold and him,' Shakespeare said carelessly. 'Do what thou wilt with both.' Tomkin oozed towards Paley. Paley screamed, attacking feebly with the hand that now held the scrip. Tomkin's claw snatched it without trouble.

'There's more within,' he drooled.

'Did I not say thou wouldst do well in my service?' said Shakespeare.

'And here is papers.' He looked towards the fire with a sheaf of them. Then he went to the grate and offered them. The fire read them hurriedly and converted them into itself. There was a transitory blaze which played music for shawms.

'Not all the papers.' Shakespeare took the rest. 'Carry him to the Queen's Marshal. The stranger within our gates. He talks foolishly, like the Aleman that came before. Wildly, I would say. Of other worlds, like a madman. The Marshal will know what to do.'

'But,' screamed Paley, grabbed by strong shovels of hands, 'I am a gentleman. I am from Norwich. I am a playwright, like yourself. See, you hold what I have written.'

'First a ghost, now from Norwich,' Shakespeare smiled. He hovered in the air like his portrait again, a portrait holding papers. 'Go to. Are there not other worlds, like unto our own, that sorcery can make men leave to visit this? I have heard such stories before. There was one came from High Germany −'

'It's true, true, I tell you.' Paley clung to that, clinging also to the chamber door with his nails, the while Tomkin pulled at him.

'You are the most intelligent man of these times! You can conceive of it!'

'And of poets yet unborn also? Drythen, or some such name, and Lord Tennisballs, and Infra Penny Infra Pound? You will be taken care of like that other.'

'But it's true, true!'

'Come your ways,' growled Tomkin. 'You are a Bedlam natural.' And he dragged Paley out, Paley collapsing, frothing, raving. Paley raved: 'You're not real, any of you. It's you who are the ghosts! I'm real, it's all a mistake, let me go, let me explain.'

''Tis strange he talks,' growled Tomkin. And he dragged him out.

'Shut the door,' said Shakespeare. Tomkin kicked it to. The screaming voice went, over thumping feet, down the passageway without. Soon it was quiet enough to sit and read.

These were, Shakespeare thought, good plays. A pity the rest was consumed in that fire that now, glutted, settled again to sleep. Too hot today for a fire anyway. Strange that the play he now read was about, so far as he could judge, a usurious Jew. This Norwich man had evidently read Marlowe and seen the dramatic possibilities of an evil Lopez kind of character. Shakespeare had toyed with the idea of a play like this himself. And here it was, ready done for him, though it required copying into his own hand that questions about its provenance be not asked. And there were a promising couple of histories here, both about King Henry IV. And here a comedy with its final pages missing in the fire, its title *Much Ado About Nothing*. Gifts, godsends! He smiled. He remembered that Aleman, Doctor Schleyer or some such name, who had come with a story like this madman (mad? Could madmen do work like this? 'The lunatic, the lover and the poet': a good line in that play about fairies Schleyer had brought. Poor Schleyer had died of the plague). Those plays Schleyer had brought had been good plays, but not, perhaps, quite so good as these.

Shakespeare furtively, though he was alone, crossed himself. When poets had talked of the Muse had they perhaps meant visitants like this, now screaming feebly in the street, and the German Schleyer and that one who swore, under torture, that he was from Virginia in America, and that in America they had universities as good as Oxford or Leyden or Wittenberg, nay better? Well, whoever they were, they were heartily welcome so long as they brought plays. That *Richard II* of Schleyer's was, perhaps, in need of the amendments he was now engaged upon, but the earlier work untouched, from *Henry VI* on, had been popular. He read the top sheet of this new batch, stroking his auburn beard finely silvered, a fine grey eye reading. He sighed and, before crumpling a sheet of his own work on the table, he reread it. Not good, it limped, there was too much magic in it. Ingenio the Duke of Parma said:

> Consider gentleman as in the sea
> All earthly life finds like and parallel
> So in far distant skies our lives be aped
> Each hath a twin each action hath a twin
> And twins have twins galore and infinite
> And een these stars be twinn'd

Too fantastic, it would not do. He threw it into the rubbish box which Tomkin would later empty. Humming a new song of the streets entitled 'Leave well alone', he took a clean sheet and began to copy in a fair hand:

The Merchant of Venice, A Comedy

Then on he went, not blotting a line.